GAELEN FOLEY

Duke of Shadows

MOONLIGHT SQUARE, BOOK 4

Also by Gaelen Foley

Moonlight Square
One Moonlit Night
Duke of Scandal
Duke of Secrets
Duke of Storm
Duke of Shadows

Ascension Trilogy
The Pirate Prince
Princess
Prince Charming

Knight Miscellany
The Duke
Lord of Fire
Lord of Ice
Lady of Desire
Devil Takes a Bride
One Night of Sin
His Wicked Kiss

The Spice Trilogy
Her Only Desire
Her Secret Fantasy
Her Every Pleasure

The Inferno Club
My Wicked Marquess
My Dangerous Duke
My Irresistible Earl
My Ruthless Prince
My Scandalous Viscount
My Notorious Gentleman
Secrets of a Scoundrel

Age of Heroes
Paladin's Prize

Harmony Falls
Dream of Me
Belong to Me

Gryphon Chronicles
(Writing as E.G. Foley)
The Lost Heir
Jake & the Giant
The Dark Portal
The Gingerbread Wars
Rise of Allies
Secrets of the Deep
The Black Fortress

50 States of Fear
(Writing as E.G. Foley)
The Haunted Plantation
Leader of the Pack
Bringing Home Bigfoot
Dork and the Deathray

Anthologies
Royal Weddings
Royal Bridesmaids

Credits and Copyright

Table of Contents

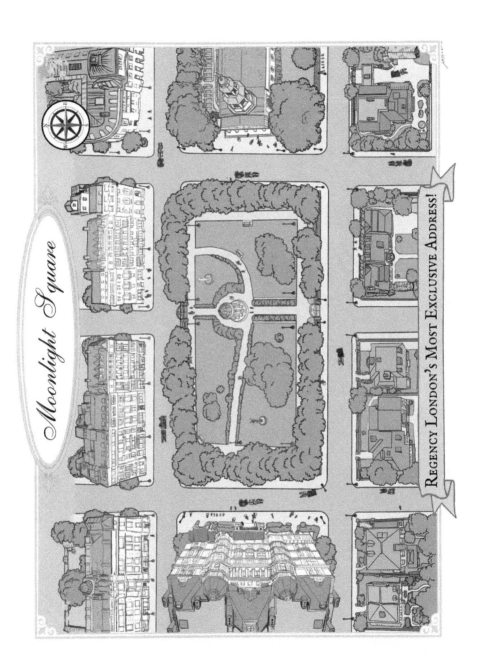

Moonlight Square

Regency London's Most Exclusive Address!

Part One

CHAPTER 1

The Highwayman

$\mathcal{L}$ady Portia Tennesley clutched the leather hand-loop to keep
from bumping her head as the carriage pitched along slowly.
The horses could proceed no faster than a walk now that they'd
turned off the road into the dark woods.

As the way before them narrowed to a leaf-strewn trail barely wide
enough for the coach, she could hear the wheels grinding, the fine
wooden chassis creaking in protest as the town coach labored along over
the rough ground.

All the while, heart in her throat, Portia stared out the open window
at the silver blades of moonlight piercing the thick tangle of black,
twisted trees that hemmed them in on all sides.

Pale shafts of moonbeams pierced the forest's inky gloom here and
there, angling in through the ancient oaks' thick, gnarled branches,
winding vines, and masses of leaves.

The effect was eerie, menacing, while the June frogs croaked and
chirped on endlessly in the hot, humid night. Their undulating chorus
was deafening inside the airless woods.

There had been a breeze out on the road, but the wall of trees blocked
it now; the heavy air stank of mulch and moss, layers of rotting leaves,
and lush vegetation.

It was hard to imagine that this wild place lay just a few miles
outside of London. Tonight, the moonlit barrens of Hampstead Heath
felt like another world.

A dangerous one.

Everybody knew the place had been the haunt of highwaymen for centuries, as surely as Cornwall equaled smugglers and pirates. At that thought, a bead of sweat trickled down her nape and soaked into the collar of the black lace mourning gown she had donned to help hide her identity.

"Ach, my old bones can't take much more o' this," Mrs. Berry said grimly beside her, likewise holding on for dear life as the coach lurched along.

"It can't be much farther now." Portia gave the old woman a brave nod before glancing out the window again, her senses on high alert.

For all she knew, spies in the trees might've already noted their presence and were even now carrying news of their approach to their underworld captain.

She sincerely hoped she and the servants would not all be murdered—though it was a little late now to be having second thoughts about the wisdom of her scheme.

Holding her dread in check, Portia peered out the window, keeping watch for a telltale light through the trees ahead that might prove to be the bandits' forest hideaway.

It had to be here somewhere.

As she searched the darkness, a moth fluttered haplessly into the coach, since the windows were down. Twin clouds of the creatures had been drawn to the feeble lanterns mounted on either side of the driver's box.

This one took a clever shortcut, passing through the coach's interior to go and explore the other light. It brushed past Portia's nose on its way, tickling her with light, silky wings, teasing her.

She waved it off, scowling—insects made her think of her fiancé— but a moth was nothing. Up on the driver's box, the mosquitoes were apparently feasting on poor Cassius and Denny, by the sound of it.

"Ow!" she heard Denny mutter. Tonight, the husky young footman played driver. "Little bastards are eatin' me alive."

"Mind your tongue!" scolded Cassius the valet, also seated outside. "There's a lady in earshot, you dolt."

"Oops, forgot. Sorry I cursed, Lady Portia!" Denny called back.

"Shh!" Mrs. Berry retorted, poking her mob-capped head out the window to scold him. "Keep your voice down, Thump! Or forget the mosquitoes; you'll have us surrounded by criminals. Young numskull," the portly old housekeeper huffed, drawing her head back into the vehicle.

Mrs. Berry had long worked for Portia's former beau, the Honorable Joel Clayton. Along with his valet, Cassius, and trusty (if dull-witted) footman, Denny, a.k.a. Thump, all three of the missing dandy's devoted servants wanted their handsome young master back nearly as bad as Portia did. Once the inspiration for tonight's risky venture had flooded her mind about a week ago, she'd had a feeling they might be willing to help in her mission, so she had sought them out and told them her plan.

Sure enough, the trio had been eager to join in her quest.

In truth, she got the feeling that Joel's servants had been rather lost without some highborn person giving them any orders for over a year now, though they'd kept his fashionable bachelor apartments in tiptop order—as if the handsome rogue might come breezing in at any moment with a funny story about where the devil he'd been all this time.

Joel's servants were all the more willing to heed Portia's orders knowing *she* would have likely become the future lady of the house, if only their beloved Mr. Clayton had not disappeared without a trace.

Portia's inspiration for how they might yet find and rescue him had filled them all with newfound hope, long after all hope seemed to have died.

And so here they were, creaking along through the woods.

On their way to a meeting with a notorious brigand.

While Denny drove, slim, tidy Cassius played navigator. Sharp-eyed as he was—at least in matters of gentlemen's fashion—the valet was in charge of following the mysterious instructions that the bespectacled newspaper reporter, Mr. Townsend, had entrusted to Portia in strictest secrecy about how to find the mysterious highwayman's headquarters.

Townsend alone knew how to get messages back and forth to the legendary Silversmoke. Anyone wanting to plead for the famed outlaw's help had to go through him. He was always the first to publish the latest tales of Silversmoke's derring-do.

It was almost as if the reporter had inside information, and clearly, he did, for it was he who had set up tonight's meeting for Portia.

No names, of course. It was also Mr. Townsend who had furtively given Portia all of her instructions on what to bring and where to go.

Apparently, Silversmoke trusted him. And so, the date and the time of their meeting had been set.

From the moment they had left Moonlight Square in London's opulent West End tonight, Cassius, with Townsend's directions in hand, had been directing Denny on which turns to take with the same meticulous care with which he would've ironed one of Joel's fine bespoke shirts.

A sigh escaped Portia when she thought of her lost beau's sartorial distinction, especially compared to her fiancé's sad lack thereof.

Ah well. It was too late for *her* now, pledged to wed the duke, but if Joel was still alive and could be found, then at least his servants could keep their posts.

For her part, Portia would simply have to content herself with knowing he was safe. That would have to be enough.

But if the news was darker, if it turned out that her former favorite really was dead, then she didn't care what became of her, so she might as well marry Fountainhurst as planned.

Such a grand match would be of great advantage to her family. Indeed, if she became a duchess, she might even be able to use her influence to help her wild elder brother reenter Society after his banishment.

If he ever came home to England, that was.

In any case, Portia knew perfectly well deep down that it was too late to back out of her lofty match now. She had stalled for as long as she possibly could, pushing the wedding back twice already with whatever excuses she could muster.

His Grace had barely noticed, thankfully. He seemed to shrug off her delays. At least, his letters gave no indication of annoyance, but it was hard to say, since the two of them had only been in the same room a total of three times.

Lucas Wakeford, the Duke of Fountainhurst, rarely came to London, so he'd written to her in reply, merely dashing off a line, saying: *As it pleases you, my lady.*

Beyond that, her rich, powerful future husband could not be bothered with her much.

Which was probably just as well. It seemed they both understood what this marriage signified: a typical, loveless alliance between two great houses.

And so much for her girlish dreams of ever finding true love.

It was foolishness, anyway, she supposed. Like Mama said, that was not how life worked. And so, months ago, resigned to her fate, Portia had thrown herself into planning her wedding instead of deluding herself with juvenile fantasies. She was a practical woman, after all, even a bit of a cynic.

If she could not have the *man* she really wanted, then she figured she would at least have the wedding of her dreams. Now the big day—the last Sunday in June—was exactly twenty-six days away, and nearly everything was ready.

But the moment she had completed her massive project, all of her gnawing questions about what the blazes had happened to Joel Clayton began returning to haunt her. Filling the void of her once again somewhat empty, if privileged, life.

Then, out of nowhere one day about a fortnight ago, she had noticed the Silversmoke stories right there in the newspapers.

Staring her in the face this whole time...

The idea had struck like lightning.

Whereupon she had become obsessed with the notion, as she was wont to do when some new project struck her. At once, she had dived into careful research on the gallant highwayman with the same attention to detail she'd given to planning her wedding day.

The idea was madness, of course; she knew that.

Yet, somehow, she could not resist pressing on. Poring over the stories in the papers about him, Portia had come to believe in him.

In Silversmoke, the legend.

To believe that he might really help her.

Heroes were in short supply these days, to be sure. But the mysterious outlaw would sometimes help people who had nowhere else to turn...

Finally deciding she had nothing left to lose, Portia had gone to see Mr. Townsend. A few days later, the reporter had sent back the thrilling answer that yes, Silversmoke would hear her case.

Of course, there were no guarantees about this night.

But she would be happy to pay him if only he would agree to take up her quest and find her missing beau—before she had to marry the odd, reclusive duke.

As the carriage crept on through the dark, mossy woods, suddenly, Cassius called out in a hushed voice, "There, ahead—I see a light!"

At once, both Portia and Mrs. Berry poked their heads out their respective windows. For her part, Portia could see nothing but more brambles, more trees.

Mrs. Berry, acting as chaperone, also pulled her head back in, then looked askance at her. "You still want to do this, milady?"

"It's coming into view!" Cassius whispered loudly.

One of the horses let out a nervous whicker.

"Should I stop, ma'am?" Denny called back in a low tone. "I don't think there'll be enough room up there to turn around if we go much farther."

She could feel the servants' fear now that they'd found the place, could hear it in their voices, and though she was acutely aware of her own, it was up to her to set the example.

"Courage, everyone," she told them. "There'll be no turning back. Silversmoke himself promised us safe passage."

"Not sure what the word of a highwayman's worth," Mrs. Berry muttered.

"Silversmoke is no ordinary highwayman, Mrs. Berry. If he were, we wouldn't be here. Drive on, Denny," Portia ordered him. "They're expecting us. Delay will only look suspicious. Don't worry, everyone, it'll be all right. We have to do this. For Mr. Clayton."

"For Mr. Clayton," Denny echoed with resolve. "Aye, milady. If anyone can find 'im, it'll be Silversmoke."

Let's hope so, Portia thought, and the coach rumbled on.

Tense with the knowledge that she was staking not just her own safety, but that of three other people on her faith that all the swashbuckling tales about the heroic outlaw were true, she decided with a gulp that this seemed as good a time as any to review them.

Before she lost her nerve.

He had gained the moniker of Silversmoke, they said, by his tendency to vanish or appear in a swirl of fog, always readily available in England.

How dramatic, she thought in sardonic amusement. Realistically, though, foggy nights must be perfect for robbing coaches, she decided.

Well, he was no Robin Hood, of course, but Silversmoke had developed into something of a folk hero because he only robbed from the rich and gave a portion of his proceeds to the widows and orphans of hanged criminals.

Nobody knew who he really was, but the poor had nothing to fear from him.

Indeed, one famous tale had recounted how he'd once come upon a wagonload of peasants heading north to find haymaking work. They'd been stranded on the roadside when their cart had lost a wheel.

They had been terrified of him and his gang, but instead of harming them, Silversmoke had ordered his men to help the humble folk. Once their wagon was fixed, he'd given them some money to buy food and sent them safely on their way.

An almost lordly gesture.

When he *did* stop coaches of the wealthy, he never took wedding bands or items of sentimental value.

And he never resorted to violence, unless some gentleman or his driver made the foolish mistake of trying to attack him first. The force he used in such cases was never known to be excessive.

He had never *killed* anyone that she knew of. Indeed, if he had, she would not be here. That would be too dangerous even for her.

In any case, all of Silversmoke's heroics had inspired even the lawmen to turn a blind eye to his roguery—especially since the outlaw had been known to leave villains far worse than himself bound and gagged on the constable's doorstep.

Like the savage apprentice master who'd been whipping his poor boys without mercy. Or the fraudster who had cheated an elderly couple out of their pension.

Or the trio of spurned swains who had ambushed and assaulted the coquette who'd rejected them all, leaving the poor girl unspeakably used and beaten unconscious.

Silversmoke had deposited all three of her attackers bruised beyond recognition and full of broken bones outside the local jail, neatly packaged for the gallows.

The magistrates always knew when it was his work because of the little domino game piece that they would find hanging on a string around the neck of each miscreant.

His calling card, as it were. One that even the illiterate criminals could read.

The man had *style*, Portia mused. Even Joel would have agreed, and he would know, having been a leading dandy in Society.

It was said that the criminal class feared Silversmoke like the devil himself, but ladies swooned when he robbed them—and not from fear.

From what she had read in the papers, it seemed like half of the highwayman's female victims became infatuated with him after some midnight encounter on the roads.

Portia shook her head. No doubt the famed outlaw cut a dashing figure when he emerged in the moonlight astride his equally famous black horse, Tempo, and bellowed those fearsome words every traveler dreaded to hear: *"Stand and deliver!"*

But how could these fainting ninnies in the papers swear he was such a beautiful man when he worked under cover of night and wore a mask?

That was what *she* wanted to know.

Poppycock, she decided, for she had always prided herself on being a very practical, clear-headed, down-to-earth sort of person.

Well, except for tonight, of course.

No, indeed. Tonight's little jaunt to a meeting with the brigand in his hideaway was not at all the sort of thing that a young lady betrothed to a duke would normally do.

Fountainhurst had better never find out about this, she thought uneasily.

Eccentric or not, he was still a duke. A jilt from the likes of him would end any girl in Society.

As for Portia's parents, she knew they would positively lock her in a tower until her wedding if they had any idea where she was right now. She hated to disobey them—especially after all the trouble Hunter had caused them years ago.

But perhaps if her brother had not sailed off halfway around the world chasing fortune and adventure, then *he* could've helped instead of her having to turn to a blasted highwayman.

Not that she resented him for his absence, she quickly amended.

But, heir to the title or not, Hunter was quite the black sheep of the family, which was why Portia always did her best to make her parents happy—insofar as two such discontented souls *could* be made happy.

Fortunately, they were both preoccupied tonight. Mama was out getting tipsy once again with her glamorous friends, and Papa had nodded off in his favorite chair, as usual, after another prodigious supper.

The Marquess of Liddicoat was presently snoring with his feet up on the ottoman back at their home in Moonlight Square in the company of his parakeet, with no idea that his youngest daughter had tiptoed out to sneak off to a reckless tête-à-tête with an outlaw.

Which just went to show how desperate her situation had become, how acute her distress.

Silversmoke was officially her last hope. But would he accept the mission?

Was he really a hero under that mask, or just another villain?

It seemed she was about to find out. *We'd better not be late.*

Eleven o'clock was the time set for their meeting. Glancing at the locket watch she had worn around her neck, she saw with relief that, so far, she was on time.

While the carriage crawled along through the dark forest, Portia pondered the question of exactly *how* Silversmoke might set about finding Joel once he'd considered the matter.

He had his ways, she supposed.

He must have friends in low places, given his criminality. No doubt he could ask questions and make inquiries where a highborn lady had no hope whatsoever of succeeding. God willing, he could succeed where even Bow Street had failed.

If he agreed to help her, that was.

Instead, he might have a hearty laugh at her gullibility for believing all those florid tales, and order his men to butcher the four of them and dump their bodies in the woods.

Cheerful thought, that.

Her heart lurched, but she quickly warded off dread with a cheeky mental jest. *At least then I won't have to marry Fountainhurst.*

Would His Grace even notice, I wonder?

That grim bit of levity helped shore up her resolve as the light among the trees ahead finally materialized into a little thatch-roofed pub with a dozen saddled horses tied up outside.

"Would you look at that," Mrs. Berry murmured, staring.

It seemed they had reached the outlaws' hideaway at last—either that, or this was some magical trap conjured by woodland fairies.

Scanning the dodgy place while Denny drove the carriage right up to it, Portia wondered if she'd lost her wits entirely. *Come, you don't actually mean to go through with this, do you? You* cannot *go into that hellhole.*

Hunter wouldn't even go in there.

The decrepit tavern sat alone in the middle of the forest, sullen under its sway-backed thatched roof. A chipped, painted placard hung above the door pronounced it The Blind Badger.

A pair of small windows flanked the gabled entrance, and feeble orange light glowed through their panes. The roof's straw thatching hung low over the windows so that they resembled the heavy-lidded eyes of a mean drunkard, peering out upon the world waiting for someone, anyone, to pick a fight with him.

Portia pressed her lips together as a bead of sweat slipped down her cheek.

"Are you going to get out, milady?" Denny called nervously. "Or should I just drive 'round?"

To her relief, she now saw that escape was an option, after all—thank God.

There was a sort of rough drive that encircled the building. They could still go around it and hurry back out of this criminal-infested wood the same way they'd come in. Drive hell-for-leather back to London.

And leave Joel to his fate...

"Milady?" Denny repeated, sounding even more worried.

Portia didn't answer, debating with herself. For another long minute, she just sat there like a lump, paralyzed with last-minute jitters.

"Are you all right back there, ma'am?" Cassius asked, his crisp voice tight with alarm.

"Um..." she said, gripping the handle of her reticule. The night was much too hot, and all the air seemed to have been sucked out of the coach.

In the small clearing around the bandits' hideaway, though, she could see the night sky, feel a hint of a breeze.

High above, the white moon half-masked its face with a scarf of wispy clouds, and the stars twinkled merrily around it.

This is it, she told herself, chewing her lip. *Yes or no? Go or stay?*

Glancing around, she saw a couple of ill-made carriages parked out of the way. A battered whiskey gig, a farmer's wagon.

A curl of smoke rose from the chimney poking up through the roof's mass of mangy-looking straw. They must be cooking for their patrons.

Portia grimaced. She could not imagine eating anything in such a place. The food was no doubt revolting. Indeed, the whole place looked altogether dodgy—but who was she fooling? This entire misadventure was dodgy.

She'd be lucky if she didn't go in there and get herself killed.

But all the newspaper stories she'd collected, everything she'd read about Silversmoke, gave her one last shred of hope that there might still be a way to find out what had become of the young man she had *expected* to marry.

She simply had to know once and for all what had really happened to him, if she was ever going to be able to move on with her life. The answer to this mystery, no matter how gory or grim, would at least bring the matter to a close in her heart. This ignorance was torture—being left in the dark, only given answers that she could not bring herself to believe.

Her parents said to let it go. Papa had never liked him anyway. Oh, he liked her fiancé well enough, though; Lord Liddicoat had once served on some boring Parliamentary committee with the duke's late father, ages ago.

Since he had respected the last Duke of Fountainhurst so well, her sire hoped the apple would not fall too far from the tree.

Mama, for her part, claimed that having a duchess for a daughter would be the crowning achievement of her life. Besides, Portia *was* already twenty-three. Why, her elder sister Sarah (the perfect one) had already birthed two children by the time she was Portia's age, and even though Mama would admit that Joel had been dashing, Fountainhurst was a man of consequence.

Even Portia's best friend, Serena, the Duchess of Rivenwood, had gently pointed out that Joel's courtship of her hadn't seemed all that serious, anyway.

"But he was never serious about anything! That's why I liked him. He was fun!" Portia had exclaimed, but Serena just sighed.

Blast it, what the devil had happened to him?

A grown man could not simply vanish off the face of the earth without explanation, without a note, without a reason, without a body being found!

It didn't add up!

Yes, she knew he was impulsive—it was part of his charm—but to stay away for a year without contacting anyone, even his mother? It wasn't like him.

Something was wrong. Very, very wrong.

Where had he gone? If someone had done something to him, she wanted to know who, and what, and why. She had always been intensely curious, even as a child, annoying her parents and tutors alike with the endless questions that streamed from her lively mind: *Why is the sky blue? How do birds fly?*

Can I fly, too? How long is forever?

How big is the world?

To think that this, the most important question of her entire twenty-three years, should still go unanswered was more than she could stand.

Well, she might have been pledged to wed another in the meanwhile; so be it. But she refused to let the world just forget about poor, rakish Joel and move on as though he had never existed.

It was awful to see how people just stopped caring as time passed, but not her. She refused to let him simply fade away like an old castle ghost.

If he was alive out there somewhere, the way her intuition swore he was, then someone had to find him and *help* him.

That someone was Silversmoke. The bold stranger who defended the weak. Protected the innocent. Lent his strength to those who seemed like lost causes.

There was just one problem.

If she was wrong about him, and dared set foot inside The Blind Badger...she might never come out alive.

Gulp.

The servants were asking what to do, but Portia wasn't listening. For it was then that a bit of motion in the shadows under one of the huge old trees near the tavern caught her eye. She turned, homing in on it.

A silver beam of moonlight slanting down from the sky illuminated a magnificent black horse tied up there, saddled, grazing.

He was the color of midnight, with four white socks, and Portia drew in her breath with wonderstruck recognition.

Tempo!

Why, the highwayman's trusty steed matched the papers' description exactly! With that, her hopes surged and her heart started thumping.

There, you see? The horse at least is real. And if that part's true, the rest of it is probably true, as well. Suddenly, her trek out here tonight did not seem as mad as it had moments ago. This might actually work!

For Joel, she decided. And with that, she pulled her black lace veil down over her face, opened the carriage door, and climbed out.

"Whatever happens, do *not* leave without me," she said.

"Never, milady," Cassius vowed.

Denny swung down from the driver's box. His artless eyes were wide with fear, but his jaw was squared. "Shall I go in with you, milady?"

Portia was taken aback by the young footman's brave offer. He might not be overly bright, but what a kindhearted fellow. "Thank you, Denny, but no. His message said to come alone."

Mrs. Berry reached out and squeezed Portia's hand. "Oh, be careful, dear."

"I will." She nodded back with gratitude.

Resolved on her course, Portia turned to face the bandits' hideaway and ignored her pounding heartbeat. Lifting her chin, she took a deep breath, squared her shoulders, and marched bravely toward the door.

To her surprise, it opened before she reached it, swinging on its hinges with a loud creak. Portia froze as light poured out from inside the tavern, along with the rough, idle clamor of men laughing and enjoying their ale. A cloud of tobacco smoke wafted out, and the sound of music sawing away on a fiddle.

Then a slim, sinewy figure appeared in the doorway: the long-legged silhouette of a rugged older man in a slouchy coat, with a halo of longish pewter hair and a silver mustache to match.

"Well, girl?" he grunted. "Ye comin' or not?"

Portia faltered, clutching her reticule as a belated wave of dread besieged her.

Faced with her first real live outlaw, she couldn't answer for a heartbeat, her voice stuck in her throat. But she refused to show herself a coward. So she steeled her nerve, straightened her spine, and walked briskly toward him.

"Yes, ahem. Thank you."

The silver-haired brigand waited, tall and lean. As she neared him, she saw he had piercing dark eyes and a grim, harrowed face tough as leather.

Though he was armed to the teeth—pistols, dagger—she sensed neither hostility nor particular interest from him; he merely held out his hand, waiting.

Portia realized with a blink that she was meant to give him the little ivory domino that Townsend had entrusted to her. "Oh—er, one moment, please."

She reached into her reticule and fished around inside it for the token, the journalist's warning ringing in her ears, that the game piece was imperative for her safety in these parts.

First, the domino would certify to Silversmoke that she was indeed the visitor he had agreed to see. Second, Townsend said that if any other gangs bothered them out on the roads, she need only show them the token and the domino's four black dots—one for each member of her party. This would serve as a sign to even unlettered criminals that she and her attendants had business with Silversmoke, and must be allowed to pass unharmed unless said criminals wished to deal with *him*.

Blast it, where is it? She groped around for it frantically amid the contents of her crowded reticule, to no avail. *What if I can't find it? What then?*

Just when she started to panic, her searching fingers found it at the bottom of her bag. She clasped the ivory game piece in relief, pulled it out, and placed it shakily in the older fellow's palm.

Through the black lace of her veil, she saw him glance down at its four black dots, then at her coach, narrowing those shrewd, canny eyes.

"Three servants and you, ma'am. That's all you're cleared for."

"Yes," she forced out, nodding.

"Hidin' anything?" He flicked a skeptical glance over her, and Portia suddenly realized he was asking if she was armed.

"Oh, goodness, no!" She did not see fit to tell him that even if she had a gun hidden somewhere on her person, she'd have no idea how to use it.

Now, if it was a ladies' archery set, that might be a different matter, but she only shot at straw targets, anyway, never people.

He harrumphed but took her at her word. "I'll not search a lady."

I should think not. She stiffened indignantly, remembering her station as the daughter of a marquess and a future duchess.

He did not look impressed.

"Name's Gower. Follow me," said the man. She thought he said Gower, anyway; it was hard to hear his low rumble of a voice as he turned away. "Don't mind the boys. They won't harm ye unless they want their throats cut."

Her eyes flared at such casual talk of violence, but Gower stepped inside, and she knew she must follow.

Casting one last, uncertain glance over her shoulder at the coach and staring servants, Portia hesitated, on the brink of ghastly regret for ever starting this. But, bracing herself, she quickly hurried after him.

When she stepped over the threshold of the tavern, she beheld a snug, low-ceilinged tavern with a bar on her right and a few long tables in the middle, where some twenty rough-looking men were eating, smoking, playing cards.

Others threw darts at a board on the left-hand wall, while the fiddler perched atop a stool in the corner played a melancholy tune.

The moment the men saw her standing there, dead silence dropped.

The music stopped, the gang of highwaymen turned, and Portia faltered as she got a better look at them through the screen of her black lace veil.

Egads, they looked dangerous. Highly disreputable, all. Lowlifes, even. Messy, dirty, bearded. Disheveled, tattooed. Young and old alike, they were tough men, mean-eyed, hard. Every last one of them, staring at her.

Portia's mouth went dry. *Oh, Lord Jesus, help me.*

She began shrinking back instinctively against the door, which now bumped her in the backside and shoulder blades as it swung shut behind her.

Gower beckoned impatiently to her, and she took two swift steps after him, doing her best to ignore the rest of the wild tribe.

Unfortunately, they started smiling at her from all directions—and that was more terrifying still.

"Well, what 'ave we 'ere?"

"Welcome, darlin'."

They began getting up off their barstools and rising from their seats, creeping closer, tankards in hand, flashing broken-toothed smiles as they leered.

"Buy you a drink, love?"

"What's ye look like un'er that veil?"

Without warning, raucous catcalls erupted, and lewd offers were hurled at her from all directions of acts she'd never heard of, terms whose meanings she did not know and did not care to learn.

Overwhelmed by this onslaught of crudeness aimed at a lady who had been sheltered by her parents like a pearl in a velvet box since her childhood, Portia suddenly feared she might cry from overwhelming dread at their attentions.

She had never encountered such people before, not directly. Not up close.

They were pressing in around her on all sides like a hungry pack of wolves, and in her moment of hesitation, the clear path between her and Mr. Gower had vanished, leaving her surrounded by over-friendly criminals.

One leaned closer, actually sniffing her. "Mmm, smells good."

Suddenly, a deep voice boomed like a thunderclap out of the back of the pub: *"Touch her and you're dead!"*

Portia jumped, but the bellow brought instant silence.

"Clear a path for her. Now," the man said in a whiplike tone full of ruthless authority.

Portia could not yet see the owner of that voice on account of the men blocking her view.

"The lady is here to see *me*," he added darkly. "She is under my protection. You've been warned. Bring her to me, Gower."

"Just havin' a little fun, sir," one of the ruffians mumbled as the horde melted back from her path.

Portia's pulse was still pounding as Gower stomped back to seize her by the wrist. The pewter-haired man shot her a look of annoyance.

"Told you to keep up," he muttered, then led her safely the rest of the way through the tavern. "Keep yer eyes to yourselves!" he barked at the brigands, who slunk aside and returned to their drinking and darts, snickering at her, as though they had only been testing her mettle, anyway.

Portia was shaking as Gower pulled her toward an inglenook in the back.

It was sectioned off from the rest of the pub by a shoulder-high oak partition topped by wooden spindles that reached to the ceiling.

A dark red curtain hung across the opening where this partial wall ended, but it was pushed to the side like an open door.

Gower hurried her through it, and as soon as she stepped into the dimmer, lower-ceilinged inglenook, she found a booth tucked away there; a lantern hung above a dark wooden table full of nicks and scars.

The smallest of cooking fires burned in the nearby hearth, where a large, black-clad man stood leaning in the shadows, one arm braced on the rustic log mantel.

He turned at their arrival—large, muscular, imposing—and the second Portia saw the black half mask concealing the upper portion of his chiseled face, she knew she was in the presence of Silversmoke himself.

He nodded to Gower, who seemed to understand his young chief without a need for words; the silver-haired man instantly turned around and pulled the curtain shut for privacy, remaining with them just long enough to toss the domino to Silversmoke.

The highwayman caught it out of the air in a black-gauntleted fist, glanced at the game piece, then at Portia.

He studied her for a moment from behind his mask with searing intensity. "I see you found your way to me all right," he murmured, his voice taut, low.

"Y-yes," she said with a terrified gulp.

"And you're aware that revealing this location would be…a serious breach of trust." The slight pause, as though searching for the right words, made her think this was a speech he gave to everyone who came seeking his help, but perhaps he'd softened the threat just a little for a lady.

One, especially, who'd just had the daylights scared out of her.

"I do," Portia managed more firmly, though her voice was still little more than a shaky whisper after her moment of panic in that other room. "Th-thank you for seeing me."

She felt somewhat safer now, since he had single-handedly held the others at bay with a word. In truth, this man looked even more dangerous than his followers, but unlike them, he kept a respectful distance, much to her relief.

Silversmoke nodded and gestured toward the booth. "Why don't you have a seat and tell me why you sought me out?"

"Y-yes. Thank you." As she sank down, weak-kneed, onto the bench, her back to the oaken partition, he nodded Gower's dismissal.

The older man silently withdrew. As the lusty young stallion of a highwayman took a seat in the booth across from her, Portia passed a wary glance over him, admittedly intrigued by him now that she was calming down.

All his clothes were jet-black: snug breeches with a black leather gun belt slung around his lean waist, a pistol on each hip. He'd rolled up the sleeves of his loose midnight shirt, which hung open at the neck.

She caught a startling glimpse of muscled chest, then snapped her gaze back up to his face.

Though a black silk bandanna was tied around his head, hiding his hair and hanging down his nape a few inches from where he'd knotted it at the back of his skull, it only made the firm, proud angles of his cheekbones and scruffy jaw seem all the more severe.

She could not tell the color of his eyes, shadowed behind his mask, but his sculpted lips fascinated her for an instant.

Suddenly, she could understand the swooning.

Her terror from the other room was fading fast in the intimacy of sitting three feet from an underworld legend.

She was awed by his size, easily six foot four. She marveled at the breadth of his shoulders, the girth of his chest, the power in his thickly muscled arms.

He drew off his gauntlets and set them on the table, where she only now noticed a trencher with a hunk of brown bread, a wedge of cheese, and a few slices of apple sitting beside a tankard of ale.

There was also a knife stuck upright in the table for some reason.

She stared at it, feeling as though she had stepped into another world, one where she had no idea of the rules.

If there *were* any rules.

As Silversmoke reached for his tankard, she stared at his hands. They were large, thick, and strong. Used to wielding weapons and taking what he wanted from life.

Through the screen of her lace veil, she stared at him, pondering the many dangers this man could pose. If he did anything horrible to her, even Hunter would have trouble punishing the likes of him.

The highwayman took a swig of ale, giving her a moment to collect herself after her fright. Then he rested his elbows on the table and loosely laced his fingers, watching her. "You're quite safe now, ma'am."

Portia eyed him skeptically.

"Why don't you start by telling me about whatever trouble brought you out here to see me tonight." His lulling baritone soothed her as she held his steady gaze, then his tone turned matter-of-fact. "What seems to be the problem?"

CHAPTER 2

Lady in Black

Luke waited patiently to hear what his mysterious caller had to say. He did not have a name yet, but names were of little consequence, as easy to shed as a theater mask.

He should know.

It didn't matter.

He preferred to meet those seeking his help in person first and weigh their credibility to make sure it wasn't a trap before he started wading into real-life details.

In truth, it was a test in itself merely to see if the person had the nerve to come and face him in his hideaway. Only those in serious trouble of some sort were usually willing to risk it.

The others simply went away, which was fine by him. He didn't need his time wasted.

But of all those who'd come to plead for his intervention in their troubles, he did not recall a bona fide lady ever venturing in here before. He was rather impressed she had not run out screaming after the way his men had behaved.

Yes, he mused, trailing a meditative gaze over her, he was difficult to surprise, but this was definitely…new.

Already intrigued, he remained on his guard, for trust was not a commodity that he readily shared. Instead, he observed her carefully while she collected her thoughts, drawing what conclusions about her he could.

Widow?

Perhaps. Her black garb would suggest that was the case.

Which was why, from the moment he had seen her slim, delicate figure wrapped in her mourning gown of fine jet lace, he had felt a pang of compassion for whatever loss she had suffered.

Loss he understood.

Indeed, it was the churning dynamo that powered his very soul, driving him on endlessly, relentlessly. Loss had made him what he was.

Maybe she'd ask him to catch a murderer, he thought, and a dark ripple of eagerness ran down his nerve endings at the prospect.

He liked doing that more than anything. He had many hobbies, but that was the most satisfying by far. He liked catching them, and once he'd taken all care to make sure he had the right man, he liked hurting them until they begged for mercy, of which he had none.

Especially if they'd harmed a child.

Mercy was for lawmen.

Luke preferred the more ruthless pleasure of helping victims' families get revenge. He'd finally found his own four years ago, but it hadn't been enough to slake the deep, bitter rage and the hatred still churning in the heart of him.

The hatred of evil had become his fuel. And he'd used it for years now, ever since he had turned vigilante in earnest. He reveled in wreaking havoc on those who smugly thought that they'd eluded justice. The men in the other room were thieves and brigands, but he was something darker than that behind all his masks...

Of course, most of his followers knew nothing of all that.

He and Gower alone were sworn to secrecy in their shared vow of an eye for an eye.

Luke had joined forces with the rugged Yorkshireman many years ago for vengeance, unlikely a pair as they'd made—the teenaged duke whose parents had been slaughtered, and the tough old fighter whose daughter had been raped and destroyed by the same Scottish gang.

Though it had taken several years, the two of them had finally tracked the evildoers to their lair, torn them apart, and sent that scourge of the Highlands back to hell, where they belonged.

That was a story not even Townsend dared print, if he even knew it, which Luke doubted.

No, if the journalist knew what "Silversmoke" was really capable of, he probably wouldn't be sending innocent civilians out to Hampstead Heath.

Certainly not shapely young widows.

He could already feel his heart tugging at him to help her. Maybe it was stupid of him, quixotic, but he never could resist a damsel in distress.

He scanned her face as best he could, but it was difficult through her black lace veil. Between that and the dim lighting that he deliberately used to cloak himself in shadows, the better to hide his true identity, it was hard to tell what she even looked like.

His general impression was of a well-bred young woman, rather pretty, but pale. He gathered she was still shaken up by the obnoxious attentions of his gang in the other room—he wouldn't call them friends.

They were merely camouflage, props providing him with by now well-established credibility in London's shadowy underworld. After all, as he had long since learned that the easiest way to catch a criminal was to become one.

Within reason, of course.

Across the table from him, the woman took a deep breath and blew it out, stirring the lace draping her face.

Feeling a twinge of guilt for the way his men had rattled her, Luke sought to put her at ease. "Can I get you a drink, ma'am?"

"N-no. No, thank you."

He offered a guarded smile. "Are you sure? You seem like you could use one."

"No," she repeated in a stiff tone that meant, *Absolutely not.*

He raised a brow behind his half mask. But considering all they had to offer was alcohol, he shrugged off her rebuke and decided she was a sensible female, determined to keep her wits about her.

Still. He hated knowing that he was ultimately responsible for terrifying her.

He paused, gazing at her as gently as he could. "You are quite safe now, ma'am. My men will not harm you. You are under my protection this night, and they know what will happen to them if they try."

"What will happen?" she asked faintly.

"I will geld them," he replied.

"Ah." He heard a soft gulp behind the veil, then a halfhearted chuckle, as though she wasn't sure if he was jesting or not.

Luke wasn't sure himself. He only knew that if any of those bastards made her cry, there would be blood.

She cleared her throat a little, finally calming down. "And to think they say there is no honor among thieves."

"A gentleman's honor is all he has, ma'am."

"Is that what you are?" A glimpse of blue eyes flashed at him from behind the black lace. "A gentleman?"

"I like to think so," he said with a smile, leaning back in his chair. "But only when it suits me."

Indeed.

A lineage that dated back to the Norman conquerors helped with that.

Behind her veil, he saw her smile cautiously at him. Ah, good ol' Silversmoke usually got along just fine with the ladies.

"Are you ready to begin now?" Luke asked gently.

She nodded and took a deep breath. "I am here about a missing person. I-I heard you help people who have nowhere else to turn."

"I'm listening."

At last, she launched into her tale. "His name is Joel Clayton. He disappeared over a year ago—last April. Everyone thinks he is dead, but I feel it in my bones that he is still alive."

Luke narrowed his eyes. "Your husband?"

"Oh—er, no, sir. I am not married."

His interest warmed further. "Go on."

"He was my suitor." She spoke slowly, choosing every word with care. "He meant a great deal to me. In fact, I quite expected him to become my husband in due time. But before he ever had the chance to offer for my hand, he disappeared."

Luke nodded encouragement.

"To be honest, I didn't even notice he was gone until a week or so passed. I just figured he was off somewhere...having fun with his friends. Brighton, maybe. But then another week went by and still there was no sign of him—right in the middle of the Season!"

She shook her head. "It wasn't like him. He always wanted to be in the thick of all the action. When I still got no answer to the notes I'd sent, I began to worry. So much so that I sent one of our footmen over to his townhouse to ask his servants when he might be back.

"It was then my worst fears were confirmed. His staff told my footman that they had no idea where he'd gone or what was happening. They were beside themselves with fear. I knew then I had to take action." She leaned forward a bit. "I began visiting Joel's family members to ask if they'd had word, but no one did. Not his mother, though she's sickly and they don't really speak much. Not even his uncle—he was heir to his uncle's earldom, you see."

"Well!" Luke murmured, a little unsettled to realize he was indeed dealing with aristocrats here. *Risky.* She had piqued his interest, however. He knew all too well what it was to wait for agonizing months without word of a loved one's whereabouts. "Do, please, continue."

"By now, everyone was worried. Joel's uncle took control and organized a search with all his friends. For weeks, we hunted for him everywhere, to no avail. So then His Lordship hired a couple of Bow Street Runners to take up the matter, but even they came up short. Oh, Silversmoke," she whispered, "I fear something terrible has happened to him. I am begging you to help if you can."

Luke gazed at her for a long moment, weighing the matter. "I shall have to ask you some uncomfortable questions."

"Of course. I understand. Please—anything."

He drummed his fingers on the table, gathering his thoughts, then stared at her. "Forgive me in advance for this, but is there, er, any chance this fellow could've killed himself?"

She sat there frozen by the question for a moment. "I-I don't think so." She hesitated. "No... Certainly not."

"You don't sound terribly sure."

She hesitated, then a sigh escaped her. "I'm not sure of anything anymore, I suppose." She propped her elbow on the table and leaned her head on her hand.

Luke waited.

She interlocked her fingers. "That is to say, I don't *believe* he would do such a thing. He had no reason to. He had friends, admirers, an earldom waiting for him." She splayed her hands expressively. "Looks, youth, health. Privilege. All the money he could spend."

"Friends, very well. But what about enemies?"

She hesitated.

"Yes?" Luke prompted.

"There was no one in particular that I know of," she said, "but he lived, um, a slightly...dangerous mode of life. At times."

Her reluctant admission instantly raised the alarm in Luke's mind, but he didn't want to scare her, so he kept his manner nonchalant.

"How's that?" He took another swallow of tepid ale.

"Joel was a high-stakes gambler with the devil's own luck. He nearly *always* won. He said he couldn't help it."

When a burst of raucous laughter from the main section of the pub reached them, she jumped.

"Dart game's over," Luke murmured in reassurance. "Continue."

She glanced nervously over her shoulder, twisting her clasped fingers before her, delicate wrists resting on the table. "Because of his habit of winning, he was quite often accused of cheating at cards, which he categorically denied. As a result, he'd been in no less than three duels before we met—which, thankfully, he won.

"Other challenges were made from time to time, but these accusations were retracted with apologies once the men making them sobered up. The ton learned the hard way that Joel Clayton would not tolerate any slights against his honor—or doubts about his honesty.

"Eventually, the other gentlemen in Society realized he was telling the truth—he was no cheater. He was just that good. Very intelligent. He said it had to do with mathematics and reading the other players more than the cards." She shrugged.

"What was his game? Whist? I understand that's the ton's favorite."

"Oh no, he called that an old man's game. He found it dull. He'd play a little macao, but his favorite was a two-man contest called burgundy. Have you heard of it?"

Luke shook his head.

"It's a form of piquet that's very fashionable just now. I find it confusing, myself—there's quite a bit of strategy involved. The young bucks in the clubs bet vast sums of money trying to outdo one another's hands."

"Ah," Luke said. *What a bloody waste of time.*

"Anyway, Joel was very good at it and didn't even mind the game's, er, slightly racy reputation."

"Racy?"

She nodded. He could feel more than see her smile. "I think that actually made it more fun for him."

"Bit of a rascal, eh?"

"A bit." Fondness for this man softened her elegant upper-class accent. "An honorable one, though. It got to the point where he no longer wished to play in Society because he didn't want to take his friends' money anymore. And so, to my dismay, he began visiting low, disreputable gaming hells every now and then—only for excitement, mind you—and he'd beat the players there, instead."

Her tone turned grim. "These were not nice places, Silversmoke, but dangerous establishments frequented by disreputable people. It was bad enough that he'd been in duels! But this?" She shook her head. "I implored him not to take such risks with his safety, but he said…"

"What did he say?"

"That it was none of my damned business." She lowered her head. "He cooled a bit toward me after that. But I do wish he would've listened, because the last time anyone saw him alive, he was playing cards at one of those godforsaken hells."

"Hmm." Luke did not want to dash her hopes, but if *he* were a betting man, he'd wager that her dunderhead beau had crossed the wrong people in some low gaming house and got himself killed.

The lady leaned forward. "Oh, Silversmoke, will you find him for me—or at least find out what happened to him, whether he's dead or alive? If I could just know his fate, it…would give me the strength to face my own."

"*Your* fate?" he asked, wrinkling his brow. "What do you mean?"

She let out a great sigh that stirred the fabric of her veil. "My parents pledged me to another, you see, when it became apparent that Mr. Clayton wasn't coming back."

"And you just went along with it?" he blurted out in surprise.

She bristled, startled and instantly defensive. "It's complicated."

"Right." He stared skeptically at her.

"This match will be of benefit to my family," she informed him.

"Ah, so the new one's rich and powerful, eh?" He could not help feeling cynical.

"Well, yes," she mumbled, squirming in her seat. "Very, as it happens."

"You don't sound too happy about it, though."

"Obviously not. I wanted Joel, but so be it." She waved it off. "It's fine, it doesn't matter. One has to marry someone, after all."

Luke nearly chortled. *Funny, that's what I said.* With about equal enthusiasm for the prospect of marriage.

But his sister had been nagging him for ages to choose a blasted bride, finally resorting to those cruel-but-true words: *Lucas, you owe it to Mother and Father to see to the family line.*

So now he, too, was scheduled to be leg-shackled about a month from now, the last Sunday in June, to some gorgeous highborn social butterfly he barely knew.

Unaware of this, however, his lady visitor had stiffened, mistaking herself for the butt of his laughter. "I'm sorry, does my situation amuse you?"

He could not resist, in defense of all males. "It just seems, I dunno, a bit mercenary that you're going to wed this other poor dunce when your heart belongs to the gambler. Don't you think?"

He could feel her frosty stare from behind her veil. "I daresay you wouldn't understand."

"Because I'm a man?"

"It's different for those of my class," she said primly.

He hid his smile behind another swig of ale. "I'm sorry. You're quite right, milady. I should mind m'place. My only point is, if you don't like this other beggar, then you probably shouldn't marry him at all."

"One does not jilt a duke," she informed him with admirable hauteur.

"Ohh, a duke! Well then," Luke said, hiding his mirth. "Why didn't you say so?"

"Besides, the whole wedding's already planned. You have *no* idea how difficult it is to get an open Sunday at St. Andrew's during the Season. And for your information, it's going to be spectacular," she added, lifting her chin. "All the papers will be covering it. It's sure to be the wedding of the decade."

"Well, at least there's that," he said in a droll tone.

Why did weddings seem to drive women insane? His own bride had written to him numerous times, nagging him about the most trivial details about a thing that would take, what, an hour, at most?

You would think it was the end of the bloody world.

"Anyway," she added begrudgingly after a moment, "it's not that I don't *like* him, per se. I barely know the man. His Grace is much too busy to be bothered with the likes of me." She leaned back and folded her arms across her chest. "I think I bore him," she declared sardonically.

"Not possible," Luke said with playful gallantry, raising his cup to her.

Because, after all, neither of them were married yet...

"What do *you* know?" she shot back, but gave in to his teasing with a snort of humor.

Wholly intrigued by her now, Luke pushed the plate with refreshments toward her, but she held up her hand, declining.

Damn. He had thought that if he could tempt her with a slice of apple, she'd have to lift her veil to eat it, and he'd get to see her face.

He wondered if she was as fair as she was witty. Brave, too, coming here. Loyal to her missing beau, as well, though not, perhaps, to her poor, oblivious fiancé.

As though sensing his gathering male interest, the lady looked away, avoiding his gaze to glance around the inglenook and out the open window, where the moon shone down. It made a silver square upon the flagstone floor.

A cricket hopped onto the windowsill and began to serenade them.

"Your point is well taken, though," she conceded after a moment. "You think I'm being a little unfair to the duke, and I do not deny it. But, to be frank, he doesn't love me either, and I know that. Anyway, it's not as though anyone else wants to marry him, so I might as well."

"What?" Luke scoffed. "Every duke's hunted like a fox wherever he goes by a pack of marriage-minded ladies—so I hear. Poor bleeders."

"Normally, I would agree with you, but not in this case. Believe me."

Luke frowned. "My dear lady, please tell me that your parents haven't pledged you to an ogre, or I shall have to mount a rescue at once."

"Well, thanks, but no," she said in amusement. "At least he's not an ogre."

"Are you sure?"

She had piqued his curiosity now in full force. He searched his memory, wondering who the deuce she was talking about. If only he went to Town more often, he might know...

"What's the defect, then, if nobody wants him?" Luke asked. "Is he old, fat, miserly? Demented? A drunkard?"

She started laughing, mystifying and delighting him. "He is none of those things, though if he were, I'm sure I'd never say so."

"Ah, you are very polite."

"More than you can possibly imagine," she said wryly. "But in all fairness, my parents aren't *forcing* me to marry him, not exactly. This match will make them happy, and, well, one does not wish to end up a spinster, in any case."

"Naturally." Smiling, Luke leaned his jaw atop his fist. She was the most amusing creature, with her splendid tact. "You're worrying me, though," he said. "What's the problem with this chap? Come, you can tell me. Is he awful? Don't worry, your secret's safe with me. Ol' Silversmoke's a vault."

"Why ever would you care?"

He shrugged. "I don't want to go to all the trouble of helping you, only to have to worry for your safety with this ogre of a duke."

"Well, that's very sweet, but trust me, there is nothing to worry about. I could probably thrash poor Lucas myself if I tried."

Wait, what?

Luke went very still.

She sighed. "No, my fiancé isn't cruel or miserly or anything like that. He's just...extremely awkward and, well, rather embarrassing. I mean, His Grace is a highly intelligent man. But I fear excessive study and a scholar's isolation have made him altogether odd."

"Odd—how?" Luke asked in a strangled tone, his heart pounding all of a sudden.

A wave of disbelief had formed somewhere in his belly and began making its way north.

"Well," she confided, leaning closer, "try not to laugh, but His Grace is enchanted with: insects."

Luke was gripping his pewter tankard, but it was fortunate he had not taken a mouthful, or he'd have spewed ale all over the table from sheer astonishment.

But not for the reason she'd assume.

"Insects?" he managed. "No!"

"Yes! Creepy, crawly, horrid little bugs! Can you believe it?"

"Who could like bugs?"

"As I said, he is terribly eccentric." She shrugged. "They say he is a genius, but I have yet to see much evidence of that. For in everyday life, the poor thing is quite hopeless."

Luke snapped his jaw shut.

"His love of science and study leaves him no time for fashionable society—or for me, it would seem. So...yes, entomology. God help me," she said in worldly amusement tinged with despair.

"I-I'm speechless."

It can't be. His brain refused to accept it.

"I was, too, when I first found out!" She laughed wistfully. "Ah well. Gentlemen of means must have their hobbies, I suppose. Some fancy art, some breed horses, some collect snuffboxes—and I assure you, any of those would have been perfectly fine with me. But the duke—my duke, my Lucas—he collects little winged creatures." She dropped her head in a humorous show of shame.

Luke leaned back in his chair, giving a masterful performance, considering he had barely just collected his wits once it sank in who, exactly, was sitting across the table from him.

"Well, damn," said Silversmoke, "I hardly know what to say."

"Quite," she agreed.

"What will you do?"

A cynical note of laughter came from behind her veil. "Marry him and have a typical, polite Society marriage, just like my parents, I should think. Unless…"

He swallowed. "Yes?"

She leaned closer, her blithe veneer vanishing to reveal the desperation just beneath the surface. "Unless *you* can find Joel alive for me. Oh, Silversmoke! That is why I've gone to all this trouble to see you. I fear you are my last hope of ever knowing real love."

Luke held his breath as his dilemma came into startling focus. "I see. So, you want me to bring this chap back to you…*before* the wedding."

"If it's possible, yes. It's probably not, but who knows?"

"Who indeed," he echoed, barely audible.

She folded her hands imploringly. "Will you do it? Will you help me?"

Well, this is a bit of a pickle, i'nt?

Luke was silent for a moment, staring down at the table as he struggled to contain his angry bewilderment. He barely knew what to say.

For he was now fairly certain that he was sitting across from his soon-to-be bride.

Oh, God. This was a disaster. His future duchess was never to have known about Silversmoke! He prayed that he was wrong, though he didn't see how.

Then it dawned on him that a rare opportunity had presented itself here, to question her and find out what *else* the little darling might not have been telling him that a girl's future bridegroom ought to know.

Indeed, this might be his only chance to find out what else his far-too-beautiful fiancée might be hiding.

He lifted his masked gaze to her veiled face. "Tell me everything, and I will consider the matter."

"But I already have," she said, sounding puzzled. "What else do you want to know?"

"First and foremost, just to be clear"—he pinned her in a fierce stare—"am I to understand you're still in love with him? With this *Joel*?"

CHAPTER 3

Hard Questions

*P*ortia pulled back a little, surprised at the question itself, but even more so by the sharp edge that had crept into Silversmoke's voice, the vehemence that now tinged his demeanor.

"In love with him?" she echoed. The question was slightly embarrassing, for she was not the sort of woman to wear her heart on her sleeve.

Ever.

That was not the Tennesley way.

She shrugged. "I don't know. Maybe?"

"Love is not a maybe sort of matter," the highwayman replied, his stare challenging her from behind his mask.

His strange reaction threw her. "I'm sorry, how is that pertinent to you finding him for me?"

"It's not. I just want to know. Humor me," he ordered. "You are asking me to risk my neck for this man, after all." He paused. "I mean, would you consider him the love of your life or what?"

"I don't know!" She blushed behind her veil, baffled by his nosy questions.

Large, broad-shouldered, and brooding across from her, Silversmoke had gone very still. One elbow on the table, he rested his chin on his thumb and obscured his lips with two fingers, waiting implacably for her to elaborate.

At a loss, she saw she had no choice. "I was beginning to think he might be, but then he disappeared!"

"And so you got engaged to someone else."

"My parents set it up!" she cried, becoming defensive and quite confounded by his bizarre line of questioning.

He shrugged. "And you just went along with it?"

"Silversmoke—try to understand." She strove for patience. Blazes, this was difficult, telling him the secrets she preferred to keep close to her heart. "I-I just didn't care what happened to me anymore in the weeks following his disappearance. I don't know if you've ever lost someone who meant a great deal to you, but I was in a deep fog of misery for months after all of our searches failed."

She shook her head. "Depression, I suppose. By the time my mother started matchmaking with the duke's sister, I saw no reason to make some big dramatic stand. What was the point? So, yes, I did just 'go along' with it. I won't apologize for that. My first loyalty is to my family.

"My parents aren't perfect, but I try to be a good daughter. They've been through a lot, and this match made them happy, and he wasn't odious, so, yes, I acquiesced," she said angrily. "Besides, marriages among those of my class are about bloodlines and useful alliances. It doesn't really matter how we feel about each other in the least..."

Luke stared at her as her words trailed off. It seemed she had not quite convinced herself, either.

Though she had not uttered one word that came as news to him, all the same, he didn't like it.

He did not like this one bit.

He felt offended, territorial, and damned if he wasn't just a wee bit jealous of this stupid bloody gambler who'd won the heart of a woman like *the* Portia Tennesley, then gone off like an idiot and got himself killed.

Luke had half a mind to decline her request.

On the other hand, he could see how much it meant to her. And there was such a thing as honor, hang it all.

Honor...

Suddenly, an alarming question bloomed in his mind. It appalled him, but he knew this was his only chance to ask, beautiful as she was. His pulse jumped.

He tried to hold himself back, aware that to ask such a question would be altogether sneaky; besides which, he wasn't sure he really wanted to know the answer. But he had to. He needed to know what he was getting into with this woman he was a month away from marrying.

"Were you lovers?" he asked bluntly.

"*What?*"

"You heard me. Did you sleep with him?"

"God, no! What do you take me for?" She recoiled with ladylike ire at the suggestion. "I'm sorry—how is this relevant?"

"Come, we are both adults here," he said. "I'm not judging you." Actually, he was. "It would be understandable. You thought you were going to marry this man. Of course, he hadn't asked you yet, but... Well?"

A huff of embarrassment fluffed her veil. "My parents raised me better than that," she said with cold disdain. "However...since you insist on being nosy, I will admit to kissing him. Twice. So there."

"Oh really? And?" He stared at her until she squirmed.

"What on earth does this have to do with anything?" she cried. "It's really quite beyond the pale!"

"It's pertinent," he lied. "Come, you want me to believe that this high-stakes gambling-hell thrill-seeker was content with mere kissing? I'm not a fool, ma'am."

"Very well!" She harrumphed, leaned back against her seat, and folded her arms across her chest, mirroring his pose. "Fine. I'll tell you. Yes, he wanted more, but I would not allow it. Honestly! I am not some harlot, thank you very much."

"Ah." Lucky for her, he believed her.

Mentally, he grumbled over it, but he supposed he could live with a couple of kisses. *Still,* he thought, *this fop doesn't sound all that honorable to me.*

"Are you going to help me or not?" she demanded, no doubt red-cheeked beneath that irksome veil. She snatched her reticule off the bench. "If it's a question of money, I can pay—"

"Don't be absurd. I don't take ladies' gold. If you really want my help, there's only one thing I require."

"And what is that?"

"Take off your veil," he said. "I want to see your face." Luke knew he was pushing his luck, but he needed to confirm his theory about her.

Seeing was believing.

Her posture turned wary; she shrank back a bit in her seat. "Why?"

He arched a brow. "Madam, if you are suggesting ungallant motives on my part, you are mistaken. Because I, for one, unlike your gambler, actually do know how to be a gentleman."

"Ohh, well, pardon me! I must've become confused on that point by the fact that you are, technically, a criminal!"

Luke narrowed his eyes, perversely amused at her defiance in spite of himself. How different she seemed here tonight, with him, than she was in her glittering Society ballrooms, always surrounded by friends and admirers, and dressed in the first stare.

Basically, the opposite of him.

Anyway, Luke knew he had brought her cheeky sarcasm on himself with his impertinent questions. But he could not deny that he was enjoying sparring with her. The chit was made of far sterner stuff than he'd had any idea.

"Criminal, my dear?" he drawled, feigning a wince. "Such an ugly word. I prefer liberator of other men's gold. Or even that fine old term, knight of the moonlit highway."

She scoffed at him—charmingly.

Luke quirked a smile. "For your information, I meant nothing improper. I merely want to look you in the eye and determine for myself whether I can trust you. For all I know, you could've been sent here by one of my enemies, or this could be a trap meant to send me to the gallows."

"Oh." She paused. "I hadn't thought of that." Then she tilted her head. "If I lift my veil, will you take off your mask?"

Lord, she amazed him! Of all the scores of people who'd crept in here, hat in hand, begging his help, none of them had ever dared demand such a thing of him.

Clearly, this girl was born to be a duchess.

"No," he answered with a patient smile.

"Why not? Are you hideous under there?"

"Very," he said dryly.

"Oh, come on," she coaxed in a satiny murmur, rousing his blood.

"Why should I? No," Luke retorted. "I'm the one being asked to risk my neck for this bounder; it's only fair that I should get to see the person doing the asking. How else am I to trust you?"

She tapped her nails on the table for a second, as though this were a card game here between the two of them, and she was debating her next move. "Very well. I see your point. Fair enough."

With that, she laid hold of her veil's hem and lifted the fragile black cloth back from her face, revealing an arch smile. "Voila."

Luke went very still, hiding his reaction to the sight of that exquisite face.

The confirmation of his suspicions could have knocked the wind out of him, but he absorbed the blow without moving a muscle.

He was not sure he even breathed. Incredulity sang in his blood. And awe at her classic beauty.

But, as always, he refused to show how her golden loveliness bowled him over. He already knew that Liddicoat's beautiful youngest daughter could've had her pick of men with so fair a face, and he did not want it going to her head.

Truly, though, the girl was a prize worthy of the Fountainhurst line.

His gaze traveled hungrily over that smooth brow, that soft, milky skin. Arctic blue eyes. The fine bone structure. Those lips, like tender pink rose petals.

He wanted her more than he ought to. It was the main reason he'd agreed to the match.

He caught a glimpse of her smooth flaxen tresses pulled back from her face. She must have tied it in some sort of bun, but her widow's veil, folded back now, covered the rest of her shining hair.

She looked at him matter-of-factly. "Satisfied?"

God, no. He would not begin to feel satisfied until he claimed her on their wedding night. Luke blinked out of his daze. "Yes," he said coolly. "Thank you for cooperating, ma'am."

"Of course. Once you explained it, I suppose it's only fair." She shrugged. "Well? Do you have any more questions for me?" she asked, evenly holding his gaze without replacing the veil.

Oh, he had a thousand of them, suddenly.

They darted every which way through his mind like a school of fish wildly scattering when someone threw a stone into a pool. His heart was thumping.

Bloody hell.

He must have been blind not to have recognized weeks ago how intelligent she was. All he would've had to do was look, really look at her.

But he'd refused.

Refused to see her for who she truly was. Refused to let himself fall, to let himself feel.

Refused anything that might ever make him truly happy.

Because that would only give him something new to lose, and he couldn't go through that again. He had nearly lost himself to the darkness once before. If he risked it again and life dealt him another cruel blow, the darkness would surely swallow him.

It was easier just to stay numb behind his wall of solidified anger.

She frowned at his silence. "Are you going to help me or not, Silversmoke?"

Watching her, Luke slowly took a drink. He wanted to turn her away.

The last thing he wanted to do was to find her missing jackass and then lose his bride to the gambler.

But refusing that face, those eyes, was beyond him.

What if it had been his mother out there somewhere, pleading for help from some stranger, only to be turned away?

"Very well. You've piqued my interest," he said coolly. "I will find him for you. Dead or alive. At least, I'll do my best." He nodded to her before he changed his mind. "You have my word."

She lit up like Easter morning, sucking in a breath. "Oh, truly? You'll do it?" Her hand flew up to her heart.

He masked his pleasure at her gratitude with a cynical snort. "Well, I could hardly risk the papers saying Silversmoke turned down a damsel in distress, now, could I? One has a reputation to maintain."

She was positively beaming. "Oh, thank you, Silversmoke—whoever you are. I mean it. I am in your debt. If there's anything I can ever do to repay you, just say the word. Remember, I shall soon become the wife of a very powerful man."

You most certainly shall.

"If you ever find yourself in a scrape where influence or patronage could save you—"

"Eh, never mind that," he said. "You owe me nothing."

"Really?" She fell silent, studying him. "You're just that kindhearted?"

"What can I say," he drawled. "I have a soft spot when it comes to true love."

"Is that so?" She tilted her head as her pale blue eyes turned inquisitive. They sparkled with mischief, and Luke was enchanted. "Goodness, Silversmoke, do *you* have a true love? Say it isn't so! Half of female London will be crushed."

"God, no. Love is something I admire from a safe distance, ma'am—like a painting or a statue. One a blackguard like me can't afford."

"Whatever do you mean? Love doesn't cost anything."

"Are you mad? Love costs everything," he said. "Me, I don't need the headache."

"I see," she said in amusement. "So, you rob coaches for a living, and yet you consider love to be the dangerous thing?"

"I rob coaches for fun, and from what I can tell, love is more dangerous than you comin' into this pub."

She arched a brow. "You are a strange man."

He couldn't help smiling. "Not as strange as your fiancé, I hope?"

She chuckled. "Oh, no one could be as strange as my poor Lucas."

They gazed at each other, sharing the jest.

If only she knew.

Luke dropped his gaze, veiling his roiled emotions behind his mask. "Very well. I still need the rest of your gambling friend's details. Full name, address, and so on. Highborn chap, I assume?"

"Yes, the Honorable Joel Clayton. He's the heir of the Axewood earldom. His uncle has no sons."

"And what was the name of that gambling hell where he was last seen?"

"The Blue Room. In Covent Garden. He was last seen there on the twentieth of April, last year." Her manner turning businesslike, she reached for her reticule and opened it. "I brought a picture of him to show you. I thought it would help you to see who you're looking for."

"Good. Yes, that's very good," he said in approval as she shoved her hand into her reticule and pulled out a small oval cameo wrapped in a piece of paper with writing on it.

She handed him the miniature portrait, and he took it, masking his cynicism about the chap as he studied it.

The tiny painting showed a dark-haired dandy with bluish eyes and a perfect cravat. He appeared to be a few years younger than Luke, maybe twenty-six or so. "Handsome fellow."

She nodded, and the little lovelorn sigh that she let out quite impaled him with a flaming arrow of pure, savage jealousy.

It came out of nowhere and startled him entirely.

Doing his best to ignore it, he turned his attention to the piece of paper she'd had wrapped around the picture. He nodded at it as she started to tuck it back into her bag. "What's that?"

"Oh—it's just a sweet little note that Joel sent me once."

"May I see it?" Luke put out his hand.

She hesitated, blushing slightly, then surrendered it. He unfolded it and read the few lines. *Smarmy bastard. Can't even spell.* What sort of idiot thought there were two Ms in *tomorrow*?

Then he reached the best part and sent her a mischievous glance. *"Buttercup?"*

At least she had the decency to look embarrassed. "That's what he called me sometimes."

"I see." Luke barely managed to hide his mirth.

"What?" she demanded.

"You don't much strike me as a Buttercup, is all."

"Well, you don't really know me, do you?" she said archly. "I might be very Buttercup-like, for all you know."

"I'm seeing more of a wild, climbing rose."

She gasped with half-offended humor. "Are you accusing me of social climbing, sir?"

"Well, you *are* marrying a man you don't love just for his blasted title."

"So?" she retorted. "Everybody does it, and he doesn't love me either, so who cares!"

"Sorry," Luke mumbled. It seemed he'd touched a sore spot.

She must've realized in hindsight that he was only teasing, and that she'd overreacted a bit. She heaved a sigh, and Luke ventured a rueful glance across the table at her.

"I'm sorry," she mumbled, waving off a mosquito that had flown in the window and was trying to get a wee bite of her.

Much as he would've liked to do.

"I don't mean to snap at you, truly. It's just...hard."

"What is?"

Her eyes glazed over with a faraway look. "This past Sunday, I had to sit there at yet *another* friend's wedding, and watch my dear Maggie, this time, walking down the aisle to wed her true love. It was so beautiful. She looked like an angel, she adores Connor, and he adores her. At Christmas, it was my best friend, Serena—same thing. And before that, Felicity married Jason, and before that, it was Trinny marrying Gable— well, those two eloped. But they're all so perfectly matched and so happy together, and now my wedding's next, but for me, it might as well be the

Great and Terrible Day of the Lord's Returning."

"The apocalypse?" he exclaimed.

She shrugged, innocently nodding. "Yes. Because, unlike my friends, I won't be marrying someone I love. That's why I am so desperate for answers, you see. The man I *thought* I was falling in love with is likely dead or"—she stopped herself—"or something else. That's why I need so badly to know."

"So you can resign yourself to your doom?" he said slowly.

"Well, doom's a strong word. But yes. More or less."

"Huh." Ol' Silversmoke was now officially reeling.

He lowered his head and tried to gather his thoughts, then cleared his throat. "Well," he said, "I think I'd better keep these items for now. I might need them. The picture and the note, if you don't mind."

A crestfallen look dropped over her beautiful face. "Even the note?"

"Handwriting sample." He shrugged. "You never know."

"Very well. If it helps in your quest. But I *will* get them back?"

"Of course." He lifted his gaze to meet hers. "Are you sure you'll want them back? If you need, as you said, to close this chapter of your life so you can move on and try to be happy in time with the duke, a picture and a love note from a past beau might only serve as painful reminders—"

"No! I need them." She shook her head, looking alarmed. "Tokens of remembrance."

Damn, she really was not ready to let this fellow go. Luke felt his own mood turn increasingly grim. "Very well."

"Will you keep me apprised of your progress?"

He nodded absently, assessing her. "I must say, you are very loyal coming here, risking your safety for a chap who might well have been a bounder. You do realize that, don't you? I don't wish to make this any worse for you, my lady, but if no body was ever found, it is not outside the realm of possibility that he's alive somewhere. That he walked away from his whole life—people do that sometimes for any number of reasons. The possibility's remote, but it must be said: he might've abandoned you."

Brutal truth, he knew, but by now he had seen she had the spine for it.

"There might've been gaming debts you didn't know about he needed to escape from. That famous dandy, Beau Brummel or whatever his name was—he had to flee to France just last year on account of the same, I heard. People do run away to escape their creditors sometimes."

"But that doesn't make any sense in his case." She shook her head. "Joel won all the time. If he had one bad night, he could make up for it within a few weeks. Even if he'd fallen into dun territory, he could always ask his uncle for help. Lord Axewood is a very rich man."

Axewood. The name sounded vaguely familiar. *Father might've known him.* Luke couldn't remember for sure.

"But yes," she conceded, "I take your meaning. You're trying to warn me about him, just in case what you learn is unpleasant. You want me to brace for the worst, and I appreciate it, I do. But whatever the answer is, it's all right."

"What if it turns out that he ran off with another woman?" He did his best to ask the harsh question gently. "I trust you have considered this possibility."

"Oh yes." With a pained look, she lowered her gaze and toyed with the handle of her reticule. "Extensively. I wouldn't like that, obviously. But the truth is, I'm here for my own sake as much as Joel's."

"In what way?" he asked softly.

"I should hate to find out I could be *that* poor a judge of character. I don't think I am. Usually, I have a good sense about people..." She paused. "Obviously, I pray that Joel is alive and well somewhere, that no one has harmed him. Yet if he is, how could the man I cared about walk away from me without a word?" Her pale blue eyes could have pierced through him with their intensity. "There was no one that I know of. I should think I would've heard. Mother follows all the gossip in Society." She looked away. "Of course, gentlemen of means do sometimes keep mistresses, I'm told. But even if he'd had...*dealings* of this sort, I hardly think a future earl would throw me over for such a creature."

She looked at Luke imploringly.

"But perhaps I was deceived entirely about him. Could he have been so cruel and I didn't see it—that he wouldn't even tell me he was leaving? Could I have been worth so little to him? I don't know." She lowered her head. "It shakes one's faith in oneself."

Finally, Luke understood. The girl did not know for certain if she had been bereaved or abandoned. He could see how such unanswered questions could fray a person's nerves. Especially someone with a mind as lively as hers.

"You do deserve answers," he murmured, and meant it. "And I'll find them for you if I can. I have only one question."

"Yes?" she asked.

"If you even *suspect* that he was capable of doing that to you, why waste your tears? I admit, I am mystified. I should think most women would curse him and gladly marry the duke. Yet here you are."

A tender smile tugged at the corner of her lips. "Love forgives, does it not? Love is patient. That's what they say at all those weddings I attend. Love doesn't jump to conclusions. It doesn't cast judgment; it tries to understand. That's all I want. To understand."

Luke could barely believe what he was hearing. Her words cast a spell on him, but she might as well have been speaking in Swahili.

"Besides," she continued, "if Joel's alive and he left me by his own volition, then at least I can ask him what I did wrong. In what way I wasn't enough…"

She bit her lip, and for a moment, a bright sheen of tears jumped into her eyes, but she blinked them away with a smile, and Luke's heart went out to her.

"My dear lady," he said gently, "are you sure you have ever even *seen* real love? Up close, I mean."

She paled, looking upset at the question. Her voice faded to a whisper. "Why do you ask me that?"

He stared at her. "Because no man who really loved you would ever make you feel that way. Ever make you doubt your own worth. That much I know."

The tears returned, more thickly now. She held his gaze, and Luke could not look away.

"What does a highwayman know of love?" she forced out, trying to sound worldly, but her gaze was locked on his in desperation.

He shook his head reverently. "I learned it from my parents. They shared a love rarely seen on this godforsaken earth. 'Twas…a sort of miracle to behold."

A miracle that he refused to let himself have, precisely because their love had been torn away from them too soon, along with their lives.

Refusing to let himself have that was his lone, bitter protest born of rage at the injustice of their fates.

Besides, how could he dare to seize such a holy and sacred thing after all his sins, all the pain he'd meted out to bad people? How could he even think of it?

It would be like claiming the Holy Grail for his drinking cup at some low alehouse. No, he was supremely unworthy to own such an artifact.

His sister pooh-poohed his resistance, not realizing how deep the wound still went in him, or how far into dark territory he'd strayed.

Tavi was fond of telling him, *"Luke, you will never be happy if you don't let someone love you."*

To which, his standard reply was: *"Octavia, I am perfectly happy. Now leave me the hell alone."*

Lost in his brooding, Luke had drifted off from his visitor momentarily.

Her tears had vanished as she shook her head.

"You're right," she admitted. "I've only seen that kind of love from a distance, my friends' marriages. But I was hoping that someday, I, too, might... Well, never mind." She dropped her gaze, but her brow had furrowed with determination as she laid hold of her usual poise.

Luke felt hollow inside. God, he wished she'd never come here. That he'd never heard her say that...

"It's foolish to want what one cannot have." She lifted her head with a forced smile. "That way lies misery. Life is life and you live with it. That's what I learned from *my* parents."

Luke barely knew what to say. Hearing such things, he just wanted to give her a hug, the good little soldier, taking on a loveless match for the good of her family.

But alas, fierce highwaymen didn't go around hugging their visitors.

Instead, he reached for his tankard and somehow kept his tone even. "You are a very interesting woman, Lady Portia Tennesley."

"Thank you...I think." Then she suddenly tilted her head. "Wait— you know my name?"

"I saw it on the letter," he lied, gesturing at Joel's love note.

"Oh—right. Of course."

"Anything else I ought to know?"

She shrugged. "That's all I can think of."

"Very well. If anything more comes to mind, you know how to reach me."

"Through Mr. Townsend?"

"Yes. It was clever of you to seek him out," he added, relieved when she looked mischievous again. Her sorrow, that glimpse of her loneliness, made him feel terrible.

Not only because it mirrored his own. But because he was the reason this fine woman would have a loveless future.

"I had a feeling our journalist friend might've had direct

communication with you somehow," she said with a smile. "He seems to know all your stories before any of the other writers do."

Luke managed to smile back. "We send the tales of our latest exploits to him, and in turn, he knows how to get messages to me. But for his safety's sake, please, Lady Portia, do not make our link widely known. I have enemies, and I wouldn't want them harming the little fellow as a way to find me. For that matter, be sure and tell your servants that this meeting never happened, yes?"

"I understand. Don't worry; they can be trusted. But yes," she said with a firm nod, "I will do it."

"Good. Then I shall bid you goodnight. Do not linger on your way back to Town. There are dangerous men in the area, I'm told." He gave her back the domino.

She took it from him, and Luke's blood leaped at the slight touch of their hands.

The zing of sheer magic took him off guard. He glanced quickly at her, wondering if she'd felt it, too.

If so, the cool patrician belle gave no sign as she rose from her seat. "Thank you for doing this."

Luke nodded and stood up as well. "I'll send word when I have news."

"Good luck. You know..." After taking a step toward the curtain, she paused, turning to him. "You really are everything the newspapers say. Possibly more." She gave him a speculative half-smile that must have stopped hearts in the ballroom. "I didn't think you'd actually live up to the legend, but I daresay you do."

His mind went blank at her compliment.

He knew Silversmoke should say something cocky, but much of that swagger was part of the mask; Luke's inward reaction to such praise from this beauty was closer to that of his other persona, Lucas the bumbling, eccentric duke.

The bold highwayman just stood there for a second floundering like a quiz.

She arched a brow at him. Thankfully, he recovered, flashing a wide, roguish grin.

"Nah, milady, you just have me on m'best behavior. It's not every day a future duchess calls on the likes of us here, to be sure. For that matter, don't come back here again, you mark me? This is no place for a lady. Next time, I'll come to you."

"I'd appreciate that. I live in Moonlight Square—"

"Yes, I know. I saw your address on the love note. I'll send word, and we'll meet someplace more suitable next time."

"I shall be looking forward to that," she said softly.

Luke stared at her, stunned. *Is she flirting with me?*

He wasn't sure. The one thing he knew was that he would be looking forward to their next meeting, too—with extreme anticipation.

With that, he stepped to the edge of the booth and pulled back the curtain.

"Clear a path!" he bellowed at his men. "And be polite this time! Or else." Then he turned back to her. "Off you go."

Still concealed from his men behind the oak partition, she gave Luke one last smile before lowering the veil over her face again.

That sweet look of trust, of faith in him against all odds, imprinted itself somewhere deep down in his heart.

"Farewell," she whispered.

He bowed his head. "Until we meet again, Lady Portia."

Then she stepped past him. He stood at the ready, making sure no one bothered her as she strode across the pub. The men were silent, respectful this time. Gower got the door for her, then she hurried out into the night.

Once she was gone, only then did Luke step back into the inglenook.

Letting out a long exhalation, he sank down into the booth in lingering shock. Gower rejoined him shortly thereafter, frowning as soon as he saw him.

"What the hell's wrong with you?"

Luke stared into space. "Gower, I think I've got a problem."

"Why? What happened?" The old fighter glanced out the window as her coach rumbled past it, circling the pub. "Who the hell was that, anyway?"

Luke looked up at him, still dazed. "*That* was my fiancée."

Meanwhile, many miles away, Joel Clayton floated on a laudanum sea of regret, watching the stone-block ceiling of his dungeon cell billow and wave weightlessly above where he lay inert on his dirty cot.

Beyond the iron bars over his lone window, the moon gleamed like an ill-gotten coin in the black sky, and he could hear the breeze haunting the wooded valley below like a gathering of ghosts.

But though the night was fair and his crutch leaned within easy reach, he no longer bothered getting up and limping over to the window to scream down into the valley for help.

Help wasn't coming. He knew that now beyond doubt, beyond any further hope. He was alone.

And, as of his botched escape attempt two weeks ago, now he was crippled, too.

The pain from his shattered foot radiated upward through his entire body. The opiate they doled out to him twice a day at least made it bearable, but he wished he had never tried to run away.

If only...so many things. Aye, he should make those two little words his bloody middle name.

If only he had not lived for twenty-seven years as an arrogant, hedonistic jackass. If only he had not blinded himself to the treachery around him.

If only, most of all, he'd been mature enough to recognize the treasure he'd possessed before it was too late.

Portia. Funny how things became so obvious in hindsight.

If only he had not let fury overtake him when he'd finally found out about her engagement to some duke. But he'd panicked.

For the hope of being reunited with her somehow, someday, had been the only thing keeping him going, just as the threat against her — that something might happen to her if he didn't cooperate — had forced him into compliance.

Having long since realized how he'd taken her for granted, Joel had sworn to himself that if he ever saw his sweet Buttercup again, he would fall to his knees and beg her to give him another chance.

But then, two weeks ago, there it was: a mention in a very out-of-date London paper (one of the rare rewards he received on occasion for being a cooperative prisoner), advising the ton that Lady Portia's wedding to the Duke of Fountainhurst had been rescheduled for the end of June.

The revelation that the girl he'd eventually meant to marry was about to slip through his hands for good had pushed him over the edge.

And so, two weeks ago, at last month's Carnevale, he had tried, foolishly, to escape. He still shuddered at the memory of being captured and punished.

Until that moment, he had never dreamed that ol' Captain Hatchet was capable of such barbaric violence.

"Your ballroom days are over, my lad," he had snarled. Then he'd ordered some men to hold him down and, ignoring Joel's pleading, had personally smashed his foot with one of the wooden mallets they used to hammer the tent pegs into the ground.

The last thing Joel remembered from that night was the bloodcurdling scream that had torn from his own lips and the echo of jeering laughter from the ruffians standing around before he'd passed out in a blinding wave of agony.

And now here he was.

Forever, it seemed. A prisoner, a slave. Ruined, maimed. Forgotten by the world. Even his own mother would've given him up for dead by now, surely. And Portia, beautiful Portia, his reason for holding on, had snared herself a duke.

All things considered, it was safe to say that the mad son of a bitch had finally broken him.

At that moment, Joel tensed, hearing the heavy wooden door at the top of the dungeon stairs creak open. He sat up slowly and did his best to clear his head, reaching for his crutch. He gripped it like a weapon.

In the next moment, his jailer came tromping down the dim stone stairs, looking like he'd just emerged from the mists of time, or stepped out of that barbaric era centuries ago when this castle had been built.

A day of warlords and Viking raiders, and nasty modes of death.

Joel bristled as the brute approached, right on schedule, to collect the tray of what they dared to call food.

Captain Hatchet's mighty henchman was a towering wall of muscle, with a shaved head sporting a serpentine dragon tattoo along one side. God knew why.

His fashion choices were just as regrettable: big, ugly boots that laced up the front. Rough woolen breeches that would've given any gentleman a rash. A brown leather vest quaintly medieval in its cut, worn, as always, over a loose, sweaty shirt with stains whose origins Joel did not care to ponder. Nor had the creature ever heard of a neck-cloth. Instead, the world was treated to a view of his ruddy throat and dark chest hairs poking out of the top of his shirt like the bristles of a boar.

His name was Rucker, but Joel had amused himself for the past year making up nicknames for him, like Attila or the Troll.

Unfortunately, Rucker took these titles as compliments, so there was no point, but that hadn't stopped Joel from baiting him. God knew there was nothing else to do, nobody else to talk to.

Besides, Joel conceded as Rucker stalked toward his cell, the brute was not without his own primitive form of wit. Sometimes they had even bantered, enjoying mocking each other through the bars.

Of course, there had been none of that since last month's disastrous Carnevale.

Joel's failed escape attempt and the savagery that followed had changed everything. Rucker knew it as well as he did.

Arriving outside his cell, the ogre bent down to lift Joel's tray off the flagstone floor, but paused when he saw it. "You didn't eat your gruel."

"Obviously not. I wouldn't give such vomitous fare to a dog," Joel said in a deadened tone.

Rucker straightened up slowly and studied him through narrowed eyes. "Well, you'd better eat it if you want your next dose of laudanum."

"Now hold on—"

"Eat!" The giant kicked the tray toward him with the toe of his boot. "You're wastin' away to nothing, ye wee skinny bastard. I don't want His Lordship thinkin' I've forgotten to feed you. You need to eat."

"I can't. Just give me the medicine," Joel said in a taut voice. "I'm ill with pain, and that bowl of shite is even more disgusting now that it's cold."

Rucker stared at him for a long moment.

Joel got the feeling that, as his daily caretaker, even Rucker had been taken aback by his employer's act of rage, though, of course, he hadn't lifted a finger to stop him.

He shook his shaved head. "You brought this on yourself, you know. This all could've been avoided if you'd lent him the money when he asked you nicely. You can't expect a man like His Lordship to let a little pisspot like you mock him to his face and do nothing about it."

Joel flinched, but let out a cynical laugh. "You can both go to hell."

Rucker scowled at him by the light of the single lantern in Joel's cell. "Fine, suit yourself, then. Starve to death for all I care. But you'll need your strength if those bones are goin' to heal. So bang the cup on the bars when your plate's clean, *then* you can have the laudanum." He pivoted and started to stomp out.

"Rucker, wait!"

"What?" The brute turned around impatiently.

Joel stared at him in misery through the bars. "Why don't you just kill me and be done with it?"

"Oh, believe me, young master, nothin' would please me more," Rucker said sarcastically, half in jest. "But it's like His Lordship says: you don't kill the golden goose. Now shut up and eat your food. Bone-appeteet," Rucker added with a rude wink before clomping out again.

Joel closed his eyes with welling despair and wanted to die. *I'm never getting out of here.*

But no. In truth, there was still one way left for him to outsmart his captors, if he dared.

One final act of defiance that could still win him the last laugh, if nothing else.

Next time, the golden goose could lose.

CHAPTER 4

His Grace Goes a-Courting

The next morning, Luke started the day as usual, training against Gower at his sprawling country estate of Gracewell, six miles north of Hampstead Heath.

The neo-gothic castle, neatly landscaped and recently equipped with all the latest modern conveniences, was not the largest of his holdings. But it was the closest to London, and therefore convenient for his Silversmoke pursuits, as well as his occasional Parliamentary duties.

Indeed, these were the only two things that could drag him to Town, for the most part. The crowds in London annoyed him.

In any case, the heat and humidity from yesterday had clung on into the morning, so he had doffed his shirt some time ago and could feel the sweat trickling down his bare back as he parried Gower's brutal blows with the quarterstaff.

All the tall, arched windows were open, and the picturesque pond visible beyond them looked inviting, beckoning Luke out for a swim.

Maybe afterward, he thought. For now, there was no sign of a breeze as the loud clacking of their fighting sticks and the fast, heavy pounding of their footwork rebounded off the walls.

Gower swung the staff at him from the right, coming in for a mighty whack, but Luke ducked and struck back with controlled force. Gower grunted and pressed his attack, and on it went.

The gymnasium was a large, rectangular room originally built by one of Luke's ancestors as a lavish indoor tennis court. In more recent centuries, it had served as a ballroom.

It had parquetry floors, high ceilings, and a huge fireplace, over which hung a nearly life-sized portrait of his parents in a gilded frame. Luke had placed it there as a constant reminder of why he did what he did.

Any time the training grew too grueling, or he injured himself doing too much of one thing or another, all he had to do was look over the mantel to remember why he pushed himself so hard.

He hadn't been able to save them, but there were other people out there he could still help. Those who had no one else to fight for them, no one else who'd even care.

Knowing that was the only thing that had kept Luke from being swallowed up by the darkness that he had made his mortal enemy.

When he'd had this space converted into a gymnasium and training studio for his purposes, he had spared no expense, outfitting it with every piece of weaponry and equipment to be found at the best boxing and fencing studios in London. From the rubber mats on the wooden floor, to the mirrors allowing him to mind his form; from the iron dumbbell sets to the targets for knife-throwing practice affixed to the four marble columns near the corners of the room; from the racks of swords, sabers, cutlasses, clubs, pole-arms, daggers, and, of course, the trusty old quarterstaffs, to the long, zigzag balance beam — atop which he now vaulted, moving the practice fight aloft.

Gower followed nimbly. Gray-haired he might be, but the wiry fifty-seven-year-old shed any trace of age when he became engaged in a match.

Aches and pains were for later, and bloody hell, the Yorkshireman was still fast. He kept Luke on his toes.

Gower had honed his milling-match skills in the Navy long ago, but it was his shrewd watchfulness as a fighter that made him so effective.

Nothing got past him; nothing surprised him. Truth be told, Gower was starting to get the better of Luke today, despite being nearly twice his age. But hell, Luke had already lifted weights for an hour before they'd started this, and was admittedly distracted.

He couldn't stop thinking about the alluring lady in black and what she had asked of "Silversmoke" last night.

Thud!

Suddenly, Luke's head snapped back as Gower punched him in the jaw.

"Ahh!" Waving his arms, Luke lost his balance and had to leap off the balance beam to keep from falling. He landed with a self-disgusted laugh.

"Dammit." He tossed his quarterstaff aside and rubbed his jaw, panting. "You're a mean old bastard, you know that?"

Gower snickered and landed lightly on the mat beside him. "You give up, boy?"

"Yeah, yeah, you won today."

Gower poked him in the shoulder with his quarterstaff as Luke walked away. "'Cause you're not payin' attention."

"Well, how could he?" exclaimed the third person in the room, who had been taking care to keep out of the way all this time. Oliver Finch served as Luke's archivist here at the castle and was, in fact, the real-life model for his, er, unusual Lucas persona.

The ginger-haired young scholar watching their practice had never met an insect that did not genuinely fascinate him. Finch was startlingly bright, though, and could memorize a page he'd read by glancing at it once.

Although he was prone to producing bizarre inventions — sometimes useful, usually not — the freckled twenty-six-year-old was diligent in his duties of keeping Luke's various collections in tidy, well-cataloged order.

This included the thousands of books and archived newspapers in Luke's library, but also maintaining careful records on his collection of antique weapons, many of which were displayed on the walls of the gymnasium.

Fortunately, his post left him plenty of time for conducting his own quizzical research, for, indeed, Finch was the real scientific gentleman here.

Luke had hired him straight out of Cambridge, impressed by the younger man's wits and amused by his cheerful eccentricity. Finch was as garrulous and whimsical as Gower was taciturn and fierce. It also helped that he'd had a bit of medical training in his varied scientific background.

The three of them made a fairly good team. Luke chose the cases, led the way; Finch did the research, patching them up when they needed it; and Gower assisted Silversmoke in breaking heads when the occasion called, and keeping the rest of the gang in line.

"Honestly, it's extraordinary when you think about it!" Spectacles resting on top of his head, Finch hopped off the heavy table where he had been perched and tossed Luke a towel.

Luke caught it and blotted his face, while Gower went over to the table and took a swig of the waiting lemonade.

"What the hell's he talkin' about?" the old fighter mumbled.

"Lady Portia, of course!" Finch could hardly contain his excitement over what Luke had reported regarding last night.

He hooked his thumbs into his suspenders, for he had not bothered with a waistcoat in the heat. Instead, he only wore a loose white shirt, and his favorite red suspenders holding up his tan trousers.

They were not very formal here at Gracewell; indeed, the master of the house was naked from the waist up at the moment. Luke wiped the sweat off his brow.

"You're telling me that your future duchess hired you to find her lost beau?" Finch exclaimed. "That's the maddest thing I ever heard!"

"That's my life," Luke said with a sigh.

Finch shook his head. "Females...! Are they not the most confounding creatures on the Earth?" He rubbed the back of his neck, as he always did when he was pondering things. "I say, Your Grace. Did you know about this suitor of hers before you became engaged to the young lady?"

"No, I did not. I assumed she'd have plenty of admirers, beauty that she is, but I certainly didn't know about *him*."

Finch squinted at him. "So what are you going to do?"

Luke sighed and lifted his right hand to his left shoulder, squeezing a sore muscle there. "Find him, I guess."

"Oh, but you mustn't, sir!"

"Why?"

"What if she picks him over you? Well, not *you*. Over...Lucas. Believe me, she will, if you based him on me."

Gower snorted and went to put his quarterstaff away.

Luke smiled at the younger man's artless humility. "Nonsense. Any girl would be pleased to have you, Finch. Besides, I gave her my word." Then he tossed the towel over his shoulder, went to the table, and poured himself a glass of lemonade. "Anyway, the question is what are *we* going to do. That's why I wanted you in here today, too, Finch."

"Right. What shall I do?" Oliver lowered his glasses off his head onto his nose and began rolling up his sleeves.

"I need you to start reviewing newspaper entries regarding Joel Clayton's disappearance. Start with April of last year and scour them for anything you can find regarding the man himself, or murders or other crimes tied to gambling houses. Also, anything about missing persons. Contact Townsend if you think he can be of help. But, as always, be discreet."

Finch nodded.

"Gower, you meet me tonight at Charing Cross. Let's say eleven."

Gower nodded. He knew to avoid coming to Luke's residence in Moonlight Square unless it was an emergency, lest anyone recognize him as Silversmoke's right-hand man, and thus tie the duke to the highwayman.

Instead, Gower lived here at Gracewell, as did Oliver. While the scholar had rooms inside the castle, Gower's private quarters were above the stable, where Tempo was housed among the dozens of horses on the estate.

Gower raised a brow regarding the night's venture. "What's the plan?"

"We'll visit that gambling hell that Lady Portia mentioned—The Blue Room."

Gower nodded. "What'll you be doin' in the meanwhile?"

"I am going to London." Luke gave them a wry look. "I daresay it's time that His Grace paid his fair betrothed a proper courting call."

"Oho!" Gower said.

They laughed.

"Good luck, sir!" Finch called as Luke headed for the door.

"Who needs luck?" he answered with a wink, then strode out of the gymnasium, leaving by the side door that opened outside onto the grounds.

He walked straight out to the pond, took off his boots, and waded in up to his thighs, then dove in, letting the silken green pond swallow him.

The cool water felt heavenly gliding over his skin. He savored the bubbling quiet under the surface.

A few minutes later, greatly refreshed, he walked out of the pond, pushing his hair back from his face. He paused to look around at the morning, enjoying the birdsong, the kiss of the air on his chest.

Then it was back inside to wash and transform himself into bumbling, eccentric Lucas the quiz.

But as he pulled the water chain in his bathing room and let the tepid shower flow over him a short while later, he still had to chuckle, half wincing to recall Portia's scathing words about her fiancé.

He had invented his Lucas character years ago as a means of keeping the hordes of tuft-hunting ladies away from him. They would've pestered him relentlessly every time he set foot in London and would've made his work as Silversmoke quite impossible.

He'd had to do *something* to keep them at bay, and to adopt eccentric habits had seemed like a lark.

Unfortunately, when it came to his chosen bride, it appeared that his ruse had worked just a little too well.

Before long, Luke was riding in his luxurious coach-and-four on his way to London. As the vehicle sped down the flat, smooth drive between green pastures fragrant with blooming clover, he smiled at the sight of his countless blood horses grazing.

But when the carriage turned out of his drive and onto the road, his churning thoughts returned. He folded his arms across his chest and leaned back against the squabs in his unfashionable, ill-fitting "Lucas" coat, hair deliberately tousled, eyeglasses at the ready, his eyebrows knitted.

Damn it all. He could not stop pondering Lady Portia, and the more he thought about her, the more confused he became.

Who the hell *was* this girl, anyway?

With the wedding less than a month away, perhaps it was time he started putting forth the effort to find out.

Because, clearly, he had misjudged her.

He had thought he was getting exactly what he wanted in this match: a shallow, fashionable beauty without much of a brain. A girl so uninterested in her bumbling quiz of a husband that she would keep her distance with pleasure—and thus stay out of his way.

He had not wanted to get married, or rather, had been indifferent to it, up until the day his sister Tavi had cornered him with the skillful application of guilt.

"If you want to honor our parents' memory, Luke, then start a family. Have a child of your own and carry on the family line before you get yourself killed!"

Elder sisters were bossy, he had long since concluded. But he shrugged off Tavi's well-meaning protectiveness. Hadn't she noticed that her "little brother" stood a foot taller than she did these days, and had done so for years?

She always warned he'd fall prey to disaster, thanks to his highwayman pursuits—what she knew of them. But Luke always cheerfully answered that he could take care of himself, thank you very much.

Ah well. He had grumbled compliance on the wife issue and sent his nosy sister to work.

Refusing to interest himself in any sort of match beyond what the obligation of his rank required, he had tasked her with doing a preliminary review of the available debutantes.

He himself couldn't be bothered.

Once Tavi had presented her findings, he'd glanced over the fillies for sale with a cynical eye, even ventured to Town for a closer inspection, and then deliberately picked one he'd thought would give him no trouble.

Ha. He shook his head at his poor judgment. *You're a blind man.*

He did not want his future duchess even *knowing* about his Silversmoke pursuits, let alone meddling in them.

He had gone for a girl he was certain would give him a wide berth. A socialite, surrounded by friends and admirers, who'd be at ease in a crowd, like he never was. Someone shallow and fashionable, who'd do her duty and keep her distance.

Lady Portia Tennesley had seemed perfect. Good bloodlines. It did not hurt that she was stunningly beautiful, as well. She was a trophy, he could admit, and really, a woman like that had been born to wear a duchess coronet.

Luke had also taken care to study her mother. You always had to look at the mothers if you were wise, since girls so often became them in time.

Her mother's type was perfect for his design. Lady Liddicoat was at the epicenter of Society, rail-thin and worldly and blond, and frequently tipsy, to boot, from what he could tell. She greeted her friends with exclamations of *"Darling!"* and little faux-kisses on each cheek. She was completely absorbed in herself, and that suited him fine.

He had sought an introduction to the daughter only then. And when he had met the fair Lady Portia Tennesley, she had gazed right through him and barely said a word; she'd seemed a thousand miles away.

Alas, he had mistaken her for some shallow, biddable dimwit. But her skin glistened like vanilla candy, and she'd smelled like an apple tree in bloom at the height of spring. One of those heart-stopping explosions of gorgeous, pinkish-white flowers that drew bees for miles around to come and revel in its dizzying perfume.

In short, she had captivated him in some inexplicable manner that had immediately made Luke back away, even as he had known from the start that she was the one, although they'd barely spoken.

Mind made up, he'd moved on in the process, businesslike, speaking first to her parents, of course. They'd been thrilled. Who wouldn't be? Not that he himself was some prize, but his title was, his huge fortune even more so.

He had not thought to ask himself *why* the girl had seemingly gazed right through him during their brief conversations; he'd barely noticed the fog that she'd told him last night she had been in at the time.

Luke shook his head. What an utter ass she must think him, asking for her hand while completely oblivious to her feelings. There she was, grieving, while he'd come along expecting her to rejoice that a duke had chosen her for his mate.

He snorted with disgust at himself. Yet that wistful vulnerability in her had tugged at his heart, made him want to protect her, he supposed. She had seemed so fragile, so delicate, and he, like a fool, had taken her quietness for docility.

In hindsight, he could understand his mistake, after what she had told him last night in the pub.

That haunting, faraway quality he had found so intriguing had been grief—or, at least, the utter distraction of a girl sick with worry over the disappearance of the man who'd already won her heart.

Luke stared uneasily out the open coach window. *What have I got myself into here?*

Lulled by the sound of the wheels whirring over the well-kept road, he draped his arm out the window to feel the slight breeze as the green landscape unfurled on his right.

By God, he'd completely misjudged her. The girl he had *thought* he was marrying would never go traipsing off to meet with a highwayman in his lair. He shuddered. As her future husband, it was horrifying behavior to contemplate.

Such a woman could not be protected with any sort of convenience. Besides, if she would do that, then what else might she do?

What other secrets might she keep from "Lucas" in future?

God, what a headache, he thought, and harrumphed. This alliance appeared liable to take far more of his attention—and effort—than he had ever anticipated.

I'll bet that's why Tavi picked her. His sister was sly like that.

As his mind drifted back to the stinging remarks Portia had made last night about her fiancé, Luke did not take them too personally.

They were enough to get his attention, to be sure, but he knew that he rather deserved it. After all, he'd been laughing up his sleeve for years now, ever since he'd created the part of the quirky, scientific duke.

It had proved an effective repellent to the cloud of well-bred mosquitoes and their matchmaking mamas, who'd have pursued him relentlessly otherwise.

He'd had to come up with *some* means of escaping them, but not for the world did he wish to be mean to them or hurt their delicate feelings. It had been far easier to invent a way to make *them* avoid *him*, rather than the other way around.

And so, "Lucas" was born, with his fascination with bugs.

Luke supposed that a part of him had foolishly hoped that the right girl would not be put off by the shy, bumbling, fumbling, stammering eccentric, might love him anyway.

Then he could know beyond any doubt that his lady's affection was not for his wealth or his rank or the pleasure that he could give her. If she could love poor, awkward Lucas, then he—the real Luke—knew that he could love *her* with all the passion in his nature.

Of course, all that was moot now. He had made up his mind long ago that love had no place in his life.

Only, now, his fiancée's tender confession last night of wishing she could know someday how true love felt stuck like a knife in his heart.

He had never wanted to hurt anyone with his deception. But now, after the things Portia had said, he was beginning to feel like a miser, hoarding his gold from the sweet young bride sold to him by her parents. Denying her basic necessities, like the simple human need…to be loved.

Luke stared out the window and could only wonder what he would feel when he saw her today. It was strange knowing things he was not supposed to know about her. Strange having secrets from her, and knowing that she, too, had secrets from him.

It put him on edge, moreover, to know that, for once, he did not have total control over the situation, as he'd assumed.

God knew, above all, it was bloody strange being asked to help his own fiancée find the man she really loved, or supposedly did. She seemed unclear herself on that point.

But he would do it. He would find out what had happened to this *Joel*.

And soon.

Luke wanted this resolved before their wedding day, because if the man was alive, then Portia must choose between them for herself.

He did not want to be married to a woman who would pine for another man for the rest of their lives. If she wanted the gambler at that point, far be it from Luke to prevent their being together.

He would not like it, of course, but it wasn't as though he was in love with her himself, and a duke could easily find another willing bride.

For his part, he had no intention of backing out of the match, or his mother would haunt him from beyond the grave. If Luke jilted Portia because of this Joel, she'd be disgraced in Society. He could never do that to her.

Besides, he had given his word, and whether as highwayman or as duke, his word was his bond.

When the skyline of London finally materialized on the hazy horizon ahead, Luke felt his pulse jump. Having slouched down on the squabs, lounging in boredom, he now sat up and stared at the dome of St. Paul's in the distance, the towers of Westminster, the white spires of countless Wren churches.

The trace of a speculative smile formed on his lips. It had been ages since he had last visited his grand house in Moonlight Square.

But that was not why his heart skipped a beat as his carriage rolled on; it was knowing that every yard of road they covered brought him closer to Portia.

I wonder what she's doing right now…

At that very moment, in fact, Portia was chasing a ball across the glossy emerald grass in the garden park at the center of Moonlight Square, laughing and slightly out of breath.

"Simon! We really must work on your aim," she exclaimed as she ran in a rustle of pale skirts and cotton petticoats.

The five-year-old standing several yards across the lawn from her giggled maniacally.

Catching up to the ball just in time to stop it from crashing into a bed full of delicate, candy-colored violas, Portia set a hand on her hip and gave the boy a look of mock indignation.

"Are you doing this on purpose? Making me run every which way just for fun?"

"He would," her friend Felicity interjected from over by the gazebo, where the blond young duchess was minding Simon's little sister, Annabelle, age three. "Takes after his papa, that one. Pure rogue. Miniature-sized, at least for now."

Portia laughed, enjoying the carefree afternoon. "At least I'm getting my exercise."

Simon hopped about impatiently on his end of the lawn. "Kick it back!"

Oh, he was the son of a duke, all right, she thought in amusement, hearing him already giving orders. Lucky for him, the lively, dark-haired lordling was too cute to resist, in his little waistcoat and short trousers.

"Ready? Here it comes!" she called, and her skirts swung as she kicked it back to him.

The leather ball rolled, Simon hurried to intercept it, and right on cue, Serena's little white Westie, Franklin, raced after it as well, barking and trailing his leash.

The wee terrier was already great friends with the children, so Serena, upon joining the game with Portia and Simon, had let go of her pup's leash to let him run about. Franklin was determined to tackle the ball this time, never mind that it was almost taller than he was.

"I hope he works off some of his energy," Serena remarked, shading her eyes with her hand in the sunny spot where she stood on the lawn.

"Which one?" Portia replied, glancing at her raven-haired best friend.

"Both!" Felicity chimed in from the gazebo.

They laughed as they watched the boy and the dog compete for the ball.

Portia thought it an altogether pleasant way to spend an afternoon, and the day was so clear and fine. Golden sunlight dappled the lush green carpet of grass, filtering in through the leafy branches of the old plane trees all around the park.

The trees rippled and swayed gently in the soft breeze that had finally arrived to start driving off the humidity. The flowers planted all around the white gazebo were in full bloom, a riot of pinks and purples, waving with peach-colored poppies and tall blue foxgloves. The rosebuds were swelling as well, nearly ready to burst, since June had come at last.

Their friend Trinny had also come out with baby George in the pram. Presently, the cheerful red-haired viscountess sat on a park bench near the gazebo, bouncing her four-month-old son on her lap.

She adjusted the bonnet she had put on the infant to shade his tender face from too much sunshine, while Felicity hovered over Annabelle.

The talkative three-year-old, clad in a frilly dress that reached to her shins, found it great fun to hop up and down the gazebo's few wooden steps under her stepmama's watchful eye.

Felicity called to Simon to ask if he was ready for a snack yet, then Serena hurried to stop her curious terrier from digging in a flowerbed that had arrested his attention.

Portia watched all these proceedings with fond interest. These pets and children certainly kept her friends busy, to say nothing of their husbands, who were currently doing whatever it was that the gents of Moonlight Square did on an ordinary day.

She supposed they were hearing speeches in Parliament or arguing over horse races or other manly matters at the club.

Meanwhile, the ladies had been enjoying the sunny day and each other's company, chatting about nothing in particular, wondering aloud how their friend, Maggie, was enjoying her honeymoon with her new husband, Connor, the Duke of Amberley.

Much of the time, though, in truth, Portia was only half listening to all the idle chitchat.

As she waited to see if Simon would kick the ball back to her or opt to take a snack instead, her mind continued to wander. Of course, she was thinking about Joel and her own upcoming wedding, but a new subject had taken hold of her imagination.

Silversmoke.

She found herself oddly obsessed with him today. She could not stop thinking about him—so much so that she was actually tempted to confide in her friends what she had done last night.

They would think she was mad for setting up an appointment with a highwayman. In all reality, though, she was quite sure that every one of them would've done the same thing in her place.

As much as she longed to confide in them about the delicious outlaw, she would not want them telling their husbands what she'd done, or word might get back to her parents—or worse, to Fountainhurst himself.

She knew her friends kept no secrets from their men, and she was worried that one of their husbands might be concerned enough about Portia's reckless visit to Hampstead Heath to inform her father.

The gentlemen could be a little overprotective that way.

Portia wasn't taking any chances. For that reason, she kept her adventure of last night to herself, at least for now. Yet she could not deny that the entire world felt different around her today.

Silversmoke had changed everything.

She had awakened this morning full of newfound hope that she might actually get the answers she craved someday soon.

What a boon it was to know that, at last, there was someone involved in Joel's case who would really take matters in hand and finally start to get to the bottom of this.

Why the Bow Street Runners had failed, she did not know, but she was confident that Silversmoke would not be afraid to follow whatever clues he found, even if they led him into dark places where others might fear to venture.

Indeed, she could not think of much that would scare him.

Lowborn criminal or not, he was a remarkable man. He had asked insightful questions, and had truly listened to the answers.

Which was more than she could say for her fiancé—or even for Joel, for that matter. Joel had never been the best listener.

Moreover, Silversmoke had said some astonishing, beautiful things. *"Love costs everything."*

Does it? she wondered, then her heart sank, for she'd probably never know.

"Lady Portia!" Simon kicked the ball with all his might, and it bounced right past her in her distraction.

With a startled cry, off she went running, with Franklin scampering after her and yipping at her heels. Portia chased the ball into a cluster of bluebells, and had to reach gingerly past the thorns of a rosebush to reach it.

"Sorry!" she called back with a chuckle. "I wasn't paying attention."

Meanwhile, Annabelle had crouched down and was examining the gravel on the walking path that wound through the park. She began digging in the dust and poking at the pebbles with a stick.

At Portia's feet, Franklin wagged his tail and waited for her to kick the ball.

This time she kicked it to Serena, and the Westie darted off after it as it rolled toward his owner.

As soon as Portia kicked the ball to her best friend, her thoughts returned to Silversmoke. It was astonishing to have seen for herself that he really was as handsome as the seemingly overblown tales in the papers claimed.

She wished she had been able to tell the color of his eyes, but it had been too dark in his oaken booth there at The Blind Badger. In all, she could not help wondering how such a being as he had come to exist. Who was he, really?

He spoke like an educated man, yet his deep voice had held the tinge of a lower-class accent. With all his pretensions to chivalry, perhaps he was, like little Simon, the illegitimate son of a lord?

Both Simon and Annabelle were the products of Naughty Netherford's youthful dalliances with famous actresses. That particular duke had indeed been the King of the Rakehells for a while before Felicity had straightened him out and tamed his wild ways.

In any case, it was impossible to guess Silversmoke's origins, or his real name. Perhaps when he contacted her with news from his search, as promised, he might be receptive to answering a discreet question or two about himself—though she doubted it.

He was a mystery. An alluring one. All too well, she remembered the curve of his lips when he smiled and that lovely square jaw with its intriguing dark stubble.

Gentlemen of the sort she was accustomed to did not go about unshaved.

Joel, for example, had kept his face baby-smooth, except for the sideburns he so carefully sculpted. Admittedly, the dandy had been a bit vain...

Without warning, the disturbing thought unfurled in her mind that yes, even Joel paled in comparison to Silversmoke.

"Ahem!" Serena said pointedly in Portia's direction.

Amid her daydreaming, Portia had not even realized she had been staring up into the branches of the huge tree nearest her, watching the leaves flicker silver and green in the wind.

When she looked over at Serena, who was tossing the ball in one hand, her friend nodded discreetly toward the gravel path leading from the nearest entrance of the park, where the wrought-iron gates stood open.

"Expecting someone?" Serena asked quietly.

Portia followed her glance, and her eyes flew open wide as she spotted her fiancé ambling down the path toward them.

Fountainhurst?!

Serena arched a brow at her.

What on earth is he doing here? was Portia's first thought.

Her second was: *Ugh.*

Oh, be kind, she scolded herself at once. Her scientific duke couldn't help his oddness. Besides, he meant well enough.

"Good luck," Serena whispered.

"Thanks," Portia mumbled. Stifling a sigh, she pasted on a smile and went to greet her disappointing future mate.

CHAPTER 5

The Awkward Intruder

$\mathcal{S}$auntering down the graveled path into the green, pleasant garden park, Luke let his gaze drink in the idyllic scene before him with a sense of pure delight.

He could've sworn Botticelli's *Three Graces* along with *Venus Rising from the Sea* had all stepped out of their paintings, put some clothes on for once, and escaped to London to frolic about the garden park before his eyes, with three little cherubs and a tiny white dog in attendance.

Long tendrils of hair wafting, pale skirts blowing, ribbons fluttering in the breeze, they laughed and talked and played with the children.

He'd been watching the innocent scene for a moment now in silent wonder, half feeling as though he'd been run through. How beautiful they were, these young wives and their children, bathed in sunshine, surrounded by flowers.

A redhead, a black-haired beauty, and two goddess-like blondes, one guinea-gold, one flaxen…

The last of which he had somehow, miraculously, snared for his own.

He had been enchanted watching the future mother of his children kicking a ball back and forth with the wee boy. By God, this was *life*. Joy as he'd once known it, long ago, before everything went wrong. But it struck him as he stared wistfully at them that he had long since become a stranger to all the beauty that still existed in the world.

Then Lady Serena had spotted him, and Luke's awe turned to sardonic amusement when he saw his fair fiancée blanch to note his arrival.

Well-trained deb that she was, though, Portia quickly hid her dismay to see him behind a forced smile.

Ouch, he thought, though this was exactly how he'd wanted it for reasons that, at the moment, escaped him.

Resolutely, his bride donned a façade of ladylike cheer as readily as he would put on his Silversmoke mask when it was time to go a-robbing or, rather, catching villains.

Luke winced privately, half in humor, at her reaction, well aware he'd done this to himself. *Oh, she doesn't like me at all.*

That had been the intention, had it not?

It seemed he might've succeeded all too well. But as lovely as she looked right now, in this shining, foreign world before him that she seemed to inhabit, and in light of the new qualities she had displayed last night—qualities he respected—perhaps it was time he tried a little harder to make his future duchess like him.

First, though, after learning that his bride was still fixated on another man, Luke jolly well needed to assess where things currently stood between the goddess and the bumbling Duke of Fountainhurst.

He donned a grin that was no more authentic than hers and lifted his hand in a hesitant Lucas wave. "Er, hullo, ladies! Good day!"

Portia waved back, but her reaction to the sight of her fiancé after months of barely any contact filled her with a curious mix of emotions.

She felt taken off guard and a little nonplussed at his unannounced arrival.

Frankly, she did not appreciate His Grace thinking he could just show up like this out of nowhere, giving her no warning and leaving her no chance to prepare herself mentally for a visit with the quiz.

But that was dukes for you. They thought the world revolved around them. Even the eccentric ones.

Humph. Maybe she was in no mood to be charming to her bridegroom. *What the devil is he doing here, anyway?*

As Lucas ambled closer, shuffling through the gravel and looking shy and self-conscious, Portia regarded him with puzzled annoyance. If he had come to change the wedding plans on her, last minute, after refusing to get involved until now, she would strangle the man.

Then Serena's dog went running over to investigate the intruder, barking his little head off. But Franklin was no attack dog. Indeed, the Westie's piercing yips sounded more like a greeting than a threat.

The sound made all her friends turn and look. Portia's heart sank as she envisioned her betrothed through their eyes.

No, her duke was not Trinny's sophisticated, understated Gable. He was not Felicity's smoldering, powerful Netherford, nor Serena's cunning and elegant Azrael, and he certainly wasn't Maggie's bold, mighty major.

Her Lucas was a quiz, to be honest. A scholarly oddment with his head in the clouds, who would probably fall into a ditch without a woman of sense looking after him.

His longish, sandy-blond hair was permanently tousled, its thick waves sticking out in all directions. His rumpled brown coat should've got his valet sacked, if he even had one, and his tortoiseshell spectacles sat slightly askew on his admittedly well-formed nose. He'd brought along a few books, tucked under his arm. At least he was tall and well-proportioned. If only he'd do something with himself!

Joel could have fixed him in a trice, told him what to wear. Indeed, Fountainhurst wouldn't have been half bad-looking if he'd try, but bookish chaps like him apparently frowned on fashion as some shallow pursuit beneath their superior intellects.

Ah well. It was tempting to think she could go to work on him once they were married. But Portia did not approve of trying to change other people.

Either accept him as he is or don't marry him at all.

She had chosen acceptance, because trying to change others was pointless, anyway. It was hard enough to change oneself.

Yet it was difficult not to compare Lucas's halting mannerisms and haphazard appearance with poor lost Joel's witty banter and debonair style.

Comparing Lucas to Silversmoke was an even stronger contrast: night and day. The only thing her fiancé had in common with that fierce, dangerous outlaw was that they were both about the same height.

Unfortunately, she then remembered Silversmoke's reproach about her marrying a man for his rank and was stung out of her comparisons game.

"Don't you think you're being a little unfair to this poor beggar?" he'd demanded.

She hated to say it, but the highwayman was right, blast him.

The Honorable Joel Clayton was not the one she was engaged to. In fact, there might even be a chance that he would prove to be the bounder that Silversmoke had warned her about.

After all, Joel had not seen fit to propose to her when he had the chance, never mind that he'd wanted to touch her body in ways that he knew full well were reserved for a husband.

Remembering that encounter made her distinctly uneasy, especially with Lucas headed toward her, so she shoved it away, just like she had Joel's wandering hands.

With the wedding only a month away, maybe it really was time to let him go. She was marrying Lucas. Silversmoke was looking into the matter of Joel's fate, and that would have to be enough.

At least her future husband had a good heart, a fact that he demonstrated clearly as he bent down to greet the tiny terrier, which was now hopping around him, clamoring for attention and yipping away.

"Why, hullo, little fellow!" he said bending down to pat Franklin's head. "I say! Aren't you a good boy?"

Serena arched a brow at her, a smile twitching at her lips; Portia let out a long-suffering sigh.

Her best friend gave her a bolstering look; Serena was the only one of Portia's friends who already knew Lucas. She, for one, had a soft spot for odd people—she'd have to, to have married Azrael.

Portia was grateful for her best friend's moral support in facing Lucas. They both hurried over to collect their respective pets.

"Franklin, get down!" Serena scolded as she approached. "Sorry about that, Your Grace. He's such a little troublemaker."

"Not at all, not at all, Lady Serena. He's a fine beast, what?"

Portia winced at Lucas's blunder with her best friend's title, but Serena was too polite to remind him that her rank had been elevated to duchess ever since her marriage to Azrael this past Christmas.

Since her friend let the oversight go, so did Portia.

Then he smiled at Portia and finished patting the dog, rising to his full height again. "Good day, my lady." He sketched a shy bow.

She curtsied. "Your Grace."

A cage of awkward silence promptly slammed down around all three of them. Serena scooped Franklin up in her arms while Portia looked at the ground, casting about for any crumb of conversation.

"Well," Portia said, lifting her head, "this is a pleasant surprise.

What brings you to London, Your Grace?"

"Why, you do!" he blurted out. "In part. Some, er, business also needed my attention here in Town. S-so, of course, I wanted to pay my respects to you, as well. I-I hope that's all right? Your butler told me I-I might find you here."

"Of course." *I would never presume that you'd come all this way just to see me,* she thought, but willed her smile to remain, and mentally cursed the butler.

Lucas glanced around at their leisurely pursuits of the day. "I hope I am not interrupting," he said in dismay, perhaps sensing her lack of enthusiasm.

"Not at all," Portia answered, smiling harder with a will.

"So these are your friends?"

"Yes!" Thank God, something to talk about. "Come, allow me to introduce you around. You really ought to meet them, since they are our neighbors, after all."

"Oh, er, yes. Good point. I-I'd be delighted." He did not sound delighted. He sounded nervous about meeting new people.

Truly, for a duke, the man had zero Town bronze.

Serena asked him how he'd been as they walked over to Trinny, still seated on the bench. The redhead now had her baby son resting on her shoulder. She greeted them with a wide smile, but held a finger to her lips.

"He's just now fallen asleep. Naptime," Trinny whispered.

Hearing that, Serena held her dog's snout closed. Franklin shook his head, trying to free himself from her light hold, while Portia whispered introductions.

Lucas bowed to the viscountess and smiled warmly in the direction of her dozing son. "Congratulations. He's a beautiful child."

"Thank you," Trinny whispered back, beaming at this praise for the new, tiny god of her world, as of three and a half months ago.

Unwilling to risk waking up the baby, Portia beckoned her fiancé silently over to Felicity, who was now standing near the base of the gazebo, her hands planted on her waist as she watched Annabelle digging in the dirt with the stick she had found.

Simon, meanwhile, began kicking the ball alone, letting it bounce against the inside of the tall wrought-iron fence girding the park. Felicity was keeping the boy in view, but smiled at them as they approached.

"Felicity, allow me to present my fiancé. This is Lucas, the Duke of

Fountainhurst. Lucas, this is my good friend Felicity, the Duchess of Netherford."

He bowed to her. "It's an honor, Your Grace."

"I'm delighted to meet you, as well—Your Grace," Felicity said lightly, but when she offered her hand, Lucas looked down and realized he was still carrying his books.

"Did I bring these?" he cried, as though they had appeared in his arms by magic. He gave Felicity a blank look from behind his spectacles. "I-I forgot to set them down inside. So frightfully absent-minded," he mumbled with an uncomfortable laugh.

"It's all right," Portia quickly reassured the quiz, stepping forward to help. "Let me take those for you. We can just set them down here." She spoke to the naïf as kindly as though she were helping one of the children.

Lord, she thought to herself, hiding her amusement as she smoothly intervened to free his hands.

As he accepted Felicity's offered handshake, Annabelle stopped digging to watch Portia alight the gazebo steps, where she'd had such fun hopping around a while ago, the little monkey.

A built-in bench ran the perimeter of the dainty garden folly; Portia set Lucas's books down on it, not far from where Felicity's servant had left the picnic basket containing the children's snacks.

He glanced worriedly after his books.

"Don't worry, Your Grace. No one will steal them, I'm sure," Portia said. Especially when she saw the titles: *Life Cycle of the Gadfly* and *On Slugs.*

Portia gave a mental whistle. Gripping reading, indeed. She should suggest them for Lady Delphine's next book-club meeting.

Think I'll just pretend I didn't see that.

To set his mind at ease, though, seeing his look of distress, Portia moved his precious tomes to the opposite side of the folly, away from the picnic basket, and well out of the children's possible drink-spilling zone.

Relief washed over his face, and he smiled gratefully at her, looking almost handsome. Then he glanced down at Annabelle, who'd been watching the adults with a serious look in her big, dark eyes fringed with velvet lashes.

She was a beautiful child, doll-like in her pale dress, with fair skin and sable curls down to her shoulders.

From what Portia could tell, Annabelle missed little of what was going on around her, and, at the moment, she was studying the duke.

He looked way down at her and smiled.

"And who is this little person?" Lucas bent down to be at eye level with the child.

"This is Annabelle, and she is very industrious today," Felicity said.

"How do you do, Miss Annabelle. I'm Lucas. What's this you're doing, may I ask? Golfing with gravel?"

"There's an anthill!" Annabelle said, pointing at the grass on the edge of the path. "The ants are making a line, and they keep going in and out of that little hole on top. They're trying to steal our picnic!"

Without warning, Annabelle jumped up and started stomping her feet in the dirt, still gripping her stick like a sword and whacking at the wee ant hill with it.

"Ack!" Lucas said. "No, no, my dear! That's their home," he told her gently.

She kept jumping, though she largely missed the line of ants hurrying by. "Hannah says that ants are naughty!"

"Who's Hannah?"

"Our cook!" the child said.

"Oh—well, yes, I suppose one doesn't want ants in the kitchen. But they're outside here, and that's fair enough, i'nt? They're not hurting anyone. Come, you don't want to wreck their little kingdom like a big, scary giant, do you?"

Annabelle stopped jumping and turned to him in wonder. "Their *kingdom*?"

"Why, yes. They have their own little palace down there, with a queen and all. And this path they're all following, you see that? That's the trail they must take to find their way home, or they'll get lost and wander off forever into the dark forest—I mean the grass."

Annabelle gasped, staring at him, then she looked back down at the ants.

When she peered up at her stepmother to see if she thought any of this might be true, Felicity gave the child a smile. "It's not nice to destroy things, sweeting."

"She was only trying to save the picnic," Portia mumbled, folding her arms across her chest.

"You know," Lucas said to Annabelle, "I'll bet it would be fun to golf with this gravel, though. Want me to show you how?"

Annabelle turned to him with a curious stare.

"May I borrow your stick?" Lucas held out his hand to borrow her twig, which Annabelle obligingly gave him.

Lucas held it as though it were a tiny golf club and knocked away a piece of gravel. "Ha!" he said as a pebble flew.

Annabelle laughed uproariously at this new game. Lucas handed her the stick back, and the child set about copying his motion.

The ants were saved, forgotten in moments.

"Bravo!" Lucas said, clapping at Annabelle's efforts while Felicity arched a brow discreetly at Portia as if to say, *Good with children. How about that?*

Portia pressed her lips together, then Simon came racing over, unwilling to miss out on the fun.

He beamed at Lucas, wanting to be included. Felicity introduced him, and Lucas gave the boy a courteous bow.

"Hullo, young man."

"Sir," the boy said, bowing back, just as he'd been taught. Then he burst out, "Watch me! I can do it, too!"

Simon ran off to find a stick that would serve as a golf club, but he had scarcely returned and joined in the game before he and his little sister began bickering.

"Stop that, you two. Well!" Felicity smiled warmly at Lucas, her eyes dancing as she looked askance at Portia. "I'm sure the two of you have better things to do than play in the dirt here with us."

"I am quite fond of playing in the dirt, actually," the duke said.

The children laughed that any grownup would say such a thing, and Felicity chuckled, too; Serena had already wandered back to the park bench to keep Trinny company.

Portia could not deny that Lucas's ability to amuse the children plucked at her heartstrings. So when he turned and smiled hopefully at her, all earnest and awkward and sweet, she could not help smiling back.

"Would you, um, care to take a turn about the square with me, Lady Portia?"

"Certainly, Your Grace."

He blinked as though he'd expected a rejection. "Excellent. Right! Well, then. Good." He gestured toward the wide gravel path. "A-after you, my lady."

Portia sent her friends the most discreet of sardonic glances, then sallied forth down the path alongside her future mate.

This should be interesting.

CHAPTER 6

A Genteel Promenade

*L*uke really was having too much fun with all of this, admittedly, though he knew it was bad of him.

Now that he had Portia all to himself, however, it was time to get serious. Things needed fixing between them if this marriage was ever going to work. If not, then he figured they had better quit now, before anyone got hurt.

As a gentleman, he knew it was the lady's prerogative. Today, he meant to give her a chance to back out, or, at least, open an escape hatch and see if she used it to flee.

Carefully guarding his heart, as always, Luke had mixed feelings about either option. Portia Tennesley intrigued him intensely with her beauty, her courage, her wit.

But she was far cleverer than he had counted on, and that could be a problem. So if he had to let her go, then he would, he supposed. And find himself a proper dimwit to marry.

One who'd leave him alone, do as she was told for the most part, and, above all, *not* pry into his secretive nocturnal pursuits.

This shrewd little lady already knew too much and had proven herself far too curious for his peace of mind.

Yet, for all that, as they strolled along, he dearly hoped she would still choose to marry silly, bumbling Lucas. The poor chap did need a lady, after all, lonely soul.

If not, Luke wouldn't really be surprised. Who could blame her? He saw now that he had neglected her shamefully and underestimated the woman to a degree that probably would've made her feel insulted if she knew.

Not to mention he was not exactly being terribly honest about himself, either. That obvious fact needled his conscience even as he worried about the clever girl figuring out his deception.

The last thing Luke had ever wanted was for his future duchess to be dragged into his dangerous activities. But Portia had made a point of seeking out his alter ego, enlisting his help.

Now that she had Silversmoke on the hunt for her precious Joel, she might jump at the chance to escape this match—and him.

The thought of missing out on a future with her gave Luke a pang in his heart that he could not account for. But no matter.

In light of all this new information about his future bride, he needed to know where things really stood between them now.

There was only one way to find out.

Portia gave up on waiting for Lucas to start the conversation. Instead, she dove right in. "I had no idea you were so good with children, Your Grace."

He flashed a smile as the breeze further tousled his dark blond hair. "I have a little niece and nephew. Bartram and Katie. They're such amusing youngsters. We get on well. I do hope you get to meet them soon."

"Bartram?" she asked.

"His courtesy title. His first name's actually Michael. We all call him Bartram, though. Or Bartie."

"Ah." She gave him a friendly smile as they ambled along the path, but when silence dropped again, blast it, it was his turn to think of a topic.

He cleared his throat a bit, searching, she gathered.

"What a fine day, what?" he said emphatically.

"Oh, yes, very fine," she agreed with all haste.

He pushed his spectacles higher onto the bridge of his nose, then clasped his hands behind his back in gentlemanly fashion as he strolled along beside her.

"And you are looking lovely as ever, Lady Portia, if, er, one may say so."

"Why, thank you, Your Grace." In spite of herself, she found his bashfulness rather endearing.

He seemed taller than she remembered. Walking by his side, it was the first time she'd noticed that his shoulder was higher than the top of her head.

Then he glanced over, his green eyes earnest as he peered down at her through his glasses. "And, um, what have you been doing of late?" he asked innocently, doing his best to chat with her, it seemed.

Hiring highwaymen.

"Oh, nothing in particular," she said with a smile, then gestured toward her friends, ignoring the pang of guilt. "As you can see, I am altogether idle."

As Mother often said, men did not need to know everything a woman did.

"Ah," he murmured.

"You?" she asked.

"Oh, the usual fare. Studies, business, adding to my collections." He held up a finger as though inspiration had struck. "I did manage to capture a splendid monarch butterfly that was sitting atop a bloom of Queen Anne's lace last week! Capital specimen. Capital."

"Really? How interesting." *Your Grace is a fearless hunter.* She cringed at the thought of a grown man prancing through a meadow catching butterflies.

Ah, but it was all in the name of science.

"I pinned it myself," he declared. "Told my assistant to have it mounted and framed, so I can hang it on the wall. You should see it. I think you are going to be *very* impressed."

"I already am," she said sweetly. But when she began to ponder it, the thought of some poor, helpless butterfly dying a slow and agonizing death with its wings nailed down began to make her slightly queasy.

"What is it?" Lucas asked, clearly sensing her dismay.

"Well…it just seems a little heartless, is all."

"Heartless? How?"

"Catching the poor, innocent thing and nailing it down till it dies. Why, it's rather sad, don't you think?"

He blanched. "Good God! Well, no. I-I never really thought of it that way."

She shrugged. Someone had to stand up for the butterflies of the Earth, after all.

Lucas frowned at her in confused disapproval, and they walked on.

If it were possible, the awkwardness now grew even thicker between them.

Unfortunately, she did not know her fiancé well enough to sense him holding back mirth.

And so, with a valiant mental effort, Portia set out to resurrect their conversation. They reached the edge of the path and turned a corner down the next one. "So, um, was there some particular reason you wished to see me, Your Grace?" Forcing a smile, she brushed a lock of her hair behind her ear as it blew against her cheek.

His eyebrows lifted. "Does a chap need an excuse to call on the lady he's set to marry?"

"Well, no... It just seems out of the blue. I haven't seen you in months."

His smile faded to an uneasy look. He nodded in acknowledgment of her subtle reproach. "Yes. About that."

Something in his voice made Portia's ears perk up.

He glanced nervously at her. "I, er, was wondering—don't take this the wrong way—but I was starting to wonder if I should ask you if..."

"What?" she prodded, sensing trouble. *Out with it, man!*

"If, um, you'd like to postpone the wedding a bit?"

Portia stopped in her tracks. *"What?"* She whirled to gape at him, aghast. *"Postpone* the wedding? Why? Don't tell me you're getting cold feet!"

"No, no, it's not that! Nothing like that." He took a step back as though she had frightened him, the big oaf. "It's just—"

"What?" she demanded. "What is wrong, Lucas?"

"Well, it just occurs to me that we barely know each other!"

Portia set her hands on her waist and glared up at him. "And whose fault is that?"

Lucas lowered his gaze like a guilty schoolboy. "I should think it was both of ours," he mumbled, and scratched his cheek.

"No. You're the one who never comes to Town. I've been here all this time, making all the wedding arrangements...by myself." She gestured toward her parents' home on the square. "You could've come to see me anytime. But you apparently had better things to do. Like murdering poor butterflies."

He looked into her eyes, and she got the feeling he was biting his tongue.

His silence gave her a sinking feeling. She held his gaze, wondering in despair if she was about to be jilted by a man she didn't even want to marry in the first place.

Don't do this to me, Fountainhurst. I've already been through enough.

"Fine," he said, "we won't postpone it, then."

Relief washed through her.

"All I meant to suggest was that perhaps you and I ought to start spending a little more time together." They walked on slowly, and he kicked his way through the gravel. "I mean, how will we ever learn to live together if we don't at least *try* to get to know each other better?"

She swallowed down her frustration and gave him a grumpy look. "Fine. That sounds sensible enough. It's not as though I have a very busy schedule. If you are willing, so am I. It is your doing, though—at the risk of sounding like a shrew. The gentleman is the one who must call on the lady. It is not normally the other way around. I don't know if you know that—"

"Yes, yes, of course I-I know that. You're quite right. I've been most dreadfully neglectful." He bobbed his head in acknowledgment, then shoved his hands into his pockets. "And you don't sound like a shrew."

A fashionable equipage came clattering down the street, and when Portia spotted Lady Dinton peering out the window at them when it passed, she remembered the neighbors.

The two of them had better move on unless they wished to find themselves the topic of local gossip.

The path Lucas and she had taken ran parallel to the road, which meant they could easily be observed from the street or the houses nearby. Although a genteel promenade was permissible for an engaged couple, their discussion had grown rather heated a moment ago.

If they were seen squabbling in the park a month before the wedding, that would make a tale the gossips would love sharing over scandal broth.

Quickly summoning a smile, Portia nodded politely at Her Ladyship as she passed. The aged baroness waggled her fingers in reply as, thankfully, her carriage rumbled on down the street.

Upon turning her attention back to her fiancé, Portia found him studying her with surprising intensity from behind his spectacles.

For a heartbeat, he almost reminded her of someone…

She couldn't think of whom.

But then that haunting possibility that Silversmoke had pointed out last night wafted through her mind, concerning Joel's possible abandonment of her. And as self-doubt rippled across her insecurities, a blunt question for Lucas arose in her mind, and she simply had to ask it.

After all, if Joel had indeed deserted her and her own fiancé never bothered with her either, maybe it was *her*.

Maybe she was just terrible with men.

"Is it that you don't like me very much?" she asked bravely, glancing at him, braced for any answer.

He turned to her, looking appalled. "No! No—nothing like that!" Genuinely shocked, it seemed, Lucas laid his hand on her arm, his touch gentle. "Please, do not jump to such awful conclusions, my lady. I-I like you very much. Why else would I propose?"

She stared at him; he seemed sincere. "But you always stay away," she said in a small voice.

He lowered his hand from her arm and, head down, averted his gaze. "That's not your fault. Believe me. It's just…this courtship business was never really my forte."

I never would've guessed it. Portia bit her tongue. "Are you sure it isn't me?"

He nodded. "Very sure. Please, forgive me. I should never wish you to feel that way because of me. I-I will try my hardest to do better."

It really was impossible to stay annoyed with him when he said such humble, artless things.

Ah well. If she wanted anything resembling domestic harmony once they were wed, Portia saw now she had better take matters in hand herself.

This was unconventional, perhaps, but she didn't mind helping him along, if that was what it took. He'd catch on eventually, with that big brain of his.

Of course, she never would've had to do this with Joel. The worldly, fashionable side of her gave a mental humph. But then again, Joel never would've lowered himself to teach a little child how to gravel-golf.

Grr. In spite of herself, her vexation with Lucas melted at the thought of his sweetness to Annabelle.

At least he'd be a good, kindhearted papa to their children, if they had them.

"Very well, I have a notion," she ventured. "Why don't you come to the ball at the Grand Albion this week?" She nodded over her shoulder toward the opulent hotel that stood behind them, on the north end of Moonlight Square, its stately façade visible through the trees.

The Grand Albion had a gentlemen's club on the first floor—where Fountainhurst would have a membership, since he lived on Moonlight Square. The elegant assembly rooms upstairs, however, were the site of an exclusive weekly subscription ball, second only to Almack's itself.

Every Thursday night throughout the Season, it welcomed the crème de la crème of Society.

"It's tomorrow night at eight, same as always. Can you make it?"

Lucas winced. "I am truly sorry, but I cannot, my lady. Not this week. There is other business that brought me to Town, and I'm afraid it demands my urgent attention. But I could come next week! And, in the meantime, um, I have an idea of my own for an outing we might take together, i-if you like."

"Yes?" she asked, encouraged by his participation.

"I should like to take you on a picnic," he said. "Won't that be nice? Weather permitting, of course."

If this involves bugs, I'll kill myself. But he needed encouragement, clearly. So she smiled and gave him a guarded nod. "That sounds very pleasant. When shall we go?"

"Could it possibly be Monday or Tuesday of next week?"

"Either day would be acceptable, yes, Your Grace. Thank you for thinking of it."

"Monday, then." He gazed at her for a moment, then they walked on.

Though silence had returned, it was different this time, not uncomfortable like before. Some relief had eased the tension of earlier, with these plans made.

Portia was happy that her future husband now seemed prepared to put forth at least a little effort in their dealings with each other.

A marriage was not a solo performance, after all, but a duet, and learning how to harmonize together would take ongoing effort.

While true love might be beyond her reach, whatever happened, she did not want to end up like her parents, strangers living cordially under the same roof, with nothing in common but their three now-grown children. They teamed up in amicable nonchalance when duty required, but other than that, the two mostly went their own ways.

Silversmoke's description of his parents' epic love whispered in her heart as she strolled along with Lucas. *"Twas a sort of miracle to behold,"* he had said.

"Are you all right?" Lucas murmured, apparently hearing the

wistful sigh that escaped her.

"Oh—yes. It's nothing."

As they arrived at the south end of the park, Portia glanced over at St. Andrew's church, where their wedding would be held, and was suddenly inspired.

She seized hold of Lucas's arm. "Come with me! Now that I have you here, I want to go over a few things concerning the ceremony."

He spluttered as she began pulling him toward the church. "But—"

"Come, this won't take long, I promise. I've worked out almost every detail by now, but I need decisions from you on a few final matters. Don't worry, this won't hurt a bit."

Lord, she had been trying to get answers out of him on certain wedding matters for weeks. Now that she finally had him in her grasp, the bridegroom was not getting away until he'd answered her questions.

She shepherded him out of the park and across the street toward the simple, white-steepled church. It sat opposite the Grand Albion down the long rectangle of the garden park. Built of brick overlaid with Portland stone, it had a couple of white pillars holding up a modest portico. A shallow set of stairs led up to the heavy oaken doors.

Despite the simplicity of the church, St. Andrew's was considered one of the most fashionable places to get married in London, second only to St. George's in Hanover Square.

When they reached it, Portia hurried Lucas up the steps, lifting the hem of her walking dress a bit with one hand; with the other, she still held on to her errant bridegroom, half expecting him to balk. Instead, he got the door for her, curiously scanning her face.

Then they went inside.

CHAPTER 7

Big Decisions

*I*t had been a long time since Luke had set foot in a church. He and God were not on the best of terms.

He would not go so far as to say he did not believe the deity existed. But from what he'd seen of life, the Almighty either wasn't listening or was too fed up with fallen man to care anymore. No, Luke ascribed to the respectable, old view that the divine clockmaker had designed nature to run on its own with exquisite precision, while He himself had wandered off to greener pastures, leaving humans to their fates.

That was why, to Luke, human beings must take matters into their own hands, exactly as he'd done with his own life. Men could not play God, but they could at least try to serve as one another's guardian angels now and then.

Still, religion had its place in maintaining order in society, he knew, so he did not argue against it, did not wish to see it torn down the way the Radicals did these days, that mad lot. He wondered what Portia's opinion of it all was as he followed her in. He'd have to ask her the next time their conversation lagged.

No doubt he'd get another chance soon, he thought wryly as he stepped over the threshold, into the dim, quiet vestibule at the back of the church.

Then they went through a second set of doors, into the sanctuary itself.

His soon-to-be bride marched ahead of him into the nave, all business.

Luke trailed obediently after her, glancing around at the place.

A long, red-carpeted aisle stretched ahead to the altar, flanked by rows of dark wooden pews. Stout white pillars at regular intervals held up the barrel-vaulted ceiling. They were Corinthian columns, and the flowery ornamentation around the tops had been gilded.

He could imagine how they must twinkle in the candlelight of the large, multi-tiered chandeliers that hung over the center of the aisle. For now, of course, the candles were unlit.

Sunlight streamed in through the high arched windows set behind the symmetrical galleries overlooking the nave.

A reverent hush filled the empty church, broken only by the creaking of the heavy door closing slowly behind him. When it bumped shut, the soft sound echoed into the cavernous space.

They passed the elaborate organ in the back, while, ahead, the white marble altar waited, draped in sumptuous green cloth. A sturdy gold cross sat atop it, flanked by a pair of large white candles.

Portia strode about halfway down the aisle, then turned and began explaining her plans to him, but Luke, alas, was only half listening, momentarily arrested by her beauty.

She looked like a windblown angel, slightly mussed from playing with the children, her golden hair sparkling in the filtered sunlight streaming in through the high, clear windows.

She did not seem to notice his distraction, busy explaining things to him about how the ceremony would play out, telling him where everyone would stand, where family members would sit, and passing on some basic instructions the pastor had already given her.

Pointing here and there, her plans well memorized, she reminded him a bit of his sister playing stage director back when they were children, concocting the home theatricals they had delighted in putting on to amuse their parents.

Since Tavi had always managed to end up as both director and star of the show, that had left Luke to play all the other roles in their scripts, a task he had not shrunk from even as an eight-year-old. He had, admittedly, been a bit of a ham.

Jumping from hero to villain, he'd found it a jolly lark to rush behind the scene sets for a quick costume change, and when he couldn't remember his lines, he was cheeky enough to improvise—a habit that irritated his sister to no end.

But the raucous applause from their doting parents and hugs afterward had made all their efforts worth it.

As his mind drifted back to the present, where Portia was giving him his stage directions for the wedding day, Luke was more than happy to rehearse the part where the vicar said, *"You may now kiss the bride."*

"...so the front pews with ribbons on them will be reserved for our families. Mine are on the left; yours will take the right. You'll have to go over the guest list one more time and make sure we haven't forgotten anybody. People do have a way of surfacing once invitations go out. We can still add a few more if you need to. I don't want to cause any awkwardness for people who might be important to you.

"Now then." She turned, fists planted on her hips as she surveyed the chapel. "We'll have garlands woven through the chandeliers and also festooning the galleries up there, along with swathes of fabric." She pointed this way and that. "There will be large bouquets in tall urns at the edges of the altar and at the back of the church, flanking the aisle. But the flowers are what I wanted to talk to you about."

He blinked back to awareness. "Yes?"

"I want you to know, first, that I searched high and low trying to fulfill your request about flowers that would not disturb the bees—"

"Huh?" Luke did not recall saying that. But it did sound like something Finch would tell him, Lucas-like, to say.

Portia turned around with an incredulous look, which turned to a glare. "You don't remember?"

He blanched at her angry stare. "Sorry."

She took a step toward him. "Your Grace, you were very specific about it. You wrote it in your letter that there should be no garden flowers, no roses—I could show you!"

"N-no, I-I believe you. Sometimes I forget things. Very sorry." He gave her a hapless Lucas sort of smile, mentally cursing himself for forgetting a detail of his Town persona.

His bride scowled at him. "Well—as I was saying—the solution that I finally came up with was that we could have *wildflowers*. They grow back quickly, so your precious bees will not go hungry, and lucky for you, they are abundant this year and many species are entirely beautiful. We should have no trouble collecting hundreds of white daisies and other field flowers, too."

He gazed at her, impressed. "That sounds charming."

The compliment mollified her slightly. "I was worried it would seem like some sort of peasant wedding in the countryside…but then I realized that, if it were artfully done, and skillfully planned, that it could actually be a gorgeous theme."

"Theme?" he echoed, marveling at this unanticipated artistic side of hers.

She folded her arms across her chest, still looking a wee bit defensive. "I've sat through so many weddings over the past year—sometimes, you know, they really start to seem all the same. I wanted ours to be a little different, but when you gave me this stipulation of no garden flowers, no roses, I nearly panicked—"

"I really am sorry. I didn't realize—"

"It's all right." She paused. "Of course you didn't. You're a man. Anyway, at first, I was at a loss—but I wanted you to be pleased. And once I started working on the problem, I thought of the wildflowers. I hated it at first. But it was the best I could come up with. So then I went out walking in some meadows to investigate the notion. And when I spotted a clump of lovely white daisies with yellow centers waving in the sunshine, the whole picture blossomed in my head of how it could be."

"Really?"

She nodded, a smile tugging at one side of her mouth. "Turns out this vexing rule of yours inspired the perfect way that I could create a very unique wedding day for us."

Luke said nothing. Until now, he'd had no idea that he had inconvenienced his bride so much with his arbitrary ban on garden flowers. He had nothing against them, of course; it had merely been part of his Lucas role.

A look of alarm filled her face at his silence. "I'm sorry if you hate it, but it's too late to change it now. Your Grace, you never mentioned any objections in your answer to my letter on the last round of questions, but—"

"No, no, I love it. I think it's a wonderful idea, my lady. I am silent only because I am amazed. Please, tell me more."

She eyed him warily. "Very well. It'll be a celebration of the countryside, right here in Town. A pastoral fantasy, as it were."

"Aha…like some of Shakespeare's plays? *Much Ado About Nothing*…"

"Exactly! *A Midsummer Night's Dream*." She nodded, her blue eyes sparking with approval at his answer. "Besides, the picturesque is all the rage right now. I've been looking at paintings from artists who specialize in the style, as well as sketches from famous gardeners and architects considered masters in it."

"You're a genius," Luke informed her.

She laughed. "You really like it?"

"It's wonderful. The irony is also amusing. A duke marrying his duchess in a peasant-style wedding."

She clasped her hands joyfully. "I thought so, too!"

They gazed at each other, laughing. Portia was radiant with pleasure at his admiration—and his cooperation, no doubt. Luke was simply in awe.

He dropped his gaze, worried that his enchantment with her would make him fall out of character. "Now I am all the more anxious for the big day to come."

She rapped him on the chest with playful scorn. "And to think you wanted to postpone it!"

He smiled shyly at her. "It can't arrive fast enough for me now."

"Well, we need time to let enough daisies grow, don't we? Then collect them all. I shall have an army of servants out picking wildflowers for two days in advance—my own, and some of Serena's."

"I could dispatch some of my staff to help—"

"No, no, yours already have all their assignments!" she warned, holding up her hand. "Don't go changing anything unless you consult me first. This whole day will run like a delicate piece of clockwork."

"Thank you for all your hard work, my lady."

With a wave of her hand, she leaned against the nearest pew. "I suppose I've enjoyed it. I'm just so relieved that you're pleased. I want it to be a beautiful day for everyone."

"It will be if you're there," he said.

Her eyebrows lifted. "That's very sweet."

He pressed his lips together and lowered his head, outwardly bashful, but inwardly beginning to wonder if he could resist using his charm to try to get on her good side. As Silversmoke, she had offered him a whiff of flirtation, but there was none of that for oddball Lucas.

It was absurd to be jealous of oneself, was it not?

"Oh!" She snapped her fingers. "Before I forget: the music."

"Yes?" He leaned his hip against the nearest pew and folded his arms across his chest, peering through his plain glass spectacles at her.

"Normally, of course, a couple chooses songs for the wedding ceremony that have a particular significance to them, provided the vicar approves. I chose the music I wanted for the entrance processional, but I left certain music slots empty so you could choose some, too. I thought…" She hesitated.

"Hmm?"

"Since your parents are no longer with us, I thought you might have some song of particular significance that could be played to honor them in spirit."

His gaze homed in on her with sudden intensity, and his jaw tightened.

Luke had been trying very hard not to contemplate his parents' absence on his wedding day. Because it enraged him and filled him with more than his usual melancholy.

Perhaps that was why he had made a point of staying uninvolved. He figured he would just show up, sign his name, and put the ring on her finger.

"Any particular song that would be meaningful to you, in honor of their memory?" she asked, searching his face.

Floundering at the question when he had not been braced for it, Luke lowered his head. "Um…I can't recall one they'd have wanted at the moment. I should like to think on it a bit, if you don't mind."

"Of course," she murmured, studying him.

"Thank you." Luke kept his gaze averted. "I'll have to ask my sister. She'd remember better than I."

Portia saw that her question had touched a nerve. She had not meant to upset him, but now that the topic had been broached, she took a step closer, scanning him with compassion. "Lucas, it must've been so hard for you, losing them both at a young age."

"It was terrible," he said quietly, with a subtle nod.

She studied him, wondering if Joel would've had the emotional courage to admit something like that. Admit to weakness. Show any hint of vulnerability. It touched her.

Fountainhurst might be an unusual man, but he was humble. He did not put on airs, and that was almost unheard of for a duke.

She laid her hand cautiously on his arm. "Your Grace, I hate to be indelicate, but since I am about to join this family, I really think someone ought to tell me what exactly happened to them. I have heard just a hint in Society that there was violence, but I have not sought out the whole story. I did not wish to pry. I would much rather hear it from you than from the rumor mill. But, you see, I dread the thought of accidentally saying the wrong thing to one of your relatives at the wedding, out of ignorance. Besides, I-I think I have a right to know."

He frowned at her, though his face was stamped with reluctant understanding. Behind his spectacles, she saw a wounded look in his green eyes, then he turned away, as if to hide it.

She watched his every move as he stared at the altar.

"A not unreasonable request," he admitted. "Very well." He squared his shoulders and crossed one arm behind the small of his back in a formal pose as he stood tall. He was silent for a moment.

She waited, watching him in the hush of the empty church.

"They went on holiday to Scotland to celebrate their wedding anniversary. Twenty years, I believe it was. Alas, they were beset upon the road, robbed, and murdered by a gang of filthy bandits in the Highlands."

Portia's eyes widened. She leaned against the pew behind her with a gasp.

At once, an overwhelming wave of guilt flooded through her. How furious her future husband would be if he knew that only last night, his intended duchess had sat across the table from a bandit—the very sort that had robbed him of his parents and his childhood!

Not that Silversmoke would ever do such a thing.

For the first time since she'd dreamed up her plan to seek the highwayman's help to find Joel, all the secrets she'd been keeping from Lucas suddenly stung, sharp and prickly as a clutch of nettles in her heart.

"I'm so sorry," she uttered, shaking her head. "My God."

He still avoided her gaze. "My father could fight, but…they were so outnumbered. The driver, the footmen. The gang left none alive. Even my mother." He paused, his back to her. "But perhaps that is a blessing. That they killed her, I mean. She was a great beauty. It…could've been worse."

Portia closed her eyes.

"Such torture as women may be subjected to, she was spared. Though I'm sure nothing could have been more horrible than seeing her soul mate killed before her very eyes. They ran my father through."

Portia shook her head, speechless, as her eyes filled with tears.

Lucas let out a long breath, his shoulders slumping only for a moment before he cleared his throat and stiffened again. "It is my hypothesis that once the criminals began to rifle through the belongings of these wealthy English travelers they had stopped, they discovered confirmation of my parents' identity, understood that they had just killed a very powerful man, they knew then how badly they'd erred. But the damage was already done.

"At that point, I figure they realized they could not afford to leave his wife alive, even as their plaything. From what I understand, they cut her throat to stop her screaming. A witness was found. That's how I know all this."

Portia sat down abruptly on the nearest pew and pressed her hand across her mouth.

"You have no idea how I wish I could've been there." His low murmur rang through the church, and his voice sounded different, hardened with an echo of cold rage.

Her heart went out to him. The tears thickened in her eyes, but she managed to blink them back as he turned around abruptly.

"Were the men who did this to your family ever caught?"

"Not by the authorities," he said slowly. "Apparently, there was an enemy gang that had it out for them up there in the Highlands somewhere. And I am glad to say that what they had served out to my family came 'round to them again in full measure. Every last one," he added softly.

An undertone of menace in his deep voice sent gooseflesh running down her arms. It seemed most un-Lucas-like.

Then he stared up at the altar and the rose window above it, the only stained glass in St. Andrew's. "'Tis so strange to me that there are actually people in this world who don't believe that evil is real." He turned to her. "Do you?"

She nodded somberly.

"So do I," he said in a steely tone that struck her as oddly familiar. "And I hate it."

"I am so sorry for your loss," she whispered. "Perhaps I should not have asked."

"No. It's all right." He lifted his chin, the dark shadow of pain and fury gradually lifting from him. "You have a right to know, as you said. After all, a month from now, you'll be part of the family. Or what's left of it."

The permanency of the covenant they were entering into shook her as she contemplated it there in the church, where their vows would be exchanged before God and man.

She repented of ever having asked Silversmoke to find Joel, in that moment of realization. Lucas was a good man, and he deserved better than that from her, after all he had been through.

She rose to her feet, and where her next words came from, Portia barely knew, as she took a step toward him. "I realize nothing can change the past for you. But if it's any consolation, Your Grace must remember that in due time, God will bless you with sons and daughters of your own."

He stared bleakly at her. "And so the world continues."

She nodded. "Life is life, and you do your best to live it."

"Thank you, my lady." He lowered his head, staring at the floor. "She would have liked you, I daresay."

Portia winced, gazing at him tenderly.

Then Lucas lifted his chin and squared his shoulders with a decisiveness she had not seen in him before. "Now that I've told you what happened, I will not speak of this matter again."

"But—"

"If there are no more wedding details to discuss, I shall wait for you outside." With that, he stalked past her with a hard look on his face, heading for the back of the church.

Portia did not have the heart to argue with him. Best to let him regain his composure, for there could be no more upsetting subject than the murder of one's family.

As he marched toward the vestibule, she gazed after him, noticing how tall and broad-shouldered he actually was in comparison to the heavy oak doors framing him. He stopped when he reached them, however, and seemed to gather himself, his back to her.

"Do you care to join me, my lady?" he asked without turning around.

Still marveling over having witnessed her gentle scholar-duke angry, she shook off her daze and murmured agreement, hurrying after him.

By the time she reached his side, Lucas appeared to have recovered his amiable composure.

He pushed the door open for her and waited for her to walk through it. But when she brushed past him, she noticed his shrewd green eyes watching her closely, with a scrutiny far too intense for some absent-minded eccentric.

Who is *this man?* she wondered, suddenly feeling unsettled about it all. But since she had clearly pressed her luck enough for one day, asking nosy questions, Portia kept her mouth shut.

But she was suddenly mystified by the man she'd pledged to wed.

CHAPTER 8

A Brief Visit to Hell

That night, Luke took off his spectacles, set them on the dressing table in his bedchamber at Fountainhurst House, and stared hard at himself in the mirror.

Shadows from the candle nearby covered one side of his face. He was not in the best of moods. How in the hell had his life grown so complicated?

All day he had been pondering his exchange with Portia in the church, his emotions churning like a dark sea from the moment they'd parted ways.

The day had been uneventful after he'd taken his leave of her. Around teatime, he had sent his empty coach-and-four trundling back to Gracewell, yet another ruse—this time, to make his future wife and any nosy neighbors believe that "Lucas" had returned to his estate in the country.

Lucas was no longer needed. But Silversmoke had dark business to see to tonight. He would begin pursuing the answers he'd promised his mysterious lady in black.

Whoever she was.

Portia Tennesley was becoming more of a mystery to him with every hour that passed. Why had she forced him to talk about his parents?

Why had she promised to give him children to somehow fix the broken circle of the Fountainhurst generations, when he knew perfectly well that the minute that he found her precious Joel for her, if he was alive, she'd retract her offer, change her mind about going through with that pretty wedding she'd described, and leave poor quiz Lucas in the dust?

Little two-faced deceiver. But wasn't he one, too? An even worse one, at that? For even now, he was preparing to darken his hair with the old theatrical trick of ashes mixed into a men's pomade. It covered his sandy-colored waves and washed out easily enough when he was done.

Bloody hell. He thrust Portia out of his mind, turned away from the mirror, and pulled off his shirt.

It was now ten thirty, fully dark outside, and time to rid himself of the scholarly clothes that he donned playing Lucas. Bare-chested, he reached for his ruffian clothes instead, pulling a dark shirt out of his wardrobe. He slipped it on over his head, tucked it into his black breeches, then pulled on his boots.

Nearby, his canopy bed was shrouded in shadows. Luke wondered if he'd ever get the chance to roger her there. He refused to think of it any more romantically than that now, since he knew he probably wouldn't.

No use dreaming.

After slinging his usual weapons belt around his waist, he buckled it, then pulled on a dark gray leather jacket. Finally, returning to the mirror, he slicked his hair back with the blackening preparation.

There was no need for the mask tonight—the dark hair and the day's beard darkening his jaw would provide him with enough of a different look.

He gave his roughed-up appearance a brief once-over. *Welcome back, Silversmoke.* Turning away from the mirror, he swiped his highwayman hat off the peg where it hung and prowled out of his room.

His old, sphinxlike butler, Howell, waited for him at the bottom of the servant stairs that Luke always used in Silversmoke mode. The hidden staircase was convenient because it led down to a service door, through which Luke could disappear discreetly out of the back of the house.

"Any special instructions for tonight, Your Grace?" Howell asked, handing him the little pewter flask of whiskey that he liked to take with him on his adventures.

Luke gave him a sardonic smile and slipped it into his breast pocket. "If anyone should call, His Grace is not at home."

"Very good, sir." Howell bowed. With wisps of gray hair combed across the pale dome of his head, and fleshy bags underneath his shrewd, deep-set eyes, the stately old butler had seen too many things in his decades of service with the family to question his master's shadowy comings and goings.

Besides, Howell had been a fixture here since before Luke was born. Why, Luke could remember when he'd been no taller than little Simon, and had had to tilt his head back to look up at Howell.

Now nearing eighty, the butler seemed diminutive and frail next to Luke's much larger frame, but Howell had always been ferociously loyal.

He had served Luke's grandfather and then his father, and like every servant in their employ, he had grieved for months right along with Luke and Tavi when their parents had been murdered.

Therefore, when the title had fallen to Luke, instead of trying to prevent his quest for vengeance, Howell had assisted him—above all, by covering for him at every turn. Inside the household, Howell made sure the staff under him asked no questions. And to the outside world, he helped Luke continue his charade with Society.

"Right. Well, I'm off, then." Luke gave Howell an affectionate clap on the shoulder—but took care to use restraint, not wishing to knock the ancient fellow across the room. "Don't wait up for me. I've no idea where the night might lead, but I should be back by morning."

"As you wish." Howell opened the door and offered one of his rare smiles. "If I may say so, Your Grace, it is very good to have you home."

Luke smiled back. "It's good to see you too, Howell."

With that, he squared his shoulders, took a deep breath, then marched through the door. He heard it close quietly behind him as he strode across the grounds. At the back of the garden, he slipped out the waist-high gate into the cobbled mews, then crossed to his stable.

Inside, the smell of hay greeted him, along with the soft snuffling of a dozen horses, bored and lazing in their stalls. Sauntering down the stable aisle, he considered which horse to take tonight. Tempo was housed at Gracewell and would stay there; Luke wasn't taking any chances of his equine partner in crime being recognized in Town.

He decided on Orion, a tall liver bay with a scattering of three small white stars down his forehead. The gelding was fast, with a steady temperament; he seemed eager for adventure, too, judging by how he swung his head around and pricked up his ears when Luke paused outside his stall.

Luke smiled at the big bay. "Evening, boy. Tell me, how do you like gambling?"

Orion took a curious step toward him, rustling the hay under his hoofs.

Since all his horses were groomed daily, all Luke had to do was fetch the tack. Eschewing the role of the pampered aristocrat, he saddled Orion himself, working by the moonlight that streamed in through the stall window.

After a final adjustment of the girth, Luke led Orion out of his stall, then swung up into the saddle and gathered the reins.

Orion seemed eager to go. Luke squeezed the bay's sides with his calves, and they left the stable. Guiding his horse out of the mews at a walk, Luke frowned at the sky. *This weather can't make up its mind.*

The humidity was back, but now in the form of a damp evening fog.

Wisps of vapor curled down from the pregnant skies. Moisture hung in the air; he could see faint swirls of mist where the wrought-iron street lantern shone, the feeble ball of light around each attracting its own shimmer of moths.

As Luke rode quietly down the street, unnoticed, he listened to the clip-clopping of his horse's hooves bouncing off the buildings. In short order, he left Moonlight Square behind, turning right onto Knightsbridge, paralleling Hyde Park.

Gower would meet him at Charing Cross, as they'd planned that morning, and accompany him to this gambling hell that Portia said was the last place Joel Clayton had been seen alive.

God's truth, Luke was beginning to feel slightly jealous of the bleeder. And that would not do.

He urged Orion into an easy trot, blending into the shadows, anonymous, and lowering his head to mask his face in shadow when a carriage drove by in the opposite direction. Nobody paid him any mind, neither driver nor occupants.

The shops along Knightsbridge were dark at this hour, but the homes of the well-to-do were lit up throughout the West End as fashionable folk flitted from one social event to another, enjoying the Season.

He could hear the music playing in some of them, could even smell the food.

Their gaiety brought back his bad mood, an irksome reminder of what an outsider he had chosen to become. Determined to ignore the revelers, he rode on, staring down the dark street over his horse's bobbing head.

Reining to a halt, he paid his toll at the Hyde Park turnpike, and the chap on duty there swung the creaky metal bar to let him through. Luke rode on as Knightsbridge turned into Piccadilly, and this, in turn, swooped up above Green Park.

Here he passed even larger and grander mansions, even louder parties in progress. Denizens of the first circles lounged on dainty wrought-iron balconies, sipping wine and enjoying the moonlight.

His mood darkened further.

But when an aged night watchman lifted a hand in greeting as he rode by, Luke waved back. A typical Charley, overweight and nearly seventy, hobbling along the pavement with his staff and lantern in hand.

There was London's police force for you, dear old things.

Of course, there were also the Bow Street Runners, but these were rather few and far between, given Britons' instinctual distrust of anything that could grow into the sort of tyrannical secret police that had formed in France under Napoleon.

With a pistol, a rapier, and a trained pair of fists, it was a man's duty and his right to fend for himself, guided by natural law and, of course, the legal commentaries of trusty old Blackstone.

In any case, the old Charleys didn't give the criminal folk of London much cause for concern. If anything, they were more often used as the butt of pranks for drunken young rakehells. With such heroes as these, no wonder the downtrodden kept Silversmoke so busy. Not that Luke minded.

In a way, he mused, turning right at St. James's Street, he needed to be Silversmoke as much as the people that he helped needed *him*.

Being a normal duke would have been too boring for him to contemplate.

Besides, if he didn't have these pursuits to occupy his mind, he'd have far too much time to ponder the past and, admittedly, the whisper of guilt that haunted him now and then ever since he had wreaked bloody vengeance on that Scottish gang.

Cool-nerved as he generally was, this was the one thought that had the power to make Luke uneasy. But, hell, they deserved it for their crimes.

As Orion's hoofbeats lulled him into a mild trance, he let his mind drift back to those terrible days…

His parents had been missing for a fortnight before he had even heard that something might be wrong, that they had never reached their destination. Luke had been oblivious, away at Oxford, a typical wellborn lad of seventeen.

Due to the distance of his parents' planned holiday up in the Scottish Highlands, and the fact (as he would learn only years later) that the MacAbe gang had hidden the bodies and burned the coach to cover up the crime, it had been months before the world could safely conclude that the vanished Duke and Duchess of Fountainhurst were dead.

Murdered somewhere along the way as they journeyed to celebrate their wedding anniversary. For the better part of a long, agonizing year, though, no one could say for certain what had become of them.

Just like Joel.

In the midst of all this, Luke had dropped out of school, bewildered and paralyzed with disbelief and horror. Much like Portia's state of mind, he supposed, at about the time when he had proposed to her.

It was six months before he could even start to function normally again. Every day felt like the end of the world, and he had been lost.

Tavi had been the strong one then; as the firstborn, she saw it as her duty to be the rock for them both. But, eventually, Luke's paralyzing shock had worn off, along with his mind's utter rejection that such harrowing injustice was even possible.

Then the rage had set in…and never really left.

It had focused his mind, helped him think, helped him start to plan. By his eighteenth birthday, any trace of the boy in him was gone.

As the heir of a dukedom with every resource at his disposal, Luke had vowed to find his parents' killers and destroy them utterly.

It had taken no less than four years to zero in on the MacAbe gang, for there were hundreds of miles of ground to search, countless false leads to follow; frankly, the entire first year had been a waste of time, since he was alone, blind and bumbling, and had no bloody idea what he was doing.

During the second year into his search, however—shortly after turning nineteen—he had met Gower, and together, they had finally started making progress.

It was only in the third year, after his parents' remains had been found quite by accident by a man out hunting with his dog, their identities confirmed by some of the items buried with their bodies, that Luke and Gower managed to home in on the right county in which they'd been waylaid.

From there, it was only a matter of time before they tracked down the gang responsible.

The murderous MacAbe had plagued the Highlands throughout that area for decades. Gower's daughter had been snatched from a coaching inn within their territory while on her way to take a post as a chambermaid, and upon digging, Luke and Gower discovered that the same nightmarish thing had happened to other girls, as well.

Some as young as twelve.

Once Luke had found his target in the MacAbe gang, some thirty thieves and criminals strong, he had no desire to put them out of their misery quickly. With revenge now in sight, he meant to savor it.

Having found the evildoers, he and Gower had enjoyed picking them off for a while one by one, terrorizing them. The gang had no idea for weeks why they were being killed, let alone by whom.

They had thought it was a rival clan with an old grudge. That had been amusing.

But, eventually, on that bloody night when Gower and he had launched their massive final attack to destroy the rest of the gang, the last surviving member had said something to Luke that had haunted him ever since.

The red-bearded man had been struck with shrapnel from the grenades Gower and he had lobbed into the gang's headquarters as an opening salvo, so he'd been unable to run outside with his comrades— directly into the line of Luke and Gower's rifle fire.

Some did push through the hail of lead—they were Scots, after all, tough as nails—so the next step had been hand-to-hand combat. Luke and Gower had both arrived prepared to die, however, and fought accordingly.

The poor MacAbe gang thought a pair of demons had attacked them.

It was only after the battle, when Luke stalked into the smoking ruins of the gang's headquarters, splashed with blood, his sword drawn to finish off any survivors, that he'd found that wild-eyed bastard impaled on a wooden stake.

Apparently, the long shard sticking out of the braw Scot's middle was all that remained of the table where he'd been sitting drinking his whiskey when the explosives landed in their pub.

Unable to rise or flee, and already feeling the life leaving him, no doubt, the last surviving gang member pleaded for Luke to help him.

Luke asked why he should. He then explained why he was there. Why this judgment had befallen the gang member and his mates.

The dying man had let out a brief, hysterical laugh. "Ye think we did that on our own, ye bloody Sassenach?"

"What do you mean?"

"He hired us, you ass! One of yer own countrymen." He began jabbering about some rich man who'd paid them to carry out what sounded like a carefully plotted assassination, but the bastard died before Luke could get a name or confirm that his tale was anything but lies.

There was no one left to corroborate his claim, since Luke and Gower had just wiped out the rest of the gang.

An eye for an eye.

Luke shuddered at the memories, but still refused to believe the dying criminal had been telling the truth. Trying to bargain for his life, that red-haired devil would've said anything.

It was nothing but a final swipe at him, a parting blow tipped with poison that would taint Luke's blood for the rest of his life.

What else could he do? He could not pursue it further. Besides, even Luke knew deep down that he'd already gone a little too far with his revenge.

The thing was over now; it had to be.

After all he'd done, he had to believe that the crime was the simple robbery gone bad that it had always appeared. Otherwise, he might go mad.

He could not afford to slip back into the depths of dark obsession, where he'd spent so much time in the past.

Wiping out the MacAbe gang had to be enough to slake his wrath, and really, what choice did he have at this point than to shrug off his doubts?

It was too late now. He and Gower had killed them all. He supposed he'd never know.

But it seemed a bitter waste to have gone to such lengths, most likely forfeiting his soul by what he'd done, only to wreak bloody vengeance on the hirelings and leave the man behind the plot alive.

He wondered, though, as he clopped along on Orion, if the past could ever really be over for him while that haunting question remained unanswered.

Come to think of it, it was not too different from Portia's situation.

She could not move on emotionally into their married future until she knew what had become of Joel. He, of all people, understood that.

Likewise, Luke did not see how he could ever be the sort of husband she wanted when he remained so full of cold, hard hate for all the evil in the world. He wanted to hurt the evil more than he cared about embracing the good.

Where that put him, he supposed, was probably somewhere between the two. Somewhere in the shadowlands between dark and light…

Ah well. Fortunately, the phantom of guilt, for all its haunting, was easily brushed away.

Turning left onto Pall Mall, Luke rode past the prince regent's sprawling home of Carlton House, with its long row of tall pillars.

From there, he took the flowing right-hand turn onto Cockspur Street, and spotted the ancient stone monument of Charing Cross ahead.

Beside it, Gower waited on his trusty blue roan.

Luke rode over to his friend with a nod of greeting. Gower nodded back and turned his mount around, then both of them headed up the Strand.

Gower's horse fell into step beside Orion. Their hooves clopped over the cobblestones. The roads were fairly empty at this hour. People who had social events to attend were already there, Luke supposed, and those who didn't were home sleeping.

He wondered what his fiancée was doing tonight.

"So what's the name of this place again?" Gower asked.

"The Blue Room."

The Thames was on their right now, and though the fog had thickened near the river, Luke could see and hear a noisy, lantern-lit barge of revelers floating out on the water, complete with a brass band for entertainment. Damn it, was he the only man with serious business to attend to in London tonight?

Gower arched a brow as Luke grumbled wordlessly under his breath. "What's wrong with you?"

"Nothin'."

Gower smirked. "Is that right?"

"What do *you* think?" Luke retorted. "My future bride has sent me off to find her former suitor so she won't have to marry me."

"Don't do it, then."

"I gave m'bloody word! So either I find this idiot alive and he steals her from me. Or I find out he's dead, and then I have to break the news to her somehow. News that'll probably crush her. But then I've got to marry her as dunderhead Lucas, pretending I know none of this—while she pretends she was never in love with someone else... Ah, it's all a bloody mess."

Gower shrugged. "So find another girl."

"Leave her at the altar?" Luke scoffed. "Are you mad? What kind of bounder would I be?"

"Well, you're stupid if you knowingly get yourself into a bad match. Take it from me," Gower muttered with a bitter edge in his gruff voice.

Luke glanced at his friend with sympathy. Gower was unofficially divorced. His marriage had crumbled after their daughter's abduction and murder. His wife had blamed him for not being there to protect her, poor bastard, never mind that the man had been at sea, making a living for his family. No matter. His wife had thrown him out and found somebody else.

They rode on in silence.

After a moment, Luke shrugged, unconvinced himself. "It's not a sure thing we'd be unhappy. It's just—she was the last bloody soul I ever expected to come waltzing into The Blind Badger asking for Silversmoke's help." He glanced around warily. "What if she figures it out? She's rather a clever girl."

Gower shrugged.

Luke blew out a long exhalation. "I have to admit, though, the fact that she would do such a thing has made the young lady a good deal more interesting in my eyes."

Gower snorted, then looked askance at him. "You're a pain in the arse, you know that?"

Luke laughed in spite of himself. The tough old curmudgeon had been telling him that since he was a lad, pestering the older man to teach him how to fight dirty, like Gower had learned in the Navy.

None of this fencing-school stuff.

Luke had already had all the usual training for a highborn boy by the time his parents died. But there was a time and a place for the finesse he had learned from his sword master, and there was a time to make an enemy wish he had never been born.

Gower had spent his youth picking up new tricks and foreign fighting techniques from the many ports he'd visited, especially in the Orient. As a sailor, he had gained valuable experience in brutal shipboard battles, not to mention the regular brawls among the crew.

Enemies always underestimated him because of his gray hair and wiry build, but fights were also about brains, watchfulness, and dogged endurance.

Hopefully, neither of them would have to use their skills tonight. Instead, the mission was simply to start making inquiries.

At that moment, the entrance to Southampton Street appeared in the darkness, and there was no more time for conversation.

They exchanged a guarded glance, then made the turn and headed the short distance up the street to Covent Garden.

It was time to find The Blue Room.

Meanwhile back in Moonlight Square, Serena turned around and stared at Portia in astonishment. "You did *what*?"

The raven-haired duchess was still standing before the cheval glass, holding up the gorgeous ball gown that she meant to wear to the Grand Albion tomorrow night.

She had wanted Portia to see it, since they were both devotees of fashion. And since neither of the two best friends had anything else to do tonight, they had enjoyed an evening in at Rivenwood House, chatting and having a glass of wine together.

Azrael had been at home earlier, but after bidding Serena adieu with a kiss, the pale-haired duke had stepped out to go and play cards with the gents at the club for a couple of hours. Once her husband left, Serena's real purpose in inviting Portia over had become clear.

The gown had merely been the little slyboots' excuse to get Portia over here so Serena could interrogate her on why she'd been acting so odd for the past few days.

Portia had bitten her lip and floundered.

Alas, there was no lying to the Duchess of Rivenwood.

So, against her better judgment, Portia had broken down and confessed to Serena about seeking out Silversmoke.

To be sure, she had not expected this reaction. Presently, her best friend's mouth was hanging open.

Why, Portia had thought Serena unshockable—especially after she'd married someone like Azrael.

"You hired...a *highwayman*?" Serena tossed the gown onto her canopy bed and propped her hands on her waist. "No wonder you've been acting so bizarre!"

"I haven't," Portia said meekly, cuddling fuzzy little Franklin on her lap. She sat perched on the satin ottoman in Serena's luxurious boudoir.

Serena marched over and bent down to scrutinize her, narrowing her dark hazel eyes, her long black lashes bristling with disapproval.

"I know what I'm doing!" Portia said. "He's not an *ordinary* highwayman."

"Oh, indeed?" Serena straightened up again, ignoring her dog wagging his tail at her. "You have others to compare him to?"

"That's not what I meant. He's...very agreeable," she insisted. "And gentlemanly, too." *With the most irresistible, roguish grin.* "Well, it isn't as though he's going to hurt me!"

"He'd better not, or he'll have to deal with me." Serena plopped herself down on the armchair across from the ottoman, still scowling at Portia, though only with fond protectiveness.

"This is a good thing," Portia said.

"Maybe." Serena arched a brow. "One wonders, though, what Fountainhurst would say."

Portia's eyes widened as she held the wriggly terrier still. "He must never find out, Serena! No one can. Not even Azrael."

Serena winced. "Hold on, my dear. My husband and I have a no-secrets policy. Whatever you tell me, I am honor-bound to share with him, if he asks. I am sorry, but I have no choice. It's the only way I can make sure he's being open with me in all things. That's not easy for him."

"Then that's all I'll say. I don't want to put you in a bad position. But I don't want your husband trying to stop me, either!" Portia added. "Silversmoke is a good man. I trust him. You would too, if you'd just look in the papers and read about all the people he's helped. He's a hero!"

"Hero? Ah, so the papers never lie to sell more copies, hmm?"

Portia ignored the cynic. "It's a wonder Silversmoke can even make a living, come to think of it. Seems like he hardly ever robs anyone..." She waved this off. "Anyway, we had a very interesting conversation. He's rather charming."

"Oh, really?"

As Serena tilted her head, still skeptical, Portia felt a telltale blush creeping into her cheeks.

"Oh my!" the duchess murmured suddenly as understanding dawned in her eyes. A smile tugged at her lips. "You wicked girl."

"I'm sorry, but the man is ridiculously handsome. I can't help it!" Portia cried as a laugh escaped her. She could feel her blush deepening.

Serena laughed, too. "I see. All well and good, but why is this stranger willing to do this for you? To help you find Joel? There must be something in it for *him*. If you know what I mean." She waggled her eyebrows.

"No!" Portia said. "He's far too honorable for that."

"Right. A hero."

"I believe he merely enjoys the adventure of dealing with such things. Besides, in the matter of me and Joel…" Portia let Franklin climb over to his mistress, whose lap he clearly preferred. "He says he has a soft spot for true love."

"Well!" Serena took the little white dog into her arms and scratched him under the ear for a moment. "I suppose if he said that, he can't be *all* bad."

Portia waved a hand. "Don't worry. The dangerous part is already done. He said that when he has any news, he'll come and meet me in a safer place. He's gallant like that."

"And when do you suppose you might hear from this mysterious hero of yours again?"

Portia took another sip of wine and shook her head. "No idea."

But if she was honest, she could hardly wait.

CHAPTER 9

High Stakes

*L*uke and Gower rode up Southampton Street to the outer edge of Covent Garden square, where they paused to glance around. Cloaked in darkness, as though ashamed of aging badly, the once-proud piazza awaited them in all its dilapidated grandeur. Nearly two hundred years ago, Inigo Jones had built the Italianate square and its tall, terraced houses with vaulted colonnades to serve as upper-class dwellings. But as the wealthy had migrated west within London, Covent Garden had begun its long slide into squalor.

Nowadays, the once-fashionable square had become a chaos of costermongers by day: flower sellers, poulterers, and tinkers hawked their wares from stalls, booths, and handcarts. By night, however, the market dissolved away, and the square became the haunt of Cyprians and sinners, drunks and cut-purses—and, of course, sharps and gulls alike pouring into the gambling hells, brothels, and pubs that had taken over the once-aristocratic houses.

The dampness lay visibly thicker in the dark, empty space of the square; it felt heavy in Luke's lungs. Vapor wafted like ghosts, curling around the ramshackle wooden stalls and semi-permanent sheds of the daytime market sellers, while in the center, swathed in mist, an old church presided over the slow decay that had long since set in here.

Gower and he urged their horses into motion and circled the square until they spotted a house with a royal blue door tucked away beneath the arched colonnade.

They exchanged a look, knowing that they'd found the place, then dismounted and hired an idle boy to mind their horses.

Walking under the archway of the colonnade, they found a large, rugged man with a flattened nose posted by the door to The Blue Room.

Stationed there to bar undesirables from entry—and to help remove sore losers, one presumed—the fellow had the look of an ex-boxer, but he did not attempt to deter the two of them from going in. He merely flicked a glance over them, making sure they were not beggars, then nodded as they passed.

When they stepped inside the raucous gaming house, Luke was momentarily dazzled by the stabbing light from the brass chandeliers after being out in the ebony night. He blinked a few times as his eyes adjusted, then took in his surroundings.

Tawdry, he decided, but in all, the place was not as bad as he'd expected after the way Portia had described it. A young lady probably had higher standards of elegance than a part-time highwayman, though. His lips curved at the thought of her.

Then Gower and he walked in.

The Blue Room stretched ahead of them, long and narrow, like most terrace houses. The place was packed to the rafters with gamblers and their hangers-on. But it was easy to see how The Blue Room had gotten its name.

Though the sticky floor beneath their feet was of scuffed black marble, the walls surrounding them were covered in slightly tattered blue damask. The ornate pattern of garlands and peacock feathers was wrought with gold and silver thread, so that the walls glistened in the chandeliers' glow.

Every so often within the florid pattern, however, there was a recurring flower shape that oddly resembled a human eye. It gave the disturbing illusion of a thousand eyes watching everyone. The effect sent an eerie shiver down Luke's spine.

Indeed, beneath the noise and gaiety, he could feel the undercurrent of reckless desperation in this place like a fever. Convex mirrors flanked by spindly candle sconces added to the general sense of distortion. Overhead, he noticed naughty murals painted inside the ceiling coffers.

Out of nowhere, a waiter hurried by carrying a platter of greasy chicken. Potboys likewise wove through the crowd, keeping the liquor flowing to all the players. Bad food, cheap drink, Luke mused, and the flatteries of the soiled doves sauntering through the crowd combined to make the men feel lucky.

Aye, it only took a moment to comprehend what this fast-paced place was all about: the elusive hope of easy winnings, when anyone with sense knew the house always won in the end.

Gower nudged him, and both men moved on, staying on their guard as they walked deeper into the gambling hell's kaleidoscope of gaudy color and motion. Here, the dice flew across the hazard table; over there, stone-faced dealers at the vingt-et-un tables shuffled cards with deft expertise.

The air was thick with the jubilant exclamations of the winners, the hissed curses of the losers. Moneylenders trolled the crowd, ready to rescue the losers with their loans at cutthroat rates of interest. The ladies of the evening, heavily rouged and scantily clad, were also on the prowl for clients.

Luke glanced at the audience that had gathered to watch several sharpers try their luck at faro, where colorful tiles depicting the thirteen cards in a suit were set into the table. Other gamblers counted out their chips and placed them in the diamonds across the *rouge et noir* table.

A fairly newfangled game, that. Luke was no frequenter of gaming houses, but he understood *rouge et noir* was becoming quite a craze—a recent import from France.

They passed a bookmaker busily taking wagers on the derby races to be held throughout the coming weeks. Behind a metal grill near the back, the aproned clerk looked surly at having to pay out the winners.

All the while, tucked away in the nook beneath the staircase—which led up ever so conveniently to the brothel—the illegal and thus wildly popular EO wheel continued spinning like a torture device, clicking and whirring, and taking all its eager devotees down the road to ruin.

There was a reason that one was against the law, thought Luke, then he remembered he was a highwayman, and had no room to talk about laws being broken.

With that thought, he took care to mind his wallet amid the jostling of the crowd. No doubt there were pickpockets in their midst, taking advantage of the crush.

Sure enough, it was only minutes later when he felt a light-fingered hand creeping up, trying to reach inside his jacket.

Lightning-fast, Luke grasped a slender wrist and yanked its owner roughly in front of him.

He found himself face to face with a startled brunette harlot of indeterminate age. Bare-shouldered and big-breasted, she could've been anywhere from thirty to fifty.

But the moment that he caught her, she tried to pretend she had only been caressing his chest in admiration of his body, instead of trying to get her sneaky little fingers on his wallet.

"No need to play so rough, darling," she said, sidling closer. "My, you're a big boy, aren't you?"

Irked but amused, Luke loosened his hold on the woman's wrist but did not let go, plucking her hand from inside his coat. "You should be more careful choosing your mark." He leaned closer. "Next time, avoid picking a fellow thief."

The brazen creature feigned innocence. "How dare you accuse me!"

Luke smirked. "Ah, there's no shame in it, dear. I've made off with a few borrowed goods in my day, too."

Her lips curved as she gave up the game and tilted her head coyly. "Humph. I knew we must have something in common. I'm Esme. Why don't you come upstairs where we can, um, talk?"

Gower snorted, and Luke glanced sardonically at him. Esme looked at the pewter-haired man with interest, too. At least Gower was closer to her in age.

"Tell me something, lovely." Luke decided that this little schemer might be of use to him. "You study people for a living, do you not? You'd have to, in your trade."

She waved her fan across her bosom. "That is true. Why do you ask?"

"Because I'm looking for someone, and I'm thinking you might be able to help me."

"Oh, indeed, there's lots of ways that I could help you, love." Esme laid a hand on his chest and stepped closer. "Just tell me what you need."

Luke ignored her practiced seduction. "Have you been working here long?"

"A couple of years or so. Why? Are you looking for someone with lots of experience, hmm? Because I can assure you, I've got that in *spades.*"

"Not exactly." Luke reached into his coat and took out the miniature portrait of Joel he had taken from Portia. He showed it to her. "Does this man look familiar to you? Highborn chap. I understand he used to come in here a lot."

Esme gave it a wary glance. "Oh. You mean Clayton."

"You knew him?"

"Not well. And not in the biblical sense," she added wryly. "But yes. I used to see him around here quite a bit. He doesn't come here anymore." She glanced from Gower to Luke with a wary look in her dark eyes. "They say he disappeared."

"What can you tell me about him?"

The courtesan shrugged. "The boy knew how to win—at least, until the night it seems his luck ran out."

"And would you know anything about that?" Luke asked.

"Why do you want to know?"

"A friend of Clayton's asked me to look into the matter. So?"

Esme put out her hand and stared at him in expectant silence. Luke's lips twisted, but he took out his billfold.

The harlot only spoke after he had tucked a five-pound note into her hand. "I know who Clayton was playing against the last night he came in. There was quite an unpleasant scene."

"Really?"

"Yes. He's right over there." She nodded discreetly to a large, curly-haired man playing hazard. "That's Dog. Clayton crushed him at burgundy."

Gower frowned. "Dog?"

She shrugged. "Martin Osgood, but that's what we all call him. Used to be Lucky Dog when he first started coming here, but that doesn't fit him anymore. Poor fool; he's been on a hellish losing streak for ages. Doesn't know when to quit." Esme sighed and shook her head. "So few of them do."

"Did Clayton beat him that night?"

She scoffed. "Oh, that haughty little prick always beat everyone. That's why nobody liked him. Well, the girls liked his money. But that night..."

"What?" Luke asked.

Esme put out her palm. Luke frowned but coughed up another fiver while Gower looked on, scowling.

As Esme tucked the bank note into her bosom, her manner turned uneasy. "That night—the last night we saw him—Clayton cleaned out everyone at the speculation table, then sat down for a burgundy match against Dog. They set their wagers high, and Clayton laid him low. Only, this time, Dog threw a temper tantrum. It was, er, rather memorable," she said. "I remember because I dreaded having to go upstairs with him afterward. He was one of my regulars at the time." She looked away. "I

106   *Gaelen Foley*

don't like it when they get violent."

Gower narrowed his eyes. "He hit you?"

"It happens, love. Part of the game, I'm afraid."

Luke and Gower exchanged a dark glance.

Esme quickly hid her feelings on the risks of her profession and looked away with an air of nonchalance. "Dog has a temper, but his bark is worse than his bite, provided he's reasonably sober. When he's drunk... Well, that's all I have to say on the matter, and you didn't hear any of it from me.

"Now, you must excuse me, loves. It's been nice chatting, but a girl's got to make a living. I'm sure you understand."

"You're doing pretty well so far," Gower said with a snort, but Luke slipped her another pound note for her time.

She tucked it into her barely-there bodice with a wink, then glided off to find another mark.

"Huh," Luke said, turning to his friend. "Quarreled with Joel publicly the night he disappeared?"

"Let's go have a word with this Dog," Gower mumbled.

Luke nodded and put the cameo of Joel back in his breast pocket, then they made their way over to the hazard table where a tall, raw-featured fellow in his forties continued rolling the dice.

Martin Osgood, a.k.a. Dog, had a broad, husky frame and a hard-living countenance with deep-set eyes, blunt features, and fleshy jowls. A bushy pelt of brownish curls rose above his receding hairline, while thick sideburns stretched down before his ears.

Despite the losing streak Esme had mentioned, he seemed to be having a good night, laughing as the dice cooperated.

Luke and Gower joined the crowd watching the fast-paced play at the hazard table. Eventually, Dog's luck took a turn for the worse, and he had to bow out.

He left the hazard table muttering a curse. But as he bent his head to count whatever money he had left, he must've noticed Luke and Gower watching him, for he looked over at them pugnaciously.

"You two got a problem?"

"Are you Dog?" Luke asked.

"Aye, who's asking?"

"We'd like a word." Luke took a step closer, and Dog took a step back, glancing from him to Gower with deepening suspicion.

Luke pulled out the cameo and showed it to the gambler. "Recognize him?"

Luke caught the man's fleeting blanch before his expression locked down. "No. Never seen him before."

"Not much for the bluff, eh?" Gower asked, lifting his chin.

"Excuse me?"

Luke pushed the cameo closer to Dog. "Maybe you ought to take another look."

Dog bristled, taking a step back. "I don't know what your game is, boys, but whatever you're sellin', I ain't buyin'. Now get the hell away from me." He started to turn away.

"We're not finished yet." Luke clamped his hand down on Dog's shoulder while Gower slid in front of the man, blocking his path.

Luke turned him around forcefully, and Dog's ruddy cheeks flushed with anger.

"I want to know about your fight with Joel Clayton on the night he disappeared."

Dog's mouth snapped shut at that, and the ruddiness drained from his face. He glanced nervously from Luke to Gower. "Now look here. I don't know who you are or what all this is about, but I have no idea what you mean."

Luke looked at Gower. "He's not cooperating, is he?"

"No," Gower agreed. "He really should."

"Tell me, friend," Luke said, edging closer to Dog. "Have you ever heard of a chap called Silversmoke?"

Dog looked baffled. "Wot, the highwayman? Why on earth would you ask me that?"

"Let's just say I'm a personal friend. He's asked me to look into the matter of Joel Clayton's disappearance."

"Shite," Dog said under his breath.

"Indeed," Luke answered, then he tried a bold tactic. "Word has it you killed the poor bastard."

"Me? No! I didn't kill him. I never killed anybody!"

"So you claim," said Luke.

"Go to hell. I don't have to answer you!"

"Would you rather Silversmoke come looking for you personally?" Luke gave him a hard, cold stare that helped the man figure out for himself who he was already talking to.

Dog went very still, and his eyes slid from Luke's face to Gower's and back again. He lifted his hands a bit. "I don't want any trouble here."

"Then I suggest you start talking."

Dog stared at them, hesitating as he visibly battled with himself, then he gave in. "All right. Come with me." He turned away, nodding to them to follow.

Gower looked at Luke, his weathered brow furrowed. Luke nodded to acknowledge the possibility that the gambler could be leading them into a trap. No matter. They were both ready.

But when they stepped outside into the little alleyway behind the building, Dog turned to them and glanced around nervously. The noise from the gambling hell faded as the door swung shut.

Luke set his hands on his hips and looked at Dog expectantly. "Well?"

Dog ran his hand through his poodle-like curls, looking cornered and afraid.

"Did you kill him or not?" Luke demanded.

"No! I mean, I was thinking about it, to be perfectly honest with you. I was *so sick* of his smug face." Dog shook his head. "That coxcomb! He just kept winning and winning. I was sure he was cheating, but of course I couldn't prove it. Plus, I might've been...a little drunk." He hesitated, putting his hands in his pockets. "I guess I lost my temper."

"So you killed him," Gower said, restraining himself, though Luke could tell he wanted to hit him back for Esme.

"No! I only wanted to get my money back. I needed that blunt."

"Shouldn't have gambled it away, then," Luke told him impassively, folding his arms across his chest.

"Yeah, yeah. A highwayman can tell me all about virtue." Dog waved him off.

"What happened?" Gower said.

Dog eyed him nervously. "It was getting late when Clayton left. Maybe one. I followed him out, kept real quiet. He went out the front door, walked up from the arcade a little, and started to cross the square. You seen those buildings out there, all the market stalls?"

Luke and Gower nodded.

"Well, uh"—he gave them a sheepish glance—"I thought I was gonna give him a good clout on the costard once he was out of sight between a couple of those stalls. Where no one would see. It was very dark. There was no moon. I wasn't gonna kill him, though! I only meant to knock him out and take my money back. He had enough blunt of his own! Point is, I never got the chance."

"And why is that?" Luke asked with a skeptical stare.

Dog grew more agitated, glancing around uneasily. "Before I could catch up to him, some coach comes flying down the street. Nearly ran me over. Halts right beside him. Door flies open, some big bald bastard jumps out and grabs Clayton, right before my eyes. Shoves a sack over his head, then throws him in the coach and drives off, hell-for-leather."

His eyes were wide. "It was over before I could even react, and Clayton, he didn't even have time to scream. But I did see another pair of hands reach out from inside the coach to help pull him in, so there must've been two of them, at least. One inside, the bald one driving. It's like they were waitin' for him."

Luke stared at him, taken aback. "You're telling me you saw Joel Clayton get abducted?"

"Aye! That's exactly what I'm sayin'. The coach went flying out the north end of Covent Garden just as fast as it had come." Dog gestured northward, looking bewildered. "He was just gone. There was nothing left to see but the damned flower he wore in his boutonniere lying on the ground."

"Flower?" Luke asked.

"He always wore one when he played, cocky bastard. Said it brought him good luck. Seemed to work." Dog snorted. "I almost thought of tryin' one myself."

"What kind of flower?" Luke persisted.

"What do I look like, a florist? I have no bloody idea. It was red; it had petals."

"A rose?" Gower asked.

"Not a rose! That I'd know. I'm not an idiot. Some other kind. I didn't go and sniff the damned thing. Anyway, I'm no fool. I figured I'd better make myself scarce and hope like hell that the bastards who took him didn't come back for me on account of what I seen. I don't think they noticed me, but I wasn't takin' any chances." Dog leaned a shoulder against the grimy wall. "Whoever they were, I guess they must've killed him, though, 'cause he never came back again."

"Do you have any idea who these people might've been?" Luke asked.

"Not a clue."

"And the carriage? What did it look like?"

"Plain black. Like ten thousand others in this city. No markings on it that I could see. But it was one o'clock in the morning, pitch dark."

"And you were drunk," Gower reminded him.

"Not that drunk!" Dog huffed. "Anyway, it doesn't surprise me. Cocky son of a bitch like that goes around taking people's money, he's bound to make a few serious enemies. All I know is that I had nothing to do with it—and I'd just as soon *not* cross the people who did."

"Did you tell the constable what you saw?" Luke asked. "I understand the family hired a couple of Bow Street Runners to investigate his disappearance."

"Hell no!" Dog scoffed. "You think I'm going to talk to that lot when I only followed the bastard out the door to bash him on the head and steal my money back? Hardly. We all know how that'd go. I'm the one they'd hang for this, but I swear I didn't do it."

Luke had to admit that he believed the man. He glanced over at Gower, and could see in his friend's eyes that he concurred. "Anything else you can tell us?"

"No!" Dog shot back. "That's all I know. Now leave me alone. I want nothing more to do with this. It's the big bald fellow and the other one inside the coach that you—I mean, that *Silversmoke* should look for—but I don't know who they were, and frankly, I don't want to know. I got enough problems of my own."

With that, Dog hauled the door open and stomped back into the gaming hell.

Gower looked at Luke, his harrowed face grimmer than usual. "Abducted? Didn't see that comin'."

"Nor did I," Luke murmured. "But by whom? And why?"

Gower nodded thoughtfully at the questions. They pondered them in silence as they walked back out to the square.

Upon reaching the horses, Luke tossed the lad another coin.

"Thank ye, sir!"

As the boy scampered off, Luke untied Orion from the post. Gower went around to do the same to Mercury.

"Maybe it was someone like Dog," Gower said, "another gambler who wanted his money back. Could've been a simple robbery after someone noticed Clayton havin' a good night."

"Yes, but then what?" Luke said. "Kill him or keep him alive? They could take his money and cut his throat—but no body was ever found. Plus, he's worth more alive, isn't he?"

"His accounts weren't touched, I thought."

"True. But who needs his accounts? Any man with Clayton's *skills* could be viewed as a lucrative investment opportunity among the more unsavory classes—rather like a winning racehorse."

Gower looked askance at him. "How do you mean?"

"A winning gambler must seem like an easy source of income, if you're mad enough to seize him. Well, you'd also need some way of forcing him to comply."

Gower squinted. "Didn't we hear somethin' once about some underworld gambling tournament…black-market stuff?"

Luke frowned, searching his memory. "Sounds familiar. What did they used to call it…Carnevale or something?"

"That sounds right," Gower said.

Luke stared at him. "I thought that was just a legend."

Gower gave him a dark look in return. "Maybe not."

A carriage rattled by, and Luke gazed into the piazza, trying to envision the kidnapping taking place.

"Well," he said at length, "I think it's pretty clear who we need to speak to next."

Gower snorted at the reference to one of their best underworld informants. "Shop's closed. We'll never find him at this hour."

"What?" Luke jested. "Need only look under the nearest rock. I'm sure I'll find him under there with all the other vermin."

Gower chortled. "Tomorrow, then?"

Luke nodded. "Say, noon? Meet me at Seven Dials."

Gower swung up onto his horse. "See you then—Yer Grace."

Luke sighed. "Aye. Back to it."

"Give my best to Lady Portia," his friend goaded. "You gonna tell her about this kidnapping story, by the way? It's bound to upset her."

Luke thought it over for a beat. "I'm not looking forward to it, but I don't see that I have a choice. Besides, she might know something about a 'big bald man' connected to Joel. She'll be all right. She's tougher than she looks." He shrugged. "I'm not going to lie to the girl."

"Oh no, you'd never do that." Gower sent him a taunting glance.

Luke scowled in reply. But he said not a word. It wasn't as though he could deny it. With a harrumph, he climbed back up onto his horse, then they headed homeward, Gower still snickering at Luke's uneasy conscience.

CHAPTER 10

Tryst with a Highwayman

oncentrate! The next morning found Portia lying on a white wicker couch in the morning room, attempting to read the novel they'd been assigned for Lady Delphine's book club next week. But, for some reason, her mind was impossibly distracted.

Perhaps her inattention was partly due to the cheerful morning sunlight streaming in through the high arched windows. Its warmth made her lazy.

That was her only excuse, for there were no interruptions she could claim, no one to bother her. Her only company at present were her mother's flourishing plants in stands and hanging baskets all around the morning room, and her father's pet parakeet, or budgie, Mr. Greensleeves.

The bird sat content in his large, ornate wicker cage nearby, grooming his feathers and flicking his tail as he hopped about.

They were both enjoying the pleasant June morning. The windows were open, and the light curtains billowed gently in the breeze.

The showy green, blue, and yellow bird let out an occasional boisterous squawk, or yelled, "Pretty bird!"

A dandy, that one. He rather reminded her of Joel sometimes, preening over his plumage. Portia sighed, turned another page, and kept on trying to concentrate on the book.

Lord knew she had nothing else to do until it was time to get ready for the ball at the Grand Albion tonight.

Well, that should be fun, at least. Perhaps she would dance with smiley Lord Sidney, a dear friend. The cheerful blond viscount always made her laugh...

Damn and blast! she thought as she caught her mind wandering again. *You had better pay attention,* she warned herself.

Lady Delphine Blire, hostess of the Moonlight Square book club, was a formidable woman, and this particular book she had all but shoved down their throats. It was by some anonymous female author, and when it had first been published four years ago, it was all the rage.

Both the first and second printings had quickly sold out, which was why Portia had missed it until now.

Never fear; when Lady Delphine caught wind that a third edition of *Pride and Prejudice* was scheduled for release, she had ordered copies for the entire book club in advance, so that, this time, none of them should miss out.

Whoever this mysterious lady author was, Delphine was surely her biggest devotee. To be sure, Portia wanted to see if stubborn Mr. Darcy would ever come to his senses, but it was difficult to concentrate on *his* romantic woes with her own incessantly plaguing her mind.

She had to go back and read the same page three times in a row, in her distracted state. Her eyes kept skimming over the lines, but her brain wasn't listening.

Wait, who was Mr. Collins again?

Just when she started getting back into the story, Mr. Greensleeves squawked and startled her into nearly dropping the book on her nose.

Portia scowled, glancing over at the birdcage. The budgie dinged his little bell with his beak. It was impossible to get annoyed at such a funny little thing—and that made her think of Joel again.

Ugh, maybe I should just give up. Portia gave herself permission to take a short break. She rested the open book on her chest for a moment and closed her eyes, ignoring the fact that she was still not officially dressed for the day.

She was clad in her white muslin morning gown, her hair loose around her shoulders. Lounging through a late breakfast, she had not even bothered donning a corset yet.

So be it. She'd be dressed up enough tonight for the ball. For now, she allowed herself to rest her tired eyes. She had not been sleeping well, and that was due to nerves, obviously.

She was jittery with expectation of news from Silversmoke. Jittery with guilt over Lucas. Jittery with dread at finding out what had really happened to Joel.

She must've stared at the ceiling in her chamber for three hours last night before finally falling asleep. It was altogether vexing.

But though her body was weary, her mind continued spinning with thoughts of the three men with whom her life was now entangled.

First: her fiancé. Poor Lucas. He was such a gentle soul. It was so sad, beyond horrible, what he'd told her in the church, about his parents being murdered—by bandits, no less.

It made her feel all the more guilty for her secret dealings with Silversmoke, man number two—as if she didn't feel guilty enough already for going behind the duke's back to try to figure out what had happened to Joel, man number three.

Well, someone had to try!

The Bow Street Runners his uncle had hired seemed to have given up all too easily. She wasn't sure if they'd even bothered tracking down witnesses who'd been the last to see him at that gaming hell.

At the same time, she was trying to prepare herself mentally for whatever answer Silversmoke might bring back—provided he actually kept his word and did some sleuthing, as promised.

She knew she must be ready for the worst.

How would it feel to receive confirmation that Joel was dead? Would all of the awful emotions of mourning take hold of her again?

She dreaded being plunged back into that cold, drowning lake of misery.

But what if he was alive? What then? Should she break it off with Lucas while there was still time to reserve her hand for Joel?

Because the one thing she knew above all was that she would never become an adulteress. Better a spinster than that. A woman had honor, too, and that mattered greatly to Portia.

Right. Where was I, now? Warding off distraction with a will, she picked up the book again and made a heroic effort to dive back in to the Bennet sisters' woes.

Ah, but it wasn't long before her thoughts strayed once more back to her own worries. Such as having told Serena about Silversmoke. She hoped she didn't regret it. Then her thoughts traveled back to what poor Lucas had been through. Maybe it was losing his parents at a young age that had made him so eccentric...

Suddenly, Portia remembered that Felicity had also been orphaned at a young age, though not in a violent way, and not losing both parents at the same time. She wondered if her friend would take it amiss if she were to ask her—tactfully, of course—what it had been like to go through such a thing as a youngster.

Maybe that would help Portia to better understand the man she was about to wed, because the Duke of Fountainhurst was dashed hard enough to figure out.

She decided to take Felicity aside after book club and see if she was willing to talk about this sensitive subject.

She probably would. The easygoing blonde was patient and understanding. *Well, she'd have to be, to have married the King of the Rakehells.* Portia liked Jason, but he used to have a seriously wicked reputation.

As a bachelor, he had been one of the gentlemen Papa said she wasn't allowed to dance with.

Just then, the family butler stepped over the threshold of the morning room, paused, and cleared his throat politely.

"My lady; so sorry to disturb."

"It's all right, Stevens." Rejoicing at the interruption, she sat up, swinging her stockinged feet down to the floor. "What is it?"

Before he even spoke, her eyes flew to the small silver tray he was carrying. "A note arrived for you, ma'am."

Portia leaped to her feet. *Silversmoke!*

"Who's it from?" she asked, already whooshing across the morning room to seize it.

"It doesn't say, ma'am," the butler replied, sounding startled as she snatched it off the tray.

Her heart was suddenly pounding. "Thank you, Stevens. Um, you may go."

The puzzled butler bowed to her and withdrew.

Portia's fingers trembled as she broke the plain wax seal and unfolded a small piece of paper. She stifled a gasp. It *was* from Silversmoke!

My lady —

I have news. Meet me at quarter past eleven tonight at the gazebo in Moonlight Square. Alone.

— S.

Portia's eyes widened. *Alone...oh my.*

Her heart lurched. She read the message again with a gulp. Now that she knew the highwayman's smoldering appeal, the prospect of being alone with him in the moonlight presented an altogether different kind of danger.

One that sent a thrill all the way down to her toes.

She gulped as she thought of his smile, and their easy banter together. The secrets they'd shared, two strangers from two different worlds.

Her pulse started racing with anticipation to see him again. She knew full well he was totally and completely inappropriate, but blast it, she found him more attractive than Joel and Bug Boy combined.

Eleven fifteen tonight. She bit her lip. She would be at the Grand Albion then, enjoying the ball. *I'll have to sneak away somehow.* She could do it. She'd figure out a way. This was too important not to.

Her heart quaked at wondering what news he might bring her. If it was the worst, hearing it from the man who was secretly her hero would at least soften the blow.

At once, she grabbed her novel and snapped it shut, then strode out of the morning room, pounding up the stairs to her chamber and calling for her lady's maid.

Idiot that she was, she wanted to choose one of her most alluring gowns for her meeting with the charming outlaw.

After all, she wasn't married *yet*.

Shortly past noon, Luke, or rather Silversmoke, walked into Foy's Rag-and-Bone Shop, tucked away in a Seven Dials rookery.

Gower waited outside, standing sentry with the horses.

The moment Luke opened the door into the dim, cavelike space, a wave of unpleasant odors wafted out: the mustiness of greasy, much-used rags. The moldering smell of old books and rotting leather. The eye-watering pungency of cat piss rolled up in the ancient used carpets for sale that leaned in the far corner.

The pawnshop was packed with the detritus of countless anonymous lives.

Crammed into the shelves on one wall were used clothes in various states of disrepair, used boots and shoes. Some weapons on offer. Belts, bags.

Across from these sat a tarnished collection of pewter mugs, chipped crockery, rusty pots and pans, and various kitchen implements.

Amid forlorn furniture and a sad gallery of low-quality paintings and ill-made figurines, there were glass bottles by the dozens and not a few candlesticks.

Some of the latter were of surprisingly good quality, for the pawnshop was a cover for decidedly more dubious activities on the part of the owner.

Not only did Junius Foy supplement his income as a fence for the local thieves, but more importantly—at least, for Luke's purposes—the grubby pawn lord operated a whole spiderweb of unnoticed spies.

His lowly agents were the dozens of rag-and-bone pickers who wandered the streets of London, eavesdropping everywhere they went as they rummaged amid the trash, seeking anything of value they could bring back to the shop for a few pennies.

As a result, the most valuable item Foy had for sale was information. Luke had consulted him on numerous occasions in the past for that very reason.

If anyone had heard a whisper or a hint of a rumor about who in the criminal underworld had abducted Joel Clayton, it was the owner of the rag-and-bone shop.

Still, as useful as the man was, Luke took no pleasure in entering Foy's dank, dismal junk heap. Wrinkling his nose at the smell, squinting in the shop's forbidding twilight, and stepping over piles of junk waiting to be sorted—nearly knocking over a precarious tower of boxes with his shoulder on the way—he finally reached the scuffed wooden counter, where the shop cat looked at him and let out an insolent meow.

It was a handsome animal, large and black, with white under the chin and oddly hostile green eyes. It mewled like it was starving, but it was a plump creature. No doubt it ate well, with no shortage of mice to be found scampering around in its master's hoard.

Giving the cat a dubious look, Luke rang the bell and waited.

Junius Foy soon emerged from the back, a grimy bandanna hanging around his neck. Beneath a mop of wild gray hair, he had a weathered face with dark, shifty eyes and a bulbous nose. He wore a work apron and had his shirt sleeves rolled up, revealing thick forearms covered with wiry gray hairs.

He wiped his hands on his apron and extended one to Luke, greeting him with a guarded mumble. "Silversmoke. Been a while."

Luke shook his hand.

"What brings you in today?" Foy asked.

"I've got a client who's interested in the disappearance of a Mr. Joel Clayton. He was heir to an earldom with a fondness for the gaming tables. Word has it somebody kidnapped him out of Covent Garden one night last April. No one's heard from him since, but no body was ever found. I wondered if you'd heard anything about the matter."

Foy scratched his cheek for a moment. "Read about it in the papers. But no. Sorry. Nothing's come in about it here."

"No rumors? That's odd. You must've heard something." Luke searched Foy's face carefully.

Foy shook his head. "Not a peep. Probably dead."

"Probably so," Luke agreed, pausing. "Wasn't there an underworld gaming tournament that used to meet from time to time in different locations? I once heard about it, but never any real details... I thought it was a myth. It was said to be like some sort of traveling circus or smugglers' fair that brought entertainments and a black-market bazaar for all manner of trade in illegal goods."

"*And* services. Aye. Mercenaries. Gunrunners and whatnot. Whores of all kinds. Even white slavers, I've heard."

Luke's brows rose. "Yes. That's it."

Foy nodded discreetly. "You mean the Carnevale."

He stared at Foy in dark amazement. "What can you tell me? Specifics?"

The man's lips twisted. "It'll cost you."

Luke smirked. "How much?"

"For you, twenty quid."

"Twenty quid!"

"For anyone else, it'd be double that, mate. Take it or leave it." Foy pushed the cat away when it returned again. It sprang down with an indignant *reer!*

Grumbling, Luke reached into his waistcoat and pulled out his billfold. He shook his head and peeled off a couple of ten-pound bank notes. It was as much as he paid the average footman at one of his houses. "This had better be worth it, Foy."

Foy pocketed the money. "Wait here."

Luke frowned as the junk collector disappeared into the back of the shop. He leaned on the counter to try to see through the doorway as he heard Foy rustling around in the back.

A moment later, Foy returned. He glanced furtively past Luke, making sure no one else was in earshot, then produced a card printed with a long list of names.

"Here's the latest wager card for the big game, the elimination tournament. You've got your top-ranked players, each one's odds. They meet once a month. Location changes to keep ahead of the Home Office. They've been wanting to break up this little gathering for years."

Luke skimmed the card. Listed were about thirty names of rated players, or rather nicknames—strange titles like the famous prizefighters adopted to shield their true identities.

The Cardiff Comet, Johnny Phoenix, The Spaniard, The Prophet of Manchester, Sir Doom…

Luke wrinkled his nose. *Where do they come up with these?*

Not that he could talk: Silversmoke.

He looked up from the betting card. "Where and when's the next one?"

Foy gave him a greasy smile. "That'll be another ten quid."

Luke huffed and scowled but gave him the money.

"You're in luck," Foy said. "It's two weeks from yesterday. They're having it Wednesday night, June eighteenth."

"Where?"

"Buckinghamshire. Find your way to a little village in the Chiltern Hills by the name of Fergus Wood. When you get there, you'll inquire at The Goat's Head Inn and give the password *Fortuna*."

"Fortuna?" Luke echoed. Well, that was appropriate for a gambling tournament.

"Once you give them the password, you'll be given more detailed instructions on where exactly to go within the local area. The fair starts at nightfall and goes until dawn. That's all I know. But watch yourself if you go. This thing attracts a nasty crowd."

Luke thanked him with another handshake, then went back outside, rejoining Gower.

Once they had cleared the dodgy environs of Seven Dials, Luke told Gower what he'd learned and showed him the card.

It was troubling information, but at least the next move was clear.

"Looks like we're going to Carnevale," he told the Yorkshireman.

If they got there and found Joel being forced to play against his will, they'd confront whoever had him and rescue the poor beggar. Get him out of there, nice and easy. It might get bloody, but Luke liked a clean, uncomplicated plan.

Until then, he'd continue exploring other routes in case the Carnevale track amounted to nothing.

One way or the other, with any luck, he'd have Joel back to his Buttercup in no time.

Somehow, that thought gave him little joy.

Luke smiled anyway, eager to see her again at their rendezvous tonight in the gazebo. Silversmoke could get away with things that Lucas wouldn't dare, after all, and he had plans for her.

Until tonight, my lady.

That night, sure enough, Portia attended the ball at the Grand Albion with her parents, just as they did every Thursday evening in the Season.

They arrived at eight o'clock, as usual, when the evening sun had turned the western sky to a blaze of pink. Then they waited in the queue on the red-carpeted stairs leading up from the grand marble foyer to the ballroom.

When it was their turn to be announced by the Assembly Rooms' master of ceremonies, they stepped into the ballroom, peeked around at the crowd, and promptly went their separate ways.

They had never really been a close-knit family.

Papa ambled off to join his friends in the refreshment room, sampling biscuits and cucumber sandwiches. Mama, arrayed in diamonds, sailed over to join her haughty coterie in swigging champagne.

Portia located her usual group of friends and told them all how beautiful they looked. It was true—and each of their husbands seemed to know it.

Azrael was kind enough to fetch Portia a goblet of punch without even a nudge from Serena. It was most endearing how the quiet, pale-haired duke had taken it upon himself to look after his wife's best friend almost like a brother. Which was lovely of him, since her own brother was halfway around the world, doing God knew what.

Portia was still trying not to think too much about whether Hunter would make it back to England in time for her wedding. So be it. She knew he'd at least try.

The evening passed in the usual way. Trinny chatted about the baby, while Gable was drawn off by his father, the stately Lord Sefton, to talk politics again with some of the graybeards. He was clearly being groomed for positions of importance in the future.

As the night proceeded, Portia got around to dancing with her charming friend, Lord Sidney, one of the most beautiful men in all London, to be sure.

He was elusive as a husband, though, a committed bachelor and consummate flirt. The suave, golden-haired heir to a marquisate very much enjoyed his single state—for now.

No doubt it would be a different story, however, when he inherited his father's title. Though he seemed on the surface to be naught but an idle ton buck with perfect hair and a brilliant white smile, Portia had often been on the receiving end of Sidney's solid common sense and genuine compassion.

He had been extremely kind to her when Joel had first gone missing, smoothly redirecting awkward questions from others away from her, shielding her from too much attention, noticing when her emotions grew wobbly and whisking her away to take a moment's privacy to collect herself.

The most interesting thing about Sidney, though, was how he always seemed to know the latest gossip.

"I heard Fountainhurst has resurfaced," he remarked as they promenaded down the aisle between the two standing rows of dancers awaiting their turn. "You must be so pleased."

When he looked askance at her, Portia could not miss the glimmer of amusement in his cobalt eyes.

She chuckled with uneasy humor, suddenly feeling guilty for those occasions now and then when she had made irreverent remarks to her friends about her eccentric fiancé.

"He means well," she said.

Sidney tut-tutted her. "He ignored you for months, *cherie*—when you needed him most, I daresay. Don't think I didn't notice."

"Oh, nothing escapes your notice, I am well aware," she replied.

He winked at her, conceding this.

"But don't worry," Portia said. "There is hope for us yet. His Grace feels we ought to start spending more time together, and I've agreed to work with him."

"Gracious lady."

Portia snorted at his wry tone as they turned and joined the row of dancers walking, hands joined, in the opposite direction. "He is taking me on a picnic on Monday. Isn't that sweet?"

"Adorable," Sidney drawled. "Will there be insects involved?"

"I sincerely hope not."

He laughed.

"Oh, be nice, Sid," she chided with affection. "He hasn't had it easy, you know—unlike some people."

"You are brutal!" he exclaimed.

Portia laughed.

"But for your sake, my dear, very well," he said with a teasing glance. "I shall withhold judgment on the quiz, at least until I hear from you how it went, this picnic."

"You always seem to find out, anyway."

"True. It's astonishing, the things people tell me."

"Well, everybody trusts you."

"That's my evil plan," he murmured, looking askance at her.

Portia laughed, but given all she had to hide lately, she changed the subject. Telling Serena about Silversmoke was one thing. Telling Sidney: never.

She dreaded to wonder what a protective male friend like him would do.

"Enough about me and Fountainhurst. What about you, sir?"

The rake gave her a curious frown as the figures of the dance sent them to stand in opposite rows, facing each other. "What about me?"

Portia arched a brow at him. "When are we going to find you a wife, eh?"

He scowled at her from beneath his golden forelock, then whisked off with a cheerful "*Adieu, ma petite.* So sorry, I must go," as their lines began to move in opposite directions.

She could hear him laughing as he danced away.

"Rogue!" she said over her shoulder as the dance separated them.

Sidney blew her a cheeky kiss farewell.

Portia scoffed, still smiling, but by the time the country dance ended, she glanced at the clock and her eyes widened.

Time had flown in his company. It was now mere minutes till eleven. *I need to get out of here!*

Suddenly breathless with excitement, Portia slyly retrieved her reticule, finished the last swallow of punch in her goblet to bolster her courage, then slid a furtive glance toward a side door leading off the ballroom.

She began moving toward it in perfect nonchalance—but then disaster nearly struck.

Felicity's handsome elder brother, Major Peter Carvel (dubbed "Danger Man" by Trinny), was making his way toward her as the next dance was called.

Portia saw his dashing red uniform coat amid the crowd, saw him searching her out with those shrewd, flinty eyes.

He lifted his square chin and scanned the throng, absently running a hand through his light brown hair.

At that moment, Major Carvel spotted her, and though he didn't smile—the stern military veteran wasn't much of a smiler—he raised his hand to flag her attention as the next dance was called.

Portia blanched.

She hated to flee him—Peter Carvel was a most intriguing fellow, not to mention a war hero. The last thing she wanted was to seem disrespectful.

Rather than reject him, and certainly not daring to explain why she had to go, Portia ducked down behind a cluster of ladies, feeling just a wee bit ridiculous.

What choice did she have? Danger Man had hunted deadly wild animals in India after leaving the army; he would easily find one mere blonde if she did not get herself out of here at once.

She refused to miss her meeting with Silversmoke.

If she was late, the highwayman might not wait for her. They were both taking serious risks here, meeting like this. She had to go.

Slipping away through the crowd before Peter could spot her, she left the rugged major furrowing his brow and looking around in confusion, as though wondering where she'd disappeared to.

In the next moment, Portia sneaked out the side door, looked around wildly for the best route, then darted down an unobtrusive staircase used by the hotel staff.

The next thing she knew, she was fleeing out of the lavish hotel, feeling rather gleeful. Hitching up the hem of her ball gown, she bolted across the street as discreetly as possible.

The liveried footmen stationed at the grand front entrance took notice of her, and no doubt wondered what on earth she was about, but Portia did not look back.

Instead, she raced alongside the black wrought-iron fence that girded the park, heart pounding in horror and hilarity at her own daring.

At last, she came to one of the gates in the tall, spiked fence. She fumbled to get her family's key out of her reticule—the park gates were locked after dark, but residents of Moonlight Square could visit if they liked.

For a fleeting instant, she worried that Silversmoke might not be able to get in. But on second thought, she doubted locked entrances would pose much problem to the likes of him. The man was a hardened outlaw, after all.

Yet even knowing that, her heart pounded with triumph to have escaped all the elegance behind her as she ran to meet the roughest, toughest, most electrifying man she had ever encountered.

As an afterthought, she hoped he did not decide to rob her of the jewels she had worn to impress him. But she laughed at the prospect. He could have them.

He could have nearly anything from her...

The thought of being with him again nearly made her forget that the whole purpose of this meeting was to discuss Joel.

All that mattered was this moment. She did not care to ponder it; all she knew was that she had never felt this way before.

He was so full of passion and feeling. So alive...

The little white gazebo came into view ahead, ethereal in the moonlight. Breathless and eager, Portia ran down the graveled path toward it.

Her heart leaped when she spotted a dark, broad-shouldered silhouette waiting for her there in the shadows.

CHAPTER 11

A Test of Loyalty

Waiting in the gazebo for their rendezvous, Luke had once more donned his black half mask, skipped a couple of shaves, and transformed back into Silversmoke.

He leaned against a white post in the whimsical garden folly, listening to the wind soughing through the trees, and watching the play of starlight and shadows dapple the park's pleasant acreage.

He'd been a few minutes early, admittedly eager to see his lovely bride again, but he was not at all eager to tell her what he'd learned. That part of his task tonight was bound to be difficult.

Gaining access to the park after nightfall had been easy, however, since, well, he lived here and had a blasted key.

Thanks to his conversation with her in the church as Lucas, he had known where she'd be tonight and what she would be doing. After the resourcefulness she'd shown in finding her way to him at The Blind Badger, Luke figured it should be relatively simple for her to slip away from the ballroom for a short while.

Sure enough, a few minutes after eleven, he heard light, running footfalls pattering over the gravel.

Then the girl herself came into view, holding her skirts up prettily as she hurried toward him. Long tendrils of her upswept hair had escaped the coif in her haste and bounced around her shoulders.

He stared, charmed, a smile playing over his lips. God, she was a dream in motion.

Her pale gown must've been made of watered silk, the way it

shimmered in the moonlight. It had a modest V-neck and short puff sleeves.

Her flaxen hair shone in the dark with the brightness of moonbeams, and since her ball gown skimmed her ankles for ease in dancing, he caught a glimpse of pale kid slippers as she flitted up the stairs.

Invading the gazebo with nimble delicacy, she came to stand, panting, right in front of him.

"I'm here!"

Luke's mind had gone quite blank, faced with her loveliness. *I really get to marry this fairy princess?* She was as magical as starlight.

"I hope I'm not late." She ventured closer with dainty ballerina steps.

He blinked, shaking off his daze.

"No, you're right on time," he answered gruffly.

"Oh, good. I'm afraid I can't stay long." She cast a nervous glance around. "You said you have news?" She could not seem to hold back her enthusiasm. "I did not expect to hear from you so soon! Oh, Silversmoke! I knew contacting you would be the right thing to do. Gracious, it's been a year, and Bow Street made no progress whatsoever! For you, it's been, what, just a couple of days and already you've found something?"

He gave her a cautious smile as he took a step closer. "I don't know how happy you'll be about it once you hear what I have to say, my lady."

She froze, her eyes widening.

"Perhaps you should sit down," he added gently.

She didn't move, but he saw her brace herself. Her shoulders stiffened and her chin came up a notch. "Is he—dead?"

"No. Not that I've confirmed," Luke said in a somber tone. "But I managed to find a witness who says he saw Joel abducted from outside that gambling hell in Covent Garden."

"Oh my God."

Luke put out a hand to steady her, but she had already drifted out of reach, going over to alight on the bench that ran the perimeter of the gazebo.

He stood before her, watching in concern as she stared at the floor planks for a moment, then she lifted her gaze to his. "Abducted? Then that could mean he really *is* alive somewhere..."

"It could." Luke sat down beside her, holding her in a somber gaze. He decided on the spot that there was no reason to tell her about the Carnevale. It would only frighten her, and he didn't know for sure yet. "That is why I needed to speak to you again. I have a few questions."

"Yes? Anything." She turned to him in distress.

"The witness I spoke to—"

"Who was it?" she interrupted.

"A fellow gambler at the gaming house. It's best if I don't share his name and risk endangering you, but he's one of the regulars there. Anyway, he told me he saw a large bald man toss Joel into a plain black carriage and drive off. That doesn't leave me much to go on, so I wanted to ask if you can think of any particular people around Joel who might've fit that description. Especially enemies."

She furrowed her brow, searching her memory. "A big bald man?"

"Anyone like that who might stand out in your mind?"

"No one," she murmured, clearly upset to hear this.

Luke chose his words with care, torn between the desire to shield her from unpleasantness and his commitment to be honest with her.

At least in this.

She shook her head. "I-I'm sorry, I can't think of anyone who matches that description. I could try asking his friends—"

"Don't," Luke ordered. "It's too dangerous. If these enemies of his are capable of kidnapping a future earl, God knows what else they might do. We need to move carefully. If you start going around asking questions, it could get back to them." He nodded with reassurance. "You leave this to me."

She gazed at him and, slowly, the dread receded from her eyes.

"What is it?" he murmured.

She laid her hand atop his, much to his shock. "You really are helping me, aren't you?"

"I said I would."

"Yes, but..."

"You weren't sure." It saddened him that she seemed so used to people failing her.

She lifted her hand away, but gave him a wan smile. "Oh, Silversmoke, I feel as if you're the only person who has truly listened to me about all of this since it happened. I'm more grateful than you know."

"You're welcome." He sat back on the bench with a tender half-smile.

She still looked distressed, though, and her unhappiness plucked at his heart.

"Try not to worry, my lady. I'll keep working on it. I've got a few promising leads. That reminds me. The witness also spoke of a red flower

Joel was frequently seen wearing on his boutonniere when he gambled. Does that mean anything to you?"

"Oh, I wasn't usually with him when he gambled, and he didn't talk about it with me much, since he knew I didn't like it." She shrugged. "He often wore a flower in his boutonniere, though." She cast him a rueful smile. "He was always a bit of a dandy."

Luke smiled back, but he was puzzled, trying to make sense of her attraction to this rakehell.

She must've noticed the wheels turning in his brain. "What is it?" she murmured as she rested her arm along the railing.

Luke paused, not wishing to overstep his bounds. "You won't like it."

"What? Please, speak freely. It's the best way, and I can take it, whatever it is."

Debating with himself, Luke rose to his feet, took a step away across a creaking floorboard, then turned to face her with a shrug. "What is it about this chap that so entranced you?"

She lifted her eyebrows, looking startled and wary at the question.

"Was it that he always won?"

"No, of course not."

"Was it that he'd become an earl?"

She laughed. "I'm the daughter of a marquess, my friend. An earl's a step down for me, to be perfectly blunt, so no. It had nothing to do with his rank or anything like that."

Luke stared at her. "Does he look like a god, then?"

She furrowed her brow with puzzled amusement. "You saw him. I gave you his picture."

"That's my point." Luke shrugged, unimpressed. "He's no better-lookin' than me."

With a mischievous twinkle in her eyes, she ran an appreciative glance over him. "I think you might have him beaten, actually, but it's hard to say with the mask. Why don't you take it off?"

He snorted, ridiculously pleased at her compliment, but what she asked was impossible. "What'd be the point?" he tossed back. "If an earl's beneath you, I might as well be an ant. I just wondered...why him?"

He watched her well-manicured fingers drum the railing, then she sighed. "People said we made the perfect couple."

"Oh really?" Feeling his mood sour as if someone had squeezed a lemon over him, Luke folded his arms over his chest.

His betrothed nodded. "We had—*have* a lot in common. Similar tastes, compatible temperaments."

"I doubt that."

"You do?" She looked up at him.

"Doesn't it bother you that he had this whole other life, gambling in seedy places until the wee hours of the morning?" He gestured impatiently. "Gambling too much in *good* clubs is bad enough. Men with such habits put their whole families at risk. They can end up in debtor's prison. That doesn't sound to me like the sort of chap any lady of sense would want for a husband."

"*You*, of all people, disapprove?" she asked with a pert smile.

Luke scowled. "I question your judgment, is all."

She sat up straight. "Does this mean you're not going to quit looking for him?"

"No, no. I gave you my word, didn't I? I just...wondered." He turned away, feeling a trifle stupid for asking personal questions. "Never mind."

But, honestly, if some dandified cardplayer had tried courting his sister, Luke would've tossed him out the window on his arse.

Where the devil was her father, anyway?

"I hope I've not offended you," he mumbled.

"No, I suppose it's a fair question. There were a couple of things I didn't like about him, to be honest." She fell silent, gazing out at the garden park for a moment, pondering with that faraway quality that had so captivated Luke when they'd first met.

He waited. "Such as?"

She seemed loath to speak ill of her missing beau, scanning the landscape. "I did not like his gambling to excess, and I really hated his duels. I am not fond of violence. But nobody's perfect... You think me a fool?" She looked over at him imploringly, her patrician profile limned in moonlight.

Luke shook his head.

She looked away again. "Perhaps I knew deep down that Joel Clayton would never propose to me. Maybe that was just part of the game we played."

"Game?"

"I don't know..." She sighed. "I will say, my father never liked him. My sister said he was an idiot. Mama thought he was charming, though, and she always gets the final say in our house. If I wanted him, I could have him. Except that he never asked before he disappeared, so I never had to think about it yet in a serious way."

"Well, you may soon have to, if it turns out he's alive," Luke murmured, trying not to sound too glum at the prospect.

She waved this off. "No, I already have a fiancé. No," she said again with a weary sigh. "That door is closed."

He winced at her defeated tone. *Ouch.* "Don't sound so disappointed."

She smiled wryly. "Even if, by some miracle, Joel came back before the wedding, who knows if he'd even want to marry me?"

"Why in the world would he not?"

She seemed taken aback, but pleased. "Why, Mr. Silversmoke"—she tilted her head coyly—"did you just pay me a charming compliment?"

"I did nothing of the kind."

She gave him a kissable pout.

He grinned. "Sorry, you're not my type."

"Oh really? And what sort of lady is, dare I ask?"

"The kind that ain't a lady." He flashed a wicked smile.

She laughed, blushing. "You are bad."

"Wanted in three counties," he murmured, holding her gaze.

Her smile was radiant at his teasing. She bit her lip as though attempting to dim the pleasure emanating from her.

Luke thought of all the ways he'd like to teach her bliss as they gazed at each other in charged silence.

Suddenly, the wedding could not come soon enough for him. Especially the wedding night. They stared hungrily at each other, until, hit with a thunderbolt of yearning, Luke had to look away.

Portia did the same.

They both seemed dazed.

"So what's next?" she finally asked.

Kissing you senseless, he thought, then ordered himself to behave. They only had a few minutes before she had to sneak back into the ball.

He tried to sound nonchalant and leaned against a post. "Next, I will start homing in on any particular enemies Clayton might've made. Hopefully, one of them is a big bald bruiser who's got no idea I'm comin'."

Her eyes widened. "Do be careful, Silversmoke."

"Eh," he said, and flashed a roguish smile.

She frowned at the hint of his readiness to brawl. "You will keep me apprised of your progress?"

"Of course."

"Are you sure there's nothing I can do to help? Any funds I could contribute—"

"No, my lady. Thanks, but I've got it all in hand."

"This is really so kind of you." She studied him. "May I ask you a question?"

"Depends on what it is."

She rose and began sauntering toward him. "Why do you do this? Why would you risk your own safety and put in the time helping a perfect stranger?"

"Because you're bloody beautiful?"

"Oh, come." She tilted her head, as though impatient with his praise of her looks. No doubt she'd heard every compliment that men could dream up by now. "I know you'd still help me even if you didn't find me so."

She stepped right in front of him and lifted her chin, gazing into his eyes. "I want to know what compels you. What's the real reason you put yourself on the line for others this way?"

He shrugged, his senses filled with her apple blossom perfume. "Somebody has to do it."

"But why you?"

"Because I can. And because I don't like it when bad people get away with bad things."

She nodded slowly. Luke could feel the warmth radiating from her sweet body. Her nearness was beyond tempting.

"It's taking a lot upon yourself, trying to right the wrongs of the world. To punish the wicked all by yourself."

If she only knew.

"You think me arrogant to presume?" he asked.

She shrugged, watching him. "I daresay you'd have to be, a little."

"I suppose that's probably true." The topic was suddenly making him uncomfortable. He had not come here to talk about himself, and if she hated it when gentlemen dueled, he could not imagine how she'd react to savage killers who wiped out whole Scottish gangs.

Yet, as much as he had to hide, this delicate creature was far too alluring to resist. He didn't want to leave her, didn't want to let her go.

The glittering necklace around her throat caught his eye.

It was a butterfly with a sapphire body and diamond-crusted wings and antennae. The fine gold chain that it hung from lay across her lovely collarbones.

Determined to change the subject away from his darker pursuits, Luke lifted his hand and boldly traced the light chain of her necklace, skimming his finger along where it lay on her creamy skin.

He heard her breath catch at his touch, felt her chest rise beneath his fingertips.

He flinched with yearning.

"This is pretty," he murmured, noting her quiver at his touch. No rebuke followed. "Who gave it to you?" Luke captured her gaze with a penetrating stare from behind his mask. "Clayton?"

She shook her head. "My father gave it to me for my birthday. Why?" she whispered faintly, mesmerizing him. "Are you going to steal it from me, highwayman?"

Luke's heart thundered. "My dear young lady, if I were going to steal anything from you, I can assure you, it would *not* be your necklace."

He heard her intake of breath at his husky whisper, then she wet her satin lips with a quick pass of her tongue, and his blood caught fire.

His brain was spinning to see that, indeed, his future duchess *wanted* the highwayman to kiss her. That did not bode well at all!

But though she was failing his test of loyalty spectacularly, Luke was past caring, could not stop the wave of desire crashing through him.

He captured her dainty chin gently on his fingertips and tilted her fine-boned face upward. "I'm stealing *this*," he whispered in a playful challenge. "Try and stop me."

She shook her head ever so slightly—and Luke feared she owned him in that moment.

Unable to chide his darling, unfaithful fiancée, let alone stop himself, he bent his head and claimed what *he*, at least, knew was already his.

Portia did not care if it was folly. She cast all consequences to the wind.

All her life, she'd been sheltered and caged like her father's blasted parakeet. But for one moment, in the arms of this thrilling rebel, this hero in black, she was free.

She slid her hand up his chest as he deftly captured her lips. As he kissed her lips apart, she clung to his massive shoulders, going weak-kneed with desire. He slid his arm around her waist while he amazed her with the intoxicating pleasure of his tongue swirling over hers.

As she realized how this was done, she began kissing him back in open-mouthed hunger, her pulse pounding.

The stubble roughening his jaw chafed her chin slightly, but she didn't care. All her skin tingled, acutely alive.

He gripped her harder as his kisses consumed her mouth. His open hand, splayed on the small of her back, moved in a series of heated caresses as he held her tightly against him. His big, warm body was like iron against her, his rock-hard abdomen pressed against her middle, and Portia yearned to do indecent things with him.

She could feel his heart thumping as she caressed his chest. It made her toes curl to think there was nothing but one layer—his dark cotton shirt—between her palm and his skin.

Emboldened, she reached up and molded her hands over his shoulders, then explored her way down his arms with her touch. The strength in his bulky muscles made her giddy.

Yet, as he kissed her ever more deeply, again and again, Portia could not escape the instinctual feeling that this was so right. There was something so familiar about him, so reassuring somehow.

Which made no sense, considering he was a brigand.

She did not even know his real name. She had spent less than one hour, all told, in his presence, and yet she felt as though she had known this man all her life.

Maybe, in the end, she was as much of a gambler as Joel.

Then her lost beau dissolved from her memory like a gray morning fog in the wanton pleasure of kissing Silversmoke.

The one who did not disappear, though, was Lucas.

The image of her future husband's face exploded in her mind all of a sudden. *Oh my God, what am I doing?*

She suddenly pulled back from the highwayman. "Stop. I can't do this! Please—I'm sorry—I can't."

"What's wrong?" he panted, searching her eyes. "I'm sorry—did I frighten you?"

"No. No," she repeated with a gulp for air, her chest heaving while he searched her face in concern.

It took all her strength to step back from his embrace. Her body cried out at the denial, but she refused to waver this time. "It's not your fault. I shouldn't have done this. I-I must go."

"But my lady—" He took a step toward her, but she held him at arm's length.

"I have a fiancé!" she cried. Then she whirled around and fled from the extreme temptation that he posed without looking back.

Shame and remorse flooded through her.

"Lady Portia!" he called after her.

She ignored him, rushing down the gazebo steps then hurrying down the path, shaking. She could feel his baffled gaze trailing her, but she didn't dare look back. For she knew he could have her all too easily.

No, it was not him, but herself she mistrusted.

He was too delicious. She'd been a fool to meet him out here.

And to flirt with him! How could she?

How could she do that to gentle, trusting Lucas?

Lust entwined with self-recrimination as she fled homeward, too out of sorts to attempt to go back to the ball, at least for now.

To her relief, Silversmoke did not try to follow her.

God, *she* must seem like the quiz at the moment, running off like this in a burst of irrationality. She hoped that her bizarre exit did not cost her Silversmoke's help in the end—but what business did she have doing all this, anyway?

Joel's family should find him! His uncle, at least! What business was it of hers? It wasn't as though the two of them had ever been engaged.

Unlike her current betrothal to the Duke of Fountainhurst.

In less than one month, she would be married to him—a good man. She had pledged him her troth, given her word.

Besides, maybe he needs you! Did you ever think of that? Look at all he's been through! Tears filled her eyes when she thought of him in the church, telling her in stark tones how his parents had been murdered when he was just a lad.

God, I am a horrible person. How could I have been so cavalier? She fumbled with the key to let herself out of the park as the tears thickened in her eyes. *I nearly betrayed him.*

She sobbed with disappointment in herself.

No, Lucas wasn't exciting and dangerous like the outlaw. And no, he did not make her want to shove him down on the nearest piece of furniture, tear his shirt off, and have her wanton way with him, the way Silversmoke did.

But he has a kind heart, and by God, he does not deserve this.

With that realization, Portia burst into tears. And she resolved from that moment forward to do her best to love him, eccentric or not.

Because, deep down, she knew that she and Lucas had one thing in common: they were both unutterably lonely.

Luke watched her running away from him, still dazed, his pulse still pounding, his cock still throbbing with need for her like he'd never experienced for any other woman. But as the chaos of his hunger for her finally started to clear, a smile, nay, a lusty grin slowly spread across his face.

She passed the test. By God, Lucas, ol' boy, you did it. You picked a good woman. Luke wiped the lingering moisture off his lips with the back of his hand, but could not wipe away his rascally grin.

He was jubilant, in fact. Her refusal of him just now meant more to him than she would ever know.

As much as her kiss had bowled him over, her rejection of him was sweeter still.

"You are mine, Portia Tennesley," he whispered. For he knew now she was everything he had ever wanted in a woman.

Maybe it's time I start to win her in earnest.

This arranged marriage might've begun as an alliance between two great houses, but after that kiss, and after seeing her heart in all the ways she'd placed her trust in him, Luke could no longer deny that he wanted so much more with her.

Aye, he wanted it all. Mind, body, and soul—and he wanted her all to himself. The thought sobered him, for he was well aware of the stakes of this gamble. He still had to beat the competition, after all.

The great cardplayer.

Dead or alive, there was still Joel to contend with, either as a living rival or a ghost. Luke would not tolerate sharing his lady with either.

Yes, he had promised to get her the answers she deserved, and he would.

But standing there in the shadows, he realized that he was ready to risk his heart for the first time in his life. To set aside hatred and darkness and reach out for the only kind of love worth bothering for.

All or nothing.

The love that cost everything, God help him.

The only kind he had to give.

Part Two

CHAPTER 12

A Proper Courtship

*T*he sun played coy with the clouds, weaving in and out from behind their big silver masses, but Monday afternoon was bright and balmy.

The breeze tickled the tall grasses and made the wildflowers nod all across the sloped face of the meadow as Lucas led her up Primrose Hill for the promised picnic.

He was carrying the large wicker basket, which he'd taken from a servant. Portia held the folded blanket tucked under her arm, and by some miracle, they were permitted by their escort of chaperones and servants to go off a short distance by themselves.

Still within view, of course. There would be no impropriety.

Unlike a few nights ago. She thrust the guilty thought of Silversmoke away, still disgusted with herself for her own moral failure.

She refocused her attention once more on Lucas, instead, who was marching up the hill, hefting the heavy basket in one hand like it weighed nothing.

"I wasn't sure what sort of food you like," he was saying, "so I had my kitchen staff prepare a variety of items for the day's menu."

"That's thoughtful of you."

Upon reaching the brow of the slope, he turned to her with a solicitous gaze behind his spectacles. The wind tousled the dark blond waves of his hair and sported with the tails of his fawn-colored coat.

"How does this spot look?" he asked.

Portia glanced around. "I think it a very good spot. We shall have a fine view of London from here," she added, turning toward the city that sat in the distance in a haze of dreamy pastels.

"Are you sure? If you prefer shade, we could dine under that tree." He pointed to a lone oak of massive age and girth that had probably stood there since the days of Good Queen Bess. "Ladies must attend to their complexions, I am told."

"As it pleases you, Your Grace. I have my bonnet." She had chosen a wide-brimmed straw hat for the occasion. It had a ribbon around the brim that trailed behind her, waving in the breeze.

Lucas passed a protective glance over her, then said, "The shade, I should think."

On he marched.

Portia stared after him for a moment, mystified. *What on earth has got into him today?*

His newfound resolve to behave as the exemplary suitor had been in evidence since he'd fetched her and her attendants a while ago, but Portia remained puzzled as she followed him over to the pleasant green umbrella of shade beneath the magnificent old tree. Their new spot still gave them a good view of London, which was the whole point of picnics on Primrose Hill—so she'd been told.

She'd never been on one before. No suitor till Lucas had ever suggested it. Such a sweet gesture never would've even occurred to Joel.

And a bandit like Silversmoke had surely never made a picnic for a girl.

Maybe Serena was right, Portia's heart whispered. Maybe "different" *could* be a good thing.

Lucas set the picnic basket down, and Portia tossed her reticule onto the grass, then they worked together to spread out the blanket, laughing as the wind luffed through it like a sail being unfurled.

When they finally wrestled it to the ground, laughing, they smashed down a few daisies that she would've rather saved for the wedding, but it could not be helped. Still barring any memory of the smoldering outlaw from her mind, Portia leaned down, bracing her hands on her thighs, ready to assist in the picnic proceedings.

The duke, her future husband, was busily at work in a crouched position, taking items out of the basket and arranging them in front of her with care. "Now then. Here is the roasted chicken. This is, er, pickled cod, I believe. There's a selection of light sandwiches here if you're not *very* hungry. Fruit, bread, cheese..." Head down, he lifted his gaze and peered hopefully at her through his spectacles.

Portia smiled, warmed by his solicitude. He seemed different, she couldn't say exactly how. A little surer of himself. Friendlier, perhaps. More open. But then, the whole point of this outing was to help them get to know each other a bit better before they walked down the aisle and made this thing permanent.

She noticed then that his eyes looked especially green, nearly emerald. And he looked happy.

He was in his element out in nature, she supposed.

"Does any of this appeal to you?" he asked, still waiting for a response.

"Oh yes! Sorry." She brushed off her distraction and knelt opposite him, amused. His desire to please her was rather astonishing. She decided to press her luck. "Do you have any salad?" She took off her bonnet, since she was now protected by the shade.

"Two kinds, no less! Oh, yes, yes, we have salad, indeed..." He started looking for them, poking around among the items in the basket. "I made sure of that. Just in case. Ladies and their salads, I know... Where are you, now? Salad, hullo?" He continued pulling various food items out of the hamper until he came to a wooden bowl with a lid. "Here you are!" He handed the bowl to her in triumph.

The quiz.

She could not deny she was charmed. "You've thought of everything, Your Grace."

He grinned. "I hope."

For a fleeting instant, there was something so familiar about that roguish smile. Portia accepted the bowl and looked under the lid to discover a nice fresh salad of crisp, in-season vegetables. The jar he handed her next proved to be a fruit salad sprinkled with walnuts.

"Well! These are so tempting, I shall have to try them both."

"Yes, I noticed," he said under his breath.

"Pardon?"

Lucas quickly sent her an innocent smile. "They both seem delicious, what?"

"Yes." Portia smiled uncertainly at him, her conscience needled over the kiss in the gazebo. They *were* talking about salads, weren't they?

Oh, come, there's no way he could've found out. She looked away. "Why don't you sit down and make yourself comfortable, Your Grace?"

"Don't mind if I do. Um—would it be all right if I took off my jacket?"

"By all means. The day's a bit warm. Please do."

"Thank you," he said woodenly.

While he stood to remove his tailcoat, Portia took over the quaint task of setting their nonexistent table. But as she laid out the silver, she sneaked a few furtive glances at her fiancé.

The first thing she had noticed when Lucas had come to fetch her earlier was that he hardly looked rumpled at all. As he pulled off his coat, her gaze trailed over his long-sleeved white shirt and the silk waistcoat he'd selected for their outing. It had pale pinstripes of muted green and light blue.

Very elegant, she thought, amazed. On his bottom half were faultless ivory trousers of summer-weight wool and brown leather shoes.

In short, there was nothing objectionable about his attire. Sidney himself could not have done better.

Maybe he hired a new valet. Whatever the cause of his sartorial transformation, he was clearly making an effort here today, as was she.

After smoothing his tailcoat neatly over his arm and setting it aside, he sat down beside her, one knee bent, the other long leg sprawled out before him.

Leaning back on one hand with casual elegance, the duke paused to admire the view. Portia studied him more closely, intrigued. *Definite potential there,* she admitted in spite of herself. She liked the angle of his nose, the firm line of his clean-shaved jaw.

At least they wouldn't have ugly children.

"Oh!" Lucas said suddenly. "Something to drink, my lady? I forgot. Iced tea? Lemonade? Wine?"

"What will you be having?" she asked, with no idea why she found his absent-mindedness...cute. For the moment, anyway.

"I think lemonade," he said with a judicious wrinkle of his nose.

"I'll have the same, then. Shall I pour?"

"If you like."

Eager for some task to perform to help ward off the continuing undercurrent of awkwardness between them, Portia applied herself to lifting the corked decanter of lemonade out of the hamper and pouring them each a generous goblet full.

"I hope it's sweet enough for you," he said worriedly.

"Everything's lovely, Lucas," she said with a fond laugh. She could not resist reaching out to lay a hand on his arm in reassurance, and was startled at the muscles she felt under her casual touch. "You don't have to try so hard to impress me."

He looked at her in dismay. "It shows?"

"Just a little." She smiled at him, then took a sip of her lemonade and changed the subject. "Oh, this is good."

He followed suit and nodded in approval.

They sat for a moment, uncertain again.

"So what now?" He glanced at her. "Shall we eat?"

"In a bit—though, if you're hungry, you need not wait for me. I should like to just sit here for a moment and enjoy the day." Portia made herself more comfortable on the blanket, shifting from her kneeling position to lean on her hip with her legs bent to one side.

She planted a hand behind her to steady herself, sipping her cool drink. "June is such a pleasant month, don't you think?"

He smiled ruefully at her. "It is. But perhaps we can think of something more interesting to talk about than the weather."

She arched a brow at him, but did not bother denying that things had been rather stilted so far. "Like what?"

Lucas brought up his other knee and loosely clasped his hands around his bent legs, feet planted wide. It was a surprisingly boyish pose, almost rascally, but it was his hands that drew her attention.

They were larger and more rugged than she had noticed before. "Let's play a game," he said.

She smiled with interest. "Cards, you mean? I'm quite good at cribbage, I should warn you. My grandmother taught me to play. I can be *quite* a shark."

Lucas smiled, studying her. "Apparently so. Because you're already winning, and you don't even know what the game is yet. Very clever, my lady. Very clever indeed."

"What are you talking about?" she asked, laughing. "By my troth, Your Grace, half the time I cannot make heads or tails of you."

"You know, I hear that a lot," he said. "I wasn't talking about cards, though." He looked away. "I don't think I even own a deck, to be honest."

Oh no. Portia suddenly froze. Did that shadow of disapproval she detected from him on the topic of card games have something to do with her former suitor?

Had Lucas finally heard something about Joel having courted her? It oughtn't surprise her if he had. It wasn't as though she had been trying to hide it.

Oh God. All the same, she intensely hoped he did not ask about it on their picnic today, and she couldn't help wondering *how* he might've found out. It wasn't as though the man could be persuaded to spend two minutes in Society. And a bookish, absent-minded genius didn't seem the type to go around ferreting out the latest gossip.

"Here is the game I propose," he said, breaking into her nervous thoughts. "I will ask you a question and you will answer it, and then you will ask me a question and I will answer it, and so on. And we must answer truthfully, of course."

"Well, that goes without saying." She tucked her chin and brushed a lock of hair self-consciously behind her ear.

"Hmm."

They stared at each other. Portia cursed the blush that crept into her cheeks at the thought of her secrets. Still seeking Joel. Burning with crazed hunger for Silversmoke.

She thrust both other men out of her mind. Today was all about the Duke of Fountainhurst.

Her future husband.

He looked away, almost as though he, too, had certain topics himself that he would rather not speak of. "Would you like to begin, or shall I?"

"You outrank me." Somehow, she managed a light, teasing tone again. "Why don't you start?"

He nodded, looking amused. "Very well. Never fear, Lady Portia; I'll go easy on you. I should not wish to be ungallant on our very first outing together."

Portia giggled, albeit nervously, and took another sip of lemonade. She had to admit that Lucas was more affable than she had expected.

"Favorite color?" he asked.

An innocuous question, thank God.

"Um...green. No, yellow. No, blue! I don't know. I like them all. You?"

"Red," he said firmly. "Hmm. She likes them all."

"How's a girl to choose?"

"Yet choose she must," he said sweetly.

She swallowed down her guilt behind a smile. "All right, my turn."

"No, I just told you my favorite color was red," he interrupted before she could start. "That was your question."

"What?" She gasped, laughing as she scowled at him. "That didn't count! I was only being polite by asking you back!"

"Oh, yours doesn't count and mine does?" he taunted, laughing roguishly. "Very well. I see how this goes. You *did* warn me you were a shark."

"Trying to steal my turn," she said, shaking her head.

His grin widened. "I wasn't! It was legitimately— Never mind. Go on, you big bully. I'll get you next time."

"Humph. Let's see…" She narrowed her eyes. "I have one for His Grace."

"Uh-oh," he said, eyeing her warily from behind his spectacles.

Portia ventured out on a limb, since their laughter had dispelled a good deal of the tension. Besides, she really wanted to know the answer to this one.

"What's the big draw with insects? Please tell me. Why in the world do you like them so much? Do you have any other hobbies besides that? Slightly less crawly ones, maybe?" She looked at him hopefully, then took a nonchalant sip of her lemonade.

Unfortunately, Lucas comprehended from the question that she was not thrilled with his favorite area of study. "You do realize that was four questions?"

Portia nearly spewed lemonade at his droll tone.

He arched a brow at her, smiling. He had an oddly knowing look in his eyes. But he couldn't know. Could he?

"Well?" she persisted, refusing to pay her doubts any heed.

Leaning back with a sigh, he gazed up into the branches above them. "Oh, I don't know… They fascinate me, I suppose. Well, really, they're amazing, aren't they? Their variety. Nobody likes them, but we wouldn't have any of these beautiful flowers around us without them. Or the fruit in your salad if we didn't have the bees. Did you know that one humble ant, for example, can carry fifty times its own body weight? You try doing that."

"I had no idea," she said with a smile, recalling his kindness to Annabelle. "Does this mean that if the ants try to carry off our picnic, you're going to let them?"

He laughed. "No, for your sake, they can fend for themselves, my dear. But…look around you. The whole world is full of wonders. And these little creatures, why, they get no thanks, yet we can't live without them. Nothing would grow if it weren't for earthworms aerating the soil."

"Ew," she said with a smile.

"Of course, they're not insects, but to a girl, just as repulsive, I'm sure."

She nodded with a wry smile.

"But what survivors they are. You know?" he mused aloud. "You chop a poor, lowly worm in half by accident with a spade out in the garden, and both sides will grow into two separate new beings from a wound that would've destroyed any other living thing. I find that absolutely...incredible." He slowly took a drink.

Portia gazed at him, too mystified by the man and his strange opinions to answer. Instead, she lifted a strawberry out of the bowl, gave him a thoughtful nod, and ate it to avoid having to respond, for she truly did not know what to say to such a comment.

Lucas seemed to realize that his eccentricity was showing. A crestfallen look sank over his face as it apparently dawned on him that the topic of cutting earthworms in half was not exactly what the poets would suggest for a courting swain trying to impress a fashionable belle.

He really was hopeless, Portia thought fondly. Yet, once again, she found his boyish enthusiasms endearing.

He looked so awkward again all of a sudden, probably cursing himself, that she took pity on him, selected a strawberry, and offered it to him.

He accepted it, and she took another for herself.

"To the earthworms," she said, holding up her strawberry like a wineglass.

He smiled, and a glow crept into his emerald-green eyes. He clinked strawberries with her, then they both ate them in silence.

"What about you?" he asked at length. "Don't you have any unusual hobbies, my lady?" He took another swig of his lemonade.

"No, I am perfectly ordinary," she said. She dabbed her lips with her napkin after the strawberry.

"Balderdash. Tell me something you like. Something you're good at."

Portia considered as she scanned the horizon. "Well. As it happens, Your Grace, I am remarkably good at archery. If I say so myself."

"Aha, are you?" He looked pleased and impressed. "How did that come about?"

She swirled lemonade in her cup. "I was born with excellent eyesight—even in the dark, I don't mind saying—and that gives me frightfully good aim. Lots of practice, as well, though not so much recently. It's not a suitable hobby for Town, in general, but I do find it, hmm, rewarding."

"How?"

"It helps to calm the mind. When I focus on the target, it forces me to push all my worries to one side. And there's just something satisfying about landing that arrow in the bullseye."

He grinned. "Remind me never to make you angry."

"Never fear, Your Grace. I'm on your side—a stout-hearted English archer. I stand ready to defend the castle." She gave him a salute, and he laughed.

Chuckling with him, Portia watched him intently. It was remarkable how well he had put her at ease, for a quiz—or perhaps it was she who had put him at ease?

She couldn't tell at the moment, but was glad they were getting along.

Today, the match between them no longer felt like a looming apocalypse.

"Shall we eat?" Lucas asked gently.

Portia nodded, resolute on marrying the quiz, come hell or high water. "Let's eat."

Be yourself was the advice Luke had received from his father as a young lad who tended to get tongue-tied around pretty girls.

Though he had long since overcome his youthful shyness, taking Father's advice wasn't so easy when he had split his real self into different personas. Exactly whom should he be?

Did he even know who the real Luke was anymore?

A liar, for starters, his conscience opined.

He was feeling increasingly guilty about that as he sat enjoying their picnic. His dilemma was becoming ever more clear. The love that he now understood he wanted required openness, did it not?

And yet the moment he spoke up and told the truth—if he ever decided to—the lady he'd lied to was going to be furious at him.

Not to mention mortified.

She probably wouldn't trust him anymore—either version of him.

Even worse, she might feel betrayed because of this game he had played.

Surely the smartest thing to do was just to keep the darker side of his life hidden from her, as he had always intended, make sure she never saw Silversmoke again, and continue gradually easing up on the eccentricity he'd mastered as Lucas.

He'd already cut it down by about twenty-five percent today, determined to win her heart before he found and rescued Joel.

If he could maintain the right balance, then he saw no reason why he could not have the best of both worlds: the love of the woman he wanted, and his freedom to still wreak havoc on the world's evildoers.

He did not expect Portia to understand about the latter. It was one thing for a lady in distress to come to him seeking Silversmoke's help. It would be another thing entirely for a wife to accept such a dangerous hobby in a husband.

Given the choice, Portia probably would have preferred the hobby of silly ol' Lucas netting butterflies like those flitting from flower to flower throughout the meadow around them, rather than Silversmoke thrashing villains.

Women as a species didn't like violence, he had noticed. To be sure, his own sister had made her disapproval clear.

Thankfully, Tavi had given up long ago trying to dissuade him from his ongoing battle for justice. She knew that it was pointless.

Luke's sense of guilt increased when he thought of his sister, as if it wasn't already strong enough, sitting here across from his gorgeous fiancée, lying through his teeth.

At least he knew for a fact that he wasn't the only one feeling guilty today.

Lady Portia had warmed by several degrees toward "Lucas" this afternoon, and cynically, Luke could only conclude she was inspired by remorse for what she had got up to the other night in the gazebo.

Little did she know.

At the same time, it was all he could do to rein in his rampant reaction to her after having had a tantalizing taste of her kiss.

Talk about butterflies. He got them like a schoolboy around her.

The bliss he'd felt holding her in his arms that night left him needing to remind himself repeatedly today not to stare. But God, he wanted her. Every inch of her lovely self fascinated him. Her creamy skin made his mouth water. Every curve of her lips when she smiled filled him with soft delight.

How easy it was to imagine the rest of the world fading away. If they were really alone, he'd have laid her down on this blanket and...

She sure likes those strawberries. He winced, watching her languorously savor another one of the ripe, luscious fruits, so freshly in season.

Ignoring the lively response inside his trousers, he looked away and focused on his ham sandwich, slowly chewing, dazed once again by his desire for her.

God, he believed he was well and truly smitten.

"Archery, eh?" he said at length, glancing over at her, still amused, though the topic had passed several moments ago.

Portia lifted her napkin to her lips, but her azure eyes twinkled. She nodded.

By God, if he'd had any idea that she was so easy to be with, he'd have married her months ago. How different she seemed now from the withdrawn, quiet waif he had met at their first introduction.

To think he had judged her as mousy! A mousy young lady did not go about hiring highwaymen.

Ah well. He understood now that she'd been in a state of mourning and shock at the time, even though no one had breathed a word to him about Joel.

Luke had signed the papers pertaining to dowry and marriage settlement and all that without asking too many questions.

He wondered what she had thought of *him* at the time, and whether her opinion had changed.

She stabbed a radish from the helping of salad she'd taken and lifted it on her fork. "So," she said, "your spectacles. Nearsighted or far?"

Careful, Luke thought as he realized their game of questions continued. Though he smiled at her, he hated the necessary lie. His spectacles were just plain glass, after all.

"Unfortunately, I need them for both." He quickly changed the subject. "My turn. Planning our wedding: misery or fun for you?"

"Oh, a bit of both." She gave a charming little shrug. "It all just depended on the day, really."

Luke gazed at her. "I'm sorry I made things more difficult for you with all my requests. If you really want, you can have different flowers—"

"No, no, it's all settled now, as I told you in the church. Besides, I don't mind accommodating Your Grace's *quirks*."

"Quirks, eh? What about you? Any foibles or flaws I should know about?" He crunched a carrot.

"Tell you my flaws?" she exclaimed. "What girl in her right mind would answer that?" She played more worldly than she was, he noticed. "I daresay you'll have our whole lives to learn them. Wouldn't want to spoil the surprise."

"Now you're scaring me."

Portia laughed, the dappled sunlight glinting on her bright hair in the places where it made its way through the tree's leafy branches.

Luke shook his head, swallowed down his mouthful with a drink of lemonade, and then informed her, "You are too lovely to have any flaws."

"La, such flattery, sir," she said, but her smile soon faded, as if she were uneasily remembering a recent flirtation with another man.

In a gazebo, perhaps?

Luke all but watched her chase the memory of kissing Silversmoke out of her mind. Her fleeting, pensive look was quickly replaced by the same mask of cheer he had seen her don during their stroll in the park last week.

"How was the ball?" he asked idly, still just a wee bit annoyed to know his little vixen had cheated on him with himself.

She paused. "Why do you ask?"

"No particular reason."

"It was fine. Same as always." She shrugged, then watched a finch land on a stalk of goldenrod. "Are you coming to the one this week, Your Grace? I so wish you would."

"If I must," he said with a smile of concession. After all, he supposed, she never would've sneaked off to meet Silversmoke if her fiancé had been there.

"I think it's my turn for a question," she said, the playfulness fading from her voice.

"Yes?"

She curled her hands in her lap. "Why do you hardly ever come to Town?"

Luke considered his words carefully. They were straying onto dangerous ground now, far from a simple exchange of favorite colors. He sat up straight from his lounging position and lowered his gaze. "It makes me uncomfortable sometimes."

"Why is that?" she asked softly.

"Because when I come here, I cannot forget that I'm the Duke of Fountainhurst."

She stared at him, her fork with a lettuce leaf paused halfway to her lips. It remained in midair. "Why would you want to forget your own title?"

Luke stared down at his toes. "Because it should still belong to my father."

"Ah," she said softly. She put her fork back down on her plate.

Luke squinted against a shaft of sun that angled in between the oak's branches. "He should still be alive. And my mother."

"I am sorry," Portia said faintly.

He shrugged. Then his gaze homed in on her. "My turn."

"Yes?" she murmured.

He braced himself for any answer. "Why did you agree to marry me?"

Her eyes betrayed a startled flicker as she lifted her head.

"Is it *because* I am the Duke?"

She went very still, but, to her credit, did not look away. She held his stare gravely. "My parents suggested it. My father spoke highly of your line. Then I met you, and I had no objections. So I agreed."

Luke arched a brow, but said nothing.

"Of *course* any family would be fortunate to make an alliance with a ducal house. I won't lie to you."

"I should hope that you would not," he said softly. "You can tell me anything, Portia."

She lowered her head, and Luke held his breath as he realized she meant to elaborate.

"Well...as it happens, your timing was good, too," she admitted.

"Oh?"

"You may have heard I had a suitor that I was quite fond of before you and I were introduced."

"Yes, I did hear something about that. The young man who disappeared." He flicked his gaze downward, barely daring to breathe. But he was encouraged that she was finally confessing this to him without his having to ask.

He hadn't been sure if she was capable of real honesty until this moment.

For that matter, was he?

Luke ignored the question that echoed in his heart. He kept his eyes lowered as he nodded. "I recall reading something about the case in the papers."

He sneaked a scrutinizing glance at her and saw her nod stiffly, her gaze downcast as well, beneath long velvet lashes.

"We weren't too terribly serious—just so you know."

I think you were. He said nothing.

She took a deep breath. "But we were frequently seen together, and there was talk... Anyway, when he vanished, after a time, his uncle called on me."

"His uncle?" Luke asked, startled. This he had not been expecting to hear.

She nodded, meeting his gaze. "Lord Axewood. You see, my suitor, Mr. Clayton, was his heir. His nephew."

"Ah."

"The earl has no son of his own, obviously. So, about four or five months after Joel disappeared, His Lordship came to call on me. He knew that his nephew and I might well have proceeded to marriage at some point. He said he felt awful for me." She paused with a slight grimace, then continued in a delicate tone. "Well, since his heir had disappeared, the earl found himself in need of a new one, and for that, he would need a bride.

"Lord Axewood told me he had not planned on marrying again— apparently, he'd had a wife long ago, but she died. I'm not sure how. Unfortunately, with Joel's disappearance, and fearing the worst, he said he had no choice but to marry a second time in hopes of producing a son."

She shook her head, looking slightly embarrassed. "His Lordship meant well, I'm sure. The day he came to visit me, he spoke with great sincerity. He said that since Joel's disappearance had also left me in need of a new suitor, I ought not to lose my, um, opportunity to become the Countess of Axewood if I wished. Therefore, he said he'd be willing to offer for me himself."

"The uncle proposed to you?" Luke asked, amazed. "What did you say?"

"That I'd think about it." She gave him a wide-eyed look. "I was shocked, to be honest. But I didn't dare reject him outright without at least pretending to think about it. He is a very proud man. To avoid offending him, I told him I would need some time to contemplate his offer. But then my parents told me you had asked for my hand as well.

Thank God you proposed when you did, Lucas. That's all I can say. I had no interest in Axewood, obviously. He's over twice my age."

Luke furrowed his brow, studying her.

"It was a little disturbing, to be honest."

"I should think so," Luke said darkly.

"His Lordship meant well, I'm sure. He was only trying to help. He felt sorry for me, because he knew for a time there that I was lost."

"Mm-hmm. Well. I suppose that was good of him," he murmured out of politeness, remembering he was Lucas just now.

But the Silversmoke side of him did not like this at all.

"So, you see?" she said with a guarded smile. "You rescued me without even knowing it, Lucas."

"Surely your parents would not have pledged you to him if you had objected."

"Well, no. But they were pressuring me to wed *someone*." She bit her lip, worry in her eyes. "You do realize I am already twenty-three?"

He laughed all of a sudden in gentle delight. "Oh yes, you're quite elderly, my dear."

She burst out laughing with apparent relief, and smacked him on the arm.

Luke couldn't stop smiling. "I think you're perfect," he whispered, and, leaning across the plates and platters, he kissed her on the cheek.

Portia blushed, but Luke was slow to pull away.

"Lucas?" she murmured.

"Yes, Portia?" he whispered, still leaning near.

"Are you angry that I had this ulterior motive for accepting your suit? To escape Lord Axewood?"

"Hmm. Well, it's better than you accepting merely for my title."

She shook her head. "That had nothing—well, *almost* nothing to do with it. I'm not stupid, after all."

He laughed quietly and lingered near, noting that she made no effort to pull away.

She gave him a demure little smile. "You and I are closer in age, and when I met you, you seemed…a kind man. I know now for certain that you are, and that is perhaps the most important quality that a…" Her voice trailed off as she held his gaze.

Inches apart, he could swear they both sensed that tingling awareness that had charged the air between them that night in the gazebo. He'd had the luxury of acting on it then, but not now.

His Grace was a gentleman.

The highwayman, not exactly.

The real Luke, he supposed, was something in between.

"I am glad I was able to spare you from that fate, anyway." He drummed up the discipline to withdraw back to his side of the blanket.

After all, there were a horde of servants and her chaperone waiting and watching discreetly from the base of the hill.

"Oh, that reminds me!" he said as he managed to snap back to his senses. "I have an important message to convey to milady."

"You do? From whom?"

"My sister. Octavia, Lady Sedgwick, cordially invites you and your esteemed parents to dine with our family on Sunday."

"Does she? How nice!"

He nodded. "It's past time we all sat down for a meal together, don't you think?"

"I agree wholeheartedly."

"Do you think your parents will be able to come?"

"Certainly. What time, and where does your sister live?"

"Actually, she is inviting you all to *my* estate north of Town. Gracewell."

"Oh?" Portia said with a startled laugh.

Luke noted how her eyes lit up at the prospect of finally taking a tour of her soon-to-be home. Really, it was shameful that he had neglected this step until now.

Leave it to Tavi to give her errant brother a much-needed kick in the trousers. "Yes," he mumbled, "she's bossy that way. At least to *me*."

"Believe me, I understand. I have an elder sister, too."

They exchanged a knowing look full of humor.

"Anyway, Tavi thinks it would be a perfect chance for you to see your future home, as well. She scalded my ears for not inviting you sooner, to be honest. I am sorry about that."

Portia smiled and gave his arm a reassuring squeeze. "It's all right, Lucas."

He thrilled to her touch—and to the speculative glint that he saw flit through her eyes as she felt his biceps.

She held his gaze for a moment. "We'll move along through all this marriage business the best we can, yes? We're both new at this, after all. I think we'll be all right, as long as neither of us asks for perfection."

He smiled at her, moved by her warmth. "You are far too pretty to be so wise."

"And you are far more charming than you let on at first glance."

"Don't be absurd." He looked away with a self-conscious scoff, in Lucas mode. "I'm terrible with women. It's a fact."

"No, you're really not!"

"Now you're the one being kind."

Smiling, she studied him. "What time would you like us to come?"

"Whatever time suits you and your parents. Perhaps around noon or one o'clock? Tavi says we'll eat at two or three. You all are welcome to stay overnight i-if it's more convenient." His slight stammer was genuine at the thought of having this luscious vixen snuggled into one of his bedchambers. "That is, er, the house has plenty of guestrooms."

"Thanks, but I doubt they'll want to stay. Papa likes his own bed. We'll need directions. How long does it take to get there?"

"From Moonlight Square, about an hour or so. It just depends on the weather. I hope you all can come, but if not, there's always next Sunday—"

"No, no, with the wedding just three weeks away—do you realize that?—I am sure my parents will have no higher priority than attending. Thank you," his future duchess added. "I shall be looking forward to this."

"As will I, my lady. But"—Luke hesitated, unable to resist—"do be careful on the roads passing through Hampstead Heath. I hear there are highwayman about."

Her eyes widened, but not with fear.

No, indeed. A quick flare of excitement rushed into their blue depths, and when he saw it, it was all he could do not to push her down on the blanket and steal a hundred lawless kisses there and then.

"Oh?" she asked, feigning nonchalance as she tucked a lock of hair behind her ear. Except that her voice sounded just a trifle breathless, much to his delight.

Luke shrugged. "I wouldn't worry, my lady. I've never seen one myself. I have my doubts they exist at all. But, you know, one hears stories."

"Indeed," she said faintly. With a somber nod, she looked away, a slight blush in her cheeks. "One certainly does."

CHAPTER 13

Surprises Great and Small

*W*hen Wednesday came, Portia discovered that, for the first time in Moonlight Square history, Lady Delphine had taken the unprecedented step of inviting gentlemen to the ladies' monthly book club.

For this, the wealthy spinster made no apologies. It was all part of her ongoing effort to make the entire world read *Pride and Prejudice*. Indeed, she continued promoting the anonymous female author with such devotion that Portia sometimes wondered if Lady Delphine might've written the thing herself.

It would not have surprised her.

Lady Delphine Blire was one of the most formidably intelligent women Portia had ever met. Truth be told, Portia was rather in awe of her. She and several of her friends found the no-nonsense heiress decidedly intimidating.

The daughter of a duke, Lady Delphine was a renaissance woman with wide interests and innumerable hobbies, all of which she had the time and the means to pursue, thanks to her being the heiress to a fortune in her own right.

Though she was unmarried at thirty-something (her exact age was a closely guarded secret), she did not fit the dreary image of the typical spinster in any way.

She dressed with independent style and sophistication; she even rouged her lips—in the daytime, no less—but not to lure a man. She could've had one or several of those with a snap of her fingers.

In fact, there were even rumors that Lord Sidney himself visited her on occasion. Alone. After dark.

Everybody knew the two were good friends. But if the eagle-eyed brunette and the suave ladies' man had a use for each other after midnight, that was hardly Portia's business.

Lord knew she had enough problems of her own. Besides, if Sidney really were Lady Delphine's occasional paramour—and who would put it past him?—wouldn't he have come to her first official book club meeting open to men?

It wasn't like the viscount to miss an opportunity to mingle, let alone flirt. But Sidney wasn't there.

Only a few gentlemen were, thanks to the club's most loyal members doing their parts to drag in whatever males they could snare. Felicity had conscripted her brother, Major Peter Carvel.

Danger Man sat there looking uncomfortable and bored, like he'd rather be tracking tigers through some misty Himalayan jungle.

Trinny, meanwhile, had left the baby at home with her mother and pulled in her father, the distracted but endlessly amiable Lord Beresford.

Though Serena did not attend book club as a rule, her mousy Cousin Tamsin never missed a meeting. Tamsin had brought along Serena's former suitor, Mr. Tobias Guilfoyle, who was an author in his own right, assembling amusing collections of old peasant superstitions and fairy lore from around the British Isles.

Maggie's portly and good-natured brother-in-law, Edward, Lord Birdwell, had also ambled in, if only to escape his termagant wife, Delia, for a while. To be sure, Delia's pregnancy had only made the redheaded marchioness even more moody than usual.

Everybody loved the gentlemanly Edward, though, and since Maggie usually came to the book club, everybody asked him if he'd heard from her and Connor, but there was no news from the honeymooners yet.

No doubt they were *busy*, Portia thought with a wicked half-smile.

Then Lady Delphine cleared her throat, looked sternly over her smart little reading glasses, and brought the meeting to order.

"Now then," she said firmly. "I want to know what you all thought of Lizzy Bennet and Mr. Darcy. Who wishes to begin?"

At first, there was an awkward pause as everyone debated what to say that might not make them look daft. Then Lady Delphine waved a commanding gesture at one of the more talkative matrons present to get the discussion going, and it soon became clear that everyone seemed to like the story, thank God.

Otherwise, their hostess might've done a violence to the dissenter.

When the discussion came around to the male newcomers to state their impressions, Portia's full attention returned. They were a novelty, as if someone had brought in orangutans. Who knew that they could even read? she thought with irreverent humor.

Only her fiancé was the bookworm, as far as she knew.

"Personally, I'd have shot Wickham," Major Carvel said bluntly. "Bounder."

Then the soldier-adventurer looked at his sister as if to ask whether he had contributed enough with this remark and could go home now.

Felicity scowled at him in reply.

"Er, if I may, I thought the writing was extraordinary," Tobias Guilfoyle ventured, glancing around politely at the ladies, as though unsure whether he was permitted to speak yet. "The style is really quite sophisticated."

"Isn't it, though?" Trinny burst out, as though she could no longer contain herself. The redhead beamed, glancing around at them all. "It's so beautiful how Darcy swallows his pride and devotes himself to Lizzy at the end!"

The women nodded, though Danger Man arched a brow at such romantical nonsense.

"I felt sorry for her sister, Jane," Felicity offered.

"Jane?" Lord Beresford said with a teasing glance at Trinny. "What about the girls' poor father? Five daughters? Who could bear it?"

"Oh, Papa," Trinny said, elbowing her sire. After all, Lord Beresford had six red-haired daughters of his own.

"And what did you think, Lady Portia?" Delphine inquired, turning to her.

"Um, well…" Portia didn't dare tell her hostess that she had barely been able to follow the ending due to all her own trouble with men. So she opted to be vague. "I liked Mr. Bingley very much. But I will say, I mostly wanted to strangle Lydia Bennet."

"Hear, hear!" everyone in the room agreed.

"If you're going to elope, at least let it be with a good man. That's what I advise my own girls, anyway," Lord Beresford said dryly, glancing again at Trinny, who had eloped with Gable to Gretna Green some time ago.

"Papa! I am leaving you at home next time," she scolded with a blushing laugh. "Honestly."

"Humph. Bingley," Major Carvel grumbled, as though drawn in against his will. "I suppose he was agreeable enough. But he struck me as entirely immature. Lacking a spine. Oblivious to boot, if he couldn't tell how poor Jane felt about him. I don't think he deserved her, frankly."

"What about that meddlesome sister of his, trying to spoil things between them?" Lady Delphine said.

"Oh, and that sickening Mr. Collins!" Cousin Tamsin chimed in. "Even I wouldn't marry him. I cannot fathom why Lizzy's poor friend Charlotte would ever agree to it. Prudence is all very well, but surely nobody's *that* desperate..."

When the discussion moved on to include the delicious scene of Miss Bennet's defiance of the tyrannical Lady Catherine de Bourgh, Portia could no longer keep her mind from drifting. Her gaze wandered out the window to Fountainhurst House.

I wonder what Lucas is doing today.

She hadn't seen him since that darling picnic he had put together for her.

Reflecting on it, she did not believe that any man had ever treated her with such solicitude. Not Joel, not anyone. To her surprise, Portia was looking forward to being with him again tomorrow night at the Thursday ball.

The ball. *Hmm.* She hoped he didn't embarrass her or himself in front of her friends. She'd have to keep watch so she could rescue him if the poor thing stumbled into any faux pas.

As her gaze trailed over the square, the sight of the distant gazebo tweaked her conscience, bringing back the memory of the highwayman who had stolen a kiss that had shaken her to her core.

She had not heard from Silversmoke again. She was not sure she wanted to. Or how she might feel when she did.

It had been nearly a week since she had escaped the ball to meet him, and there had been no word from him since.

What that meant, Portia was not certain. Cynic that she was, she half believed the supposed hero had abandoned her case, losing interest after she'd refused his advances. Only time would tell.

Refusing to think of him anymore—or of Joel, for that matter—she pulled her yearning stare back into the drawing room, lowered her gaze to the rose-colored carpet, and said little more until the meeting was adjourned.

When it finally ended, she turned her attention to her mission of the day: to ask Felicity what it was like being orphaned at a young age.

Maybe Peter would be willing to talk about it, too, she thought. His perspective as a male might be especially helpful.

She caught up to the Carvel siblings outside after filing out of Lady Delphine's townhouse with all the other guests.

"Well, Danger Man, you survived your first book club," she said with a smile as she joined them.

They were strolling down the pavement toward Netherford House.

Major Carvel snorted at the nickname Trinny had made up for him, but Felicity smiled at her as Portia fell in step with the pair, not waiting to be invited.

"What did you think of the experience?" Portia asked him.

"Not bad," he said. "Lady Delphine is, er, an interesting woman."

Felicity gave her brother a nudge. "Maybe next time I can get Jason to come along, now that you've bravely waded in."

"Only if the book has lots of pictures," he replied.

Felicity laughed and shoved her brother halfheartedly into the wrought-iron fence that flanked the pavement.

"You see how she treats me?" he exclaimed. "The two of them always ganging up on me, these Netherfords. To say nothing of the little ones climbing on me half the day."

"Oh, you love it, Uncle Pete. Ignore him. He's a clod," Felicity said pleasantly to Portia, ignoring the roguish twinkle in her brother's teal-colored eyes.

They ambled past flower boxes burgeoning from every window in the row of terrace houses.

"If I'm such a clod, then why do you keep pestering me to buy one of these houses, hmm?"

"Oh, you should!" Portia said.

"I know! He's always here anyway," Felicity agreed.

Listening while the two siblings bantered about nothing in particular, Portia found herself wishing again that her own brother would come back to England and rejoin the civilized world.

The thought gave her heart a pang.

Refusing to get her hopes up—after all, Hunter might not even have received her letter telling him that she was getting married—she fixed her attention on her friends.

"Are you really thinking of moving to Moonlight Square, Major?" she asked as a phaeton rolled by. "Because if so, I heard the Chapmans may soon be putting their house up for lease. Mama said they're even considering dividing it into two or three separate units, as there's more need in Town for smaller places these days."

"Really?" Felicity said. "That sounds like it would be perfect for you, Pete. Have you heard why they're leaving?"

"Mama heard they, ah, need to retire to the country for a while. *Dun territory.*"

"Oh dear," Felicity murmured.

"Which house?" Peter glanced around.

"Three doors down from ours, on Marquess Row." Portia gestured.

He frowned. "Do you have to be a marquess to live there?"

She chuckled. "No, it's just a nickname, since a few of them already do. Lord Birdwell. My father."

"You may qualify soon, anyway, brother, if Cousin Charles doesn't recover this time," Felicity said.

"Oh no," Portia said. "Is he unwell again?" She was not well acquainted with their flamboyant cousin, Charles Carvel, but she knew he'd been previously styled Viscount Elmont until last year, when he had inherited his father's title as the Marquess of Sandonhelm.

She remembered Felicity telling her some time ago that Cousin Charles had moved to Portugal for the weather after being diagnosed with consumption. He was a young man—only in his thirties—but frail and slight of build. As was standard with consumptives, his physician had ordered him to seek out a warm, dry climate for his health.

"I thought all that sunshine was supposed to make him better," Portia said in dismay.

"Up to a point, yes. But he's still taking snuff!" Felicity shook her head in exasperation.

"Are you jesting?" Portia exclaimed.

"I wish," Peter muttered.

"He refuses to break the habit," said Felicity. "A man with weak lungs has no business putting that rubbish up his nose, but he likes it too much, and, as a rule, Cousin Charles does what he pleases."

"Never mind if he's coughing up blood." Peter harrumphed. "Absurd."

"Hmm." Portia glanced at the major. She knew he was next in line for his uncle's title. "Perhaps we'll be seeing you on Marquess Row after all."

Peter's smile was grim. He did not look terribly enthused about the prospect of being elevated to the peerage. Technically, he was now Major Lord Elmont, but he never used the courtesy title.

"Portia, why don't you come over and dine with us?" Felicity suggested, putting an arm around her with a fond smile. "It's already one o'clock now; we're eating at two. We're keeping country hours for the children's sake. You're welcome to join us."

"Oh, that's all right. I don't wish to impose."

"Never!" Felicity said.

"I did want to speak to you, though, if I may. Both of you, if possible." Portia hesitated. "If you don't mind, I was hoping to ask the two of you what I truly hope will not be an…indelicate question."

Both Carvel siblings stopped and turned to her in surprise.

"What is it?" Peter asked.

"Is something wrong?" Felicity's brow furrowed.

"No, nothing like that." Portia glanced awkwardly at both of them. "I beg your pardon in advance if the topic is too painful. Feel free to tell me if you'd rather not discuss it. But, um, Felicity, I remember you mentioning that your parents passed away when you were both quite young."

Felicity nodded. "Yes."

"Well, I just recently learned the same thing happened to Lucas when he was seventeen. I've been trying to fathom what it's like to go through something like that to help me understand him better, and I was wondering if you two might be willing to shed some light on your experience, and how it affected you. But only if you're comfortable discussing it," Portia added hastily. "Not for the world would I wish to pry—"

"No, it's fine," Felicity assured her with a light touch on her arm, and, thankfully, Peter did not look put off by the question either, though his tanned, handsome face saddened a bit.

The two Carvel siblings exchanged a glance full of painful, shared memories. Peter gave his sister a nod, and Felicity spoke first, her tone searching.

"I was sixteen when our parents died. I was sent off to live with my elderly aunt, Lady Kirby."

"The one who left you her fortune?" Portia asked as they walked on at a slower pace.

Peter hooked his thumbs into his pockets thoughtfully, escorting the ladies.

Felicity nodded. "I miss her dearly, even though she really was a difficult old dragon. She helped me get through the loss somehow. I thought I would die of sadness at first, especially after Mother passed. Then we were truly orphaned."

"Our parents died a few years apart," Peter explained. "We had barely recovered from our father's death when our mother fell ill."

"How awful. I'm so sorry for you both." Portia shuddered. "I can't imagine."

"At least we still had each other," said Felicity.

"And Jason," Peter added. "Rogue or not, he was there for us both. It's the only reason I let such a scoundrel marry my sister."

Felicity chuckled and gave her brother a nudge of reproach; Peter smiled with affection, then glanced earnestly at Portia.

"What my sister says is true, though. Losing our parents made us depend on each other all the more."

"Which is why I hated him going off to war. But *that* is another story." Felicity linked arms with Portia as they strolled on. "Looking back on it, I have often thought that my dragon aunt's no-nonsense ways were actually a great help to me, even though I didn't much enjoy it at the time. She imposed rigid structure on my day-to-day life, but all of her rules and regimens gave me something else to occupy my mind, instead of leaving me idle to wallow in my grief. Aunt Kirby had been widowed herself, you see, by the nabob who left her his fortune. She always insisted from firsthand experience that life must go on."

Felicity glanced at her brother. "Frankly, I think Peter got the worst of it." The major furrowed his brow. "It made him intensely responsible and even more serious than he already was."

"You think so?" he mumbled.

"Absolutely! If it weren't for Jason and all his roguery, you'd have forgotten entirely how to laugh."

"And if it weren't for me, he'd have never grown up," he drawled, though his eyes glowed with appreciation of his wild friend, the Duke of Netherford.

"Peter and my husband were the best of chums from the time they were Simon's age," Felicity told her.

"Yes, I was always the boring one next to him." Peter harrumphed. "But what choice did I have? Our parents' deaths forced me to grow up early. As the firstborn, I had many decisions to make, many matters to settle upon our father's death."

"My point exactly," Felicity exclaimed. "You had barely just become a man yourself, when suddenly, you were heaped with adult responsibilities."

Peter shrugged, hands in pockets. "I had no need to be sheltered."

"Well, I still find it odd that as soon as you had sorted out everything with our solicitors, you went running off to join the war."

"Army life is very structured, too, sis. It helped me."

"Hmm." Felicity looked amazed that her strong, quiet brother had just admitted that. "I thought it was because you meant to go and put Boney in his place personally."

Peter's lips crooked. "Well, a bit of that, too."

Felicity gave her brother's shoulder a caress, then smiled haplessly at Portia. "I'm not sure any of this is very helpful."

"No, it is," Portia said with a nod. "Thank you for sharing it with me. I admire you both for coming through your losses as well as you did."

"Well," Peter offered, his tone reflective, "I think the loss of a parent can affect people in any number of different ways. But there is an important distinction between our situation and Fountainhurst's." His expression darkened. "Our parents died of natural causes, but Fountainhurst's were brutally murdered."

Felicity gasped and turned to him. "They were?"

Portia winced and nodded. "Lucas doesn't like to talk about it."

"Who would?" Peter answered, then glanced at his sister. "Such dark tales are generally kept from young girls, which you both were when this happened. I heard they were attacked by highwaymen somewhere up in Scotland."

"Oh my God," Felicity whispered. "I had no idea! Poor Lucas."

"Indeed," Peter said. "What we went through was bad enough. But what he must have suffered, I shudder to contemplate. What that might do to a young man, I can barely imagine."

"No wonder he's eccentric, the poor man," Felicity murmured.

"If it were me, I wouldn't rest until I'd had revenge," Peter said.

Portia felt a chill run down her spine at his words.

"Don't upset her," Felicity scolded him, noticing how Portia had paled. "Don't listen to him, darling. Lucky for you, Lucas is not a ruthless warrior like my brother."

"There is a proper time and place for ruthlessness," Peter said in a menacingly mild tone. "Like when some pack of beasts kills your family."

"I can't say I disagree," Portia admitted.

Still, she was glad that Lucas was a gentle soul, not a trained killer like the major.

He passed a searching glance over her face, apparently noting her uneasiness about his deadly capabilities. "Sorry."

"You have nothing to apologize for," Portia said. "I appreciate your honesty."

The major nodded, but perhaps he was used to people being just a wee bit afraid of him, for he dropped his gaze and smoothly changed the subject.

"So, how did Fountainhurst escape the book club, anyway? What's he doing today?"

"Actually," Portia said with a smile, grateful for this safer topic, "now that you mention it, I have no idea."

At that very moment, as it happened, Luke was in the library at Gracewell, listening to Finch report on his research so far.

The ginger-haired archivist had assembled piles of relevant newspaper articles that he'd found following Joel's disappearance.

"I put together this list of all the places they searched for him. But it's just as Lady Portia told you, sir. Everywhere they looked, they turned up empty." Finch shook his head, sifting through the papers. "There's a tearful interview with his mother here. Quotes from many of his friends.

"The uncle organized the search, held vigils at their church. He even hired men to dragnet the Serpentine—the most fashionable place to drown yourself in London these days, in case you were wondering—but, thankfully, the dragnets did not produce a body."

"Hmm." Luke tapped a pencil on his desk while the afternoon sunlight spilled in through the tall windows in the library.

"I was also able to identify the two Bow Street agents Lord Axewood hired to pursue the investigation. It would be possible to go and talk to them, I should think," Finch said, but Luke winced.

"I'd avoid that if I can." He glanced dryly at Gower. "I'd just as soon not bring myself to the attention of the Bow Street offices—all things considered."

"Oh...right," Finch said.

Gower grumbled in wordless agreement. The pewter-haired fighter was lounging on a nearby chaise, sharpening his knife on a length of iron while he listened to Finch's report.

Luke rose, twitching the pencil between his fingers as he walked across the room. "What about his money? I would think Joel must've generated quite a fortune of his own, with all his winnings."

"Yes...I have that, too." Finch nodded and shuffled through a few pieces of paper until he found the one he wanted. "It looks like the uncle got control of his accounts a few months after he went missing."

"Oh really?" Luke murmured, turning to him and resting a hand on his hip.

"Well, not to confiscate his money—that wouldn't be legal," Finch said. "But from what I can tell, Lord Axewood is acting in a fiduciary capacity for his nephew. Making sure his financial obligations are being met. Servants given their wages. Creditors paid off. Tailors, bootmakers, pub tabs, and whatnot."

"Hmm." Luke propped his elbow on the mantel of the unlit fireplace. "Why the uncle?"

"Well, he's the patriarch of the family, and actually became Joel's legal guardian after his father died when he was a child."

"Really?"

Finch nodded, scanning the pages laid out before him on the library table. "Apparently, Joel's sire died when he was nine. He was Lord Axewood's younger brother. Axewood became Joel's guardian and chief trustee of his estate upon his father's death."

"I see." Memories of Luke's own board of trustees, who had overseen his fortune until he came of age, flitted through his mind.

Half a dozen solicitors and older relatives, they were trusted men appointed by his father in his will to oversee Luke and Tavi's inheritance, should anything ever happen to him.

Which, of course, it had.

Luke had had little contact with them as a lad, except for the occasional interviews when he was required to sit down before the panel of his keepers and answer dozens of prying questions on every subject from his health to his academic progress, his future plans, and even his dealings with any particular girls that might be of concern to them.

Tavi had known how much Luke despised having to answer to this whole panel of judges, so she'd gone out of her way to act as a buffer between them. She spoke to them more frequently than he did, and indeed, still kept in touch with them today out of gratitude.

As an adult, Luke also appreciated their service to his family, but he could not deny he had always resented their control over him as a lad.

He wondered if Joel had experienced the same sort of sentiments toward his uncle.

"Ah!" Finch found the one he was looking for. "This one's interesting. More proof of the uncle's refusal to give up on finding his nephew. This article tells how Lord Axewood chose to keep Joel's household open and running for him, in case he returns unexpectedly."

"You mean they all considered this lad flighty enough to do something like that?" Gower asked with a dubious squint. "Just disappear without a word and then show up again without so much as a by-your-leave?"

Luke shrugged. "Probably more a matter of hoping against hope. But Finch is right about the money. Though that's always my first thought as a possible motive, the uncle's control over Joel's fortune must be very limited. After all, without a body, you can't declare someone dead until they've been gone for seven years, so it isn't as though his uncle could've seized his accounts."

Finch nodded, straightening up from where he'd been leaning. "That's my understanding, as well."

"What do we know about the uncle, anyway?" Gower asked.

"Other than the fact that he proposed to my fiancée?" Luke said dryly.

"He did?" Finch exclaimed.

Luke nodded ruefully. "That was one of the main reasons she accepted my suit. To avoid having to marry the earl."

"Hold on just a minute." Gower swung his booted feet back down onto the floor and frowned at Luke. "The nephew disappears; the uncle takes at least partial control of his money, then asks the boy's lady for her hand?" He snorted. "Well, that's not too suspicious!"

On the face of it, Luke couldn't disagree—except that Dog had witnessed Joel being kidnapped.

That would mean that Axewood would have to be involved in the abduction, and why on earth would a wealthy and respected peer of the realm kidnap his own blasted nephew?

Intrigued by the notion, but doubtful all the same, Luke turned to his assistant. "Any record of the uncle being light in the pockets, Oliver?"

Finch shook his head. "Nothing that I've found, sir."

Luke gestured toward the bookshelves. "Check *Debrett's* on him. Just out of curiosity. Let's see what they have to say."

"Yes, sir."

Luke waited while Finch located *Debrett's Peerage* and looked up Lord Axewood.

"Ah, here it is… Vincent Clayton, the fifth Earl of Axewood. Born 1765 in Shropshire. Married 1790 to Lady Catherine Wheeler. Oh—it says here the countess died without issue in 1805."

Luke nodded. "That's the reason he proposed to Portia. Joel's disappearance left him without an heir, just as it left her without a suitor. Axewood needs to have a son in case his nephew turns up dead, otherwise his title reverts to the Crown."

"No wonder he searched so hard for him," Finch murmured.

Luke nodded. "Thus his sudden search for a bride. For what it's worth, Lady Portia, at least, was convinced that Lord Axewood was only trying to help."

"Well, I ain't convinced," grumbled the misanthropic Gower.

Luke's lips twisted at his mentor's typical curmudgeonly response. "Without knowing the man personally, it's hard to guess his intentions. Perhaps Portia can introduce us sometime in Society, then I can size the earl up for myself."

"Oh God, that'll be awkward," Finch muttered. "I mean if he proposed to her, too."

Luke waved this off. "Beautiful as she is, half the men in the ton are probably in love with her. I've already accepted that."

"But that makes it all the stranger, don't ye see?" Gower said, frowning. "How high an opinion of himself does this ol' goat have, thinkin' a girl like that would ever give him a second thought?"

"Maybe he thought the title alone could carry him," Luke said.

"Especially if he's rich." Finch folded his arms across his chest.

"But if he is, then what does he need with Joel's money?" Luke said.

Even Gower conceded this with a nod.

"No," Luke continued. "Our original theory still seems stronger to me. We know from Dog that someone kidnapped him out of Covent Garden. Given our missing person's dangerous habit of trawling these low gambling hells, I still say he must've run afoul of some ruthless party from the criminal class who saw an opportunity. We just need to figure out whom."

Finch nodded in agreement.

"Gower, why don't you visit a few more such places and keep asking around? Maybe he made other enemies at some of these hells, especially a 'big bald man.' But go during daylight hours and watch your back. Could be dangerous, so keep it discreet. If you find any leads, let me know, and I'll go back there with you.

"Finch, you keep digging. Just for fun, get me a list of Axewood's holdings, as well. It might come in handy, if things take an unexpected turn.

"As for me, I am leaving for London tomorrow. I promised Portia I'd show up for this ball on Thursday night. While I'm there, I'll see if I can find out the size of Axewood's fortune—just in case. Since the earl's on a bride hunt, rumors of his worth should be easy to come by. Point is, if he's in dun territory, that could change the picture.

"Whatever the two of you find, put it aside and I'll look at it when I return on Saturday. Tavi's bringing the children on Saturday afternoon, so I'll be back that morning. Any questions?"

They shook their heads.

"Good! Then you and I should get a round of practice in while we can, Gower. Are you game?"

The Yorkshireman cracked a smile. "Always happy to give you a thrashing, my lad."

Finch grinned. "Go easy on him, Gower. Don't send His Grace into the ballroom sporting a black eye for Lady Portia."

Luke laughed. "Aye, that'd be hard to explain. I'd have to say I ran into a tree chasing a cricket or something."

Gower harrumphed. "Silversmoke at a ball! Or are you going in full Lucas mode?"

"Actually, I've been thinking about that," Luke said. "I've decided my best course is to keep toning Lucas down gradually. After all, I rather fancy this girl." That was putting it mildly, but he held to his bravado. "I don't much care for the notion of losing her to Clayton once we've rescued him."

Gower rose, shook his head, and drifted toward the door.

"What?" Luke said, grinning self-consciously. "Fashionable young lady like that? I don't want to embarrass her in front of Society by being *too much* of a quiz. I went about three-quarters Lucas at the picnic. For the ball, I think I'll bring him down to half."

"Wish I had that option," Finch said wistfully.

Hands in pockets, Luke smiled as he sauntered toward the library door. "Maybe it just takes the right girl, Oliver. Because, you know, quiz or not, I think I'm growing on her."

She was definitely growing on him.

Then he left to go get ready for practice, while Finch called after him, "Have fun at the ball!"

CHAPTER 14

Thursday Night Intrigues

nother night, another ball. Wednesdays was Almack's, of course, but Thursday evenings belonged to the Grand Albion Assembly Rooms in Moonlight Square.

The ball started at eight o'clock, just an hour from now.

As the glow of evening filled his chamber, Vincent Clayton, the fifth Earl of Axewood, stood before the mirror in his dressing room, idly buttoning his white lawn shirt.

Though he lived in St. James's, he had taken care to get a voucher for all the best subscription balls the ton had to offer, determined as he was to secure a willing young bride before the Season was out.

It wasn't easy.

By now, his search was well underway, but it continued at a snail's pace mostly because he was picky. Admittedly, there was stiff competition from younger men for the few girls he deemed worthy to stand by his side.

Well, his rivals might be more dashing, but he was more powerful.

The real problem, he feared, was that these young milk-water misses could tell how bloody boring he found them.

He pulled on his striped silk waistcoat and let out a sigh. God, he never thought he would find himself at the age of fifty-two searching for another wife, but the disappearance of his irritating heir had left him no choice.

Instead of buttoning his vest, Axewood paused to take a casual sip of wine, mentally reviewing his criteria for the bride in question.

He wanted a girl with a sizable dowry, of course. Good bloodlines. He preferred looks or at least generous curves: ample bosom, good hips made for breeding.

Obedience was a must, but he could instill that in his next countess if need be.

Above all, the girl must be fertile. He did not have time anymore to wait and see. He was even considering trying to find a young widow with a proven ability to produce a son.

It was damned inconvenient, Joel's exit from the ton. For all his many flaws, at least his nephew had spared him from having to bother with any of this.

Axewood took another world-weary swallow, then set his wine back down on his dressing table. It was then that he heard a commotion in a distant region of his quiet Town mansion.

He cocked his head and listened for a moment, arching a brow at the sound of a woman's voice invading his house.

Shouts and angry protests rose from the direction of the entrance hall.

What the devil? Puzzled, Axewood left his dressing room, crossed his bedchamber, and went out to the top of the landing.

He peered over the railing down the two stories into the black and white marble entrance hall far below. The voices grew louder, echoing up to him under the domed space.

"I demand to see Lord Axewood this instant!"

"Now look here, this is a decent house and His Lordship has no use for the likes of you."

"How dare you? You don't know me—"

"I've got eyes! I can see what you are. Now, you need to move along before I call the constable. Shoo!"

"I am telling you, your employer will want to see me! It won't go well for you if he hears you turned me away again!"

"Begone, ye trollop!"

"Why don't you just go and ask him?" she cried. "I've got information His Lordship will want—"

"Aye, and I'm the Duke of Wellington."

"Now, you listen here, you insolent little prick—" The female intruder proceeded to give his servant what-for in language one would think she'd picked up in His Majesty's Navy.

Intrigued and rather amused, Axewood was already walking down the curved staircase to the entrance hall.

When the front door came into view, he could see the footman, a new hire, trying his best to get rid of the woman who was standing at the door in a natty feathered hat.

At that moment, she stood on her toes, peered past Jacobs into the house, and saw Axewood coming down the stairs.

He, in turn, recognized her at once.

A lewd memory instantly rushed into his veins—and heated his loins. It was that dark-haired harlot from the gaming hell. Her name escaped him, but he certainly remembered her skill at the hornpipe...

"There you are! My lord, would you please tell this cretin you know me?"

Axewood narrowed his eyes as he reached the bottom of the stairs, surprised indeed to see her there after all this time.

She pointed to herself as he crossed to the door. "It's Esme! From The Blue Room! In Covent Garden? Pardon my intrusion, but you said you'd pay for any news. Well, I've got some for you. Are you interested or not?"

Axewood went very still. He had hired her as his eyes and ears at The Blue Room, in case any news arose concerning Joel's disappearance.

"Of course," he said at once. "My apologies for my staff. Jacobs, let her in. Now."

The footman turned to him in astonishment.

Axewood stared back at him matter-of-factly, needing no words to express his blunt reply: *Yes, she is a whore. What of it?*

A country lad, Jacobs looked slightly scandalized, but he knew where his bread was buttered. "My deepest apologies for my error, sir. Ma'am, I beg your pardon." He stepped aside at once and held the door for her.

"Humph." Esme lifted her chin and swept grandly into the marble entrance hall.

Axewood eyed her in hungry amusement as Jacobs shut the door behind her.

What a mess she was, with her worn scarlet gown and her cheap, showy hat, he thought. But her worldly manner appealed to his baser instincts.

He might have to marry a virgin, but this curvy little disaster was his kind of woman. More his age, as well.

He had first encountered the cheeky hoyden on one of his several visits to The Blue Room with the Bow Street officers he'd hired to help search for Joel.

Wandering deeper into his entrance hall, Esme stared all around her at his sumptuous home, her eyes wide. He suspected the luscious pickpocket was wondering what she might be able to steal.

His kind of woman indeed.

Let her try it. He'd have fun punishing her.

Flicking a glance over her and wondering how easily that gown might come off, he was surprised she had dared to come to his house, but she was a clever minx. That was why he had hired her to keep an eye on things for him at the gambling hell.

"Well?" Axewood prompted.

She turned around, in no hurry to reveal whatever information she had to sell. No doubt she planned to withhold it until she could get the maximum payment out of him.

"This is the third time I've been here to see you, my lord." She gave the footman a dirty look. "I tried twice last week, but you weren't at home, and your staff refused to let me in to wait."

"Terribly sorry, my dear." Axewood looked at Jacobs in disapproval.

The young footman clasped his hands behind his back and lowered his head. "I beg your forgiveness, sir. I thought she was lying."

"Dismissed," Axewood said. "You." He looked at Esme, then nodded toward the staircase. "Come with me."

The seductive little smile she offered him in response pleased Axewood. He liked it when they did what they were told.

And this one was a professional.

There was a very good chance he would be late to the ball.

It had been thirty years since her harlot mother had sold Esme into the trade at fifteen, auctioning off her virginity to the highest bidder.

Now she was forty-five, clients were harder to come by, and the prospect of the future terrified her. But she was nothing if not a survivor.

She had learned to supplement her dwindling income by thieving when necessary and—always—living by her wits.

Esme felt a twinge of conscience for coming here to tattle on Silversmoke, but if she sensed there was more to Lord Axewood than met the eye, it was not her business to say so.

A woman had to do what she had to do.

She could feel the earl's appreciative stare sliding over her rump as she strutted up the staircase ahead of him. His interest was clearly genuine, and it gratified her.

After three bawdy decades of making her living on her back, it was rare for her to come across a man who piqued her thoroughly jaded sexual interest, but for some strange reason, Axewood did.

Polite as he acted, he could not disguise the hard, brutal edge in him that she viewed as strength, albeit of a ruthless variety.

Combined with his wealth, she found it a potent concoction. What she wouldn't give to have a man like that as her protector. Forget carte blanche; she'd be happy with a secure roof over her head and food in the pantry.

Ah well. With any luck, she'd be able to sell him more tonight than just her information.

He had a magnetic presence and, she suspected, a bit of a mean streak, as well. But such men, in her vast experience, made the most exciting lovers. They might scare the hell out of her, but at least they made her *feel* something, anything, when she had long since gone utterly numb.

She glimpsed him practically salivating over her ass like a ravenous wolf when they passed the pier glass in the hall. She twitched her hips all the more as she walked, determined to entice him, and not just for the money.

The fact was that Esme wanted him too. Just a few years older than her, he had dark hair with gray at his temples, dark eyes, and a rugged, rectangular face.

He was solidly built, a little thicker around the middle than he had probably been in younger years, but the elegant cut of his clothes flattered his mature body with long, clean, well-tailored lines.

He led her upstairs to his bedchamber, where she continued to marvel at the opulence everywhere she looked. Art and statues as fine as any in a museum. Rich carpets and glossy mahogany furniture. Fresh flowers in vases. Not a speck of dust anywhere.

She felt a twinge of envy for his easy life, but found it a crime that he had no woman here to satisfy his needs.

He ought to; Esme would be happy to volunteer. Perhaps if she played her cards right...

Her heart beat faster as Axewood gestured her into his chamber.

She stepped in and found herself in a vast room with muted gold walls, a patterned red carpet, and ebony furniture. She glanced at the bed while he closed the door discreetly behind her.

The headboard boasted a gilt-trimmed medallion with his coat of arms; rich bed-curtains of red velvet swept down from the canopy rails.

The sight of it made her tremble with anticipation, even though she knew it was potentially dangerous for her to be here.

Well, it was always dangerous, but that was why she carried a knife in her reticule.

Axewood sauntered past her. "I was just having a glass of wine. Care to join me?"

"Why, thank you, I will," she said absently, then took off her hat.

She had a feeling she'd be taking off a great deal more before he let her out of this room.

Axewood went to pour her a glass of wine. "Well, my dear? What news?"

She propped a hand on her hip and flashed a smile. "How much will you give me for it, first?"

He sent her a sardonic glance, then set the bottle down as he finished pouring. "How much do you want?"

"Ten quid," she said without blinking an eye. He could afford it.

He looked at her in amazement.

"Ten shillings is more like it!" he said, then laughed to himself, shaking his head. "Little mercenary."

"Well, never mind, then, if you're going to be stingy!" She gave a blithe toss of her head. "I'll just be on my way—"

"Not so fast." He grasped her arm as he approached, bringing her the wine.

"Hmm?" She looked at him.

"Maybe we can negotiate."

She shook her head. "Ten pounds firm. We both know it's but a trifle to you."

He eyed her in amusement as he handed her the glass of wine. She accepted it with a coy smile, and Axewood clinked his glass against hers. They stared at each other in open speculation as they drank.

"You have a beautiful home, my lord."

"And you have a beautiful body." He lowered his head and kissed the crook of her neck with sudden boldness, wrapping his arm around her waist. "How much for *you*?"

Esme laughed gaily and steadied herself by holding on to his shoulders. "We did have fun last time, didn't we?"

"We did," he growled against her neck. "It's rare for me to find a woman as lusty as myself."

"Oh, my lord," she purred, "you'd be mistaken if you think just any man has that effect on me."

Axewood pulled back and looked into her eyes, soaking up the compliment. "God, you are tempting." He bent again and kissed her chest this time, brazenly squeezing her breast.

She stopped him. "Now, now, we haven't come to terms yet."

"Very well, how much do you want?" he asked roughly. She could feel him already getting hard against her belly.

"Depends on what you want me to do." She peeked up at him through her lashes.

"Whatever I please," he whispered, squeezing her nipple this time.

She didn't stop him. "Twenty, then."

"Done." He hooked a finger in the bodice of her gown, rousing a tremble of eagerness from her. "Now then. You were saying?"

"Right." She took a breath to clear her head. "A man came to the gambling hell last week asking questions about your nephew's disappearance."

He paused in playing with her décolletage and looked at her in question.

Esme caressed his chest at the open V of his crisp white shirt. His chest hairs were shot through with gray. "He said a friend of your nephew's asked him to start looking into the matter."

"Really?" Axewood furrowed his brow. "Which friend?"

His nephew had many loyal companions. At least, he used to.

"He didn't say, my lord."

"Well, what manner of man was this fellow? A private investigator of some sort?"

"Not exactly." Esme hesitated. "That's the strangest part. I don't know who the friend was, but the man who came looking for your nephew was that highwayman, Silversmoke."

Axewood went motionless.

Indeed, from the instant she said the name, the earl's whole demeanor changed.

He stepped back and stared at her. She could swear that he paled. "Did you say Silversmoke?"

She nodded.

"Are you sure it was he?"

"Fairly sure," she said. "He didn't tell *me* his name, but after he left, there was talk in the gaming hell that that's who he was. Silversmoke! Right there in our midst."

Axewood's eyes flared with anger. "Who all did he talk to? What did they tell him?"

Esme was taken aback by his sudden intensity. "I don't know," she said, instantly on her guard. "Several different people."

"Did he tell any of them who it was that hired him?"

"Not that I'm aware."

The earl gripped her arm and scanned her face as though searching for lies. "What did he look like?"

Esme veiled her uneasiness, confused. This reaction was not what she had expected. Axewood seemed rattled, as if the topic of Silversmoke signified more than just reopening the wound of his nephew's disappearance.

That, she had been prepared for. Indeed, she'd been eager to comfort him in his loss, just like last time.

She'd found it quite touching, how upset the worried uncle had been when he'd come to the gambling hell with the Bow Street men, distraught over his missing nephew.

But his reaction now felt different. Almost like fear at the name of Silversmoke.

All Esme knew was that, in her experience, men were most dangerous when something scared them. That was when they lashed out.

On the spot, she decided that the best thing to do was to try and calm Axewood down, then back the hell out of this before she got hurt.

She had come here eager to sell her information, but now the thought of saying too much filled her with dread.

After all, if Dog had told Silversmoke something that Axewood didn't want him to know, there was no point admitting that *she* was the one who had pointed Dog out to the highwayman in the first place.

"Did you speak to Silversmoke yourself?" Axewood prompted, impatience harshening his face.

She nodded. "Just for a moment or two."

"And? What did you tell him?"

"The truth." She shrugged innocently, drawing on a lifetime of telling men what they wanted to hear. "That Joel came into The Blue Room many times, but that nobody really liked him, since he always won.

"He asked if your nephew ever, er, patronized my services, and I told him—as I told you—that, no, he never did." Esme paused and tried a reassuring smile. "There's no need to worry, my lord. I don't think he learned anything of importance."

Axewood narrowed his eyes at her. "Then why did you set the price for your information so high, my dear?"

"Well...because I'm a sharper." She slipped him a guilty little smile and caressed his chest. "And because you can afford it."

Axewood pondered this for a moment, staring at her. But he seemed to calm down at her touch and her cajoling tone.

"Who all did he speak to?" he murmured. "Give me names."

"I'd rather give you something else."

"Esme. This is no trifling matter. A bloody criminal is now hunting my nephew."

"Oh, he didn't seem so bad," she said with an optimistic smile. "Maybe he really can help."

"Who all did he speak to?"

"I don't know!" she lied. "He moved around the tables chatting up a dozen of the regulars. Then he left."

"Oh really?"

"But what they discussed, I have no idea. I was *working*. I didn't hear much. It sounded like general inquiries. If anyone knew him and so forth. How much longer do you want to keep talking about this, my lord?" She slipped her fingers inside his shirt. "Wouldn't you rather do something else?"

He captured her wrist. "Tell me what he looked like. Nobody's ever seen Silversmoke without his mask on."

"Well, he wasn't as handsome as you."

"Esme!" He seemed to know she was working him, for he jerked her by her arm and made her slosh some of her wine on herself.

She huffed with indignation.

"Describe the man!"

"Very well! He was young—maybe thirty. Tall, muscular. Dark-haired, with a scruffy jaw. Very much like a brigand. Light eyes. Maybe blue, maybe green, I couldn't tell."

"And what was his bearing? How did he speak?"

She shrugged. "Ordinary enough. Not as common as some, not as fine as others—say, your nephew."

"Was there anyone with him?"

"Oh yes! I nearly forgot. A nice-looking silver-haired chap, older than him, not as tall." Esme had liked the rough-and-tumble look of that grizzled gent almost more than the herculean young stud.

"Did you catch the friend's name?"

She searched her mind, but couldn't remember it. "No, sorry. I don't know if I heard it. I only chatted with them for a moment or two, as I said." She did not see fit to explain that she had only been trying to pick their pockets.

Axewood released his hold on her, shoving her slightly and turning away with a curse of frustration under his breath.

Esme caught her balance, but more of her wine sloshed onto the floor this time. *Oh shit.* She stepped over the wet spot on the fine carpet to hide it, since the earl was already cross at her.

She was not leaving this place with a black eye.

Lord, this was not working out at all as she had envisioned. Axewood intimidated her more than she'd expected, and she feared she had ruined her prospects for this night.

She hesitated, staring at his back and trying to salvage it. "Did I make a mistake in coming here, my lord? I'm sorry if all this has upset you. It was not my intention. I-I just thought you'd want to know that one of your nephew's friends has apparently decided to renew the search."

She took a step closer. "If Silversmoke returns, I'd be happy to press him for more information, if you wish. Just tell me what you want me to do."

Axewood turned around slowly. He read the anxiety in her eyes, then relented with a rueful half-smile. "You're a good girl, Esme. It's all right."

Relieved, she offered a weary smile back. "I'm many things, my lord, but good ain't one of 'em."

"That must be why I like you." The smolder returned to his dark eyes, to her relief.

She tilted her head, holding his gaze. "Do you?"

The earl set his wine aside and moved closer, taking her chin between his finger and thumb. "Now, look here. If Silversmoke returns, I want you to send for me immediately. Use your wiles to keep him there till I arrive. Have you got that?"

The order startled her, but she dared not ask why, merely nodded.

His breath warmed her lips as he leaned closer. "Mm. Now let's see about you earning your fee."

A searing look in his dark eyes, Axewood hooked his arm around her waist without warning and pulled her closer abruptly. Esme stumbled against him; knocked off balance, she dropped her half-full wineglass on the fine rug and gasped at her own clumsiness.

"I'm sorry!" At once, she bent down to get the glass and try to blot up the puddle she'd made with her handkerchief.

She could feel Axewood watching her. A heartbeat later, his hand clamped down on her shoulder.

"Leave it," he ordered her in a rasping tone.

As she looked up, he joined her on the floor, lowering himself onto his knees, straddling her. He was already unbuttoning his formal black trousers as he pressed her down onto her back. Her heart beat wildly as he tugged at her bodice, so rough and hasty with lust that he tore the front of her gown.

No matter. She knew then that he'd buy her a new one.

As he freed his rigid cock from his trousers, Esme eagerly lifted her skirts for him. She still did not understand his strange reaction to her news, but it was his own affair. For her part, she gave herself over to wanton enjoyment as the earl ravished her on the floor in a puddle of wine.

Portia watched the doorway of the Grand Albion Assembly Rooms, waving her fan in the crush and trying not to keep looking at her locket watch.

There was still no sign of her fiancé.

Lud, she had not felt so nervous at a ball since her debut.

She had not seen Lucas since Monday at their picnic, and now that Thursday night had come, she waited on tenterhooks to see if he would indeed keep his promise and appear.

It was not so much the prospect of seeing him again that had discomfited her, but how he would fare here tonight if he showed up.

It would be the ton's first chance to get a look at her fiancé, and she dreaded the thought of anyone mocking him. They could be so judgmental. Perhaps it had been wrong of her to insist that he come if he was not comfortable with it.

He had apparently gone back to Gracewell for Tuesday and Wednesday. There was a good chance, of course, that the absent-minded scholar might forget he was supposed to come back to London for the ball, but she supposed she'd soon see.

It did not help her tense state of mind that the ballroom felt like an oven this evening. Hundreds of fans waved in the hands of fashionable ladies and gentlemen alike.

The staff of the Grand Albion were doing their best to mitigate the heat from the great fireball of the mid-June sunset glaring into the ballroom through the tall western windows.

Having already opened the French doors, two liveried fellows were now climbing up ladders to push the upper parts of the massive windows open to admit the breeze.

This, in turn, caused a comedy of errors that Portia observed with amusement. As soon as they opened the top parts of the windows, the draft blew out the candles on the chandeliers.

Other servants rushed forth to lower the chandeliers so they could relight them. This process was repeated three times, until the guests standing around put it to a jolly vote amongst themselves and loudly decided that the servants should leave the candles unlit for now. It wouldn't be dark for another hour, anyway.

The chandeliers were duly run back up to their proper stations near the high ceiling, and the servants climbed back down to move the ladders and repeat their task.

Watching all this, sweating like a wineglass herself, Portia crunched on the ice chips in her goblet of punch. Which, of course, she knew was quite improper, but she wasn't speaking, anyway, only half listening to her friends' amiable chitchat.

But she kept one ear cocked toward the entrance of the ballroom, monitoring the names that the master of ceremonies intoned as each guest arrived.

Welcome to the oven, she thought as she watched the crème de la crème of Society parading in.

She felt sorry for the gentlemen in their layers of shirts and cravats, waistcoats and tailcoats. Though her palms felt sweaty in her white elbow gloves, she was happy to be wearing the light zephyr silk ball gown that her modiste had delivered earlier that day—the same woman who was doing her wedding gown, for which, incidentally, Portia had the final fitting tomorrow afternoon.

Tonight's wispy, opal-colored ball gown was sleeveless and cut above the ankle for ease in dancing.

Dancing...

Perhaps it was the thought of having to stand up with Lucas for a dance or two that had her half dreading the night ahead, or feeling the heat more acutely than anybody else.

She had reason to be uncomfortable, though. *She* was the one who had insisted on his coming to the ball, but now that the night had arrived, she was desperate at the thought of her gentle Lucas making a fool of himself in front of the ton.

With that innocent quality he had, she did not want him to get his feelings hurt. But she knew her duty if he did: to stand by his side, smooth things over as best she could, and put anyone in their place who dared mock him.

Infused with a sense of protectiveness toward her dear naturalist duke, she would not allow anyone to hurt him, after he'd already been through so much.

She did not fancy making enemies of anyone in Society, but he was *her* quiz, and nobody here had better mock him.

As she took another ice chip to suck on while she waited for him to arrive, a snippet of conversation nearby got her attention.

"So how are all the animals?" Major Carvel was asking Azrael, Serena's husband.

"As it happens, your friend Bertie the chimp got loose the other day and scrambled up a tree," the pale-haired Duke of Rivenwood replied.

As Peter laughed, Portia turned to them. Azrael's stories about the menagerie of animals he'd inherited from his infamous father were always quite colorful. Serena grinned as her elegant husband shook his head.

"Oh, our Bertie was having a grand time swinging from tree to tree across the grounds," Azrael continued. "I'm told he stayed aloft for several hours and thought it a fine game to scamper away, every time one of his keepers climbed the next tree to try to get him."

"Were they able to retrieve him?" Peter asked.

Azrael nodded. "Finally coaxed him down with a bunch of bananas."

Peter grinned. "Well, everyone gets hungry sooner or later, don't they?"

"Lucky for us," Azrael agreed. "Otherwise, there'd be a wild monkey roaming the English countryside."

"I daresay that would give the villagers a start," Serena chimed in.

"To be sure, my dear," Azrael said with a laugh.

Just then, Felicity called to her brother from over by the column, where she was talking to some other friends.

"Peter!"

When he turned, she beckoned him over. "I have to ask you something."

"Pardon," the major said, then left them.

The moment he had gone, Azrael turned his ice-blue eyes to Portia and stared at her with a chilly look of disapproval.

Portia stopped chewing her ice, then swallowed the melting fragments. "What?"

Azrael arched a silvery-blond brow. "What's this I hear about you hiring a highwayman?"

She gasped and looked at her best friend. "Serena! You told him?"

"I had to! Please don't be angry at me, P." Serena winced, but the look in her brownish-green eyes was as stubborn as ever. "I told you, I keep no secrets from Azrael. You know I only have your best interests at heart, and when your best friend tells you she's been consorting with a highwayman, one cannot help but be alarmed!"

Portia folded her arms across her chest and scowled at her. "I knew you were going to blab."

Azrael regarded Portia with his usual enigmatic reserve. "Suffice to say, I've been looking into him for you."

"What? No! There's no need!" she said in exasperation. "I've already done my research. Well—unless you find out his true identity. That I would like to know."

"His name is not so much my concern, merely whether he is dangerous to *you*."

"He isn't!" Portia shook her head. "I appreciate your concern, both of you, but I'd really rather if you'd just stayed out of this."

Azrael lifted his chin, looking startled at her reproach. Then he frowned. "It's too late," he said, his tone matter-of-fact. "I've already sent forth my inquiries through my own, er, unique channels. Don't worry, I'm very good at keeping secrets."

No doubt, Portia thought. The heir to a dark occult family must be rather an expert on that.

"Thus our no-secrets bargain," Serena told her, glancing at her mysterious husband.

"My wife was worried sick," Azrael informed Portia, then kissed Serena's hand. "When Her Grace has a problem, I solve it. That's my job. In any case, I should hear something back very soon."

Portia strove for patience. "Very well. What's done is done, but beyond this, please, leave Silversmoke alone, Azrael. He's a good man. He helps people. Yes, I know, strictly speaking, he's a criminal, but nobody's perfect, are they? If you go stirring up trouble for him, who knows what it could lead to?"

"The Duke of Fountainhurst!" the master of ceremonies suddenly announced from the distant doorway.

Portia turned to look, her pulse lurching. Through the crowd, she caught a glimpse of Lucas in black and white formal attire, standing alone at the entrance to the ballroom.

Her cheeks flushed with guilt to think that here she was, dabbling once again in the dangerous topic of Silversmoke, just when her sweet fiancé had arrived.

She knew she had to go, but glanced at the Rivenwoods one last time. "I must go."

Azrael gave her a discreet nod. "Whatever I learn, I will bring you the information, and you can decide for yourself what to do with it."

"Thanks," Portia mumbled.

Then she took a deep breath and hurried off to welcome her oblivious duke to her little corner of the ton.

CHAPTER 15

A Night at the Ball

Scanning the glamorous crowd from behind his spectacles, Luke resisted the urge to hang back in the shadows outside the ballroom doorway.

He was only there for Portia's sake, but he did not yet see her.

Instead, he beheld scores of well-dressed strangers turning to stare at him as though he were a freak from the traveling circus show. Their scrutiny filled his whole body with pins and needles.

Judging by the murmurs he detected and the odious pity and morbid curiosity that came into the eyes of the many who turned to gawk at him, it was obvious that, oh yes, they remembered the terrible story of his parents' murders in grim detail.

Their attention set Luke's teeth on edge. He'd been getting those pitying looks for as long as he could remember, and he hated it.

No wonder he avoided coming to Town.

Only slightly less unpleasant were the smirks and snickers from those who had bought into his scholarly ruse as the reclusive eccentric all too well. That much, at least, he had brought on himself.

Years ago, cheeky as he was, he had decided that if he was going to be whispered about like a freak, he might as well embrace the role and throw it in their faces.

But tonight, it was time to water down Lucas, because he did not want his beautiful bride feeling ashamed to be seen with him.

Where the blazes was she, anyway?

His gaze swept the long, colonnaded ballroom, but he did not see her. Oh God, what if she had stood him up and he was stuck in this opulent hellhole alone?

After a slight pause in the doorway, as was customary, Luke took a few steps into the ballroom, trying to pretend like he wanted to be there, and feeling like a fraud.

He smiled politely at people here and there, strangers all. In truth, his heart was pounding more than it did when he waited in the woods beside some lonely road, preparing to hold up some approaching coach all to satisfy the criminal urges of his men.

Feeling slightly strangled by his cravat, Luke squared his shoulders, lifted his chin, bent one arm politely behind his back, then began strolling into the glittering space as if he belonged there.

It was the longest thirty seconds of his life, but then he saw her hurrying toward him.

Portia. Luke drew in his breath at the brilliance of her golden beauty in the fading light of evening. She flashed a dazzling smile as she fought her way through the crowd to come and save him.

The woman was radiant. Her pale hair was sleekly piled atop her head. Diamond earrings dangled from her kissable earlobes, and the slender white column of her neck was exposed all the way down to the V of her pale silk gown.

He stared in wonder at her exposed arms as she hastened toward him like some petite, earthbound goddess out of Greek myth, somewhere between virginal Diana and lovely Aphrodite. The pink flush in her cheeks from the ballroom's warmth entranced him.

As his future duchess wove through the throng, Luke stood motionless, waiting for her to come and claim him—his fair guide in this foreign land.

In the next moment, she flitted through a final knot of chatting people and alighted before him, whereupon she grasped both of his hands.

"Lucas! I'm so happy to see you here." Her arrival and her affectionate touch sent a cooling wave of relief through his tense, sweating body.

Luke smiled back at her, then remembered to breathe.

If she'd been amazed at how well they'd got on at the picnic, Portia was astonished at how smart Lucas looked tonight.

Not that a man's looks were the be-all and end-all of life. But given his usual rumpled state, his appearance thoroughly impressed her.

His evening attire, crisp black and white, was beyond reproach, his sandy hair just tousled enough to look charming, and, wonders to behold, his cravat was on straight.

Most importantly of all, he was here. He had come—for her sake, she knew. That was all that really mattered.

"What is it?" he murmured, smiling back at her as she blushed. She couldn't seem to peel her gaze away from his.

She laughed. "I wasn't sure you'd remember, to be honest."

"What, miss seeing you in all your glory? Never. You look magnificent, my lady. I am truly unworthy of y—"

"Nonsense! You look altogether handsome. But thank you for the compliment. I'm so glad you're here."

Releasing his hands, she stepped back and gave him a proper curtsy, since countless bystanders were observing their exchange. Lucas bowed in return with gentlemanly grace.

Relieved that he had not only shown up, but seemed prepared to comport himself like a relatively normal human being tonight, she took his arm and led him off rather proudly to greet her parents.

It was a suitable mission to help them break through the initial awkwardness of his entry into the ton after all this time.

Besides, Mama would want to preen about her ducal future son-in-law.

Sure enough, her mother made a fuss over Lucas as soon as she saw them coming.

"Oh, here he is…!"

Samantha Tennesley, the Marchioness of Liddicoat, had never had the slightest trouble thinking up what to say in Society, so Portia, still feeling a little shy, herself, was all too happy to let her mother take over.

Lady Liddicoat began presenting her future son-in-law to all of her friends.

Papa joined them a moment later. "Fountainhurst," he said. Which was about as much conversation as one could expect out of the portly, white-haired Marquess of Few Words. He put his arm around Portia briefly, though. "Having a good time, butterfly?"

"Yes, Papa," she said. "Are you?"

"Tolerable, tolerable." He studied Lucas and seemed pleased that he had come.

The two shared a brief exchange and a handshake, but before long, Portia took hold of her fiancé's arm again. Grateful as she was for Mama's vivacious help in breaking the ice, she did not want the woman monopolizing Lucas for half the night, and she would, left to her own devices.

Portia suspected that Mama was ever so pleased to have a substitute son to fill the void her star, Hunter, had left behind when he'd sailed off from England.

Fortunately, Lucas didn't seem to mind her parents' attention. Perhaps it pleased him, since he no longer had living parents of his own. But he tolerated it like a saint.

After what seemed a suitable amount of time paying their respects to her parents and their friends, Portia led him away to meet her own.

Well, he'd already met her female friends, but he had not yet been introduced to their husbands, his fellow dukes around Moonlight Square.

Azrael and Serena were right where she had left them, so that was where she started. In truth, she figured that Azrael would be one of the easiest for Lucas to get along with—one reclusive eccentric to another, albeit of two very different varieties.

Portia was gratified when Serena greeted Lucas warmly, and then introduced him to her husband. The two men exchanged polite bows and studied each other with wary goodwill.

While Serena informed each man of the other's peculiar area of interest, wild animals for the one, insect life for the other, each seemed intrigued by the other's hobby.

Serena sent Portia a twinkling glance as they asked each other strange questions about animals and insects in turn; however, they seemed to make perfect sense to each other.

"Where do you find suitable veterinarians for all these exotic creatures?" and "How long can you actually keep them alive in a terrarium?"

Portia fought back a chuckle as she listened to their exchange.

I told you different could be lovely, Serena's dancing eyes seem to say. Portia smiled back at her, unable to stay cross at her for having told Azrael her secret.

Silversmoke who? Portia thought. For when Lucas was near, she couldn't even remember why the highwayman had fascinated her so.

Before long, Felicity joined them, bringing both husband and brother over to meet Lucas.

"How do you do," Lucas said as he shook Jason's hand. "I say, Netherford, I had the honor of meeting your children in the park recently with Her Grace."

Jason grinned. "I hope they didn't try to bite you."

Lucas laughed. "Not at all. Most impressive youngsters."

"He taught them how to gravel-golf," Felicity chimed in.

"Oh, right! I remember hearing about that." Jason laughed. "They couldn't stop talking about it for days. It's their new favorite game."

"You must be very proud," Lucas said.

Jason beamed, his brown eyes aglow. "They're impossible, but they own me, I'm afraid."

Major Carvel was also most gracious to Lucas. Portia remembered his comments after the book club and realized that sympathy must've inspired the no-nonsense major to treat her fiancé with a bit more welcome and warmth than he normally showed.

Portia appreciated all her friends' kindness toward him—at least, until Sidney arrived.

Unbeknownst to her, the golden-haired viscount had hung back, observing Lucas skeptically for several minutes before he came forward and joined them.

The moment the suave, impeccably dressed wit sauntered into their midst, she sensed trouble. He cast cordial greetings around to the circle of their friends and then smiled broadly at Lucas.

Portia's suspicions increased, for she saw that rapier gleam in her friend's eyes and sensed an edge to his careless demeanor.

Oh no, what is he up to?

She stared at Sidney, trying to capture his gaze, for she feared he was winding up for some sort of blow.

Not that an innocent like Lucas would ever see it coming. Because with Lord Smiley, there was friendly, and then there was friendly with daggers.

"Congratulations, Your Grace! On your pending nuptials, of course," he said, smooth as fine steel.

"Why, thank you," Lucas said, more warily than she would've expected.

Was that a good sign or a bad one?

Sidney smiled at Portia, though speaking to Lucas. "You are a lucky chap. She is an enviable prize, this young lady, is she not?"

Portia narrowed her eyes at her friend in suspicion, but Lucas seemed startled, as though temporarily unsure if Sidney fancied her, himself.

Which was not at all the case.

They were like brother and sister. For that matter, all the men in their group seemed to treat her like a younger sibling.

"I, er, I am indeed most fortunate," Lucas said, looking a little nonplussed.

Portia glared at Sidney, trying to rein him in by sheer dint of will, but he continued ignoring her, stubborn mule.

His smile never wavering, he looked her fiancé up and down. "You know, you're taller than I expected."

Oh God. Here it comes. Portia tensed and gripped her fiancé's arm, for while Sidney could be sweet as custard pie on the one hand, on the other, he was one of those impeccable dandies of whom it was said he could give you a cut and you wouldn't even know it until a week later, when your head fell off.

Lucas's eyebrows had risen above the rims of his spectacles. "Am I?"

"Yes." Sidney idly buffed his nails on his waistcoat. "I thought for certain that only a *small* man could neglect so charming a lady."

Portia gasped; both Serena and Felicity's mouths fell open.

Even Azrael blinked.

"Sidney!" Portia cried the instant she found her tongue.

Lucas stood frozen.

"Yes, my dear?" Sidney turned to her with utter nonchalance.

"Apologize at once!" she demanded, turning scarlet.

"Whatever for?" He gestured at Lucas with flawless aplomb. "It's so nice he finally managed to drag himself up to Town to see you. I mean, you've been engaged for what now, a year? It's not as though you've had to stand around by yourself at these events, week after week, month after month, feeling foolish while everyone wondered if he even—"

"That will do, Sid," Jason ordered. As the former King of the Rakehells, he did not hesitate to reprove one of his most loyal henchmen.

Seeing the tide go against him, Sidney let out a blithe laugh and turned it all into a lark. He held up his hands in idle surrender. "No offense intended, my dear fellow! Far be it from me to take issue with how a man wishes to treat his future wife—"

"No—you're right," Lucas forced out abruptly. "I'm the one who must apologize. My behavior has been wanting in the extreme, for which I beg your forgiveness with all my heart, Lady Portia." He bowed to her. "And I apologize to you, her friends, as well, who I see now I've also offended."

All three women instantly began to protest, desperate to smooth things over after this outrageous rudeness from their otherwise beloved Sidney.

"Your Grace, Lord Sidney is only being protective," Felicity said. "We are all very fond of Lady Portia, as you've inevitably gathered."

"Only, some of us have a dashed strange way of showing it." Serena scowled at the viscount, who still seemed perfectly at ease.

Sidney regarded Lucas with an aloof smile, his eyes still bright with challenge.

Portia wanted to strangle him by his perfect cravat.

Lucas nodded at him. "No, the gentleman is quite right. I should have come to pay my respects to my bride's friends and family long ago."

"This is not necessary, Lucas," Portia said. "You don't need to explain yourself!"

"Yes, I do. You deserve that, my dear. But my absence wasn't due to any lack of regard for my fiancée."

"Oh really?" Sidney lifted his chin, his unflappable smile never faltering, his disdain palpable. "Were you just too busy for her, then? With what, dare I ask? Saving the world or something such? Because that excuse would at least go toward explaining—"

"Sidney—enough!" Portia said fiercely, stepping between him and her fiancé.

Even so, Lucas hung his head. "No. It was nothing so impressive as that."

"Indeed," Sidney drawled before finally relenting. "I thought not."

Jason shook his head at the viscount; Peter scowled at him.

But Portia was shaken. "If you'll excuse us," she said, directing her withering tone at Sidney, and taking her fiancé by the arm. "I, for one, could use a drink. Come, Lucas. Let's get some punch."

With that, she led him away toward the safer environs of the refreshment room, her heart still pounding with anger at her friend's shocking rudeness.

"I am so, so sorry," she said as soon as they were out of earshot. "I had no idea he was going to do something like that! I am beyond mortified. Please accept my apologies—"

"Darling, it's all right."

"No, it's not! You're my Lucas and he had no right to talk to you that way! It's none of his business." Grasping his lapels, she gazed up earnestly at him. "Please don't take his words to heart. You had your reasons for staying away from Town, and I understand that now."

"You do?"

She nodded. "They don't realize how it is for you, with all you've been through. But I do."

He looked at her in tender surprise. "But he was right. I *was* in the wrong. You don't need to make excuses for me, darling."

"Well, I'm utterly embarrassed that one of my friends would be so rude to you. Even if he was only being protective."

"Ah, it's all right. I, for one, am grateful to the man for being such a loyal friend to you. I'm not angry at him for this. On the contrary, I respect him for standing up for you."

She searched his face, amazed at his calm reaction.

She'd been afraid that the viscount's obnoxious attack might drive Lucas away from Town all the more. But as he glanced back toward her friends, he looked intrigued by Sidney's willingness to confront him for her sake.

"Are you sure he's not in love with you?"

"Not in the slightest." She followed his eyes and saw the entire group of her friends scolding Sidney now.

Arms folded across his chest, Sidney lifted his patrician nose in the air, obviously convinced that he was in the right, no matter what they said.

The strange thing was that Lucas seemed to agree.

All of a sudden, he laughed quietly and began shaking his head.

Portia furrowed her brow, glancing at him. "What is it?"

"Man's got a spine, to be sure."

She lifted her eyebrows. "That's one way of putting it. Come now, let's see about that drink. But I'll tell you one thing…"

"Yes, my dear?"

"Anyone else who dares give you grief is going to have a problem with me," she declared. Then she linked her fingers through his and guided him toward the refreshment room.

Lucas followed, eyeing her with amusement.

When they stepped past the columns adorning the wide doorway of the refreshment room, a gracious salon adjoining the ballroom, a busy hum of conversation filled the air, but it was always quieter in here, because of the lower ceiling and carpeted floor.

It was very crowded, however, as people wandered about in search of drinks and crossed paths with countless friends.

Around the walls, long tables lit by candelabra presented the night's initial offering from the Grand Albion's excellent kitchens. An array of light foods and cheeses on boards surrounded an elegant epergne of fruit. There were cucumber sandwiches, petite oyster rolls, tender asparagus stalks, and little finger-length whets of fried anchovies on breads drizzled with melted cheddar and a sprinkling of parsley; other tiny, crisp breads were laden with paper-thin slices of ham adorned with pickled red cabbage shredded fine.

Later, at precisely eleven, the hotel staff would bring out more substantial fare to allay the guests' hunger after they'd worked up an appetite dancing.

But for now, it was hors d'oeuvres alongside colorful sweets that were, as always, beautiful to behold. There were biscuits and bonbons, custards and little iced cakes, ratafia drops and petite cheesecakes, as well as Portia's favorite—dainty drop cakes flavored with orange-water.

Alas, the fluffy whipped syllabubs were already starting to melt in the heat, along with the ice cream. The waiters were quietly debating what to do, while the tabletop wine fountain lilted nearby.

Lucas and Portia discussed the food for a minute or two, both feeling awkward as half the people in the room turned to snoop on them.

To be sure, Society had long awaited the entry of Portia's alleged bridegroom into their midst.

She'd heard jests along the lines that spotting the Duke of Fountainhurst at a fashionable gathering was nearly as rare as a unicorn sighting.

Other catty souls liked to say that perhaps he didn't even exist—that perhaps she'd invented him to explain why she wasn't married yet.

Well, the duke was here now, in the flesh, and as she steered him carefully toward the punch bowl, she was torn between gloating and worrying that they'd be unkind to him.

At least Sidney had had good intentions. The same could not necessarily be said of other ton folk, who simply liked making fun of everyone and everything.

Joel had been that way, come to think of it.

She hadn't liked *that* about him, either...

As they drifted along the edge of the tables, inspecting the food and wondering aloud what to eat, a waiter passed on his way back to the kitchens, carrying a large tray full of empty glasses.

Just as he marched past Lucas, he shifted his tray to avoid a knot of guests who weren't watching what they were doing.

At that moment, a wineglass plunged off the back of the tray.

Before Portia noticed what was happening, Lucas swooped down, shot out a hand, and caught the falling glass in midair before it hit the ground.

She stared at him in astonishment.

He straightened up with a smooth motion, cleared his throat, and set the glass back politely on the tray.

The waiter had stopped, gaping at his lightning-fast reflexes. "Thank you, sir!"

Lucas gave an absent nod and tugged self-consciously at his waistcoat. "Not at all."

Still dazed by his display of prowess, the waiter shook off his amazement and continued on his way. When Lucas turned to Portia, looking a little chagrined, she was nearly speechless.

"How did you do that?"

"Oh, um, probably just from catching flies. For study, you know."

"Right," she said.

He popped a grape into his mouth and chewed earnestly.

Shrugging off her disbelief, Portia gave an uncertain laugh.

He swallowed his mouthful. "What can I get for you to drink?"

"Oh..." She turned toward the wine fountain—and nearly ran right into dear old Mr. Barnaby Lynch.

A diminutive elderly gent with twinkly blue eyes, he was sipping his customary raspberry cordial.

He beamed with a grandfatherly smile when he saw her. "Lady Portia, my dear! How lovely you look, as always."

"Mr. Lynch, it's good to see you." Glad as she was to see the charming little old man, she eyed his purple drink nervously. Between falling glasses and jostling crowds, she did not want to end up wearing it for the rest of the night. "How have you been, sir?"

"Oh, capital, capital. And you, my dear? I say, the wedding must be any day now."

"Seventeen days away, to be exact. You are coming, I hope?"

"I wouldn't dream of missing it!"

"Well, good. As it happens, I have someone here for you to meet." She turned to her fiancé, happy to introduce him to a kindly soul like Mr. Lynch. "Allow me to present—"

"Fountainhurst!" the old man burst out before she could even finish, his eyes widening.

Lucas swallowed his second grape and grinned uncertainly. "Yes? Hullo."

"Zounds, but you are the spitting image of your father, my boy!"

Lucas lifted his eyebrows. "You knew him?"

"Indeed! Not terribly well, but in Society, of course. And your mother, too. Such a gracious lady. Such a dreadful loss. But let us not speak of that. Best to remember the good, I always say."

"Indeed, sir." As Lucas gazed at him, appreciation of the old man's mention of his parents crept across his face.

"Barnaby Lynch at your service, Your Grace." He thrust out a bony hand.

Lucas shook it gently, careful of the man's frail bones. "Very good to meet you, Mr. Lynch. Lucas Wakeford, the Duke of Fountainhurst—but it seems you already know that."

He chuckled. "Well, the resemblance is unmistakable."

Portia watched their exchange, thoroughly pleased. Funny, but Lucas did not seem inclined to stammer or bumble in any way just now.

"We call Mr. Lynch the Christmas elf around here," she informed him. "He organizes a marvelous charity fundraiser every year at Yuletide."

"For widows and orphans." The little fellow poked the much larger duke cheerfully in the chest. "And this year I'll be calling on you, as well, mark my word! I hope you don't mind."

"I shall be looking forward to it, sir," Lucas said with a warm smile.

Gazing up at him in wonder, the little man shook his snowy head again. "You really are so like him. I say, would you mind taking off your spectacles for a moment, for comparison's sake? Satisfy an old man's curiosity about a long-lost friend, won't you?"

Lucas hesitated as the old man beamed at him, then glanced at Portia. She nodded encouragement, curious indeed to see her fiancé without his glasses on, for she had long since noticed that her lovable quiz had the potential to be very good-looking, indeed.

"Ahem, um, very well. As you wish." Lucas obliged him, taking off his glasses briefly.

The entire Grand Albion faded away as Portia's eyes slowly widened. She suddenly felt a trifle faint.

Sweet heaven.

Without the vexing screen of his spectacles to hide behind, she discovered in that moment that, lo and behold, her bumbling fiancé was...

Why, he was something of a demigod.

Her stunned gaze trailed over his strong, chiseled face.

Good Lord, am I blind? How in the world could I not have noticed this till now?

How handsome he was. The square jaw, the proud nose. The healthy bronzed complexion. The feathered symmetry of his dark eyebrows framing intense and almost cunning moss-green eyes.

She was utterly taken aback, gaping at him in disbelief.

In a flash of hindsight, she realized she must have been blinded by her own biases and preconceptions about him—conclusions she had drawn over those long, dreary months when all she'd cared about was finding Joel.

Joel who? she thought, shaking her head in a daze.

This man, her own future husband—simple, goodhearted—outshone the proud dandy in every way.

A hint of a memory tickled at the back of her mind. He reminded her a little of someone she knew...but she couldn't think of whom.

Ah well. It didn't matter. She bit her lip as her shock began melting into a sense of giddy delight. *Shame on you, darling! Hiding behind those funny little spectacles all this time.* But thank God he had, or surely some other, more clear-sighted woman would've long since come along and snatched him up by now.

Yes, she thought suddenly, still staring at him in wonder. Thank God that he stammered and tripped and laughed belatedly at people's jokes.

Thank God for the insects, as well, dear little creatures!

They had reserved him for her, the cloud of them driving all other ladies away with their buzzing and their stings, keeping him free for *her* to come and claim him.

Lucas. While Portia studied him in shock for that fleeting instant, Mr. Lynch let out a merry laugh.

"Upon my word, it's as I thought, Your Grace! You are your father all over again—and his father before him, I daresay."

"You knew them both?"

"Oh, I'm a fossil, lad. I've seen generations come and go around here all the way back to Adam and Eve."

Lucas chuckled. "Well, er…" He noticed Portia's smitten smile, and glanced away self-consciously. "I'd better put these back on. Otherwise, I-I'll get a headache."

"Of course. Good lad." Mr. Lynch clapped him on the biceps. "Thank you for indulging an old man's memory."

"Not at all, not at all," Lucas mumbled, quickly putting his spectacles back on, hooking a wire arm over each ear.

It was then that a familiar, lilting series of music notes sounded from the ballroom.

"Ah, there is a sound that must fill all young hearts with delight." Mr. Lynch rocked sagely on his toes.

"Why do you say that?" Lucas asked, his glasses now perched in place on his handsome nose.

Portia couldn't stop smiling. Maybe she was shallow. But a woman did want to feel a certain…chemistry toward her mate.

"That's the signal that the dancing is about to begin," Mr. Lynch told him. "You two are going to dance together, aren't you?"

Portia and Lucas glanced at each other in hesitation.

"But you must! You have to practice for the wedding," the old elf teased, his eyes twinkling.

"Mr. Lynch, I fear you are determined to make mischief this evening," Portia evaded, feeling rather put on the spot.

"Pish," he replied. "Go and dance, you two lovebirds. Shoo!"

"Well." Lucas recovered first. "Ahem. You heard the man, my dear. Shall we?" With a brave look, he offered her his arm.

This time, it was Portia who balked.

Her feet shrieked silently in terror. Without his spectacles, Lucas might be a tall, strapping, handsome bit of business, but that did not mean she trusted him not to crush her toes.

In truth, it was not even the physical pain that alarmed her as much as the thought of people making fun of him or shaking their heads in pity at her.

Then she caught the drift of her own thoughts. *Good Lord, when did I become so concerned about what other people think?*

An uncomfortable observation swam through her mind: perhaps a vain sort of insecurity was what she and Joel had *really* had in common long ago.

Well, such petty concerns clearly did not trouble Lucas. He did not seem to care one iota if people thought he was eccentric and awkward; he was too busy simply being himself.

Admiration for that trait filled her. Perhaps she had more to learn from her unusual future husband than she'd realized.

So be it, she decided.

If he was prepared to make a fool of himself, she would do the same, right by his side—and Society be hanged.

"I would be honored," she said primly.

"There you are," Mr. Lynch said, then shooed them off with a broad smile of approval. "Enjoy!"

They smiled back, turned away, and had barely taken a step toward the ballroom when someone cut across their path.

"Oh—pardon me." The man glanced absently at them: a sturdy lord in his fifties, with piercing dark eyes and short-cropped sable hair graying at the temples.

The moment Portia met his gaze, they both stopped in surprise.

"Lord Axewood!"

"Lady Portia." Surprise broke across his weathered face.

She flashed an automatic smile in turn, but inwardly, she tensed. *Oh God, can this night get any more awkward?*

Recalling the proud earl down on one knee, asking for her hand, she cringed at the thought of having to introduce him to Lucas, but there was no escaping it.

"How nice to see you again, my lord," she managed, while Lucas looked on curiously.

"The pleasure is all mine." Axewood bowed to her, but when he glanced at Lucas, she noticed that, for a moment, he went very still.

The reason was obvious.

"Um, may I introduce you to my fiancé?" She glanced imploringly at Lucas, praying he would not say anything untoward. "Your Grace, allow me to present Vincent Clayton, the Earl of Axewood. My lord, this is Lucas Wakeford, the Duke of Fountainhurst."

Lucas feigned ignorance of the whole story, bless him, and bowed his head politely to the earl. "How do you do, sir."

Axewood suddenly blinked off his consternation and gave the young duke a polished smile. "It's an honor, Your Grace."

As Lucas studied him, she could feel his guarded interest in the man;

no doubt he was recalling the anecdote she had confided during their picnic.

To her relief, Axewood did not linger.

"You must forgive me," he said. "I arrived a bit late, and a certain young lady promised me the first dance tonight. I must go and find my partner."

"Of course." Portia nodded, still holding her smile in place.

"Nice to meet you," Lucas added as the earl hurried off.

Wonder who he's dancing with. For a moment, she watched Axewood snake his way through the crowd, then she shrugged off the question. *Whoever it is, better her than me.*

When she turned to Lucas in chagrin, he gave her a reassuring wink.

Just as they started to walk on, Mr. Lynch tapped him on the shoulder. "Fountainhurst!"

He turned to him. "Yes, sir?"

Mr. Lynch pointed discreetly after Axewood. "Did he tell you he worked with your father in Parliament?"

"Lord Axewood did?" he asked in surprise, and Mr. Lynch nodded.

"He and your sire served on one of the finance committees ages ago. Dashed if I recall which one. Axewood could tell you if you're curious. They worked on several bills together, too, if memory serves."

"Is that right," Lucas murmured, glancing after the earl, who had now vanished into the crowd. "I thought that name sounded familiar."

The old man chuckled. "Ah, London's just a small town in a big body, m'boy. Especially in Society."

"Apparently so."

"Well, run along, you two. I shan't keep you. You'd better go and find a good spot before you miss out!"

They smiled at him, then went on their way, hand in hand. Lucas seemed intrigued to hear that Lord Axewood had been a political ally of his father's.

In any case, the dance floor was filling up fast. Portia could not see much through the crowd, but Lucas used the advantage of his greater height to scan the ballroom, then he spied her friends forming a quadrille square.

"I think they're waiting for us," he reported. "The duchesses are looking around."

"Oh, let's go and join them! That is, if you don't mind."

"I don't mind if they don't," he said.

"They won't, my dear! They're not angry at you, Lucas." His humility gave her heart a pang. "Even Sidney will be back to his usual happy self by morning, I promise!"

Or I'll wring his neck.

Lucas gave her a skeptical glance, but they wasted no time in hurrying toward their waiting companions.

As Portia trailed Lucas through the crowd, clinging to his hand, she could not deny that, after all those weddings she'd attended, it was gratifying that, finally, she could join a dance with her own soon-to-be husband by her side.

"There they are!" Felicity saw them coming and beckoned to them as the introductory music began.

In the next moment, they claimed their spot across from head couple Felicity and Jason, with Serena and Azrael on their right, and Trinny and Gable on their left—the Rolands must have only just arrived.

"Dragged yourself from the wee monsieur, I see," Portia teased, greeting the redhead with a squeeze of her hand from their posts on the square.

"Barely," Trinny shot back with a grin.

The elegant, black-haired Gable, Viscount Roland, also nodded in greeting. Portia smiled at him.

While the introductory music played, she noticed Lucas glancing around and got the feeling he was again looking for Lord Axewood.

It must be quite disorienting for him to be meeting strangers who used to know his parents. All the more reason to be patient with him, she thought, although, in truth, he was doing extremely well so far tonight.

As for the dancing…we'll see.

At last, the music began, and the lively movements of the opening quadrille commenced.

To her surprise, Lucas had no trouble following with the various figures, merely keeping an eye on the men's role as he went along.

Not once did he trip, nor stumble, nor send anybody flying.

It reminded her anew of his impressive reflexes, deftly catching that falling wineglass out of midair. Indeed, Portia soon concluded that Sidney couldn't have carried himself more nobly in a ballroom.

Miracles abound: her future husband could dance.

Her friends noticed, as well. Serena sent Portia a saucy but discreet look of approval when all four ladies had to skip into the center, join hands, and revolve like an elegant pinwheel.

Returning, pink-cheeked, to her station, toes tapping in time with the rhythmic melody while the gentlemen circled their ladies, Portia tried to hide her sense of triumph, but she was altogether pleased.

She blushed as Lucas smiled at her, then took his hand for the next courtly motion.

It was then, despite all her concern about Lucas being clumsy, that she herself nearly tripped when her foot strayed across an especially slick spot on the polished floor.

Lucas caught her with ease.

When she touched his chest to steady herself and grabbed his arms, she nearly choked at the marvelous feel of hard male muscles beneath his clothes.

Oh my.

"I've got you," he murmured as he steadied her. "You all right?"

She gulped. "Fine." Her voice sounded decidedly breathless.

Lucas met her dazed glance and seemed amused. Having helped her regain her balance, he lifted her hand over her head and waited for her to execute a turn. She whirled around, her heartbeat quickening, and she blushed when she met his stare.

Indeed, this entire night was causing her to take a new look at her fiancé. A closer look.

Very well, a lustful look.

She ran a speculative glance down from his wide shoulders to his lean waist, and his long legs in neat black trousers. A little shiver vibrated through her.

Frankly, she blamed the highwayman.

That brash kiss Silversmoke had stolen last week in the gazebo must've awakened these sensuous feelings. Feelings that now had her eyeing her unsuspecting fiancé like some carnivorous predator salivating over its prey.

This newfound attraction to Lucas, of all people, seemed as bizarre as it was welcome.

Honestly, my dear duke, she thought as they circled intimately a moment later, their gazes locked, his hand on her waist, *the better I get to know you, the more of a puzzle you become.*

CHAPTER 16

An Unannounced Visitor

The next day, bright and early, Luke went to call on Lord Axewood—and it was fortunate he'd come when he had, for a traveling chariot was parked outside the earl's pillared monstrosity in the busy heart of St. James's, not far from White's.

A trio of liveried footman marched in and out of the mansion, carrying fine traveling trunks and loading them into the vehicle's boot.

Another was busily stocking the carriage interior with hampers of food and bottles of drink, while a pair of grooms went around making their final checks of the six black horses under harness.

Clearly, the master of the house was headed out on a journey somewhere. No matter, Luke thought. This wouldn't take long.

But when he went to knock on the door, it suddenly opened before he could land a blow, and the next thing he knew, Axewood himself was there, gazing at him in surprise.

"Why, Your Grace!" the earl blurted out, having only just opened the door to see how his servants were progressing at their task, apparently. "To what do I owe this honor?"

"Do, please, forgive the intrusion, my lord. I was just—"

"Nonsense, it's no intrusion." Quickly masking the initial flash of alarm that Luke could've sworn he'd seen pass across the man's face, Axewood opened the door wider and beckoned. "Come in."

"Thank you, sir." Hat in hand, clad in well-rumpled clothes—in full Lucas mode—Luke stepped over the threshold into the earl's sumptuous home. "I-I won't take up much of your time."

"Not at all." Axewood waved the footman out the front door with his burden, while Luke glanced around discreetly at the high-ceilinged entrance hall.

Quite a showplace. Red walls adorned with gilt-framed Old Masters stood proudly over pristine white wainscoting. The floor, treacherously shiny, sprawled a checkerboard of black and white marble all around them.

An opulent curved staircase snaked up to the next floor, while a ponderous crystal chandelier hung down over a round center table with a large china vase full of flowers on display.

Impressive. Yet it was odd and disturbing to think that Portia could have become the lady of this house if it weren't for him.

"Your timing is fortunate, Fountainhurst," Axewood was saying as he waited for the footman to pass. "As you can see, I am headed out of Town for a while. Business to attend to at one of my estates, don't you know."

"Ah."

"It never ends," he added wryly. "The duties of our station."

"Indeed, sir."

Axewood shut the door, then gave Luke a bright smile that did not quite reach his dark, shrewd eyes. "Come. Follow me."

His Lordship's sure footfalls clicked over the perilous stretch of highly polished marble as he led the way to a place where they could talk.

On his guard, Luke followed him past a showy blue and gold anteroom that overlooked the street.

Instead, Axewood led him into a quiet library farther back off the entrance hall. When Luke stepped over the threshold, his eyes traveled around the rich, wood-paneled room.

An illuminated manuscript lay open on a book stand in the corner, while fine bronze figurines graced pedestals between the four windows.

On the massive desk sat a small, ancient Greco-Roman statue of Janus displayed on a black rod, its stone faces staring out in two directions.

Judging by the art treasures and finery everywhere, this was obviously a very wealthy family, even by aristocratic standards.

I wonder how they made their fortune. If Axewood was short on funds, there was certainly no sign of it here.

Once Luke had crossed onto the jewel-toned rug, Axewood shut the door, then turned to him with an almost insipid smile. He could not quite hide the suspicion in his stare, however. "What can I do for you, Your Grace?"

"Well, um, sir, it is a-a matter of some delicacy, I'm afraid."

"I see." Intrigued, Axewood lifted his chin. Though his jaw was square, a little saggy flesh hung beneath it due to age.

He was indeed over fifty, and Luke mentally harrumphed at the nerve of this man, proposing to a girl half his age.

"May I offer you a drink, by the by?"

"No, thank you, sir. I-I know you are leaving, so, um, I'll be brief."

"As you wish." Looking amused, Axewood passed a glance over him that seemed to say, *My God, this chap's a nervous wreck.*

Good. Then he suspected nothing.

Going over to lean an elbow on the mantel, Axewood gave Luke an encouraging nod. "Please, feel free to speak, Your Grace. What seems to be the matter?"

"Um, well…" Luke frowned with an awkward show of distress. "Sir, it's about your nephew."

An almost imperceptible coldness crept into Axewood's demeanor, and his bland smile thinned. "What about him, Fountainhurst?"

"Well, I-I know that he and m-my betrothed, Lady Portia, as you know, were, um, quite fond of each other. Before he, that is, before he disappeared."

Luke paused while Axewood studied him in open pity for his lack of Town bronze.

"It appears that, um, Mr. Clayton's absence h-has affected my intended quite deeply, and I-I wondered, you see, that is, well, it's just— she is not the easiest girl to impress!" he finished in an awkward rush, then laughed self-consciously.

The earl tilted his head. His sideburns were pewter, but the rest of his hair was the color of black coffee, shiny and sleek with some sort of dressing oil.

Luke forced out another halting laugh. "One may possess a title, after all, but that does not necessarily win fair lady's heart."

"Oh, I understand, believe me," Axewood said, his tone dry, his gaze tracking him as Luke began to pace, making plain his anxiety.

He hoped he wasn't playing it too ham-fisted, but he did not trust this fellow one bit, though he scarcely knew why.

Somehow his instincts had already made their decision while his brain was still trying to gather information.

The introduction to the earl that he'd received last night had made this visit possible, and, indeed, would've been reason enough to go to the blasted ball.

Which had not been as terrible as Luke had expected, aside from Sidney's curious attack.

At least it had given him the luxury of spending time with Portia. Besides, it made her happy, and he *had* promised to go.

Meeting Axewood there had been an unexpected boon, one that Luke had decided to take advantage of immediately.

Strike while the iron is hot, as they said.

When Axewood glanced meaningfully at the mantel clock, Luke cleared his throat. "Well, sir, um, you see, the reason I needed to speak to you is because, er, I-I have unfortunately noticed that my future duchess may, ah, still harbor a slight, er, *tendre* for your nephew."

Luke feigned a wince. "Since no body was ever found, I realize that it could mean your nephew might still be alive out there somewhere. And I-I just, I suppose I just wanted to know if there is any further information you might be able to share with me about that. For my own peace of mind—if you take my meaning."

Axewood cocked a brow. "Hmm?"

Poor Lucas gave a gulp, nearly crushing his hat. "My lord, if there's *any* chance that your nephew might return and try to come between me and my future wife, I would just as soon know it now. So that I m-might brace myself, you understand. At the very least, I-I should like to be prepared—mentally—should Mr. Clayton reappear...and try to win Portia back.

"Therefore, if there's anything you could tell me, anything at all, that might shed light on my, her, our situation, I-I should be most grateful. *Most* grateful."

Axewood gazed at him for another long moment, looking slightly mystified. "I daresay you are smitten with the lady, Fountainhurst."

"Painfully, my lord. Who wouldn't be?" Luke looked away. "She's altogether perfect. Thing is, she doesn't really quite believe your nephew is dead, I'm afraid."

Axewood narrowed his eyes slightly. "Doesn't she?"

"No." Luke shook his head.

"Why ever not?"

He shrugged. "Women's intuition?"

"Well," Axewood said decisively, dropping his skeptical gaze and pushing away from the mantel. "I can see why you'd be concerned." He folded his arms across his chest, then lifted a hand to skim his fingers along his jaw. He passed a probing glance over Luke's face, taking his measure.

"If there is any insight you can share, sir, I would be eternally grateful," Luke said with an earnest stare.

Axewood paused. "I knew your father from our work in Parliament. Did you know that?"

Luke shook his head. "No, sir. I was a boy at school, absorbed in my own life. I did not know nor much really care at that age about my father's political life in London, to be honest."

Axewood crooked a sad half-smile. "He was very fortunate to have a son like you. He spoke of you all the time to anyone who'd listen, you know. How clever you were. How brave a lad."

Luke stared at him, genuinely shocked.

"For your father's sake, I am willing to confide in you, Fountainhurst. But I must have your word that I can trust you. For this is a highly sensitive matter. It cannot leave this room."

"Of course," Luke said at once, though his conscience prickled at the lie, given his charade here, deceiving a friend of his sire's.

Father would not have approved.

"Your Lady Portia is a very clever girl," Axewood said.

Luke leaned against the nearest bookshelf, listening intently.

"Things are not always what they appear. Her woman's intuition is right." The earl sent him a cunning smile. "My nephew is alive."

Luke tensed at this revelation. He had truly not expected that.

"However. I wouldn't worry one bit if I were you about him coming back from the dead and causing trouble between you and your duchess. In fact, if you swear Lady Portia to secrecy, as well, on what I'm about to tell you, I am rather certain that upon hearing it, she will despise my nephew as much as I do."

Axewood drifted over to the liquor cabinet and lifted a crystal decanter. He held up the bottle. "Changed your mind about that drink?"

Luke shook his head. "Too early for me, sir."

"For me, as well. But if we're going to discuss the subject of my nephew, I'm bloody well going to need it." With that, Axewood splashed a generous shot of whiskey into a small glass. "Joel Clayton was, still technically *is*, my heir. Did you know this?"

He glanced over his shoulder at Luke, who nodded.

Axewood corked the decanter. "Unlike your father, I have no son of my own at the present time, but I am seeking a bride these days to amend the lack. I have a few young ladies in mind at the moment, and I trust that, by this time next year, I will finally be a father. Then I can wash my hands of the feckless Mr. Joel Clayton for once and for all."

Axewood turned around, swirling a draught of golden whiskey in the glass. "Fountainhurst, I should not like the following information to leave this room."

"I understand, sir. You have my word."

Axewood nodded and slid his free hand into his coat pocket. "It is, I'm afraid, an untidy situation. One that reflects quite poorly on my family line. However, you have my blessing to share it in confidence with Lady Portia, if you think it would help her and your future match. I know for a fact the girl can be discreet. Consider it my wedding gift to you both, for the sake of your future happiness. To be sure, the poor lady has suffered enough for no reason, God knows."

As Axewood tossed back half of his whiskey, Luke pondered his words.

Axewood sighed and then bowed his head. "Please tell Lady Portia I meant no harm withholding this information. I would've told her eventually if… Well, never mind that. It's just so terribly unpleasant to have one's family's dirty laundry aired in public."

Luke knew it all too well. "One hates to be the topic of public discussion, to be sure."

"Indeed." Axewood glanced at him again, his lip curling in disgust. "Yes, Fountainhurst. My nephew is alive. But I have disowned him. And, frankly, I don't care if I never see that smug face of his again. However, *you* may rest assured that he cannot steal Portia away from you. Not legally, anyway."

Luke lifted his eyebrows. "And why is that?"

"Because…" Axewood rubbed the center of his forehead. "He is already married."

"*What?*"

"He eloped to France with his mistress!" the earl burst out with a glare. "A totally unsuitable woman. A Creole, for God's sake, fit for nothing but bed sport. Some high-priced courtesan!"

Luke's jaw dropped.

"But, by God, if he thinks that *creature* will ever become the next

Countess of Axewood, I will shoot him myself. How dare he? Forgive my outburst, Your Grace, but his behavior is quite beyond the pale. The gambling was bad enough—but this? Is unforgivable."

"He's married?" Luke murmured in shock.

Axewood gave a weary nod. "As you can imagine, I have been trying like hell to keep this matter quiet to minimize damage to the family's reputation. Apparently, she's some exotic beauty of mixed Jamaican extraction, much in demand among the younger rakehells. He was so pleased to have won her favors all to himself. For a price, no doubt.

"If it had remained at that, so be it. I care not. A man can sleep with whatever sort of woman he fancies. But to think that he actually went and married her?" Axewood stared at him in horror. "Why, we are descended from Norman conquerors, and he would introduce slave blood into the family line!"

Luke blinked at the earl's vehemence on the matter.

Lord, no wonder the couple had run away, if that was how the patriarch of the family felt about those of other races.

Well, Portia *had* said the earl was proud, Luke thought. But at least this secret attachment to his Creole mistress explained why Joel had never proposed to Portia.

Oh God…

Luke's heart sank at the prospect of having to tell Portia she had been involved with a two-faced deceiver, while Axewood ranted on.

"I don't care how fine the chit's supposed to be. A whore's still a whore. So let them go to France, where such matches are supposedly better tolerated. I'll have none of that here." Axewood shook his head, his face livid. "No. My nephew threw himself away on this misalliance, and when he did that, he threw away the title, as well.

"Let the jackanapes support himself and his gutter bride with those gambling skills of his in Calais, or Paris, or wherever they are now. I wash my hands of them. Where he is, exactly, I cannot tell you. All I know is that my own heir betrayed me, Your Grace.

"Therefore, when I let the world assume he's dead, he might as well be dead—for dead he is, to me. Joel betrayed this family, his class. And you are welcome to break the news to Lady Portia that he betrayed her, too, if you have the heart. Me, I could not bring myself to do it, gentle as she is. But at least then, you won't have to live with a wife who might otherwise waste her time pining over a scoundrel. My nephew never deserved her."

Axewood shook his head. "As you yourself said, she is quite perfect, as aristocratic brides go. If I were you, I'd tell her to forget she ever met my nephew and move on with her life."

"I see..." Taking it all in, Luke struggled to square the earl's story with the one he'd heard from Dog.

Faced with this equally convincing explanation of Joel's disappearance, he found himself flummoxed.

One or the other man surely had to be lying. So which one should he believe?

Oh come, who's more credible? he thought. *A rich and powerful friend of my father's or some poor, drunk loser at a gambling hell?*

The answer seemed obvious, and yet something wasn't adding up here. He could not deny that Axewood's fury at his nephew was obviously genuine. But then again, Dog had been very convincing...

Luke furrowed his brow. Was there any way they could both be telling the truth?

Determined to figure it out, he pressed Axewood a bit. "I heard Bow Street got involved in the search."

The earl sighed and rolled his eyes. "Yes, well. I had no choice, for the sake of keeping up appearances. To protect the family name, don't you know. Anyone in my position would do the same in my place, I'm sure."

"Ah." Luke nodded, hiding his skepticism.

"I admit, I panicked, early on." Axewood gave him a glum frown. "Even though I already knew where my idiot nephew had gone and why, I went through the motions of hiring a couple of Bow Street agents to pretend, as it were, to try to find him. The search went nowhere, which was exactly as I'd wished. I certainly didn't want the truth coming out." He shuddered. "Would you? It would've meant a scandal for the family, and public humiliation for poor Lady Portia—and for that very reason, I trust you, too, will keep it quiet, Fountainhurst."

He was right, Luke realized. It wasn't just Axewood's family that would've been disgraced by Joel's reckless actions, but Portia, too.

After the ballroom last night, it was all too easy to envision the cruelty she would've had to endure as Society's tongues wagged about how Clayton had duped her.

The chill that crept over Luke as he pictured the mockery and shame the woman he loved could've suffered must've been written all over his face.

It made him want to kill Clayton, not save him.

Axewood studied him. "Perhaps it would be kinder simply to tell her you've found out Joel is, in fact, dead. For I very much doubt the bounder will ever show his face again in England. Certainly, if he does, he'll get no welcome from me." The earl downed the rest of his whiskey.

Luke was still a bit shocked over what could've happened to Portia—while she went on to mourn him for over a year! *That bastard.*

"How could he put her at risk this way?" Luke exclaimed. "Simply leave England, never saying a word to anyone about where he was going? Not even his mother, his friends?"

"If you knew him, it would not surprise you." Axewood shook his head with a jaded air. "He is vain and utterly self-centered, Fountainhurst. He wanted to punish us all for not accepting this woman—he knew Society would never sanction this match. He did leave me a nasty little note when he left, though. Would you like to see it?"

"If you don't mind," Luke said, startled at the offer.

Axewood marched over to the desk and opened the bottom drawer. He pulled out a letter and unfolded it, frowned at the page, then handed it to Luke. "Here is his juvenile attempt to justify his disgraceful actions."

As Luke began to read, there was a light knock at the door.

"Come in," Axewood said.

The butler opened the door and leaned into the room. "Forgive me, my lord. There's a question regarding needed items for your journey?"

"Of course. Would you excuse me for a moment?"

As Luke nodded politely, Axewood stepped out of the room to see what his servant wanted.

The moment he pulled the study door shut behind him, Luke reached into his waistcoat and hastily took out Joel's love note to Portia.

Determined to compare the two, he unfolded the one Portia had given him at The Blind Badger, already scanning Joel's letter to Axewood.

Uncle:

With these lines, I hereby bid you and miserable England adieu. I do not expect you or anyone else in this land of cold fish to understand my ardent devotion to my darling Antonia.

The lot of you are incapable of passion, but she is more vibrantly alive than any other woman I've ever met. I choose love over everything, even your wretched title.

So do what you must. Disinherit me to your heart's content. It makes no difference. I don't need you or your money, only the hand of the woman I love, and if the family cannot accept her, then you're no kin of mine.

Good riddance and farewell to you all.

— J.C.

Well! Luke's eyebrows rose. Such defiance was impressive. The gambler did indeed sound head over heels in love with his Antonia — and the letter was clearly genuine, for the handwriting matched.

The similarities were obvious in the slant of the t's, the narrow ovals of the a's and o's, the flourish underneath the y's, and the oversized J on his signature.

Seeing this, Luke was fairly well convinced that Axewood really was telling the truth.

Yet it nagged at him. For Dog had seemed very credible, too…

Good God, he suddenly thought. Seeing that Axewood's fury at his nephew was undoubtedly real, could the earl have hired criminals to dispose of the rebel and his Creole bride in order to protect the family name? Might the earl then have merely played the worried uncle, leading a search that Axewood himself had just admitted was only a charade?

Could he have had his own heir killed?

He'd have to be damned cold-blooded to do such a thing.

With that thought, Luke realized it could not be, for Father never would have been friends with such a man.

Besides, if the Bow Street officers the earl had hired had caught wind of such a crime, Luke doubted any bribe would've sufficed to buy their silence.

As for Axewood offering for Portia, most likely, he had only been trying to clean up the mess his nephew had left behind.

Still unsure, Luke hastily tucked Joel's love note back into his breast pocket as he heard the earl's footsteps approaching.

Seconds later, the door opened and Axewood stepped in with a wry smile. "Back again. Pardon the interruption, Your Grace."

"Of course. I should go. I've delayed you long enough. As for this" — Luke handed Axewood back his nephew's letter — "I scarcely know what to say, sir. These are some very cutting words. I'm truly sorry for what he's put you through."

"That's kind of you, Your Grace. It is shocking, I know." Axewood sighed. "His exit left me in the lurch, to be sure. But for all my disappointment, Lady Portia has no doubt had the worst of it, poor thing. I should have told her, I know, but I...I just couldn't do it, knowing how hurt she would be. How ashamed she would feel."

Luke nodded. "I will take good care of her. She'll forget him in time."

With an absent nod, Axewood hooked his thumbs into his pockets and lowered his head, hesitating. "I, er, I suppose I ought to just come out and tell you, if you didn't already know, that I offered for Lady Portia myself, after Joel disappeared. But please don't mistake me; my motives were pure. I fear my nephew led her on. I felt it my duty to make good on whatever promises he might've implied in his flirting. She said no — obviously." Axewood smiled ruefully.

Luke smiled back, though the moment was awkward. "Quite honorable of you, sir."

Axewood waved this off. "She'll be better off with you, though. You are closer to her in age, and you seem well matched. I wish you both happy."

"Thank you, sir. I wish you all the best in your bride hunt, as well."

"Right! Well." The earl clapped his hands together. "If there's nothing further, Your Grace, I really should be on my way before the sun climbs any higher. I've many miles to travel before nightfall."

"Of course. I appreciate your time."

"As I appreciate your discretion."

"Understood."

"I knew I could trust you, Fountainhurst. Just as I trusted your father." Axewood clapped him on the back, then walked Luke back out across the opulent entrance hall.

"If there's ever anything I can do for you, don't hesitate to call on me," the earl said warmly when they reached the front door. "I know you do not often come to Town, but perhaps your marriage to such a popular belle will help to change that."

Luke gave a small laugh. "We'll see."

Axewood's smile was pure cordiality. "Either way, if I can ever be of assistance in political matters, call on me anytime. After all, we are in similar straits, are we not? I'm an old man without a son, and you're a young man without a father. Misery loves company, eh?"

Luke smiled and nodded.

Axewood opened the door for him.

Pausing on the threshold, Luke turned and looked sincerely at the man. "Thank you for shielding my fiancée from this scandal as best you could."

Axewood nodded. "If you eventually decide to share the truth with her, I'm sure her attachment to you in time will help to take some of the sting out of my nephew's perfidy."

"Or at least her attachment to the duchess coronet," Luke said wryly, and shrugged.

Axewood scoffed at the jest, and Luke put on his hat.

"Safe travels, my lord. Good day."

"Your Grace," Axewood replied, still chuckling at the quip.

With an easy wave, Luke walked out, passing the fat gray pillars holding up the portico overhead.

In the shadow of the mansion, the earl's traveling chariot waited at full readiness to spirit him away.

Upon reaching the pavement, Luke just stood there for a moment, unsure of his next move.

His mind churned, and his head felt almost foggy with all the stunning information he had learned, none of which fit his expectations.

Standing beside the man, he'd become convinced of Axewood's innocence, but now, as soon as they'd parted, he began to question some of the things he'd been told…

He wasn't even sure why.

He stared unseeingly at the traffic clattering up and down the cobbled street.

Bloody hell. Glancing back at the mansion, Luke was now officially all the more confused.

Either that chap's telling the truth or he's an even better liar than me.

Bloody odd duck, that one, thought Axewood after closing the door behind him. To be sure, the new Duke of Fountainhurst seemed nothing like his iron-willed father.

Thank God for that.

Why, Axewood had nearly had an apoplectic fit when he'd gone to the door and found that self-righteous bastard's son standing there on his doorstep.

Looked just like him, too. Uncomfortably so.

Somehow, Axewood had hidden his shock and managed to charm Lucas. But in truth, he'd been astonished at what a weakling the younger Fountainhurst had turned out to be.

His father would be so ashamed, after all his bragging.

Humph. Axewood could only conclude that the family tragedy in his youth must've ruined the lad, for truly, the younger Fountainhurst had grown up into a stammering, pitiful ball of nerves.

Well, anyway, he was gone now, and—Axewood was sure—none the wiser. *So much for that rumored genius intellect.* His lips curved in a smirk as he stepped into his blue-and-gold anteroom off the entrance hall. Crossing to the bow window, he inched the curtains aside and peered out discreetly.

Fountainhurst was just standing there, staring into space.

Axewood narrowed his eyes. *What the hell is he doing?*

The eccentric young magnate stood motionless outside his house, as though still trying to absorb what he'd been told.

Axewood shook his head. The man was a naïf. Clearly, when it came to worldly cunning, the current duke had none.

Axewood was pleased to have befriended him, though, for this *new* Fountainhurst was his favorite sort of person: rich, powerful, and weak.

Easy to manipulate, control…

Watching his new chum finally saunter off down the pavement, Axewood reflected on how strange it was when fate bestowed such abundant blessings as title and fortune on an idiot like that.

Ah well. He let the curtain fall and turned away, then strode off to make sure that everything was ready for his trip.

He did not imagine he'd be coming back to Town until the end of next week, when he returned from the Carnevale.

With a fresh infusion of gold in his coffers, hopefully.

Why, what remained of his debts from the damned canal project would be paid off in no time.

For now, however, Esme's alarming news before the ball last night, warning him that Silversmoke—of all people!—was searching for his nephew made it imperative that he get to the castle without delay and beef up security at once.

Axewood wasn't afraid of much, but the name of Silversmoke admittedly struck dread into his bones.

As well it should. After all, he knew better than anyone what that mad highwayman was capable of.

Whoever he was.

Axewood had never laid eyes on the mysterious outlaw, but had followed his illustrious career in the papers, given their connection.

A connection to which he prayed the ruthless highwayman remained oblivious.

Silversmoke.

The name sent a prickle of dread down his spine, for it was the *nom de guerre* of the very outlaw who'd conveniently disposed of that Scottish mercenary gang that Axewood had dealt with all those years ago…

With Fountainhurst's son having just left his house, the drift of his thoughts was so unnerving that Axewood left the room, eager to get out of Town.

Minutes later, he stood in the entrance hall as his butler handed him his hat and coat, then opened the door for him.

"I'll be back next week," Axewood said without further explanation. Not even his own upper servants knew about the *other* side of his life. The side he truly relished, far from the tedium of his Parliamentary duties and his status as an upstanding pillar of society.

"Very good, my lord." The butler bowed, then Axewood marched out to his waiting coach.

He stepped up into it and sank down into the luxurious cushions, resting an elbow on the pillow that his servants had provided.

As the large, smooth-riding carriage glided into motion, muscling its way through the traffic and heading out of Town, he propped his feet up on the divan-like seating, crossed his ankles, and made himself comfortable for the journey.

Axewood put the pillow behind his head and closed his eyes, intent on resting to wile away the time. He hadn't slept well last night after Esme's news, and uneasy questions continued gnawing at his innards.

It was not lost on him, of course, that Silversmoke wasn't the only one asking about Joel these days.

So had that ridiculous quiz of a duke just now. *Damned strange coincidence.* Given that nobody knew Silversmoke's true identity, for a moment, Axewood wondered…

Could it be remotely possible?

Oh, come. Scoffing at his own absurdity, he punched his pillow into a somewhat better shape for his neck. *That innocent — Silversmoke? The blackguard who nigh single-handedly wiped out the entire MacAbe gang? No. Not in a million years.* The notion was laughable.

The young Duke of Fountainhurst seemed like an overgrown choirboy, while the masked highwayman was known throughout the underworld as a hardened killer.

Even Axewood respected Silversmoke's bloody handiwork, and he didn't respect much of anyone or anything.

Don't be an idiot. It was merely his own secret life making him paranoid, he concluded. *He* was the one with the dual identity, not Fountainhurst's son.

God forbid it!

Because if that were the case, then Axewood had far bigger problems than he even wanted to think about.

Get some sleep. Your wits have obviously gone missing. With that, he shut his eyes, determined to ignore his inane misgivings.

Instead, he indulged himself with bright visions of gold coins parading and pirouetting across his mind. A man had to measure the game of life somehow, after all, and Axewood liked knowing that he was winning.

True, the thought of Silversmoke catching up to him frightened him a little, but at the same time, perversely, he found the danger invigorating. It was only under dire threat in his experience that a man felt truly alive.

Besides, why should he worry? He always got away with everything and always would.

Always.

"Will you be seeing Lucas tonight?" Felicity asked as the four ladies marched back to Moonlight Square after a brisk morning constitutional in Hyde Park, a few streets away.

Portia smiled at her from beneath the brim of her bonnet. "We don't have plans until Sunday. My parents and I are going to spend the day with his family at his estate."

"Oh, how exciting!"

Her friends cooed over this, and Portia laughed with agreement. She couldn't wait, herself.

After the success of the ball last night, her mood was unshakably cheerful. Her feet barely seemed to touch the ground as the four friends marched past a row of shops in the shade.

The sun was climbing higher now, but it had been a beautiful walk around the Serpentine. The day was fine, and a little tribe of quacking ducks had followed them along the waterline as the ladies circled the lake.

There weren't many fashionable carriages on the graveled roads of the park in the morning hours, but they had seen plenty of smart riders out exercising their blood-horses. Their glossy mounts had frolicked over the green, kicking up chunks of turf as they galloped by, gentleman and horses alike showing off.

Portia had smiled at everyone they passed, her dreamy musings still on the memory of dancing in Lucas's arms last night.

It was de rigueur after every ball or other grand event to meet and discuss the latest gossip in the ton, and that morning, to her delight, her friends could not stop raving about her future husband.

"He's adorable!" Trinny said.

"I told you so," Serena boasted with a smile under the wide, beribboned brim of her pretty straw hat. "He just needed time to come out of his shell."

"But Sidney was so awful to him!" Felicity said. "You should've seen it, Trin. You weren't there yet. My eyes nearly popped out of my head when he went on the attack."

"Oh, Sidney can be terrifying in social situations if one gets on his bad side," Trinny agreed with a wide-eyed nod.

"Thank goodness Jason was there to rein him in," Felicity said.

"Well, Lucas responded with such manly grace, I nearly swooned myself." Serena nodded decisively. "I like him well, P."

"So do I." Portia flashed a joyous smile at her friends.

"My Lord, she's in love," Felicity murmured with a twinkle in her eyes.

Am I? Portia wondered.

"I say, is Gunter's open yet for ice cream?" Trinny asked, glancing in the direction of Berkeley Square as they continued homeward.

The ladies burst out laughing.

"Trinny!"

"Temptress!"

"No. We mustn't."

"That would ruin the whole point of this walk," Felicity said sternly.

"Yes, but…"

"Oh, come on, you." Serena took Trinny's arm and steered her safely past the intersection where the temptation of the most delicious ice cream in London beckoned. "You haven't even eaten breakfast yet."

"All right," Trinny grumbled. "I'm the one who's got to lose the baby fat, anyway. But I will say my husband likes my giant bosoms. Aren't they splendid? He says I'd better watch out for the Regent."

They laughed as the redhead looked down at her previously modest chest, but Felicity shushed her, lest the couple of footmen attending them overhear.

Upon reaching Moonlight Square a few minutes later, the friends parted ways, each returning to their houses.

Portia was still smiling when she opened the front door to her family's home on Marquess Row. At once, she noticed the house seemed especially quiet.

Indeed, she had even managed to come in without gaining the attention of the ever-vigilant Stevens. The entrance hall was empty, and afternoon shadows had begun to fill the house.

The tick-tock of the long-case clock by the wall filled the silence, and as she took off her bonnet, she noticed that it read nearly noon.

As Portia began walking toward the stairs to go up to her room, she suddenly stopped in her tracks.

In the quiet, she heard something that instantly alarmed her: the sound of someone crying.

Low sobs were coming from the morning room.

Mama? Casting aside her book, reticule, and bonnet, Portia ran toward the sound in a flood of dread.

"Mama, where are you?" She checked the other rooms on her way, not seeing even a servant, then reached the back of the house, dashing to the threshold of the morning room.

There, she froze, astonished by the unprecedented sight of her glamorous, always well-coiffed and perfectly dressed mother, Samantha, the Marchioness of Liddicoat, bawling her eyes out on the wicker couch, while the parakeet looked on in solemn silence from his cage.

"Mama, what's wrong?" Portia rushed to her side in a panic. Instantly, she thought of her father and sucked in her breath. "Where's

Papa?" Dread gripped her. "Has something happened?"

They all worried about his heart, with that potbelly of his. It wasn't healthy.

Alas, the elegant lady was too much beside herself to answer coherently. She was trying to stifle her sobs, now that her daughter had invaded her privacy, but it was no use. Tears streamed down her face, streaking the makeup she claimed not to wear.

Sitting down beside her, Portia barely noticed the letter on her mother's lap. "Mama, tell me right now why you are crying! Is it Papa?"

"No, no, my dear." Gulping for air, her mother dabbed at her patrician nose. "Don't worry. Everything's fine," she said with a sniffle. "I'm crying—from h-happiness!"

"What?"

"Oh, darling! We've had the most wonderful news." She gave Portia the letter, her hand trembling. "My son is coming home! Hunter's on his way. He promises he'll be here for the wedding!"

Portia stared at her. For half a second there, she had thought she was going to hear that her father had dropped dead.

As this positive news sank in, she could have fainted in relief.

"Mama, you scared the blazes out of me!"

"What? Oh, I'm sorry, dear. No, as I told you, everything's fine."

It took Portia a moment to calm down, then she glanced at the letter. "Hunter's really coming home?"

Her mother nodded, wiping her eyes. "He would've been here already, but the winds have not cooperated. They've delayed his journey a bit, but he swears he'll be here in time."

At last, the full force of the news hit her. Portia looked at her mother in amazement. "Hunter's coming home."

Mama nodded, and fresh tears brimmed in her eyes. "At last, I shall have my whole family under one roof again."

When she sobbed, Portia hugged her, still marveling. Mama had always doted on her roguish son, but these tears from a glittering Society lady who never showed excessive emotion took Portia aback.

Not only did they reveal her mother's vulnerable side, they also made Portia wonder if, perhaps, the cordial distance all of her family members kept from each other might not be what her mother truly wanted.

They had never been a close-knit family. It was just normal life as they'd grown accustomed to it. But that didn't mean Mama found it fulfilling. And in that moment, Portia realized it certainly wasn't what she wanted for herself.

Oh, there had been a time when she would've been content—or at least not *too* discontent—with an arranged match devoid of love.

But Lucas had come along and changed all that.

"I told you he'd never miss your wedding," Mama said with a sniffle, pulling back at length to blow her nose. "Even with all he'll have to face in returning to London."

"Well," Portia said slowly, "Hunter's never lacked for courage."

"True." Her mother dabbed at her eyes. "I'm so happy, darling. We must shower your brother with love when he comes home, so this time, at last, he might stay," she whispered.

Portia nodded, her eyes watering for her mother's sake. "We will, Mama. At least, we can try. But do you think Papa will be able to do that?"

At least this explained why the house had seemed so deserted when she arrived. Papa had probably had one of his once-in-a-decade explosions, then stormed out of the house to go collect his thoughts at his club. The servants must all be lying low.

"Your father had better not scare him away," Mama vowed. "No matter what he's done, Hunter's still our son."

"What happened wasn't *his* fault, anyway. At least, not all of it."

"I know, dear. It's time your father accepted that, too."

Portia agreed, but, unfortunately, Papa wasn't the only one who had banished her brother. Though the legal aspects of the tragedy had long since been resolved, many people in Society—particularly Hunter's ex-friends—would no longer have anything to do with him.

Even Sidney could not seem to forgive him.

"I can't wait for him to meet Lucas, Mama. Do you think they'll get along?"

"I'm sure they will, darling, for your sake."

Portia smiled, but as happy as she was at the news, she could not deny feeling hugely relieved that her mild-mannered fiancé was nothing like her dark and dangerous brother.

Not in a hundred years could she ever imagine Lucas killing another man.

Not even by accident.

No, her darling quiz wouldn't even hurt a fly. *Literally.*

"I must look a fright." Mama pulled back with a sniffle. "What time is Mrs. Bell delivering your gown? I can't let her see me like this."

"Not until two, Mama. You have plenty of time to compose yourself." Touched by her rare moment of vulnerability, Portia gave her mother another comforting hug.

Then the two of them continued rejoicing tearfully together over Hunter's long-awaited return.

CHAPTER 17

An Unexpected Ally

*A*fter leaving Axewood's residence, Luke wasn't entirely sure what to do with himself. Though it was now midday and he could use something to eat, he had a knot in his stomach that came from not knowing *what* to believe.

At a loss, he returned to Moonlight Square, but decided to avoid his fiancée until he figured out what the hell he was going to tell her—as Silversmoke, that was.

As Lucas, he was not supposed to know about any of this.

But as someone who cared desperately about her, he could not deny that, whichever story was true—kidnapping or elopement or both—this was bad.

Ah, damn, the whole thing was a mess.

Not to mention lying to her was growing increasingly uncomfortable.

With a growl under his breath, Luke ordered his driver to let him out at the Grand Albion. Might as well go in and have a meal at the club, where no lady could intrude and ask him questions to which he still had no answers.

Alighting from his coach, he had dismissed his driver, telling him he would walk home after a spot of lunch.

Still in a brown study, Luke marched into the same opulent hotel where he had danced with Portia last night, but instead of going up the red-carpeted stairs to the Assembly Rooms, he crossed the ground floor lobby to a quiet corridor that led toward the back of the building.

The hallway ended ahead at a pair of double doors flanked by potted palms. Through those polished wooden doors lay the exclusive gentlemen's club at the Grand Albion.

Luke rarely visited, but was a member there by virtue of his residence on the square.

When he walked in, he was immediately greeted by a maître d' who sped out from behind his wooden stand beside the door with a look of alarm.

The little fellow was relieved when Luke informed him who he was, then offered needless apologies for not recognizing His Grace, bowing and scraping, and telling Luke to make himself at home.

The maître d' was clearly relieved that Luke was not some sort of intruder.

Having passed this pesky little guardian at the threshold, Luke shrugged off the unexpected encounter and, with newfound caution, proceeded into the club.

The dim, wood-paneled, masculine refuge was done in dark jewel tones with brown leather furniture and patterned carpeting. A row of windows along the back wall overlooked a terrace and the hotel's sculpted grounds.

There were about twenty gray-haired gentlemen dining at present, about four to a table. To Luke's right, some portly chap had dozed off reading a newspaper on one of the leather couches by the unlit fireplace.

As he sauntered toward the dining area, the pleasant clinking of dishes and silver and the murmur of conversation blended with the tantalizing smells of the food on offer.

Uniformed waiters scurried past, pouring wine, removing finished plates, delivering more courses to the tables.

Luke's mouth watered as a waiter hurried by carrying a tray with a kingly dish of roast beef and gravy alongside a Yorkshire pudding.

He caught a glimpse of a steaming meat pie with a flaky golden crust, another of filleted sole with a side dish of tender spring vegetables, artfully arranged.

The diners at the middle table were already onto the sweets course. Luke stared as a waiter served the oohing and ahhing gentleman a golden rum cake piled with strawberries and dusted with powdered sugar.

Luke's stomach growled in response. Maybe all of this would make more sense after he'd had a good meal. It was strange, though. He did not trust Axewood for one moment, yet he did not dislike the man as much as he wanted to.

Then he paused at the edge of the dining area, standing there awkwardly for a moment, unsure where to sit. He did not know anybody there, and all the men he saw eating together were of the older generation, deep in discussion of politics, by the sound of it, enjoying their grumbling in general disapproval of modern times and younger folk.

He was not eager to join them, which was just as well, for they ignored him.

But then, beyond the main dining area, Luke spotted one familiar face, and promptly tensed.

Sidney.

The blond viscount was shooting a lonely game of billiards by himself and looking very bored, indeed.

At that moment, Sidney saw him. Having just made his shot, the viscount straightened up and, to Luke's surprise, his expression brightened. He lifted a hand in greeting.

Luke sent back an uncertain wave, happy to let bygones be bygones, if the other man was. After all, he'd only acted like a bastard toward him for Portia's sake.

Sidney beckoned him over to one of the high, round pub tables near the billiards table.

Luke shrugged off his confusion and made his way warily toward the fashionable rakehell.

"Fountainhurst," Sidney said in an amiable tone, as if nothing had happened. "Fancy seeing you here. Care to join me?" He gestured toward the wooden cue stick holder on the wall.

Luke looked askance at him. "Actually, I'm starving. I came in for a meal. But I'll keep you company, if you like."

"Please do. It's dull as dust around here! As you can see, it's the hour of the Old Ones." Sidney cast a sardonic glance toward the diners, only to frown back at one crusty old gent with gray side-whiskers, who was scowling at the viscount with particular zeal.

"I say," Luke murmured, noting the old man's glare. He pulled out a high-legged stool from one of the tall tables around the billiards area. "Do you know that fellow?"

Sidney snorted. "That would be my father. The Marquess of Valliers. We don't exactly get along."

"Oh," Luke said in surprise.

"I'd have left by now if there weren't some perverse part of me that didn't enjoy baiting the ol' goblin. But then, I'm ornery like that." Sidney paused. "As you've probably noticed. Sorry about last night, ol' boy. It had to be said."

Luke sent him a wry look as he sat down on the stool. "You were protecting Lady Portia. I can respect that."

Sidney studied him for a moment, and it seemed a truce was achieved.

"So," Luke said, glancing toward the green baize table. "Billiards."

"Yes. Playing with myself as usual these days, now that my mates have gone and got themselves leg-shackled. It's tiresome. But I reckon you're next for the vicar's mousetrap, eh?"

"Sixteen days," Luke replied.

"God, must be something in the water," Sidney grumbled, then beckoned the waiter to come and take Luke's order.

After Luke requested the roast beef and a pint of ale, the waiter withdrew.

Luke took off his spectacles, since they became uncomfortable after a few hours. He tucked them into his breast pocket, then watched Sidney drift around the billiard table, sizing up his angles and sinking several admirable shots.

The waiter brought him his drink, and Luke decided to take off his tailcoat. As he stood, removing it and draping it over the low, curved back of the leather-padded stool, he continued mulling Axewood's claims about Joel.

"You seem preoccupied, Fountainhurst."

When Sidney reached for the chalk, Luke suddenly noticed that the viscount had been studying him again with shrewd intensity.

Though the stylish man-about-town might've been evaluating his wardrobe, Luke didn't think so. No, he got the impression that, once more, Sidney was sizing him up for his worthiness to wed Portia.

Luke bristled at his polite but no-nonsense scrutiny.

He got the strangest feeling that, unlike Lord Axewood, this chap could somehow see right through his façade, and he wasn't quite sure how to react.

On his guard, Luke sat down again, freed of his coat. Thankfully, he did not sense any more hostility from Sidney, just a healthy dose of skepticism.

He supposed he could not blame the man for being suspicious of him. After all, he had gone out of his way to cultivate an eccentric reputation simply to keep the ton at arm's length.

Nevertheless, he realized he had better be careful with this too-perceptive fellow, since he had so much to hide.

He recalled Portia telling him once that Sidney always managed to find out everything that happened in Society. The risk to Luke's ruse was obvious, as a man living a double life.

But on second thought, if Sidney really did know the secrets of the ton, maybe he had some useful information about Joel's disappearance.

Suddenly, Luke had questions. *Very well.*

If Sidney wished to interview him to gauge his worth as Portia's future mate, then maybe Luke could interrogate the viscount, in turn, and learn something that might just help in his quest.

Because, so far, he had hit nothing but dead ends.

"Troubled about something?" Sidney asked with nonchalance, then he set the chalk aside.

"Actually, I am." Luke took his spectacles out of his breast pocket and toyed with them.

"Hmm?" Sidney arched a brow.

Luke regarded him intently, wondering how to begin and how much he could safely say. "Portia tells me you know everyone who's anyone in London."

"Well. One doesn't like to brag." Sidney cast him an arch look, then sized up his next shot.

"Did you know Joel Clayton?"

"Certainly. Not well, but yes. We were friends." He bent over the table. "Gambled with him once, too. Big mistake."

"He was as good as they say?"

"Better." A sharp crack sounded as Sidney took the shot. The cue ball slammed into the nine and sent it careening into the corner pocket. "How he did it, I can't fathom. It was impressive, though. He had the devil's own luck, as they say."

Chewing the arm of his glasses, Luke brooded for a moment. "Do you know if— Ah, never mind," he said, waving it off.

"What?" Straightening up, Sidney turned and glanced curiously at him.

Luke knew he had to tread carefully, since Sidney and Portia were close. He drummed his fingers on the table, then decided to chance it.

"For reasons I would rather not go into, I'm trying to find out if Clayton had a mistress on the side while he was courting my fiancée."

"Aha." Sidney's golden eyebrows lifted. "Reasons pertaining to Lady Portia's happiness, dare I ask?"

"More like her peace of mind." Luke paused. "I, er, I've heard a rumor that he had taken a Creole demirep under his protection. Would you happen to know anything about that, my lord?"

Sidney held his tongue, for just then, the waiter arrived, delivering Luke's food. As Luke got himself situated with his napkin and silver, and assured the waiter he did not need anything else at the moment, Sidney sauntered over to the table and perched on the stool across from him.

He called after the waiter to bring him another glass of iced tea with an extra sprig of mint and lots of sugar. The man nodded and sped away again. Though he could not wait to dive in to his meal, Luke hesitated, not wishing to be rude by eating in front of his new acquaintance.

Sidney waved this off. "Go on."

Not needing further encouragement, Luke cut away a forkful of gravy-drizzled roast beef that all but melted in his mouth.

"Mm!" He nodded in approval.

Sidney's lips quirked at his enjoyment. "To answer your question, Your Grace, I hadn't heard about one particular mistress, but I could believe it. Most men do keep a ladybird these days. *Don't* they?"

Sidney fixed a firm stare on Luke, who stopped chewing.

His eyes widened as he caught Sidney's meaning. "Well, I don't!" he exclaimed. "Do you?"

Sidney let out a cynical snort. "God no. I have never had to pay a woman to sleep with me. Why do you want to know about Joel's love life?"

Luke washed down his swallow with a mouthful of ale. "Because I'm wondering if his choice of companions might've had something to do with his disappearance. As you may have noticed, Portia was deeply hurt by all that happened—"

"Oh yes. I know. I was there." Sidney looked meaningfully at him, and bristled with the slightest hint of warning.

Perhaps it was perverse of him, but Luke decided on the spot that he liked this fellow well. If Sidney was willing to pick a fight with him for the sake of protecting their lovely mutual friend, they were going to get along just fine.

"She told me she fell into a depression when he could not be found,"

Luke said.

Sidney's patrician face saddened. "Yes. I thought we'd nearly lost her there for a while."

Luke's heart sank, hearing that. Had she loved Clayton so much? She *had* said they made the perfect couple.

He rallied, though, warding off the dispiriting thought. "Well, I can tell she's very fond of *you*, for what it's worth. Thank you for being a real friend to her when she needed one."

"It was my honor," Sidney answered quietly, then again, looked at Luke as if to say, *And where were you?*

Luke set down his fork, beginning to lose patience.

It seemed there was only one way he was going to be able to settle this matter, and that was by telling Sidney the truth. Otherwise, this stubborn mule might never let it go.

And, after all, Luke admitted, it was a perfectly reasonable question.

He decided there and then to come clean with the man, insofar as he was able. "The reason I am asking about Joel's love life is that I mean to find out what really happened to him," Luke said. "For Portia's sake."

Sidney looked startled. "What do you mean?"

"Portia seems to think he might still be alive out there somewhere."

"Really?" Sidney murmured.

Luke nodded. "I'm trying to find the truth for her. I know the world has largely given him up for dead, but I need to know for certain. Preferably *before* the wedding."

"Oh! Oh..." Sidney repeated, frowning. "I see." His piercing blue eyes turned icy. "You mean to jilt her because of any lingering feelings she might have for him?"

"No! Of course not." Luke sat up straight. "I would never do that. You misunderstand me. If Joel's alive and she would prefer him, then I simply want her to know she still has a choice."

Sidney furrowed his brow, staring skeptically at him.

"If I can bring him back safe and sound, and she still chooses me at that point, then I'll know it's because *I'm* the one she genuinely wants. If not, then so be it. All I want is her happiness."

Sidney gave him a mystified look.

"Do not say anything to her about this," Luke warned. "The whole topic of this bounder has already caused her enough pain, as far as I'm concerned."

"I agree." Sidney sat back slowly. "Very well, Your Grace. You needn't worry. I'm a vault."

Luke could believe it. He knew that Portia trusted Sidney explicitly. But a strange look had settled over the man's face. The wariness had faded from his cobalt eyes, leaving an almost wistful expression.

"Damn," Sidney said. "You really love her."

Luke wasn't sure how to react, for Portia and he had not exchanged any sort of love words yet. Perhaps they never would, if Joel returned.

But, for his part, Luke knew how he felt about her.

Sidney laughed softly at Luke's increasingly cagey scowl. "Never fear, Fountainhurst. Your secret's safe with me. You love her. That's all I needed to know."

Luke mumbled under his breath and shifted in his seat, then picked up his fork again, embarrassed.

Sidney watched him with amusement as the waiter returned with his iced tea. The viscount thanked the man and waited for him to leave, then looked at Luke. "So how can I help in your search?"

Luke glanced ruefully at him. "Ever heard of a top Creole demirep called Antonia?" he asked. It seemed as good a place as any to start.

Sidney thought for a moment. "No. But there's somebody I could ask."

"Oh really? Who?"

"Friend of mine. She happens to be a charming Creole demirep herself. Name's Marta. She works at an exclusive little nunnery called Wanderlust. Ever been there?"

Luke shook his head. "Never even heard of it."

"What?" Sidney laughed at him. "My God, man, you really need to live a little!"

Luke frowned.

Sidney leaned closer. "They're known for the quality of their, shall we say, *imports*." He sat back again with a mischievous look, swirling the ice in his glass. "They bring in exotic beauties from all over the world. Even the Regent visits occasionally."

"Really?" Luke gave him a dubious look.

"Oh yes. Admittance by personal referral only. But I can get you in, if you're interested. 'From sultry señoritas and Greek Aphrodites to graceful Asian dancers, lovely as the lotus...'" Sidney offered his sardonic rhapsody as though he'd memorized it from a flyer advertising the place. "'From Nubian princesses to Nordic Valkyries, the gentleman of means will always find a cultured companion at Wanderlust, whatever his taste.'"

"I thought you never paid for it," Luke said dryly.

Sidney grinned. "Carvel drags me there! It's his favorite place."

"Who, the major? He seems like such a paragon."

"Ah, Pete's a roving nomad at heart. He likes the travel theme as well as the beautiful women. I merely tag along to amuse m'self and, er, enjoy the sights."

"Right. Anyway?"

"Yes—as I was saying. Knowing Joel, he would only accept a high-priced courtesan like one of the girls at Wanderlust. Since I doubt there are that many *filles de joie* of Creole descent running around London, I think there's a fine chance that my friend Marta might know this Antonia of yours." Sidney shrugged. "I'll talk to her tonight. Easy enough to ask. Of course, I'll have to bring the major along, or he'll never forgive me."

"Can he be trusted?"

"More than either one of us," Sidney retorted. "Man's a damned war hero, you know. Why don't you come along? We'll get you in."

Luke let out a knowing laugh and wagged a finger at him, shaking his head. He knew a trap when he heard one. This smooth invitation was no doubt just another test of his worthiness for Portia.

Fortunately, it was one that he had no trouble passing. "I am getting married in two weeks, Sidney. I am *not* going to any damned brothel, no matter how exclusive it may be. But if you do manage to track down this Antonia, please let me know as soon as possible. It's important that I speak to her. Fully clothed. And remember, when discussing this with Marta, you need to be discreet."

"Discreet's my middle name." Sidney waggled his eyebrows. "Just ask the ladies."

Luke harrumphed and took another tangy bite of roast beef. He chewed thoughtfully for a moment. "Tell me something, Sidney. If you care so much for my fiancée, why didn't you offer for her yourself?"

"Who me? No." Sidney scoffed. "She's like a sister to me, man. I mean, I might've done so eventually, if I'd had to watch the poor thing flounder around for much longer. But if it had come to that, she would never have accepted, anyway."

"Why not? She's very fond of you." Luke took a bite of bread.

"No female alive wants to marry for mere *fondness*, you great dolt. Don't you know anything about women?"

"Not really."

"Secondly, your bride has heard me make fun of the married state one too many times. She'd have known I was only offering out of chivalry, and pride would've forced her to decline."

Sidney seemed finished, but, peering philosophically into his glass, he added, "To be honest, I didn't much fancy the notion of having Hunter Tennesley for a brother-in-law, either. Watch your step with him, Fountainhurst—if he ever shows up again. Evil bastard."

Luke stopped chewing, then gulped down a hasty swallow of ale. "Why do you say that?"

Sidney hesitated, then shook his head. "You'll have to ask Portia."

"Evil bastard?" he echoed.

Sidney lifted his hands. "It's just my opinion. But I'm not the only one. It's not my place to tell you why. Portia can do that."

"Huh." Before Luke could press him about Portia's brother, Sidney changed the subject. "So, what other leads are you pursuing on Joel's disappearance? The mistress angle and anything else?"

Luke passed a wary glance over Sidney's face as the viscount swirled the ice in his tall glass, making it clink. Although the subject of Axewood was even riskier, Luke decided to trust him with this part, as well. "I am also looking at the uncle." He sawed off another bite of beef.

"Aha. Axewood. Yes, he is...something else." Sidney laughed ruefully.

"What do you make of him?"

"Well, he's got a bit of a dodgy reputation, I can tell you that."

"Oh?"

Sidney nodded. "Always coming up with some daft investment scheme or other. Dragging half the men of the ton into it with him, and telling them they're going to make a fortune."

"Swindler?" Luke asked, astonished, after seeing all that wealth on display at Axewood House.

"Put it this way—Joel's not the only gambler in the family. Only, with his uncle, it takes the form of business investments instead of cards."

Luke frowned. "Hmm. Sounds like a vulgar pursuit for so top-lofty a lord."

"True. Still, few peers will overlook the chance to line their coffers, if the opportunity is tempting enough. Sometimes his schemes are profitable, from what I hear, but not always. My old man nearly lost five thousand last year in some canal thing Axewood put together. It must've worked out, though, because Father got his money back after a while."

"Glad to hear it." Damn, but all of a sudden, Luke was positively itching to talk to Axewood again, in light of this revelation.

Alas, their second chat would have to wait, for he had seen for himself that the earl had just left Town. Luke suddenly wondered with intense curiosity exactly *where* Lord Axewood had gone.

"Er, Fountainhurst?"

"Yes?" When Luke snapped back to attention, he found Sidney studying him again with that all-seeing stare of his.

The viscount's expression was polite, his jaw resting on his fist, but the sharp look in his eyes worried Luke. "The gig's up, man."

"W-what?"

"Sorry, but I must ask—you don't really give one damn about insects. Do you?"

Taken off guard, Luke floundered for a heartbeat. "I-I don't know what you mean."

"Oh come, what's the game?" Sidney leaned closer. "It's all some sort of bam, i'nt? You're having everyone on."

"Wh-what are you talking about? And why do you keep staring at me like that?" Luke retorted, alarmed.

"All right, fine." Sidney pushed back from the table. "You really want to know?"

"Yes!" he said. Only, he didn't.

"Very well, I'll be blunt. If I am looking at you strangely, Your Grace, it's because I cannot help but sense that there is something...deeply untruthful about you."

"Oh really?" Luke said, his heart pounding.

Sidney gave a placid nod. "I am merely trying to decide if it's malicious or benign."

Luke clenched his jaw. *Bloody hell.* He saw that he was trapped.

Dammit, he had long since realized this was bound to happen sometime, that someone would eventually catch on to his ruse. And so he had prepared a range of denials and excuses with which to misdirect or allay others' suspicions.

But now that the dreaded moment had arrived, Luke realized that lying to a canny bastard like Sidney probably wouldn't work.

Moreover, if he took him into his confidence, the man could potentially be a valuable ally.

"So which is it?" Sidney prompted with a blunt stare. "Malicious or benign?"

Luke studied him for a moment longer through narrowed eyes. "Very well. I'll tell you. But if you repeat this to anyone, I will kill you," he said, sounding most un-Lucas-like.

Sidney's eyes widened as he realized Luke wasn't jesting. "Oh really?" With an uneasy scoff, the viscount sat up straight, his expression sobering. "Well, you can try."

"I will succeed. Trust me," Luke said.

"Aha. So, malicious, then."

"No. Just a great deal more serious than I suspect you're used to." With that, he cast off his Lucas façade altogether.

Sidney set his drink down and studied him shrewdly. "Very well. You have my attention. Consider me sworn to secrecy, Your Grace."

Luke nodded in approval, took a drink of ale, then gave Sidney a hard look and set his tankard down. "Ever heard of Silversmoke?"

Sidney furrowed his brow. "What, that do-gooder highwayman up in Hampstead Heath? What about him?"

Luke stared at him.

Quick-witted as he was, it took Sidney a moment to catch Luke's meaning. Then his jaw dropped. "Oh my God. *You?*"

Luke nodded slowly.

Sidney gaped at him, speechless.

Luke hoped he wasn't making a mistake.

"No."

"Mm-hmm."

The viscount leaned forward in his seat, incredulous. *"The* Silversmoke?" he whispered.

"In the flesh," Luke murmured, fighting a grin.

"No, you're not!" Sidney fairly shouted, on the verge of hilarity.

His outburst attracted still more disapproving scowls from the graybeards.

"Keep your voice down!" Luke muttered, glancing over his shoulder at them. "I am. I swear it. Have been for years." He began laughing quietly as Sidney shook his head in disbelief.

For, of course, it really was absurd. But such was his life.

Elbow on the table, Sidney rested his cheek on his fingertips, gazed at Luke in astonishment for another heartbeat, then jumped off the stool and took a few steps toward the billiard table, striving to absorb the news.

After putting things together for a second, he spun around and stared at him. "So that's why you never come to Town!"

Luke nodded. "Too busy."

He marched back to him, amazed. "And the whole bumbling, eccentric routine?"

"Cover," Luke replied.

"I knew it! I knew there was something... But— Jove's balls, man!" Sidney let out a raucous laugh and suddenly punched him in the arm. "That's the maddest thing I ever heard!"

"Ow."

"Why in the hell would you take up a sword as a—"

"Shh! Because somebody murdered my parents when I was seventeen," Luke said in a low voice.

"Oh...right." Sidney hesitated. "Sorry. I forgot about that."

Luke waved off his apology. "That's how it all began. I swore revenge, and then, after a while, righting wrongs just became, I dunno...a habit. Like a hobby."

"A hobby!" Sidney echoed, shaking his head. He plumped back down into his stool and laughed. "And to think, I took up drawing."

"Drawing's a fine hobby," Luke mumbled with another wary glance over his shoulder to make sure that none of the graybeards were listening. They'd probably call the constable on him if they knew who was sitting in their club right now.

Sidney's humor had faded at the mention of Luke's parents. "I truly am sorry for your loss, Fountainhurst. It's nightmarish, what happened to them. I've heard the story."

Luke nodded his thanks.

"I can certainly see how an experience like that would make one feel compelled to do something about all the evil in the world. God knows there's never any shortage of it. But it's still mad, you know."

Luke sighed. "Yes, I know."

"Well, I'll be damned. Silversmoke!"

"You cannot tell a soul," Luke warned. "I move among a rough class of men in that capacity, and believe me, I've made enemies."

"I'd imagine so." Sidney gazed at the ceiling, then looked at Luke. "All those stories in the papers. Are they true?"

"For the most part."

"Huh. What can I say but bravo, Your Grace." Sidney began applauding slowly, grinning from ear to ear. "Well played. You missed your calling. Truly. You should've trod the planks at Drury Lane. You'd outshine Mr. Kean."

Luke smirked.

"Hold on—does Portia know?"

"No! And I don't want her finding out."

"Why not?"

"Sidney."

The viscount lifted his hands. "Don't worry, I'm not going to tell her. It's hardly my place. But she is a clever woman, neither blind nor stupid."

"Believe me, I know." Luke hesitated, uneasy to recall the way she'd stared at him last night, when Mr. Lynch had asked him to take off his spectacles. His fear of her catching on was the reason that Silversmoke had not sought another meeting with her.

Thank goodness they had only been together twice, both times under cover of darkness.

"I'm not actually sure yet how I'm going to handle the whole highwayman business once we're wed," Luke murmured. "I'll probably just quit the whole business."

"Seems a shame to give up such a fine *hobby*."

Luke snorted.

"Well... Now I'm finally starting to see the whole picture." Sidney leaned back in his chair. "It's not just the Duke of Fountainhurst trying to figure out what happened to Joel. Silversmoke is on the hunt."

Luke nodded.

"Very well. So how can I help?"

Luke gave him a grateful glance. "If you'd speak to your friend Marta, like you said, that would be helpful."

"Done. What else?"

Luke frowned at him. "Are you sure you really want to get involved in this? It could get messy."

"For Portia? Of course. And besides, honestly, my God, I have nothing meaningful to do. You must let me help, Fountainhurst."

"Very well. Given that you seem to know everyone in the ton, it might also be of use if you could do some discreet asking around about Axewood."

"Oh, this I can do," Sidney said, eagerly leaning closer. "What sort of information are you after?"

"I dunno... I want to gain a sense of what he's really like from those who know him well. His character. Personal history and so forth.

Whatever you can dig up."

"Very well, I understand." With a sly grin, Sidney sat back in his chair. "You've got yourself a spy in Society, Your Grace. How soon do you need the answers?"

"As soon as possible, I should think. Certainly within sixteen days," Luke added wryly.

Sidney laughed. "I'll be in touch the moment I hear anything." Then he raised his glass in a toast. "To the future Duchess of Fountainhurst."

"Hear, hear. I'll drink to that." Luke clinked glasses with him. "To my bride."

"What's she doing today, anyway?"

"Actually, I don't know. But I think I'll go and see her after this."

The viscount laughed at him in worldly amusement. "Stupid, bloody love."

"Aye," Luke said, but regretted it not a bit.

Portia, meanwhile, was standing on a footstool in her chamber, staring at her reflection in the cheval glass.

"Oh, Mrs. Bell," she said in awe, "you have truly outdone yourself."

"I am glad you are pleased, my lady." The famous dressmaker inspected her work on her client's slim figure.

Mama leaned against one of Portia's bedposts nearby, gazing at her in her wedding gown in teary-eyed silence.

The poor marchioness had barely just recovered from her crying bout this morning over her son; now she was choked up again over her youngest daughter.

"I can't believe my baby is getting married."

Mrs. Bell smiled at her. "There will be grandchildren to occupy you soon, Lady Liddicoat, God willing."

"Yes." Mama nodded. In truth, though, the glamorous lady was never too fond of being reminded of that, as young as she looked, she was indeed of a grandmother's age.

Portia smiled fondly at her in the reflection, then ran her hands down over herself, smoothing the cream lace she had chosen as part of the pastoral fantasy theme of her wedding.

It truly was perfect.

The slim-fitting gown had a scoop neck and short sleeves with a dainty ruffle above her elbows. A short train hung down from the footstool behind her.

Nothing too showy—it had to go with the wildflowers and simple ribbon garlands that would be hanging everywhere in the church—but elegant enough for a woman about to become a duchess.

This really is happening, Portia thought in wonder.

At last, after all the delays and the distance that had existed between them, her marriage to the Duke of Fountainhurst was beginning to feel real.

"Do you want to try the veil now, my lady?"

Portia smiled at Mrs. Bell and nodded eagerly.

As Mrs. Bell helped Portia put it on—the veil was also made of lace, and trimmed with narrow blue ribbon—a discreet knock sounded on the chamber door.

The maid standing by to assist went over to answer it, then Portia heard Stevens' voice.

"Is Lady Portia at home?" the butler asked. "His Grace of Fountainhurst is in the entrance hall."

"Ack!" Portia said, though she was delighted to hear that he had come to call.

"Oh God, don't let him see her!" Mama pushed away from the bedpost. "It's dreadful bad luck!"

"Relax, Mama, Lucas can't see me all the way from the entrance hall. But I'll bet he could hear me—Stevens, open the door wider. Don't worry, I'm decent."

"May I look, ma'am?" the butler asked Mama.

"Let him see," Portia said. After all, Stevens had known Portia and her siblings since they were little. She could still remember the excitement among all the servants when she had been arrayed for her debut in that ridiculous court dress that all debutantes were required to wear to make their curtsies to the Queen, complete with panniers and a giant white feather on her head.

This was much more reasonable, and altogether pretty, she decided.

Smiling, Mama gestured to the butler to have a peek. The maid pushed the door open wider, and Stevens poked his graying head in.

Portia turned around, and when the butler saw her, he beamed.

"Ah—!" He seemed speechless for a heartbeat. "Magnificent, my lady. Shall I tell His Grace so?"

"If you like. But maybe…" Suddenly, Portia raised her voice to an indecorous but happy shout: "Lucas?"

"My lady?" he called back in a curious tone, his deep voice resounding up the staircase from the entrance hall. "Is that you?"

"Don't come up!" she warned. "I just wanted to say hullo! I can't see you right now. I'm trying on my wedding gown!"

"Oh!" he exclaimed.

"She looks radiant!" Mama chimed in, amused to join the shouted conversation.

"I'm sure she does!" Lucas yelled back. "Shall I come back tomorrow, then?"

"Please do!" Portia could feel the blush warming her cheeks, especially with so many witnesses to their jolly exchange.

"Very well. I can't wait to see you!" he called.

"Likewise, Your Grace," she replied, laughing. "Now, go away before we get bad luck!"

She heard him laugh. "If I must."

Stevens chuckled, already on his way. "I will show him out."

Mrs. Bell smiled coyly at Portia. "Looks like someone's in love."

Indeed. Portia looked at her reflection again in her wedding dress, and when she thought of her soon-to-be husband, she couldn't stop smiling.

CHAPTER 18

Friday Night Answers

*H*alf Moon Street was far too fine for the likes of rough-and-tumble Silversmoke, but that night, after full darkness descended, Luke and Gower arrived on the doorstep of Joel's bachelor lodgings.

He knew the address, thanks to Joel's love letter to Portia. That was twice today the thing had come in handy.

While Sidney went to talk to Marta at that exclusive brothel, Wanderlust, Luke meant to interview Joel's servants.

Still unsure whether to believe Dog or Axewood, he hoped the missing gambler's staff might know something about Dog's "big bald man." If not, perhaps they could verify the uncle's claim about Joel falling in love with his mistress.

His valet, in particular, seemed the perfect person to ask about Clayton's dalliances with other women.

Gentlemen *did* tend to confide in their valets about such matters, much as gentlewomen entrusted their secrets to their lady's maids.

Leaving the horses tied up in the pitch-black alleyway next to the missing dandy's fashionable townhouse—a stuccoed affair two window bays wide—Luke knocked firmly on the door.

Gower stood silent beside him. His visits to the other gambling hells so far had yielded no results.

As they waited for someone to answer, Luke chuckled over his brief visit to Portia's house today. Their shouted conversation had been amusing, but he couldn't wait to be with her again.

God's truth, it was getting harder and harder to lie to her. He thought of the Janus statue he had seen on Axewood's desk this morning, and brushed off a twinge of conscience.

"Where the hell is everybody?" Gower muttered.

They exchanged an impatient glance, then Luke rapped again, harder this time.

"Coming!" a male voice called from inside. They heard heavy footfalls approaching, then the door creaked open, and the clean-shaved face of a husky young footman peered out over the candle in his hand.

He glanced suspiciously from Luke to Gower and back again. "Can I 'elp you gentl'men?"

"I'm here on behalf of Lady Portia Tennesley. I trust you know who I am," Luke said in a dark tone.

The footman's eyes grew round. "Mr. Silversmoke?" he whispered. His awestruck gaze traveled over Luke—dressed all in black, heavily armed, the upper part of his face hidden by his half mask.

"In the flesh." Luke hooked a thumb at Gower. "This is my associate. Mind if we come in and ask a few questions?"

"Of course!" The door swung open wider, and the strapping lad beckoned them in. "By all means, come in, sirs, please. You are most welcome. Lady Portia said you might want to come and talk to us. Cassius! Mrs. Berry! Come quick!" he hollered.

Luke stepped warily over the threshold into Joel's townhouse; Gower followed.

It gave Luke a very odd feeling to be visiting the home of the man who might well have married his fiancée—who might yet steal her away from him, if Axewood was lying.

The thought sat like a stone in Luke's stomach.

"I'm Denny," the footman said. He quickly shut the door behind them, then hurried over to the pier table, where he turned up the lamp.

As the dim light rose to full brightness, Luke looked around at the small but elegant entrance hall. Gower remained silent, on his guard, thumbs hooked into his gun belt.

"I'm happy to help any way I can, Mr. Silversmoke," Denny said earnestly.

Before Luke could answer, two other servants came running in answer to the lad's call of a moment ago.

A plump, aproned woman rushed out from the probable direction of the kitchens, and a slim, tidy man came springing down the stairs.

"What's the matter, Denny?" the latter asked.

"Has our master come back?" the woman cried.

Their faces promptly fell when they saw two rough-looking strangers standing there instead of their beloved Mr. Clayton.

Gower's smirk grew even more sardonic at their disappointment.

"It's Silversmoke, Mrs. Berry," Denny said in wonder, gesturing at him. "He wants to ask us questions!"

"Silversmoke! Bless me, is it really you?" Mrs. Berry seemed torn between amazement and a twinge of worry as to whether she ought to hide the silver.

"Never fear, ma'am, I'm here to help." Luke gave her one of his most dashing highwayman smiles, and she lit up.

The tidy little man had paused cautiously on the stairs, meanwhile, but now continued walking down. His eyes were shrewder than the others, his expression warier.

"Well, of course, we're glad to help, dears," Mrs. Berry said, apparently won over. "Would ye like to sit down? Don't just stand there! Make yourselves comfortable. Can I get you fellows anythin' to drink? Perhaps a bite to eat?"

Poor woman, it seemed she had not had anyone to mother-hen in over a year.

"That's very kind of you, ma'am, but we'd better stick to business," Luke said in amusement.

"Aw. Well, all right, then. But if you need anything a'tall, dears, you only have to ask. I'm Mrs. Berry, this is Cassius, Mr. Clayton's valet, and we're ever so grateful you're helpin' Lady Portia find our master."

She beckoned him down to her, lowering her voice as Luke bent toward her ear.

"You know," she said, "if you succeed in findin' him before the big wedding, the dear girl might not have to marry that dreadful duke. So? Any luck yet?"

Gower hid his amusement; Luke hid his wince.

"Making progress," he said vaguely, straightening up again.

"Would you like to have a look around?" the valet suggested. "We could show you the house, if you think that it would help."

Luke nodded, then all five of them traipsed through Joel's small but well-appointed townhouse.

"Tell me," Luke said as they went from room to room, "have you ever seen a big bald man lurking around here, or know anyone of that description connected to Mr. Clayton?"

The servants shook their heads.

"No, sir. Why do you ask?" Denny ventured.

"Just following leads," Luke said with a reassuring smile. He did not want to say too much yet. He didn't want to panic them.

The tour moved on to Joel's snug study, with its shelves of uncracked books, then they filed back out to the foyer and marched up the stairs.

Joel's bachelor residence was exactly the sort of dwelling that Luke would've imagined a spoiled dandy would keep. Everything was in the first stare of fashion. Heavy velvet curtains. Leather couches. Sleek Egyptian-style seats in the dining room.

Yet the place felt lonely. No doubt that came from the servants, who'd spent the past year fighting off despair as best they could, Luke supposed.

"His Lordship—Lord Axewood, I mean—will probably close the house down soon," Denny said.

"It's a wonder he's kept it open this long," Cassius agreed with a look of misery. "But the earl shares our hope that Mr. Clayton is alive and might still return."

"Do *you* think he might, Silversmoke?" Mrs. Berry asked, her bright eyes hopeful under her white house cap.

"It's possible," Luke said guardedly. But he dropped his gaze as he realized something.

It was damned cruel of Axewood not to tell these poor people about Joel's supposed elopement. Here they were, heartbroken over their young master's disappearance, when the cad was alive and well, living in France with his new wife.

Surely Axewood could have told them the truth in confidence so they needn't have suffered all this time.

Luke supposed Axewood was one of those callous aristocrats who didn't see his servants as real human beings, but mere functionaries, tools.

Well, hell, Luke thought, for that matter, why hadn't Joel told them himself, if he intended to elope?

Because maybe it's a lie. Luke frowned at his own churning thoughts.

"I'm afraid my next question is indelicate, but it's important." He turned to Cassius.

"Yes?" the valet asked. He eyed Luke mistrustfully. Cassius, for one, still seemed unsure about the wisdom of letting two brigands into the house.

"Do you know anything about Mr. Clayton having a mistress?"

Cassius' eyebrows lifted.

Mrs. Berry looked offended at the question; Denny cracked a grin.

The valet hesitated.

"Well?" Luke prompted.

Cassius shifted his weight. "Sir, the secrets of a gentleman's dressing room are sacrosanct."

"Do you want me to find him or not?" Luke retorted.

"Go on," Gower urged, staring at Cassius.

"Oh, very well," the valet mumbled, glancing at Mrs. Berry with an apologetic look, as though he wished she would cover her ears. "There were, um, several ladies the master was dallying with, as far as I know. Well, not *ladies*."

Mrs. Berry let out a small gasp; Denny blushed.

"Were you aware of Mr. Clayton forming a particular attachment to any one of these women?" Luke asked.

"No, not at all."

"Did he ever mention someone named Antonia?"

Brow furrowed, Cassius shook his head. "Not that I recall. The only one for whom he had any real feelings was Lady Portia, in his fashion. He meant to marry her in time. Only, he wasn't ready yet."

"I see," Luke murmured, hiding his flinch.

Gower sent him a rueful glance, but Luke was feeling increasingly confused.

Though he had held Joel's defiant letter about Antonia in his hands and read it with his own two eyes, he was still beginning to doubt Axewood's account.

"How did he get along with his uncle?"

"Lord Axewood?" Cassius asked in surprise.

All three servants hesitated, glancing at one other. They looked nervous.

No wonder. Axewood was the one paying their salaries.

"There was sometimes tension between them," Mrs. Berry said cautiously.

"But all families fight," Cassius said.

Denny kept his mouth shut.

"What did they fight about?" Luke asked.

Silence.

"Gambling? Women?"

"Well…" Cassius scratched his temple.

"Not really…" the housekeeper began.

While the other two stalled, Luke sent the footman a dark glance. "Denny?"

The young man gulped, then blurted out, "Mostly it was money, sir."

Luke stared at him. "You don't say. Did Clayton gamble his way into a bit of debt, then?"

"Oh no, sir. 'Twas the other way 'round," Denny said, hunching his shoulders. "His Lordship wanted to borrow some money from our master. Again."

"I see." Luke hid his shock. "And did Mr. Clayton lend it to him?"

"I'm sure he did—they're family," Cassius said, frowning at Denny. "Plenty of people borrowed money from Mr. Clayton. He was always happy to help a friend."

"Generous to a fault," Mrs. Berry agreed, nodding.

Luke looked at the valet. "Do you have any IOUs he might've collected from these friends of his?"

Cassius lifted his eyebrows. "Surely you don't think one of the young gentlemen could've…"

Luke pinned him with a hawklike stare. "It would help to know who owed him money."

Denny nudged the valet.

"Very well," Cassius said. "He kept them in a locked drawer with the good silver in the dining room. This way."

They followed Cassius into the dining room, where Gower pointed to the painting of a smiling young lad above the mantel. "Is that him?"

"Oh yes, sir." Mrs. Berry beamed. "He was just ten there. Wasn't he a handsome little tyke?"

Gower scoffed at any man who'd hang his own portrait in such a place of honor. Mrs. Berry frowned. Denny stepped out of the way, while Cassius took out a key and unlocked the drawer where the silver was stored. The valet lifted up the box of silverware, reached under it, and took out an envelope.

Luke, however, was staring at the vase of red flowers adorning the dining room table.

He forgot all about the IOUs as Dog's words from the gambling hell went rushing through his mind.

The luckless gambler had described the dark, empty street down which the unmarked coach had fled after Joel had been thrown into it.

"All that was left of him was the red flower he wore in his boutonniere."

Dog hadn't known what kind of flower it was.

Luke pointed at the vase. "What's this?"

"The carnations?" Mrs. Berry seemed startled at the question, but Gower glanced at Luke, recognizing that tone of voice that meant he was onto something. "Oh, we always keep a vase of those around the house, sir, just in case he comes home," she said sadly. "That was Mr. Clayton's favorite flower."

"And his lucky charm," Denny added. "He always made us keep them on hand so he'd have one to wear to his card games."

"I see," Luke murmured, another detail tugging at his memory.

He reached into his vest and pulled out the wager card he had received from Junius Foy. As he skimmed the list of outlandish nicknames for the players who would be participating in the gambling tournament at the next Carnevale, his hunch grew stronger. *I know there was something here...*

What was it? *The Cardiff Comet, Johnny Phoenix, The Spaniard, Sir Doom...* No, no.

There. His gaze homed in on an alias halfway down the list.

And there it was.

The Red Carnation.

Gower glanced curiously at him.

Luke stared at the odds by that name. The Red Carnation was the best-ranked player in the whole bloody tournament. He stared into space for a moment, as the pieces finally started sliding into place. *Well, I'll be damned.*

Found you.

"Everything all right, sir?" Denny was watching him with a worried look when Luke blinked back to awareness, his pulse still thumping.

"Oh yes," he said absently. "I think we've got all we need now."

"Don't you want to see the IOUs?" Cassius held up the envelope.

"That won't be necessary. Thank you all. You've been most helpful." Luke headed for the door. He needed to think.

Gower arched a brow and trailed him.

"Good luck, sirs." Denny hurried after them to let them out. "Would you mind letting us know if you learn anything?"

"Yes, of course." Luke said a hasty goodnight, then Gower followed him outside.

"I take it you've figured it out?" the Yorkshireman said.

As soon as the door had closed behind them, Luke showed Gower the nickname on the betting card. "That's him. Right there. It's got to be."

Gower peered at the list of names by the light of the lanterns flanking the door.

Luke tapped the name on the card. "It all fits. Damn it, Axewood lied to me!"

Gower glanced at him in surprise, then they began striding down the dark side alley where they'd tied up the horses.

Seething with anger, Luke wrenched off his mask. "That son of a bitch stood there and lied to my face. He's the one behind *all* of this, I warrant."

"How do you figure? If Joel really is the Red Carnation, maybe his uncle doesn't know."

"He knows," Luke said. "I'm not sure what the hell is going on, but trust me, he knows. I can feel it in my bones."

Gower frowned at him. "So you're tellin' me you really think the Earl of Axewood kidnapped his own damned nephew?"

"Yes, Gower, that's exactly what I think."

"All right," he said, resting a hand on his pistol. "And why would His Lordship do such a thing?"

"You heard what the servants said! They argued sometimes."

Gower shrugged. "So does everyone."

"Axewood pressured Joel to lend him money."

"So? Servants said he gave it to him, end of story."

Luke scowled at Gower's playing the devil's advocate, as usual. "Well, maybe it happened more than once."

"Why would it? You said Axewood's rich as Croesus."

"Well, he certainly wants to appear so!" Luke searched his mind for possibilities. "Maybe he's not as wealthy as he looks… Maybe something went wrong with one of these investment deals of his. Sidney told me his father nearly lost five thousand last year in a canal scheme gone wrong. Last year was also when Joel disappeared. Timing fits. And Axewood's arrogant—the type who'd do whatever it takes to save face."

Gower frowned. "All right. But couldn't Joel have done this of his own free will?"

"What, kidnapped himself?" Luke retorted.

"Dog could be lyin'. The uncle at least showed you some possible proof in the form of that letter. Think about it," Gower said with a speculative stare. "Maybe seein' that the high world would never accept the Creole girl, he figured to join her in the low world, instead. So he decided to become this underworld champion gambler called the Red Carnation."

"Throw himself into his addiction?"

"Right."

"All right, that's possible," Luke said. "But for all we know, Axewood might've forced Joel to write that letter at gunpoint—or the big bald man."

"Huh," Gower said.

They continued walking more slowly over the uneven cobblestones. The horses turned their heads and pricked up their ears, waiting for them.

Luke hooked his thumbs into his gun belt. He snorted. "And I suppose Axewood leaving Town just days ahead of this Carnevale coming up next week is just one big coincidence?"

Gower frowned at him.

"But maybe he really did have business to take care of at one of his estates," Luke said in a cynical tone. "Because how could some top-lofty lord like the Earl of Axewood know about an underworld gathering of thieves and mercenaries, right?"

"Except...I know a duke who plays a highwayman," Gower said, "and is rather adept at moving about in the low world."

"Thus the dilemma," Luke said. "Don't you see? This morning, Axewood told me—well, Lucas—the perfect sort of cock-and-bull tale to make me go away and stop asking questions. One that would make even Portia wash her hands of his nephew. Why would he let me read so personal a letter unless it was just a prop? I knew that was strange. Meanwhile, Dog's story just got more credible, as far as I'm concerned." Luke rested his hand on Orion's soft muzzle. "Dog told us about the red flower, and that just turned out to be real. I'm afraid we must now assume he was probably telling the truth about the rest of it, as well."

"So, boil it down for me," Gower said. "What's your theory?"

"Whoever kidnapped Joel has forced him into *this*." Luke lifted the wager card. "It's like we said from the start. They found a way to harness his talents, poor bastard. He didn't elope with anyone. Only now, I don't think it was just random criminals behind it. Mad as it sounds, I'm betting it's the earl. Oh my God—Axewood tried to marry Portia! Remember? She told me."

Luke turned away, stunned as old information struck him anew. His heart pounded with sickening force at what her fate could have been. If Axewood turned out to be guilty of these things, it meant that Portia could've wound up married to a monster.

When Luke turned back to Gower, he found the Yorkshireman squinting at him again. "What is it?" he asked.

"It don't add up," Gower said.

"What doesn't? What do you mean?" Luke asked.

The old fighter shook his head, his hands on his hips, his expression darkening by the second. "I thought you told me Axewood was a friend o' your father's."

Luke stared back at him, the blood draining from his face.

A knot promptly formed in the pit of his stomach as the implications of that began to emerge. He shook his head dazedly. "You're right, Gower. There's no way they could have been friends. My father would have seen right through him. If anything"—he looked at his mentor in alarm—"they would have been enemies."

And that changed everything.

Sidney, meanwhile, wove through the Friday night crowd at Wanderlust, searching for Marta.

Tucked away at the end of a quiet lane north of Piccadilly, the place did not look like a brothel from the outside.

But for the stately gilt sign above the entrance—and the exotic music that spilled out discreetly whenever the door opened—it could have easily been mistaken for a small, expensive hotel or a fashionable house.

Inside, however, it offered an endless variety of sensory delights. Why, a man could take the whole Grand Tour without ever having to leave the West End. Beautiful women of every shape, color, and creed waited to oblige the wealthy gentlemen, and each successive chamber was decorated to simulate different cultural styles.

Sidney searched them all. His charming Jamaican friend wasn't in the Roman dining room, with its green marble columns, alabaster statues in niches, and long banqueting table fit for a Caesar.

Nor did he find her in the Egyptian drawing room, dominated by its giant, seated statue of Ramses. Here, painted hieroglyphs adorned the faux-stone walls, and dog-headed Anubis figures held up brass torchieres.

At the back of the house, Sidney glanced into his favorite room: the conservatory. The whimsical glasshouse had been turned into a lush South American jungle with vines and palm trees, burgeoning orchids, and an indoor waterfall that ran into a fountain where the ladies liked to frolic naked.

No Marta. Still, he lingered there for another mischievous moment, enjoying the sights before moving on again.

He had already lost Carvel somewhere along the way. The last he'd seen the major, Peter had ducked through the sumptuous swaths of tentlike curtains draping the Moorish parlor.

There, he had been pushed down onto one of the low red couches by a belly dancer, who proceeded to entrance him with her gyrations.

Good, Sidney thought as a smile quirked his lips. His friend was far too strict and serious most of the time, strung as tight as a bow, with all his military discipline. Sidney couldn't even imagine trying to live up to Pete's standards for one day. The mere thought was exhausting.

Making his way up the staircase, Sidney greeted half of White's Club, until, at last, he found his lovely, mocha-skinned friend in the Chinese music room, where Marta was in the middle of displaying her skill at the pianoforte.

The Oriental style of decor was all the rage these days, and the music room bore all the usual motifs. Hand-painted wallpaper wrapped the room in peacocks and pagodas, with woven bamboo furniture to sit on and dragon lanterns flying overhead. A jolly Buddha statue perched atop the pianoforte, where Marta's nimble fingers raced over the keys.

Her spine ramrod straight, the ebony-haired beauty was playing a lively and whimsical sonata.

A few of the other girls twirled and danced with their companions for the night, dressed as fine as the ladies in any London ballroom, only, laughing louder and showing considerably more skin.

Sidney leaned against the doorframe and admired Marta's talent.

After all, gentlemen of means like the clientele here expected the women on whom they lavished their funds to be able to entertain them, and not just in bed.

At last, she played the final, tinkling trill of her sonata, and applause filled the air. Sidney grinned, clapping loudest of all.

Marta rose in a rustle of silk from the piano bench and gave the room an elegant curtsy.

"Thank you, ladies and gentlemen," she said in the most proper accent, far from her adorable Jamaican patois, which Sidney had insisted on learning—at least a few simple phrases. "I am glad you enjoyed it. The honor was mine," she told her audience.

After another quick, demure bow, Marta stepped aside for the next girl's turn.

Sidney pushed away from the wall and sauntered toward her, still applauding loudly. "Brava! What talent!"

Marta saw him coming, and lit up with a smile as sunny as the Caribbean. "Lord Sidney!"

"You just keep getting better every time I hear you, I swear."

"Pshaw!" She pressed her hand modestly to her heart, her velvety brown eyes twinkling. "I am honored by your praise, my lord."

He bent down and kissed her on the cheek. "Wah gwan, girl? How yuh stay?"

She laughed in delight at his attempt to speak her language. "Everyt'ing is everyt'ing! You gud?"

"Everyt'ing nice," he replied, and they both laughed for a moment in mutual affection. Then Sidney took her by the elbow. "I need to speak to you, my darling."

"Good Lord, you sound serious! That's a first."

"It *is* serious, I'm afraid."

Marta read his eyes with a worried glance, then nodded and led him out onto a small balcony overlooking the garden.

There, Sidney quickly explained the situation.

Marta heard him out, nodding now and then.

"Well?" he asked at length. "What do you think?"

"Antonia?" Brow furrowed, Marta shook her head. "Well, of course, I remember Joel Clayton. And yes, there are a few of us girls from the West Indies who've taken up the life here in London. Certainly, I'd know her. We'd move in the same circles. But I'm sorry, my lord, I've never heard of anyone called Antonia."

"Are you sure?"

"Believe me," she said with a cynical smile, "if one of our own had eloped with a future earl, the entire demimonde would know. But I've not heard even a single rumor about this." Marta shrugged. "You want my opinion? It's poppycock, my dear. This Antonia doesn't exist."

❖

Far away, at that same moment, deep in the bowels of Darpley Castle, Joel lay on his bug-ridden cot in his dungeon cell, his arms folded under his head. His armpits stank, his clothes were filthy, and the disgusting beard that had sprouted from his jaw itched, but the erstwhile leading dandy of the ton no longer gave a damn.

Watching the dim flicker from the lantern play over the craggy stone ceiling above him, he wondered where he'd be, what he would have been doing on this fine Friday night at the height of the Season if his uncle hadn't ruined his life.

The sun had set about an hour ago, so it must be, what, a little after ten? In that case, he'd still be having drinks with his friends before heading out in a good-looking pack together to some ball, soiree, or fashionable rout in the West End, toying with the ladies.

The lads are really missing out, he thought with a smirk.

At least his foot was doing somewhat better. He could go longer spells between doses of laudanum now, and, by some miracle, his untreated injury had not grown infected in this dank, dismal hellhole.

Nevertheless, Joel had not changed his mind about his fate. He was still resolved to die at the next Carnevale.

Rucker had told him it would be next week, so Joel supposed he ought to get his affairs in order.

Ah well. It wouldn't be pleasant, but it would be over soon enough. Anything was better than the future that stretched out ahead of him living as his uncle's slave.

The golden goose, he thought bitterly.

Then his mind drifted back to the argument that had put him here in the first place.

"Of course you will help me cover my losses, nephew," Axewood had said on that fateful night last April. "If you don't, the whole family will be disgraced. Is that what you want?"

"Uncle, you will not get another farthing out of me," Joel breezily replied, washing down his haughty declaration with a swig of the expensive champagne that he liked. "You still owe me a thousand quid from last time, remember? You called it a loan, but I very much doubt I will ever see that money again."

For a moment, Joel was amused at the look of shock stamped across the earl's rugged face.

His uncle's posture stiffened. "That thousand took you, what, ten minutes to win?"

"Less than five, actually. But that is not the point."

Unfortunately, Joel had failed to notice the deadly malice that had sparked to life in Uncle Axewood's dark eyes at his effrontery.

Fool. He shook his head at his own blind arrogance, in hindsight.

He should've realized it was dangerous to taunt so vain a man when his back was up against the wall. But, damn it, he was sick of bailing out a grown man who ought to have known better!

"Surely you will reconsider, nephew," Axewood had said, his voice sounding so constricted that he could barely force the words out. "You are my heir. We are flesh and blood, and I am facing ruin."

"Again? And whose fault is that? Sorry, Uncle, but this is not my problem. You should not have started spending your investors' blunt until you had a sense of how the project would go."

"It is done! What do you expect me to do?" Axewood cried.

Joel shrugged. "Learn to live within your means, like anybody else."

"We are not just anyone in this family," the earl said coldly. "Perhaps you have forgotten that. We have standards to keep."

Joel had waved this off. "Ah, you're as bad as the Regent, spending other people's money. I am sorry, Uncle. You got yourself into this, and you'll have to get yourself out, too. You always seem to land on your feet. For my part, I'm done."

"I see." Axewood tilted his head in a certain, conclusive way that Joel now recognized in hindsight as the moment that his fate had been sealed.

He remembered it clearly, how the chandelier's light had danced on the gray hairs scattered among the earl's dark, short-cropped waves.

Even more strongly he recalled his uncle's next words. "So be it. But if that's how you feel, then perhaps you are not worthy of my title."

At the time, Joel had ignored the frisson of uneasiness that ran down his spine at his uncle's ominous tone.

Instead, the half-bottle of champagne he had already drunk must've been the reason he laughed at the insult. "Well, you have no other, so I'm afraid you're stuck with me, old man."

The earl had stared at him. "Am I?"

Four nights later, Joel had been abducted.

He had long since come to understand that it was not simply his refusing his uncle the loan that had brought this retribution; it was the manner in which he had done it.

To be fair, he had not realized his uncle would have been facing the gallows for fraud and embezzlement without a fast infusion of funds to help him cover his tracks and pay back his highborn investors.

At that moment, Joel heard an ominous noise outside. He glanced toward the window in surprise. It was usually so quiet at the castle that any sort of activity was easy to detect.

The sound grew louder, coming from the direction of the long drive that snaked up through the woods. A rumble and a rhythmic pounding...

His stomach tightened with dread as he sat up and listened intently.

Oh, he knew that sound. His heart began to pound with fear.

It was the cavalcade of the earl's traveling chariot, drawn by its usual team of six horses, clattering up the hill toward the castle. Joel swallowed hard.

He's early.

Joel sat very still in the gloom, wondering with his heart in his throat what could've brought the bastard all this way from Town days ahead of the Carnevale.

Then he frowned, for the clamor of approaching hoofbeats sounded too loud for just his uncle's six horses. Reaching for his crutch, Joel heaved himself up in a hurry to see who had come. Limping over to the window, he peered through the bars, trying to view the drive as best he could.

A starry summer sky unfurled above the wooded hills, but there, suddenly, through a gap in the trees—just for a moment—the moonlight showed him half a dozen riders flashing by, following the coach.

Who the hell is that? Joel wondered as they all thundered on toward the castle.

They had already disappeared from view, but their presence filled him with foreboding. His heart thumped as he stared on into the darkness, listening for all he was worth.

Something's going on.

"You're home early, milord," Rucker said as he got the carriage door for Axewood.

Rucker had walked out to greet him carrying a torch, and had lit both braziers alongside the castle's entrance to illuminate the courtyard. By the flickering light of the flames, Axewood saw him cast an uneasy glance around at the extra henchman he'd brought along.

"Weren't expecting you back yet for another couple o' days."

"No." Axewood stepped down from the carriage and gave his trusty bodyguard a grim look. "We have a situation, Rucker. That's why I stopped to hire these lads on my way. Gentlemen," he said to the six hard-eyed mercenaries who had just swung down off their horses, "this is John Rucker, my head of security.

"Rucker, let them see to their horses, then I want them posted on the battlements, keeping watch from the towers, and standing sentry over the castle grounds. They will be here, on duty, until we leave for our, ah, engagement."

Rucker's expression darkened at the news. Axewood sent him a communicative glance; he'd explain the nature of the threat soon.

"Yes, sir," the giant said. "I'll show them to their places while you settle in. You lot, follow me." He beckoned to the hirelings to bring their horses, then led the line of them back toward the stables.

Axewood had told the men they would have to look after their own mounts, for he kept only a small staff at the castle: two grooms, a housekeeper, a footman, and homely maid, all of whom were related in some way to Rucker.

While the mercenaries walked their weary mounts toward the stables, Axewood marched into the castle, loosening his cravat. It had been a long, grueling day of travel, and he was worn out from the tension of knowing he had a ruthless killer on his trail.

Finally, here, he could relax.

Well, he could've arrived hours ago, but he had stopped at an unsavory pub he knew along the way to engage the services of those lowlifes. Also, he had taken a circuitous route to make sure he hadn't been followed from Town.

Admittedly, the news that Silversmoke was on his trail had him spooked.

Indeed, he was tempted to take Esme under his exclusive protection, considering the woman might well have saved his life with her warning.

But no matter. He was taking every precaution to neutralize the threat. And doing his best not to choke on the irony of finding himself hunted by the very man he'd cheered all those years ago, when he'd first heard the news that Silversmoke had wiped out the MacAbe gang.

Typical tribal warfare between rival gangs, he'd assumed. Hell, he saw that sort of thing all the time between criminal bands at Carnevale.

Some of those fellows could not cross paths without falling upon one another in snarling packs, trying to tear each other apart on sight like rabid dogs.

It was most amusing.

Axewood figured it had been just the same with Silversmoke and the late, great MacAbes.

As for him, why, he'd toasted the victor with the finest champagne when he'd heard the news, laughing up his sleeve. Axewood had lifted a glass to the masked outlaw, whoever he was, and thanked this Silversmoke for the great favor he had unwittingly done him.

By wiping out the last human beings on Earth who ever could have tied him to the Fountainhurst deaths, Silversmoke had neatly covered Axewood's tracks for him.

Axewood had toasted Silversmoke's health and slept like a baby ever since.

But never had he dreamed that he himself might one day become the highwayman's next target. The mere thought of it put him in need of a drink.

Stepping into the entrance hall of the castle, Axewood found his staff scrambling over his unannounced arrival. The gawky young footman was lugging his traveling trunks up the stairs, the maid was hurrying around lighting candles ahead of him, while the portly, gray-haired housekeeper rushed out, winded, to ask His Lordship what he'd like to eat.

"Oh, nothing for me at this hour," he said. "I dined at a tavern on the way. Draw me a bath, though. And make the water good and hot, the way I like it."

His muscles were aching after a whole day of clattering along over the roads, which grew steadily bumpier the farther one drove away from Town.

"Here." Axewood turned, and the housekeeper bustled over to help him with his coat. "Oh," he added, as she slipped it off his shoulders, "we'll have six more mouths to feed for breakfast in the morning and every meal thereafter for the next few days. I brought some extra" —he hesitated— "workers."

The housekeeper's eyes widened at this information. But she asked no questions, merely nodded. "Yes, milord."

Axewood dismissed her, then continued on his way. While the housekeeper fled to the kitchens to begin heating water for his bath, he marched up the staircase, eager to make himself more comfortable.

When he reached his chamber, unfortunately, the maid was still freshening his bed, so he threw his tailcoat on the chair and crossed to pour himself a large draught of brandy from his liquor cabinet.

"Let me know when the bath is ready," he ordered the girl.

She curtsied, and he left, stalking through the dim medieval rooms with their faded tapestries and iron chandeliers. He went into the nearest corner tower and climbed to the top of the spiraling steps, where he then walked out onto the breezy ramparts to wait for Rucker.

Either Rucker or his bath—whichever was ready first.

Far from civilization in his ancestors' moldering castle, Axewood went over to the battlements and did his best to soothe his frazzled nerves with a deep breath of the cool night air.

True, the news about Silversmoke had him feeling slightly paranoid, but he trusted that, by now, he had matters well in hand.

Untying his cravat the rest of the way, he unbuttoned the top of his shirt, then leaned his elbows atop the weathered stone of one of the crenelated battlements.

He stretched his back a little as he leaned against the stone wall in front of him. Gazing at the dark familiar landscape, he finally began to unwind. The night was calm, and he fingered the pleasantly rough surface of the cool stone wall as he drank.

Somewhere in the depths of the castle, he supposed his nephew must be eating his heart out with curiosity.

Too bad. Axewood had no intention of letting Joel know that a rescue effort was apparently underway. A real one, this time. Not another charade, like the one he'd had his useful cronies inside the Bow Street offices carry out, when his nephew had first gone "missing" over a year ago.

With that, Axewood made a mental note to warn the entire staff not to mention the mercenaries to the prisoner. Not that the other servants had much contact with him, and Rucker could always be trusted.

Still, Joel was clever enough to figure out what their presence here signified. There was no need for anyone to go giving the boy false hope.

At last, Axewood let out a sigh as the soothing effects of the brandy seeped into his bones. Safe atop his ancient fortress, he looked up at the moon, marveled at the likeness of a face in its shadows, then shrugged it off. Instead, he stared out into the serene darkness, where the indigo sky met the black trees.

Suddenly, a bat rocketed out of the darkness and flew by with a screech just a few feet overhead. Axewood ducked with a startled curse, but the creature was gone again as quickly as it had appeared, chasing moths for its supper.

"Bloody hell," he muttered, then shook his head and finished his drink in a single gulp.

It was about then that Rucker came out, showing two of the men to their stations atop opposite towers. He stayed with each one for a moment, pointing here and there as he explained features of the landscape, making sure that each understood they were to monitor a full one-hundred-and-eighty-degree view.

At last, Rucker headed for Axewood, and as he stomped toward him, the earl couldn't help thinking that his trusty brute looked like he belonged to this castle. Some sort of modern-day medieval warrior.

Ugly as hell, of course, but staunchly loyal to his lord.

Rucker had been devoted to him for the past two decades, after Axewood, in a rare moment of pity, had used his influence to save the poor devil's life.

Rucker had been an aimless soul, headed for a life of hard labor in a penal colony in New South Wales. Caught and jailed as part of a housebreaking team in London, in truth, he had only been the lookout.

It was his cannier mates who had actually burgled the houses, but in court, the knaves had managed to pin much of the blame on him.

The jury was all too happy to believe Rucker had been the main culprit because of his fierce looks.

Axewood had only heard about the case by chance. He wasn't sure why he'd felt sorry for the big lug, but he'd known for certain that a man like that could be very useful, so he'd pulled a few strings.

The next thing he knew, he had himself a bodyguard, while the prison ship headed for Australia was missing one passenger.

Axewood had never regretted taking the giant under his wing. One glare from Rucker could back off any number of common thieves. Best of all, he did whatever Axewood said.

"So what are we dealing with, sir?" Rucker hitched up his belt as he approached, his rough-hewn face stamped with grim resolve.

Axewood pushed away from the battlements, massaging his forehead with his fingertips for a moment. "Does the name Silversmoke ring any bells?" he asked dryly.

"Silversmoke?" Rucker furrowed his brow, then shock bloomed across his granite countenance. "Surely you don't mean…"

"Oh, but I do. The selfsame blackguard who wiped out our old friends, the MacAbes. It seems someone's hired him to locate my nephew."

Rucker cursed. "Who would do such a thing?"

"Lady Portia Tennesley, that's who." Axewood shrugged. "At least, that is my surmise. I thought about it the whole way here, and, impossible as it sounds, it's the only damned thing that makes any sense."

"Blind me," Rucker mumbled.

"Well, I have it on good information that the lady is about to marry a man she does not love," Axewood said, recalling his odd meeting with the eccentric duke. "I can only conclude she must've hired the highwayman as a last-ditch effort to escape her match and be reunited with her beau before her wedding day."

Rucker pondered this with a brooding frown. "We'd better hope to hell he doesn't find him."

"That's why I brought the extra men." Axewood paused. "How is he, by the way? Our golden goose?"

Rucker pursed his lips. "Not good, sir, frankly."

"What, is the foot infected? He's lucky I didn't cut it off."

"It's not so much his injury that pains him, from what I can tell." Rucker hesitated. "Looks to me like he's close to giving up."

"Is that right?" Axewood stared at him, brushing off a sickening memory of the crunching sound Joel's bones had made when he'd brought the wooden mallet down on them.

He was a little shocked, himself, that he had done that.

Very well; he could admit he had lost his temper with the lad over his stunt at the last Carnevale, and that was regrettable. But at least now, he would never have to worry about the cheeky little bastard trying to escape again.

"It's his spirit that's broken, sir, not just the bones."

"Eh, he's a weakling," Axewood grumbled, and looked away, warding off the half-forgotten image of his nephew as a rambunctious little boy running through the castle. "We may need to hide the evidence soon, Rucker, if you take my meaning," he said quietly.

His bodyguard frowned. "Kill your nephew?"

Axewood nodded. "'Tis unfortunate, but if this Silversmoke starts closing in... Well, I'm not going down for this."

"Understood." Hands on hips, Rucker held him in a steady gaze. "Still, there's no need to do anything hasty, sir."

"I suppose the boy is valuable," Axewood admitted. "But, soon, we may have no choice. Better that we should get rid of Joel after the Carnevale and hide the body than risk the highwayman rescuing him and setting him free to tell the world what we've done. I don't care to hang. Do you?"

Rucker frowned. "No, sir. How do you want to handle it, then? The threat from Silversmoke, I mean."

"Well, I brought these other men along for extra eyes and ears—and guns—if he should find us over the next few days. Which I very much doubt, but better safe than sorry. Once we reach the Carnevale, I intend to hire one of the assassins there to eliminate Silversmoke for me. It's the simplest solution."

Rucker frowned. "You think you'll be able to find someone willing to go after the likes of Silversmoke, sir?"

"For a price, why not?" Axewood retorted, bristling. He turned back toward the battlements and gazed cynically into the darkness, hands on hips. "Don't worry, Rucker. After all, it worked last time, didn't it?"

"Not for the MacAbes," Rucker said under his breath.

Axewood looked at him and laughed.

CHAPTER 19

Bullseye

*O*n Saturday morning, Portia decided to amuse herself by pulling out her old archery set. It was better than sitting around feeling restless and impatient to see her fiancé again.

As she'd told him on their picnic, it was not a hobby she often practiced in Town, but today, the morning was so fresh and fine that any excuse to spend time outdoors would have sufficed.

Better still, the large, sculpted garden behind her parents' house would have shade until eleven. After all, not even an experienced archer like herself could shoot well with the sun glaring in her eyes, no matter how excellent her eyesight.

So, at about ten a.m., Portia dragged out a hay-stuffed target and set it up against the wooden privacy fence along the back wall of the garden, then took out her bow and white leather quiver of arrows.

It had been ages since she'd practiced. She wondered if she would still be any good. Of course, even if she botched it, there was no one to see. The fashionable folk of Moonlight Square would only just be rising about now.

Glancing around, she concluded they were truly missing out on a lush June morning; the sky was cerulean, the grass glossy emerald. Mama's flower borders were burgeoning, especially the peach-colored climbing roses that grew up the fence.

The only sound was the buzzing of the bees flying around the jasmine bush; its perfume sweetened the air as she pulled the shooting glove onto her right hand to protect her fingers.

The bees made her think of her darling Bug Boy, and she smiled. He had promised to call today. She could barely wait. She hadn't seen him since the ball Thursday night, except for yesterday's shouted conversation while she'd been trying on her wedding dress.

Hefting the familiar weight of her bow in one hand, Portia selected an arrow and drew it from the quiver. It slid out with a slight, eager hiss.

Pacing off her distance, the skirts of her walking gown swirling against her legs, she turned and eyed up her target, stepped into ready stance, and planted her feet firmly on the wet grass.

As she started to pull up into the anchor position, she noticed how very tight her shoulders were. She rolled her neck a few times and shrugged to loosen up the muscles. Then she nocked the arrow and lifted her bow, elbow cocked high—then higher still.

Balance the draw, she reminded herself. *Use your back muscles, not your biceps.*

Blazes, I'm out of practice.

Minding her form, she pulled the bowstring back until her fingers grazed the corner of her mouth; she peered over the sights to her target, remembered not to favor the right like she tended to do, and released.

Well! Her lips crooked. It was not the best shot ever fired on England's green isle, but it had felt bloody good.

She bent down to take another arrow from her quiver on the grass and repeated the ritual a dozen times, gradually starting to regain her skills, and feeling confident to try a few different angles.

From time to time, she marched back to the target, pulled out her arrows, and then went and fired another volley.

Soon enough, the skill she'd worked years to develop came creeping back to her, no matter how long it had been. Her left hand's grip on the sleek, polished wood of the bow was secure; her fingers remembered how to curl around the string and manage the tension. She breathed in the way that helped to ground her, and her sharp eyes sized up angles and distances.

Her shots grew more accurate; it was all about balance and spatial relations, but mostly, it was fun. After a while, she played the old games with herself, walking here and there about the garden, then turning suddenly and firing in a trice, as though a foe were sneaking up on her. Then it happened: a bullseye.

"Yes!" She grinned and punched the air with her gloved fist.

But when sudden applause sounded behind her, she spun around, startled, only to gasp with delight.

"Lucas!"

"Brava, my lady!" Her darling duke was standing at the top of the few short stairs below the French doors that led up to the morning room. He wore an astonished grin, and had handed off the bouquet he'd brought her to the butler so he could clap. "Don't shoot!" he added, laughing as he held up his hands. "I am unarmed!"

Portia burst out laughing self-consciously, but could not hide her joy at the sight of him.

Lucas swiped the flowers back from Stevens. "I'll take those."

"Lady Portia: the Duke of Fountainhurst," the butler intoned.

"So I see," Portia said. "Thank you, Stevens, you may go. Don't worry—we'll be on our best behavior."

"I can't stay long anyway," Lucas said as he walked down the three steps to the grass. "My sister and her family will be arriving at Gracewell later this afternoon. They're coming a day early for tomorrow's festivities and spending the night at my estate. I've got to be there to greet them. I'm leaving this morning to make sure everything is in order before they arrive. But I couldn't leave Town without seeing you first, of course. I came to say goodbye."

"What a good fiancé you are." Portia chuckled warmly. She set her bow down, then straightened up, admiring her tall, strapping beau's impressive physique as he marched toward her, flowers in hand.

She still couldn't get over how graceful he'd been when they'd danced. Or how beautiful he was without his glasses.

When Lucas stopped in front of her, she tilted her head back to smile at him, gazing fondly into his green eyes behind those funny little spectacles.

"For you." Earnestly, he offered the bouquet, and hang the bees, apparently. Why, there were even roses in there—an elegant posy of fragrant white roses and pink, starlike astrantia.

Portia took them, smelled them, then glanced at him in wonder. "They're beautiful. You're so thoughtful, Lucas."

"I missed you," he said softly.

Diamonds could not have pleased her more than that one simple sentence. She beamed. "I missed you, too."

Lowering the flowers, she demurely offered her cheek.

He leaned down and kissed it, lingering close to her for an added heartbeat. Portia savored the warmth of his breath on her skin.

Her pulse quickened at his nearness. He must have been feeling the attraction as well, for when he pulled back, a smolder had leaped to life in the depths of his eyes.

Gentleman that he was, though, he stepped back and, instead of ravishing her, alas, cast about for a safer topic to distract them. "Ahem, I say…" He gestured at the target bristling with arrows. "I had no idea you were so deadly."

"I warned you," Portia said serenely.

"These were not idle boasts, I see." He grinned. "You're rather terrifying, actually."

She shrugged, pleased with his praise. "I enjoy it. Don't worry, Your Grace"—she captured a button on his coat—"I won't hurt you."

"I daresay."

She offered him her bow. "Would you care to give it a try?"

"Me? Egads, no! I wouldn't want to embarrass m'self after your display of prowess. You'd unman me."

"Nonsense. Come, I'll show you how." She slipped him a flirtatious little smile.

By Jove, if her innocent quiz was too shy and polite to make the first move, she wasn't. "Stand close here behind me and just…follow my lead."

It took him a second, but then his eyes widened behind his spectacles as he got the message in her come-hither look.

"Right! What's this you want me to do, then?" He ventured closer.

"Hold on." She set the bouquet aside, then picked up her bow again and fetched an arrow, bending gracefully while Lucas eyed her backside.

As she stepped into position across from the target, he moved toward her with eager obedience.

Portia nodded to him to stand right behind her. "Place your hands lightly on my elbows and I'll show you how it's done."

He obeyed. She felt a wild thrill run down her spine at the solid warmth of his big, hard body so close behind her, the smooth touch of his fingers alighting on her bare arms.

She blushed with a silent gulp.

A faint memory tugged at the back of her mind: Silversmoke holding her in his arms on that wicked night in the gazebo. His iron body against hers, his tongue in her mouth…

Stop thinking about him! Lord, woman. You're with Lucas now. The man you're going to marry.

"So, what do you do next?" he murmured, his voice warm and seductive close to her ear.

"Next comes the anchor position." Feeling breathless, she lifted the bow. "Note the angle of my elbow."

"Oh, believe me, you have my complete attention," he purred.

Sometimes she could swear he even sounded like Silversmoke. No wonder she secretly got them confused sometimes.

"Are you sure you've never done this before?" she asked, furrowing her brow at the smooth steadiness of his warm, sure hands when he touched her.

"Once or twice. But please don't stop. Your tutelage is...most instructive."

She smiled wickedly. "Very well." Her heart pounded as she drew the string back farther and farther until it was ready to snap with delicious tension. She licked her lips. "Release comes...suddenly."

"Show me," he breathed, sliding his hands from her elbows, down her arms and molding her sides.

She nearly cried out with pleasure when she let the arrow fly. It leaped into the air—and missed completely.

No wonder. He had her quite distracted. He slid his hands around her waist.

Portia was acutely aware of them, her body throbbing with pent-up need. "Well, that wasn't a very good demonstration," she said in a trembling voice.

"Nonsense. You are my own little cupid," he whispered, then, without warning, kissed the side of her neck.

Portia nearly cried out with desire. A giddy explosion of longing went off softly inside her. She leaned back against him slightly, her skin tingling.

She tilted her head back against his muscled shoulder, nigh panting for him to touch her more. He pressed his splayed hand against her stomach, driving her closer to his body until she felt the swelling bulge of his manhood throbbing against the small of her back.

Oh God. She licked her lips, eyes closed, chest heaving. If it were possible, she'd have taken him upstairs and straight to her chamber at that moment for a practice run at their wedding night.

As he caressed her, she forgot all about the bow in her hand.

"You're not giving up, are you?" he whispered, holding her body against him. "Do it again. Please."

"I can think of something I'd much rather do." Portia turned around boldly and stared up at him, offering a very plain if unspoken invitation to him to kiss her.

Lucas whipped off his spectacles, revealing gold chips in his green eyes that glowed like kindling about to burst into flames.

Once more, the sight of her future husband without the vexing screen of his spectacles filled her with longing. She knew that if he would just kiss her once, passionately, she would never think of Silversmoke again.

The highwayman had awakened her desire, but Lucas had won her heart, and she hated herself for this dishonesty.

Desperate for her duke to kiss away all memory of Silversmoke, she offered her lips, wetting them with an eager pass of her tongue. Lucas leaned down with a ravenous stare, captured her chin on his fingertips, and tilted her head back gently.

"Portia," he breathed. His lips were warm and soft and so familiar somehow as they alighted atop hers, magical as dreams.

Behind her closed eyelids, her heart soared. But the second he stroked her lips apart with the tip of his tongue, a voice in the nearby morning room made them both freeze.

"Ho there, Mr. Greensleeves! How are you today?"

"Pretty bird!" the parakeet rasped through the open door.

Portia gasped, tore her mouth away from her fiancé's, and planted a hand on his chest to push him away. "It's my father!"

A stifled oath escaped Lucas as they stepped apart. At once, he turned his back on the house, sparing the marquess the telltale evidence of his genuine regard for his daughter.

Portia's heart pounded. While His Grace struggled to will his most manly parts back under control, she shook herself, dazed and panting,

Good Lord. Her hand was still wrapped around the wood of her bow. She'd forgotten she was even holding it.

Lucas quickly put his glasses back on.

They exchanged a sideways glance like two roguish thieves who'd nearly got arrested in the middle of some magnificent heist.

Soon, he told her with a soothing gaze that made her want to rip his clothes off him, now. She bit her lip, but thankfully, the madness began retreating.

To be sure, if Papa disapproved of the waltz, he would be most displeased with this new dance they had begun. She was nonetheless astounded that Lucas could have this effect on her.

He looked askance at her. "Parakeet, eh?"

She nodded. "My father loves that bird almost as much as you love your insects. In fact, if you want to find yourself in Papa's good graces, all you need do is make friends with that bird."

"Oh really?" His eyes twinkled. Then he nodded toward the morning room door. "I should go and pay my respects, if you don't mind. I need to make sure he knows where he's going tomorrow, as well."

"Be my guest." Portia gestured toward the house. "I'm sure he'll be happy to see his future son-in-law."

Indeed, she knew her father could use some cheering up after his grumpy mood of yesterday, after the news that Hunter was indeed coming to the wedding. One would think his heir's return would make him happy, but the whole situation had put him in a foul humor for a few hours.

Poor Hunter couldn't win with Papa. She just hoped the two would be civil to each other at the wedding.

"Very well, then. I shall bid you adieu." Lucas sketched a bow with a lingering gaze. "Until tomorrow, my lady."

"I'll be counting the hours," she whispered, using her wiles on him once more. After all, raised in the ton, Portia knew how to flirt; she had merely figured that her skills would never be needed with the quiz.

But, as of this moment, everything between them had changed. To like him was one thing; to want him was something else altogether.

Why, she had expected nothing more than a grand, loveless match with the Duke of Fountainhurst. But, for the first time, as she watched Lucas walk away, it finally sank in that she might just get her chance at true love after all.

Luke had known that coming to see Portia would put him in a better frame of mind after last night's ominous realization that Joel was the Red Carnation and had most likely been kidnapped by his own damned uncle.

That in itself would have been grim enough, but, for Luke, the implications for their match made it even worse.

After all, with this fairly sure confirmation that her precious Joel was indeed still alive, and soon to be rescued by Silversmoke and his gang at the next Carnevale, Luke could not deny he'd begun to feel a twinge of anxiety about how Portia would react once she got her gambler back safe, as promised.

However.

After that winsome encounter in the garden just now, with the taste of her ardent kiss still lingering on his tongue, he was walking on air, feeling wonderfully certain that, come what may, the wedding was most definitely on.

For it to be otherwise at this point would simply tear his heart out.

Determined to become a true part of this family, he sprang lightly up the stairs into the morning room.

"Good morning, Lord Liddicoat!" He strode in with a smile. "How are you today, sir?"

"Ah, Fountainhurst." The portly marquess turned to him with a sleepy-eyed blink. "Didn't realize you'd popped by."

Luke nodded and joined his future father-in-law before the budgie's spacious wicker cage. "I came to pay my respects to your daughter before I leave Town. I'm off to Gracewell to make sure everything's in order for our gathering. Did my coachman send over the directions for your drive tomorrow?"

"Oh, yes, yes, we're all sorted."

"Excellent," Luke said.

Then the marquess fell silent, standing there, hands in pockets, gazing at his little pet bird, who stared back at him.

As the seconds ticked past without another word from the man, Luke wasn't sure what to do, what this silence might signify—if he was supposed to go away now, dismissed, or if Lord Liddicoat was standing there stewing with disapproval.

Perhaps Portia's father had seen more than either of them had intended.

Like Luke's hard cock pressed against her lovely derriere.

Luke gulped at the memory as the silence stretched thin. To be sure, that flaxen-haired vixen and he were both feeling the springtime today— and Luke would've been overjoyed at her newfound desire for him, if only he had some assurance that he had not just outraged her father.

He must apologize if he had, for that was no way to start off their relationship as father- and son-in-law. He did not want Liddicoat thinking he'd treated his daughter dishonorably, for as far as Luke was concerned, he had been an absolute gentleman with her at all times.

Even as Silversmoke—though perhaps slightly less so.

Anyway, she was the one who had started it today.

For his part, Luke knew he was more prude than rakehell.

Still, he did not want Liddicoat taking him for a cad. He studied the portly old chap from the corner of his eye, trying to read him.

Liddicoat seemed fairly peaceful. By all observation, his bride's sire was a man of very few words.

Portly and placid, sedate under sail as a thirty-ton merchant ship laden with cargo, the Marquess of Liddicoat had white sideburns to match his snowy eyebrows and what was left of his hair—the sort of white hair that had probably been jet-black in his youth.

He sported the round potbelly of a true gourmand, and, from what Luke could tell, was about a decade older than his rail-thin, glamorous wife, in perhaps his mid-sixties.

Portia clearly took after her mother, with her slim build and sociable nature. Her father, by contrast, was the sort of inert chap who could sit at a party all night, still as a boulder, arms crossed, and barely utter a word. Not having a *bad* time, perhaps, but showing no signs of having fun, either.

Luke could not fathom what the man was thinking right now.

If anything.

He was having trouble thinking, himself, after seeing the come-hither sparkle in Portia's blue eyes. By God, if he had not been smitten enough with the girl, her sheer adorableness this morning had made him her slave.

Little did she know that their butler had allowed Luke to stand there for a few minutes before making his presence known. He'd been utterly tickled watching his lovely future duchess prowl back and forth across the lawn and then turn suddenly and fire, as though hearing an enemy closing in—and she usually hit the target! She had reminded him for all the world of a kitten stalking through the grass, pretending to be some fierce lion in a jungle.

Adorable, he thought. *Just adorable.*

Oh, and when she had turned around and seen him there, the way her face had lit up... Luke knew he would remember that smile forever.

Now, *that* was the way a lady was supposed to look at the man she was set to marry in a fortnight.

Finally! he thought. Why, it was beginning to look as though he had truly won her—even as Lucas, awkwardest chap in the ton.

It hadn't been so long ago, after all, that she'd rolled her eyes whenever she saw him coming, and then tried politely to hide her exasperated boredom with him—or rather, with Lucas.

What am I going to do about Lucas? he wondered with a frown, because he did not intend to play a stammering quiz in Town for the rest of his life. If Sidney, for one, had already seen through his ruse, others were bound to start noticing, too.

There was also the small fact that Luke had begun yearning to fully be himself with Portia.

Maybe with everyone.

But that was a question for another day.

Right now, he still had her father to deal with.

Liddicoat hadn't spoken, though he made a little chirping sound to his budgie, and the bird hopped about.

Perhaps the marquess had seen nothing and was simply that quiet—more awkward than Lucas himself.

Say something, Luke scolded himself. *Don't just stand there like a lug. He's about to become your father-in-law.*

At least make sure he doesn't despise you.

Besides, Portia was watching now, too. Bow and arrow in hand like some wayward Artemis, she hung back in the garden, peeking through the door and spying on him with her father. It was clear she wanted the two of them to bond a bit if they could.

If that was ever going to happen, Luke saw it was up to him. *Here goes nothing.* "Ahem, I say, my lord. Lady Portia tells me this is your budgie. I had one myself as a lad, as it happens."

"Did you, now?" Her father turned to him with genuine interest, and no sign of rage in his eyes, to Luke's relief.

"Indeed." Convinced now that her father had either seen nothing or, at least not enough to alarm him, Luke proceeded to tell him about Snowball, the blue and white budgie that his grandmother had given him for his tenth birthday.

They chatted for several moments on this topic, and, finally, just as Portia had promised, her father started coming out of his shell.

"Does yours talk?" Luke asked.

Liddicoat smiled mysteriously. "Hmm, ask him if he likes Napoleon."

At the mere sound of the conquered emperor's name, the bird

squawked. "Hang Boney! Hang Boney!"

Luke gasped with astonishment, then started laughing. "That's fantastic!"

Liddicoat beamed, hands in pockets. "Mr. Greensleeves, what's your favorite holiday?"

"Happy Christmas!" the bird squawked.

Luke laughed merrily. "Are you the one who taught him?"

"Over time," Liddicoat said with a chuckle and a nod.

"Speaking of time, I really should be on my way. My sister is bringing her family out to Gracewell a day early, since they have a long drive."

"Ah, very good, very good." Liddicoat bobbed his head. "Mr. Greensleeves, say goodbye to the duke."

"Cheerio!" the parakeet rasped.

Luke grinned. "Nice to meet you too, Mr. Greensleeves." He started to turn away, but a thought struck him. He'd done well with Liddicoat discussing birds, but the older man's potbelly gave him a hint that there might be something even dearer to the marquess's heart.

"I say, sir, before I go, do you have any suggestions for what I might tell my chef to serve for the sweets course? It would put my mind at ease if I could be sure in advance that my table will offer selections that everyone likes. Any particular favorites I could arrange for, hmm?"

He gave the marquess a conspiratorial smile, and Liddicoat grinned, looked flattered and pleased at the question.

"Well, my wife likes lemon meringue. Portia barely touches sweets; she usually takes fruit instead."

"And for you, sir?"

"Actually," he confessed, "I have always been fond of a good trifle."

"Me too!"

"Yes? Splendid. All sat atop sweet Naples biscuits and mounded with custard, then topped with a cloud of whipped syllabub, what?"

"Damn me, that sounds delicious right now," Luke said, and he wasn't jesting.

Liddicoat snorted. "Too bad Samantha won't let me eat 'em. Says I'm too fat." He clapped both hands to his belly, but Luke waved this off.

"She should look at the Regent."

"That's what I tell her!" the marquess exclaimed.

"Well, if my chef were to make a trifle for us tomorrow...?" Luke suggested, elbowing him.

Liddicoat grinned. "'Twould be rude to refuse."

"Exactly." Luke grinned back. "Consider it done, sir. Mum's the word."

Liddicoat laughed and clapped him on the back. "You're a good sort, Fountainhurst—much like your father, although he was a great deal sterner, I warrant."

Luke went motionless. "That's right... My sister mentioned that you knew him."

"Oh yes." The old fellow nodded. "That's why I was so glad when you began courting my daughter. I had great respect for your sire." Liddicoat glanced past him out the open doors of the morning room, checking on Portia, who waved sweetly when he looked.

"Morning, Papa!"

"Morning, dear!" He glanced discreetly at Luke, then lowered his voice. "Such a good girl. Always looking after her mother and me. It pains us to part with her."

"Well, we'll be just down the street," Luke said with a smile.

Liddicoat nodded. "That's a blessing. I, for one, was relieved when you asked for her hand, heaven knows. She'd been so unhappy, and I just had a feeling you would take care of her for us. I know your father certainly worshiped your dam."

Startled by the mention of his mother, Luke lowered his head. "Why, yes. Yes, he did, sir. She was his prized jewel. Thank you for trusting me with your daughter. I am...humbled by your faith in me. I won't let you down."

"No, Fountainhurst, it is my wife and I who thank *you*. 'Tis a good match. Frankly, I never quite trusted that Clayton fellow of hers. Doesn't surprise me a'tall that he went off and got himself into some ridiculous scrape."

"Why do you say that, my lord?" Luke studied him, fascinated.

Liddicoat waved a hand. "Eh, you ask me, all those Clayton men are alike: all flash, no substance. Gamblers, the lot—the nephew as well as the uncle, I daresay."

"The uncle gambles, too?" Luke asked keenly, considering it was only last night he had concluded that Axewood himself was behind Joel's disappearance. Hopefully, Sidney would dig up more useful details, but Luke hadn't heard back from him yet.

"Gambles, yes," Liddicoat said, "but in a different way. His way's more respectable: business investments." He gave Luke a wry look of warning, his eyes shrewd.

"I see." Luke nodded. Sidney had told him as much at the club.

The marquess slid his thumbs into his waistcoat pockets. "You know, I never could fathom how, with his reputation, Axewood got himself appointed to that budget committee I served on with your father all those years ago."

"Pardon?" Luke stared at him, taken off guard. "What budget committee was that?"

"Eh, fairly ordinary business. It was a joint appropriations committee, with oversight on certain aspects of military spending. We had them each year during wartime."

"Is that right?" Luke murmured, searching the older man's face. A prickle of foreboding crept down his spine. The same ominous feeling that had come over him last night, once he'd reached his conclusions about the earl and the identity of the Red Carnation.

Chiefly, that his father would never have been friends with such a man, despite Axewood's claims to the contrary.

Liddicoat nodded idly. "Our committee members came from both houses of Parliament, with representatives from the Treasury and Admiralty, as well. We were the last layer of review, you see, on the proposed annual budget for the war effort before giving final approval. It then went to a vote in the full Parliament, and if it passed, the funds were dispatched, based on our recommendations."

"I see." The sense of ominous premonition grew in Luke's breast.

"Your father was chairman; Axewood was secretary. I was just a voting member." Liddicoat shrugged. "We were fourteen in all. Still, it was our duty to give the final yay or nay over budgets worth millions of pounds. That's why I was surprised they let Axewood participate.

"He always seemed, oh, I dunno, a bit dodgy." Liddicoat gave him a confidential glance. "But then again, the earl has a great deal of experience managing fortunes and choosing which business concerns will make good investments, so I suppose it makes sense.

"Of course, your father kept a close eye on him," he added. "Made sure he didn't attempt any nonsense to line his own pockets at the nation's expense. It all ran smoothly enough."

For a moment, Luke stood there trying to absorb what Liddicoat had so casually revealed. "I've been told my father and Lord Axewood were actually friends."

The marquess gave a mild scoff. "I wouldn't say *that*."

"Enemies?" Luke asked darkly, peering over his spectacles.

"No, not *enemies*, really. It's just that your father saw through his pretensions; Axewood didn't much care for that. But Fountainhurst kept him in line. He was a hard one sometimes, but fair."

"Oh, I know, believe me," Luke murmured, feeling sick to his stomach as his search for Joel Clayton suddenly led him down a sinister alley, indeed.

One he had never expected to find while hunting for the gambler. But was it possible?

With millions of pounds from the nation's coffers to tempt him—a man with a reputation for running dubious financial schemes—and with Luke's father watching him like a hawk, as he surely would have done, might Axewood have wanted, even needed, to get rid of the committee chairman?

Luke had long worried that he'd missed something about his parents' murders. That the last surviving MacAbe might've been telling the truth when he'd claimed that a wealthy Englishman had hired the gang.

For years now, he had been plagued with the gnawing fear that, somehow, for all the wild lengths he had gone to to wreak vengeance on his parents' killers, the real source of the plot against them had slipped through his fingers.

But now, after what Liddicoat had just told him, he stood there privately reeling with shock. *My God, what if it was Axewood?*

It seemed impossible. But…millions of pounds sterling earmarked for the war could certainly prove a strong motive to a man with the heart of a swindler. And Father—strict, stern Fountainhurst—would never have allowed it to occur.

Unlike Luke, Father would never have fallen for Axewood's lies. And once he'd sniffed him out, he would have exposed him, turning a deaf ear to any and all excuses.

Proud as Axewood was, the mere whiff of threat that he had been detected would've given him all the incentive he needed…

To reach out to some of the brutes for hire at this Carnevale.

Suddenly shaken, Luke needed to go home and think.

Since Lord Liddicoat apparently had nothing more to add on the topic, Luke said his goodbyes in a daze. Portia came skipping in to walk him to the front door of their family home, hanging on his arm.

"Are you all right?" she asked softly, scanning his face with a worried look. "You look like you've seen a ghost, Lucas."

"No, I'm fine," he said in distraction.

"Are you sure? Was Papa angry? Did my father see us together? Did he scold you?" she whispered.

"No, nothing like that, sweet. We spoke of parakeets...and other things. Well, I'd better go. I-I'm not sure what time my sister is arriving."

"Of course. I'll see you tomorrow." She lifted onto her toes and kissed his cheek.

Luke looked at her gratefully as she pulled away again. Her light kiss made him feel better despite his thoughts' churning like a foul whirlwind.

He could feel the same black rage he had once known so well gathering anew in his veins, all but blurring out Portia's worried face.

"Goodbye, Your Grace. See you tomorrow."

He bowed to her and mumbled something in kind.

With suspicions swirling in his brain and Liddicoat's idle comments reverberating like an earthquake under his feet, he took leave of his bride's family residence and returned to Fountainhurst House.

There, he delayed his exit from Town just long enough to take his butler aside. "Howell, I need you to find something for me."

The elderly fellow lifted his head, at the ready. "Yes, Your Grace?"

"I need you to dig out my father's old records on a budget committee he headed during the war years. It's very important. I'll send Finch to Town to review any papers you find on the matter. Check every file drawer in the study. Any boxes of his old papers up in the attic, too. I want whatever you can find on this committee—including anything that might mention Lord Axewood."

"Lord Axewood?" Howell echoed in surprise. "As you wish, sir. Anything else?"

Luke shook his head. "That's all, at the moment. If I think of anything else, I'll send word with Finch."

"Very good, sir. Oh, before you go—this letter just arrived for you. It's from Lord Sidney, marked urgent. Do you wish to see it now, or shall I—"

"Yes, give it here." Luke flicked his fingers impatiently.

The butler fetched the small envelope from his silver tray atop the pier table nearby. Luke opened the note at once, his heart pounding at what he might find.

F. —

Marta doesn't know anyone called Antonia. Her opinion (which I share) is that there's no such person. Still working on the other part. It will require me to speak to my illustrious father, and though this is a bitter pill, I undertake it bravely for the sake of our mutual friend. I'm having supper with the ol' goblin on Monday evening, after which I'll be in touch directly. Let's just hope I can get through it without being disinherited. Anon!

— S.

"Huh," Luke said under his breath. *Just as I suspected.* His fury only grew to think of how Axewood had stood there and lied to his face with that whole elopement story. *Brazen.*

At least this was confirmation that he was on the right track with his inquiry. *Good man, Sidney,* he thought, then gave the note back to Howell.

"Burn this for me, please. If another comes, lock it in my top desk drawer. I'll be back in a couple of days."

"Yes, Your Grace." The ancient fellow tilted his head back to study Luke with worry. "Is there anything else I can do?"

"No. I must make for Gracewell." Luke did his best to clear his head as he turned toward the door.

Howell quickly got it for him. "If it's no trouble, sir, would you kindly let Lady Sedgwick and the children know the staff send their best?"

Luke managed to smile at their loyal family retainer. "Gladly, ol' friend. She'll be pleased to hear from you," he said, then strode out to his waiting carriage.

Moments later, they were underway, the wheels whirring as his coach sped away from Moonlight Square.

As eager as he was to see his sister and her family, first he needed to talk this through with Gower and Finch. Needed them to hear the theory that had taken hold in his mind, and tell him it was madness.

But what if he was right? What if Father had caught Axewood playing games with the war funds?

How far might the earl go to cover up his corruption?

If Axewood was capable of kidnapping his own flesh and blood and forcing him to play in these high-stakes underworld gambling tournaments, then why would the earl even think twice about hiring some lowlife killers to eliminate a powerful foe who could've exposed him?

Father...

Stunned fury pulsed through Luke's veins at the thought that, after all this time, he might have finally unmasked the unseen villain behind his parents' deaths.

If that was the case, by God, he would punish Axewood worse than he'd done to his likely hirelings, the MacAbes. For now, however, only one thing was certain.

That smug son of a bitch was damned lucky he had left Town.

CHAPTER 20

Revelations, Decisions

"Serena, what in the world did you put in this tea?" Portia spluttered, her eyes watering.

"Whiskey," her best friend said with a wide-eyed look.

"Well, that explains it." Coughing a little, Portia patted her chest as the swallow of spiked tea burned a fiery path down to her belly. "Why, for heaven sakes?"

Serena grimaced. "You're going to need it, I'm afraid."

"Oh no, is this another of those occasions where you've invited me over with some ulterior motive, hmm?"

Serena nodded with a semi-contrite pout. On her lap, Franklin tilted his head and whined for a bite of cake.

It was about five in the afternoon, and they were sitting on the terrace behind Rivenwood House, where Serena had invited her over for tea.

Portia had been glad to receive the invitation to distract her, nervous about visiting Gracewell tomorrow.

Well into the afternoon, moreover, she had been unable to shake off her gnawing uneasiness about the strange mood that had come over Lucas when he was leaving her house earlier today.

She had never seen him like that before. He was always so cheerful and easygoing.

Well, no, she reminded herself. Once, she had glimpsed a darker side of him—in St. Andrew's, when he'd told her the terrible story of what had happened to his parents.

Obviously, that had nothing to do with his visit this morning. Yet he had looked so pale when she'd walked him to the door.

The logical conclusion was that Papa must've said *something* to reproach him for their delicious little flirtation in the garden during their archery lesson.

Lucas had claimed that was not the case, however, and Papa had seemed perfectly at ease with him, so maybe it was nothing, but she hoped all was well.

In any case, after Portia had taken the midday meal with her parents as usual in the dining room, she had received a message from Serena inviting her over for afternoon tea.

Curious but glad of this impromptu invitation, she told Serena's footman to take his mistress word that she would be there shortly.

A little while later, Portia walked into the Rivenwoods' grand but strange mansion on the corner. She had never been invited into Lucas's house, but she doubted it could be more eccentric than Azrael's.

On the outside, the classical design of Rivenwood House blended well with the rest of Moonlight Square, but on the inside, the pale-haired duke had had it decorated in the neo-gothic style, complete with suits of armor in the great hall. It was like walking into an ancient castle or some medieval abbey.

Ah well. The mysterious Azrael was an original, to be sure.

As it turned out, he was the one who wanted to speak to her.

Serena had come out to greet her, carrying her dog to restrain his yipping, tail-wagging eagerness to greet any guest.

Portia gave Franklin a pat on the head, still warmed to think of Lucas befriending the tiny terrier in the park that day with a cheerful *"Hullo, little fellow!"*

"How are you today, my dear?" she asked her friend brightly. But then she noticed the somber look in Serena's dark hazel eyes. "What is it?" Portia asked at once. "What's afoot?"

"We have news for you," Serena murmured. "Azrael has heard back from his sources. Come." With a dire look, the raven-haired duchess led Portia through the house and out onto the shady back terrace.

"Is it something bad?" Portia asked on the way, her heart already pounding as she hurried after her.

"You'll see. It's best to let him tell it. He has all the details."

Portia sucked in a breath. "Did he find out Silversmoke's true identity?"

"That? Oh, no. Sorry. Seems nobody knows who he really is."

Portia lowered her gaze. Well, perhaps that was for the best.

When they stepped out onto the flagstone terrace, Azrael was already there waiting for them, lounging in his shirt sleeves on a cushioned wicker settee. He rose at the arrival of the ladies, swinging his lean, elegant frame upright and giving Portia a polite bow.

She sketched an automatic curtsy in return. "Your Grace. You have news?"

"I do. But I doubt you're going to like it." He gestured to a chair.

"Thus the spiked tea," Serena mumbled.

"You might want to have a seat, Lady Portia."

"Oh." Portia managed a nod and lowered herself in one of the rose-cushioned wicker chairs. Dry-mouthed, she folded her hands in her lap and waited.

Serena put Franklin on the ground, then sat down in the chair next to her. She mirrored Portia's tense pose, watching her husband with trust and worry.

Azrael's ice-blue eyes were troubled as he took his seat again across from the ladies.

"Well," he said, "I've heard back from my contacts."

"And?"

"Portia, you are my wife's dearest friend," he said with a searching gaze. "Therefore, I look upon you as though you were my own sister. For that reason, I must urge you in the strongest possible terms never to go near Silversmoke again. Especially not alone."

"Oh?" She felt a bit faint hearing his grim tone. "Why do you say that?"

"He is far more dangerous than you or I or even the newspapers had any idea." Azrael paused with a cool stare. "The man is a ruthless killer."

Her eyes widened. She sat up straighter, shocked. Then she set her tea aside. "Go on."

"If I could find out who he actually is, that might help put what I've learned into context, or somehow explain what he's done. But he's been very clever about covering his tracks. Even my sources had no idea who he might be."

Her heart thumped with sickening force. "What did they tell you?"

"I'm afraid it's very unpleasant."

She waved off his warning, needing to hear whatever he had to say.

"My contacts in the low world say the entire criminal class of

London give Silversmoke a wide berth. They do their best not to cross him. And it's true, he's helped put many of them in jail. But never mind his gallant deeds, as chronicled in the papers.

"To them, what Silversmoke is most famous for is destroying some enemy gang up north. Apparently, he tracked his foes all the way to Scotland, then laid waste to their entire operation. Word has it he slaughtered some twenty men in the fight, damned near single-handedly."

Portia's jaw dropped as the air left her lungs in a whoosh. *Twenty men?*

Azrael shook his head. "I don't know the cause of their quarrel, but they say he left none alive."

"Stay away from him," Serena pleaded softly.

Portia stared at them in disbelief. It took her a long moment to form a coherent thought. "Now…just hold on for a minute. I don't believe it just because these people say so. Who are these sources of yours, anyway?"

Azrael dropped his gaze with chagrin. "You know the sorts of things my family was, er, infamous for."

Underworld dealings of all kinds, Serena had once told her.

Occult things, even.

"Let's just say we have friends in low places," he murmured.

Portia frowned. "Well, just because these lowly informants of yours claim that something's so, that doesn't mean it's true. After all, nothing like that ever showed up in the papers about him, as far as I know."

"The newspapers never print the whole story," Serena said with a chiding frown. "You know that."

Azrael gazed at Portia, his pale blue eyes full of sadness. "I'm sorry, my lady. Every hero has a dark side. Trust me on that." He looked away, but Serena laid a steadying hand on his shoulder, and he reached up and covered it with his own.

When Portia saw the silent bond of love between them, she felt a lump rise in her throat. *It's not fair!* her heart cried. *Will it ever be my turn to have that with someone?* But she blinked off the brief threat of tears.

There must be some explanation. "But I know Silversmoke is a good man. He's helped so many people."

The duke shook his head. "He's a hardened killer. Half the criminals in London are terrified of him."

Portia sat there, stunned, not knowing what to believe.

"I don't want you being alone with him again," Serena said, while Azrael stared at Portia with a warning look, as though he might go to her father, if necessary.

"But...you don't understand. He was kind! A-and agreeable. He spoke like a poet on matters of love, and I-I found him charming." Her own words sounded naïve and foolish even as she spoke them.

Azrael shrugged. "Even the devil can disguise himself as an angel of light," he said matter-of-factly, and he should know, given the spooky rumors about his ancestors' dabbling in dark, supernatural things.

Portia took a deep breath, at a loss and deeply shaken by this information.

She knew on the one hand that Azrael would not waste her time with idle accusations. But on the other, she could not make his claims fit with the gallant man she had talked to on two occasions now, let alone all those swashbuckling tales in the papers.

All the stories of the people he had helped, the villains he had delivered to the constables, asking nothing in return.

"If this Scottish tale is true, he must've had his reasons," she said halfheartedly.

"Still." Serena gave her a firm look.

"If he contacts you again," Azrael said calmly, "I urge you with all earnestness to send for me, and I will help you."

"We both will," Serena said, nodding. "I wish you would've come to us in the first place."

"Well, I appreciate it, truly," Portia said, glancing from one to the other. "I know you both mean well. But, as it happens, the whole thing is neither here nor there, because I'm fairly sure Silversmoke has abandoned my case."

"Why do you say that?" the duke asked.

"I haven't heard from him in days." She lowered her head. "And, um, the last time we met, he, er, he tried to kiss me, and I refused his advances." *Though it wasn't easy.*

"That is not the behavior of a gentleman," Azrael pointed out, but that much was obvious.

The more Portia thought about how she had put herself in jeopardy, being alone in the dark—twice!—with a possible killer, she was frightened, in hindsight.

"I wish you never would've drawn this outlaw's attention to yourself," Serena murmured.

Portia turned to her in alarm. "What are you saying? Do you think he might come after me somehow?" She felt like a traitor even asking the question.

Silversmoke had given his word to help her find Joel. He had put himself on the line for her. He did not deserve this disloyalty.

"I-I cannot bring myself to think he would ever be a threat to me."

"No, darling, we're not saying that—"

"Don't scare her, Serena," chided her husband.

"She's better off scared than hurt!" Serena said.

Azrael turned to Portia. "Nothing I heard gave me cause to believe that Silversmoke would ever hurt a woman. Still, if there's any merit to these tales, he can be a very dangerous man when he chooses. If you hear from him again, please contact me and allow me to assist you."

Portia nodded, still reeling at the news that she may have sat across the table from a murderer—even kissed him!

The sense of danger looming all around her made her wish that Lucas was there.

Not that a lovable quiz like him could have done much to protect her from the likes of rough, tough Silversmoke. Still, his gentle presence was so reassuring that even the thought of him made her feel better.

"I'm sorry, P," Serena said, touching her forearm. "I didn't mean to scare you. I'm sure you'll be quite safe."

"Especially after you're married." Azrael nodded. "Fountainhurst will take care of you. He seems a good, solid chap."

Portia nodded, then took another shaky sip of tea.

"By God, if I'm right," Luke growled at Gower and Finch as he paced across his makeshift gymnasium at Gracewell, "if it was all down to money and he had my parents killed simply to cover up his own corruption, there's no hole deep enough for Axewood to hide in. I'll find him. And, so help me, what I did to those Scots is nothing compared to what I'll do to him. I'll tear him limb from limb!"

It was now about six o'clock that afternoon. He had told Gower and Finch everything he'd learned and now suspected. The pair sat in grim silence, pondering the crime as they watched Luke stalk back and forth in restless fury.

The long, light curtains blew gently in the cross-breeze of the erstwhile ballroom. Beyond the open windows, sunlight glittered on the pond.

Meanwhile, throughout the castle, the servants scurried about making last-minute preparations for the Sedgwicks' imminent arrival. By now, the guest chambers stood ready, the kitchens were brimming with good things to eat, and the well-polished rooms smelled of lemon and beeswax.

Already dressed to meet his guests, Luke clenched and unclenched his fists as he strode past his men, then grabbed a quarterstaff and twirled it slowly in thought as he paced.

"I don't have the proof yet, but that's where you come in, Finch."

"Yes, sir?" Finch's freckled face was stamped with worry, his spectacles perched atop his head.

"I'm sending you to London to dig through my father's old papers. I told Howell to pull out anything he could find concerning this budget committee. Get to Town and start digging through them. I want you on the road within the hour." Luke pivoted and marched back the other way, his black boots leaving fresh scuffs over the parquetry floors. "Set aside anything you find that mentions Lord Axewood. Liddicoat said the earl was the secretary of the committee, if that helps."

"What should I be looking for, exactly?"

"Anything that would suggest my father discovered some sort of irregularities in the management or allocation of the war funds. Especially if his suspicions pointed at Axewood. After all, if the bastard is capable of kidnapping his own nephew, as we now believe, then he surely wouldn't have scrupled over having my father killed before he exposed Axewood's misdeeds. We already know his connection to the Carnevale could have given him the means to have hired the assassins. This budget committee might prove to have been his motivation to do so."

"I understand." Finch nodded.

"And me?" Gower asked. "What should I do?"

"Get the boys ready. We're going to Carnevale," Luke said with a slight, fierce smile.

Gower lifted his eyebrows. "Sounds fun."

"Aye. Silversmoke and company are going to show up in force. Cause some havoc. Upend the damned thing. While the boys raise hell, I kidnap the Red Carnation back from his uncle."

"Oh, the boys'll like that."

"So will I, believe me. Because then comes the best part." Luke gave them a dark smile. "I confront Axewood if he's there and punish the bastard for his treachery—if my suspicions are correct. That's up to you, Finch—confirming it." Vengeance coiled inside him as he glanced at the redhead. "You find me proof in my father's papers…and I'll do the rest."

"Anything else, sir?" Finch asked uneasily.

Luke thought it over. "Actually, yes. Get me a list of Axewood's properties. He's probably holding Joel prisoner at one of them between Carnevales."

"Poor soul," Finch murmured, nodding, then he jotted down the order in his notebook.

"I have a second task for you as well, Gower. As you may recall, the Carnevale takes place in Buckinghamshire this coming Wednesday night. I've checked the map, and it looks like a ride of about four hours.

"I want everyone who's going to be ready to leave Town on Wednesday morning, bright and early. But it would help to get a clearer notion of what to expect once we get there. To that end, I want you to get a meeting with Jimmy O'Toole as soon as possible. After all, if the Carnevale is, as they say, a black-market trading hub, he's probably been there many times."

Jimmy "the Bull" O'Toole was a smuggler and gunrunner whose gang ruled a seedy section of the East London Docklands. An Irishman with a temper.

"Find out all you can from him and his lieutenants about what goes on at these things so we can walk in prepared," Luke said.

Finch grinned at Gower. "But watch out for his wife, mate."

Gower scowled at the lad, then turned to Luke. "Shouldn't Silversmoke be the one to meet with that hothead?"

"Can't. I've got to focus on my family for the next couple of days. My sister will be here any minute, and Portia's bringing her parents tomorrow to spend the whole day. We've only got till Wednesday, Gower. Anyway, you should be fine. I'm the one she always tries to grope," Luke muttered.

"Don't worry, Gower, you're old and ugly," Finch said cheerfully. "For once, it'll work in your favor. You'll be quite safe with her, I'm sure."

The pewter-haired fighter harrumphed.

All the same, Luke was glad *he* wasn't the one going. The voluptuous Maisie O'Toole still had the morals of the tavern bawd she had once been before her devoted Jimmy had put a ring on her finger.

"If she makes eyes at you, just ignore it," Luke told him. "That's what I always do. Pretend she doesn't exist. But be polite. God forbid we should be rude to the rookery queen. The last thing we need is a war with Jimmy's gang."

Suddenly, Luke spotted his sister's coach in the distance. They were just turning in at the end of the long drive. He couldn't help smiling when he saw two young heads hanging out the coach windows: the dark-haired one of young Bartram and the curly blond locks of little Katie.

Warmed at the thought of his niece and nephew, Luke turned to his men. "You two, make yourselves scarce," he ordered. "Especially you, Gower. And make sure Tempo's in the far pasture. You know how it upsets my sister to be reminded that her brother is a highwayman. Although... I daresay she won't have to worry about that for much longer."

"What?" Finch asked while Gower frowned. "What do you mean?"

Luke hesitated. "Gentlemen, I have decided that rescuing Joel will be Silversmoke's last ride."

Finch's jaw dropped. "But you can't mean it, sir!"

"What the hell?" Gower demanded, rising from his chair.

Their shock at his rather obvious announcement took Luke aback. "I'm about to get married, remember?"

Gower huffed and folded his arms across his chest. "Not necessarily."

This stopped Luke in his tracks. "Why do you say that?"

"Hate to be a killjoy, Yer Grace, but your precious Lady Portia only came to you in the first place wantin' her Joel back—so she wouldn't have to marry the Duke of Fountainhurst. And now you're plannin' on serving him up to her on a silver platter?" Gower gave a cynical shrug. "Just sayin'."

Luke gazed at his mentor with a chill down his spine. "Surely she prefers me to Clayton by now."

"But she's not getting you, sir—she's getting Lucas," Finch said. "Isn't she?"

Gower nodded slowly. "Kid's right. She don't even know the real you yet."

Luke felt his stomach turn over. Did they actually think Portia might still call off their wedding in favor of Joel once Silversmoke rescued him?

"You should probably tell her the truth, sir. About who you really are," Finch said in a delicate tone. "If you truly care for her—"

"Impossible!" Luke scoffed without letting him finish, feeling cornered. Then he glanced toward the closed doors of the ballroom. "She'll hate me forever for lying to her."

His sister's coach continued barreling closer.

Finch frowned. "Surely nothing is impossible, sir."

Luke snorted. "If I tell her now at this late date that I am Silversmoke, there's no way she'll marry me," he said, his heart thumping. "I might as well push her right into Joel's arms!"

"No. I gave her my word that I'd find her missing person, and I shall. But after that, the game's over. You mark me? The time has come to let ol' Silversmoke retire—before my bride figures it out."

Gower shook his head at him in withering reproach. "I can't believe you'd give it all up for a woman."

"Gower!"

"He's right, sir—respectfully." Finch sent Luke a wounded frown. "The people count on Silversmoke."

"The people?" Luke cried. "Haven't I done enough for them yet? I've given them everything I've got for the past, what's it been, six, seven years? Eight? Isn't it *my* turn to be happy for once?"

They said nothing. Both studied the floor.

Luke scowled at them. "Go and see to your tasks. The Sedgwicks will be walking in the door in a moment."

When he started to go, Finch spoke up again. "But, sir, if you love her, that's all the more reason to tell her your secret. Surely it would be the height of dishonor to marry a lady under false pretenses. W-wouldn't it?"

Luke turned around in amazement.

Gower seemed amused that it should be the bookish redhead reminding Luke, of all people, about honor. "Kid's right," he drawled. "If the little wife finds out later by some other means, so much for your marital bliss."

"I can't believe the two of you are teaming up on me! Stop worrying," Luke said with a scowl. "She's not going to find out. We rescue Joel, we quit the game, and move on with our lives. I can't be doing this sort of a thing when I'm a husband and a father! Obviously."

"So you're just going to keep this secret from her for the rest of your life, eh?" Gower asked.

"I daresay she'll draw her own conclusions once she starts living with you, sir," Finch added. "That chap, Sidney, figured it out."

"That is quite enough out of both of you!" Luke barked, his cheeks flushing. "Portia Tennesley is *mine*. Do you understand me? I want her. Like I've never wanted anything before. Whatever I've got to do, whatever the cost, I will not risk this match. Don't you see? I am in love with this woman. I can't—I won't live without her. If that means burying Silversmoke after this last mission, then so be it. One way or the other, she *will* be my duchess. I won't have it any other way."

With that, he strode out of the gymnasium, leaving both men looking thunderstruck.

To hell with their advice. His pulse pounding, Luke marched down the hallway. Still impassioned, he did his best to rein in his churning emotions, but hope and the shadow of loss grappled for ground in the forest of his heart.

Yes, he'd lost his parents to a brutal, senseless murder and had been powerless to stop it. But that was in the past, and now that he knew who had hired the killers, soon his justice would be complete.

And then, by the month's end, he'd have a wife he loved by his side to help him carry on the family line at last.

He'd barely noticed it happening, but somehow, the way he felt about Portia had caused all of life to start making sense to him again. It had seemed so meaningless for so long. But maybe there really was a reason for everything…

Soothed by the thought of her smile, her eyes, her kiss, and their waiting life together, Luke paused in the corridor to collect himself. He took a deep breath, squared his shoulders, and then went to greet what was left of his beloved family.

CHAPTER 21

Dinner with the Duke

*T*he next day, Portia did her best to shake off her lingering uneasiness over what Azrael had told her about Silversmoke. It was not too difficult, thankfully, in the warmth of meeting Lucas's family.

Octavia, Lady Sedgwick—or Tavi, as she preferred to be called—was a tall, statuesque woman with a commanding figure, a loud voice, and chestnut-colored hair. Her green eyes were brighter than her brother's but just as shrewd.

Animated and highly charismatic, the countess could easily dominate any room she entered. Her husband, on the other hand, was a lean, laid-back fellow with patrician features and sandy hair.

Dressed with casual sophistication, Lord Sedgwick had a clever wit and a bit of an arrogant edge to him, but Portia had no doubt whatsoever that, behind closed doors, Tavi could put him in his place.

The Tennesleys, for their part, had arrived at Gracewell only to discover, much to their surprise, that before the traditional Sunday meal would be served, entertainment was to be provided in the form of an elaborate home theatrical.

This was apparently a beloved tradition with the Fountainhurst clan.

It took place in the music room, where no expense had been spared. There was a raised wooden stage complete with red curtains and foot lamps to illuminate the players.

Since this was a matinee performance, the special lighting was not needed, thank goodness, otherwise Portia would have been worried that someone might accidentally set themselves on fire. Especially the stars of the play, Bartram and Katie, who were only ten and seven years old, respectively.

Indeed, the entire household had their designated roles, even the footmen. Each time the red curtains closed, there could be heard great scurrying about from behind it as the duke's staff hastened to change the sets. All the while, the children's governess provided the musical score for the unfolding drama entitled *Redclaw the Terrible*.

Redclaw the Terrible, played by "Uncle Luke," was, of course, a mighty dragon.

If Portia had thought her fiancé was a quiz before, she had burst out laughing when she saw him wearing the giant green papier-mâché dragon head to indulge his niece and nephew.

How he could see from inside of that thing, she could not imagine.

He was probably peering out through the open mouth of the beast, in between the fierce jagged white teeth. His body was concealed beneath a thick green mass of cloth, hand-sewn with individual flapping scales to give the proper lizard effect, complete with a long tail that dragged.

On his hands, he wore heavy green gauntlets for the dragon's front legs. These were tipped with long ivory claws of some sort, morbidly painted with streaks of crimson to represent the blood of the many noble knights he had felled.

Redclaw the Terrible guarded a large wooden façade of a gray-painted castle. Inside was trapped Queen Samantha, briefly played by Portia's mother, who was made to walk around the back of this sturdy prop, poke her head out above the battlements, and cry, "Help, help! Someone save me! Will no one come to my aid?"

"Bravo, Mama!" Portia clapped for her, since audience participation was not just encouraged, but required.

The glamorous marchioness nodded politely. Having spoken her piece, she was then permitted to return to her seat in front of the stage next to Papa.

Even the sleepy Marquess of Liddicoat had been conscripted for a role in the show. He was the sound effects man, and his chief duty was to pound on a drum whenever the mighty dragon walked across the stage, for Redclaw the Terrible did not fly; he was one of the wingless variety of dragons.

Portia had never seen her parents having such a grand time as they watched the entire Fountainhurst family making splendid fools of themselves.

This was done, ostensibly, to indulge Bartram and Katie. They were the stars of the show.

Act one opened when King Sedgwick (their father, Portia's future brother-in-law) received the dreadful news that his kinswoman, Queen Samantha, had been trapped in her castle by Redclaw and could not go outside. To address this dreadful wrong, His Majesty sent off his most trusted champion, Sir Bartram the Brave.

Lucas's ten-year-old nephew marched about self-importantly draped in child-sized chain mail, with a wooden sword painted silver strapped to his side; the shield strapped across his back had the Sedgwick coat of arms painted on it.

But also going along on this adventure—to supervise, no doubt—was Princess Katie. Because she was of royal blood, Sir Bartram had to listen to her, and as all the world knew, big brothers did not like being told what to do by their little sisters.

Every tale needed conflict.

The curly-haired seven-year-old princess wore a tunic of chain mail over her flouncy pink dress. Not to be outdone by her brother, she, too, carried a sword and shield.

And so the heroic duo set out on their quest to save Queen Samantha, or, in Katie's case, "Queen Thamantha." (The princess had recently lost a front tooth.)

Curtain closed.

Behind the red drapery, the footmen could be heard shifting things around. Mama smiled at Portia, who beamed back at her.

While the children's governess played a brief intermezzo, servants shuffled in and out quietly toward the back of the room.

The whole staff had been invited in to watch the performance, which Portia found rather remarkable. The kitchen workers could not stay long, however, since their big performance was next, when dinner was served.

But various servants drifted in and out of the rows of chairs behind the family, or stood lining the walls. Every true actor required a crowd, after all. No star wanted to look out and see an ocean of empty seats.

When the curtain opened on act two, the audience found themselves gazing upon a mysterious dark forest with toy animals placed about here and there. A stuffed rabbit. A statue of a deer.

And here came the questing knights, tiptoeing in amongst the mossy, painted trees, on their way to the castle.

"Stay behind me, Your Highness," Sir Bartram said. "This place is ominous."

"I think we're lotht!" Katie said.

The boy knight glanced around suspiciously. "Methinks I feel an evil presence in this wood."

"There's a fork in the path! Which way do we go?"

"Quiet! Someone's coming," Sir Bartram suddenly said. "It's an old lady..."

"Oh, good! Maybe we can athk her for directions."

From out among the makeshift trees hobbled a hunchbacked crone with a crooked cane and a big, warty nose somehow pasted onto her face.

"Why, halloo, my fair young wanderers. What are you strangers doing in this neck of the woods?" the hag asked in a wheedling voice.

The heroes explained their noble quest, but the little old lady they asked for directions turned out to be a wicked witch (played by their mother, of course).

Tavi clearly had the theater in her blood. The only question was how such a stunning beauty had succeeded in making herself look so hilariously awful.

Someone here had a talent for costuming, to be sure, Portia thought.

Sure enough, the heartless crone attacked the brave children, as witches tend to do. She managed to grab Princess Katie, then lifted her off her feet and placed her right down, shrieking, into her cauldron, where the girl stood up to her waist, calling to Bartram for help.

"Hurry, I'm boiling!"

The audience laughed and applauded while Sir Bartram gently battled his witchy mama, then helped his sister climb out of the stewpot.

Together, they managed to capture the old crone and tie her to the tree, never mind her fearsome howls of protest. They threatened to leave her like that, where the forest animals could come and nibble her toes, but they took pity on her when she told them she had a potion that was their only hope against Redclaw the Terrible.

If thrown on the dragon, it would paralyze him, then Sir Bartram could slay the beast.

Although the witch was crafty, the heroes decided to trust her. They accepted her offer and let her go, then found their way out of the forest, potion in hand.

End act two.

The curtain was already closing as the heroic duo exited stage left.

As act three opened, the audience found themselves back outside the castle, where Redclaw paced restlessly, growling to himself. Soon it would be time for Portia's small part, but first, Redclaw had his big scene.

When Sir Bartram and Princess Katie reached the castle, the dragon pounded the earth with his feet. (Papa beat the drum as best he could in time with the monster's footfalls.)

Letting out terrible roars, the beast swiped at the children with his wicked claws. Katie fought not to giggle, and Bartram whacked the monster with the flat of his blade.

Portia watched in astonishment, wonderstruck and delighted.

Who is this man? She had been speechless when they had rolled up the tree-lined drive to the castle, awed that this place—with its rolling pastures full of blood horses, its stately elegance from floor to ceiling, its big windows on every hand, offering green, sweeping views—would be her home.

But for all its beauty, Gracewell was nothing compared to the treasure that would soon be hers in this whimsical husband.

He had a magic about him that cast a spell on her.

He pounded back and forth across the stage in his ridiculous costume, playing along like the best of good sports. No wonder his niece and nephew so clearly adored their uncle Luke.

Portia had never realized he was Luke to his family.

It warmed the cockles of her heart to see how close-knit they were. It was so different from her house, where everyone went more or less their own way.

At last, Sir Bartram and Katie took the potion from the witch and threw it on the dragon. (Colorful, sparkling confetti.)

Now it was Redclaw's big death scene.

He had absolutely no shame.

Portia watched, shaking her head, unable to wipe the grin off her face while her father pounded the drum, laughing, trying to match the beats with the staggering steps of Redclaw collapsing into his death throes.

Miss Claiborne, the governess, provided suitably dramatic music on the pianoforte. Pounding out an ominous tune on the low keys, she grinned over her shoulder, not wanting to miss the show.

At last, letting out a final, thunderous roar, Redclaw collapsed in a heap on the stage, belly up, though he was careful to move his tail aside before giving up the ghost. (Princess Katie could be heard giggling as he kicked up his feet one last time for good effect.)

But then came the great twist of the ending. Redclaw's fearsome dragon head popped off, and lo and behold, underneath was a handsome prince with a slim golden crown encircling his head.

Sir Bartram and Princess Katie duly gasped.

"Look!" the knight cried.

"Who is that?" Katie ventured closer toward the fallen beast-turned-man. "Sir Bartram, it's our noble cousin, Prince Galahad!"

"The one who disappeared all those years ago? But everyone thought he was dead!"

"Oh! That witch must've turned him into a dragon!" the princess cried.

"I knew she was hiding something," Bartram said, clenching his fist.

Then the children tried to shake him awake.

"Prince Galahad, wake up! Cousin, are you in there?"

"Can you hear us?"

Luke kept his eyes shut, lying there limp as they pulled his big dragon gloves off him to reveal his true hands.

Bartram unlatched a couple of well-hidden clasps on his green, scaly chest, and the costume opened, revealing the upper half of the poor prince.

"It really is him! Bartram, why won't he wake up?"

"The witch's potion only made things *worse!*" the boy said.

"Oh no, we shouldn't have trusted that mean old hag! She tricked us, and now we've killed him!" Princess Katie exclaimed, and started to cry most convincingly.

Her father, Sedgwick, chuckled.

"It's hopeless." Sir Bartram plunked down in defeat beside the faux-weeping Katie.

"There's my cue," Portia whispered to her mother, for if all else failed, a handy *deus ex machina* could still produce the needful happy ending.

Adjusting the flowery wreath on her head (her costume), she gripped the beribboned wand she had been assigned as her prop.

"Break a leg!" Mama whispered as Portia jumped up from her seat in the front row and, feeling entirely ridiculous, decided to give herself over to this absurdity as fully as the duke had. Why not?

If this was the Wakeford way of doing things, she must show her future relatives that she could be one of them.

She pranced in as sprightly a fashion as she could evoke, wafting her way up to the stage, while sweeping her wand back and forth to make the long ribbons trailing off it swirl around.

Princess Katie responded right on cue, lifting her head, drying her pretend tears. "Look, Sir Bartram! It's the fairy queen!"

Portia jumped up onto the stage and flitted over to the children, with the dead dragon-prince between them.

Her parents beamed from the audience.

"What seems to be the trouble, noble knights? It is I, the fairy queen!"

They explained their predicament.

"We don't want him to die! Please, can you help him?"

"Hmm, let me see…" Portia noticed Luke peeking up at her with one eye open, though he was supposed to be at death's door.

She rocked back and forth on her toes, swirling her wand's dangling ribbons back and forth over him, and then in a circle over his chest, and finally, she flicked the wand at him.

"Abracadabra!"

Nothing happened.

Portia frowned.

The children tried to wake him up, but he remained inert.

"Good fairy, it didn't work!" Katie said.

"No matter. I'll try again. Perhaps my aim was off." Portia spun around twice and then flicked her wand at him a second time: "Live!"

Nothing.

She nudged the rogue in the side with her toe. It was supposed to work that time. Why was he going off script?

"Is there nothing else you can do?" Katie pleaded.

Lucas was getting a little too comfortable down there on the floor, but now Portia could see him holding back laughter. His lips twitched, though his eyes remained closed.

"Psst," the wicked witch said to her daughter from the wings.

Princess Katie glanced at her mama, then lit up at the reminder. She turned back and grinned at Portia. "Why don't you try giving him true love's kiss, Auntie Portia? That always works in the *best* stories."

Startled, Portia looked around to find everybody watching her expectantly, smiling, and she gasped with a grin to realize she had been set up! They had all known in advance where this scene was leading — everyone except for her.

Her fiancé was clearly in on it, too, she realized, as he looked up at her and shrugged his dragon shoulders.

She fought a smile. *Very well.* "Do you really think that might work?" she asked the children gravely.

Their heads bobbed.

"Hurry up, before he dies!" Sir Bartram said.

"If I must." But first, Portia looked over to see if her conservative father might be frowning upon this suggestion.

Far from it. Laughing, he gave his blessing with a nod.

Admittedly, she was embarrassed, but she went down on her knees, leaned over the poor fallen prince, and gave him a demure peck on the lips.

It worked.

Back on script, Lucas sat up quickly and gasped for air, as though he'd been holding his breath for a very long time.

He clutched his chest, then started coughing. "Where am I? What happened? I had the strangest dream…"

Portia got out of the way as the children explained, pulling the rest of the dragon costume off him to reveal the true prince charming beneath.

Mama had become so entranced in watching the show that she nearly missed her cue. Portia gave the marchioness an urgent look and gestured toward the castle.

"Oh, right!" Lady Liddicoat jumped up from her seat and hurried around to the back of the castle façade while the music changed to joyous strains of triumph.

The castle door opened, and Queen Samantha ducked out, free at last.

Celebrations ensued, and all ended happily, as it should.

There was nothing left to do now but for the whole cast to take their bows. A special round of applause was offered up for the drum section and the trusty pianist. King Sedgwick and the hunchbacked crone came out together on the stage to bow side by side.

Prince Galahad and the good fairy did the same, hand in hand, and when Luke glanced over at Portia, beaming, she knew beyond any final doubt that, impossible as it seemed, she had truly fallen in love with her soon-to-be husband.

They let go of each other's hands and parted ways, exiting off opposite sides of the stage to hurry back into the audience to clap for the main stars of the show.

Bartram and Katie marched out and received a standing ovation. Portia took one of the flowers out of the wreath on her head and tossed it up onto the stage for them.

"Bravo, everyone!"

In short, it was the most fun she'd had in years. All of the adults looked on dotingly as the children ran to their parents and hugged them, proud of themselves. Then they all milled about, except the servants, who hurried back to their assignments. When Portia turned to Lucas, she found him watching her with a soft smile. His green eyes danced with delight.

"You were marvelous, my dear," he declared.

"Me? You carried the whole thing, you scary bit of business!"

"Someone has to be the villain," he said with a grin.

They laughed, gazing at each other. Portia could not look away, her heart welling up with all her newfound feelings for this man.

Never in her life had she dreamed she could be so happy in what had started as a mere arranged match.

All doubt had evaporated; indeed, she knew now that this was where she belonged—by his side, in this beautiful home, a new member of the colorful family that she was about to join. Luke lifted her hand to his lips and kissed it, since neither of them seemed to know what to say in that moment.

Portia blushed, still feeling a bit funny that she had kissed him in front of everyone. "So, um, should I be calling you Luke instead of Lucas?"

He nodded obligingly. "Or Redclaw the Terrible."

"It suits you!" She laughed, self-conscious with the smitten feeling that had come over her. "You are a man of hidden talents, Your Grace. I had no idea you were such a fine actor—or such a good uncle."

That point was proved when Bartram and Katie came running over to leap on him, hugging their towering costar for all they were worth.

"Bravo, you two," he told them. "As usual!"

"Uncle Luke, I want to sit by you at table!" Katie clung to his hand.

"Uncle Luke is going to sit next to Lady Portia!" Tavi called, somehow hearing from across the room while in another conversation.

"*I* know!" Portia smiled at the little girl. "I'll sit on one side of him and you sit on the other. Would that be all right?"

Katie nodded, but still did not let go of her uncle. She did not look eager to share him.

"I'm hungry!" said Bartram.

"Come along, you two." Tavi took off her hideous fake nose. "It's time to wash up and change for dinner."

Portia was surprised to realize the children would be joining them at the table. She did not mind, of course, though she wondered if her mother might.

After all, it was customary for youngsters their age to eat with their governess in the nursery. Portia and her siblings certainly had.

Apparently, Sunday dinner with this family was different. But on second thought, perhaps it made sense. After being orphaned herself as a young girl, no wonder Tavi doted on her children to a remarkable degree.

Life was fragile, and it was clear the woman believed in embracing the experience fully while it lasted.

Portia couldn't agree more.

While the Wakeford family theater troupe hurried off to change out of their costumes and dress for dinner, the butler approached the three Tennesleys and offered to show them around the castle while they waited for their host and his kin to return.

"If you're sure the Duke won't mind," Portia said, though for her part, she was dying to see more of what would soon be her home.

"It was His Grace's idea, my lady," Crenshaw replied.

"Ah, how nice. Yes, then, thank you. Lead on."

Her parents drifted along with her, following the butler, as he led them from one graciously appointed room to the next, explaining the significance of particular details here and there: an ancient, tattered battle flag on display, won by an ancestor during the Hundred Years' War, an ornate gold automaton clock that had been a wedding gift from King George and Queen Charlotte to Luke's grandparents decades ago; an ancient Greek bust of an unknown general in stunning alabaster.

When they came to the gilded drawing room, with its splendid red damask furniture, Portia froze at the sight of the portrait over the black marble mantelpiece. She suddenly went very still.

"Crenshaw." She turned to him, pointing up at it. "Is that the last duke and duchess?"

The butler gave a sorrowful nod. "Yes, my lady."

Portia walked closer, studying the painting. Lucas—or Luke, as he apparently preferred to be called by family—looked a great deal like his father.

The previous duke had a more serious expression and did not wear spectacles—though Luke had not been wearing them either today, on account of the play, she assumed. He had the same sandy, brownish-blond hair, the same square jaw and penetrating gaze as his father. Portia could see the resemblance between auburn-haired Tavi and her mother, as well.

The last Duchess of Fountainhurst looked thoughtful and slightly amused, with a mischievous twinkle in her green eyes. She had been quite beautiful, and seeing her picture made it all the more horrible to contemplate the violent end she had met with on some lonely mountain road.

Shaken to have come face to face with her murdered predecessor like this, Portia glanced at the butler. "Did you serve under them, Crenshaw?"

He nodded sadly. "I did have that honor, my lady."

"What were they like?"

"All that they should be, ma'am," he said with somber reverence. "Noble, generous, proud. An excellent family."

She gave him a compassionate smile. "It must've been unspeakably painful for you all when they died."

"'Twas worse for our master and Lady Sedgwick."

"I'm sure," she murmured. "But know this: for what it's worth, I will do aught in my power to make His Grace happy."

The butler smiled. "My lady, it is clear you already have."

She gave him a warm look, then the tour moved on.

Every now and then, as they drifted down the various wings of the sprawling ducal residence, Portia noticed some sort of butterfly, moth, or colorful beetle proudly pinned and mounted on the wall in one of those little glass-top display boxes.

She gave her mother a wry look with every one they found.

Mama shrugged, eyes twinkling. "Could be worse, love: deer heads."

Portia chuckled and put her arm around her mother as they walked on.

But it was when they came to a hallway on the ground floor of the east wing that Portia's innate curiosity was piqued.

Crenshaw seemed to grow uneasy as he hurried them past a long room with three different sets of double doors, all of which were closed and, as Portia discovered, locked.

"What's in there?" she inquired, testing one of the doors.

"Erm, that's the ballroom, my lady," the butler said in a judicious tone. "It is…not used."

"Oh, darling, your own ballroom at last! How exciting," Mama said. "May we see it, Crenshaw?"

"I'm terribly sorry, Lady Liddicoat. It is, um, undergoing repairs."

Repairs? thought Portia.

"Oh." Her mother's face fell. "Very well, then. Perhaps some other time." Mama drifted on down the hallway, and Papa followed.

But Portia lingered for a heartbeat, eyeing the locked doors and wondering what sort of repairs had been necessary.

She forgot about the matter a few minutes later when they returned to the entrance hall, where Luke was just coming down the stairs, smartly dressed for dinner with the family.

"There you all are," he greeted them with his usual cheer. "Did you enjoy your tour?"

"Very much. Your home is beautiful," Portia said, leaving her father's side to take his arm.

Luke tucked her hand into the crook of his elbow. "It only lacks one thing," he said. "A proper duchess. But not for long."

"La, how sweet!" Mama said as Luke leaned down and gave Portia a peck on the cheek.

Even Papa smiled. "Aye, 'tis but a fortnight till the wedding." His lack of disapproval for this show of affection amazed Portia; Luke had clearly charmed him in their chat over parakeets.

Then the four Sedgwicks returned in their neat Sunday garb, and the footman came out and murmured something to the butler. Crenshaw then cleared his throat politely to capture the chatting group's attention.

"Ladies and gentlemen," he said, clasping his white-gloved hands behind him, "dinner is served."

CHAPTER 22

A Moonlit Stroll

*L*uke hoped it had not been a mistake to show off his acting skills in front of Portia, but Bartram and Katie were counting on him to play Redclaw the Terrible. Far be it from him to leave the youngsters without a proper villain for them to smite.

The show must go on.

Besides, Portia wasn't going to put two and two together on this, Luke was certain. Who ever would?

Just because there was a fond old tradition of home theatricals in his family, that surely wouldn't be enough to make his fiancée suspect he was, well, a fraud.

Would it?

A ripple of uneasiness ran through him at the question, searing his conscience on its way. But he did his best to ignore it as he pulled out a chair for her beside him on his right, then seated Katie on his left and sat down at the head of the table.

Their little show had broken the ice and brought everyone together, he thought. That was all that mattered. His bride had made a splendid fairy queen, and even her parents seemed to have enjoyed it.

Luke surmised such antics were not part of Tennesley family life. Nevertheless, his future in-laws had managed to go along with it in the spirit of the thing. Older people did tend to unite when it came to entertaining children, especially to such charming youngsters as Bartram and Katie.

Perhaps, before long, Portia and I will have a few of our own.

While Tavi continued entertaining them all, as she was wont to do, Luke was acutely aware of Portia beside him.

He kept glancing over at her and thinking how perfect she looked here at Gracewell, his future duchess.

She belonged here, no question.

Portia had taken a flower from the fairy queen wreath she had worn during the play and tucked it behind her ear. The white bloom added to her fresh, graceful loveliness. She noticed him gazing at her and smiled back discreetly, her hair like a band of white gold held up to the sun.

Eager to have some time alone with her before the day was out, he was glad to see everyone enjoying the meal. The children were content with their favorite—macaroni salad—though Tavi had insisted that Bartram eat some of the celery ragout.

Luke watched his nephew rolling one of the hard-boiled egg yolks garnishing the ragout around his plate, innocently trying to get it onto his spoon. Alas, the boy was at that age where moments of awkwardness just seemed to happen; in the next moment, Bartie accidentally sent the egg yolk flying across the table like a tiny yellow cannonball, where it hit one of the footmen square in the face.

Luke bit his lip to keep from laughing as the boy's eyes widened. The footman blinked but maintained admirable composure as the missile bounced off his nose onto the floor and rolled.

Bartram looked over nervously at his mother, but Tavi hadn't noticed a thing, talking a mile a minute as she ruled the conversation. The child then looked over at Luke.

Luke sent him a conspiratorial wink.

The boy grinned, knowing he'd escaped punishment for his blunder.

"Honestly, you should have seen my brother in our home theatricals when we were children," Tavi was telling his soon-to-be in-laws. "What a ham!"

"Do tell!" Lady Liddicoat said, while Portia laughed.

Luke frowned at his sister, but Tavi ignored him.

"Oh, he could change characters at the drop of a hat! One moment he could be a swashbuckling brigand, and the next, a very Hamlet."

"Even Shakespeare?" Portia asked.

"She's exaggerating, really," Luke mumbled, giving Tavi a stern look. Blast her, she knew full well that she was dropping hints she ought not to be dropping.

Portia suspected nothing, he could tell. "Now Your Grace is only being modest," she teased.

"A modest actor? No such thing," Tavi said.

"What can I say? I always found it droll to be someone else for a while." He sent his sister a discreet warning glare.

"I like pretending, too!" Katie piped up.

"So do I, sweetheart!" her mother declared.

"You made a terrifying witch, Lady Sedgwick," Lord Liddicoat offered.

"Years of practice, trust me," drawled Tavi's husband.

"Sedgwick! You beast." She gave him a pout and a little smack on the arm.

Luke frowned. He had never much cared for his brother-in-law's sense of humor, even though he knew that Tavi could manage him. What his sister saw in that piece of arrogance, he could not fathom, but she had fallen head over heels for Sedgwick when she was barely eighteen.

"Tell me, who made all those gorgeous costumes?" Lady Liddicoat asked. "They were marvelous! And the sets."

"Oh, the whole staff gets involved, don't they? Tell her, Miss Claiborne," Tavi said.

"It's true, my lady." The governess set her soup spoon down politely. "Lady Sedgwick brings in seamstresses and costumers who work for the London theaters."

"No expense spared," Sedgwick murmured with amusement, eyeing his wife.

"In the *off* season," Tavi said. "What else have they got to do? One must support the arts, I always say."

"My countess missed her calling, as you may have guessed," Sedgwick said, and the marchioness laughed.

Luke, however, wanted a change of subject before Portia got suspicious about their family's theatrical tendencies.

After all, these pastimes had been his inspiration for hatching alternative identities in order to hunt his parents' killers. He never would've attempted to become Silversmoke, let alone Lucas, if he hadn't already had years of practice honing his playacting skills.

He'd known from the start that he would need to fool the criminal world, as well as the aristocracy, in order to pursue his goals. That had taken no small measure of audacity.

Along with a willingness to deceive everyone around him.

At the moment, he was not feeling too proud about it, though.

Instead, he was haunted by the thought of what might happen if Portia figured out his ruse, as Gower and Finch had warned.

Distract her, he thought, desperate to pull the conversation away from the whole subject of their home theatricals as quickly as possible.

"Are you, um, enjoying the salmon, my lady?" he asked, reverting to Lucas mode with disturbing ease.

Portia nodded and took a sip of white wine. "Very much."

Everyone agreed the meal was excellent, and Luke breathed a private sigh of relief to have successfully changed the subject.

The day's feast was a lavish midday spread of boiled salmon fillets garnished with prawns, white mushroom fricassee with a tangy touch of lemon, herb pudding, lamb cutlets with watercress garnish, and venison from right here on the estate, glazed with a delicious red currant jelly.

Although there were green gooseberry tarts on the table, Luke and his future father-in-law exchanged a conspiratorial glance, both of them saving room for the promised trifle.

"So, tell me, Lord and Lady Liddicoat," Sedgwick spoke up, "do you have other children besides Lady Portia?"

Luke noticed how his future father-in-law instantly tensed.

"Portia is our youngest," Samantha answered, her smile turning brittle. "Our eldest is Hunter, Lord Arvendon, and my middle child is Sarah, Lady Parrish. She has three children of her own now."

"Oh, why didn't I invite them?" Tavi cried from the foot of the table. "I'm so sorry! I didn't think to ask."

"No worries," Lord Liddicoat mumbled.

"They're very busy," his wife agreed. "They're still in the country at the moment. They have not yet come to Town, so never fear."

"We'll have to do this again sometime when everyone can be here," Luke suggested. "How old are Lady Parrish's children?"

For a while, both Luke and Tavi listened curiously while Samantha described her three grandchildren.

Portia, meanwhile, was watching Katie push her food around her plate until it formed a smiley face. Only then would she eat it.

"You should have your grandchildren come over and play with these two sometime, if that would be convenient. It would be so nice for them to get to know each other a bit," Tavi said, "since we'll all be family soon."

"And what of your son?" Sedgwick inquired. "Is he in the country as well?"

Even the children could not miss the awkward silence that immediately followed.

The marquess and his lady dropped their gazes, and even Portia hesitated. Luke frowned. What was it Sidney had called Portia's brother? Ah yes.

An evil bastard.

Lady Liddicoat's face had stiffened, and her smile turned even brittler. Her husband had stopped smiling altogether and lowered his gaze to his plate, his chubby jowls tensing.

Portia gave Luke a wide-eyed stare that begged for a change of subject.

"We, um, do not see my brother much," she said. "Hunter has been traveling for quite some time."

"But he will be at the wedding!" her mother hastened to add.

"Oh, good," Tavi said, no doubt sensing the tension. She then smoothly steered the conversation in a direction that could not fail to please. "Now, who's ready for cake?"

After dinner, Luke led his guests on a casual stroll outside, showing them the gardens and the castle grounds. There was time for a lazy game of croquet on the lawn. Sedgwick had a smoke while they tapped the wooden balls through the series of arches.

Luke watched Portia playing croquet in delight, sizing up her shots with that keen archer's eye of hers. Next, they stopped in the stables, where the children ran to greet their favorite ponies. Luke was relieved to see that Gower had taken Tempo out of his stall.

"Can we go riding this evening, Uncle Luke?"

"Tomorrow," Tavi told them. "It's nearly time to start getting ready for bed, you two."

They whined, but she was right. It was almost eight o'clock, and the western sky was afire with big, billowing pink clouds.

Twilight was descending as they all headed back into the house. The children reluctantly said their goodbyes, then Miss Claiborne led them off to prepare for bed while the adults repaired to the drawing room.

Sedgwick got the Liddicoats and Portia engrossed in some sort of political discussion, so Tavi took Luke aside on the pretext of planning tomorrow's activities.

She pulled him into the next room, then turned to him with a proud smile. "Well, brother, I'd say you owe me a *huge* congratulations."

"Oh?" Luke laughed softly. "What have you done now?"

She propped her hand on her waist and leaned against the wall. "I found you the ideal bride, thank you very much."

He grinned. "You have."

"Truly, I ought to win some sort of matchmaking award! You two are adorable together. I was watching you with her the whole time. Oh, you melt my heart, you're so besotted! And Portia—such a lovely creature—she couldn't take her eyes off you the whole time."

"Really?" Luke asked, beaming.

Tavi closed her eyes and gave a heartfelt nod. "I'm so happy for you, Luke—and so relieved! Finally, someone has found the chink in your armor. In short, she's perfect for you."

His smile stretched wider. "I know."

Tavi lifted her glass. "A toast to my matchmaking skills."

"I'll drink to that," he said heartily, and they clinked their glasses.

They both took a swallow, gazing at each other, needing no words to reflect together on how much they'd been through and how far they had come in building new lives for themselves since the tragedy in their youth.

"She's good for you," Tavi said at length. "You seem different."

"Do I?" Luke leaned against the doorway, musing. He glanced into the other room at Portia. "I do feel different," he admitted.

"No wonder. Dare I say it, you seem—happy?"

He snorted in acknowledgment and looked away.

Just for a heartbeat, he considered telling Tavi what he learned about Axewood's role in their parents' deaths. But this was very much not the time or place. He let it go for once. Old wounds had to start healing sometime.

"I am, actually."

"At last!" Tavi squeezed his hand. "You deserve it, brother. She is wonderful. Our parents would've loved her."

"I know." Luke lowered his head with a pang in his heart.

But with the gorgeous full moon rising over the green hills, he was not about to pass up a very special opportunity before the Tennesleys saw fit to head home.

"Do you think you could contrive to help the two of us steal away alone for a little while?" he asked in a low tone.

"Why, you rogue." Tavi's eyes danced.

"I'm not being— I just, I have that ring of Mother's I want to give her. The sapphire."

"What? You haven't given it to her yet?" she cried in a hush, then smacked him on the arm with her folded fan. "Shameful, horrid dunderhead!"

"Ow," said Luke.

"Two weeks before the wedding and you still haven't given the bride a ring? Honestly! What is wrong with you, Lucas?"

"It's been a strange courtship!"

She whacked him again for good measure. "Jinglebrains."

"Might I remind you, you're the one who shoved me into this. This whole thing started out as an arranged match. I barely knew her for the longest time, but now..."

"Now?" Tavi folded her arms across her chest and regarded him expectantly.

He couldn't help but smile. "Now, I don't think I can possibly do without her."

"Humph. Very well. In that case, you must have a moment alone with your bride."

"Think you can manage something?"

She gave him a lofty little smile. "This is me you're talking to. Of course." Then she glanced at the gathered company in the next room. "Shouldn't be too difficult. Everyone wants this match badly for you both, if you haven't noticed."

"No one wants it more than I do," he said softly.

"Aww, little brother." Tavi pressed up onto her toes and gave him a peck on the cheek. "For you, anything."

Sure enough, when they returned to the drawing room, without too much effort, she feigned a sudden inspiration and clapped her hands together. "Oh, I know! I am so craving a good game of whist! Who will join me?"

Since the game required four players, both couples sat down at the card table in the drawing room, but Luke and Portia hung back.

Once the game got underway, they exchanged communicative glances and, one by one, managed to slip out. Luke went first, inching backward out of the drawing room. No stranger to stealthy moves, he.

Shortly thereafter, Portia mumbled an excuse and walked out in a state of distraction, as though there was something important she needed to attend to.

"Psst!" Luke whispered, beckoning eagerly to her from the bottom of the staircase.

She flitted after him with a grin, peering over the polished handrail.

As she began to follow, he led her deeper into the house. They played a stealthy game of hide-and-seek until he'd led her out onto the moonlit terrace.

He gazed at her as she stepped out into the starlight through the French doors, joining him.

"There's my bride." He held out his hands to her. She glided over to him and clasped them both.

Luke held her delicate fingers gently in his grip, gazing at her for a long moment. She held his stare with magic shimmering in her eyes.

"Finally," she whispered.

He leaned down and gave her a light kiss on the lips. "Are you having a good day?"

Her cheeks dimpled as her smile grew. "*Very* good."

"Excellent. Come," Luke said, moving beside her and tucking her hand into the crook of his elbow. "There's something I want to show you."

"What is it?" she asked, her step light and graceful, as always, as she walked beside him.

He lifted her hand to his lips and kissed it. "It's a surprise."

She laughed. "Oh, indeed?"

He escorted her down the stone steps on the other end of the terrace, and out across the breezy expanse of grass, heading for the pond where he liked to swim.

"Won't you at least tell me where we're going?"

He shook his head with a mysterious smile. "You'll see."

CHAPTER 23

All That Glitters

*W*alking out across the breezy lawn hand in hand with Luke, Portia felt as though she'd stepped into a dream. On this balmy midsummer's night, the glittering constellations stretched overhead, while the full moon sat like an opulent pearl on a bed of black silk.

Luke's hand, so much larger than hers, wrapped around her fingers, his warm touch full of gentle strength.

As a delicate whiff of night-blooming jasmine perfumed the air, Portia was acutely aware of him: of his shoulder looming above her as they walked beside each other; of the wind tousling his hair and the starlight shimmering along his noble profile.

He held his head high as he led the way. He was not wearing his spectacles, to her private delight. Not that she disliked them, but he looked so much handsomer without them.

Strange, he did not seem to need them tonight.

Behind them, the lights of the castle shone in the windows. She could still barely believe that she would live in a castle soon…

Then she smiled, musing on the family meal back there. It had gone quite well. No disasters, and the food, to be sure, was delicious. The sweet flavor of strawberry pie with whipped cream still lingered on her tongue.

The host himself was most delicious, though, she decided, stealing another smitten glance at him. She reveled in the simple pleasure of being alone with him. The night sparkled with wonder, especially when a nightingale somewhere warbled a lilting melody, serenading them.

Luke and she both glanced toward the trees, but the little singer remained hidden. They exchanged a smile and strolled on, their pace slowing, their footsteps whispering through the ankle-deep grass.

A moth hurried by, tickling right past her ear.

"You seem thoughtful," Portia remarked.

"Actually, I'm wondering if I'm allowed to ask what happened with your brother."

Portia gave him a quick smile, though the topic troubled her. "I take it you noticed the awkwardness on that point."

"It would have been difficult to miss," he admitted. "Why?"

She sighed. "It was a bad business. Poor Hunter. He got into a duel and had to leave England, I'm afraid."

"Really?"

She nodded ruefully. "It was over a young lady. Unfortunately, things seem to escalate as a rule where my brother is concerned."

Luke gave her a curious glance. Since he would be her husband, he had a right to know, so Portia continued.

"A friend of Hunter's was enamored of a certain young lady. He meant to ask for her hand, but my brother knew from firsthand experience that this girl was a thoroughgoing coquette, playing his friend false. She'd thrown herself at him on various occasions."

Luke winced. "Ah."

"It turned out that to feed her own vanity, this attention-craving girl had been encouraging the suits of several different young gentlemen, behaving in a scandalous fashion, and leading his unwitting friend on all the while. She was in no wise serious about Hunter's friend, but hanging on to him just in case no one better came up to scratch."

"Lord," Luke muttered.

An owl hooted somewhere, as though agreeing with him.

Portia shrugged and pushed a lock of hair behind her ear when it blew in her face and tickled her nose in the breeze. "Well, Hunter tried to warn his friend, but Anthony wouldn't listen. Unfortunately, my brother set out to prove the point by flirting with the girl himself in front of his friend, merely as a demonstration. One thing led to another… Well, women do tend to lose their wits over my brother."

Luke gave her a look of amusement. "Handsome chap?"

"Very," Portia said proudly. "The next thing he knew, Hunter had this scandalous hussy eating out of his hand. When Anthony found out, he took it...amiss."

"I should think so."

"He was so angry he actually called Hunter out. My brother refused to fight him, but also refused to apologize, since he was only trying to help—albeit in a misguided fashion. Anthony refused to believe that Hunter had been trying to protect him from a two-faced flirt who would only break his heart and make his life miserable if he married her."

Luke grimaced. "Rather heavy-handed help, though."

"True. It's always strong medicine with Hunter. People say he's intense." She shrugged. "He meant well, but poor Hunter. The whole thing exploded in his face. Somehow he came out as the villain.

"Nor did he help his own cause, frankly, for he refused to admit any wrongdoing. Too proud. For that reason, he eventually saw he'd have to duel against his friend. And so he did."

"How awful."

"Anthony tried to kill him, but Hunter sought to miss—only, he grazed Anthony's side in the volley. I'm not sure to this day if it was infection or the surgeons' bleeding him that really killed Anthony, but my brother got the blame. Anthony died within a fortnight, and there was talk that Hunter would be arrested.

"All my brother's friends turned against him. I was still in the schoolroom at the time, but the general condemnation of him even cast aspersions on Sarah, who was just making her debut.

"My parents were receiving the cut direct everywhere. It tore our family apart for a while, and things have frankly never been the same. That's the reason Hunter left—so that *our* lives, at least, could go back to normal, even though he had all but ruined his own."

"I'm sorry," Luke said in a kind tone.

"I hope you won't think badly of my family for this—"

"No. Sounds to me like your brother had some dreadful bad luck. He didn't mean for his friend to die."

Portia nodded with a mild scoff. "Anthony brought it on himself, if you ask me. He refused to see the truth that Hunter was trying to show him. Instead of thanking my brother for opening his eyes, he'd have killed him from sheer rage, only, thank God, he missed. Those who live by the sword, as they say.

"Not that Hunter acted much better," she added with a rueful glance at Luke. "The whole situation should've never escalated to violence like that. I love my brother dearly, but let's just say he has never backed down from a fight. I don't think he even knows how." A sigh escaped her. "Of course, that trait probably serves him well in his current life."

"Why? What's he doing now?"

She gave a bewildered shrug. "He bought a ship and became some sort of privateer."

Luke paused and looked at her in amazement. "You're serious?"

She nodded, chuckling. "He always had a taste for adventure. I daresay England was too small for him. Especially when so many of his closest friends abandoned him. He became an outcast, I'm afraid. So, he embraced the role, and off he went. Even Sidney hates him now."

"Hmm."

They walked on thoughtfully.

Ahead, Portia saw a lovely weeping willow tree leaning over a pond that reflected the stars. She gazed at the tranquil sight as they walked toward it, then glanced at her fiancé.

"So, what do you think of the big family secret?"

Luke gave her a disarming smile. "Oh, I've got nothing against your brother, my dear. But I am rather wondering now if anyone's going to start throwing punches at the wedding."

She laughed. "Only my father. No, whatever sort of scoundrel he may be, I'm sure Hunter will behave himself for our sake. After all, it's just for one day. He was always a good brother to me."

She paused. "Sometimes, when it's been a long while between letters from him, I wonder if he's even still alive. He has never shrunk from danger, or violence." She shuddered and took Luke's arm, clinging to him for a moment. "I'm so glad *you're* not like that, Lucas. A violent man. It touches my heart to see how gentle you are...with me...a-and the children."

Any answer Luke might have given her withered on his tongue as her innocent comment brought him face to face with all his lies. Guilt flooded him, and he looked away, watching their path through the grass beneath their feet.

She didn't seem to notice his momentary floundering.

"It's lovely to see how well you get along with your sister, by the by," Portia added.

Luke glanced at her, grateful for the distraction. "Tavi's a good sort.

Did you like how she helped us slip away together?"

"Very smooth," she answered with a chuckle. "Her children are delightful."

He smiled.

"You seem, I dunno, different around your family," she said.

"Do I?" Luke asked uncomfortably.

She nodded. "More at ease here than in London. But I suppose that's only natural, since this is your home."

"I do prefer the country," he murmured with a vague nod, but was feeling increasingly plagued by his conscience.

He ignored it. The pond lay ahead.

"Come, we're almost there."

"Where are we going?"

"This way." He sent her a secretive smile and pulled ahead of her, releasing her hand. "There's something astonishing I want you to see."

There was a slight depression in the ground, which led down to his swimming pond with the willow tree beside it.

The simple fountain in the center splashed on in the quiet of the night; its vertical spout and circular return kept the water moving so the pond stayed fresh. It cut down on algae but did not stop the pussy willows from thriving around the edges.

Luke took Portia's hand again as they approached the pool. When she had lifted the hem of her pale skirts a bit, laughing curiously as to what he was about, he led her down the little curved path to the grassy banks.

Somewhere among the reeds, an alarmed frog plopped into the water with a splash.

"Oh!" Portia said, glancing around. "There aren't any snakes here, are there?"

"I've never seen one."

"Good." She came to stand beside him and smiled up at him in puzzled expectation.

"Now, my dear, I brought you here for a very special reason. Look closely. If you still think 'little creepy-crawly things,' as you once put it, are no fun, behold!" Luke swept a showman-like gesture at the moonlit prospect before them.

Portia stared into the dark. "What am I looking at, then?"

"Check the reeds," he whispered.

She did, silent for a moment, then: "Ohhh!"

"You see?" Luke beamed as she realized why he'd brought her down here.

In among the reeds and tall grasses around the pond, the darkness glistened with glow worms. The tiny caterpillars only came out for a few short weeks around this time of year and confined their magical performance to wet, dismal places.

"You see them?"

"Yes!"

He watched the wonder steal over her face, her lips parting slightly as she stared at the sparkling little secrets tucked away in the landscape before them. Like tiny fallen stars.

"The more you look, the more you see," he said, pointing.

On the reeds around the pond and on the branches of the stark dead tree that loomed against the dark sky, and riding the gentle sway of the weeping willow boughs, countless glow worms twinkled everywhere like a thousand fairy lights.

She said not a word, staring all around in wonder while the crickets sang and the smell of the grasses in the fields filled the cool, silken darkness around them.

The big, gold full moon glittered on the water, where a turtle poked its snout out of the pond.

"Oh, Lucas...it's beautiful." She turned and looked up at him incredulously.

"No, my darling Portia," he said in a husky voice, "you are."

Moved by the magic on her face, the dazzled innocence in her eyes, Luke captured her chin with his fingertips, leaned down, and kissed her gently.

His future duchess. Mother of his future children.

His line would be whole once more…

His lips rested on hers for a moment, but he held himself in check, though his heart was pounding. He felt her cup his elbows with a light touch, holding on to him.

"Oh, Portia," he breathed, "I've been wanting to do that all day."

"More, please." She ran her hands up his chest and put her arms around him.

Luke wrapped his arms around her waist and kissed her with fierce tenderness. Her response inflamed him. She pressed her lips to his, and when he felt her quiver in his arms, he could no longer contain his emotions.

"Portia—I'm so in love with you." The words broke from him as his chest heaved.

She stopped kissing him, and her eyes swept open. She searched his face with a look of dreamy surprise. "You are?"

He nodded slowly. "You must know how I feel. I would do anything for you. I mean it."

"Oh Lucas…" Again, her use of that name tweaked his conscience. "I…I feel the same for you."

"Truly?" he asked, awestruck.

"Surely you can tell." She reached up and stroked his hair, then caressed his face. "I've fallen in love with you, Lucas, and I—I am entirely eager to marry you."

He stared at her in shock. "I-I'm speechless."

A laugh of pure enchantment bubbled up from her lips. "That's all right, darling. You don't have to talk."

He laughed breathlessly as she slid her hand around the back of his head and started to pull him down for another kiss—except he stopped her.

"You love me? You actually said that?"

Her doting smile widened. "Yes, Lucas, I do. You are wonderful."

He stared at her, flummoxed as the truth sank in. She loved Lucas. She *wanted* Silversmoke, he'd noticed. But somewhere along the way, she had actually given her heart to the bumbling quiz.

My God. Was that not precisely what he'd hoped for, ached for, secretly dreamed of, and long since concluded he could never have? Maybe *shouldn't* have. But she returned his feelings.

And that changed everything.

Luke took her carefully into his arms, lowered his head, and kissed her with all he had in him, all the hope she'd resurrected, all the joy she'd helped him find again, and all the devotion he had learned from watching his father treat his mother like a queen.

All he had to give had just become hers.

He caressed her face, cupped her nape, and let his fingers penetrate the silken coils of her hair, running his left hand up and down her back all the while. She parted her lips hungrily for his tongue, and a small moan escaped her when he licked deep into her mouth. He was instantly intoxicated by the taste of her. But when he felt her fingers dig into his shoulders, he lifted her up off her feet, into his arms.

Still kissing her, he walked the narrow trail around the edge of the pond, taking shelter under the green dome of the willow tree, while the glow worms sparkled all around them.

She was panting when he set her down on her feet, her back to the tree trunk. At once, she drew him to her by his lapels, looking tousled and delicious in the moonlight that filtered down through the whispering branches.

Sheer temptress, with fire in her eyes and ecstasy waiting for him on her lips. Luke did not care what her parents or anyone else inside thought when they returned.

If they returned.

All that existed in this moment was his throbbing want of her, his beautiful, soon-to-be bride, her desire for him, and the mutual hunger that had swept them up in the magic of this sensual spring night.

He wanted to make love to her here and now beneath this tree with the moonlight filtering in through the branches. He knew she would not stop him. They both had been far too well behaved, too civilized for too long.

And yet, as fierce as his need was, as sweet as the curves were that she thrust into his hands, offering her breasts eagerly for his exploration, Luke's heart sank as he realized there was a stronger drive within him than even the fiery arousal throbbing at his groin.

Damn his bloody conscience!

He did his best to ignore it, having waited so long for this reward. He kissed and caressed her, stroked her breasts until her swollen nipples jutted against his palms. Panting, he moved against her till she moaned for release.

And yet…

Amazed at her eager writhing against him, Luke knew he could not proceed for one more minute with her under false pretenses.

Finch was right.

To do what he wanted to her right now without ever telling her who he really was would be the height of dishonor. His body cried out, but his conscience stood firm as he tore his mouth away from hers, panting. "I can't do this."

"Of course you can, Lucas. Trust me," she said breathlessly, and pulled him back to her. "I'll show you."

Luke could not help kissing her once more, but he shook his head, his lips to hers. Then he moved back again ever so slightly. "Portia—I really can't."

His eyes widened when she reached down and placed her hand between his legs with a naughty little giggle. "I daresay you can, Your Grace."

He flinched with lust, then took a startled half step back from her. "You don't understand."

"What's the matter, darling?" she asked, finally sensing the seriousness in his tone. She cupped his cheek, her lips bee-stung and wet.

He wanted to devour them. But this was wrong. "Portia, there's something I have to tell you."

She frowned, pouting slightly. "What is it?"

Luke could not believe he was doing this. The happiness he had yearned for all his life was in his reach. The love he had needed so desperately for so long after everything he'd been through was right before him. But, for honor's sake, he stood on the precipice of throwing it all away.

A tremor ran through him.

She was staring at him now, wide-eyed. "Did I do something wrong? Was I too forward—"

"No! No, darling," he assured her softly, cursing himself for this. Why could he not just act like a normal rakehell for once in his life?

Why did he have to be Prince bloody Galahad?

Because that's how my parents raised me. Besides, gazing into her eyes, he knew his sweet lady deserved better than this from him. She deserved honesty.

"What is it, Lucas?" She reached out and cupped his face. "Whatever it is, you know you can tell me."

Don't do this. Don't ruin it. You've finally won her and now you're going to lose her. There must be some other way.

Think.

Heart pounding, he turned away as he strove to clear his head. But his mind was so clouded with the scarlet frenzy of want that he could not come up with anything cleverer than simply blurting out, "Portia, I know about your search for Joel Clayton."

She went perfectly silent, perfectly motionless, shocked. A look of panic flashed across her face. She seemed to hold her breath as she said, "You...do?"

He nodded, avoiding her gaze.

"H-how?" she said, but the question faded into a whispered apology. "Oh my God, Lucas, I'm so sorry!"

He shook his head, pained. No, the point of this wasn't to make her feel guilty.

Damn it, for too long, the presence of this third party in their relationship hung like a phantom in their midst. Luke wanted it out, any memory of Joel out of her heart, along with his own lies out in the open, where they could not haunt him anymore.

"Truly, I-I can explain. I was upset. I-I'm so sorry, Lucas!" She sounded frantic, and he could see her posture shrinking into shame.

That was not what he wanted.

"Please don't hate me. I only needed to know what hap—"

"Portia, it's all right," he interrupted, though he wasn't sure it was.

She stared at him, looking stricken and ashamed of her earlier preoccupation with her former suitor. But it was best to clear the air before the wedding.

"H-how did you find out?" she ventured.

Oh, that was the question, indeed.

"Was it Azrael who told you?"

"No, darling. You did," he said softly. "I've known from the very start."

"I...I don't understand."

Luke held his breath and stared at her. "Portia," he finally said, "I'm Silversmoke."

She gazed at him for a long moment, clearly confused. "What?"

"I am Silversmoke," he repeated.

She narrowed her eyes with bafflement. "Lucas—no you're not."

"I am," he said wearily. "I have been all along."

She knitted her brow and studied him with deepening incredulity.

"I created my highwayman identity after my parents were slain. To help me hunt down their killers. I needed a way to infiltrate the criminal underworld."

"No! That's impossible." Shaking her head, she took a few jerky steps away from the tree trunk, brushing by him.

But she did not pass through the hanging green curtain of the boughs, remaining under the willow's dome with him.

Luke's heart pounded. His stomach was in knots as he watched her.

She stood very still, her back to him.

"I'm sorry," he whispered.

She turned around slowly. "This isn't a prank?"

"No." He shook his head slowly.

"You…are…Silversmoke?"

"At your service," he said with a nod. "The Blind Badger. The booth in the back where we first talked. The domino game pieces. That's what I do. That's who I am. Sometimes."

She shook her head so hard that the soft tendrils of her flaxen hair that had fallen from her chignon during their kisses swept across her collarbones, back and forth. "I don't believe you!"

"I'm telling the truth." He saw fury gathering over her delicate features now.

"You're the Duke of Fountainhurst! My fiancé. You're clumsy and unassuming, you're a gentle soul and— Tell me you're playing a joke on me now, Lucas!"

"I can't do that." He swallowed hard.

She whirled away again with a small cry of rage, turning her back to him, one hand on her waist, the other pressed to her brow. But again, she did not leave.

She stood very still, facing the gently swaying boughs of the willow tree that hung down around them like a great green umbrella.

When she spoke again, her voice held an odd, strained note. "That room with all the locked doors. Crenshaw said it was under construction." She turned around slowly and stared at him. "What's in there?"

"The ballroom? You noticed that, eh?" He gave a grim nod. "Why don't you go and see it for yourself? Maybe then you'll see I'm telling the truth."

Luke walked past her and put his arm out to brush aside some of the hanging boughs, parting them like the curtain door that hung over his private booth at The Blind Badger.

She walked through it in a daze. He followed her back out into the night.

When they stood under the indigo sky once more, he pointed across the lawn to the steps off the back of the house that he used every day after training to come out to the pond for a swim.

"Go up those stairs, and through that door."

Portia stalked ahead of him. Luke watched her walking away with a heavy heart. Her every step was graceful, her pale, gauzy gown floating out behind her in the night breeze.

Her slippered feet barely seemed to touch the earth as she followed the little trail that curved around the pond, and then quickly alighted the few big stones up to the meadow. She even moved like the fairy queen, he thought, aching with regret over his lies as he followed her.

He could not bear to lose her.

Neither of them spoke all the way back to the house. Portia went to the shallow stone staircase off the ballroom and swept up the few steps to the landing at the top, where she opened the door with catlike caution.

Luke followed a few steps behind, giving her a moment to see for herself that he was indeed telling the truth about his dual identity. Or was it triple now?

Hell, neither Lucas nor Silversmoke were entirely him.

He only knew that the man he really was needed and loved her.

Unfortunately, he could not imagine what she must be feeling. Betrayed? Would she still want to marry him?

He was afraid to find out, but he somehow scrounged up the courage to try to gauge her reaction as he followed at a wary distance.

She was standing inside his ballroom-turned-training studio, staring all around at the evidence that he was telling the truth.

Luke swallowed hard. "Portia?"

CHAPTER 24

Mirrors & Masks

*I*gnoring his query, Portia crept into the darkened ballroom, looking all around her in shock. The moonlight pouring in through the tall windows revealed things she did not want to see. Racks of weapons on display. Mirrors on the walls.

Some sort of elaborate zigzag balance beam where a warrior might train. Leather mats laid out across the wooden floor, like this was a gymnasium. There were targets fixed to the ballroom pillars and a heavy bag strung from the ceiling in one corner.

As the truth finally sank in, she drifted to a halt mere steps into the vast, rectangular room, reeling.

This was not a ballroom, a place for happiness and dancing.

No, this space intended for laughter and celebrating life had been transformed into a temple dedicated to violence and death.

To revenge.

Azrael's revelations of yesterday echoed in her mind like the ominous tolling of a church bell.

Twenty men dead…

The hairs on her nape bristled as she heard Luke arrive behind her. She glimpsed his reflection in the wide set of mirrors across from her, hung there, she guessed, so that a warrior could check his form from all angles.

Flabbergasted, Portia turned around slowly and saw him silhouetted in the doorway, and suddenly it was all so clear.

Of course.

How could she not have seen it before? His silhouette gave him away. In fact, his kiss just a moment ago had begun to do just that. The feel of being held in his arms. An intoxicating familiarity…

Silversmoke.

She stared at him, cursing herself as the truth sank in. *Fool!*

How could she have been so blind? He'd been standing right in front of her all this time, only she could not conceive it. Oh, but she recognized him now.

The broad shoulders. The square chin, the moonlight dancing along his rugged jaw line.

Lucas?

Her lower lip began to tremble as she suddenly realized there was no such person. Her bumbling, beloved quiz. He was just a role this stranger played. Just like Silversmoke.

Neither of them were real.

In that moment, she felt more alone than ever.

"Who are you?" she whispered, unable to keep the hint of tears out of her voice.

"Please—"

"Who in the hell am I about to marry?" she suddenly cried. "I don't even know you!"

He took a step into the ballroom after her. "Portia. You know me. You do. Please, sweeting. I'm sorry."

She took a step back, not wanting him to come any closer. "You lied to me. You've been lying all along."

"I didn't mean to hurt you."

She took another step back, unsure what this two-faced stranger might be capable of if he found himself in a situation where he could not get what he wanted.

For her part, Portia couldn't even think right now. Her head was spinning, and her heart felt as though it had been ripped out of her body.

He lifted a hand toward her. "Darling—"

"Stay back! Just stay away from me, whoever you are!"

"Portia, I never meant for any of this to happen, but then, there you were, that night at The Blind Badger, showing up out of the blue."

"Yes," she whispered. "Asking Silversmoke to find Joel for me so I wouldn't have to marry the Duke of Fountainhurst. Oh my God!" She buried her face in her hands in shame and spun away from him. "I knew this entire match was a disaster from the start."

He flinched. "Come, it's not *all* a disaster."

"Yes it is!" She turned back to him in fury. "You let me sit there and pour out my heart to you like an utter fool!"

"I remember, believe me," he answered in a hollow tone. "You said you wanted me to find the man you really loved. Imagine my surprise. My own bride."

"But you said nothing!" She dropped her hands to her sides and turned to glare at him with tears in her eyes. "You interrogated me, and you never said a word!"

"What was I to say?" he cried. "I was in shock to see you there myself! *And* to hear your request. My future duchess, still in love with someone else?"

"Why didn't you break off the match, then, if you were so indignant?" she shouted, though she kept a safe distance.

"Why didn't *you*?" he thundered back, glowering at her.

She snapped her jaw shut briefly. "Do *not* yell at me, sir."

He visibly checked his temper and blew out a breath. "It wasn't as though I could *tell* you about my dual identity. Only a handful of people know about this. Frankly, I can hardly believe I'm telling you now. But I'm going to quit, Portia. Just as soon as I rescue Joel for you, exactly as I promised."

She felt overwhelmed, dazed as she studied him. "Oh God…it really is you, isn't it? I'm engaged to a highwayman!"

Shaking her head in disbelief, she turned away and steadied herself with a hand on the balance beam.

"Are you all right?"

She looked over her shoulder, scrutinizing him as he warily approached. "Is it true you slaughtered twenty people up in Scotland?"

His face hardened in the shadows. "They murdered my parents." His voice became steel. "Don't ask me to apologize for that, for I never will. They all deserved to die."

Portia swallowed hard, for it was then that any lingering doubt she might have had dissolved. Oh, that ruthlessness in him, she recognized.

She remembered it well from their two brief meetings.

Meetings that had taken place in the darkness…under the cover of shadows.

"You must think me such a fool."

"No." He shook his head. "Never."

"So blind… How you tricked me! Every time we've been together, it's all been a lie, hasn't it?" Tears flooded her eyes. "You were laughing at me inside—"

"No I wasn't!"

"Of course you were." She shook her head, appalled to remember how she had flung herself into the handsome highwayman's arms that night at the gazebo.

Cheating on her fiancé.

Or so she thought, when, in fact, it was him all along.

It dawned on her that he must have been testing her. The bastard! A fresh wave of indignation flooded into her veins, mingling with her fury.

"Portia." Beginning to sound a bit desperate, Luke took another step toward her. "Please. I know what I did was wrong, and I admit that. But you're not entirely innocent here, either. Can you own up to it, in turn?"

She inhaled sharply through her nostrils while her cheeks flamed.

"You were engaged to the Duke of Fountainhurst in good faith," he said, "and yet you went behind my back in a final bid to try to find your precious Joel. All so you could get out of marrying me."

"You played along!" she shouted, furious that he would dare point that out right now, when he was clearly the villain here. "I suppose it doesn't matter that, in the meantime, you made me fall in love with Lucas, who doesn't even exist! You never had any intention of actually looking for Joel, did you?"

"Of course I did. I gave you my word!"

"What's the word of a highwayman worth?" she retorted. "You are obviously a colossal liar!"

"Dammit, I'm telling the truth! I've been looking for him constantly. What the hell do you think I've been doing all this time? You were right. He is alive. He was kidnapped, but never fear," he growled. "Plans to rescue your darling Joel are already in motion. You'll have him back by the end of next week, if all goes well. And then, my dear, you'll have a choice to make."

Portia was taken aback to hear this and unsure whether to believe another word that passed his too-tempting lips.

Trying to hide how shaken she was, she paused, folding her arms across her chest. "So you actually did it, then? You actually went searching for my old beau? Knowing there was a fair chance I'd jilt you once I had him back?"

He let out a curse, laughed under his breath, and angrily looked away. "You think I want to marry someone who doesn't want to marry me? You think I need to do that? I daresay I could find another as easily as you could, my sweet."

Portia stared at the coxcomb, amazed that he would dare to remind her at a time like this what a desirable commodity he was on the marriage mart—or could be, if he decided to try.

But on second thought, why was she surprised? This was Silversmoke she was talking to. There was almost nothing he wouldn't dare. She knew it well, having studied his legend.

Now she saw that all those gallant stories must have been filtered through rose-colored glasses. They had certainly never warned her he was a killer.

He stared at her, a handsome stranger. "Say something."

"What am I to say?" she replied, at a loss.

In that moment, she could feel their match hanging by a thread.

Luke's face stiffened by barely perceptible degrees.

"It's over, isn't it?" he asked softly, stoically, after a long moment.

Her voice stuck in her throat. Portia had no answer.

He lowered his head with a small, bitter laugh and turned away, hands on hips. "Of course. I understand. Do what you must, my darling. Far be it from me to stand in the way of your happiness."

"Lucas…"

"*Don't* call me that." He glanced at her with searing anger. "It's Luke," he ground out. "The people who really know me call me Luke."

"Well, I don't know you at all."

"But you do. You know you do, Portia. You know my heart. For God's sake, you own the damned thing."

She shook her head. "I feel like such a fool."

He took a step toward her. "Please. If I had it to do over again, knowing what I know now, knowing you, I never would've lied to you. It was just an arranged match at the start, Portia, and—let's be honest—neither of us really gave a damn. Your visit to The Blind Badger made that clear."

She flinched at his brutal honesty, belated as it came.

His green eyes searched her face. "You say you don't know me. Well, I didn't know you, either. What was I supposed to do, trust a girl I barely even knew with a secret that could get me hanged?"

She held her ground as he ventured closer. "Well, if that's how it stands, then maybe you shouldn't have proposed to me in the first place."

"Do you wish me to retract it?" he whispered.

She glared at him, but could not bring herself to say yes. She was furious at him and wanted to wring his neck, but that didn't mean she was ready to let him go.

Not yet.

"Come, do you think I could've helped any of those peasants if the world knew who Silversmoke was?" he cajoled her.

"You don't understand!" She threw up her hands. "I cannot marry a highwayman. It's ridiculous! I want nothing to do with this."

"Oh, but it was fine when you needed my help, wasn't it?" He let out a cynical snort and shook his head. "Figures. The beautiful Portia Tennesley, impossible to say no to. I let you use me in both of my personae, so, clearly, I'm the fool here."

Portia gasped with fury. "*Use* you?"

He shrugged.

"I have never used anyone in my life! How dare you accuse me of such a thing? You're the one who freely offers to help the public—not to mention, *you're* the one who proposed to *me*.

"Why? Why did you even bother? Because of my looks? Is that all you care about, just like every other man?" She scoffed. "You want to talk about using someone! You merely wanted a broodmare—oh, and a hostess to shield you from Society. A prop for your show! Some poor, blind fool you'd keep in the dark for the rest of our lives. That's it, isn't it?

"Yes, I see now." She nodded in amazement as the realization became clear. "You judged me too much of a henwit ever to figure out your double life. Well, I guess you were right about that, weren't you, Your Grace?"

"Damn it, Portia, at least I told you the truth of my own free will before the wedding! Doesn't that count for something?"

"Very big of you, Your Grace," she said coldly, throbbing with anger. "This whole betrothal has been a sham. My God, do you really think I ever would've accepted you if I had known that you were capable of killing all those people?"

"They murdered my parents!"

"But who appointed you judge, jury, and executioner? God, I knew dukes were arrogant—and I'd noticed that Silversmoke was, as well. I found it amusing, up to a point. But this? This is hubris. You will bring about your own destruction. And mine, if I were mad enough to marry you. But how can I marry you when I don't even know you? Right now, frankly," she said, "I'm not even sure I want to."

He flinched and lowered his head, his weight on one foot, hands on hips.

He looked hurt and thwarted, and seeing that, Portia regretted her cruel words, but she refused to take them back. He had completely misrepresented himself, and she had been duped.

A lump formed in her throat. Dammit, she had never let herself care so much for any man before.

A marquess's daughter, raised in the ton, she had always known better than to go around wearing her heart on her blasted sleeve.

But then came hopeless, bumbling Lucas. And he'd melted her defenses like no suave dandy ever could. But he might as well have been wearing a papier-mâché dragon head, for as false a role as it had been.

To think that the *one time* she had given her heart to someone, he turned out to be wearing a mask, just like everyone else in Society.

Indeed, the one time she took off her own as the nonchalant, self-assured belle, look what it had got her.

Well, I'll never do that again, she thought.

"So, the wedding's off, then?" Luke asked, scrutinizing her intensely from beneath his lashes. "Am I jilted, or does my lady prefer to delay the choice until she's had a chance to speak with Mr. Clayton?"

His question drew her up short.

The answer should have been easy, but she could not bring herself to speak.

"Put me out of my misery now if it's over—as a courtesy, if you would?"

Portia's pride seethed, but her tongue refused to answer. Let him stew on his uncertainty. It was the least he deserved.

"I'm going home," she replied. She whisked her skirts around her as she pivoted, then marched across the ballroom.

"Portia!" he exclaimed. "Can I at least have an answer?"

"Go hang! There's your answer," she retorted.

"Not the best thing to say to an outlaw, love," he called after her as she went stomping off over the leather mats.

"Don't care!" She scowled at the balance beam as she passed it on her right, then shied away from the rack full of swords and other weapons on her left.

Weapons she did not even know the name of. But Lord knew Hunter would've felt right at home here.

She knocked over a whole rack of them just for spite on her way to the door, and took great satisfaction as they fell and rolled and clanked. "Ha."

Luke just sighed.

"And I thought my brother was a killer!" she muttered as she reached the nearest pair of ballroom doors. "He only killed one man, and that, by accident. But you!" Reaching for the door handle on her right, she grasped it, but it was locked.

She shook it, then angrily moved on. "Why, you wipe out whole Scottish clans, don't you, Silversmoke?"

"They were monsters, if you must know, and I'd do it again in a heartbeat."

No remorse! She shot him a glare over her shoulder.

Thankfully, the next door had a key sticking out of it. She yanked it open. "Goodbye, whoever you are!"

"Portia, please don't go."

She flinched at the note of despair in his voice, but refused to give in. "You will not manipulate me again," she informed him, then she stalked out.

He did not bother following right away as she strode down the corridor of what was to have been her home.

She found her way to the entrance hall and rounded the newel post, hurrying up the staircase, the blood pumping in her ears.

She heard Luke's slow, weary steps some distance behind her as she reached the upper landing, and was grateful that he had at least enough respect for her to hang back and give her some breathing room.

As she headed for the drawing room, Azrael's warning echoed around and around in her head. *"He is a very dangerous man."*

More than you know, my friend! she thought. *To women's hearts and Scotsmen's health.* Well, where she might have been willing to marry a stranger weeks ago, this was different.

Everything had changed. Luke's deception cut her to the quick. And now that she knew what he was capable of, the thought of marrying the highwayman-duke simply unnerved her.

How could she ever trust him again—or herself, after falling for his ruse?

Even if she went through with the wedding, how could they ever get past this? It would probably stand between them for the rest of their married lives.

A wave of grief washed over her as she approached the drawing room, for he was right about one thing: she was not innocent here either. She was angry at him, angry at herself.

Their whole match so far suddenly seemed like nothing but a downy bed of lies.

Her chest felt hollow, her wits were still bewildered, and it was all she could do to school her face into a stiff, emotionless mask when she walked into the drawing room without her fiancé. "Mother, Father, it's time to go. Darkness has fallen, and we must be on our way."

"Oh!" Her mother looked up absently from her hand of cards. It was clear that the foursome had been enjoying their game of whist. "Are you sure, darling? Lady Sedgwick and I were just discussing the possibility of us staying the night here, after all, as the duke originally suggested."

"No, no, no, I don't think that would be a good idea at all," Portia said, aghast at the notion.

Instantly, from across the room, her father's gaze homed in on her, suddenly alert.

The Marquess of Liddicoat might be a sleepy fellow, but he always sharpened to complete awareness when one of his brood gave any sign that something was wrong.

"Are you all right, dear?" he asked, keeping his tone casual.

"Yes, Papa." She sent him a reassuring look to let him know it was nothing like he probably assumed. Far be it from the Duke of Fountainhurst in any of his personae to take undue liberties with her.

At least he had that much honor.

"I am merely tired," she forced out. "It has been a long day."

"Oh, but darling"—Mama pouted—"they have plenty of room for us here. And besides, I'm not sure we ought to travel at night. They say there are highwaymen about."

Portia bristled at that.

Indeed, from the corner of her eye, she saw one enter the room at that very moment.

So she answered in the coldest possible tone. "Oh, believe me, Mama, they won't bother us in the slightest. I'm sure they wouldn't dare."

Tavi's eyes widened at those words; she, at least, understood Portia's cryptic answer. *So. His sister knows, too.* Portia was outraged, for Tavi's guilty look revealed that she had been in on Luke's deception from the start. *A whole family of liars?* What great actors they were, these Wakefords!

Portia sent the countess a brief, withering stare for her role in the matchmaking. She wasn't sure what was worse: Luke hiding his secret identity, or Tavi knowingly pledging an unsuspecting young woman to the head of a criminal gang.

Papa, meanwhile, was studying Portia from across the room with a look of deepening concern. He pushed out of his chair and rose. "Come, Samantha, our daughter is quite right. We should not wish to wear out our welcome, and besides, I can hear my bed calling me." The marquess took his lady's elbow and lifted her firmly from her chair. "Up you go, then, dear."

"Oh, George," Mama said, fussing at him. But, gentle soul that he was, the Marquess of Liddicoat was still the man of the family. Indeed, it was from him that Portia had inherited her stubbornness.

They walked out twenty minutes later.

Mama was still at the doorway gushing with thanks to Lady Sedgwick and her brother, while Papa escorted Portia out into the night.

"What happened?" her sire asked discreetly. "Should I be worried? Especially with Hunter coming home? Should I expect another duel?"

"Oh God, Papa, no, it was nothing like that. We quarreled, is all." She did not wish to alarm him, and she certainly didn't want her rough-and-tumble brother jumping to conclusions and taking matters into his own hands.

Silversmoke versus Hunter Tennesley? That was one fight that she never wanted to see. They'd probably kill each other.

"Aha." Papa looked relieved. He sent her a sideways glance, while Mama trailed behind them, making sure she had all of her things.

"Do give the children kisses for us, darlings! Night-night!"

"We certainly will. Goodbye, Lady Liddicoat!"

"Well, try not to take it too hard, butterfly," Papa murmured as they walked toward the carriage. "Wedding jitters are to be expected. Tension does tend to build before the big day. But don't worry—it'll all be forgotten by tomorrow, I'm sure. That's how marriage is, you'll find."

I don't know about that, Papa, she thought, but held her tongue. This was not the time or place. She needed some time to absorb what had happened and figure out if she could really live with a liar and a deadly, wild barbarian for a husband.

It didn't look promising.

Before she stepped up into their coach for the drive back to Moonlight Square, she glanced back at him—Luke, Lucas, Silversmoke, Redclaw the Terrible, their mysterious host, whoever the devil he was.

The man she loved.

The stranger.

The sight of him standing there in the moonlight, so familiar and yet so completely unknown to her, made her heart ache. Her chest felt hollow, and just for a moment, she wished she had never heard of the Duke of Fountainhurst.

She looked up one last time at the elegant castle that would probably never be hers. Not now.

Nor the beautiful man.

Then she tore her gaze away from him and his lying family and Gracewell, and stepped into the carriage. She had no idea in that moment what the future held.

She only knew it would be a long, dark drive back to Town.

Part Three

CHAPTER 25

Deepening Shadows

*M*onday. Luke awoke in hell. The world looked the same—his house, his reflection in the mirror—but everything had changed.

He had not felt the weight of such dark emotions crowding around him since the days of his hunt for revenge. Damn it, this was why he had never wanted love. Because he had known what it would do to him someday.

Now that that day had come, what could he do but face it, live it, like any other day? So he did. He rose from his bed, got dressed, went down to see his family in a fog, going through the motions. His head was in the clouds. Dark clouds, murky and menacing. Thunderheads.

A storm was coming. He could feel it.

Axewood. Joel. Now Portia… Everything was coming to a head, and he was filled with a growing sense of danger. He was fairly sure he'd lost her and ruined his own life with his lies.

His trust in his own judgment had been shaken like never before, just when he needed to be sure about his next moves.

Sitting at breakfast, staring down at his empty plate, forgetting to put the usual splash of milk in his morning tea, for once, doting Uncle Luke could not abide the constant babbling of the children, and merely grimaced at the food on the table, his stomach in knots.

Beyond knots.

No, he felt like some overconfident leviathan of the deep who had swallowed a ship's anchor, which now sat in his gut like a giant hook, weighting him down in the lightless fathoms of some watery abyss.

Such a heaviness came over him, such a cold sense of doom, that he felt like he was drowning, bit by bit. Soon he would run out of air, but there was no more to be had, for she was gone.

The woman he had let himself fall stupidly, painfully in love with had stormed out and left him in front of both their families, and there wasn't a damned thing he could really say in his own defense.

She was right; he was wrong. He had lied. Pretend as he liked to be an easygoing chap, he was a killer and a stone-cold bastard, and there was no escaping it. Worse still, he wasn't even sorry about the men he'd slain up north and never would be.

Should've at least lied about that part, he thought. But it was too late now.

He had a very bad feeling that her decision was final, and he would not be given a second chance.

After all, she had never really wanted him in the first place, had she?

She had wanted Joel Clayton, and there it was.

Now Luke had given her the perfect excuse to back out of their match. He had also given her hope of being reunited with her beloved bloody suitor before the week was out.

To be sure, the writing was on the wall. He'd best start thinking about finding another bride.

Well, perhaps Portia would at least forgive him someday if he could bring Joel back to her as promised. He would rather be flayed alive than see her with that blackguard, of course, but at least then Portia might be happy.

Though it irked him that she refused to see things from his point of view, Luke had no choice but to harden his defenses and get on with his day.

Ruing the daft, reckless folly that had inspired him to bare his soul to her in the first place, he left his sister and her family to enjoy the hospitality of Gracewell while he left for London by noon.

Sitting around being sociable would have been impossible under the circumstances. His sister did not protest; she knew things had gone disastrously wrong, a mere fortnight before the wedding date.

Luke still had the sapphire ring in his pocket, but he hadn't the slightest inkling if the wedding was still on. He hoped his maybe-bride would not keep him in suspense for too long on that point, or he might well lose his sanity, and that could be dangerous for the world.

In any case, he made his apologies and left Gracewell to return to his house in Moonlight Square. He knew Portia wasn't ready to see him yet, but he needed to be near her, just in case.

Besides, he had so much to do before they left for this Carnevale on Wednesday. He wanted to see if Finch had had any luck yet going through his father's papers.

By now, of course, Luke was fairly sure that Axewood had both abducted Joel and killed his parents, and he meant to vent his current unhappiness with life on the earl as soon as he knew for certain.

And yet, with Portia having abandoned him, there was a part of him that barely gave a damn about all of this anymore. What did it matter if he finally completed his revenge down to the last jot and tittle, if he'd lost the trust and respect of the only woman he had ever loved? The only one who had ever found the chink in his armor, as Tavi had said, and captured his heart.

Well, Portia must've taken it with her, because he already felt as hollow inside as the bloody Trojan horse. Promising one thing on the outside and delivering quite something else, indeed.

You deceitful bastard. You don't deserve to be forgiven.

He stared broodingly out the carriage window for the hour or so it took his carriage to deliver him once more to Fountainhurst House. He neither saw the overcast landscape nor felt the motion of the coach this time, utterly numb.

Still moving in a daze, he got out in front of his house when they arrived.

For once, he did not bother with his stupid spectacles. In fact, when they fell out of his pocket, he deliberately crushed them underfoot, ground the glass into the pavement with his heel, and walked on, his posture rigid, his face stark, his heart in shambles.

He permitted himself the briefest of glances across the square at Marquess Row, where Portia lived. He did not see her, but worried over her, wondering how she was and what she was doing right now.

Cursing him? Crying? God, he hoped not.

Taking a breath, Luke pulled his gaze away and continued on into the house. He did not know if she'd ever speak to him again. But if it all came to nothing, he told himself that at least he had the consolation of knowing that, for a few moments underneath the willow tree, he had been his real self with her.

Maybe that was why today felt so terrible. His real self, which he'd finally revealed, was the one she had rejected. It made him want to shrivel up and die.

He willed his heart to be stony and marched inside, where Howell was startled to see him on account of his early return to Town.

The butler blanched when he saw Luke's face.

Loyal as he was, the old fellow's wrinkled countenance filled with the need to know what was troubling his master so he could help, but Luke was not in a sharing mood. Yes, something had gone wrong, but no way in hell did he wish to discuss it.

She hates me. I hurt the woman I love. What more was there to say?

Picking up on his taciturn mood, the butler politely feigned ignorance and told him Mr. Finch was in the library, so Luke walked in and joined the redhead there, trying to pretend that things were vaguely normal.

It didn't work with his trusty quiz of an archivist.

"Good God, sir, what's the matter with you?" Finch cried the moment he looked up from his papers and saw Luke's grim face.

"Nothing," Luke said in a deadened tone.

"Nothing?" Finch started to scoff, lifting his glasses onto his head to peer skeptically at him.

Luke's stare turned icy. "Never mind it. What have you found?"

"Oh…oh dear," Finch said under his breath, drawing his own conclusions. "Er, right." He cleared his throat and perched his glasses once more upon his freckled nose. "Let's see…"

Luke walked over to the stacks of boxes that the staff must've located for him. Finch had been arranging them in piles by topic and year, small towers of old records spread out across the Aubusson carpet.

"I haven't got terribly far yet, sir." Finch stepped over a stack of yellowed receipts, carefully picking his way toward the desk. "I only just now found the box of notes about the budget committee. Copies of the minutes are in there from all their meetings, but there are years' worth to go through. I'm only on 1806."

"Give me 1807."

"You're going to help?"

Luke nodded and took off his tailcoat, then accepted the folio that Finch held out to him in surprise. The task would help to take his mind off Portia, provided he could get his blasted brain to concentrate.

He sat down on the ottoman nearby and got to work.

Lord, it was dry stuff. Page after page of details and figures, projections and estimates, explanations and bygone deadlines. Dull as hell. The sheer boredom of it lulled Luke into a calmer frame of mind, but it also put him half to sleep, after his night of insomnia.

He took the odd years; Finch took the evens. They got through one box and then moved on to the next without really getting anywhere.

The sun rose high over London, and Luke finally managed to eat a little. He even admitted to Finch that he and Portia had quarreled.

Badly.

"I-I'm sure she'll come 'round, sir."

"I doubt it. I told her everything."

"But…not about Scotland, surely?"

Luke shrugged, at a loss. "She already knew. How, I have no idea."

"Damn." Finch offered a sympathetic wince.

Luke nodded, then lay back on the library floor in a carpeted patch of sunlight to keep reading.

He tried to keep his attention fixed on the folio from 1809, but eventually, he dozed off at around six in the evening, the papers tented over his face.

The material was so damned boring, plus he had hardly slept a wink last night, and, of course, he was wrung out from his own quiet, grumpy form of heartbreak.

Without even noticing he had fallen asleep, Luke drifted out of consciousness until the nearby grandfather clock bonged seven and nearly made him reach for his pistol, scaring the hell out of him.

He awoke with a jolt, pulled the papers off his face, and sat up, groggy and surprised—and not a moment too soon, for he had barely come back to his senses when he heard a light but urgent tapping at the door.

"Who is it? Come in," he said, still out of sorts.

At once, the door swung open and Howell and Finch both appeared. Luke had not realized that his assistant had left, no doubt to let him rest.

"What is it?" Luke climbed to his feet as Finch hurried into the room.

"Not to disturb you, Your Grace—"

"It's all right, I'm awake," he said, shaking himself. "I must have drifted off."

"No doubt you needed it, sir," Howell said kindly.

"What is it?" Luke pushed his fingers through his hair.

"This." Finch held up a leather-bound journal.

"Would Your Grace like some tea?" Howell interjected.

"Yes, that would be welcome, thanks," Luke replied.

Finch crossed the room and handed Luke the small book.

He took it, still disoriented. "What is this, then?"

"It appears to be a journal of your father's."

Luke stared at him in surprise, then he was suddenly wide-awake. "Where did you find it?"

"In the attic."

Howell hovered anxiously. "Your Grace, we debated extensively about whether we ought to look inside, but we had to verify—"

"Howell tried to stop me from reading it, honestly, he did," Finch said. "But I just had a feeling…"

"It's all right, Howell," Luke said, then glanced again at his assistant. "You were both merely doing as I asked. I take it you found something?"

Finch nodded, and it was then that Luke noticed the trace of regret in his eyes behind the spectacles.

"I marked the page for you, sir, where the ribbon is. You'll find, um, alarming news there about Lord Axewood—just as you suspected."

"Tell me," Luke said, his heart pounding.

Finch gave Howell a grim glance. "Apparently, your father discovered that Lord Axewood was taking bribes from certain manufacturers of war materials in exchange for his funneling fat government contracts through the budget committee to their companies. By this corruption, the earl greatly added to his fortune, but I'm afraid it's even worse than that."

"How?" Luke asked, stunned.

"One of his favorite co-conspirators in this little arrangement was called Ares Manufacturing," Finch continued. "As you'll see in your father's notes, this company became notorious for sending Wellington's army cheap goods of dreadful quality. Guns that misfired. Sabers that rusted and cracked. Boots that wore out in a month. Things that got the troops killed, or at the very least, would have made our soldiers' lives miserable."

"Holy hell," Luke murmured, staring at him. "That's treasonous."

Finch nodded. "Commanders of various ranks wrote to the committee to complain, but as secretary, Axewood merely hid their correspondence.

"Your father records in his journal how he ran into some angry colonel who'd been sent back to London for a desk job after being wounded. The officer cornered the duke, as chairman of the committee, and demanded to know if future contracts with Ares Manufacturing had been canceled yet, said their goods were getting people killed. The duke had no idea what he was talking about, but that was what first tipped him off to Axewood's mischief."

"Traitor to the nation!" Howell burst out with a glare. "Sending our brave boys into harm's way with inferior equipment!"

"And profiting handsomely by it," Finch said with a grim nod.

"Aye, it's blood money," Luke murmured, amazed. But when he opened the old leather journal to confirm this information for himself, the impact of seeing his father's handwriting hit him harder than he expected.

Reading the lines his sire had written was almost like hearing his voice again after all these years. It brought a lump to his throat.

In these pages, the previous Duke of Fountainhurst recounted what he had discovered regarding the earl's corruption, and debated with himself on what to do about it when he returned from holiday in Scotland.

But he had never returned.

Axewood must've seen to that, realized the canny Duke of Fountainhurst was on to him.

A dagger of loss twisted afresh in his heart as Luke sat down slowly. "Leave me."

Finch and Howell exchanged a somber look and then respectfully withdrew, heads down.

When they had gone, Luke gripped his father's book, reading what he'd written about his suspicions.

> *I knew Axewood was a schemer, but I never thought he'd go to these lengths…*

He read as much as he could until a tremor of fury coursed through him, an echo of pure rage.

So *this* was why his parents had been slaughtered. And the soldiers, betrayed.

It was all down to nothing but the lust of a Judas for his pouch of silver.

Luke cast the papers aside with a wrathful cry and lowered his head into his hands, elbows resting on his knees.

Profound silence filled Fountainhurst House as he struggled to absorb the awful blow. Their deaths had been meaningless.

But at least now, finally, after all these years, Luke had arrived at the truth. The who and why of it.

Axewood. To protect his reputation and his ill-gotten gains.

I'll kill him.

Luke rose abruptly from the ottoman, fists clenched at his sides. He stalked out of the library. It was time to finish this.

And Axewood was going to rue the day he was born.

By Monday evening, the "beautiful" Portia Tennesley looked a fright and didn't care. Those in the ton (and certain lying dukes) who only seemed to value her for her looks ought to see her now, she thought, staring coldly at the dupe in the mirror that hung upon her bedchamber wall.

Her eyes were red, swollen masses, her nose was chapped from crying, and her hair was a tangled wreck hanging free about her shoulders. But no matter. She had no plans of ever leaving the house again in her misery, possibly even her own room.

Why, she had half a mind to leave the ton behind and join a convent at this point. Such was her luck with men.

Turning away from her reflection with a seething huff, she supposed the shock of last night's revelations had finally worn off. But it had been followed by tears—an embarrassing flood of them, in truth. Now, however, came confusion.

And anger.

Serious anger. The sort of anger that had nothing to do with being a lady, like she usually strove her best to be. (*Why?* she wondered.)

Oh, no. This was Hunter sort of anger. She was feeling ready to fight. But so far, all she did was pace back and forth across her chamber. It was better than lying on her bed weeping like a cakehead over a lying fiend.

Whatever the case, she certainly did not look like any young lady two weeks away from her wedding.

But how could she marry a man who pretended to be something he was not? Oh, he was a proper play-actor, wasn't he? How was one ever to know where one truly stood with such a person?

Who *was* Lucas Wakeford, the Duke of Fountainhurst?

A silly quiz in a papier-mâché dragon head one moment; the next, one of the most feared outlaws in England. Baffling man! Did he really care for her, or was that part a lie, too? Was she just another prop in his play?

How could she begin to guess his motivations? Was it even worth trying? But how could she *not* try—when she was in love with at least two of his guises, damn him.

God, she felt like such a fool. How could she not have known?

Pacing back and forth across the evening shadows that stretched out on the plush carpet in her chamber, she shook her head. Such games he had played with her heart! How he must be laughing at her.

She absolutely cringed when she thought back to how she had poured her secrets out to "Silversmoke" on that very first night, holding nothing back. Now she wanted to crawl under a rock when she thought of how he'd tricked her.

Schemer. Why, Luke was even more of a sharper than Joel was at the tables. Joel merely bankrupted other men at cards, but Luke was the player who gambled with her heart.

Shaking her head in stifled wrath, Portia leaned against one of the posts of her canopy bed, her heart pounding. She had never been more confused in all her life.

She rather sensed it would have been helpful if one of her sterner friends were to come over right about then and give her a good shake.

Sidney, perhaps. He was always good for doling out doses of reality, usually with the utmost tact. But she did not feel like seeing *anyone.*

Especially her female friends. All the happily married wives! *Ugh.* Their love matches seemed so perfect; how could they possibly understand what she was going through?

She thought of Serena's pledge with Azrael: no secrets! How in the world had any woman ever procured such a promise from a man?

Ah, but Serena had always been so much better with the male species than Portia was. The raven-haired beauty had always had them eating out of her hand, while Portia had little patience for their egos.

Or maybe they just stayed away from her out of sheer terror of her brother, she thought. Then she heard her mother calling her down to dinner.

Grr. She did not want to eat, and did not care to join her parents at table. Those two! They had always treated her like a baby simply because she was the youngest, and sure enough, in the carriage home last night, they had chuckled and tut-tutted over her "quarrel" with Lucas, as if it was a joke.

Oh, but wait, she reminded herself sarcastically, *you're not to call him Lucas anymore. Very well.*

Luke the Liar. Redclaw the Terrible. Silversmoke, the unbelievably seductive and completely inappropriate ruffian. Her future husband…

Or not.

How oblivious she must seem to him, like a child! She paused in her pacing to glare out her bedroom window in the direction of Fountainhurst House. In spite of herself, she ached with missing him, desolate to think she'd never get him back, not like the way it was before he had confessed.

Things would never be the same between them now.

What's he doing over there? she wondered morosely. She knew he'd come to Town, for she had seen his carriage arrive, in her obsession with the man. Indeed, she was surprised he had not stayed at Gracewell with his kin.

She had half a mind to summon him hence and give the wayward, wicked duke a tongue-lashing he would never forget.

Tempted but skeptical of this idea—because he'd gaze at her with those soulful green eyes and she'd melt—she pivoted away from the window.

Yanking the edge of her fluffy, feather-trimmed dressing gown around her, she resumed her angry march across her chamber. She wondered if he planned on showing his face anytime soon, or if he was too ashamed of himself to try. *Coward!* Well, no. That was one thing she could not really accuse him of, after all his highwayman exploits.

And his many murders, of course.

Let's not forget that *little detail.* She huffed and paced on. Maybe he was simply too busy again to bother with her. Just like old times!

He had said he had been hard at work on bringing Joel back to her, as promised. *But I don't even want Joel anymore—I want Lucas!* her heart cried.

Only, the Lucas she had fallen in love with didn't really exist.

Silversmoke had killed him.

And now she was more alone than ever.

At her wits' end, Portia looked down at all the wedding invitations so carefully arranged by seating order on the table in her room; then she shot out her hand and swept them all away with an angry cry.

The darkness hung close that night as Gower walked into Jimmy O'Toole's domain in the Dockyards, very much on his guard. The air was thick down by the river, and the smell of old rope and the creaking of wooden planks brought him back to his Navy days.

Mixed memories. Some good, some bad. But at least there was order aboard a Navy ship. Here, the very air smelled of anarchy.

And fish.

Gower harrumphed, the sleek supposed "fishing" boats of Jimmy's operation moored on the river behind him as he marched stoically up the dock to the warehouse looming ahead.

Fountainhurst better be grateful for this.

Oh, aye, Gower could see the point of coming here to find out whatever the Irish gunrunner could tell them about this Carnevale. Nevertheless, he was risking his neck here with this lot, more than Luke knew.

The visit had better be worth it.

Warily scanning the prospect before him, Gower walked up the wooden pier at the appointed time. The pair of heavily armed Killarney boyos guarding the door to the warehouse came to attention, but, thank God, they knew to expect him.

Hospitable, the Irish. Until you crossed them.

"Mr. Gower," said the larger of the two. "Himself'll be ready to see ye in a trice."

Gower nodded his thanks, taking a silent breath to check his agitation. Then they went in.

The warehouse was not overly large, but inside, it was dark. A maze of tall shelves, hanging nets, and oilskin tarps guided Gower along behind his hulking escort. The other Killarney bruiser remained behind to guard his post.

As they wove back and forth around the dark space, Gower caught glimpses of lamplight in between these barriers arrayed to slow down intruders. Jimmy's lair proper lay at the center of the space; Gower knew because he'd been here before, but certainly not alone.

But, bloody hell, it wasn't Jimmy that made him nervous, that flamboyant fool.

It was the wife.

Maisie was far too shrewd a player to make her real preferences clear. Whenever they'd come here on business before, she hung on Silversmoke because she knew the famed highwayman had the soul of a pure, young, questing knight.

Gower, not so much.

That brazen bad girl was just his kind of woman—tough on the outside, fragile deep down—and Gower could not deny he was insanely attracted to her. Maybe part of that came from his idiotic sense of chivalry, sensing she was trapped in her underworld life, a damsel in need of his protection. Nobody ever cared about protecting a whore, but Gower's instinctive compulsion to shield her had made Maisie as wildly attracted to him as he was to her.

The fact was that Gower had fucked her several times before she'd married Jimmy. Best sex of his life—and hers. The thought of her raking her nails down his back in the middle of an August afternoon still made his mouth water.

But God help him if the kingpin's wife ever decided to kiss and tell.

As they neared the center of the maze, Gower heard voices coming from inside. He braced himself for the meeting, for Jimmy O'Toole, in his view, was something between a typical merry lad and a savage nutter.

Oh, the world was full of thrill-seekers, risk-takers. Madmen all, to some degrees. Gower would've liked to say he wasn't one of them, but any man who wound up as second-in-command to a famous highwayman obviously did not mind playing rough and loose with his life or his safety.

Such a one was Luke. And such a one was Jimmy.

Unfortunately, so was Jimmy's wife, who suddenly appeared when they stepped around the next corner.

Gower stopped in his tracks. A stupid smile skimmed his face. He could not deny the burst of excitement that went fizzing through his veins as the curvy blonde sent him a knowing smile and posed before him, one hand on her juicy hip.

"Hullo, Bernard." The sensuous purr of her voice curled his toes in his boots. It was ridiculous.

Gower gulped and ordered his cock to behave. "Mrs. O'Toole."

In the shadows of the maze, a sliver of lamplight splashed across her guinea-gold hair and crisscrossed her magnificent cleavage. She was tall and curvaceous, built on an impressive scale. Not some mousy little wisp of a thing, like his ex-wife.

Her presence made Gower crushingly aware of his loneliness. As usual, he thrust it back to the nether regions of his mind where he could easily ignore it.

Maisie glanced at his escort. "I'll take him the rest of the way."

"Aye, ma'am." The Killarney bruiser nodded but didn't leave them alone, which was probably for the best.

Instead, the big, freckled fellow merely stepped back to a respectful distance, waiting for them to go ahead of him.

As Maisie sidled over to Gower and slipped her hand through the crook of his arm, he quivered like a lad of eighteen.

God, I wish I'd met you twenty years ago.

"How've you been, Bernard?" She tugged playfully on his arm as she made to lead him to her husband, but it was then that Gower saw it.

The bruise.

He stopped, turning to her. He wanted to take her chin gently in his hand and lift her pretty face up to the light, but there was no need.

"Something wrong, sir?" their escort asked.

Dread leaped into Maisie's eyes as she realized her makeup didn't fool him. The flesh-colored cream and powder she had caked on did not quite hide her black eye.

Fury began pumping into Gower's blood. He couldn't help it. Perhaps this reaction was to be expected from a man whose daughter had been kidnapped, raped, and then beaten to death by ruthless thugs. He hadn't been able to protect her...

"Jimmy give you that?" he demanded, nodding at the bruise.

Maisie's eyes flared with fear, but her voice dropped to a whisper. "Don't. Bother."

"Huh," Gower said in murderous quiet.

"Stay out of it, Bernard. He'll kill you. Nobody can help me."

"Rubbish. Go and pack your things," he murmured in her ear, leaning closer. "Wait outside, and when I'm done here, we both leave. It's all right, lass. I'll protect you."

"Are you mad? I can't just leave!" she whispered back, pulling away. "They'll come after us. Don't you know what that could lead to?"

"Don't care. He's not gonna do this to you again. You're either comin' with me, or I kill him when I go in there. Your choice."

Maisie stared at him in dismay.

CHAPTER 26

Conflagration

By nightfall, Luke's shocked grief at his horrible discovery had hardened into cold, steely resolve.

Now that he knew beyond doubt that Axewood was the one behind his parents' murders, all he wanted to do was reach The Blind Badger, sit down with Gower, and hash out their plan for exactly how to marshal every willing member of the gang in their attack on the Carnevale two nights from now.

By God, he would rain down fire and brimstone on the earl, that smiling snake.

Eager to hear whatever his right-hand man might've learned from the colorful Jimmy O'Toole, Luke was in Silversmoke mode once again, cantering up the road to Hampstead Heath astride Orion, as he'd done so many times before.

After a day of such misery over Portia and then rage at his discovery, the cool, silken darkness was a comfort, natural to him after all his years of riding by night.

Orion knew the way to their headquarters well, and Luke listened to the lulling rhythm of his hoofbeats as they rode at an easy canter, winding their way through the moonlit landscape. Finally, after his fury of today, he had begun to calm down enough to think.

With a cynical shake of his head, Luke wondered what Gower would say when he told him that he'd finally found his parents' real killer—the hidden hand who'd hired the MacAbes.

Not much, probably. Man of few words, that one.

Then, as his thoughts drifted, Luke ruefully remembered that it had been Gower—and Finch—who had challenged him to tell Portia the truth about himself. He scoffed as he rode along.

Why the hell did I ever listen to those two? Finch had never even wooed a girl, and Gower was notorious for short-lived, ill-fated romances with disreputable women. *Guess that's what I get.*

With a snort, he urged Orion on, as though he could outride the swirling emotions that chased after him tonight like a horde of phantoms.

Perhaps what hurt the most was knowing he could not go to Portia for comfort at such a time as this. After what he'd learned today, it would've helped a lot to feel her arms around him. But after this fracture between them, the truth alone would have to suffice.

It proved a cold comfort.

Luke rode on beneath the moon, trying to compartmentalize the heartache, just as he had long separated his life out into neat boxes: Fountainhurst here, Silversmoke there. His heart packed away somewhere in the attic...

Ah well. The words he'd told her could not be unsaid. All he could do now was await his sentence from the pretty judge once she calmed down enough to issue her opinion on his case.

Whether it would be the gallows for him (she chose Joel) or a life of hard labor (a wife who never trusted him again) remained to be seen, but until then, there was much to be done.

Like rescuing Joel.

And killing Axewood.

Luke bristled with eager hatred as he rode on.

It was then, about a mile from the turn into the woods where The Blind Badger was tucked away, that he smelled the first hint of smoke on the air.

At first, he thought nothing of it, dismissed it as the scent of a cooking fire from some farmhouse nearby.

But the smell grew stronger with his horse's every stride, and as he rode up over the rise, he instantly reined Orion in.

Luke narrowed his eyes with a curse. A bright orange glow emanated from among the trees, billows of smoke rising over the dark horizon.

God's teeth, the bloody woods were on fire!

He kicked Orion instantly into a gallop, riding hell-for-leather toward the blaze while the flames lunged for the treetops. He could be wrong, but it seemed to be coming from The Blind Badger.

Racing up the dark road, Luke hauled Orion to the right at the turn, then urged the nervous bay down the path through the forest, his mouth dry, his heart pounding over what he might find when he reached his headquarters.

What the hell is going on? Have we been raided? Did one of those idiots lose control of a cooking fire? Whatever the cause, Luke prayed no one was hurt as he raced toward the blaze, already hearing shouts.

But nothing could have prepared him for what he found when he arrived at the grove.

Chaos—an utter melee in progress. His pub had become a giant bonfire, and scores of men were brawling in the smoke clouds that rolled across the clearing.

Orion reared up with a frightened whinny at the flames.

Luke steadied the horse, but could well understand why he had been spooked. The pub was an inferno, hurling showers of sparks at the indigo sky and snarling like a dragon, while the fight heaved all across the clearing.

Punches flew; head butts thunked; thrown elbows knocked teeth loose; kicks sent several blackguards sprawling. Grunts of pain and roars of fury punctuated the great round of fisticuffs. Here, a brawny fellow flipped his opponent over his shoulder; there, one of Luke's men slammed an invader flat on the trampled grass.

Though his eyes watered from the smoke, Luke scanned the seething row and noticed that some of these lads looked familiar...

Then, suddenly, near the edge of the fray, he spotted short, stocky Jimmy O'Toole. Luke recognized the muscle-bound little savage at once by his gaudy taste in clothes. His jacket tonight was emerald green, his waistcoat purple and gold, and his red hair stuck up angrily from his head.

The Irish gang leader was trying to drag his wife Maisie toward a waiting horse. "Think you can turn around and betray me, ye faithless wench? After all I've done for you—"

"Lemme go!" Maisie hollered, digging in her heels.

"You're comin' home with me!"

"The hell she is!" Gower boomed, wedging himself between them, and at that, Luke instantly grasped what must've happened.

Bloody hell.

But no matter. The ill-tempered Yorkshireman had saved Luke's life on more than one occasion. He was happy for the chance to repay the favor.

And, frankly, with the mood he was in after everything that had happened, a good wild milling-match sounded like just the thing.

With that, Luke leaped off his horse, doubled his fists, and went barreling into the fray.

❖

Perhaps the bottle of wine had not been the *best* idea.

Portia had not intended to get tipsy, but like mother, like daughter, she supposed. Given her state of mind, a glass of wine to calm her down had seemed a good idea. Then a second.

And a third.

Before she knew it, a feisty state of intoxication had snuck up on her, probably as a result of not having eaten much today.

No matter.

When, later that night, watching out the window, she saw some kind of activity going on outside of Fountainhurst House, the wine infused her with the courage to go over there and confront her lying fiancé.

Well, false courage was better than none at all, especially when facing down a part-time dragon and altogether dangerous highwayman.

Especially when you only came up to his chest.

With a hiccup, Portia slapped a bonnet onto her head to hide her face from the neighbors in her moonlit jaunt across the square.

It was, after all, eleven p.m. No sort of hour for a well-bred young lady to venture out alone. But it was a good neighborhood, she argued with herself, and she only had to go around the corner.

Nothing was going to happen to her. Except a scandal. But that was going to happen anyway if she jilted His Grace of Fountainhurst a bloody fortnight before the big wedding.

She had to see him so she could figure out whether to keep him or kick him into the gutter, the scoundrel.

Fortunately, she had decided to put on a walking gown at some point that evening, sick of being in her banyan. So at least she was dressed, though still quite disheveled. *Ha.* She didn't care.

She was sick of always trying to be what everybody else thought she should. Her fiancé surely didn't bother. Ol' Silversmoke did whatever he pleased.

Taking her wine bottle with her, clutching it by the neck, Portia tiptoed down to the morning room, took a final swig from the bottle, then set it beside Mr. Greensleeves' cage.

"Watch that for me, bird," she whispered.

"Cheerio!" the parakeet rasped.

"Shh!" Scowling over her shoulder into the house, where her parents were doing their same-old, usual, boring married-aristocrat things, Portia crept out the French doors and escaped through the garden.

Vexed as she was about everything that was going on, she could not help the hint of giddy laughter that twitched about her lips at the recklessness of what she was doing. Ah, Luke-Lucas-Silversmoke would never see her coming!

After stealing through her parents' back garden, she went to the waist-high wooden gate hidden among the hydrangeas and slipped out silently, closing it behind her.

She hurried along the passage beside their house, stumbling occasionally on the cobblestones and giggling as she scolded herself for her clumsiness.

At the end of the passage, she darted across the street, fleeing from the glow of the wrought-iron lampposts. She did not wish her neighbors to see her on this indecorous adventure, so she kept to the park side of the avenue, hurrying along in the shadows under the tall, whispering plane trees.

The cool night air sobered her up just slightly. But not much.

All along the way, she rehearsed what she was going to say to the duke. At least she knew for certain he was there now. She had monitored his house for hours today, but this was the first sign of life she had seen.

Eager to have it out with him and settle the question of their match for once and for all before she lost her nerve, she marched right up to his house.

Into which he had never invited her, she reminded herself. The bounder.

But no wonder. Lord only knew what the highwayman-duke might be hiding in there.

She lifted her hand to pound on the front door, but decided she would not give him the chance to send a servant to lie for him and try to claim that His Grace was not at home.

Instead, boldly—since, after all, she was supposed to have been the lady of the house—she grabbed hold of the door and burst in without warning.

"Fountainhurst!" she shouted, ready to fight.

Four men were standing there, right in the entrance hall.

The tallest was Silversmoke—dressed all in black, rough and dusty. Just the way she liked him.

God, he looked good. But lusting for the blackguard would hardly do, since she'd come here to scold him.

All four men turned when Portia burst in; each looked shocked at her invasion.

The smallest of the quartet, a wee bald butler, stepped toward her, sputtering with astonishment. "C-can I help you, ma'am?"

"No, but he can!" Pulling off her bonnet, Portia nodded rudely at the highwayman-duke.

As her eyes adjusted to the brightness, she did not know the skinny young redhead, but she recognized the pewter-haired man, Gower, from The Blind Badger.

For some reason, Gower had his arm draped across Luke's shoulders, as though Luke had been helping him walk into the house…

Then Portia saw the dried blood caked on Gower's clothes, realized that he and Luke both looked battered. Their clothes singed, they were coated in ash and reeked of smoke—and she suddenly realized that she had just stumbled into something dire.

"What is going on?" she demanded.

"Come in if you're coming!" Luke said impatiently. "Don't just stand there. Shut the door before we're seen!"

Though Portia was in no mood to take orders from the ruffian, at once she closed the door behind her, since there was clearly serious trouble afoot.

Even foxed, she could glean that much.

Only now did she notice a fifth person standing behind the men: a woman of about forty, whose gaudy appearance immediately marked her as, well, not a lady. But even she appeared hurt. Portia noted her black eye with a startled wave of sympathy. Clearly, there had been some sort of a row.

"Come on, Finch," Luke ordered the bespectacled redhead, who was helping him support Gower on the other side. "Let's get him to the sitting room. You've got to get that bullet out of his leg posthaste."

"Yes, sir."

"Bullet?" Portia exclaimed.

"Eh, I'll be fine," Gower grumbled. "I've had worse."

Finch was a surgeon, then? Whoever he was, the slender young chap wore respectable clothes, unlike the other two, except his waistcoat didn't match his trousers and his coat was a rumpled mess.

It gave her a pang of missing Lucas.

As Luke and Finch continued helping Gower across the entrance hall, Portia and the blond woman followed uncertainly, while the butler stood by in bewilderment.

Still supporting his right-hand man, Luke glanced over his shoulder at Portia. He looked fierce and wild, with a smudge of black ash on his cheekbone like war paint.

God, was it wrong of her to find him so incredibly desirable in his bad and dangerous state? She could have thrown him right down on the nearest piece of furniture. The wine must have faded her sense of decency.

"What are you doing here, Portia?" he demanded.

"Portia…?" the butler echoed softly, bringing up the rear, then he gasped. "You don't mean *Her Ladyship*, surely?"

"Afraid so, Howell. Everyone, allow me to present the future Duchess of Fountainhurst…or not. Lady Portia Tennesley."

"H-how do you do," she mumbled, suddenly self-conscious of her tipsy state.

"Egads!" the butler whispered.

Portia gave him a hapless smile, then the redhead craned his neck to gawk at her again. "An honor to meet you, my lady!"

"This is Oliver Finch, my archivist."

"Oh!" she said.

"And that's Mrs. O'Toole."

Portia gave the unfortunate woman as polite a nod as she could manage in her confusion.

"Whaddya mean 'or not'?" Gower demanded as they carried him toward a sitting room that adjoined the back of the entrance hall. "She jilted you?"

"Aye," Luke said.

Both the butler and Finch gasped at his answer. Portia scowled, but even the harlot arched a brow at her with a look that said, *You're mad.*

"Will someone kindly tell me what the devil's going on here?" Portia exclaimed.

"The Blind Badger was attacked and burned down by another gang," Silversmoke replied. "Gower's hurt. All hell broke loose, and we nearly got arrested when the militia showed up."

Her eyes widened. "I see."

"That's what our efforts to rescue your precious Mr. Clayton got us tonight," he added, then he and Finch deposited Gower carefully on a leather sofa in the sitting room.

Mrs. O'Toole hurried to assist, while Finch left the wounded man's side to rifle through the contents of a black leather bag on a round table nearby. It seemed to contain medical equipment.

Portia lingered at the threshold of the sitting room, unsure what to do. She refused to leave, but she did not wish to get in the way.

The butler approached her with a bow. "Your Ladyship," he said in awe. "May I be of assistance? I am Howell. It is such an honor to meet you at last. I am at your service in all things, I assure you."

"How kind," she said uncertainly. He was such an adorable old thing that she did not have the heart to tell him that the successful outcome of their wedding plans was yet to be determined. Instead, she merely gave the ancient fellow a stately nod and hoped like the blazes that she didn't look too tipsy.

It was not the ideal first impression a bride wanted to make on the chief servant of her future household, though, admittedly, the past few minutes had had a very sobering effect.

"If there is anything I can fetch for you, my lady—"

"No, no, thank you, Howell. You're very kind. I merely came to speak to His Grace."

"Perhaps Your Ladyship would prefer to come back tomorrow, when all this has been…sorted," Howell said with exquisite tact. He sent a discreet glance of thorough disapproval at Mrs. O'Toole.

Indeed, Portia knew it was scandalous for her to be in the same room with an unmentionable woman and two outlaws, but she refused to be tossed out.

No more blinders on here. Especially if all this had happened on account of the mission she had given Silversmoke.

She shook her head at Howell with a not-to-be-trifled-with smile, then returned her attention to the rogue.

Now that Luke had deposited Gower on the long couch, the rumpled redhead brought his black physician's bag over and began assessing the older man's injuries.

"Howell, I'll need hot water, and plenty of it, soap, towels, bandages, and more candles to work by. Might as well get the fire going, too. I'll have to cauterize the wound."

"I'm fine!" Gower said, and harrumphed. "Just gimme more o' that whiskey and quit makin' a fuss."

"Gower, you've been shot, and I'm fairly sure you've got a concussion," Finch said while Howell hobbled off at top speed to collect the needed items. "It's going to take more than a bottle of whiskey to patch you up this time. Honestly!"

"He's just showing off for Maisie," Luke said wryly, glancing at the woman while Gower tried to smack away Finch's helping hands. "Do you think you can get this curmudgeon to cooperate, Maisie?"

Gower let out a short bark of laughter. "Ha! That gal can get me to do damn near anything, and she knows it."

"Oh, Bernard, behave yourself," the blonde said. "I can assist you, Mr. Finch. God knows I helped stitch Jimmy up enough times."

"That would be excellent, ma'am. Thank you." Finch nodded at her.

"Helluva woman, Maisie," Gower mumbled with a bloodied, half drunken smile, gazing at her.

Maisie captured his wrist and shook her head at him with tender reproach. "You shouldn't have done it. I told you."

"Pah. At least you won't have to worry about him anymore."

"Jimmy O'Toole got nicked," Luke informed Finch, whose eyes widened at the news. "He's bound for the gallows now, I warrant."

"Good riddance," Maisie said under her breath while Finch rolled up his shirt sleeves.

Portia had no idea what they were talking about.

"Right," Luke said at last, straightening up and resting his hands on his hips. When Howell sped back into the room with the requested supplies, Luke watched him pass as though this sort of thing happened every day. "If you're all settled here, I'm going to go look after these blasted burns on my shoulder."

Portia whirled to face him with a gasp. "You're burned?"

He gave her a stern look. "If you'd kindly come with me, my lady, I crave a moment of your time."

With that, he left the room, stalking back out into the entrance hall.

Portia had no choice but to hurry after him. When she arrived in the entrance hall, he was already marching up the opulent staircase.

"Are you hurt badly?"

"No, of course not."

Relieved, Portia lifted the hem of her gown to scramble up the steps after him. Her head was reeling from all she'd heard, and, of course, all the wine she'd drunk wasn't helping.

"I can't believe someone burned down your pub all because I asked you to find Joel!" She steadied herself on the banister, then glanced up and lifted her eyebrows at the fine view of his muscled derriere in those snug black breeches as he continued leading the way.

Oh my.

"Yes," he said, "I'm afraid your ex-beau has turned into a lot more of a bother than I ever expected."

"I'm very sorry."

"Don't apologize. It turns out to have been a most valuable exercise. This way."

She followed him up another flight of stairs, where the quarter landing turned. "Why is that?"

"Because, much to my surprise, the search for Joel has led me on a winding path to the same villain who I have just learned was behind my parents' murders. This man hired the gang of assassins I 'slaughtered,' as you put it, in Scotland."

"Who?" she exclaimed.

He paused and turned to her with a grim expression. "Lord Axewood."

She was so startled by his announcement that she tripped on the landing. "Axewood?!"

"The same." Luke saw her steady herself against the wall, then narrowed his green eyes as he studied her for a moment, noting, she feared, the flush in her cheeks and the slightly glazed look in her eyes. "Darling, are you drunk?" he suddenly asked, then flashed a grin of utter roguery.

"Don't be absurd. Ladies don't get drunk," she said, then hiccupped and ruined the whole thing.

His eyes danced as his handsome smile spread wider. "Of course not. My mistake."

"Excuse me," she mumbled, cursing the hiccups. Well, she did not intend to apologize for accidentally drinking a little too much wine while he was out robbing coaches!

She quickly steered the conversation back on track. "What on earth makes you think Lord Axewood did this to your parents?"

"It's a long story, and I'll be happy to explain it to you tomorrow. I'm not entirely sure you'd follow it right now." He gave her a wry smile, chuckled under his breath, and continued up the steps, shaking his head. "I can't believe you're foxed."

"It's your fault, you bad seed! You drove me to drink! Besides, I never said I was perfect!" She scowled at his broad back.

"I see. So you thought you'd swig some liquid courage then barge in and give me a wigging, eh?"

How dare he sound amused? "I have every right to be angry at you!"

"Yes, I know." He sighed. "But as much as I deserve it, now really isn't the best time."

"Obviously not," she mumbled. "But we do need to talk, Luke."

He gave her a speculative glance over his shoulder. "I agree."

"So where are we going, then?" she asked when he left the staircase and led her down a dim hallway.

A small, punched-tin lantern glowed on a mahogany pier table midway down the corridor. Luke picked it up and nodded to her to follow. "In here." He opened a door and strode ahead of her into a cavernous, dark blue bedchamber with a huge canopy bed.

"Oh…" Portia froze at the threshold, suddenly remembering that they were unchaperoned, it was late at night, and she was no longer certain whether she was marrying this man. "Is this, er, your chamber, then?"

"Good guess," he teased, then drifted into the room with an air of nonchalance, set the lantern down, and pulled off his torn and dusty black jacket.

Before her very eyes, while she still lingered in the doorway, he peeled his black shirt off over his head, then balled it up and cast it into the corner.

Portia forgot what she was thinking.

All she could do was stare at the gorgeous expanse of velveteen skin, the smooth, sleek muscles that spanned his back and shoulders, and his chest and chiseled abdomen when he turned around to face her.

"Are you coming or not?"

CHAPTER 27

To Tempt a Lady

*L*uke could not deny that he was wildly encouraged to see her, though he was shocked she had come, to be sure. As mad as it was for any young lady to storm into her fiancé's house half-foxed near midnight, it seemed she couldn't stay away.

And that was a welcome realization, indeed. *Hmm.* He did not mind in the least that she'd only come to yell at him. She was here. That was all that mattered.

Maybe there was hope for them yet.

Nevertheless, Luke knew he must be incredibly careful not to scare her away again. Not to make her angry. Their match was hanging by a thread, if it wasn't over entirely.

But, God, her presence was a comfort to him after the hellish past twenty-four hours he'd had. Even cross at him, she was a balm that soothed all his hurts.

Of course, she was still refusing to come in the door, lingering at the threshold of his chamber, half in, half out. Just like with their match. He sighed, but far be it from him to complain. He was glad that she was here at all.

And yet, as he trailed his gaze longingly over her, it was not lost on him that this could be his chance to win her back. He must play his cards carefully. If that didn't work, well, he had other means of persuasion. Ones he really hadn't dared use on her yet, out of respect for her as his future wife and the mother of his children—not to mention basic respect for her parents.

But that didn't mean he might not still resort to that. Indeed, if he were ruthless enough to cast all honor to the wind, he could make sure that, after tonight, Portia *had* to marry him whether she wanted to or not.

In short, he could seduce her.

And the way she was staring at him told him she might just be game. The lady clearly liked what she saw, and, by God, so did he.

The flickering lantern light caressed the carved-marble oval of her delicate face; it gleamed on the spun gold of her uncharacteristically messy hair and lit up the rosy glow of wine in her cheeks. Luke knew her defenses would be lowered—her inhibitions as well.

His mouth watered at the thought of the pleasure he could give her, if she were only willing to receive. His pulse quickened over what might be possible tonight, and his gaze lingered on the sweet curves of her body, clad in a cream-colored walking dress with a print of little blue flowers.

She'd thrown a shawl around her shoulders, and her bonnet dangled from her grasp. She looked as though she'd just come tripping in from a windblown walk across the meadows somewhere.

Unfortunately, Luke was in no shape to try seducing anyone quite yet.

He needed at least a few minutes to clean himself up, tend his wounds, and generally put himself back to rights. Now that Gower was home safe and getting the care he needed, for his part, Luke was finally beginning to feel the effects of his milling match against the Irishmen.

His body felt bruised all over, every muscle leaden-tired. His lungs ached, the burns on his shoulder blade smarted, and he could not get the smell of the fire out of his nostrils, the acrid taste of smoke out of his mouth.

Leaving Portia to decide for herself if she'd be joining him or not, Luke thrust aside the swirling temptation to take advantage of her in her tipsy state, even though doing so could get him exactly what he wanted—and then some.

Acutely aware of her standing there studying his hard-won physique with a wide-eyed stare full of virginal curiosity, he turned away with a will and let her look all she pleased, though his groin heated at the admiration in her eyes.

Laying hold of his formidable self-discipline, he went over to the chest of drawers and poured the pitcher of water there into the waiting washbasin. In truth, he needed a shower or a bath, but this would have to do for now. He was just glad that he had not bothered with the charcoal concoction that he sometimes used to darken his hair as part of his disguise. He was an ashy, smoky, sweaty, blood-flecked mess as it was.

Bending down to splash his face, he welcomed the luxuriant relief of cool water, but when he closed his eyes, the timid creak of a floorboard from over by the doorway made his pulse jump.

Portia.

It seemed his bride had found the nerve to enter his lair. Luke could feel her venture into his chamber, heard her shut the door quietly behind her... His body tensed with hunger at her nearness.

He seemed to know exactly what effect he had on her.

Even so, Portia could not take her eyes off him as he leaned down, in profile to her, splashing his face and hair with the water. She marveled at his powerful arms as they flexed with his motions, scooping generous handfuls of water up onto his face and neck, the droplets trailing down the lean, sculpted muscles of his abdomen.

To be sure, it was more than just the wine that had her feeling dizzy now. Then her gaze flicked past him to the large, inviting bed.

Their bed, if she married him.

She dropped her gaze to the floor as her mouth went dry. Determined not to ogle him any more than she could help, she sauntered deeper into His Grace's well-appointed chamber, having a look around.

Rich draperies...dark, claw-footed furniture...a few small oil paintings on the walls. She strove to look at anything but him, the magnificent half-naked man who was now running the wet washcloth over his glorious upper body. But a quick, hungry glance revealed the V-shaped arc from his broad shoulders, sweeping down to his sleek waist and narrow hips, hugged by dusty black breeches.

To her chagrin, he caught her eyeing him and smiled knowingly. "Sure you want to cancel the wedding, love?"

She scoffed at his arrogant jest and looked away, her blush burning all the way down her neck. His low, husky chuckle beguiled her.

"I should go," she muttered, heading for the door.

"Stay." He turned.

"Why?" she shot back, turning to face him with impatience balled up in her belly. If she was honest, however, it was only her long-suppressed desire for this man that had her feeling testy.

"Would you mind having a look at my back for me?" he asked. "Someone bashed me in the shoulder with a burning log. I need to know if it's serious."

"What?"

"Could you take a look for me and see if it's blistered?"

Taken off guard by this alarming news, Portia rushed over to his side, her impatience forgotten. *"Hit* you with a *burning log*? Who?"

"I dunno. I couldn't see; he was behind me. One of O'Toole's men." Finished rinsing out the washcloth in the white basin, Luke turned his back to the light so she could inspect him.

Portia looked up at the wide expanse of his shoulders illumined by the lantern's ruddy glow and gave a silent gulp. What a specimen he was.

He bent his head obediently as her awed gaze followed the sinuous curve of his spine from the back of his neck down to his rugged shoulder blades.

Sure enough, there, on the muscled expanse of his left shoulder, she could see an angry red mark about the size of her palm, part bruise, part burn.

"Oh, you poor thing." Her fingertips alighted on his skin, inches away from the injury's inflamed outline. "That does look sore."

He nodded. "Stings."

In the mirror attached to the chest of drawers, she glimpsed his face. His eyes were closed, and she could see him savoring her light touch.

A shiver of want ran through her, but she swallowed hard, determined to keep her wits about her.

Ignoring her visceral attraction to the scoundrel, she ran a businesslike gaze over the rest of his body, feeling protective and searching him for any other injuries.

It was then that she noticed the dried blood flecked across his breeches, but it wasn't his, and it chilled her to wonder if he'd killed again tonight.

Would it always be this way if she married him?

"Well?" he asked, waiting.

She took a step backward. "Let me send for Mr. Finch—"

"No, he needs to work on Gower. I'll be fine. I'll just have to put some salve on it." He twisted, trying to see his shoulder blade in the mirror. "So is it blistered?"

She shook off her uneasiness as best she could. He required a little assistance—and God knew he had been there for her when she had needed help.

"I can't really tell," she said. "You're too tall. If you'd sit down, I could see it better."

Luke nodded and lowered himself wearily onto one side of the backless, upholstered bench that spanned the foot of his bed, leaving room for her. She moved the lantern closer, then braced her knee on the bench behind him so she could examine the burn.

"Well...I don't see any blisters."

"Good. Then it's nothing serious."

"If you have that salve, I could put it on there for you—and a bandage. I-I don't mind."

He sent her a soulful glance over his shoulder. "Thanks, but I don't know where it is right now. I'll find it later. It already feels better not having my shirt rubbing against it."

"I should think so. Can I at least put some water on it for you? Clean it up a bit?"

He scanned her face warily. "I'd be grateful."

Portia nodded and went to refresh the washcloth.

When she squeezed fresh water out of it onto his burned skin a moment later, he winced and made a sound of discomfort, yet he seemed to appreciate her attentions.

She dabbed at the edges of the wound ever so gently, then got more fresh water onto the washcloth, letting it rain down once more on the angry red patch on his left shoulder.

"I can't believe someone hit you with a burning log."

"Resourceful, no?"

She chuckled. His tense posture finally eased, telling her the water now brought relief instead of pain. She shook her head at the thought of what could've happened to him tonight.

Even Silversmoke wasn't invincible, after all.

He sat quietly, his eyes closed, enjoying her ministrations. Portia worked in silence, watching water droplets slide down his velveteen back, and forward, over the muscular swells of his chest.

The little glistening rivulets entranced her for a moment. To stop them from running all the way down to his waist or dripping on the furniture, she caught them with her hand, her palm flat against his damp skin.

Luke turned to her with a look of open longing.

Portia felt her breath catch with desire, but she refused to give in so easily and tore her gaze away. "How did all this happen tonight?"

"Hmm," he said, his voice low and weary. "Remember how I told you I was following a lead that Clayton had been kidnapped? Well, that turned out to be the case, but it was his uncle who was behind it all along."

"I can't believe it. Are you sure?"

"Pretty near certain. But seeing is believing. If Axewood is there on Wednesday night, at the place where we'll finally get our opportunity to rescue Joel, that will settle the matter of his guilt for once and for all."

"What place is that?"

He paused. "It's an unsavory topic to discuss with a young lady."

"Please. I'm the one who started this."

"As you wish. It seems there are these…secretive underworld gatherings known as the Carnevale. Rather like a traveling fair exclusively for cutthroats and criminals."

"Oh Lord."

"They're held monthly in all different locations, different times, as well, so that only those with inside knowledge know where and when to find them. Mainly, it's a black-market trading bazaar for smugglers and fencers and dealers in various illegal goods."

"Have you ever been to one of these? As a highwayman?"

"No, but I heard of them years ago. I thought they were a myth! Apparently, there are myriad entertainments on offer at Carnevale, but chief among them is a high-stakes gambling tournament. I believe that Lord Axewood has been forcing Joel to play in these games to add to his own personal fortune. For now, Joel is the top-ranked player in these ongoing games. He's known to the crowd there as the Red Carnation."

Portia's heart pounded at this ghastly information. Poor Joel! Dear God, what if she had never sought out Silversmoke to try to find him? He'd be trapped forever.

"Anyway," Luke continued, "I wanted to learn more about what to expect on Wednesday night when I arrive at this thing. Try to get a better sense of what exactly I'll be up against. So I sent Gower to speak to Jimmy O'Toole."

"Mrs. O'Toole's husband?"

"Yes. He is—or was, until tonight—the head of a smugglers' gang based in the Docklands."

"Really?" she exclaimed. "Smugglers, right here in London? How brazen!"

He smiled fondly at her naivete. "What Gower managed to find out before all hell broke loose—" He stopped himself abruptly.

"What? Tell me," she said.

"I don't want to scare you."

"Luke! What?"

His chiseled face grew grim. "Well, it's a good thing Clayton's such a dab hand at cards, because Jimmy told Gower that they kill the loser each month after the card game as some sort of twisted entertainment."

She stepped in front of him with a gasp, searching his smoke-reddened eyes. "You can't be serious."

He shrugged. "It's madness, I know." Then he frowned at her ashen expression. "I shouldn't be telling you this—"

"No, it's all right," she said faintly, sitting down on the bench beside him, her thoughts reeling. "I'd rather you tell me the hard things than keep any more secrets between us."

He looked askance at her, saddening at the reminder of his lies. But he nodded and continued. "It's a bad business, my lady. These are serious people. Devils might be the better word. Last month's Carnevale took place on a Devon beach in an old smuggler's cove; Jimmy told Gower the loser that night was fed to the sharks."

Her jaw dropped, and, for a moment, Portia could barely find her tongue. "My God. He must be terrified."

"Yes, but he keeps winning, so he's safe for now." He laid his hand over hers in reassurance, then withdrew his touch, as though worried that he might offend her. "I'm sure he's making a fortune for Axewood, which is the whole point, no doubt. Turns out the earl has a dubious reputation where money is concerned."

Slumped on the bench beside him, she could only shake her head. "I-I don't know what to say. He proposed to me!"

"I know," he said darkly. "I'm a little worried about that, actually."

"Why?"

There was a storm brewing behind his eyes. "I have a theory *you're* the reason Axewood got Joel to cooperate."

"What do you mean?" she asked, taken aback.

Luke said nothing, and she figured it out for herself in a wash of cold dread.

"You think Lord Axewood told Joel he would harm me unless he went along with it?"

Luke nodded, and Portia clutched her heart. "Then thank God I refused the earl's suit!"

"He'll pay. Don't worry."

A chill ran down her spine at his ominous tone. She paused. "You're going to kill him?"

"Indeed."

Portia's heart sank. More killing? But the stony resolve in Luke's eyes and the blood on his clothes made her back down from voicing her protest to hear that, once again, he would turn to violence.

With the wine still making her head fuzzy, it was all she could do to take in this shocking information. Smugglers right here in London! Criminals who killed for sport. And stuffy, pompous Axewood a ruthless villain himself.

"Poor Joel," she said softly, staring at the floor as she tried to wrap her mind around it all.

"Don't worry," he said. "I'm getting him out soon. In two nights' time, he'll either be free or we'll both be dead."

She looked up, even more horrified as Luke took the washcloth back from her and rose to put it back in the basin.

"But you asked what actually led to all this," he continued, "so I'll conclude my explanation with a fact I only just learned tonight. Namely, that my right-hand man has, er, a bit of a *history* with Jimmy O'Toole's wife."

"Ah," she said, recalling Gower in his cups doting on the woman.

"When Gower found Maisie sported a black eye, he acted accordingly. Promised her our protection and spirited her out of O'Toole's territory. Before long, the two were followed. The battle ensued."

"Hmm. Well, at least you won."

Luke gave her a rueful smile and returned to the bench. "I think it's fair to say that neither side won tonight, actually. The militia showed up and everybody scattered. It's a damned inconvenience, really."

He sighed and leaned forward to rest his elbows on his knees, hands loosely clasped. "I was planning a raid on the Carnevale Wednesday night, attacking in force. But the lawmen sent the boys running for cover, and I don't expect to see them again anytime soon. Now Gower's down…

"Well," he said after a moment, rubbing the back of his neck, "no matter. I can do it myself. I'll figure something out."

"Oh, Luke." Portia stared at him, unsettled.

The thought of what could've happened to him tonight was bad enough. But now he intended to—what, sneak into a gathering of criminals cruel enough to feed men to sharks, and try to save Joel single-handedly?

Was he mad or simply that brave, that sure of himself?

Studying him with awe, it struck her that the most amazing part of all was that it was not just "Silversmoke" doing this—it was Lucas.

Her darling dragon-head.

To dismiss him as some ferocious killer would be to ignore the other side of his nature. The sweetness, the warmth, the humility.

But the weightiest thought that sank in at that moment that Luke was doing this for *her*.

He had been, for weeks. All this time, hard at work behind the scenes, never taking the credit for all his good deeds.

On the contrary—he had disguised himself by playing the fool, the bumbling quiz, not caring who laughed at him or mocked him behind his back.

Including her, the woman he counted worthy to be his duchess.

Portia cringed to think of how she had regarded her fiancé until just a few weeks ago. How oblivious he must think her! She had never even suspected that her future husband was the very man behind all Silversmoke's heroics.

But this? Why, this mission was extraordinary, she thought as she studied his handsome face.

It wore a slightly confused expression at the moment.

"What?" he said, frowning at her.

Portia shook her head. That any man should go to such lengths as risking his life not just to save another human being, but his own rival for a lady…

She knew absolutely and entirely in that moment that it was no contest between him and Joel. Whatever Luke was, whatever his guises, his violence, his lies, she loved him, much to her despair, and she might as well accept it.

Without warning, she leaned down and kissed him softly on the lips, cupping his beloved face in her hand.

The slight prickle of his scruffy jaw made her fingertips tingle and her blood zing with wild awareness of him as a man.

"Oh my darling," she whispered, overcome, "you truly are the hero that I dreamed of."

Luke stared at her with surprise when she pulled back, ending the kiss. "So, does this mean you forgive me?" he asked slowly.

"Well, no!" She straightened up and propped her hands on her waist, startled by the blunt question.

Luke arched a brow; it seemed they both knew her answer was a lie.

"I don't know," she retorted. "Maybe?"

"Maybe?" he echoed, and feigned a slight pout, though he looked unsurprised, casting her a cynical glance from the corner of his eye.

Portia couldn't help smiling. "Yes, Your Grace. I will concede to a maybe, even though you are still a bounder and a bad seed. But...I am glad you weren't killed tonight."

"Believe me, so am I." He suddenly shot his arm out and captured her about the waist, pulling her down onto his lap. "Maybe? I'll *maybe* you, my girl!"

A breathless laugh escaped her, but she could not bring herself to object. She closed her eyes and gladly let the brigand claim the kiss he would have stolen anyway.

Parting her lips with a bold stroke of his tongue, he tasted of fire and smoke, but the strength in him thrilled her, his powerful arms encircling her. Portia slid her hand slowly across his sculpted chest, savoring every inch of him, her pulse pounding.

His green eyes glowed with seduction when he finally let her up for air. "I'm glad you came tonight. I missed you."

She shook her head stubbornly. "I only came to yell at you."

A roguish half-smile crooked his lips. "Are you sure about that?"

She huffed at his flirting and feigned an attempt to squirm away, but he tightened his gentle hold and laid her down on her back on the bench, leaning over her.

"Because *I* get the feeling you came here for something else entirely."

"What's that supposed to mean?" she retorted as he kissed her neck. She closed her eyes, dizzied by the sensation.

"Well, look at you," he said. She opened her eyes to find him sizing her up with a ravenous glance. "Waltzing in here all tousled and rosy with wine, just looking for trouble. Well, guess what, my lady? You found it," he whispered. Then he slid his hand beneath her skirts, and his fingers began gliding up her thigh.

Portia went motionless on the cramped bench, her pulse pounding.

"You're my captive now," he taunted in a silken whisper.

"No I'm not." Oh, but she was. Wholly willing, in spite of herself. Fascinated by him—and he knew it.

"Afraid so."

Her cheeks heated while she held her breath and waited to see what the gorgeous scoundrel might do next.

He nodded, holding her stare. "You've fallen into the clutches of a dread highwayman, my dear. Heaven only knows what might happen to you now."

"What might happen?" she asked breathlessly.

"You'll see. I warned you…"

She lifted her chin with a quiver of excitement. "Do your worst, highwayman. I'm not afraid."

"Mm, that sounds like a challenge. I accept." He leaned down and gave her one rich, deep, leisurely kiss after another, stealing her breath. Then he paused to nuzzle her ear. "Perhaps I shall rob you of your virtue, so you'll have no choice then but to marry me, as planned."

She turned her face away with a shiver of want, still trying to play coy, though he had her panting with desire.

"You would never do that, in any of your guises."

"Wouldn't I? Don't be too sure about that, Portia Tennesley," he whispered. "If it means keeping you forever, I could be tempted. And honor be damned."

Then he lifted her onto his bed and lay atop her. Portia's heart slammed in her chest as she caressed his sides and shoulders, trying not to touch any of his burns, cuts, or bruises. Luke's hand traveled down her belly and curved around her thigh, then he pushed her legs apart gently.

She groaned, clutching him as his warm, deft fingers ventured into the dewy wetness of her core. He whispered as he stroked her, telling her how he longed for her with intoxicating murmurs in her ear.

Her womanhood throbbed, and the crazed pleasure that his rhythmic touch stoked in her blood led her past all shame. The wine and her crazed lust for him blurred away any lingering inhibitions.

She helped him eagerly when he pulled down her bodice and feasted on her swollen nipples. She ran her fingers through his dampened hair, feeding her other breast into his hot, wet mouth when he sought it.

She arched against him, moaning with need like she'd never known.

The combs in her hair distracted her from the pleasure he lavished on her. She needed to be rid of them. Her chignon was already a mess, so she quickly removed them. As she shook her hair free, Luke lifted his head drunkenly from her breast and gazed at her.

"What is it?" she asked, panting, self-conscious.

"I've never seen you with your hair down before. You're so... I haven't the words." He captured a lock of her hair like a pale ribbon across his palm and kissed it, reverent as Galahad, to her unending delight.

Portia shook her head tenderly at him, adoring the man. "You are such a quiz."

He grinned with hapless trust, his lips damp with kisses; Portia pulled him close again and held him like she'd never let him go. Somehow, he was Lucas and Silversmoke and everything she ever could have dreamed of, all wrapped up in one.

One glorious man—her darling duke—and there'd never be another.

He claimed her lips again with unbridled enthusiasm.

Portia caressed his hair and cupped his nape as he kissed her so deeply. His tongue swept over hers with the same maddening rhythm of his tender touch pleasuring her.

She tipped her head back, her legs sprawled, Luke lying on his side next to her. Though his fingers were as deep in her core as he could thrust them, it was not enough for either of them. She hovered at the brink of a shattering climax. She was shaking as he plundered her mouth with rough, needy kisses.

Then she noticed through a haze of passion that he was unbuttoning his breeches with his left hand. She swallowed hard and tried to clear her head, half alarmed as she realized what this signified.

And yet the flicker of hesitation dissolved in a trice. Instead of protesting, she licked his lips with sensuous hunger, running her hands down his hard, delicious body, craving all he had to give.

"Ah, you drive me mad," Luke said in a ragged voice between kisses, panting.

She dragged her eyes open. How beautiful he was. His chest was damp with sweat, and the lantern's glow flickered over his stone-carved abdomen. But there, beneath his adorable belly button, she saw the ruddy, rounded head of his enormous erection sticking out over the top of his black breeches. Primal eagerness flared inside of her as he freed it.

She swallowed hard. "May I touch you?"

"Please do."

At once, she began inching her palm down his warm, chiseled stomach and went exploring. Luke moaned with anticipation; Portia felt the fierce drumbeat of his pulse as she slid her hand down his body.

His muscles were tensed, and he quivered when she grazed her fingertips cautiously over the silken head of his cock.

He whispered a ragged oath at her light touch.

His response thrilled her. "Ohhh, Silversmoke," she purred in a mischievous tone.

He laughed breathlessly at her admiration and kissed her on her shoulder. "All yours, love."

"So, um, what do I do with it, precisely?"

He laughed, his eyes sparkling in the lamplight. "Whatever pleases you, my lady."

"Oh, I see." She gave a teasing smile, curling her fingers around his hot, velvet shaft. "Do I stroke it?"

He flinched and closed his eyes with a look of bliss. "I hope so. Oh God, yes. Lots of that."

"And do I squeeze it…like so?"

A savage groan escaped him. His chest heaved as he nodded. "Fast learner, you."

"Does this make you feel better after this awful night you've had?" she whispered.

"*You* make me feel better. Just seeing your face, Portia. I fear you have no inkling how much I adore you… But hell yes. That definitely helps."

Moved by his words, Portia applied herself to giving him the pleasure that he craved. Luke slid his left arm around her waist and drew her closer, warmly cupping her breast.

As he kissed her with mesmerizing depth, Portia lost herself in caressing his pulsating member. She was fascinated by the effect her touch had on it, on him. His kisses deepened, and, if it were possible, his manhood swelled even larger, grew even harder and hotter in her hand, and he trembled with pleasure now and then.

"Come here," he said suddenly, capturing her hand. He laced his fingers through hers and pinned both her hands above her head on the mattress, rolling atop her. "Let's play."

"I don't know this game," she said with an uncertain smile, though she thrilled to whatever he wished to show her.

"I'll teach you." He held her gaze with a smoldering stare, his face sculpted by shadows.

She quivered, helplessly eager. "Are you going to deflower me now, you wicked beast?"

"Would you like that?"

Portia didn't answer for the simple reason that she didn't know. She couldn't even think as he reached down with one hand and guided the satiny head of his member against her dripping passage, teasing her with it.

She whispered a curse of utter enjoyment, absorbed in the sensation. She'd never felt such things. He held his hard, thick shaft in his hand at just the perfect angle with which to tantalize her. Toying with her, slip-sliding at the threshold of her passage, he made her want like she'd never wanted before. God, it was the most blissful torture...

"Now what's this about you canceling our wedding, my sweet? Or more importantly, our wedding night?"

"*Unh.* You are cruel," she gasped out, striving for sanity.

She felt his cocky smile against her lips. "So I'm told."

But, oh, she couldn't bear for him to stop. Her body begged for release, but still he made her wait. A cry of longing escaped her when he angled the now slippery-wet length of his massive hardness to caress her drenched mound, inch by inch.

She gritted her teeth as she arched against him. After a moment of this, she glanced down to watch in reckless abandon as he dipped just the tip of his hardness into the swollen pink folds of her passage. He watched, too, both of them panting.

She felt lawless, barbaric. God, he was driving her out of her mind. He slid his throbbing shaft slowly against her rigid center, luring her in exquisite temptation.

Oh, he knew exactly what he was about. With every illicit caress, every naughty motion, he was leading her into a veritable trap.

Marriage.

But she was past caring at the moment if he was manipulating her with his beautiful body. She wanted him, craved that closeness with him, needed him inside of her *now*.

No matter the consequences.

"Luke," she moaned, half a plea.

He looked down at her, his emerald eyes heavy-lidded. "Yes,

darling? Tell me what you want."

"You already know."

"Say it."

She licked her lips, well aware that if she did this, if she gave herself to him, then she'd *have* to take him for her husband—and live with whatever secrets he opted to keep.

Whatever illusions he created. Whatever rules he saw fit to break or bend. If she gave in right now to her own thunderous desire for him, the Duke of Fountainhurst would own her henceforth, for all practical purposes.

Alas, deep down, she feared he already did. How could any other man ever compare? It was no use. Passion would make her his slave and so be it. She looked into his eyes, burning, as the breathless whisper escaped her: *"Take me."*

Savage hunger flamed in his eyes. But he held himself back for a moment. She could see him battling himself, fighting to check his reaction.

Waiting eagerly for him to take her innocence, she could feel his pulse booming in his glorious chest. He nuzzled a kiss along her cheekbone, then leaned lower to slip a blunt reply into her ear: "No."

"What?" Portia went motionless, then planted her hands on his shoulders and pushed him back a few inches, sure she'd misheard. "No?"

He shook his head, looking dazed at his own answer. "I—could never forgive myself if I deflowered the woman I love when she's drunk. Sorry."

Portia stared at him in astonishment. "I am not drunk!" *Anymore.*

"You're not sober," he said. "No. I want to, believe me. But I won't want you forced into marrying me, then resenting me for it forever."

Her jaw dropped. He was serious!

She spluttered with confusion.

"Don't worry—there are other things I can do to you, love," he murmured, laying his hand on her hip, though he looked a bit worried at her reaction.

"Don't bother!"

"Darling, the wedding is only a fortnight away. We've waited this long."

"I don't believe you." She pushed him off her indignantly, her face heated with embarrassment at her own wanton behavior. How perfectly mortifying! "If that's how you feel, you shouldn't have started this."

"I know!" He scowled at her, looking sheepish indeed as he shoved his member back into his trousers. "I couldn't help it. I just wanted you to see what we could have together before *he* comes back."

"He, who?" she exclaimed, glaring at him as she wrenched her sleeve back up over her shoulder, still throbbing with frustration.

"Clayton! Who else?"

Portia stared at him in shock. "Is that what this was? A bloody contest?"

Luke opened his mouth, but no answer came out. He looked cornered.

At that moment, a discreet knock on the door jolted them both.

"Who's there?" Luke barked as he rose from the bed to finish buttoning his breeches.

Portia glared at the door, still smarting with shame as she yanked her other sleeve back up.

"Terribly sorry to interrupt, Your Grace," Howell said through the door.

No doubt the stately old butler was scandalized that the unmarried duke and his scheduled duchess were already in there together, prematurely enjoying the rights of the marriage bed.

Or not—as the case may be! Portia harrumphed as she scrambled off his bed and brushed down her skirts.

"You have a visitor, Your Grace."

"At this hour?" Luke muttered. "Who is it?"

"Viscount Sidney, Your Grace. He says it's urgent—"

"Sidney?" Portia echoed. "What on earth is he doing here?"

"His Lordship is insisting he must speak to you at once. He says you'll want to hear his 'information.' Are you at home, sir, or shall I send him away?"

"Tell him I'll be right there!" Luke said.

"Very good, Your Grace." As Howell's footfalls faded down the hallway, Portia shook her head.

She was now officially bewildered. "I don't understand. I thought you barely knew Sidney, aside from that one time in the ballroom when he was so rude to you."

"We resolved that. I ran into him at the club a while back. We had a good chat." Luke took a deep breath and shook himself as if to clear his head, then went to find a fresh shirt.

Portia stared at him dubiously. "So you're friends now? Has he come to take you out to some disreputable place where the rakehells—"

"No. He's here on business, not pleasure."

"Meaning?" After retrieving her combs from the bed, she raked her fingers through her hair and quickly started remaking her chignon.

"I asked him for a favor—or, you might say, sent him on a mission. Seems he's back."

"A mission?" Holding the rope of her hair in mid-twist, she sent him a puzzled frown, still peeved at him for teasing her in the most scandalous fashion. "What sort of mission?"

Luke let out a large sigh and finished tucking in his shirt. "You'll see."

CHAPTER 28

The Missing Piece

ell, that didn't quite go as planned. Bloody hell. Luke still throbbed with torturous frustration as they left his chamber and headed back downstairs. Butterflies of want tickled in his belly, and he craved her like a beast. But that was not how it ought to happen, and she knew it as well as he.

A lusty bit of bedsport was one thing—they both had wanted it, badly—but to consummate the match was quite another. Take advantage of his sweet, amorous innocent when she was tipsy and vulnerable? Deflower her when her judgment was impaired?

After he had specifically thanked her father for trusting him with his daughter?

Absolutely not. He was many things, but there was no way in hell he would ever sink so low. No matter how much he wanted to claim her and thus stop her from backing out of their match.

He'd have forfeited his honor, lost all self-respect, and probably ensured that Portia would never trust him again.

She gave him a sideward glance as they marched on toward the top of the grand staircase. Yes, yes, he knew she was miffed at him, but just walking through his house beside her felt right. His future duchess…

Or not.

Oh, she did not look pleased with him at all. Not that he could blame her. It was *his* fault their amorous play had almost got completely out of hand.

Luke felt utterly sheepish for not having better control over himself where she was concerned. Lucas, indeed. But her unexpected arrival, her jaw-dropping beauty, and his long-suppressed need for her had nearly overcome his wits.

He blew out a breath as they started down the staircase, then he turned his attention to the sound of brisk footsteps pacing the entrance hall below.

The moment they turned at the quarter landing, Sidney's golden head popped into view. "Fountainhurst!" he started, but then the worldly viscount saw the rosy-cheeked blonde beside Luke and his jaw dropped. "Why, Lady Portia Tennesley!" He burst out laughing. "You wicked girl."

"Hullo, Sidney," she answered in a flat tone, opting to brazen it out, Luke gathered, though he noticed that her blush deepened.

Sidney tsk-tsked her with mock disapproval, propping his elbow on the newel post. "I am shocked, shocked, I say. What can a lady of your impeccable reputation possibly be doing here at this hour—unchaperoned, alone with this scoff-gallows?"

Luke smirked.

Portia lifted her chin, refusing to flinch. "I might ask the same of you, my lord."

Sidney laughed merrily and tossed his wheaten forelock out of his eyes as they stepped down into the entrance hall. "Much as I adore you, dear, *that* is none of your business. I need to borrow your fiancé for a moment. Fountainhurst, a word?"

Portia shot Luke a scowl, and any thought of excluding her from the conversation withered in his brain. With Joel returning in two nights' time, Luke was acutely aware he could not risk messing up with her again.

Especially after that glorious debacle upstairs.

"It's all right. She can join us," he told Sidney, then nodded to them. "Follow me."

Sidney's eyebrows lifted. "She knows?"

"He knows?" Portia exclaimed.

"Yes, yes, you both know I'm Silversmoke," Luke said impatiently.

She narrowed her eyes, lashes bristling. "Am I to understand that you told this scoundrel before you told me?"

"I needed his help in tracking down a lead! You said yourself that Sidney knows everyone. Do you want me to find Joel or not?"

"Don't worry, my dear, his secret's safe with me," Sidney said. "You know I am a vault."

"That's not the point," she said with a humph.

"Come along, you two," Luke said with a sigh, then led them both to the library, passing the sitting room on the way.

He glanced in and saw that Gower was now dozing with Maisie seated by his side. Finch gave Luke a nod as he passed, signaling that the tough Yorkshireman's condition was stabilized.

Thank God. Things had escalated quickly in the fight. Luke did not know what he would have done if Gower had been killed. But just as Jimmy pulled out his pistol in a rage, the militia, along with a band of local farmers, had arrived in response to the blaze.

With a sigh of relief that Gower would indeed be all right, Luke gave Finch a grateful nod, then marched on, showing his guests into the library.

Both seemed puzzled by the boxes and stacks of papers everywhere, the notes and jottings arranged in piles all around the room.

Damn, he'd forgotten about this. "Er, sorry about the mess." Luke quickly bent down to lift a tower of his father's papers out of their path. He carried it to and fro, unsure where to put it, until he spotted an empty space on the edge of the massive desk. He trudged across the room and set it there.

"What *is* all this stuff?" Sidney asked as he drifted in, keeping to the clear lane along the floor-to-ceiling bookshelves. "Doing research on something?"

"That's exactly what it is." Luke rested his hands on his hips and glanced around at the boxes, each carefully labeled by year. "These are my father's old papers from his time in Parliament. You see, after a tip from Lord Liddicoat on Saturday morning, I had Finch start searching through all these records."

"The surgeon?" Portia asked.

"He's actually my archivist. The fellow in the other room," he told Sidney. "Quite a mind on that lad. He's had training in various sciences, including a year or so of medical studies. Anyway, it was in my father's old records that I found out—just this afternoon—that Lord Axewood had reason to want my sire dead."

They both stared at him in astonishment while Luke went on to explain about the budget committee. He beckoned them over and showed them the journal entry where his father had expressed his suspicions about the earl's misappropriation of the war funds.

"My father was going to expose him and launch an investigation as soon as he returned from holiday. Axewood must've realized he suspected him, so he made sure that the duke never came back alive—at least, that's my theory."

"Oh Luke, I'm so sorry," Portia whispered as she stood beside him, laying a hand on his arm.

He glanced gratefully at her. "I never would've found out about this if *you* hadn't put me on the hunt for Joel. My last unanswered question, supposing this is true, was how an earl could've made contact with a band of assassins. But if Axewood is forcing Joel to play in the Carnevale tournaments, then he'd have access to plenty of criminals. That could explain the connection."

"Actually, that ties in perfectly with what I came to tell you." Sidney leaned on the tall back of a wingchair. His blue eyes were somber. "You asked me to make some inquiries regarding Lord Axewood."

"Yes, I got your note, that you intended to speak to your father."

"I did. Yes, I endured that for your sake, my friend," he said wryly while Portia sat down on the brown leather couch. "As luck would have it, though, Lord Grant was at the house. He's been my father's best mate since boyhood. Fortunately, old Grant is much more pleasant than my sire, and he had some interesting things to say about Axewood. You'll love this. It seems the earl shares your penchant for dabbling in low-world matters under an assumed identity."

"What?" Luke took a step toward him.

"Ages ago, one of Grant's nephews was a school chum of Axewood's. Apparently, they were quite rowdy. While they were at Oxford, Axewood got a reputation as a troublemaker for leading other lads to carouse in seedy establishments, rubbing elbows with the criminal class.

"To avoid detection on these excursions, they'd adopt outlandish stage names and create alter egos for themselves, even dressing the part to try to blend in. When their antics were finally discovered by the proctor, Grant's nephew was nearly expelled. The boy's parents forbade him from associating with the ringleader ever again—the future Lord Axewood."

Luke was stunned, then he met Portia's wry glance. She said nothing, though.

He was glad. He did not care to hear either of them state the obvious aloud, that *he* should have something in common with his mortal enemy.

"So," Sidney said, "perhaps he has kept up this practice into adulthood."

"Given his financial adventuring, I'd imagine he's found it lucrative." Luke shook his head with gathering anger. "That would also explain how he found out about Carnevale in the first place."

"That could be where he hired the monsters who murdered your parents," Portia said quietly.

Luke lowered his gaze. "Aye."

"Well? What do you think?" Sidney asked.

When Luke looked up, he found the viscount studying him. Luke shook off his brooding. "Good work, Sidney. This only strengthens my certainty that I'm on the right track."

"So, what's the plan?"

Luke shrugged. "It's fairly straightforward. Go to the Carnevale on Wednesday night, find the right moment, and get Clayton out of there. I'll deal with his uncle afterward."

"You're going to kill him?" Portia murmured.

"You're damned right I am," he replied, sending her a steely glance. "My only concern is..."

"What?" Sidney asked.

"Well, it's just that now that I finally have a clear sense of what the hell's going on, I find myself a little shorthanded, is all."

"How's that?"

"My, er, band of merry men ran away tonight after a brush with the law," he said ruefully. "Figures the blackguards would scatter just when I needed them most. But never mind that." He folded his arms across his chest. "I might not have the numbers I'd hoped for, but I still have the advantage of surprise. I'll get there early, survey the ground, and figure out a plan once I see the place. Should be able to do this myself without too much trouble—"

"Nonsense," Sidney said. "You need reinforcements. I'm in, of course—"

"Wait, *you're* volunteering?" Luke furrowed his brow, unsure if the viscount was jesting.

Sidney laughed and slapped his gloves against his thigh as he stepped away from the chair. "Wouldn't miss it, my friend! The chance to ride with a real, live highwayman? Sounds like a grand time."

"This is no game, Sidney. Things are likely to get very nasty."

"Trust me, Fountainhurst. I'm meaner than I look."

Portia shot to her feet. "Well, if he's going, I'm going, too! I'm the one who started all this. It's only right that I should be there to help you finish it. I'm coming with you." She lifted her chin with a stubborn stare that dared him to naysay her.

He and Sidney traded dubious glances. Luke frowned, but Sidney, with his watchful eyes, must have noticed that not all was roses between them at the moment.

"If Joel has indeed been held captive for the past year by his uncle, we're likely to find him in a traumatized state," Sidney said.

"Especially if they kill the loser in these card games." Portia nodded. "Can you imagine the terror he's had to go through every month?"

Sidney's eyes widened. "Kill the loser?"

Luke nodded grimly.

"In that case, I think we need her to help calm the poor fellow down once we rescue him," Sidney said. "What if he panics when you show up to save him? He might take one look at you and think you're just another one of the criminals at this thing, but if she's there, that should reassure him."

"You do look very intimidating in Silversmoke mode," she said.

"Yes, well, that's rather the whole point," Luke muttered. "Sidney, don't you think if you're there, that'll be reassuring enough?"

"Joel and I were never *close* friends, but he trusts Portia. Besides, she's a woman. It's different. Women are much more soothing than men."

"Luke, you have to let me go," Portia insisted. "I'm not asking to be part of the rescue itself, but surely I can be stationed somewhere nearby, where it's safe."

His heart sank at seeing her eagerness to be reunited with her ex-beau.

But then it dawned on him that if he agreed to let her come along for the journey, then at least he would have a few more hours in her company to try to make everything right between them before Clayton returned.

When he saw the discreet, prodding look Sidney gave him, Luke realized that had been the chap's whole purpose, encouraging this.

Was it *that* obvious that she was cross at him?

Considering it, Luke had no doubt he could find a safe place to stow her during the thick of the action...

"You'd need a chaperone," he pointed out.

"Maybe Serena would cover for me—"

"No," Sidney interrupted with a sage look. "Delphine."

Luke and Portia both eyed him with confusion.

"The book club lady? I thought she was some bluestocking spinster," Luke said.

Sidney laughed. "Oh, believe me, mate, she's much more than that. But we'll need a third man to round out our party." He flashed a mischievous smile. "Never fear. I know just the chap."

CHAPTER 29

The Rescue Party

*T*hat black lace mourning gown she had worn to The Blind Badger was proving to be one of the best wardrobe purchases Portia had ever made. She had worn it on the night she'd gone to hire Silversmoke, and she wore it again early Wednesday morning as she hurried out of the house into the dewy gray dawn.

Her parents did not bother getting up to see her off; Portia had insisted that they not. The less they knew about all this, the better.

No, she had said her goodbyes last night, with reassurances that she'd see them in a day or two. As far as they were concerned, she was off to spend a couple of days in the serenity of the beach near Brighton in hopes of calming those "wedding jitters" that her parents still believed were the cause of her quarrel with Lucas at Gracewell.

"Take the time you need, butterfly," Papa had said, giving her one of his rare hugs. "All will be well. We both want you to be sure of your decision. Just know that last-minute anxieties are perfectly natural. Marriage is a big step."

"But how grand, to be a duchess!" Mama reminded her with a squeeze of her hand. "Besides, Lucas is all that's good and kind, dear. Truly."

That, she did not argue.

It was the other one that worried her—the highwayman.

Especially now that he had set his sights on murdering Lord Axewood.

In any case, her parents believed she'd be under the chaperonage of the profoundly respectable Lady Delphine Blire, and that was not a lie.

Even now, Lady Delphine's coach waited outside the house for her. Envying her parents the extra hours of sleep, Portia lugged her things as quietly as possible down to the still-dark entrance hall, the cord of her reticule draped over her wrist, a small valise in her hand, and the carrying strap for her wooden archery case over one shoulder.

Luke had ordered her to bring her bow on the trip during last night's hasty meeting at Lady Delphine's, where everyone going on this risky venture had assembled for about an hour to receive their final instructions from their fearless leader.

He had laid out a simple, straightforward plan. The three men— Luke, Sidney, and Major Carvel (who'd been all too happy to ward off his perpetual boredom with civilian life and pick up a sword again)— would infiltrate the Carnevale until they spotted Joel and Lord Axewood.

They would keep eyes on the pair and follow the earl and his prisoner as the festival broke up.

Only after Axewood was clear of the cutthroat crowd would the trio launch a surprise attack on the earl and simply kidnap Joel back.

Once they had him, they would gallop away, hell-for-leather, and deposit him in the coach, where Portia and Delphine would be waiting, along with Oliver Finch, ready to tend any injuries Joel might have sustained in his ordeal.

Finding Portia in the coach should help to calm Joel down after all he'd been through, but the moment the carriage door closed, they'd go racing off at top speed with Luke, Sidney, and Peter covering their escape. The three mounted men would block the road, ready to thwart any effort by Axewood and his "big bald man" to follow.

Portia knew Luke intended to kill the earl once she was away and Joel was in the clear. After all he'd revealed about Axewood, she couldn't blame him for wanting to. Yet it filled her with a gnawing uneasiness that had kept her awake too long last night.

That ruthlessness in him frightened her. As Azrael had said: *"Even a hero has a dark side."*

Still, the ramifications of what that could mean for both their futures terrified her. She had forgiven Luke for his lies, but his capacity for violence was more than she had bargained for. If she had known of it, in truth, she would never have agreed to the match in the first place.

It wasn't fair. He had presented himself to her as one sort of person when the truth was much more dire. It seemed the equivalent of a girl who was no longer a virgin marrying a man and trying to fool him about it on their wedding night: a betrayal of trust.

She needed some kind of tangible proof or serious assurance that Luke did not intend to go around killing people on a regular basis if she went through with this marriage. They had to figure out some way to put this behind them if the wedding was still going to happen.

For now, though, the nearness of the danger they were heading into was the reason Luke had ordered her to bring her bow and quiver of arrows.

He did not expect trouble to catch up to the carriage, he'd said, but just in case anything went wrong, he did not want her defenseless. Since her bow was the weapon with which she felt most comfortable, he wanted her to have it within reach.

Portia thought it was silly but didn't say so, afraid that if she balked, he'd say she couldn't come. But of course nothing untoward was going to happen. She'd be staying well back from the Carnevale itself, and besides, she could never shoot an arrow at another human being.

Delphine would have her pistol, anyway. It turned out the mysterious lady was as good with her elegant little double-barreled flintlock pistol as she was with a pen. All the more reason to find the woman completely intimidating, Portia thought as she trudged down the stairs with a yawn.

Bleary-eyed, she paused at the front door and checked her bags one more time to make sure she had not forgotten anything, then said a hasty goodbye to the butler.

Stevens must've found it very odd, indeed, that her chaperone did not come in to collect her, but merely sent a bored wave through the carriage window. Odd, too, that a bride-to-be heading out on a wee holiday before her wedding should choose to wear grim black widow's weeds. And odd, above all, that a marquess's daughter insisted on carrying her things out herself.

Oh no, none of that was at all suspicious.

Determined to prevent the family servants from discovering Lord Sidney waiting in the coach along with Lady Delphine—Portia did not think it proper to wonder why the two were arriving together—she waved Stevens off cheerfully.

"Don't worry, it's light, I've got it! Goodbye!"

Dodging his questions and ignoring the dear fellow's puzzled looks, she bustled out the door into the gray morning mist toward Lady Delphine's fine brown coach crouched in front of their townhouse.

The team of six smart bays tossed their heads and shook their manes as Portia hurried toward the vehicle. On her way, she said good morning to the portly lamplighter, who was going around dousing the street lights. No doubt he was shocked to see one of Moonlight Square's fashionable denizens up and dressed at this ungodly hour.

Indeed, Portia was relieved that their traveling party would be underway before the neighbors started rising. She had not even told Serena what was going on. Her best friend would ask far too many questions—questions that Portia was not at liberty to answer.

A groom jumped down from the back of the carriage to load her things in the boot for her. Though he was wearing Delphine's livery, Portia knew that he actually worked for Luke. So did the driver and the couple of footmen who'd been conscripted for this mysterious mission.

They had come up to Town from Gracewell; it seemed the duke only trusted his own people.

Then Portia sprang up into the coach, her pulse racing. It was strange to feel so jumpy and yet so tired at the same time, but this was undeniably exciting.

And risky.

"Good morning!" she said breathlessly as she slid into the backward-facing seat, across from Sidney and Delphine.

"Morning, P." The viscount barely opened his eyes. He was smartly dressed, as always, but slouched down with his head resting on the squabs, arms folded across his chest. "It looks like I'm awake, but I'm really not."

She grinned. "Go back to sleep."

"Goodnight." He closed his eyes again. "Oh—sorry not to have helped you with your bags, my dear. It goes against the grain, but, you know, we have our orders."

"No, no, it's good you stayed out of sight. Our butler can be nosy."

"Have you got everything?" Lady Delphine was dressed in a jaunty, plum-colored traveling gown, and handed Portia a lidded jar of tea for the road.

"Oh, thank you. Yes, I think so." Portia accepted the tea gratefully.

"Good. Then we're off. Cheers," Lady Delphine added, clinking her own jar of tea to Portia's.

The coach rolled into motion.

As they headed for the rendezvous point nearby, Delphine sipped her drink and studied Portia with her usual brown-eyed intensity as the carriage passed on through the swirls of mist.

Portia smiled politely at her; Delphine smiled back, unreadable as the sphinx.

The coach smelled of the cigarillos that the independent lady allegedly enjoyed, and the silence between them felt increasingly awkward—to Portia, at least.

Her so-called chaperone sat there, content not to talk. But why was Portia surprised? Lady Delphine was all business, as a rule. And, in truth, Portia had always suspected that the savvy older woman did not much respect her, thought her a blond, silly chit.

Delphine only truly respected other bluestockings, like Trinny. Which made Portia wonder why the spinster had even agreed to participate. For Sidney's sake? What was going on between them, anyway?

The nature of their relationship puzzled her. People whispered they were lovers, but somehow, Portia wasn't convinced.

Perhaps she would figure it out on this trip, while the three of them were closed up in the coach.

After only ten minutes, the coach turned in at the quaint cobbled lane of shops they had set as their meeting place with the other half of their party.

As the coach slowed, making the turn, Portia looked out the window and spotted three horsemen waiting in the grayness of the narrow street ahead.

The one in the center sat astride a big black horse.

Luke. Her heart gave a kick at the sight of him. Distressed as she was that he was fixed on more violence, she could not deny the instant attraction that rushed through her veins—especially after their brazen encounter in his chamber.

Then Lady Delphine's coach proceeded down the street toward the mounted trio. Luke rode over as it halted.

Portia met his gaze with a tremulous smile. He looked more handsome than ever, dressed for the day's travel somewhere between a duke and a highwayman.

A long, loose coat of soft black leather spilled down his shoulders. He wore a plain black waistcoat over a loose ivory shirt. Comfortably well-worn black breeches disappeared into his dusty top boots. Judging by his relaxed posture on the horse, he seemed perfectly at ease, nonchalant as ever in the face of danger. She supposed he was used to it.

"Morning, all," he said through the window with a half-smile, though his gaze lingered on Portia.

"Sorry we're late," Lady Delphine said. "It's Sidney's fault. The lazy jackanapes wouldn't wake up."

"Damn, Fountainhurst!" Sidney said, finally perking up to ogle the stallion. "Now, that's what I call a horse!"

"Ah, he's a good boy." Luke grinned and leaned forward to give his trusty steed a proud pat on the neck.

The magnificent black stallion snuffled and tossed his glossy head, as though eager to get underway.

Portia looked past Luke to acknowledge the other two. "Good morning, Major Carvel. Mr. Finch." She waved politely to them.

Peter nodded in answer from the broad back of a big, restless white horse that looked worthy of some knight headed out on a quest. Instead of his scarlet Army uniform, the major was arrayed in the rugged garb he must've worn on his wanderings—especially the soft brown leather coat that draped his muscular frame.

While Peter gave them a casual salute, Finch stammered a polite greeting. Seated astride a handsome liver bay with white stars splashed across his forehead, Luke's scholarly assistant seemed to be asking himself what he was doing there.

Then Luke swept the carriage passengers with an assessing glance. "If anyone wants to back out, this is your last chance."

"Wouldn't dream of it, ol' boy," Sidney said with a yawn.

Delphine lifted her jar of tea. "In for a penny, in for a pound."

"My lady?" Luke glanced at Portia.

"No chance of that," she replied. "I'm the one who started all this. I intend to see it through. To the bitter end, if need be."

His eyes glowed with approval at her answer, but it was time to get underway, as Major Carvel reminded them with a brisk glance at his fob watch.

"We are now twelve minutes behind schedule, ladies and gentlemen."

"Twelve whole minutes!" Sidney murmured.

Luke nodded to the major, then addressed them all. "It should be an easy ride of about thirty miles. The roads are good all the way from here through Buckinghamshire, where we're headed, and all the horses chosen for today should have no problem with the distance.

"We'll ride for two hours, take a break at the halfway point, and then press on for the final two hours. You might as well rest while you can," he said to those in the coach. "It's sure to be a late night."

"No need to tell me twice," Sidney mumbled, closing his eyes again.

Portia did not know how the viscount could doze through such excitement. Her pulse pounded as they rolled out a moment later amid rumbling carriage wheels and drumming hoofbeats. The shop façades and colorful awnings whisked by faster and faster as the horses gathered speed.

As she stared, wide-eyed, out the window, her heart lifted with anticipation for the quest ahead. *I believe I am developing a taste for adventure.*

Perhaps she would make a suitable bride for a highwayman-duke after all.

❖

Luke spent the first half of their journey preparing himself mentally for whatever lay ahead tonight.

A long horse ride always gave a man a chance to think, and he welcomed the chance, for a dozen tangled subjects vied for his attention.

While Tempo clopped along beneath him at an easy trot down a smooth, straight stretch of country highway, Luke ignored the painful burn on his shoulder, his mood equal parts grim and reflective.

The tranquil beauty of the morning was at odds with the darkness he'd have to face tonight, but it soothed him for now. As the sun rose higher, the dewdrops sparkled on the green crop fields, as though the farmers must be growing emeralds. The air was fresh and fine, and perfumed with fruity sweetness when they rode past an old orchard tucked behind a mossy stone fence.

At the head of their party, Luke glanced back to make sure everyone was all right. He'd been watching the mile markers and was mindful of the time; they'd be wanting a break soon.

A couple of paces behind him and to his right, Finch rode Orion. Luke knew the scholarly lad was frightened of the night's events ahead, but with Gower down, it was important that the junior member of their team tear himself away from the library for once and gain a bit of experience in the field.

Untried as he was, though, Finch was nervous.

He should be. They were headed toward a gathering of criminals—real ones, not revenge-obsessed aristocrats who merely took it up as a hobby.

No matter. Luke had decided that while Finch should be on hand, he would stay back at a safe distance from the fight, with Portia and Delphine. Of course, it was dangerous for the ladies being part of this, and God knew it made Luke uneasy to bring his fiancée anywhere near such unsavory company.

Unfortunately, with Axewood's location uncertain, he dared not leave Portia behind. Not when he believed the earl had only bullied Joel into cooperating by threatening to hurt her.

Maybe Luke was merely being paranoid, but the implications of that one thought alone had him spooked. After all, Axewood hadn't needed to be personally present to have his parents killed.

No. Now that the time had come to rescue Joel and complete his revenge, he wanted Portia nearby, where he could see her and protect her himself, if need be.

There was also the fact that this brief journey would be his last chance to fix things with her before Joel returned to the picture.

An urgency to secure their match thrummed in his temples, clawed at his heart. He could imagine no future happiness without her, yet he was filled with the sense that time was running out.

What if she chooses him?

Luke shoved the irritating thought aside, briefly considering all the other members of their party in turn.

Sidney was in the coach with the ladies—stationed in there to protect them, actually. Luke was still not entirely convinced about the dandy's fighting skills, but he did not take Sidney for a braggart. He supposed he'd find out the truth of his abilities tonight.

The one man whose skills were not in question was Major Carvel, bringing up the rear astride his impressive white horse.

Man of few words, that one, crisp and military-stern. Luke got the feeling that Peter rather disapproved of him and his highwayman hobby.

The gruff veteran was happy to help, though, and could be trusted to keep the secret, according to Sidney. Sidney had assured Luke that Peter was so bored with Town life that he'd be happy for any excuse to pick up his sword again.

It seemed to be so. Peter had immediately agreed to assist, and from the moment he'd arrived at the rendezvous point at dawn, he'd proven well prepared, solid, and quietly efficient. Luke already sensed he could rely on *him*, at least.

Still, he missed having Gower on hand for this dicey venture. It was strange to be undertaking something like this without his trusty curmudgeon by his side.

Luke had sent Gower and Maisie off from Town this morning in one of his extra coaches for their own safety, lest one of Jimmy's men manage to track them down. Barely healed enough to travel, Gower would continue his recovery at one of Luke's lesser estates up north. No doubt he'd enjoy having Maisie looking after him.

Amused as he was at this strange bond that had flowered seemingly overnight between Maisie and his right-hand man, Luke was not thrilled that O'Toole's runaway wife now knew about his double identity. He would have to deal with it later, though.

For the next twenty-four hours, his mind must remain fixed on rescuing Joel Clayton. It had been a long time coming, but now that the mission was here, he could not deny that he dreaded Joel's return to Portia's life.

Especially with the way things stood between them right now.

In truth, he wasn't even entirely sure how she felt about him at the moment. Amid the scramble to get ready for this journey, there had been no time to debate something as tenuous as emotions.

Everything felt unsettled, up in the air, but Luke knew it would be much easier for him to concentrate on the dangerous task ahead tonight if he had a clear notion of whether she still intended to marry him.

He hated being dangled along this way and, God knew, he would not have put up with it for any other woman but Portia Tennesley.

He decided the time had come to get his answer.

For that reason, Luke called a halt when he saw the next coaching inn ahead.

A few minutes later, they rode into the courtyard of a charming, old, half-timbered inn with three gables and a slate roof. Stout Tudor chimneys wafted smoke into the morning sky. It smelled like breakfast.

Flower baskets twisted slowly in the breeze, hung from the jutting eaves of the second story. Their colorful blooms and trailing tendrils of green adorned the simplicity of dark beams and ivory plaster. A fanciful sign over the entrance proclaimed the place The Crow and Crown.

"Halfway there, everyone. Let's take half an hour," Luke said as they all started getting down from their horses and climbing out of the coach.

Sidney handed the ladies down, then yawned and stretched a bit as he shut the carriage door.

"Did you get your beauty sleep, my lord?" Luke asked with a smirk.

"Barely!" Sidney answered. "Does it show?"

Peter eyed his friend sardonically, then offered his arm to Lady Delphine and escorted her inside. Finch grinned at Sidney's jest, and the viscount slapped him cheerfully on the back.

"Something smells delicious, no?"

"It does," the redhead agreed.

Portia waited for Luke while he turned to the grooms. "Let the horses rest and see that they have water, then you may take your leisure."

"Yes, sir," they said.

He then turned to Portia, standing there in her widow's weeds, her pale face draped in the same black lace veil she'd been wearing that first night at The Blind Badger. It was only prudent under the circumstances for her to seek to hide her identity again, he supposed.

His mysterious lady in black.

Luke would rather see her wearing a veil of white lace...but he did not yet know if the wedding they had waited so long for was ever going to happen.

He steeled himself. It was time to find out. "Shall we?"

He offered her his arm, and she accepted. But as Luke escorted her inside, Portia made a suggestion.

"Why don't we sit apart from the others so we can talk?"

"Oh—very good," he said, startled. He'd intended to request that himself, but she sounded troubled, and, unable to see her face clearly, he wondered if he should worry.

Ignoring the cold tightening of his stomach, Luke led her into the cozy common room. Quaint place, but there was hardly anybody there.

Dark beams ran the width of the plaster ceiling, and the charcoal-colored flagstones underfoot wore the mellow patina of age.

An old brown dog lazed by the wide hearth, which was currently unlit. The dog lifted its scruffy head and thumped its tail slowly, as though debating whether it had the energy to get up and greet them. Then it lay back down again.

Half a dozen wooden tables with long benches and rustic chairs sat empty in the middle of the dining room, but there were tall booths built in around the perimeter, and their four companions had piled into one of these together.

Since there would not have been room to join them even if they'd wanted to, Luke led Portia to another booth out of earshot of their friends. The others knew the two of them needed to talk, anyway.

Portia sat down while Luke remained standing to remove his long leather coat. He hung it on the peg provided as a silver-haired landlady glided out, wiping her hands on her ruffled pale blue apron, and greeting them with beaming smiles.

But when she realized their party had been broken up, she hurried over to them, her apple-cheeked face stamped with distress. "Oh, sir, madam! We can push one of these tables over with two chairs—"

"No, no, that's all right," Luke said, gesturing at Portia. "The lady and I have private matters to discuss, in any case."

"Oh! O-of course." The kindly innkeeper flicked a glance over Portia in her mourning gown. "Can I bring you anything special, dear?" she asked softly. "A nice cup of tea, perhaps? I'm sorry for your loss, if I may say so."

"Oh—how kind," Portia said. "Um, thank you very much. No, I-I'm fine. But I will take a cup of tea, please."

"Do you two know what you'd like for breakfast?"

Since there was hardly anybody there, Portia deemed it safe to take off her veil. She asked for a muffin and the day's fresh fruit, then peeled off her gloves. Luke ordered two eggs with ham and toast, a bowl of oatmeal with milk, and black coffee.

As the woman bustled off across the dining room to go and take their friends' orders, Portia gazed after her. "How do you stand it?" she asked barely audibly. "Deceiving everyone."

His heart fell at the question. She glanced across the table at him, a trace of chagrin flitting across her fine features, as though the words had slipped out of their own accord.

She lowered her gaze, sitting very still.

"It's all for a greater purpose," he said.

"I suppose." A well-trained Society belle, she was difficult to read when she chose to be. Wondering just *how* much trouble he was in here, Luke studied her.

The black gown bothered him as he realized now that she had probably bought it for the sake of mourning Clayton. He'd mistaken her for a widow the first time he'd seen her in it.

Her pale face and sleek champagne-blond hair made a jarring

contrast to where the black lace collar of her high-necked gown adorned her slender throat.

All he knew was that the widow's weeds, symbol of death, seemed so wrong when her face bespoke youth, freshness, beauty, life.

Luke did not want death anywhere near this woman.

"So here we are again," he said with a taut smile, trying to start the conversation that they so desperately needed to have, even though he dreaded the outcome.

She seemed reluctant as well. But they both knew it was necessary.

Braced to hear whatever she had to say, he sought to put her at ease. After all, her visit to his chamber the other night gave him good grounds for hope.

"Silversmoke and the lady in black," he murmured, "back in the booth once more."

She lifted her porcelain-blue eyes to his with a rueful smile. "But this time, we both are unmasked."

"Indeed." Luke nodded slowly, staring deep into her eyes. *Where do we go from here, Portia? Do you still love me? Or have you already made your plan to leave me?*

"Luke—I've had a lot of time to think since Monday night. And there's something I want to say to you." She clasped her hands, tight and demure.

"I'm listening," he said with outward calm, his pulse slamming at his jugular.

"I…I owe you an apology."

"Me?" This took him completely aback.

She nodded. "You deceived me, it's true. But as you pointed out at Gracewell, I am not innocent in this, either. I went behind my fiancé's back to seek out the help of a highwayman to find my ex-beau."

"In the hopes of escaping your marriage to me," he said with a gentle smile, for he had long since forgiven her.

"Yes." Her gaze dropped. "About that."

Luke tensed as Portia swallowed, squaring her shoulders for whatever she had to say.

Alas, at that moment, a maid came bustling out to their table with a large tray. A loud, hearty girl, she chattered as she hastily set down flatware, then served their food and drink. Luke paid no attention.

The serving girl gave Portia her tea, Luke his coffee. Portia's warm blueberry muffin arrived with a pat of melting butter atop it and slices of honeydew melon sprinkled with a handful of ruby-red strawberries.

But when the girl set down Luke's breakfast of eggs, ham, and toast, along with a steaming bowl of oatmeal, he had little hope of eating anything now.

What had Portia been about to say?

His stomach was in knots and his heart continued pounding as he waited for her to complete her sentence. Thank God, the maid sailed away a moment later to go bother their friends.

Luke could not tear his dread-filled stare off his fiancée. He hated feeling this way, at her mercy. Disgusted with himself, he strove for a more stoic attitude.

He leaned closer while Portia stirred a lump of sugar into her tea. "You were saying?" he asked in a low, measured tone.

She set the spoon down, then folded her arms, resting her hands flat one atop the other, her demeanor more self-possessed now.

"First, I want to thank you again for all you've done to help Joel."

Ah. Bloody Joel again. Luke's mouth went dry. Not good.

"Of course," he forced out. "I could not leave an innocent man to rot once I realized he was alive. That your hunch was correct."

"I know. That's what I admire most about what you've done here. Not only did you track him down, but you continued the search even though you knew that finding him might not be to your advantage."

His midsection clenched with the defiance of simple male pride. "As I told you," he said evenly, "I don't wish to marry someone who doesn't want to marry me."

Her face was a smooth white mask. "Still. It shows a truly remarkable measure of honor, and, to me, that outweighs the deception of your Silversmoke charade. I understand it is necessary. For what it's worth," she added, "I believe your parents would be proud."

He held his breath. "Does *this* mean you forgive me?"

The last time he'd asked, he'd got a *maybe* in reply.

But this time, Portia held his gaze and nodded.

Just when Luke thought he was saved, she said, "For the deception, yes."

His fleeting relief cut off like a spigot. "But?"

She ignored the question. "Furthermore, I know you said you mean to quit being Silversmoke once we've rescued Joel." She was being exceedingly careful, drumming the fingers of one hand on the knuckles of the other in deliberation. "But I don't want you to give it up for my sake."

"What?" He was taken off guard again. "You don't?"

She shook her head, staring into his eyes. "You help people. Who am I to rob them of your aid? That would be extremely selfish of me. I've concluded I don't mind if you continue, actually, as long as you're careful.

"You see, now that I've had some time to absorb it all, my main objection is the secrecy, Luke. I don't want to be shut out of major portions of my husband's life. Surely that's not so hard to understand? I want to be included. Maybe there are even ways that I could help now and then. Like I'm doing now."

He stared at her in utter astonishment. He did not know what to make of this reprieve.

But, with welling joy, he was prepared to agree to nearly anything to keep her. *Husband.* She'd said *husband.* "I-if you wish."

"I do! It's necessary, Luke. I don't want us to be isolated from one another, as we were before. I want to know the real you. I want us both to be our real selves with each other. I want for you henceforward always to be honest with me—and for me to be equally honest with you."

He started to say he wanted that too, but she held up her hand.

"That is why I must be honest with you now, Luke, and tell you that the killing…" Her voice fell to a whisper and she shook her head slowly, her eyes full of anguish. "It has to stop. For your sake. And mine. And for the sake of any future we are going to have together."

Luke reached uneasily for his coffee and wrapped his fingers around the mug handle. He felt its warmth but did not lift it to his lips, waiting on tenterhooks to see where all this was going.

"I realize that what happened up in Scotland took place a long time ago. You were younger then, and it was long before I knew you. But just the other night when I came to your house, I saw the blood on your clothes. I know it wasn't yours."

He started to huff, hating the need to make excuses, but he hadn't killed anybody that night.

"Hold on," she said. "Because of Gower's injuries, I realize that, whatever happened, it was in self-defense. I *am* aware, you know, that sometimes a man has no choice but to fight."

"Good," he said, relieved that at least she was being reasonable.

Yet a sense of foreboding filled him.

She paused their negotiations, reaching for her tea. Luke mirrored her actions, lifting his coffee to his lips. Too hot, it burned his tongue and trickled like acid down his throat. He winced and put the cup down as she did the same.

"Well?" he asked, his whole body tense.

She looked hard into his eyes. "While I've decided I can handle being married to a highwayman, I cannot share my life with a murderer, Luke. If that were so, I might as well have accepted Axewood's suit."

His jaw dropped. "A murderer?" He leaned closer and whispered, "You actually think I'm a murderer?"

"Defending yourself in a fight is one thing. But hunting down your enemies and slaughtering them—knowing full well that your rank will protect you and let you get away with whatever you please—that is something else entirely, Luke. I want nothing to do with that. It is beyond disturbing. It's but a shade away from evil."

He could barely speak. She was never even supposed to know about this. "So what are you saying?"

"Let's review. You tracked your parents' killers ruthlessly for years, then tore them apart when you found them, and you do not regret it in the slightest, as you said. Though such a deed might fill me with awe—not to mention terror of what you might be capable of—my trust in you has already been shaken by your lies.

"I need to know that the light in you is stronger than the darkness. I need to know that the kindness, the humanity I saw in you as Lucas was real, not just part of the charade. I dare not marry you until I can be sure you're not like that anymore."

"I promise you—"

"No. We are past verbal assurances, Luke. If you wish to earn back my trust, there is only one way for you to prove."

"How? What must I do?" he whispered.

Portia held his stare with iron-willed stubbornness. "Spare Lord Axewood."

CHAPTER 30

A Hard Bargain

*L*uke felt the blood drain from his face. A wave of coldness gusted through him like a winter wind. "I beg your pardon?"

"Do what you've done so many times before as Silversmoke," she said, somberly holding his stare. "Take Axewood into custody and then turn him over to the law."

Luke pushed his plate away and obscured his mouth with his fist, dropping his gaze.

That quickly, the progress they'd made this morning evaporated. Fury pounded in his veins.

"You don't know what you're saying," he said at last, his tone flinty. "He already owns men inside the Bow Street offices. And Silversmoke is, technically speaking, a highwayman. So who do you think they're going to believe?"

"But you have evidence of his wrongdoing."

"It wouldn't count as *proof!*" He checked his temper and told himself she didn't understand. "Even if I showed them my father's journal, this is the last man who deserves any kind of mercy."

"Luke—"

"Where was mercy when his hirelings cut my mother's throat? When they ran my father through? They even killed the servants. No, Portia. The bastard dies, by my hand, and I will not sit here and listen to this foolishness. Not even from you."

Her blue eyes narrowed; she sat up straight. "I see. Then you've made your choice."

He clenched his jaw then leaned closer, staring at her, willing her to understand. "You have no right to ask this of me."

"No right? You are to be my husband!"

"He murdered my parents!"

"He's a peer!" she whispered in fury. "This is not the same as hunting down lowborn bandits with long criminal records, and you know it, Luke. This could affect your entire family. Believe me, I know what I'm talking about. I already went through it once with my brother's duel, and that was bad enough. Now you're going to put me in an even worse situation, because if I become your wife, I'm the one who's going to have to live with the consequences of y-your savagery!"

"It has nothing to do with you!"

"Of course it does! Suppose justice catches up to you a few years down the road. What am I to tell our children when their father is arrested and put on trial for murder in the House of Lords?"

He scoffed, which only heightened her ire.

"You would disgrace me, my family, Tavi—you'll break your sister's heart *and* ruin her children's lives, to say nothing of orphaning your own when the court sends you to the gallows.

"Oh, *and* you'll leave us destitute," she added, "for you'll forfeit everything your parents left you to the Crown. Now, you tell me: Is killing Axewood really worth all that?"

Luke sat silent, absorbing her broadsides.

Though he glowered, at least he considered her words. "First, you assume I will get caught. That isn't going to happen."

She scoffed and shook her head. "Such arrogance."

"Then Joel can back me up and tell the court I had no choice. Self-defense. I daresay your precious beau will owe me *that* much at least. Besides, once I expose Axewood's corruption with regard to the war funds, no one will weep for him."

She paused. "What about repairing my trust?"

The quiet question skewered him.

He dropped his gaze and dug in his heels. "I don't respond well to ultimatums, love."

"That is not what this is!" she exclaimed. "I am trying to save you here! Trying to save your soul—"

A jaded laugh escaped him. "Bit late for that."

She glared at him, her cheeks flushed with anger. But she strove visibly for patience with him. "Luke, I know it wounded you, deeply and permanently, when your parents were killed—"

"You have no idea."

"You spent years doing whatever it took to destroy those who cut them down. But, Luke, what about the rest of us, who are *still here*, trying to be a part of your life now? You're so caught up in trying to fix the past, which can't be done—you'll never bring them back—that you can't even see how you'd harm us all just to gratify your wrath. Do you really think it's worth it? Because if that's the case, if that's your choice, then, honestly, I really *would* be better off with Joel."

Luke clenched his jaw, glared at her, then threw his napkin aside. "You know what? You're right," he clipped out. "Maybe you would."

They stared at each other across the table, their untouched breakfast congealing. Luke rested his elbows on the scuffed wood and steepled his hands; Portia mirrored his pose.

The seconds ticked by and neither budged, their gazes locked, walls up.

It seemed they were at a stalemate. He would not be threatened, and she would not back down.

He broke first, damn her. "So you expect me to, what, just let him get away with it?"

"*No, Luke,*" she said with a withering look. "I want him brought to justice, too, but *in the proper way.*"

"This is the proper way, damn it!" he bit back. "I deserve his head on a bloody platter after what he did."

Portia winced at his words, looking revolted, and just for a moment, Luke saw himself through her eyes.

"*Twenty men,*" she had said that night at Gracewell, horror stamped across her delicate face. "*You killed them all.*"

Indeed, he had.

A vision flitted through his mind of the last surviving MacAbe impaled on a wooden spike that used to be a table. Luke blinked away the horror, just as he'd been doing ever since he'd put the blackguard out of his misery that night.

"Luke—"

"No." He refused to break. His jaw was taut; his heart was iron. "You have no right to insinuate yourself into the middle of something that does not concern you."

"And you have no right to play God," she whispered.

He flinched at the accusation, but fixed her with a glower known to strike fear into roomfuls of brigands. He waited for her to blink.

She didn't. *Damn.*

She really was born to be a duchess.

"So that's it, then?" he challenged her. "This is the Gordian Knot you present me with less than two weeks before our wedding? If I fulfill my duty as a son, I lose my bride."

She gave an almost imperceptible nod, looking dazed herself that it had come to that. "Yes, Luke. You have a decision to make. Love or hate. Marriage or vengeance. 'I set before you life and death.' The choice is yours."

He twisted his lips cynically at the Bible quote and braced himself. "So, you'll marry Joel instead?"

"Yes," she said in a shaky voice. "If he'll have me."

"If he'll have you! I see…" Behind his bravado, panic gripped him, tightening in the pit of his stomach, but outwardly, Luke remained cool, aloof. "Well, perhaps I've changed my mind about this whole mission. What if I don't save him, hmm? If I'm so evil, maybe I'll just leave him to his fate. And what'll you do then?"

Her eyes flashed blue daggers at him, but when she answered, her voice was as elegant as frosted glass. "The great Silversmoke would go back on his word?"

He shrugged. "Why not? You're about to go back on yours."

She looked away, her fine-boned face tense with distress.

Let her worry, Luke thought, but his sense of control over this entire situation was fraying, along with his patience. The last thing he wanted was to hurt her. Desperation coursed through his veins.

"You don't love him. Not like you love me."

She shook her head. "That only means that he can't hurt me as you can. Hypocrite. You said love costs everything. Such pretty words. But I see now they were just more lies."

Luke stared at her like a trapped animal. He could feel her slipping through his fingers and didn't know what to do.

Nor could he seem to help it somehow that the more scared he got of the mess that he was making, the ruder he sounded.

"He had mistresses, you know," he said, his heart pounding. "Your precious Joel. I wasn't going to tell you that, but you might as well know what you're getting into with this 'perfect match' of yours."

She gripped the spoon by her plate, avoiding his gaze. She turned it end over end for a moment. "Well," she said with forced nonchalance, "at least he's not a murderer. So there's that."

A quick, bitter laugh escaped him as he realized that was how the woman he loved truly saw him. "Right…"

Worse, that might very well be what he actually *was*. For he could not even claim that killing Axewood was simply his duty.

No, he wanted to do it. Craved the bastard's blood. Indeed, he could barely wait to watch him die.

At that moment, the sickening thought truly sank in that Portia was right about him. Unmasked even to himself, Luke now realized what was—what he had somehow become.

And he was aghast.

For it was not just from the outer world that he'd hidden the truth; he'd hidden it from himself, as well. But his eyes were opened now, and a tremor ran through him as he saw what he must do.

Portia Tennesley must not be allowed to marry such a monster.

Love costs everything. He had to protect her.

With blinding clarity, Luke suddenly saw that he had to let her go while he had the strength.

He shot to his feet and grabbed his coat off the peg. "Very well," he said. "I wish you and Mr. Clayton every happiness together." His heart wrenched like it had just torn in two in his chest, and unfortunately, the stunning pain of this unbearable new loss brought out the bastard in him. He couldn't seem to stop himself from leaning down and whispering in her ear, "But we both know you'll think of me when you take him to your bed."

Portia gasped at his effrontery, but Luke was already leaving. He ignored their friends as he stalked off across the common room and slammed out the front door, nearly tearing it off its hinges.

Fists clenched at his sides, he was deaf to the birdsong, blind to the colorful beauty of the day. Fury had long since imprisoned him in darkness, in hate. Anger was the steel-barred cell he carried with him everywhere he went, and he was still locked inside, alone.

How much easier it was to focus on a target.

Luke narrowed his eyes, staring blindly at the verdant meadows across the road. He saw only vengeance. *Look what you've cost me now, Axewood.* His heart churned; his pulse thundered.

But Portia would no doubt be better off with the idiot gambler than a hardened killer like him, so the mission was on. He'd save the dandy as promised and watch them ride off together, the oh-so-fashionable pair.

Then he'd complete the revenge that had made him what he was. This dark, twisted creature whose whole life was apparently a lie.

At some point, he must have deceived himself into thinking he could move through the underworld among killers and outlaws and thieves and stay uninfected by its barbarity.

Good God, the underworld feared him. Did he never stop to ask himself what that might say about the man he'd become?

He hated that Portia, such a delicate soul, should have been the one to see through his façade and show Luke to himself. She should never have to look into the eyes of a killer. It was right to release her.

But it hurt like hell.

Inhaling sharply through his nostrils, Luke reached for his knife. The familiar feel of the hilt in his hand comforted him, but the pain she'd inflicted did not bode well for his enemy.

Axewood, your death just got ten times more painful.

Meanwhile, back at the table, Portia had jumped at the door's deafening bang. She could hear her friends' hushed exclamations after seeing Luke storm out, but she ignored them, as he had.

Her pulse was pounding, her hands felt like ice, and she was utterly dazed by what had just happened.

She could not seem to breathe. *It's over. He chose his hate over me.* With a belated gasp for air, she strove to steady herself, trembling now from head to foot. *My God. I've lost him.*

She'd gambled and she'd lost, staking everything on it. Delayed panic began rushing down all her nerve endings.

Dizzy with dread, she turned and glanced over her shoulder at the door, willing Luke to return.

He did not.

Instead, she saw Sidney leaning his head out of their booth. He sent her a questioning frown full of brotherly concern.

Heart in her throat, Portia shook her head, declining his wordless offer of moral support. She desperately needed a few moments alone to absorb the spectacular failure of her attempt to tame the highwayman-duke.

Oh, but she had vastly miscalculated. All she'd wanted was to save him from himself, but she'd driven him off.

Now her wedding was well and truly canceled. The love of her life would rather see her marry Joel than give up his revenge.

Her chin trembled. He might as well have run her through where she sat, but she fought the wave of grief washing over her. Stunned but quite stuck with the deal she had made, it was all she could do not to cry.

But, as she did not wish to make a fool of herself by blubbering like a child in front of Lady Delphine and stern Major Carvel, Portia turned forward again, struggling to compose herself.

It was then that she found herself gazing down at the bleak sight of Luke's uneaten breakfast. It sat there, abandoned, the oatmeal turning to paste, the coffee leaving drab brown rings on the inside of the mug.

The lump in her throat tightened, and tears flicked into her eyes. For the dismal image perfectly depicted the sort of arranged match she'd once expected to have with His Grace: herself and the absent stranger.

Now she wouldn't even have that.

CHAPTER 31

The Break

$\mathscr{L}$uke said little and kept to himself for the second half of their journey, but he seethed every step of the way.

It helped to remind himself she was not at all the sort of wife he'd wanted in the first place. He had specifically ordered a dim, biddable beauty who would stay out of his way. Not a little miss know-it-all who dared to throw down the gauntlet to Silversmoke or call a duke to account.

All he could do as the road unfolded before him was nurse his hurt and shake his head in wonder at her audacity.

Well, she was Joel's headache now.

Luke refused to regret his decision. She'd be better off. For his part, he would not be manipulated by anyone nor countenance ultimatums. Axewood deserved to die, and if the little queen bee was too self-righteous to understand that, then let her buzz off and go sting someone else.

Her refined sensibilities were a nice luxury for a sheltered young lady. But Luke lived in the real world, where real villains brought real consequences down on their own damned heads.

For too long, Axewood had got away with his crimes. But punishment was coming soon, and Luke intended to deliver it in person, no matter what she said.

Temples pounding from the headache he had given himself by clenching his jaw like a vise for the past hour and a half, Luke called a halt when they came to a country crossroads near the lazy River Wye.

An old finger sign at the intersection pointed him north: *Fergus Wood — 3 Miles*.

That was the village where Junius Foy had instructed him to find The Goat Inn. There, he must give the password in order to receive the final piece of directions to where the Carnevale was being held tonight.

Swinging down off Tempo's back, Luke checked his weapons and made sure he had his folding telescope in his knapsack of supplies. Then he slung the pack over his good shoulder and borrowed Orion from Finch.

Tempo was too showy to avoid drawing notice, and given the company gathering in the area, Luke did not want his horse getting stolen.

He ordered the rest of their party to retire for an afternoon break in the shade of the ancient oak tree that overhung the river wending its way through the meadow by the road.

The spot looked pleasant enough for a picnic, and there was food in the hampers they'd bought at the last place for nuncheon. Besides, so genteel-looking a group of travelers would not draw suspicion from the sort of people who might pass by on their way to the Carnevale.

"I'll be back in two hours," he told them, ignoring Portia's tumultuous stare. "Carvel, you're in charge. Don't let anyone wander off."

"As you wish. What are *you* going to do, Fountainhurst?" Still astride his white horse, Peter took Tempo's reins from Luke like a lead rope.

"I need to do some scouting up ahead." Luke squinted against the late morning sun. "Get the lay of the land. I'll find us accommodations we can use as our headquarters for the night. Somewhere safe for the ladies."

Peter nodded, then he turned and waved the driver toward the shady tree, as instructed. "Let's get these horses watered!"

"Yes, sir," said the driver.

Luke nodded to his servants in approval, but Peter was clearly used to giving orders. It put Luke's mind at ease to know Portia and the others would be under the major's protection while he explored the situation ahead.

As the carriage began rumbling off the road into the flat, grassy meadow, Peter turned to Luke, concern in his sober, teal-colored eyes. "You sure you don't want one of us to go with you? Watch your back?"

"I'll be fine."

Peter nodded. "Good luck."

"Thanks." Luke tugged down the brim of his hat, then wheeled Orion around and cantered on alone, riding over the old stone bridge there and up the north road.

He could feel Portia watching him from the carriage as he swept out of view.

The look in her eyes when he'd agreed with her that she might as well marry Joel haunted him. He knew she did not understand. Shock had mixed with betrayal in her sky-blue eyes as she realized she had miscalculated.

Knowing he had hurt her only underscored his unworthiness to keep her for himself.

Putting her out of his mind as best he could, Luke followed the road to Fergus Wood as it meandered through the Chilterns.

The whole time, a small tributary of the river he'd crossed at the bridge babbled along beside him, hugging the road.

After a jaunt of some twenty minutes, Luke spotted the village. Just a few hundred yards on the rise ahead, the little hilltop town waited, a hazy heap of golden-brown stone buildings surrounded by lush trees and greenery.

He could already see the square bell tower of a simple Norman church, hear the whirring of a millstone powered by the stream.

The place looked idyllic. But, knowing that the unsuspecting village was the current destination for countless outlaws and ruffians who'd soon be pouring in to attend Carnevale, Luke rode toward it very much on his guard.

Maybe someone would pick a fight with him. Some brash fool at The Goat Inn.

One could hope.

Perhaps he would happen across Lord Axewood himself.

Urging Orion onward, Luke reminded himself that the password Foy had given him was *Fortuna*.

The goddess of fate.

Figures, he thought. But what his own fortune might be in all this remained to be seen.

"Why isn't he back yet?" Portia turned to Peter in the shade of the old oak tree where Luke had ordered them to wait.

"Don't worry about Fountainhurst. He'll be fine. Shoot the tree."

"But I don't want to shoot the tree!"

"It'll make you feel better," he promised, handing her the bow and an arrow.

Portia stared at Peter, at a loss. She'd never been one to wear her heart on her sleeve, but the whole party knew that Luke and she had quarreled. They just didn't know the extent of it.

Misery aside, she was worried. "He said he'd be gone for two hours. It's been nearly four! With all of the criminals coming into the area, well, what if something's wrong?"

Peter gave her one of the same dismissive frowns he often gave his sister. "Why are you worried? He's Silversmoke."

"He'll be fine, Lady Portia," Oliver Finch chimed in with an earnest nod. "Trust me—he does this sort of thing all the time."

She threw up her hands with a huff. That hardly made her feel better!

"One of us should have gone with him," she said, but the others ignored her, their mood idle and bored.

"It's bloody hot," Delphine mumbled, fanning herself with the leather-bound journal in which she'd been writing. She sat on a large rock right beside the river.

"It is," Sidney agreed. He'd tired of skipping stones across the water some time ago and had flopped down into the tall meadow grass, where he lay serenely sprawled out on his back, eyes closed, ankles crossed, arms out wide.

"If he doesn't come soon, I am going to strip naked and go for a swim," Sidney declared. "Who's with me?"

Peter scowled. "Don't talk like that in front of the ladies."

Finch looked embarrassed at any mention of nudity, but Delphine laughed. "By all means! Have at it, boys. Diana the huntress here and I will watch with great interest."

A lazy laugh escaped Sidney, but he did not open his eyes. "You'd like that, wouldn't you, you lecherous minx?"

"More than you know," Delphine murmured, eyeing up the handsome Major Carvel again.

He seemed nonplussed by her frisky leer.

Well, thought Portia. It seemed her so-called chaperone and dear

Lord Smiley hadn't been fibbing in the coach.

In the interests of trying to cheer her up, they had finally admitted to her under great secrecy that, no, they were not a couple.

"That's what everyone thinks, isn't it?" Sidney had teased, his cobalt eyes dancing. "That Del is my mistress?"

"That he's my cicisbeo?" Delphine had slung an arm around the viscount's shoulders in a chummy fashion.

Portia had nodded, slightly embarrassed. "Those *are* the rumors." Then she'd glanced from one to the other. "Well? Is it true? Are you...together?"

They had sat there grinning like a pair of cats at the cream.

"No," Delphine had finally admitted. "That is not the nature of our...pact, shall we say. But don't spoil the fun for the gossips, dear."

"Never." Portia had furrowed her brow, grateful for the distraction. "But if you're not lovers, then what are you, exactly?"

"Hmm. Co-conspirators?" Biting his lip, Sidney had slid Delphine a mischievous glance. "Shall we take her into our confidence, Del?"

The book club hostess had shrugged. "Why not? If she can keep a secret like Silversmoke, I daresay the lady can be trusted."

Sidney had turned back to Portia and made his triumphant announcement: "We are fellow artists!"

"Artists?" she'd echoed.

"But if you tell anyone, we shall both deny it in the strongest possible terms." A roguish smile tugged at his lips. "The truth is, Del writes the most spine-tingling gothic penny dreadfuls, and I do the illustrations. Ha! What do you think of that?"

Portia's jaw dropped to hear it, and they'd both begun laughing. She spluttered. "Lady Delphine, you're an author? I had a feeling... Oh my goodness, have you had your books published?"

Delphine had nodded, her smile widening.

"Tell me a title! Why do we not discuss them at your book club? Oh—or have we?" Then Portia had gasped, momentarily forgetting Luke's perfidy. "Are you the anonymous 'Lady' behind *Pride and Prejudice*?"

"Oh heavens, no," Delphine said. "That's not the sort of thing I do at all, much as I admire it. My books are considerably...bloodier." She smiled serenely and took another sip of her tea while Sidney waggled his eyebrows.

"Del writes of murders and gore. It's delicious."

"My family disapproves with all their might," Delphine continued. "That's why I must use a pseudonym, you see. If I were to publish under my own name, I'd be cut off."

Portia's gaze had then swung back to Sidney. "And you, Sidney, you're an artist? I had no idea. How wonderful! Oh, but of course you are. Now that you've said it, it makes perfect sense. You've always had such an eye."

"Now, now, I never said that I had any talent."

Delphine had smacked him for that. "He's ridiculously talented."

Portia had sat there shaking her head in amazement. "So that explains the nocturnal visits, eh? Not trysts, but meetings of the muse."

"Just so. We do our best work at night." Sidney cast the authoress a mischievous smile. "Del gives me new challenges of what to draw for her stories—"

"And he gives me the male perspective when I'm contemplating my characters. How a man would react—"

"I help her fashion her plots—"

"Sometimes he even has a good idea or two."

"Only when I'm very well liquored," he said as she elbowed him.

They both had laughed, but Portia could only shake her head in wonder. "Why let everyone think you're a couple, then?"

"Because it amuses us," Delphine replied.

"We like to keep them guessing." Sidney grinned. "And it really irks my father."

"You two sound like Luke, with his real-life playacting." Portia let out a pained sigh. Fortunately, the two had pretended not to hear it. The wound was too raw yet to discuss it.

"That must be why we like him," Sidney had declared. "He's one of us, eh Del? An artist at heart."

"Is that why you agreed to participate in this mad venture?" Portia asked her mysterious chaperone.

Lady Delphine had smiled. "It sounded interesting. All of life is just grist for the mill, after all."

"Eh, don't let her fool you," Sidney had taunted. "Del's got her eye on Carvel, and I assure you, it's not marriage that she's after."

"Infamous rudesby!" Delphine had smacked him again, but apparently, Sidney had been telling the truth, for the authoress had continued giving Danger Man sultry looks ever since they'd started their break here in the meadow.

Sidney showed exactly zero signs of jealousy, but, for his part, the dutiful major seemed confused by her lusty glances.

Even now, Carvel turned away, looking somewhat disconcerted, Portia thought, by her chaperone's lack of propriety.

Hands on his hips, he squinted judiciously at the river, while Portia still stood beside him under the shade tree, holding her bow, at a loss.

She had pulled it out of the coach for no other reason than to while away the time with some practice, desperately needing the clarity she so often found in her hobby.

Luke might have crushed her heart choosing murder over marriage, but this was no time for weakness or tears, with the Carnevale waiting tonight. Their lives were at stake, including Joel's.

Anything might happen. She had to stay sharp.

Alas, far from succeeding in distracting herself from her churning emotions, she had lost interest after shooting a mere three arrows.

After that, it didn't take long for Peter to show her up with his skill.

"Well, I'll shoot the dashed tree if you won't," he said abruptly, doing his best to ignore Delphine's hungry perusal of his muscular body.

"But it's such a nice old tree," Portia said halfheartedly, doing her best to seem cheerful. She handed him the bow.

"Don't worry. It won't feel a thing." He stepped into position and lifted the weapon, drew back the bowstring, and took aim. His eyes narrowed.

Then he released; the arrow flew, plunging into the center of the ancient oak's trunk with a resounding *thwap*.

The shot scared a couple of turtledoves out of the branches, and the major looked up at them, alert as a hunting dog.

"Oh no you don't." She quickly took her weapon away from him. "Hide, birdies. This bow doesn't kill things, Major."

"Oh really?" He cocked his fist on his waist as the breeze ruffled through his loose shirt sleeves; the gentlemen had removed their jackets in the heat. "What's the point in having it, then?"

"For fun!" She scowled at him. *Typical.* Serving his country was all very well, but men who had killed had a look to them, she decided. A cold, pained wisdom they carried in their eyes.

Giving her a sardonic glance, he marched forward to pull the arrow out of the tree, and Delphine bit her lip and fanned herself again, watching him pass.

"I wish I had my fishing pole," Finch remarked. Seated with his arms loosely wrapped around his bent knees, he was chewing on a long piece of grass he'd picked in the meadow. He gazed at the river. "It's very peaceful here, don't you think?"

"Very," Delphine said.

"Well, I'm bored." Sidney sat up, the sun glinting on his golden hair. He leaned back and planted his hands behind him, looking effortlessly elegant, as always.

But Portia looked again at her locket watch, and with every quarter hour that dragged by, her anxiety climbed. Where the blazes was Luke?

"We should go after him," she said.

"Lud, you sound like a worried wife," Sidney muttered.

She flinched and dropped her gaze. He didn't know their marriage was canceled.

"His Grace can take care of himself, I'm sure," Peter said.

"Yes, but maybe he ran into trouble—"

"There he is!" Finch suddenly interrupted, pointing to the road.

Portia whirled around, and, sure enough, she saw Luke cantering toward them in a cloud of dust. Relief washed through her. *Oh, thank God.*

"Told you," Sidney mumbled.

"Hold on…" Finch rose to his feet with a frown, and shaded his eyes with his hand. "What horse is that? That's not Orion!"

Squinting up the road, Portia confirmed for herself it was true. Luke had left on a dark liver bay; he was now riding toward them on a palomino whose hide gleamed with the soft patina of antique gold in the sun.

Peter's rugged face instantly returned to its usual grim arrangement. "Seems Lady Portia was right, after all. He must've run into trouble."

"What's happened to Orion?" Finch cried, as if they could tell him.

The lighthearted atmosphere evaporated. Major Carvel handed Portia back her bow and strode toward the road, drawing his sword as if to defend Luke, should trouble have followed him.

Taking her cue from him, Portia gripped her bow tighter, slipping her quiver of arrows onto her back. She walked cautiously after him, searching the road behind Luke. She saw no one.

Sidney rose with a stretch, still unconcerned. "The horse probably threw a shoe or some such. You people worry too much. Honestly."

Delphine closed her notebook and let Sidney pull her to her feet.

Finch hurried ahead of Peter, more concerned about the horse than he was for his master, it seemed.

Luke slowed the palomino to a trot going over the bridge, then turned off the road, riding into the field.

They gathered around, already peppering him with questions the moment he reined in before them.

"What happened? How did it go?"

"Are you all right? What took so long?"

"Where's Orion?" Finch asked anxiously.

"Sorry, all." Luke swung down from the horse. "That took longer than I thought."

"Trouble?" Peter asked.

"No, not at all, thankfully. I found The Goat Inn and got the rest of the directions to where we must go tonight. Had a look around at their impromptu fairgrounds. Also, I stopped and got us lodgings."

"Where's Orion?" Finch repeated.

Luke glanced at the redhead. "I left him at the stable of the inn where I got us rooms. It's a perfect location for what we've got on hand tonight."

"So you already got a look at the place where they'll be holding the Carnevale, then?" Peter murmured.

Luke nodded. "That's what delayed me." He wiped the sweat off his brow with his arm, then reached for his canteen. "They're holding it in a secluded dale in the middle of the woods." He shrugged. "I would've been back a couple of hours ago, but when they told me it would be held outdoors, I wanted to study the landscape in the daylight. Check the lay of the land before it gets dark tonight." He took a quick swallow of water.

"Wise." Peter nodded.

Portia stared at Luke, but he avoided making eye contact with her.

"I take it you found The Goat Inn?" Sidney asked, only just joining them as he sauntered over beside Lady Delphine.

"I did," Luke said. "I got an interesting piece of information there, as well. About Axewood. Falls right in line with what you found out."

"Oh really?" Sidney asked, squinting in the sunlight.

"Aye. I asked the barkeep if he'd seen the Red Carnation come by yet to get the directions, just like everybody else. Pretended to be a fan. Famous as the star player is, I figured the man might've recognized him."

"Had he seen him?" Peter asked. "Proof that Clayton's still alive before we start this would be nice."

"He had." Luke gave a terse nod. "It cost me ten quid to get the information, but the barkeep said he had come in that morning along with his 'usual partner': Captain Hatchet."

"Captain Hatchet?" Sidney said, then his eyes widened. "A hatchet's another name for an ax!"

"Indeed," Luke said with a dark smile.

"His alter ego," Delphine murmured, fascinated.

Portia could only shake her head in astonishment. It was strange enough that the Duke of Fountainhurst masqueraded as a highwayman to carry out his business in the underworld. But the Earl of Axewood, as well?

She pressed her fingertips to her brow and scoffed. "What the devil is he the captain of? A ship?"

"I don't know," Luke said, warily glancing her way at last. "Probably nothing. But the nickname's enough of a clue, I think, to let us know we're on the right track."

"Silversmoke versus Captain Hatchet," Sidney drawled. "It should be one interesting night."

"There's more," Luke said. "The barkeep mentioned that Clayton was limping. He's injured, by the sound of it."

"Oh no," Portia murmured.

"If Axewood's as wicked as you say," Delphine interjected, "he might have hobbled his nephew to keep him from escaping."

Portia felt the blood rush out of her cheeks. *Poor Joel.*

"That could make rescuing him more complicated," Peter said in a low tone.

"He's also under guard. The barkeep said that the two had a 'big bald man' with them. Sound familiar?" Luke snorted. "I asked the fellow if he knew the third chap's name. He said he heard 'Captain Hatchet' call him Rucker. Said he was big as a house, with a dragon tattoo on the side of his head. I'm fairly sure that's a gang marking of some sort, but the barkeep felt Rucker was security, protecting Axewood and guarding Joel."

"Big as a house, eh?" Sidney glanced at the veteran. "You can have that one, Major."

Peter arched a brow, then looked at Luke. "What did you see when you went to preview the fairgrounds?"

Luke steadied the restless palomino. "They were already setting up for tonight," he said. "Putting up tents and pavilions. Building temporary market stalls. Gypsy-looking caravans rolling in, too. There were other workers stacking up kindling for bonfires. They put a pig on a spit and got it cooking. It's a marvel they didn't attract the notice of the locals, all this activity going on down there in the middle of the woods."

"They must've paid someone off," Peter said with a stern look.

"Indeed." Luke took another swallow of water. "After that, I went to find us a headquarters for tonight. The two main inns up the road are filling up fast with, well, the sort of folk you'd expect. I don't want the ladies anywhere near that lot, so I rode farther and found us a place.

"It's called Alpine House. Good people. I spoke to the owner, an ex-professor from the Continent—straitlaced Swiss. Moved his family here during the war, fleeing Napoleon. He closed the house for Carnevale attendees, but I explained our situation is quite different, that we're here to rescue someone, so he agreed to rent me the whole house. The inn is rather small, but we'll have it to ourselves, except for a few staff."

"You didn't tell him that you're Silversmoke, surely?" Delphine asked.

"No, I didn't go that far. Nor does he know that I'm a duke. Just an ordinary traveler trying to rescue a friend who's taken a bad path by getting involved with the Carnevale tournament—and I didn't tell him Joel had been kidnapped, either. Our host is the one who lent me this horse, by the way. Orion needed to rest. He didn't get the break the other horses did. How's Tempo? Did he behave?" he asked Peter.

"He was fine," the major replied. "Easygoing for a stallion, isn't he?"

Luke nodded, giving way to a smile. "He's a good boy. Anyway, we should go." Looking past them, he signaled to the servants to get the carriage ready to go.

"How are you all?" he then asked, glancing around at them.

"Bored!" Sidney retorted.

"Well, you won't be tonight," Luke said, quirking a smile. "I saw some rather bizarre people gathering for this thing."

"How mysterious," murmured Delphine.

"Right! Well, we should get underway." Luke put his canteen away with a weary air. "The inn is about five miles from here."

"I think I'll ride this time," Sidney said.

"Take him." Luke gestured at the palomino.

"He matches your hair," Delphine teased, then she and Portia returned to the coach, and this time, it was Finch who joined them.

Through the carriage window, Portia saw Luke walk over to Tempo and greet the black stallion with an affectionate pat. Sidney swung up onto the golden horse while Peter mounted up once more onto his big showy white gelding.

Before long, they were on the road. As the carriage rocked and rumbled over the uneven ground of the meadow, Portia brooded on Luke's chilly attitude toward her. It stung, after she had been so worried about him.

Perhaps he was disturbed by the fact that, if everything went well tonight, she would soon be reunited with Joel.

Somehow, the prospect gave her little joy.

Then the coach bumped up over the same stone bridge Luke had crossed earlier and continued northward, deeper into the Chilterns.

Twenty-five minutes up the road, they passed through the town of Fergus Wood and drove right by the dodgy-looking, half-timbered Goat Inn, where Luke had gone for directions.

"What a dreadful place," Delphine said.

Both women gazed out the window at the ominous old tavern as they drove by, then looked at each other. Delphine blanched.

Before Portia knew it, they had cleared the little town and rolled out the other side. As the carriage rumbled up the road, woods swallowed up the long, cloud-mottled vistas of the Chilterns.

Signs of civilization vanished away. The forest thickened around them, deep and green, and the tunnel of trees that met overhead cast the road in a verdant shade.

About fifteen minutes beyond the town, going up a long, gradual hill, they passed a galleried coaching inn with a sign out front that read *The Maypole*. The courtyard bustled with a rowdy crowd of sharpers and scantily clad harlots jumping out of coaches and milling about.

A festival spirit prevailed.

"It appears the guests are arriving," Delphine remarked.

Staring out the window at the raucous crowd was the moment for Portia that this whole misadventure became utterly real.

This was happening. This was what Joel had been subjected to for the past year.

Moreover, the danger was real. Especially to Luke, who was putting his life on the line for a man he didn't even know.

To dear, lovable Sidney, as well. Good God, why had Sidney come? He was no fighter!

As for Major Carvel, the poor man had already survived a war. If anything happened to him, she would never be able to look Felicity in the eye…

Sitting there, ramrod straight and tense as iron, Portia began, privately, to panic, knowing all three men were headed into the very lion's den tonight.

Because of her and the quest she had brought before Silversmoke.

"I hope he's worth it," Luke had once said to her in highwayman mode.

She swallowed hard, dry-mouthed, unsure if anybody was.

Unfortunately, it was far too late to be having second thoughts. The carriage barreled on, down a slope, then up another hill, until at last, after another twenty minutes' travel, they turned off the road onto a lonely dirt drive.

This curved a short distance through a stand of majestic pines, then a hilltop clearing opened before them, where stood their lodgings for the night. Portia stared at the inn as the coach squeaked to a weary halt.

Why, the owner must've brought his native style with him to England, she mused, for, true to its name on the picturesque wooden sign, The Alpine House was built in the fanciful style of a Swiss chalet.

This romantic new mode of architecture had started becoming popular of late for garden follies or hunting boxes, she knew, but Portia had never seen one full size, let alone spent the night in one.

A large, sturdy rectangle, it sat atop stone foundations and peaked up into a wide, A-frame roof. The sides were covered in rustic brown weatherboard. Lacy gingerbread adorned the balcony that wrapped all the way around the second story.

The big Swiss cottage seemed right at home in the woods and offered an excellent view of the valley out back—which was why Luke had secured it for them for the night, Portia realized. From here, they would have a clear view of the Carnevale down in the dell.

A frisson of premonition trickled down her spine, and the dark turn of her earlier musings came rushing back. She climbed out of the carriage after Lady Delphine and took a deep breath of the pine-scented air.

Then she glanced over at Luke as he swung down off Tempo's back. Riveted by his tall, muscular form and effortless air of command, she watched him giving orders and caring for his horse. Agonizing love gripped her as dread rose in her throat.

By God, if anything happens to him tonight, I will never forgive myself.

CHAPTER 32

Darkness Falls

After bringing everyone safely to The Alpine House, Luke finally retired to his own guestroom, where he gingerly removed the bandages from his shoulder, wincing his way through the process.

His burns hurt like hell from the constant motion today, and his body was stiff from the long day in the saddle.

Grateful for the chance to leave his wound open to the air for a while, he did not bother putting on another shirt, but lay down on his stomach and tried to get some rest. It had been an early morning and would be a late night. He wondered how Gower was doing, and eventually fell asleep.

He dreamed of Scotland. Steep green hills, castle ruins, teeming brooks, and a moody flint-blue sky fading into black. Then flames. Screams. The smell of gunpowder, the crack of his rifle, the swift flash of his blade.

He dreamed of the blood that he had shed in that place, the hell he'd unleashed. He could still see their faces so clearly, the MacAbe men, could still hear the screams.

And, always, that one blackguard begging for his life. He'd have died even if Luke had spared him, but there had been no mercy in him that night.

He reveled in the scarlet thrill of savage victory, the rush of justice, knowing he had devastated them and evened the score. But amid the smoke and chaos of his own handiwork, he somehow realized he was the monster of his own nightmare…

The realization woke him abruptly. Luke sat up with a start, disoriented, chest heaving. Beyond his chamber window, twilight had fallen.

He swung his feet down and sat on the edge of the bed, willing his pulse to slow to normal. Leaning forward, he rubbed his brow.

My God, he thought. No wonder Portia had called him a murderer.

With a knee-jerk vehemence, Luke refused to accept that label, but in this moment of stark self-honesty, he could not deny the toll that his obsession with revenge had taken on him.

It was a lot to live with on his soul. No wonder he had cloaked himself in lies and illusions ever since…

Hidden in the shadows.

He closed his eyes for a moment, took a deep breath, and blew it out. The truth was that he had already paid an enormous price for doing what he considered his duty as a son. Now it seemed that this burden had cost him the heart of the woman he loved, as well.

He couldn't even blame her. Everything she'd said had made perfect sense.

In grim silence, he rose and started getting ready for the night's mission.

As he splashed his face, the Bible verse that she'd quoted, of all things, kept trailing through his mind. Which was ironic, considering how irked he was at God even now, all these years later, for abandoning his parents to their fate.

I set before you life and death… Therefore choose life, that thou and thy seed both may live.

And, postscript: *Vengeance is mine, saith the Lord.*

Well, Portia had accused him of playing God, and perhaps she was right. But if, as he'd seen, much to his despair, the Almighty refused to lift a finger to protect the innocent, then somebody at least had to try.

At what cost? he wondered.

He caught his own eye in the mirror and stared hard at himself for a second, weighing matters, then he turned away from his reflection with a growl.

This was no time to get caught up in philosophical self-doubt.

A short while later, he left his room, once more arrayed in his Silversmoke garb. He stopped by Sidney and Peter's rooms and reminded both men they'd be leaving at nine.

Then he exited the inn and slipped down into the woods for a final round of surveillance; he wanted to see how the situation in the valley was proceeding before he and his two henchmen for the night ventured down there. God forbid he get either of them killed.

There was a path among the trees, and Luke followed it down to a good vantage point.

Crouching down atop a boulder that overlooked the valley, he took out his spyglass and studied the scene below.

The bonfires were burning, the colorful crowds already pouring in. There was a line at the liquor tent. He could hear the music faintly in the distance and saw circus performers already exhibiting their strange talents: contortionists, jugglers of flaming torches, swallowers of knives.

By the bonfires' light, he scanned the crowd for Axewood—or Captain Hatchet, he thought with a smirk—but didn't see him.

Luke wondered how he'd feel when he did. But he didn't like knowing that he had this habitual deception in common with his enemy.

Somewhere in the woods nearby, a brook babbled along through the deepening darkness. An owl hooted, crickets chirped unseen, and he could hear small animals scurrying among the leaves here and there.

The woods at night were so peaceful. One learned that as a highwayman. How he wished he could've stayed there. But he had promises to keep.

Sliding his telescope back down into the folded position, Luke rose and walked slowly back up the hill.

Somewhere along the way, his fury at Portia's request for clemency toward Axewood finally receded, after these many long hours. At least enough to let him toy with her request.

Spare Axewood.

His mouth curled in disgust at the notion, as if he had just taken a mouthful of sour, clumpy buttermilk. He wanted to spit it out at once.

But love costs everything, she'd reminded him. He was the one who'd told her that.

Until that very second, Luke had always taken his motto to mean that he would never shrink from any duty that might be required of him to avenge the parents he'd adored, and who had loved him so dearly in return. The father who had been his hero, the mother who'd thought he hung the moon…

But the more he pondered it, the more his thoughts began to take a shape he did not want to see.

An uneasy question began forming in his mind: what if he had it backward? Battling darkness was all very well, but at what point did he overstep his bounds and become something quite like the very thing he hated?

He knew full well that the darkness had nearly swallowed him after Scotland. But, dear God, what if everything he'd done to destroy his enemies was wrong and he should've taken the high road?

Like Father would've done. He stopped walking and lifted his gaze to the whimsical Swiss chalet above him on the hilltop.

Lights glowed in the windows, drawing him like a moth to Portia's light.

To her love. He needed her so much.

The thought, small and forlorn, whispered through his mind, *I can't bear to lose you.* But if his worst fears about himself were true, then maybe it was as he'd realized earlier.

Maybe his darling bride really would be better off with Joel.

Twenty to nine. Portia kept checking her locket watch, her hands trembling. She fidgeted about the chamber, making sure she had all of her bags in order.

Before he retired, Luke had said they must all be ready to go again at a moment's notice, because anything might happen down in that valley when night fell.

With every minute that passed, danger drawing ever nearer, the sense of dread that had gripped Portia's heart took her right back to the awful days when Joel had first gone missing. Or the other bad time, when her family had feared that Hunter would be arrested for dueling.

Her shoulders sore with tension, she rubbed the back of her neck and glanced around the long, narrow bedchamber, making sure she had not left any of her things lying around. But, of course, she had barely unpacked.

The rooms at The Alpine House were decidedly austere, with dark furniture brightened by lace doilies. The two twin beds were about the size of the servants' cots back home, but the chamber was cozy enough, except for a faint musty smell.

Two tallow candles had been provided, and Portia had lit them both, doing her best to drive away the encroaching darkness.

Night in the countryside always seemed coal-black to her compared to London. But tonight the darkness seemed even more threatening, when she could hear strains of wild music and sounds of general debauchery echoing up from the dale.

For a moment, she gazed at the humble little vase of wildflowers that had been left for them on the chest of drawers. It brightened the chamber's dark-paneled austerity and made her smile, reminding her of Lucas's strictures on what flowers would be allowed for the wedding.

As of this moment, it was off. She did not even want to contemplate the nightmare of canceling it all when she got home—the food, the flowers, the guests. It was too much to think about when she was still raw from her fight with Luke at the last coaching inn.

His anger afterward was to be expected, yet she had been unprepared emotionally for the chill that had come over his demeanor toward her ever since.

Routing her vexing self-doubts as best she could, Portia lifted her valise off the floor and set it on the bed, checking the clasps one more time. Lady Delphine had already gone down to see the gentleman off and have a smoke on the wraparound porch.

After both women had napped, the sophisticated spinster had been absent for about an hour this afternoon.

Portia had awoken from her nap wondering where her chaperone had gone, but Delphine had eventually reappeared, nonchalant as ever.

At that moment, a thunderous round of cheers traveled up from the valley. Portia froze and turned her head toward the sound.

There was no way to guess what the roar signified, for her room did not have a view of the valley. Instead, it overlooked the stables.

Earlier today, Luke had gone into his room to rest after recommending that they all do the same.

Portia had been too anxious to lie down. Instead, she had peered out the window and seen Tempo sticking his handsome head out of his stall.

The horse looked lonely.

With a smile, she had gone down to see the outlaw's famous steed. After all, a visit to the stables was a sure remedy to soothe anyone's nerves. She was not a great horsewoman, but the company of animals was always a comfort.

At least it was a way to pass the time, which had slowed to a crawl amid all the tense waiting.

When she'd arrived at the stables, she found Oliver Finch feeding carrots and apples to Orion and Tempo. The young scholar had looked as anxious as Portia felt.

She was glad she wasn't the only one feeling on edge with the prospect of the night ahead. Upon chatting with Finch, she learned that he did not frequently undertake dangerous actions with his employer.

"That's Gower's role," he said. "I do the research, y'see."

"Ah."

"For example, His Grace had me read every article I could find on Mr. Clayton's abduction."

"And now, here you are, in the thick of rescuing him," she said with a sympathetic smile.

"Not in the thick of it, no," Finch said with a blanch. "I'm glad he's not making me go down there with them, to be honest. My asthma tends to act up when I get scared and then I wouldn't be able to breathe."

"Oh, you poor thing." He really was the model for Lucas, she thought, hiding her amusement. "So you'll be staying up here with me and Lady Delphine?"

"Er, yes. I-I'm, um, to protect you." He gave her a self-deprecating smile, as though they were both well aware that he was more mouse than lion.

Portia had laughed fondly and patted him on the shoulder. "I'm sure my chaperone and I will be very glad to have your sword to defend us, good sir knight."

"Oh, you ladies seem quite capable of doing that all on your own, I daresay. I saw you with that bow today!" Finch had then handed her an apple to feed to Tempo.

Portia had gone over to the black stallion's stall and shyly presented her offering. Tall and powerful, with a midnight coat that shone like black velvet, Tempo had nuzzled her hand, and then startled her by taking half the apple in one bite. With a second bite, the apple was gone, and he'd nudged her with a friendly whicker, looking for more.

Delighted, Portia had begged a carrot from Finch and fed that to Tempo, as well, and from that moment forward, she was sure they would be fast friends.

That had been hours ago.

By now, of course, the riding horses were saddled again, the carriage team already hitched to the coach, in case they had to leave quickly tonight. The plan was solid, but there was no telling how it would all play out in actuality.

Portia looked at her locket watch: quarter to nine now.

I should be going down. Procrastinating about joining the others or refusing to appear was not going to cancel the culmination of these efforts that she herself had set in motion weeks ago…back when she had fancied herself still in love with Joel Clayton.

Ah well. Now that it was all coming to a head, it would not do to hide in her chamber like a coward.

At that very moment, a knock sounded at the door.

She nearly jumped out of her shoes, startled out of her distraction. Then she flew across the room to answer it, instantly fearing trouble.

When she threw open the door, there stood Luke, all in black once again, and armed to the teeth for his mission. He loomed large in the doorway of the tiny room, his chiseled face somber.

Shadows from the lantern in the corridor sculpted the planes and angles of his cheekbones and jaw, but the candles in her room illumined his brooding green eyes.

She looked up at him, at a loss. Fear for his safety clawed at her insides and nearly overwhelmed her, but she swallowed her reaction. "Yes?"

"It's time," he said. "We're meeting on the porch before we go. Come." He pivoted and stalked away, more remote than ever.

Taken aback by his abrupt demeanor, Portia stared after him for a heartbeat. *Oh, Lucas.*

There was so much to say, but the time in which to say it had run out. She could do nothing now but follow.

Hastening after him, she pulled the door to her room shut behind her and hurried down the wood-planked corridor until she caught up with him.

Luke had not slowed his pace to wait for her, marching down the main staircase of the inn and out through the rustic lobby. When they stepped outside onto the wide wooden balcony, a riot of stars glittered in the patch of indigo sky visible between the tall trees surrounding the hotel.

Just above the black woods' silhouette, a bright, waning gibbous moon shone down.

Fortunately, Portia's eyes adjusted to the darkness within a few seconds as she followed Luke down to the corner of the wraparound balcony, where their friends waited near a brazier that had been lit to keep away the mosquitoes.

Delphine was smoking a cheroot in a long-handled ivory holder, leaning against the railing and looking detached from it all.

Finch was pacing like an anxious young father-to-be, waiting for the midwife.

Major Carvel was sitting on the built-in bench, rhythmically sharpening a knife with an ominous air of intense focus. He flicked Luke a patient glance as the two of them joined the others.

But when Portia noticed the glow of satisfaction on Lady Delphine's face—and how her contented gaze lingered on the major—she suddenly realized where her chaperone had been for half the afternoon, and it was all she could do not to gasp.

Well, it seemed the major had enjoyed book club very much, indeed.

As for her chaperone, Portia decided that nothing Lady Delphine might do henceforward could surprise her.

Delphine noticed Portia's slightly scandalized glance, smirked without a trace of shame, shrugged, then blew a line of smoke toward her conquest.

Peter ignored it, his mission already accomplished there, it would seem. The major stood, all business once again, and slipped his knife into the sheath by his side.

"Where's Sidney?" Luke asked.

"Coming!" The sound of boot heels striking the wooden planks resounded through the darkness as the viscount strode out of the inn toward them and presented himself with a flourish. "Well? What do you think? Do I look convincing?"

When Portia saw the always well-dressed Sidney transformed into his own showy version of an outlaw, a giggle escaped her.

The sartorially savvy rake had obviously prepared his highwayman apparel for the night with great care before they'd left London. Sidney wore a flashy purple waistcoat over black breeches and knee boots, and had donned not just a scrolled-brim black hat with a red cockade, but a flowing black cloak.

He showed it off with a proud turn. "Now *this* is how a highwayman's supposed to look," he informed Luke, who was gazing at him in wonder.

"My God, you're more Silversmoke than I am."

Finch looked impressed, too. "Why didn't *you* ever dress like that, sir?"

"Lucky he didn't," Portia said. "It would've caused mass hysteria among the ladies of London." Then she began applauding for her friend. "You are beautiful as ever, Lord Sidney!"

"Thank you, m'dear." He gave a courtly bow, and Luke laughed all of a sudden—loud and abruptly—a delayed laugh that came straight from his Lucas side.

Mirth poured from the feared highwayman at the pretend one's antics, and he stepped forward to shake Sidney's hand, clapping him on the shoulder. "Brilliant, mate. Just brilliant."

Sidney chortled, pleased with himself.

Portia shook her head, watching them laugh with affection for them both. She never would've guessed it, but she now realized that they were two peas in a pod—a pair of hams who would likely do anything for a lark.

Peter merely arched a brow. But at least Sidney's antics had helped dispel the tension over the danger they were about to face.

The major hooked a thumb toward the valley. "You do realize there are hundreds of actual criminals only a furlong away, and we're about to go down and socialize with them?"

Sidney smoothed his waistcoat. "I can hardly wait."

"Did you at least remember your weapons?" Peter asked dryly.

"Pistols loaded, dagger at the ready. I must say, the sword nearly ruins the line of my cloak. But yes, I've brought it."

Finch gave a nervous giggle at that jest, but Peter just sighed.

Delphine glided over to her co-conspirator and gave Sidney a kiss on the cheek. "You are so brave, darling!"

"Aren't I, though?" Sidney eyed at Peter's outfit. "Mock me as you like, but what the hell are you supposed to be? A cattle driver?"

Peter glanced down at himself. "What? I look more authentic than you do, y'coxcomb."

The major had exchanged his military uniform for dusty brown garb, which, along with his brown leather coat, made him look very realistic for a brigand, Portia thought. He'd have fit right in with the ruffians at The Blind Badger.

Leaning an elbow on Sidney's shoulder, Delphine studied Peter with casual admiration. "Looks like everybody's ready."

"Oh! Except for one thing." Finch opened his satchel. "I have something for you gentlemen." He reached into the leather bag, pulled out two black bandannas, and handed one to each of them.

"What's this?" Peter mumbled as he shook the square cloth open.

"You use it as a mask," Finch said.

"Oh, that's fantastic!" Sidney snatched it out of his grasp, quickly folded it in half to form a triangle, and tied it around the lower half of his face, then held out his hands. "Well? Am I terrifying?"

"Stand and deliver," Peter drawled, doing the same—giving in, it seemed, to Sidney's determination to relish the adventure.

Luke glanced sardonically from one to the other. "You don't actually need to put those on yet."

Portia and Delphine burst out laughing at that, though it was perhaps nervous laughter. Finch chuckled and folded his arms across his chest.

The two amateur highwaymen pulled their borrowed masks down to hang around their necks, revealing grins on both handsome faces.

"Trust me," Luke added, "you'll be glad you have those masks once we get down there." He looked around at them, his expression sobering. "Now then. Let's go over the plan."

They all stepped closer and gathered around as he lowered his voice.

"We three ride down and join the Carnevale. Blend in. Confirm that Clayton is there. We keep our distance for the time being, but follow him and Axewood when they leave.

"Once they're away from the crowd, we wait for our moment to attack, then we grab him, get him out of there, and take him to the coach. After that, I will deal with Axewood personally."

Portia winced at the reminder of his choice and dropped her gaze to hide her hurt. So much for her ultimatum.

Folding her arms across her chest, she bit her lip and did her best to tuck the pain aside for now, determined to concentrate on the deadly situation at hand.

Luke glanced at Finch, Delphine, and Portia. "You three who'll be staying up here at the hotel, you need to be ready for anything," he said. "We might end up sleeping here, or we might have to leave quickly. It all depends on how this unfolds. If we do need to leave, Finch, you settle up with the landlord under your own name. You've got the funds I gave you?"

"Yes, sir."

"Lady Delphine, your job will be to alert the driver and grooms to bring the carriage and horses out, and Portia, you keep those eagle eyes of yours fixed on the Carnevale below.

"Stay alert and watch for any signals I might send you to keep you abreast of what's happening down there. Here, use my telescope." He handed it to her. "I want one of you keeping watch the entire time we're gone. You can take turns, but no lapses. This night is bound to be unpredictable.

"I've noticed, by the way, that although these trees do crowd the view, there's a clear line of sight down the hill from this corner of the balcony." He pointed, the light from the brazier gilding his black-clad form.

Portia went over and checked the view, since he had specifically assigned her to keep watch. It was true. There was a brook that ran down through the woods, and its course was clear of trees.

Peering through the spyglass, she was surprised that the dale below really wasn't all that far away. But she held her breath at the sight of tents and colorful gypsy wagons, half-naked carnival performers illumined by the glow of bonfires, and countless ruffians milling about, enjoying the night.

Uneasy, she lowered the telescope from her eye.

Luke glanced around at everybody. "Any questions?"

They all shook their heads.

"Please, just be careful, all of you," Portia said.

"Don't worry, my lady. I'll watch his back for you." Peter sent her a reassuring smile, then nodded at Luke, whose face remained stony.

She gave the major a grateful smile, then Sidney clapped his hands and rubbed them together eagerly. "Well, gents, I think we're all set! Shall we?"

"Aye, let's go to the Carnevale," Luke said.

The trio walked over to the wooden steps that led down from the balcony to the graveled courtyard, where their hired saddle horses waited; the landlord's animals were fresher than the ones they had ridden all day.

Besides, neither Luke nor Peter wanted to risk bringing their prized steeds down to a gathering of thieves.

Moreover, the horses from The Alpine House stables no doubt knew the ground here better, and it would be very dark indeed on that path leading down through the woods.

Delphine and Finch drifted over to the top of the wooden stairs, but Portia followed the three men down to the courtyard.

"Goodbye, Major," Delphine called in a flirtatious voice, blowing smoke in his direction as she leaned against the railing.

Peter turned and sent her a private little salute. It was obvious by the appreciative look they exchanged what had happened between them this afternoon.

And it certainly wasn't lost on Sidney. He laughed as he swung up onto the palomino. "Ah, I see Del got herself a slice of Peter pie today, eh?"

"What?" Luke exclaimed, turning where he stood beside his horse, adjusting the stirrup.

"Shut up, Sidney," Peter mumbled.

"Careful, mate," the viscount taunted as he gathered up the reins. He sent Delphine a cheery wink. "She's a man-eating tigress."

"Fine by me." The major shot her a decidedly wicked parting smile.

Delphine laughed, but Finch turned scarlet at such talk.

Portia shook her head, amused by their banter, but by no means surprised after seeing her chaperone ogle Danger Man all day. Even now, Delphine watched the handsome major mount up on his horse with a gaze full of remembered pleasure.

Luke shook his head, finished lowering the stirrup, and visibly decided to mind his own business. Then he noticed Portia standing there in awkward silence.

"Was there something you wanted?" He glanced over at her in the darkness, his chiseled face stubborn, distant, hard.

"Please be careful."

"I'll be effective."

They stared at each other with so much unsaid. Portia's heart pounded.

"Thank you again for doing this," she forced out, if only to detain him. For now that it had come to it, knowing what he faced, she wished with all her heart he would not go.

Luke stared at her for a long moment, then set his highwayman hat atop his head. "Don't thank me yet. I'll have your beau back to you soon."

She flinched, hearing the reproach in his tone and aching that they should part this way at such a time.

But he was fixed on his task. "If you'll excuse me, my lady." Abruptly, turning away, he swung up onto his horse and beckoned his comrades with a nod.

Then he rode right past her without another word. Portia stood there, at a loss, while he led the men toward the trailhead that opened into the dark woods, while the crickets sang and the coals glowed in the brazier.

The flickering orange glow sent grotesque shadows writhing through the trees, like phantoms haunting the forest. It made the woods seem all the more threatening, as did the hoot of an owl hidden somewhere in the branches above.

Sidney tipped his hat to Portia as he followed Luke, obviously relishing his brief stint as an outlaw. Peter brought up the rear, saddle leather creaking softly as he passed, weapons glinting in the light.

Portia wrapped her arms around herself and remained on the graveled courtyard, watching the riders file into the woods at a slow, plodding walk.

One by one, they were swallowed up in darkness, and she was left standing alone, trembling with dread over what she'd set in motion.

CHAPTER 33

The Golden Goose

The Dunstan Arms, a creaky wooden coaching inn with moss growing on its roof, perched atop a wooded ridge overlooking the secluded valley, where the Carnevale crowd awaited the arrival of the famed Red Carnation.

Naturally, Uncle Axewood had rented the finest apartment to be had in the half-decrepit place.

Their suite of rooms had its own private balcony, where Joel presently stood, leaning on his crutch, gazing out upon the starry night and collecting his thoughts before it was time.

He savored this, his last taste of freedom, while the sound of raucous laughter and lively music floated up to him from the clearing below.

An accordion. Pipes and drums.

He could smell the smoke from the several bonfires that had been lit here and there among the striped canvas tents down in the grassy dale. The rugged attendees sat around them on logs, or milled about, watching the strange, colorful performers who gyrated, flipped, and tumbled with mesmerizing acrobatics, juggled flaming torches, or danced alluringly by the fanciful gypsy wagons.

Countless scores of rough-and-tumble men wandered from tent to tent and stall to stall, perusing the black-market goods on offer.

Joel noticed that a crowd had already started gathering around the main pavilion, where he would soon sit down to play for the last time.

Feeling the excitement in the air, he could not deny he felt a flutter of eagerness in his belly for the contest ahead, but his mind was made up.

Whatever happened, he was *not* going back to that dungeon cell ever again.

Oh, he could be terrified if he let himself. But he could not afford it. That way lay ruin.

With all hope of escape shattered by the blow that had crippled him, tonight was his best chance for getting back at his uncle in a way that not even Axewood could prevent.

Joel glanced over his shoulder at the earl, who was in the room behind him, finishing his final swig of a pewter pint of ale.

He'll fit right in tonight, he thought, eyeing his uncle's ridiculous attire.

Once again, the earl had arrayed himself as his alter ego, long known to the cutthroat gents of the Carnevale as Captain Hatchet.

Axewood wore a deep-brimmed hat to shadow his face, but it was curled up on one side, pinned in place with a red cockade. In his long coat and knee boots—sword and pistol by his side—he looked for all the world like some ruthless pirate captain.

Rucker stood by, waiting for the order to go. The massive henchman had donned a green and black plaid kilt and a loose natural linen shirt— clean for once. He had his woolen socks pulled up over his sturdy legs. Thick work boots hugged his mighty shins.

Joel rolled his eyes. It had been generations since Rucker's family had moved down from Scotland, as the tattooed giant had once told him in one of their idle exchanges through the bars. Yet he insisted on dressing himself up in full Highland regalia. Rucker was also armed to the teeth.

No surprise in that. Any moment now, it would be time to head down to the festivities.

Humiliating as his situation was, Joel must somehow don his usual, calm, confident demeanor. Play the part of the star he was supposed to be at these godforsaken events.

Until the moment he threw the game and finally turned the tables on his uncle.

That thought alone got a slight smile out of him. Till then, he must do the only thing that any mortal ever could in this life: play the hand he was dealt.

Inside the room, "Captain Hatchet" set aside his pewter tankard and wiped off his mouth with the back of his hand like a true brigand. "Time to go, boys! Let's go win us a fortune, shall we?"

"Coming, Uncle." Joel glanced up again at the bright shilling of the moon. *Heads or tails?* Then he tucked the fragile red carnation into his buttonhole.

"*Now* I'm ready," he said in a deadened voice. Gripping his crutch under one arm, he limped back in from the balcony.

His uncle nodded in approval, his dark eyes full of that wild glint they always took on when he changed into his alter ego.

Then they filed out of the suite, but of course, Rucker had to carry Joel down the stairs, as though he were some kind of invalid child.

Clenching his jaw against both the physical pain of the jostling and the shame of his helplessness, he promised himself anew that it all would end tonight.

His uncle might've won their battle of wills, but by God, Joel would get the last laugh.

Axewood led the way, eager to get down to the valley. He had friends down there, friends in low places. Well, not *friends*, exactly.

Those lowborn ruffians had no idea who he really was, and probably would not have believed it if someone were to tell them. They fascinated him, though, these swashbuckling savages with their complete unconcern about all the rules and mores by which men of honor were bound.

He envied their freedom.

For Axewood, it had always been such a boon to be able to walk away from the charade of aristocratic life for a while—from the weariness of being an upstanding pillar of the ton and all the duties of his rank.

But this was no simple masked ball.

Everybody down in that valley was the genuine article. Cutthroats, mercenaries, gunrunners, smugglers, slavers, assassins for hire.

Nasty fellows, all.

The kind of people with whom he could really be himself, he thought, laughing up his sleeve.

More importantly, it was always profitable coming to these things.

Dark happiness bubbled up from inside him as he wondered how much his nephew's winnings tonight would add to his coffers.

After marching down the creaky wooden steps, Axewood reached the loud, crowded lobby. He stepped aside to make room for Rucker, who set Joel back down; the lad balanced himself on his good foot and his crutch, his face pinched.

Axewood frowned, hoping the laudanum they'd been giving his nephew for the pain had not dulled his wits for the night's play.

He looked all right, Axewood supposed. Joel was dressed in his dandyish attire—black and white formal clothes for the occasion, as always—with his trusty red carnation tucked into his lapel.

Unfortunately, even Axewood could admit that his nephew was only a pale shadow of the hearty young coxcomb he'd been just a year ago. Warding off a faint twinge of guilt for the lad's gaunt, hollow-eyed condition, he nodded for them both to follow, then marched out the back door of the lobby.

Joel dutifully limped on his crutch, and Rucker brought up the rear, keeping a watchful eye on the golden goose.

When they went out to the flat, grassy area behind the building, transportation was already waiting. Eager to keep their criminal guests happy, the innkeepers had provided conveyance down to the vale. A couple of rustic hay-wagons trundled back and forth through the woods, taking a dozen Carnevale-goers at a time down to the festivities.

As an earl, Axewood never would've dreamed of lowering himself to ride on such a thing. But as Captain Hatchet, such experiences amused him.

He climbed up onto the wagon and took a seat with the same jolly nonchalance as all the lowlife criminals and their already tipsy women.

Their fellow travelers eagerly made room for the famed Red Carnation, honored to find themselves sharing a ride with the champion of the tournament.

As Rucker helped Joel up, a painted woman whose gown barely covered her cleavage smiled. "What happened to you, love?" She nodded at his crutch.

He snorted and gave her the lie they'd agreed upon: "My blasted horse stepped on my foot! No luck in that, eh?"

They laughed to hear that even a champion gambler could run into such folly, then Rucker stepped up onto the wagon, and the whole vehicle tilted slightly under his weight.

Everybody looked at him in surprise, but no one dared make a jest on his size. A moment later, they were underway, a cheerful, unpretentious company. Axewood took pleasure in the smell of the hay, the music of the crickets on a fine summer's night, and the rocking of the wagon as it rumbled down the wooded escarpment in the dark.

There was not a proper road down to the fields, just a working farm path for plows and carts. The ground was uneven, and he heard Joel suck in his breath with pain as the cart bounced over a rut.

With the game soon to start, Axewood dared not give the boy his laudanum. Instead, he took out his flask, offering him a swig of whiskey.

Joel refused.

"Suit yourself," Axewood muttered. He knew the boy hated him. Couldn't blame him, really.

He warded off a faint twinge of guilt. It was the lad's own fault. He shouldn't have tried to run away at the last gathering when Axewood's back was turned and Rucker had been distracted by a harlot.

Indeed, Joel had brought all of this on himself by his refusal to cooperate when Axewood had asked him politely to lend him the money.

That unlicked cub should've realized that his clever uncle always got his way in the end.

After that, Axewood ignored his prisoner, gazing ahead down the hill until the Carnevale came into view between the trees.

The scene below struck him as almost quaint. Last month's gathering in an old smugglers' cove on a Devon beach would have been hard to top, but the country festival waiting below intrigued him more the closer they went.

Tall torches were stuck in the ground here and there. Garlands of colorful pennants had been strung up between the tents. The brightly painted gypsy caravans had pulled up to one side, bringing the entertainers.

The music, though humble, was merry, and the delicious smell of the barbecue floated on the air.

Minor vendors sold their wares from wheeled carts or the backs of heavily laden donkeys, while the serious traders carried out their business from within closed tents or makeshift market stalls.

Various games awaited, as well: vicious arm-wrestling matches, drinking contests, and a perilous knife-throwing challenge where someone might well lose an eye.

Strange to think that by tomorrow, it would all have vanished again like the morning mist.

Axewood's spirits were light when the wagon finally halted at the edge of the Carnevale. He jumped down off the wagon, leaving Rucker to help Joel.

"Ho, Captain Hatchet!"

Acquaintances hailed him jovially here and there. They were always glad to see him, even if it was mainly for the money he threw around like a generous pirate captain flush with booty.

"Evening!" he called back, giving kingly waves and nods, and relishing every ounce of their attention, damned glad to be there.

Never mind the fake name—these men knew him better than any of his fellow parliamentarians or his late wife ever had.

The people of his own class had never understood him. But here, why, he moved amid the crowd with a veritable glow in his heart.

This was where he truly fit in, and it felt good, better than he could say. Finally, he felt like he could breathe. Was it his fault he'd been born a scoundrel? At last, he was among his own kind, and the long-anticipated night was underway.

"Hurry up," he said to his nephew.

Rucker had just finished helping the cripple down. Once Joel had steadied himself on his crutch, nodding to their fellow wagon riders who wished him luck in the tournament, Axewood led them over to the largest tent with a swaggering stride, greeting his acquaintances and puffing out his chest.

Even Joel lifted his chin as they approached the high-poled pavilion where the main event would soon be held, for the rough-and-tumble crowd waiting to watch the tournament started clapping and cheering in a rowdy fashion when they saw the star player. They parted to make way for him, and the lad smiled at that.

Even Axewood had to admit it was a relief to see him smile for once. But the crowd adored him. After all, the Red Carnation had often won money for many of these lowlife bastards—and Joel, for his part, certainly ate up the adulation.

Even in his damaged state, the former London dandy could not resist preening a bit at their applause. Ah, he'd had always been vain.

Axewood smirked but let his nephew soak up their attention. It might do him good after his ordeal these past few weeks.

A few of his fans tried to strike up a conversation with the champion, mainly asking what had happened to his foot, but Rucker stepped in with a scowl, making sure they stayed back.

"You must excuse me. I have to go sign in," Joel told his admirers.

They accepted this cheerfully. "Give 'em hell, lad!" they said, clapping for him as he limped off.

Then the three of them continued into the sprawling pavilion, while the canvas roof overhead flapped gently in the slight breeze. There were tables set up where a starting group of thirty-two players would face off in a cardplayers' version of a duel.

The losers of the first round would be eliminated, the winners paired with fresh opponents. Round after round, half of the players would be cut until it came down to just two men.

One would win a fortune worth twenty thousand pounds while the other lost his life.

It was terribly exciting, Axewood thought with a shiver of anticipation.

They headed over to the organizers' table, where Joel signed in for the tournament, as usual. Axewood, or rather, Captain Hatchet, had already paid the thousand-pound entry fee at the last gathering.

He chatted with the organizers while his nephew scanned the list of players and odds displayed on the bookmaker's large chalkboard.

"How does the competition look?" Axewood asked, turning to him, a hand resting casually on the pistol by his side.

"I've played most of them before," Joel said, staring at the chalkboard.

Axewood noticed he looked troubled. "What's the matter? You see a name on there that worries you?"

"No. But there are never any guarantees."

"Eh, don't worry about it." He slapped his champion on the back. "You always make it to at least the second tier."

"Well, Uncle," Joel murmured, lowering his gaze, "there's a first time for everything."

Before long, Joel took his seat under the big tent for what he already knew would be the last time.

He had to be helped into his chair by Rucker on account of his injury. His foot hurt like hell, and every atom of his being cried out for laudanum.

But Uncle Axewood wanted him sharp, up to his usual self, and Joel did his best to keep up appearances in front of his fans, despite his shattered pride.

He wondered if it was merely the shadowy half-light of the lanterns that kept them from noticing just how bad he looked, but Joel knew he looked like a wraith. Pale from being in his dungeon cell. Gaunt. Dark circles under his eyes.

Crippled. Ruined. Enslaved.

He still could not believe his own uncle had done all this to him. Blood meant nothing to the man, but clearly, Joel had overplayed his hand where Axewood was concerned with his failed attempt at escape.

Ah well. After tonight, he would no longer have to worry about his uncle's cruelties. Indeed, he would no longer have to worry about anything, because he would be dead.

He did not know nor care what nasty mode of death the monsters who planned these gatherings had chosen for their victim this night. But he'd find out soon enough.

It didn't matter.

The Red Carnation was done. His face was grim, expressionless, as he picked up his first hand of the night while the eager crowd looked on from the perimeter of the tent.

He ignored them, their drunken cheers and jeers alike, well-wishes for good luck along with the taunts. He blocked out all of it.

To hell with them.

They did not give a damn for him. Just like his bastard of an uncle, they only cared about what funds he could generate for them.

Well, tonight, they would all lose their blunt, because this time, Joel was going to do what he had never before attempted.

He was going to lose.

Suicide by card game. Let the savages kill him for their entertainment.

At least then he would finally be free.

As the game began, Axewood watched from the front row of the crowd ringing the edge of the tent, still troubled by his nephew's dark mood. Joel's face was impassive now, as it always was when he was gambling, but he had seemed a bit rattled beforehand.

It wasn't like him.

Eh, bloody hell, perhaps Axewood had come down too hard on the erstwhile dandy, punishing him as he had for his escape attempt last month.

Well, he shouldn't have tried it! I didn't want to break his bones, I had no choice. If he got free, he could destroy me.

I warned him.

Still worried, Axewood watched Joel's first couple of hands, but after a time, he was satisfied with his nephew's play for the night.

Thank God, the laudanum they'd been giving him did not appear to have damaged Joel's abilities. Still, Axewood decided, they'd have to wean their gold-plated prisoner off the medicine soon before it addled his wits.

In any case, Axewood did not intend to hover about watching every turn of the cards like some of these gambling-mad devotees did. He had business to attend to. The other half of his purpose here tonight was to find some mean-eyed fellows willing to eliminate his Silversmoke problem.

There had been no sign of the do-gooder highwayman at Darpley Castle, but Axewood had been glad to have the guards on hand anyway. He had dismissed them at the end of their few days' service, unwilling to let them in on his secret that the Earl of Axewood was also Captain Hatchet.

The question of who Silversmoke might actually be made him restless, but he assured himself it wouldn't matter soon. There were people here who would take care of his problem for him gladly, if the price was right.

Axewood nudged Rucker, who was planted beside him, arms folded over his chest. "Keep an eye on him," he ordered, nodding at Joel. "I'm going to have a look 'round."

"Yes, sir." Rucker gave him a slight nod, ignoring all the annoyed people of ordinary size who were trying to see around the giant.

By the time Axewood left the gaming tent, there must've been fifty men standing around watching the contest. They all had their favorites, sometimes changing their wagers as the three hours of the tournament unfolded. Ah, but the other players were usually of little concern to the Red Carnation.

Wipe 'em out, nephew, Axewood thought, rather proud of the lad as he walked away in confident assurance.

His mood was expansive as he greeted friends and acquaintances here and there, buying rounds of drinks for some, exchanging jests with others, and, all the while, keeping an eye out for some of the better-known assassins for hire.

He wandered around the Carnevale until he came across some of his underworld acquaintances congregating by one of the bonfires.

He joined them for a while to hear about their latest schemes and adventures, propping a foot up on one of the logs they had rolled up to the fire as benches.

With the drink flowing and the pleasant summer breeze making the fire dance, he watched one of the men harassing a gypsy girl while the others talked. He downed another pint of ale and sampled a puff of the opium smoke from the latest shipment they were passing around, but declined the offer of a roasted turkey leg to eat.

The antics of the rogue with the gypsy girl intensified until she finally punched her captor in the chest with a cry and fled, running back to her people up by the wagons, amid much raucous male laughter.

After she had gone, Axewood decided it was time to get serious. He lifted his cup to get his mates' attention.

"Listen up, you lot!" he said with easy cheer. "Who wants to do a job for me? Pays five hundred pounds."

"Five 'undred?" they said.

A murmur of interest ran through their midst.

"Wot's the job?"

"You've heard of the highwayman, Silversmoke? They say he operates out of Hampstead Heath."

"Oh, everyone's heard of him, Cap," the man beside him grunted.

"Well, I want him dead." Axewood scanned their rugged faces slowly by the firelight. "I will pay five hundred gold guineas to whoever will hunt this blackguard down for me and send him to his Maker. Who'll bring me Silversmoke's head?" he boomed, expecting an eager response.

Dead silence dropped.

Not a single volunteer leaped at the chance, despite the fortune he had just offered.

Axewood looked around in amazement. "What, no takers? 'Tis a princely sum!"

Still nothing. None of his cutthroat friends said a word, but all stared dubiously at him.

Axewood frowned. "Shall I double it, then?"

But not even this plum prize could move them. Men he knew for a fact were hardened killers, like Onyx and Diablo, lowered their heads at the mention of the legendary highwayman, put their hands in their pockets, and kicked at the grass with the toes of their boots.

A few muttered inaudibly, while others turned away, shaking their heads.

"What's the matter with you all?" Axewood exclaimed.

"Ain't worth it, Cap."

"I wouldn't cross him," a thief known as Shroud mumbled.

"Aye," his partner agreed, "I'd sooner cross the devil himself."

Axewood stared at them in astonishment. "I've never taken you men for cowards!"

"Not cowards!" one rough-looking mercenary retorted. "Everybody knows what happened to the last lot you hired. What was the name again, them Scots?"

"The MacAbes," Sly Bill supplied. "Poor bastards."

"Aye, everybody knows the story. Silversmoke wiped 'em out," Onyx said with a guarded smile, then took a swig of ale.

A smuggler friend standing beside him laughed at Axewood's stunned expression, his gold tooth flashing in his dirty face. "What's the matter, Hatchet? Why you want him dead? Is Silversmoke after *you* now?"

The others, realizing this must be the case, began backing away from him slightly. As though he were either contaminated...

Or marked for death.

"Better make a will, mate," Diablo said.

Outraged by the jest—and hurt by their indifference to his plight— Axewood steeled his spine and turned away. "Fine, you useless bastards. I'll do it myself."

His gold-toothed friend arched a brow at him. "And how do you propose to do that?"

"Bugger off!" Axewood muttered, leaving them in a huff to continue his search. God's bones, there must be *one* capable assassin around here who wasn't a bloody coward.

After all, Axewood had yet to meet a problem that an ample sum of money couldn't solve. Indeed, that was the whole point of nearly everything he did, his entire modus operandi. He was not about to let it fail him now.

One way or the other, he wasn't leaving here tonight until he'd made arrangements with some hard bastard and his crew who could promise him that Silversmoke would soon be a dead man.

CHAPTER 34

A Losing Hand

"**A**nd here I thought I was the one having all the fun living m'life of leisure in Town," Sidney drawled under his breath as they approached the Carnevale.

Moments ago, they had tied up their horses inside the edge of the woods, out of view. Now the three of them walked warily under the gaudy wooden archway welcoming criminal revelers to the underworld fair.

As they entered into the merriment and chaos, Luke's senses were on high alert, but Sidney continued making jests.

"If I'd have known being an outlaw was this amusing, I'd have tried it long ago."

"Stay focused," Peter ordered in a gruff tone as they advanced down the torch-lined center aisle between two rows of small merchant tents.

Amid the sounds of laughter, shouts, and vigorous rhythms on the drums, they drifted through the rowdy, jostling crowd, scanning constantly for Joel—and for Axewood.

"Glad you gave us those masks, mate," Sidney murmured to Luke. "I wouldn't want this lot getting a look at our faces."

"Agreed," Luke said, watching the dangerous crowd with his hand resting on the hilt of his knife.

Fortunately, they were not the only masked brigands at this event. Half the crowd saw fit to hide their faces. As for the ones who didn't...

"These are nasty bastards," Peter mumbled, sizing them up on all sides, his piercing teal eyes full of suspicion under the brim of his brown hat.

"I'll say." Sidney paused to stare at a knife-throwing game that Luke probably could've won if he were in any mood for fooling around.

But he wasn't. No, he wanted this done and over with so he could get on with his bloody life and start trying to forget he'd ever heard of Lady Portia Tennesley.

Sidney had asked him what the devil had happened between them on their way down the hill, but Luke had just growled. He did not feel like explaining it. This wasn't the time or place.

"Come on." He nodded to his temporary henchmen.

Sidney turned away from the knife game with a shudder while Peter lingered nearby a moment longer, tilting his head to follow the movements of a scantily clad contortionist who had painted her wiry body blue and bent herself in the most obscene fashion.

"Damn," he mumbled, obviously impressed, then followed Luke.

All throughout the underworld fair, Luke sensed a blend of jollification and cruelty. He knew the mood well from his own band of merry men.

Those cowards. He shook his head in disgust at the thought of them. So much for storming the Carnevale in force. He still couldn't believe the blackguards had abandoned him like that and scattered, but so be it. When it came to criminals, loyalty only ran skin-deep.

He was just glad to have the help of his two comrades here tonight, though he hoped he had not overestimated the carefree Sidney's capabilities.

We'll see how he does. At least the rake's keen powers of observation proved helpful right away.

"I think that's the place we want." Sidney nodded at the tallest tent, an open-sided pavilion of red and white striped canvas set atop on high poles. It seemed to have gathered the largest crowd.

Sure enough, when they made their way over to it, trying to seem casual, they found the infamous high-stakes gambling tournament in progress.

Sidney tensed, staring into the tent. "Damn me..."

"What?" Luke asked in a low tone.

"That's Joel." Sidney's voice was taut, his lean frame bristling. "I can't believe it. It's really him." He stared in shock over the fold of his black bandanna. "Christ, he looks like death warmed over."

Luke followed his gaze, and it was then that he caught his first glimpse of the famous Red Carnation.

"That's him?" Peter asked.

Sidney nodded. "You'd hardly recognize him, though, he's so changed."

Luke heard both anger and compassion in the viscount's voice, but for his part, he felt a strange mix of emotions as he studied his rival.

The Honorable Joel Clayton sat at a green baize table, a gaunt young man with brown hair and a glazed, ill-kempt appearance. His formal black and white evening attire looked sadly tattered, and he wore a small red flower in his boutonniere.

Luke stared at him with an odd sense of amazement. So this was the man he'd spent the past fortnight searching for...

The blackguard who was about to take Portia away from him.

Aye, her first choice of husbands.

The beau she had sought out Silversmoke to save.

Well, Luke had finally found him, and he was here to do just that. No matter how dead he felt inside at the prospect of losing her to another man.

Surely I can have my way on both counts, his ruthless side opined. *She'll get over it if I kill Axewood. She doesn't really even want Joel anymore. She wants* me.

But if this is who you are, you don't fucking deserve her, his conscience retorted. *Look around. You fit right in here, and that's all the proof you need that she should stay the hell away from you.*

Portia should marry Joel because it was safer for her than marrying a killer and a highwayman.

Never mind that the thought of giving her up made him want to tear down the world. Starting with Joel Clayton.

Luke took a deep breath and set aside the ferocious jealousy that mingled with his pity for the earl's underfed captive. He reminded himself again that both he and Clayton were victims of Axewood in their own ways.

"Who is that old ghoul over there with the potbelly, and why the hell is he staring at us?" Peter muttered, breaking into Luke's thoughts. The major nodded discreetly across the tent.

Luke followed his gaze and caught sight of a face in the crowd that made his blood run cold.

Axewood.

The sounds of the crowd faded as his stare locked on to his enemy.

The blood thundered in his ears. Hatred seethed in his veins.

The earl had looked away the moment he realized that Peter had spotted him; why he'd been staring at the three of them, Luke did not know. Had he recognized them somehow?

Luke doubted it. Now Axewood pretended to peruse the crowd with a casual air. But when, a few seconds later, his speculative gaze crept back to the three of them, Sidney laughed beneath his mask and nudged the major.

"I think he fancies you, mate."

"Oh Jesus," Peter hissed in disgust, and turned away while Sidney snickered.

Luke barely listened to their irreverent exchange, his murderous stare fixed on the earl. God, how he hated him. Now he had all the more reason to. Not only had the man destroyed his family, but he'd cost him his hoped-for marriage, as well.

If Axewood had been a decent human being, then Luke might never have learned how it felt to take a life, never have had to carry that on his soul. Never turned into this dark creature he'd become.

Portia had shown him a glimpse of who he could've been under different circumstances. What he could've had.

Fists clenched by his sides, it was all he could do to stop himself from launching across the tent and settling his score with the bastard for once and for all, in front of everybody there.

"What the hell is he wearing, anyway?" Sidney asked.

"Good question," Luke muttered, eyeing his enemy.

Axewood had arrayed himself like some sort of aging pirate captain sunk in middle-aged dissipation.

Cold scorn filled Luke. *What a fool.* Then he frowned.

If it wasn't disturbing enough to find out he had this kind of deception in common with the man he hated most, Luke hoped like hell that *he*, at least, didn't look that stupid as his alter ego.

"Captain Hatchet, I presume," Peter muttered.

"It would seem so."

Sidney cast Luke a worried glance. "You all right?" The viscount turned his back to Axewood to avoid being recognized.

The earl knew Sidney from the ton, but had never met Peter, on account of the major's having been away at the war.

Axewood also knew Luke—or, rather, Lucas.

Thinking back to the day he had visited him at Axewood House,

Luke tasted bitterness in his mouth as he recalled the earl's claim of having been such great friends with his father. *Liar. You're the one who set him up to die.*

Sidney rapped him on the arm, pulling him back to the present. "Easy, mate. Remember, we have a plan."

Luke growled. "Right."

"He seems well liked here," Peter said, nodding at the earl's many acquaintances greeting him. "We'll have to be careful."

He was right. Ol' Captain Hatchet was clearly in his element, while the three of them were strangers, unsure of the customs among these savages.

"Well? What do you want to do while we wait?" Peter turned to Luke.

Luke glanced at them, then back at his enemy.

Axewood had lost interest in them, fortunately, and was now absorbed in a furtive discussion with a small group of menacing-looking fellows on the far side of the tent.

"We lie low and follow the plan," Luke finally replied in a cold monotone. "Don't talk to anyone. Avoid eye contact. Let's get a pint. It'll help us blend in. Then we'll come back here and, I suppose, watch the Red Carnation win another tournament."

"Good enough." Sidney nodded, then Peter led the way to the wagon selling ale.

For the next couple of hours, Portia continued tracking the trio through the rough-and-tumble crowd, as Luke had instructed.

The telescope pressed to her eye, she had a clear view of the Carnevale from her perch on the railing, where she had wedged herself securely into the corner, like a child lounging in a tree, her feet braced on the built-in bench.

Everything seemed to be going smoothly down there, as far as she could tell. The gents had joined the crowd without incident. They seemed to fit right in.

Even Sidney's showier garb looked more or less at home, thanks to the presence of circus performers who were far more bizarrely arrayed. Some of those colorful costumes were impressive.

Now and then, she let her disk-shaped viewer linger on their exploits. Acrobats, jugglers, fire eaters, just like at a proper fair, or even Vauxhall.

She wondered, though, what the big, human-shaped wicker basket sort of thing was that they had wheeled out a while ago. It towered alone in a distant corner of the field.

Maybe something for one of the games, or a structure on which a performance of some sort is going to take place?

Warning herself not to be distracted by insignificant details, she shrugged it off and located Silversmoke in her viewer again, then adjusted the focus slightly.

Hullo, handsome. Despite all the tumult between them, it was reassuring being able to see for herself that he was still safe.

She watched the trio meander around, nursing their pints, their demeanor outwardly casual, but she knew they were studying everything happening down there. After the first hour, they bought another round of ale off a wagon loaded with barrels, but soon sauntered back to the largest pavilion to observe the card game.

Portia had a surprisingly good view of the main event taking place there, thanks to the structure's open sides and thirty-foot poles atop which the fanciful striped canvas roof hung. She couldn't see everything under the tent, but she could see Joel because the people running the tournament kept the crowd back from the gaming tables.

He sat in profile to her across from his current opponent, well lighted by the many lanterns under the tent.

For her part, Portia had been shocked when she first spotted him limping out on a crutch, to be helped into his chair by a big bald man.

The pitiful sight of her once-arrogant beau after all this time had brought tears to her eyes and filled her with a complicated brew of emotions. Intense relief that he really was alive, after all. *I knew it. I always said so.* But sorrow had also wrenched her heart at seeing the battered state the proud dandy had been reduced to in his captivity. Anger at Axewood for doing this to him pounded in her blood—along with a great deal of fear about the rescue ahead.

What if something went wrong? Yet she knew she had to set all her roiling emotions aside and stay focused on the task at hand.

For now, it was a waiting game.

About every half-hour, she watched each successive round come to an end, and half the men would leave. Soon, there were four pairs of players, then two pairs, and still Joel remained.

He was playing well and had made it nearly to the final round. Portia's heart beat fast with excitement for him.

Seeing how awful he looked, the least he deserved was a win. She wondered how much money he—or rather, Lord Axewood—stood to gain from all this.

When the second-to-last match ended, Joel did not rise, but reached up to shake hands with the other two players, who then left the gaming area.

Her eyes widened as she realized it was down to just him against one other man.

But then something strange happened.

Again and again, after every hand, Joel showed his cards, and the scorekeeper added the points to the two final players' columns on the chalkboard.

Portia stared at the scrawled white numbers in astonishment.

Joel was…losing.

Perhaps his injury had tired him out, muddied his concentration. Yes, he had always been a master of the bluff, but he did not appear much perturbed about losing the first hand of the game.

Or the second.

It happened again on the third, and it was then that Portia started to worry.

She did not know what was going on down there, but this should not be happening. If the Red Carnation didn't lay hold of his old luck soon, he was going to lose the game.

And that would be unthinkable.

Maybe this is some sort of strategy? She frowned as she watched through the telescope. *That's it—he's up to something. He's got to be. He never loses.*

But when he slid yet another hand of poor cards into the middle of the table with a smirk on his face, a chill ran down her spine.

Hold on.

She knew that smirk. What it meant. That particular look of defiance… That was always the look he wore when he'd decided to cast caution to the wind and lay it all on the line.

"Oh no," she whispered as a terrible hunch began forming in her mind. "No, no, no…"

He wouldn't.

But her heart began to pound. For she knew deep down that,

actually, he might, if he thought he had nothing left to lose.

"Would this Joel of yours ever kill himself?"

It had been Silversmoke's first question about the case, and Portia hadn't been sure how to answer at the time.

Now she had the most dreadful feeling that she was watching Joel commit suicide right before her eyes.

He knew the price the loser must pay, surely.

Lowering the telescope from her eye, Portia turned toward the hotel and shouted, "Delphine, Oliver, come quick! We've got a problem!"

Down in the big tent, the crowd could not believe what was happening. The Red Carnation was trailing, badly.

Joel was flush with a reckless sense of self-destructive glee, his heart pounding, his stomach in knots as he prepared to show his cards.

It was too late to regret his decision. He had passed the last opportunity to save himself three hands ago, when he had willfully thrown down a queen that could've saved him.

He was past saving, no longer wanted to be saved, a man resolved to die.

All around the big pavilion hung a hush of disbelief.

His uncle had given him a nod of approval when he made the final round, but then wandered off again with his cutthroat friends and had not yet noticed what was happening.

Well, he'd soon find out.

Joel, for his part, had discovered the fate planned for tonight's loser in the meantime. It wasn't going to be pleasant.

The organizers had rolled out a big humanoid form made of woven reeds. It was a burning man—in honor of their ancient ancestors, he supposed.

Once the victim had been selected, he would be locked inside the massive hollow figure, which would then be set on fire.

It was an extraordinarily nasty way to die, but it could only last so long, he figured. Maybe Rucker would slip him a last dose of laudanum as a final token of mercy; once he downed it, Joel wouldn't feel a thing.

He refused to think about it.

Meanwhile, a ghastly silence had fallen over the watching crowd as the gamesters around the table played their final hand.

Joel's was murderously awful: an off-suit range of rubbish cards from two to nine. He could not have done much worse if he were that loser, Dog, back at The Blue Room in good old Covent Garden.

He watched his opponent declare *carte blanche* and take the game. Some young upstart out of Wales, styling himself The Cardiff Comet. Joel had never played him before.

Beginner's luck, maybe. He was welcome to it.

On his last turn, Joel laid down his cards. The crowd actually gasped at how bad they were.

By design.

"Look at that! Not so much as a pair o' twos!"

"I'll be damned, his luck's finally left him."

"Why didn't he fold?"

Word spread quickly: *"The Red Carnation's lost!"*

"What's the matter?" Finch said as he and Delphine came running out onto the porch in answer to her shout.

"We've got a problem," Portia said with a gulp.

Delphine glanced swiftly toward the dale. "Are the boys in trouble?"

Portia shook her head. "No, not them—it's Joel. He has thrown the game!"

"What?" Delphine's jaw dropped.

"I fear he means to die! They kill the loser for sport down there," Portia said, on the verge of panic.

As if they needed reminding.

Finch furrowed his brow. "You mean he's lost *on purpose*?"

"But that's madness!" Slack-jawed, Delphine peered toward the valley. "Surely, he wouldn't—"

"He would. Trust me, I know him," Portia interrupted. "The rogue courted me for months, and this is exactly the sort of reckless thing he'd do if he was backed into a corner. His final act of defiance against his uncle?"

"But that's not part of our plan!" Finch cried, his voice growing shrill. "What do we do?"

Portia threw up her hands. "I have no idea!"

She glanced down into the valley again, at a loss. She felt like she could be sick. To think that they had gone to all this trouble to save the bounder, only to have him throw himself into the jaws of death—well, it was just pure, typical Joel Clayton.

I can't believe I ever wanted to marry him.

Luke would never give up if their places were exchanged.

You didn't track your parents' murderers for years on end and punish them to a man, only to cry defeat after one broken foot.

Portia shook her head, furious at Joel, of all people, for letting Axewood break him.

"Well…what are we to do? I don't believe this!" Even Delphine looked rattled. "The boys are right there—they're this close to saving him."

"I know." Portia nodded vigorously.

Finch went to the railing and stared down into the dark valley. "Maybe Silversmoke can get to him first," he said in a tight voice, then looked at the ladies. "Do we at least know how they plan to kill the loser this time?"

Portia shook her head, shuddering at the question.

But Delphine slowly lifted her arm and pointed at the distant meadow. "I wager *that* has something to do with it," she said, her tone grim.

Portia and Finch both followed her finger and saw she was referring to the big wicker burning man standing alone in the field.

The blood drained out of Portia's face. "Oh, you can't mean…"

"Why not?" Delphine turned to her with a dazed look. "In pagan times, they burned people alive in those things as human sacrifices to the gods. Maybe…"

"No!" Portia clapped her hand over her mouth in horror.

Finch panicked. "What do we do? This is not in the plan! Joel was supposed to win! His Grace and the others weren't going to move in to grab him until they got him away from the crowd, but now—"

"Now the crowd is going to burn him," Delphine said in an ominous tone. She sat down abruptly, as though all of this had just got a little too real for a writer's mere story research. "They're mad. They're all mad down there if they do this…"

Portia turned away. *Think.*

With the other two panicking, she knew Luke was counting on her. "He's going to need a distraction."

Burning, she suddenly thought. From the corner of her eye, Portia noticed the brazier of coals nearby…

The idea came in a flash.

"Oliver! Run and get my archery set. Quickly!" she said. "Bring it here, then go settle up with the landlord like His Grace told you. Delphine, go tell the driver we need to be ready to leave."

Her chaperone looked at her in question.

"Any minute now," Portia explained, "chaos is going to break out down there. Because Luke's not going to let them take Joel away to burn him. He's going to make his move. And when he tries to stop them, there's going to be violence."

Finch shook his head, looking queasy. "This is awful. They're too outnumbered."

"I know. But I think I can help. At least I can buy them some time."

"What are you going to do?" Delphine asked.

"Give them the distraction they need so they can grab Joel and get out of there safely. Hurry, there's no time. Go!" Portia shouted abruptly.

Startled out of their terrified paralysis, Delphine and Finch ran off to carry out the tasks Portia had assigned them.

For her part, Portia remained at her post, heart pounding in dread. Lifting the telescope to her eye, she watched the scene unfolding below. But she never would've dreamed she could be so grateful as she was in that moment for how dangerous Luke was.

If that made her a hypocrite, so be it.

I don't care what you have to do, my love. Just come back to me alive.

"The Red Carnation's done for!"

The news was spreading fast, and Joel savored every moment of their shock.

"Wot? I don't believe it..."

Murmurs of astonishment rushed through the audience in the main pavilion, and for that brief taste of victory in defeat, he reveled in the crowd's dismay.

Up until the moment that the same pair of brutes who had dragged so many other players off to their doom appeared on either side of his chair.

Each grabbed him by an arm.

"You're goin' to have to come with us, mate."

"Don't make a fuss now. You know the rules."

At that moment, his uncle came shoving through the crowd, his face a mask of horror. "What is going on here?"

The two brutes holding Joel's arms looked innocently at Captain Hatchet.

"Why, he lost, sir," the larger one said.

"*What?*" the earl uttered.

"Wit' all due respect, Cap'n Hatchet, we're bound to take 'im, sir," the smaller one said. "We got no choice."

Axewood turned to Joel, aghast. "You *lost*?"

Joel's lips slowly curved into a smirk, and his uncle gasped with understanding.

"You did this on purpose!"

"Who, me?" Joel drawled.

The stunned look on the earl's face nearly made it all worthwhile. "How could you do this to me?"

Joel let out a hollow laugh. "Guess your goose is cooked, Uncle."

Axewood's face filled with rage.

Shoving aside the nearer thug, Axewood gripped Joel by the arm. "Now look here, you cheeky little snot. You don't have permission to die until I give you leave—"

"Hands off, Hatchet! He's ours now." The larger ruffian thrust the earl back.

"But he lost the game on purpose!" Axewood shouted, then turned toward the announcer's table. "It doesn't count!"

Arguments broke out on all sides. Rucker shoved his way into the crowd to make sure he was by his master's side to protect him while the throng surged like an angry sea around them.

Thieves and murderers sloshed ale over the brims of their mugs, howling their drunken opinions as to whether or not the loss counted. But Joel just stood there wearily, his weight balanced on his good foot, one thug still holding onto his arm. What else could he do? It wasn't as though he could run.

Meanwhile, tempers were escalating quickly, with large sums of money made on wagers now at stake. Everyone was yelling.

"Take him away!" some shouted. "He's got to pay the price, just like anybody else!"

"Leave him be!" yelled others who had bet on him, but they were outnumbered by those who wanted their gory entertainment, as usual.

"This is outrageous!" Axewood was insisting, while the other players hollered that Joel had lost the match fair and square.

The organizers marched over and tried to reason with his uncle, as if any of this was reasonable.

"Now look here," Axewood began, turning to them, his face flushed.

Joel, meanwhile, motioned to his captor amid the clamor that he needed to sit back down. His foot hurt, and he did not know how long this was going to take. The man let him lower himself back into his chair.

Both of the organizers frowned at his uncle, unmoved.

"With all due respect, Captain Hatchet, I don't care if he is your partner—he'll get no special treatment from us."

"But ask him yourselves if he didn't lose on purpose!" Axewood turned wildly to Joel. "Say something, boy! Do you really want to die?"

"This is no life, Uncle." Joel looked at him with hatred. "And frankly, you can all go to hell."

With that, the organizers washed their hands of him.

"Take him away," the senior of the pair said. "The Red Carnation is hereby declared the loser!"

Joel cried out when the two ruffians wrenched him up onto his feet before he was ready. He shouted with pain, his eyes watering.

"Enough dawdling," one captor said. "Come on, you."

When they lurched him off balance, Joel put too much pressure on his crushed foot.

This proved to be a dire mistake.

Joel yelped and fell awkwardly against his chair, tipping it over and making his own suffering worse with his clumsiness. His captors weren't ready for his stumble and accidentally dropped him like a sack of grain— and at that, the sheer agony that shot up his leg stole his breath.

For a moment, sprawled on the ground, he felt sickened by the wave of blinding torment that raced through his entire body from the multiple broken bones in his foot.

They're going to burn me alive.

The world went wavy, the crowd dimmed, and when he thought of the fate awaiting him, he lost the ability to focus on what the two brutes trying to lift him to his feet were saying.

"What's the matter with him?"

"Is he drunk or somethin'?"

The voices seemed faraway, whooshing off down a long black tunnel as he swooned with pain. The last thing Joel saw before he passed out was the billowing tent roof high above him.

But there, he found a mystery. Why did the tent suddenly glow like a chandelier in spots, little candles burning here and there?

Are those flames? he wondered, dizzy as he lay broken on the ground, half trampled by the angry mob. Then the darkness enfolded him, and the world disappeared.

CHAPTER 35

Unmasked

"*I*t's working!" Finch cried, watching eagerly from the railing. "Quick, my lady, fire another one!"

"On my way." Portia had already taken the next arrow from Delphine. She held it over the nearby brazier while her chaperone hurried to prepare their little missiles.

Delphine had sacrificed one of her linen shifts, tearing the garment into long strips of flammable dry cloth. She was busy wrapping a strip of fabric around each arrow tip, and then dousing it in the lamp oil they'd collected from the lanterns in their rooms.

While Delphine worked and Finch watched through the telescope, reporting on the spread of the fire and suggesting new targets, Portia held the next arrow over the brazier until the prepared tip burst into flames.

With great care, she nocked the arrow and steadied herself in position, just like she'd practiced so many times. Planted in her post at the corner of the deck, she took a breath, lifted her elbow, and looked down the sights with her dominant eye.

The whole festival was almost out of range, but at least the roof of the sprawling pavilion made a very big target.

All he needs is a distraction…

The flames provided that, and the smoke would give him cover.

At once, she released, then watched as the arrow flew up and up and up into the black sky.

Joel did not know for how long he had lain there unconscious. Surely it was just for a minute or two. But when full awareness returned, everything had changed. The air around him was thick with smoke.

Did I miss something? For a second, he wondered if he'd passed out and hadn't even noticed if they'd already thrown him in the wicker cage of the burning man.

But no. He was still on the ground beneath the tent, where panicked confusion had seized hold of the crowd.

Men were running in all directions, knocking over gaming tables as they scattered. There was chaos everywhere, and, to Joel's surprise, everybody seemed to have forgotten all about him.

Coughing slightly, he sat up, groggy and confused. He looked around, but there was no sign of Rucker or Axewood.

"Get out of here! Move, move!" people were shouting at each other.

What the hell happened? Joel thought, then he looked up and saw.

The whole bloody tent was on fire!

❖

Luke couldn't help it. He had never felt prouder in his life than he did at that moment, turning with a grin from ear to ear as he watched yet another flaming arrow arc down gracefully out of the night sky—as if it had been fired by some blond avenging angel perched atop a cloud.

He whooped as she set yet another of the smaller tents ablaze. "That's my girl!"

It was obvious what had happened. Portia must've been watching through the telescope, as ordered, and seen how their plan was about to go awry. With her usual quick thinking—and skill as an archer—she had scattered the crowd of thugs trying to drag Joel off to his doom.

"Brava, bella," Sidney murmured, watching the fiery darts continue raining down, setting fires all around the Carnevale.

Even Peter was impressed. "You should definitely marry her, man."

Luke winced at the reminder. "Come on. She bought us some time. Let's go get this bounder while we can."

Though he was not eager to brave another fire with the burn still healing on his shoulder, he secured the bandanna over his mouth and nose to filter out the billowing smoke clouds everywhere.

People were running in all directions; it was every man for himself. The thieves, naturally, were taking their chance to steal whatever they could on their way out. The gypsies were laughing at the absurdity of it all and calmly moving their wagons farther back.

As the trio strode toward the main pavilion, a circus performer streaked by the other way, shrieking, because her big plumed headdress had caught a spark and was smoking.

It was the only thing the painted woman was wearing as she ran past, screaming, tassels twirling on her bosoms.

"Well, you don't see that every day," Peter remarked, glancing over his shoulder.

"More's the pity." Sidney lifted his eyebrows as the dancer passed. "You think we should help her?"

"Ah, she'll be fine," Peter said, and indeed, she paused, simply tore the burning plumes off her head, then fled again, quite unscathed.

"Did anyone see what happened to Axewood?" Luke scanned the crowd as they pressed on. The earl and his hulking pet ogre had vanished in the smoke.

"Not I."

"Me neither."

"Let's keep an eye out for him," Luke said.

They advanced, moving against the stampede. They had to fight their way through the frenzy under the big tent until they finally spotted Joel.

The poor devil was on the ground, trying to pull himself up using a toppled chair. He was coughing but doing his best to shield his nose and mouth with his arm.

As they approached, a shifty band of thieves started closing in on the famous Red Carnation, treacherous as wolves.

"Come with us. We'll save you," Luke heard one say.

But it was plain what they wanted. Just like the poor fellow's uncle, they saw a lucrative opportunity in the chance to control the Red Carnation and make use of his inimitable talents.

Right in front of Luke's eyes, they tried to carry him off.

"Oh no you don't!" Sidney shouted, then the three of them rushed the miscreants.

Luke flattened the first, Peter smashed the second a facer, and Sidney jabbed the third with a neat, fast blow to the throat that left the would-be kidnapper choking.

A brief skirmish ensued, but while Luke and Peter dealt with the others, Sidney bent down to greet his wounded friend.

"I say, Clayton, ol' boy." He pulled his mask down to reveal a cheery grin. "Remember me?"

Joel's jaw fell open. "Sidney! Is it...really you?"

"In the flesh, my friend!" Sidney laughed. "The three of us are here to help you." He nodded at Luke and Peter, who were still dealing out punches and holding the crowd at bay. "What do you think of that?"

Joel was clearly overwhelmed with emotion. "I-I..."

Sidney laid a hand on his shoulder. "Take courage, mate. Your friends have not forgotten you. We're here to get you out."

"Lady Portia sent us," Luke added over his shoulder, for the battered rakehell looked like he needed reassuring.

"Portia's here?" Joel choked out.

"Nearby," Luke responded. "Don't worry. She's safe." Then he blasted another menacing chap with a straight punch to the nose and sent him reeling.

"Who do you think set the fires?" Peter added, giving Joel a wry smile in between battling foes.

"This was all her idea," Sidney said.

"We need to get out of here." Luke gestured at the spreading blaze above them. "What's left of this pavilion's coming down any minute now."

"Righty-ho," Sidney said. "Clayton, if you'd care to come with us?"

"More than I can possibly express—and thank you all so much for doing this," Joel said. "But I'm afraid I can hardly walk. And I certainly can't run."

The three exchanged grim glances.

"I've got him," Luke said, since he was the brawniest of the three. "You two clear a path."

Peter nodded and drew his second pistol.

"Sorry for the indignity, mate," Luke mumbled. Then he bent down and heaved the wounded man over his good shoulder, much as he'd done to Gower just a couple of nights ago.

Having been kept in dungeon conditions for the past year, Clayton weighed less than Finch. Luke carried him out of the tent without much trouble, not sure if Joel was even fully conscious.

Then Luke strode back out through the mayhem, Portia's ex-suitor slung over his shoulder like a blasted sack of flour.

I have the strangest life, he thought, not for the first time, and shook his head to himself, but kept going, marching through the billowing clouds of smoke.

Peter and Sidney did a fine job of clearing a path. They slashed and shot, shoved and punched their way efficiently through the crowd, making short work of anyone who tried to stop them.

Luke quickened his pace and focused on reaching the tree line, where the horses waited. *Almost out.* So far, frankly, this had been easier than he'd expected.

But in his experience, that was never a good sign.

Of course, they weren't finished yet. They still had to get to the horses. But it worried him that they hadn't seen Axewood for a while.

Where the devil had he gone?

When the first tentpole came crashing down, trailing with it a large swath of blazing canvas, it landed on the organizers right in front of Axewood and set them afire. It would've crushed him, too, except that Rucker hauled him out of the way in the nick of time.

Screams immediately erupted, and half a dozen other men leaped out of the way. They toppled the chalkboard where the bookies kept the odds and scrambled over the tables in their crush to flee the scene.

"Yer Lordship, come!" Rucker held him fast. "We need to get you out of here!"

"Never mind me, fetch my golden goose!"

Rucker shook his bald head. "I'm *your* bodyguard, sir! Nephew's on his own. I'm not gonna let you die." With that, his devoted henchmen seized Axewood's arm in a viselike grip and dragged him out the far end of the crumbling tent to safety, tossing aside anyone who blocked his path.

Axewood was too angry at his situation to appreciate Rucker's good deed. "Unhand me, you oaf!" he said as soon as they'd reached a clear section outside the tent, then pointed at the fire. "Now get back in there and bring me my nephew!"

Rucker glanced from him to the inferno and back again with a wounded look. "But, sir...the whole thing's comin' down."

"Coward!" Axewood snarled.

Crestfallen, Rucker took a halfhearted step or two toward the blaze, but then just stood there looking at it, tilting his head, as though trying to pick out a survivable path. There wasn't one.

Dammit, if Joel was still in there, he was as good as dead!

But then, suddenly, Axewood spotted a large, black-clad man carrying Joel away from the conflagration. Axewood waved away the smoke, trying to see him more clearly.

The tall, brawny stranger had two accomplices aiding him, keeping the horde at bay. Already, they had cleared the main chaos in the meadow and were making their way toward the woods.

"Rucker!" Axewood shouted.

"Yes, my lord?" His large bald friend spun around, looking hopeful for a reprieve.

"Those men have taken my nephew. Look! You've got to go after them." Axewood pointed. "Hurry—they're getting away!"

Rucker followed Axewood's finger and squinted through the smoke at the three strangers absconding with the golden goose. "Who the hell is that, sir?"

Axewood looked grimly at Rucker as he realized who the masked bandit must be. "Silversmoke."

Rucker turned to him in surprise.

But something inside Axewood snapped when he saw that damned highwayman making off with his prized possession. He had to do something to slow him down.

"I guess the fire wasn't enough to stop him, Yer Lordship."

"Apparently not," Axewood said coldly. But he was nothing if not a quick-witted fellow, and a smile curved his lips.

The solution was simple.

He suddenly jumped up onto an abandoned table nearby and bellowed at the frightened crowd, "Everybody, calm down! Listen to me! The fire will burn itself out! It's already starting to dwindle."

"Shut up and pay attention, you lot!" Rucker boomed.

A few of the panicked brigands nearby looked over at the two of them, somewhat willing to heed, since the organizers were dead, after all.

"We've got a bigger problem than this fire, ladies and gentlemen!" Axewood announced.

"What's that, sir?" Rucker shouted on behalf of the crowd, playing along.

"At this very moment, we are all in extreme danger, because this gathering has been infiltrated by *Home Office agents*! They're the ones who started the blaze!"

"What? Who? Where?" the criminal revelers murmured.

This got their attention.

"Who do you mean, Cap'n Hatchet?" one called.

"Those men over there, headed for the woods!" Axewood pointed. "They are government spies working undercover, and believe me, if you let them get away, they are going straight to Whitehall to lay an information against everybody here! They're taking the Red Carnation for a witness!"

They looked around, but the highwayman had already vanished into the smoke.

"I don't see anyone. Who does he mean?"

"Over bloody *there*!" Axewood pointed angrily again in the direction he'd seen them go. "Now, I suggest you pull yourselves together and *catch* those bastards before they get away, or they'll be back here in short order with the militia to arrest us, and hang us, every one! There is no time to escape!"

"The Home Office?" a few people echoed, turning to one another. The crowd seemed astonished at this claim.

"Of course!" Axewood said in exasperation. "Don't you people read the bloody papers? The bloody prime minister is cracking down on crime like it's Judgment Day! They've probably got troops waiting up in these hills even now!"

The brutish attendees looked around at the forested hills, suddenly paranoid. The crowd forgot its panic over the fire compared to the possible threat of the gallows.

"Hurry! You've got to stop them before they reach whatever troops have been assembled in the area! Well, don't just stand there. Go!" Axewood roared at his audience.

At that moment, a puff of breeze parted the smoke clouds and revealed exactly whom he meant. Silversmoke and his accomplices had nearly reached the edge of the dell.

"Understand this!" Axewood continued. "If they force my partner to stand as a witness against this Carnevale, we all swing from nooses. Now, do what you do best, you nasty sons of bitches, and *cut their bloody throats*!" he howled, every inch the pirate captain in that moment.

It was exhilarating. Especially when the dangerous mob turned with a collective growl and fixed their sights on the designated target. Every ruffian there reached for his weapon.

Axewood smiled as they charged.

Luke and his companions had made it to the edge of the woods, where another band of robbers had tried to steal the Red Carnation from them. They were forced to stop and fight their way through the pack of miscreants.

But when a great roar rose from somewhere in the smoke clouds behind them, Sidney was the first to turn around.

He glanced slowly over his shoulder, his chest heaving from the exertions all three of them had been putting forth to ward off another gang of miscreants who had taken it into their heads to try to steal the Red Carnation from them.

Joel, for his part, was now sitting on the ground behind them, his face stamped with fright as they battled to protect him. He was merely doing his best to stay out of the way and avoid being re-kidnapped until they could continue their escape.

"Er, gentlemen," Sidney said, "I...think we may have a problem."

Luke was brawling with a couple of nasty chaps at once, but reached enough of a break in his battle to send an inquiring look over his shoulder.

Sidney gestured toward the Carnevale.

"Bloody hell," Peter muttered when he turned to look, wiping the sweat off his brow.

Luke glanced back as well, and saw the entire horde of criminals now charging out of the smoke billows, running straight at them like a barbarian army.

"Um..." Sidney started walking backward. "Perhaps *now* would be an excellent time for us to make our bows, what?"

"Couldn't agree more." Peter wiped the blood off his saber on a fallen foe.

Luke eyed the approaching mob grimly. *Damn. Knew it was too easy.* Well, this night had just grown considerably more interesting.

"Let's get the hell out of here," Peter said.

"No time," Luke said. "We won't make it to the horses." He gripped his sword harder and got into position. "Close ranks. Stay behind us, Clayton."

I'm not leading them straight to Portia.

Weapons drawn, the three of them backed into a tighter formation around Joel as the crowd came barreling toward them.

"Bloody Home Office!" one of the brigands yelled.

"Get 'em!" shouted many more.

"Home Office?" Luke echoed.

"What the hell are they talking about?" Peter said.

"My uncle must've told them a cock-and-bull story about you three!" Joel exclaimed.

Sure enough, Axewood himself came striding behind the seething mass of men, the general in command of this criminal army.

No surprise there, Luke thought in simmering hatred.

Axewood gestured impatiently at his minions. "Cut them off before they reach the woods! Don't let them escape!"

Over his shoulder, Luke glimpsed several more men sidling into place behind them. "We're surrounded," he informed his friends in a low tone.

Peter scanned the force hemming them in, ignoring the ridiculous odds against them. "We can fight our way out of this," he said through gritted teeth. "No problem…"

"That might not be necessary. Hold your fire, boys," Sidney murmured. "Let me try talking to them first."

"Sidney!" Luke whispered in alarm, but, of course, the scoundrel didn't listen.

The blond viscount took a step forward and lifted his weapon in a show of non-hostility. "Ho, there! Evening, everybody! Let's just calm down here. What seems to be the matter?"

He tossed his cape over one shoulder with a flourish and faced down the crowd with flawless aplomb, looking more of a storybook highwayman than Luke would ever be.

Luke and Peter exchanged looks of bewilderment.

"What's he doing?" Peter murmured.

"No idea," Luke replied.

Sidney had taken the horde off guard as well.

Their steps turned more cautious as they neared, but the sight of their many fallen comrades strewn across the ground around the trio no doubt gave them pause.

"Pray tell, why are you attacking us?" Sidney asked, confusing them with his friendly tone.

The thugs and miscreants looked at each other uneasily.

"You're Home Office," someone accused them.

"Home Office?" The charming rogue let out one of his merry laughs. "Don't be absurd, gents! You really don't know who you're dealing with, do you? Home Office? Come, you don't even recognize the greatest highwayman in all England when he's standing right in front of you?"

"Ah hell," Luke said under his breath. His heart sank as Sidney gestured dramatically at him.

"Ladies and gentlemen, allow me to present the one, the only, the one and only, the great and terrible Silversmoke—in the flesh!"

Well, they weren't expecting that, Luke thought dryly. Suppressing a sigh, he lowered his blade.

"Is this true?" a tattooed fellow near the front demanded, and a few echoed his sentiments.

Seeing that he had no other choice if he wanted to save his friends' necks and his own, vastly outnumbered as they were, Luke made a bold decision in that moment.

"It's true." He stepped forward, took off his highwayman hat, and tossed it onto the ground.

Let Axewood discover the truth for himself, Luke thought.

Then "Silversmoke" finally lowered his mask and showed the criminal world his face by the light of the distant blaze.

A murmur of amazement ran through the crowd.

Luke knew the rest of these low villains would never put it together that he was the reclusive Duke of Fountainhurst. But Axewood would see his face, recognize him, and realize his profound mistake.

He was Fountainhurst's son.

"I am Silversmoke!" Luke looked around at the criminal horde, doing his best to appear as fierce and threatening as possible. "You know my reputation. And I say to you, if it was Captain Hatchet who told you this daft Home Office story, he lied.

"But that's to be expected when it comes to that coward. Isn't that right, *captain*?" he said defiantly as Axewood stepped closer, staring at him in shock.

His formidable bald giant followed a step behind.

"Hatchet's told you all manner of lies," Luke said, then gestured at Joel. "As for this young man, he's been Hatchet's prisoner all along. We are here to free the Red Carnation. Nothing more! We're not Home Office, and we don't give a damn about the rest of you. Do as you please." He paused. "But if you want a fight, you've got one, my boys."

Peter nodded, gripping his sword.

Sidney stood tense, still hopeful that reason might prevail.

All the while, Axewood's stare was clamped on Luke, his face turning ashen.

Oh, he recognizes me, all right. Luke stared back at his parents' killer with vengeance singing in his blood like the silvery hiss of a blade.

He fairly watched Axewood putting it all together in his mind...

That Lucas, the bumbling Duke of Fountainhurst, was Silversmoke, the same killer who had wiped out the gang of assassins Axewood had hired to carry out their bloody assignment all those years ago.

Before Luke's very eyes, Axewood realized he was caught—and that he was a dead man.

Suddenly, the earl panicked.

"Kill them!" Axewood shouted at the mob, pointing at the three outsiders. "Why are you just standing there?"

"Easy!" Luke barked. "Nobody else needs to get hurt. Just stay out of my way! I've no quarrel with you lot. This Home Office story is pure bollocks, and you know it. I've come for no other reason than to take this lad back to his family. He's suffered enough."

"Oh, don't listen to him!" Axewood scoffed, looking around at the crowd. "How long have you known me? Who are you going to believe? I'm telling you, Silversmoke's a fraud!"

The crowd murmured uncertainly.

"Use your heads!" Axewood insisted, pointing to his temple and then gesturing angrily at Luke. "Why do you think Silversmoke never gets arrested? Why is he always handing over good, honest criminals like us to the magistrates? Because he's a fraud! He's a government agent, not a real highwayman!"

"*You're* the fraud, Hatchet," Luke shot back. But he did not dare reveal Axewood's real name, for, no doubt the bastard would do the same to him in a heartbeat.

"Well, I don't know about Silversmoke being a gov'ment spy," a grimy, toothless fellow spoke up, then pointed at Peter. "But that one there, that's a soldier if I ever seen one."

"A soldier gone bad!" Sidney assured them. "He served once, it's true, but they booted him out for being a ruthless brigand—not to mention a terrible debaucher of ladies."

Peter glanced at him indignantly; Sidney's blue eyes twinkled with mirth above his mask.

"What about that one?" a fat thug said, gesturing at Sidney with his knife. "Talks like a toff, 'n' he's dressed like a dandy."

"Can't a criminal have a little style?" Sidney retorted. "Really, you could all take a lesson."

"Who *are* you people?" a scarred barbarian demanded, narrowing his eyes.

"Does it really matter?" Axewood said. "Whoever they are, we all know these three don't belong here. Traitors, I say. They've come to sell us out. You ask me, we better kill 'em while we can."

It was the big fellow, Rucker, who decided the matter for the crowd.

"Hatchet's right, lads. Better safe than sorry." Axewood's towering bald henchman glanced back at the burning Carnevale. "This fire didn't start itself. I don't trust 'em."

With that, the ogre drew his blade, and the mood of the crowd darkened. Luke could feel their hesitation dissolving as the criminal mob fell back on its baser instincts.

"Bloody hell," Peter mumbled as the horde bristled anew for the attack.

"Well, I tried." Sidney raised his blade and widened his stance, moving back into formation with them.

"For the love of God, somebody give me a weapon!" Joel pleaded from the ground behind them.

Luke parted with his last loaded pistol, tossing it to the wounded man, so he could at least defend himself. Portia had said her ex-beau had fought in duels, after all; perhaps he knew his way around a gun.

"Deeply sorry about this, chaps." Drawing a dagger, Luke stayed shoulder to shoulder with his two allies.

"Nonsense," Peter said. "Most fun I've had since India."

Luke snorted. "Just don't anybody die."

"What, and miss the wedding?" Sidney drawled.

Luke smiled in spite of himself.

Then the battle exploded on all sides of them.

They brawled with swords and fists, ducking bullets on occasion. The smell of black powder added to the smoke around them.

When another pistol shot cracked out beside him, Peter shoved his gun back into its holster and ripped off his bandanna.

"Damn thing's gettin' in my way." Giving up anonymity for efficiency, he threw it to the ground and pulled out a sword, promptly running a man through.

Others started backing away, seeing the major's ferocity. Sidney, too, showed surprising skill; he had a straight punch like he'd been trained by Gentleman Jackson himself. But when an enemy blade nicked Sidney's cheek, he turned away and cursed.

"Not the face, you blackguard!" With that, he pulled out a gun and shot the beggar.

All the while, Luke was busy battling several men at once. The air was thick with shouts and curses, grunts and *oofs*, panting and bellows and the clash of blades.

In the distance, horses whinnied and men yelled to each other, trying to put out the fires.

Luke drove an elbow backward into the gut of a man who had flung an arm around his throat from behind and was trying to squeeze the life out of him.

Another charged at him from the front, and Luke was hard-pressed to avoid being skewered. He kicked the man back, then twisted to the side, flipped the bastard off his back, and parried with his sword.

Overhead, the clouds parted to show the moonlight, and, just for a second, Luke paused to catch his breath.

Glancing up at the hotel, he hoped to God that Portia wasn't seeing this, even though he'd ordered her to watch.

What was he to do, stand there and let these blackguards kill them? Well, damn, it wasn't as though Luke had any real hope of winning her back. Not now. She was about to be reunited with her precious ex-beau.

In the next instant, another ugly criminal ran at him, and once more, Luke was fighting for his life.

And for bloody Joel's.

CHAPTER 36

The Highwayman's Lady

"They're in trouble," Portia said grimly to Finch and Delphine, the telescope pressed to her eye, every muscle tensed as she watched the melee below.

Luke, Sidney, and Peter were now facing what she feared were insurmountable odds: three of them against some thirty criminals. No matter how many of the enemy they felled, more kept coming.

Meanwhile, Joel was elbow-crawling as best he could away from the fray, dragging himself toward the woods.

Though the tree line was just a few yards off, he could not seem to get there with the battle whirling around him. It was all he could do not to get stepped on or skewered while the others brawled, but Portia could plainly see that his presence was distracting Luke, splitting his attention between the need to protect the wounded man and ward off the throng trying to kill *him*.

Seeing Luke embattled and badly outnumbered — realizing the man she loved could be murdered right before her eyes — Portia cursed herself for daring to reproach him. What hypocrisy on her part! What blind arrogance! Who did she think she was, setting nice, tame, gentlemanly rules of engagement for him?

She wasn't the one who had to fight those savages, after all. He was down there risking his life — for her sake! — while she stood here safely on the hilltop. And she'd had the audacity to judge him? She shook her head with self-disgust.

You don't deserve him, Portia Tennesley.

She flinched as another ruffian slashed at Luke with a sword, but, thank God, he parried the blow. She could hardly stand to watch and yet couldn't bear to look away.

Instead, she scanned around the rest of the fight, her pulse pounding, the telescope shaking slightly with the trembling of her hands.

Through the round viewer, Sidney and Peter appeared to be holding their own. But as the fight intensified to new levels of barbarity, she noticed that Joel had been left practically unguarded.

At that moment, she spotted Lord Axewood sidling around the back of the fray, trying to get to his nephew—whether to recapture or kill him was anybody's guess.

She gasped.

"What's happening?" Finch said while Delphine stood by in alarm.

"It's Axewood. He's trying to steal Joel back." Finally, Portia gave them the spyglass so each could have a look. "We've got to do something. We've got to help them!"

"How?" Delphine asked, turning to her while Finch peered through the telescope. "You're down to your last arrow."

"I know…" While Portia racked her brain for some clever new solution, Delphine lost patience and snatched the telescope out of Finch's hand.

"Let me see!"

"Please tell me that Axewood hasn't got to Joel yet," Portia said.

"No, he's being cautious. He's at the edge of the woods. I believe 'lurking' is the word," Delphine reported.

Finch's eyes were wide, glazed with fear. "What do we do?"

"That's it," Portia declared. "I'm going down there on horseback and fetching Joel myself. If he's captured again, then this was all for nothing."

"Wait, what?" Finch said with a startled blink.

"You heard me."

"B-but that's not the plan!"

"The plan has gone to hell, if you haven't noticed, Mr. Finch! Joel's practically defenseless down there. If he keeps distracting them, somebody's going to get killed. But if I go down there and quickly remove him to safety, Luke and the boys will be better able to fight their way free. It's safest for everyone that way."

"Not you!" Finch said, then he grimaced. "I-I-I should really b-be the one to…"

"It's all right." Portia waved him off. "I'm the one who started this, remember?"

Delphine sent her a dire look. "Do it. Just don't be seen."

Portia nodded. "I'll keep to the cover of the woods. Both of you, be ready to go as soon as I return. I'll be back in a few minutes with Joel, and then we're getting out of here. The men can catch up with us later somewhere down the road."

With that, she whisked her black skirts around her and started marching off.

"Oh, but you mustn't, my lady, it's much too dangerous! His Grace will be furious— My lady?"

"Take this, Finch." Delphine handed off the spyglass to him while Portia hurried toward the stairs.

"Wait!" A moment later, Delphine grasped her arm from behind.

"Don't try and stop m—"

"Here," Delphine interrupted, handing Portia her bow and last arrow. "Better take these with you. Just in case." Delphine gave her a meaningful stare.

Portia hesitated but accepted the weapon. She could not imagine shooting anybody with it, but it would be foolish to go down there completely unarmed.

She nodded her thanks and slung the bow over her shoulder. Gripping the arrow, she ran down the wooden steps to the graveled yard. She marched right over to Tempo, who was already saddled in expectation of his master.

The big black stallion whickered gently as she approached, as if she'd only come to spoil him with more apples. "Sorry, my friend. I need a favor."

After tucking her last arrow into the empty leather sword sheath attached to the saddle, Portia hiked up her skirts as she lifted one foot up high to reach the stirrup.

The saddle creaked as she heaved herself up. But she didn't dare attempt to ride sidesaddle. Stallions were skittish, and she had no intention of falling off the horse. Besides, the time for propriety was far behind her now. In for a penny, in for a pound.

She gave Tempo's velvety neck a pat. "Promise you'll behave for me. We'll do the best we can, yes?"

Tempo tossed his head, champing at the bit.

Although she had never ridden so large a horse before—Tempo stood at least three hands taller than her spirited mare back at her parents' country estate—Portia felt instinctively, somehow, that Silversmoke's trusty steed would take care of her.

With her black skirts draped about her knees, Portia turned Tempo's nose toward the same path into the woods the men had taken earlier.

But when she clicked her tongue and gave him a light squeeze with her ankles, the mighty black stallion took off like a shot.

It was all she could do to keep her seat as the powerful steed charged into the woods and carried her down the crooked slope. He followed the winding path without her having to guide him, crashing through a stream along the way, as if he sensed the urgency of their mission.

Portia held on tight and didn't look back.

What Luke was going to say when he saw her, she hardly dared wonder. No doubt Finch was right: he'd be furious to see her.

But she wasn't turning back. She pinned her courage into place and rode on through the darkness.

The forest thinned as she approached the meadow below. The clamor grew louder, shouts and cries, the ring of blades, the sharp report of gunshots now and then. Her heart pounded as she gripped the reins. After splashing through another little stream that flowed along the bottom of the slope, she arrived at the edge of the action.

Still shadowed in the relative safety of the woods' edge, she reined Tempo to a breathless halt. From here, at the bottom of the path, she had a view of the three men's backs as they fought.

Peter was hacking down hordes with ferocious energy. Sidney fired a pistol at one man and held another at bay with his sword. Luke was battering some unfortunate fellow's face with his fist and dodging a blade to the ribs.

Portia then looked beyond them in amazement: the tents were burning heaps of canvas and wooden poles. Crowds of people were running to and fro. The gypsy wagons were rolling away to safety, drawn by panicked horses.

Everywhere was chaos, and she could not believe that she, of all people—mild-mannered Society belle Lady Portia Tennesley—had caused all this mayhem.

I did this.

Hunter would be proud, she thought wryly. Then her wide-eyed gaze homed in on Joel just as he spotted her, in turn, from his undignified position on the ground.

His jaw dropped, and, for a heartbeat, he gaped at her in disbelief, then he suddenly yelled over his shoulder, "Sidney?"

It was probably the only name of his three rescuers that he knew.

Sidney glanced over, saw her waiting there, and gestured to Luke. "Er, Silversmoke? You have a visitor."

Luke dropped the man he had been thrashing and followed Sidney's nod in her direction.

She saw the savage snarl on his face, the fury gleaming in his green eyes when he looked over — but he froze to find her sitting there astride his horse.

Portia pointed at Joel, then gestured to Tempo, indicating she had come to give Joel a ride up the hill.

Luke nodded. "Be right back," he told his allies, chest heaving. He sheathed his sword, marched over to Joel, and helped him up off the ground, half carrying him toward her while Sidney and Peter held off their foes.

"Portia!" Joel said once Luke had sped him over to Tempo's side. "I can't believe you're here."

"Neither can I," Luke muttered.

She ignored his sardonic comment, giving Joel a look of reassurance. "I've come to get you out of here. Luke, can you help him up?"

He was already doing just that. "We will discuss this later, you madwoman. You should've sent Finch."

"Just help him onto the horse and I'll be gone."

"Ready?" Luke asked Joel.

Joel nodded and seemed to brace himself.

As Luke gave him a leg up onto Tempo's back, Portia struggled with her own shock at her ex-suitor's woeful condition. It was one thing to have seen him through the telescope, but up close, she was shaken by his transformation.

The once-proud dandy looked awful: gaunt, drawn, and grim. His face was pale, his eyes glazed with pain. He was a changed man, and she was furious at Axewood for doing this to him.

"Hold onto my waist," she instructed him, but Joel barely seemed to hear, moaning with pain at the jolt to his injury with the change in positions.

Tempo wasn't helping matters either, shifting restlessly beneath them. Not to mention Joel had her bow poking him in the face.

"Steady, boy." Luke took hold of the bridle and laid a soothing hand on his horse's ebony neck. "You take care of her for me," he murmured to the stallion.

Joel finally recovered enough to speak. "Portia—I can't believe it's really you."

"Told you she was the one behind all this," Luke said, but when Joel tightened his grasp around her waist, his stare zeroed in on the motion, and his eyes turned frosty.

"They said you were the one who set all this up," Joel continued. "I don't know how I can ever thank you, my lady. Truly."

"Don't thank me—thank Silversmoke." She nodded at Luke, but he was all business as he fixed her with a grim stare.

"Get on the road as soon as you're up the hill," he said. "Head for London. We'll find you later."

"Where?"

"The inn where we stopped earlier today?" he suggested. *The one where you called off the wedding,* his eyes seemed to say.

Her heart flinched, but she gave him a nod. "Be careful."

He harrumphed at that. "Off you go, then, you two lovebirds. I'm sure you have plenty of catching up to do."

"Luke!" She glared at him.

"Get to safety," he ordered her, reloading his pistols with smooth expertise. He didn't even need to look at what his hands were doing. "I'll find you later." When another enemy screamed somewhere behind him, he glanced over his shoulder, then sent her a hard look. "Get out of here."

"Going." *I can't lose you,* she thought, terrified of him returning to the fight, but Sidney and Peter needed him.

"Nice work with the arrows, by the way," he said as he marched back toward the fray. "Remind me not to make you angry."

"Little late for that!" she retorted as she gathered up the reins.

He let out a hearty laugh at that, not looking back. Instead, he drew his sword, then launched himself at the next enemy with a war cry. Watching over her shoulder, Portia could barely tear her gaze off him. She marveled that she could fall even more deeply in love with the barbarian at a time like this.

Then Luke noticed her lingering. An exasperated look flashed across his face. "I said *go!*" he shouted through the battle.

"Hold on tight," she told Joel, then turned Tempo's nose back around toward the trail.

Her ex-beau clung to her waist. She squeezed Tempo's sides with her calves, and the stallion charged straight at the hill.

Luke stared after her in lingering amazement, making sure she got away safely. God, that girl never ceased to surprise him.

Burning down the Carnevale. Riding to the rescue.

What a sight she had been astride his midnight horse, her blond hair pale against the dark forest. He was in awe of ever finding such a creature—indeed, in that moment, he had never loved any living thing more.

Truly, Portia Tennesley was meant to be his bride.

But that was not to be, he reminded himself with a pang. Especially now. He had done as she asked of him. He had reunited her with the gambler.

So be it. If Clayton was the one she wanted, Luke wished them every happiness. She deserved it.

As for him, he had enemies on whom to vent his churning emotions. Eager to finish this so he could go after Axewood and complete the quest that had driven him since he was seventeen, he redoubled his efforts in the melee, clashing blades with another ruthless brigand.

Embroiled as he was in the heaving fight, Luke nearly missed Axewood taking leave of the meadow.

But there, beyond the edge of the fray, he suddenly spotted the big bald henchman holding a horse steady for the earl.

Axewood swung up into the saddle. Catching Luke's angry stare from beyond the fray, the earl smirked and sent him a crafty little salute.

To Luke's fury, Axewood urged the horse forward, cantering into the woods.

Following Portia.

Rage rushed into his veins as Luke turned and watched Axewood ride past. To his fury, the earl was too far away for him to do a damned thing about it.

For a heartbeat, all he could think about was his mother having her throat slit by men of this ilk, even though his logical mind realized it was probably just Joel that the earl wanted.

Half panicked all of a sudden, Luke turned to his comrades. "We have to get to the horses."

Panting, he quickly told them what he'd seen.

Sidney kicked a blackguard in the stomach and sent him flying backward. "You go. We'll finish here."

Peter gave Luke a quick nod, then blocked a strike and smashed the thug a facer in return.

As much as Luke hated to abandon them, he mumbled grim thanks, then broke away from the fight and sprinted into the woods.

He could only pray that Tempo would spirit the pair up the hill well ahead of the earl, that their coach would then race away and lose Axewood before he could find them in the darkness.

History must not be allowed to repeat itself tonight.

Lungs still burning from the smoke, Luke pounded into the woods, his steps cradled by fragrant pine needles. Ahead, he heard the babbling of the brook.

He slowed his pace just long enough to slide his sword and dagger back into their sheaths, then untied his rented horse from the tree, doing his best to soothe the skittish animal.

It was then that he heard a shot rip through the forest—the sound came from somewhere up the hill, the same way Portia had gone.

He lifted his head and stared up the trail, aghast.

Portia would not carry a gun, he knew. Joel had one, but he'd long since run out of ammunition. That left only Axewood as the one doing the shooting.

Luke's stomach twisted. *God.* He had lost his parents to that murderer. He would not lose the woman he loved as well.

A rage unlike he'd ever felt gusted through him, firing every vein. But no. He *had* felt it before, this rush of frenzied hatred.

In Scotland.

Axewood, he thought, *you're a dead man.*

Then he swung up into the saddle and charged his frightened horse straight up the hill.

CHAPTER 37

Deep, Dark Woods

Tempo's powerful strides ate up the steep trail ahead. Portia's heartbeat pounded in time with the stallion's surefooted lunges. She leaned forward in the saddle to assist the horse in climbing the slope, while Joel clasped her waist, never mind propriety. They were running for their lives.

The path snaked ahead of them, winding up the hillside. There were boulders here and there, gaps in the ground. Tempo sprang right across them.

They had splashed through the brook near the bottom of the hill and now clambered over a small wooden footbridge where a meander of the same stream crossed the path several yards higher.

Portia murmured a warning to Joel, and they both ducked under a low-hanging bough; a few strides later, the horse gave a little leap, clearing a fallen log.

They barreled on.

Joel was grimly silent. Portia got the feeling he was concentrating on not sliding off Tempo's back.

Some sections of the path were steeper than others. The stillness in the pine-scented woods seemed uncanny compared to the chaos behind them in the meadow.

Moonlight angled in through the trees around them, adding to the eeriness, but there were few sounds beyond the stallion's hoofbeats and the faint squeaking of his leather tack.

Behind them, the gunfire and shouts were fading, along with the smell of smoke. The pine needles muffled the noise, filling the air with a deep forest hush.

"I can't believe you came for me," Joel said. She could feel him shaking and hear the emotion that choked his voice as he held on to her.

"Just stay strong a little longer," she replied, not looking back. "We have a coach waiting at the top of this hill, then we'll get you out of here."

Suddenly, a shot rang out behind them. She felt her fellow rider jolt with fright.

"Are you hit?" she cried.

"No, it just startled me. I'll bet you anything that's my uncle," he said grimly. "He'll kill me to silence me. Maybe both of us. How much farther?"

Before she could tell him that they were about halfway there, a second shot rang out.

Tempo screamed; Portia felt the horse stumble and realized in horror that the stallion had been shot. He kept running, though, so perhaps he'd only been grazed.

But now she had a different problem, as the powerful steed went veering angrily off the path and crashing through the underbrush.

She heard Joel cry out, but could not get control of the horse.

Pulse pounding in her ears, her whole world narrowed down to just one thought: the dizzying need to stay astride the spooked stallion's back.

Tempo wanted them *off*.

He reared up the moment they reached a small flat clearing, and to Portia's horror, she felt Joel slide off behind her, tumbling backward over the horse's rump.

Joel let out a bloodcurdling scream as he fell to the ground and rolled several feet away, but there was nothing she could do. Tempo bolted again, barreling sideways along the hill, taking her with him.

The next thing she knew, thorns were tearing at her arms and shoulders, she had all but lost the reins, and Tempo brushed so close to a tree that she felt the trunk pull at her leg. Any closer and it would have wrenched her out of the saddle.

The hurt stallion barreled through the underbrush in a blind panic. Yet she could not be sure if the bullet hadn't struck Joel, with the way he had screamed when he fell off.

Unable to bring the horse under control, she felt panic taking over, but Luke was counting on her.

So was Joel—and his uncle was on his way.

Somehow she kept her wits about her but was not sure how many minutes passed before she finally managed to pull Tempo to a shaky standstill.

"Whoa, whoa, boy…" She had no idea how far they had just fled to the right of the trail. Joel was back there somewhere, wounded.

As poor Tempo stood trembling in the aftermath of his wild run, Portia stroked his neck with a shaking hand and struggled to calm him down.

"It's all right, it's all right, g-good boy…" Even her voice shook. She could not tell who was more petrified, her or the horse. She did her best to gulp down her terror and turned around in the saddle. "Let's have a look at you…"

A dark streak of glistening wetness cut alongside the muscled swell of the horse's right thigh. The fact that it looked like a cut instead of a hole suggested that the wound was nothing more than a nasty graze.

It was less than what Gower had incurred, to be sure. Still, Luke was going to be furious. She stroked Tempo's neck. "Good boy, you're all right," she kept telling him. *At least, I hope so.*

That only left Joel to worry about. She had to find him—before Axewood did.

At last, rustling through the underbrush, she managed to get Tempo turned around. Calmer now, the horse allowed her to guide him back the way they had come.

It was easy to find the way back. She merely had to follow the path of broken twigs and branches.

A cut on her cheek began to sting. She hadn't even felt it till now, but a thorn must've scratched her when she'd gone whipping by. Her heart still thumped like a frightened rabbit's. She scanned the forest floor continually for Joel, but dared not call out to him.

Not with Axewood on the way.

Now she had seen for herself what the earl was capable of.

Finally, she spotted some white clothing ahead in the thick darkness of the woods and urged Tempo toward it. They found their way back to the glade where he had reared up.

The little clearing was on relatively flat ground, ringed by a few massive oaks and towering pines. But dread filled her when she saw Joel lying facedown, motionless on the grass.

"Please behave yourself this time," she begged the horse as she slid down off his back, landing on still-quivery legs.

Tempo did not appear inclined to run off again; he stood meekly now, as though ashamed of his moment of cowardice. He never would have fled like that with Luke, she suspected.

Hurrying over to Joel, Portia dropped down on one knee by his side and said as quietly as possible, "Joel, can you hear me?"

He did not move or answer. She shook him gently by the shoulder but got no response. Perhaps he had bumped his head or, God forbid, broken his neck in the fall, for he slept like the dead.

Terrified at what she'd find, she forced herself to press two fingers to his neck and felt for a pulse.

Relief filled her. *Alive.*

She glanced grimly at Tempo. Clearly, that bullet had been intended for Joel.

Well, she had found him, but now Portia was faced with a serious problem. Unconscious, Joel was a dead weight. How was she to lift him all the way up onto the back of a wounded, seventeen-hands-tall horse by herself?

She shook him harder, her desperation rising. "Joel, you have to get up. We need to go."

It was then she heard a rider approaching.

She looked up, her throat constricting with fear. It had to be Axewood, for she knew that Luke was still embroiled in the fight below.

Heart pounding, she looked down at Joel again. A bead of sweat rolled down her cheek as she realized she had no choice but to defend them both.

She rose to her feet, took hold of Tempo's reins, and pulled him nearer to Joel as she heard the rider cantering closer, breaking twigs, shaking branches.

I can't possibly do this, she thought, staring wide-eyed in the direction of the sound. *I am just a Society belle. A lady. I'm not a fighter, an adventurer! That's why I hired the highwayman in the first place!*

But what choice did she have?

Axewood was coming. This was not the time for hesitation.

With no other choice, she pulled her last arrow out of the holder on the saddle, then reached over her shoulder for her bow.

She nocked the arrow and planted her feet in position, just like she'd practiced so many times.

Taking a protective stance in front of Joel's body, she trained her weapon in the direction of the sound just as the murderous earl burst into the grove.

❖

Axewood forced his horse into the small clearing, his chest heaving with exertion, his blood pumping. He felt so intensely alive in moments like these, staring down danger.

But he laughed at the sight that greeted him in the grove. "Well, what have we here? If it isn't Lady Portia Tennesley!"

Her fair face was taut with a deadly serious stare, and she stood very still in front of his nephew, the arrow in her bow trained on Axewood.

"Good heavens, what manner of accomplishment is this for a young lady?" he taunted. "I know you debs must have your talents to display, but this is taking things to a bit of an extreme, don't you think, my dear?"

"Stay back!" she ordered, but just beneath her icy tone, he detected pure fear.

Good.

She held her pose with admirable steadiness, though. Such a lady. Her face betrayed nothing as she pinned him with her stare.

Why, she was nearly as good a cardplayer as his nephew, sprawled on the ground, unconscious behind her.

Axewood wondered for a moment if he had succeeded in shooting the lad after all. From his vantage point atop his horse, he could not see any wound on Joel's back.

He supposed if his nephew were dead, Portia would not be standing guard over him like that, ready to defend him like a little she-wolf.

"Now that's love," Axewood said dryly. "But really, my dear, shouldn't you be protecting the other one? I speak of your fiancé, of course. Fountainhurst." He saw her absorb this information. "That's right. I know who he is now. Imagine my surprise."

"Then you know he is going to kill you," she said in a shaky voice.

"I'm sure he would've liked to, but I'm sorry to inform you that he's dead."

She drew in her breath. *"What?"*

"Yes, after you rode away with this wretch, he and his comrades were torn to pieces by the crowd, I'm afraid." Axewood sighed. "Pity. They fought like lions for a while. Fine men. His father would've been proud. But, you know, they were terribly outnumbered. Sorry to be the bearer of bad news."

Her face turning milky white in the darkness, she shifted her feet, adjusting her archery stance. "I-I don't believe you. We all know now what a liar you are."

Axewood shrugged. "Believe what you please, my lady, but how awkward it will be for you in Society, now that you've lost two suitors instead of just the one. You should've taken my offer for your hand while it lasted. Because, unlike these fine lads of yours, you see, *I* always manage to survive." He swung down from his horse.

"Stay on the horse and keep going, if you plan on surviving the night," she warned.

He smiled. "I'll do that, dear. But I'm taking this one with me." He sauntered toward her, determined to retrieve his nephew.

She tracked him with her arrow pointed at his chest. Axewood doubted she would use it, but he did not want to startle her into accidentally releasing the damned thing.

For his part, Axewood carried a pair of long dueling pistols; he had already unloaded one on them while riding up the hill. Presently, he drew its mate and kept it trained on Portia as he left his horse's side. He did not have time to waste, and she did not look sufficiently intimidated yet.

Though she licked her pretty lips nervously, the little blonde held her ground. As he remembered proposing to her, he could not help but chuckle. Why, he'd never dreamed she had such a steely spine.

"Tsk, tsk, my dear, do your parents know where you are?"

"*Stay back!* You're not taking him."

"Lady Portia, if you think I will not hurt a woman, you are mistaken. I actually…enjoy that sort of thing. Now, here is what's going to happen." He strolled calmly toward her, the pistol steady in his hand. "You are going to be a good girl for me, lower your weapon, and move out of the way. You and your horse."

Joel groaned softly, beginning to rouse.

"Wake up, nephew!" Axewood called to him. "We're leaving."

"Stay back, you filthy murderer!" she cried. "Not another step closer!"

"Murderer?" he exclaimed, offended. Best to keep her talking until he could figure out a way to get around her. "What are you talking about?"

Truly, he did not want to kill her. He was not *that* low. At least, he liked to think so. He was still the much-respected Earl of Axewood; Captain Hatchet did not possess him entirely.

Yet.

Did he?

"That's exactly what you are," she goaded him. "A liar, a killer. A kidnapper. God only knows what else."

"Oh dear, oh dear." He shook his head chidingly at her.

"You deny it?" she exclaimed. "Then let me ask you a question."

"Can I have my nephew back if I answer truthfully?"

"No. But answer or I'll shoot you."

He chuckled. "Oh, will you, now?"

"Did you hire the MacAbe gang of Scotland years ago at one of these twisted Carnevales to kill the Duke and Duchess of Fountainhurst?"

Axewood stared at her, oddly taken off guard.

It was the first time that anyone associated with his aristocratic life in Town had ever confronted him directly about his dark side.

The secret side of his dual existence.

His usual glee over how he continued to fool them all evaporated with stunning speed as he stood there across from her, ringed in by the grove. The huge black trees, oak and pine, seemed to be closing in on him, and the damned crickets wouldn't stop chirping, so loud he could hardly think.

Axewood realized then that he was indeed going to have to kill the girl whether he wanted to or not. Gentleman or not.

He could not have the daughter of a marquess going back to Society and telling people what he'd done.

Who and what he really was.

"It's over, my lord. Lower your weapon and go. I'd leave the country if I were you—unless you fancy a trial in the House of Lords. Followed by the gallows."

He flinched to hear such a thing spoken aloud, his worst fear. Indeed, that was why he'd had to have the last Duke of Fountainhurst killed.

To silence the self-righteous bastard from exposing Axewood's necessary-at-the-time but not-entirely-legal misdirection of the war funds.

So he'd made certain secret, highly lucrative arrangements with a key manufacturer or two, ensuring rich contracts for weapons and equipment went to his allies in exchange for a cut of the funds to be awarded. So what? It happened all the time, this sort of thing! It wasn't as though he'd invented the practice.

But the chairman of the committee had not been the type to sympathize with one's financial predicaments or heed logical explanations that it could all be paid back. No, the Duke of Fountainhurst was not one to forgive.

Unfortunately, it was now clear that the son was exactly like him.

Correct that, Axewood thought. The son was something far worse.

"You see, Luke found evidence against you in his father's old papers," Portia informed Axewood coldly as she held him at bay with her bow. "All that's left for you in England now is ruin and disgrace, my lord. Especially when Joel takes the witness stand against you."

He narrowed his eyes as she taunted him.

"My God, what if they make it a public hanging? To a proud man like you, that would surely be a fate worse than death."

She had read him well with those piercing blue eyes of hers. Axewood hesitated, feeling trapped.

Her fingers flicked around the bow as she adjusted her grip. "But if it's death you choose, then rest assured, Luke will be here at any moment to deal it out to you. You and I both know he's on his way. So I suggest you flee while you still have time."

She turned her head ever so slightly. "Is that hoofbeats I hear? Why, yes," she murmured with a little smile, bluffing, he suspected, for he heard nothing. "Even now, he comes."

Luke stood slightly in the stirrups, leaning forward to help the horse go thundering up the slope. The trees flashed by as fast as the thoughts whirling through his mind.

It was like so many moonlit gallops he had known in his career as a highwayman. But somehow, everything in his life had led to this night, this moment. He had not been able to save his parents, but by God…

If you harm one hair on her head, I will make you beg for death.

As he murmured to the horse, urging him onward up the winding path, all his thoughts were trained on one simple task: killing Axewood.

This moment was the culmination of years.

It was revenge that had transformed him into a highwayman, and his shadowy existence as a highwayman, in turn, that had led to this night. Now the ultimate fulfillment of his quest to avenge his parents was at hand, so close he could taste it. All these years, it had been Axewood behind their murders. A smiling traitor who'd pretended to be his father's friend.

Tonight, Luke would make him pay for it all. Every tear his sister had shed. Every hollow Christmas he'd spent after their deaths. Every time he could not ask his father for advice. Every time Tavi had had to seek out other matrons to soothe her anxieties about her babies. Even her wedding day, when he, her blasted younger brother, had had to walk his sister down the aisle because their father was dead.

And now that same son of a bitch who had done all this to them now dared, *dared,* shoot a gun in Portia's direction?

No. Any trace of mercy Luke might've considered showing the earl for her sake had dissolved the moment he had heard that gun go off in the woods.

Oh God, what if he's already killed her? What will I do? How will I live?

Potentially losing her to Joel was bad enough, but if she was no longer on the Earth, he saw no point in remaining himself.

Especially when it would be entirely his fault if she was murdered.

His own selfish doing, bringing her here, so he could have just a few more hours with her to try to convince her to love him.

Please, God, I haven't asked you for much. I know we're not on the best of terms. A cold sweat dampened his face. *But don't make her pay for my selfishness. Punish me all you like, but she's done nothing wrong. I'm not asking for miracles. Just let me get there fast enough to save her.*

His horse leaped over a fallen log, straining up the hill, when suddenly, Luke thought he heard voices ahead. He tilted his head and listened more sharply, straining his ears.

Axewood's voice—and Portia's. *Oh thank you, Christ.* She was still alive. He caught sight of an opening to a small clearing ahead off to the right of the trail and realized he'd found them.

He wrenched the horse to the right and went galloping down the twenty-foot path toward the clearing just in time to catch the tail end of their exchange.

"He's coming, Axewood," Portia was saying. "You're through."

"Perhaps." The earl surely heard him barreling down on them. "Let me leave your duke a parting gift to slow him down, then: his bride's body."

Before Luke's horrified eyes, Axewood cocked the pistol to shoot her; at the very same moment, Portia let her arrow fly.

Instantly, it slammed the earl back against the fat oak tree behind him and pinned him there like one of Finch's prize beetles.

Portia dropped her bow and shrieked in horror at what she had just done while Axewood let out a bloodcurdling scream, and Luke stormed into the grove astride his horse.

As Luke jumped down from the saddle in wrath, the earl tried reaching down for the pistol he'd dropped, but he could not move, nailed in place to the tree trunk through his right shoulder.

Defenseless.

"Please!" Axewood wailed, holding out his hand as Luke drew his dagger, already stained with the blood of the foes the bastard had set upon him in the valley. "Don't kill me, Fountainhurst!"

"You dare ask me for mercy?" Luke roared in his face. He grasped Axewood by the throat with one hand, pressing his blade against the man's fleshy neck with the other. "My mother asked for mercy as well, but your men had none for her. Did they?"

"I had no choice! You don't understand! H-he was going to have me arrested," Axewood said, bleeding from the shoulder and trying helplessly to hold Luke at bay.

"Well, I'm going to do much worse to you, Axewood. Portia, move his gun away." Luke wouldn't put it past the earl to tear his way free from the arrow, even if it made his wound worse. Like some rabid wolf that would gnaw its own paw off to escape from a trap.

He heard her jagged breathing as Portia edged closer. With fearful movements, she bent down and retrieved Axewood's gun. She picked it up, then quickly backed away, carrying it out of range.

"Set it down," Luke ordered her. She had no experience with a pistol. He did not want to end up accidentally getting shot in the back.

She obeyed.

"Now get on my horse and go," Luke said, not taking his eyes off his enemy. "When I'm finished here, I'll see to Joel."

Portia didn't move. Perhaps she was in shock. He wouldn't be surprise.

Luke then disarmed the earl of his knife and sword, tossing these weapons onto the ground.

This done, he laughed softly, bitterly, at the stark terror etched across his enemy's face.

"Well now, look at you, my fine Lord Axewood. Or should I say

Captain Hatchet? Trapped like an animal. Nice shooting, my love."

"I didn't mean to do it!" Portia was sobbing quietly behind him. "Why didn't you leave when I told you to?" she shouted at the earl.

"Don't weep for him, darling. He'd have killed you without a second thought. And that…was his greatest mistake. As he'll soon learn."

Luke nicked Axewood's neck with his dagger just to scare him.

The earl yelped and started blubbering, begging for his life, much to Luke's annoyance. "Please, Fountainhurst!"

"Shut the hell up. You're already dead, don't you understand? You aimed a gun at my fiancée. That is not allowed. Portia, leave. Now. This won't take long."

"I-I wasn't really going to shoot her!"

"Yes, you were. And you killed my parents."

"I had no choice! I panicked, don't you see? H-he was asking too many questions! I-I didn't want to do it, but I had to silence him."

"And now I'll silence you." Luke grasped Axewood's jaw and struggled to pry his mouth open. "I don't really feel like hearing your excuses. Let's get rid of that lying tongue first, eh?"

Eyes wide with terror, the earl struggled to turn his face away from Luke's grip on his jaw.

"Open your mouth! No more lies, Captain Hatchet! What, you refuse? Would you rather I take an eye?"

It was then, through the hatred, that he heard Portia's horrified whisper: "Oh, Luke, what are you doing?"

Joel flicked his eyes open and found himself staring up at black tree branches crisscrossed overhead, the starry sky behind them.

He had caught a little of their exchange, but was still groggy, his foot throbbing.

As full consciousness returned, he recalled with chagrin how he'd passed out from pain a second time tonight after falling off the damned horse. In front of Portia, too. What a weakling he'd become.

With a mental curse, he swore this would be his last humiliation.

Wincing as he sat up slowly, Joel was delighted to find his uncle pinned to a tree with the last of Portia's arrows.

Silversmoke, whoever the devil he was, had struck the very fear of God into the arrogant bastard, and now Axewood was groveling.

Joel savored the sight, a bitter smile spreading over his face. *Well.* It seemed Captain Hatchet had finally crossed the wrong man.

But who was this towering stranger, exactly?

More importantly, who was he to Portia?

As a gambler, Joel was an expert at reading people's faces, and he had not failed to notice the way the mighty outlaw and Portia had looked at each other when she had arrived on the horse to spirit him away.

Fountainhurst, he'd heard his uncle call him a moment ago, as he'd swum his way back to awareness. Why did that name sound familiar...?

Good God!

Awe filled him as Joel suddenly realized who the highwayman-duke was.

Portia stood watching Luke with tears in her eyes. He'd gone very still at her whispered question, calling him back to himself.

He now turned uncertainly to her, though he kept one hand planted on Axewood's shoulder, holding him in place, the other wrapped around his knife. Cruelty hardened his handsome face in the shaft of moonlight that angled through the trees to find him in the shadows.

"Why are you still here?" he demanded in a low, hard tone. "I told you to go."

She shook her head and refused to budge. "I won't leave you. Please, my love," she said, half terrified of him after what she'd just seen. "You don't have to do this. I'm all right. He didn't hurt me," she assured him, her throat constricted with tears. "Just let him stand trial."

Luke let out an anguished curse and shook his head. "You don't understand what he's done to me," he said. "He has to pay."

"My darling, I know that no one will ever truly understand what you've been through," she whispered, striving to be the voice of reason here in the midst of his barbarity. "You lost your family, your childhood, your innocence. And all that followed... Oh, Luke. I know what you sacrificed.

"You've given up so much to try to make it right. But this isn't the way, my darling. You're better than this. Please, don't give in to the darkness. Don't let it claim you. Come back to me, Luke. I need you. Spare his life. He is an evil man, but your father would not have wanted this."

He stood there stock-still for a second, staring at her.

Portia held his gaze, riveted, barely daring to breathe.

Axewood was blubbering quietly, begging Luke to listen to her.

Luke shuddered, then suddenly threw his head back and screamed at the black sky in wordless fury.

Portia jumped at his roar, her heart thumping.

As his howl of rage echoed down into the valley, the grove went absolutely silent. The breeze quit—even the crickets stopped chirping.

Portia held her breath, feeling as though she had just stopped a force of nature.

Axewood stood frozen with terror. He had stopped struggling to free himself, had swallowed his whimpers.

Luke's nostrils flared as he inhaled angrily, glaring at her. "Why should I spare him?" he asked, pointing at the earl with his knife. "He admits he was the one who set them up! He deserves to die."

"Not like this. Luke, please, this isn't you."

"Oh yes it is," he said darkly. "It *is*. That's why I allowed you to call off the wedding. You shouldn't be around me. You certainly shouldn't marry me."

"But Luke—"

"No. You were right about me, Portia. I've gone too far, done too many bad things. You wanted to know why I do what I do? Well, the reason I help the people who come to me, as you did, is simply because that's my penance."

"No." She shook her head emphatically as the tears thickened in her eyes. "You are Silversmoke. One of the last true heroes left in this world. To so many people. Especially to me," she whispered while he held her in a lost stare.

"I still believe in you, Luke. I want to be with you. I *don't* want to cancel the wedding. But please. I know you have good reason to hate this man, but he's already beaten. A hero doesn't kill an unarmed man. Dark or light, Luke. You need to choose. You can't keep living in the shadows."

He glared at her for a long moment, the barest pinprick of tears glistening in his eyes. Then he looked at the earl.

The whole grove seemed so filled with his hatred for Axewood that Portia half expected him to pivot and plunge his dagger into the man's guts.

Instead, he bit out a curse and hurled his knife away without warning.

486   *Gaelen Foley*

It stuck viciously into the ground, bloodied and shuddering in the moonlight.

Portia exhaled with relief. Luke lowered his head with a shaky breath and took a few steps away from the earl, as though to distance himself from the sore temptation to turn and finish the job.

Without a second's hesitation, Portia rushed into his empty arms, refusing to let him brush her aside. She wrapped her arms around his waist and held him until he gave in, encircling her in a sorrowful embrace.

He tightened his hold, and they clung to each other.

"I love you," she told him. Lifting her head, anxious to read his reaction, she saw the stark, haunted look on his face, the despair in his eyes.

It wrenched her woman's heart.

"Oh, my darling." She reached up and cupped his jaw tenderly between her hands, then wiped a smudge of black powder off his cheek with her thumb.

His posture was stiff, still bristling and angry, but she pulled him down and kissed him softly on the lips, tears spilling down her cheeks. "You did the right thing, sweeting. It's over now. It's going to be all right."

Luke finally kissed her back, clasping her waist.

But at that moment, a cold voice broke the silence, startling both of them.

"Well, *he* might be better than that, but I'm not."

Joel.

Portia looked over at her former suitor with a gasp.

He had regained consciousness and, powered by hatred, dragged himself over to where she had set Axewood's pistol in the grass.

Luke tightened his hold on Portia as Joel raised himself up on one knee, the weapon in his grasp, harsh victory stamped across his face.

"No!" Axewood shouted as Joel lifted the pistol in both hands.

"Now it's your turn to be the prisoner, Uncle. In hell." Joel squeezed the trigger.

Portia jumped as the shot cracked across the grove.

Axewood shrieked, and Joel smiled grimly. Portia buried her face against Luke's chest with a small cry of horror. Then the earl slumped against the tree.

Dead in seconds from the bullet lodged in his black heart.

CHAPTER 38

A Ride by Moonlight

*L*uke cradled Portia's head to his chest. He felt her shudder, but the gurgling sounds from Axewood ceased.

The earl was dead.

For Luke, the moment was profound. Holding Portia in his arms, he looked across the grove at Joel.

The two men exchanged a hard look of tacit understanding.

Joel did not seem to begrudge him the lady's affection, and to be sure, no one there would grieve for Axewood.

At the moment, though, Portia had obviously had all she could take for one night. She was trembling in Luke's arms and trying but failing to hold back her sobs.

Luke caressed her and held her in a protective embrace. "It's all right, sweeting. I've got you," he whispered. "He's gone. It's over now."

Silently, he sent Joel a look; the gambler nodded, then turned away to give the two of them a moment alone.

Luke kissed Portia on the head, then rested his cheek atop her hair and closed his eyes, exhausted. Through the smell of smoke and sweat that clung to him, he caught a hint of the apple blossom fragrance of her hair.

God, she was so precious to him, and he felt so strange as he pondered what she'd done. She had broken through the barricade he'd built around himself against the threat of any more hurt than he'd already experienced in life.

And now here they were.

It truly was over. Joel was rescued. Axewood was dead. And in the space of an hour, everything had changed.

Luke heard Portia's soft exhalation as she nestled her cheek against his chest, finally calming down. As he stood there wearily, the woman he loved wrapped in his arms, he could feel the rage and hatred he'd held onto for so many years seeping out of him, dissolving into the night.

Leaving him for good.

The release of such bitter poisons from his system left him feeling spent, heavy, and bone-tired down to his soul from carrying that burden since his youth.

He realized that the life he had known for so long was over, as of this moment.

He needed to believe that a better one awaited him, with Portia. She'd said she wanted to be with him. That she did not want to cancel the wedding. And hearing that, Luke dared to believe that this fierce, dainty little creature would find the strength to love him until all the broken pieces inside of him mended one day, and he'd be whole again.

Finally, Portia lifted her tear-stained face and gazed up at him, her skin pearlescent in the moonlight. "I'm proud of you, Luke."

He cupped her cheek and wiped away the trace of a tear with his thumb. "I'm proud of *you*, my little lioness. Thank God you are so handy with that bow. What is it?" he murmured when her blue eyes filled with fresh tears.

Her lips trembled. "I was so scared you would be killed. I couldn't bear to lose you."

"Ah, I'm all right." He pulled her into his embrace and kissed her forehead. "I love you so much, Portia Tennesley."

"I love you too. Oh, Luke, can we please just go home and get married now?"

He laughed wearily as she lifted her head and smiled up at him through her tears. "My darling bride," he said, "nothing in this world would please me more."

Then he slid his arms around her waist and claimed her lips in a heartfelt kiss.

Unfortunately, he remembered his allies at the foot of the hill and, all too soon, forced himself to end the kiss.

"Darling. I have to go back down the hill—"

"*What?*"

"I've got to make sure Peter and Sidney are all right."

"Oh! Oh, of course. You're right. Yes, go," she said unhappily.

"You and Joel take Tempo back up to the inn. Come, I'll help Clayton onto the horse." Luke released her, he knew not how, but just as they turned, they suddenly heard the sound of horses moving through the woods, voices approaching.

Luke reached for his gun, unsure who it might be, but in the next moment, Sidney and Peter rode into the grove.

They were all greatly relieved to see one another. The two men dismounted, their hands bloodied, their faces grim, their clothes torn in places, but they were alive.

To be sure, it was the most disheveled that anyone had ever seen Lord Sidney. Thankfully, the cheery viscount's smile flashed back into place as they all looked around at one another in belated shock over the night's events.

"Well!" Sidney said at last. "We're all still alive, I see."

"Not all of us." Joel hooked a thumb toward his uncle pinned to the oak tree.

"Egads." Sidney frowned at the gory sight.

Luke watched Sidney and Peter's faces with undeniable satisfaction as both men realized it was one of Portia's arrows holding Axewood in place; his pride in their lovely archer swelled as both men looked at her with astonishment.

"You did this?" Sidney exclaimed.

"What can I say?" She shrugged and grinned at him. "I'm Hunter Tennesley's sister."

"Apparently so," he murmured, then he gave her a little hug. "You all right, P?"

"Not really," she said with a wry smile.

"Hmm. Well, Silversmoke will look after you, I'm sure. Well done, my dear."

"Thanks for saving our necks," Peter added, giving her a cautious pat on the shoulder as Sidney released her. Then he gestured at Axewood. "So what do we do with the body?"

"Eh, let his henchman find him," Luke said with a dismissive wave of his hand.

"Can't," Peter answered. "Sidney slew the beast."

"What?" Luke turned to him in surprise.

"Aye, you should've seen him," said the major, looking askance at Sidney. "Didn't know he had it in him. For a rakehell."

Sidney rested his hands on his waist and smiled serenely. "I told you, I'm meaner than I look."

"I'll say," Peter mumbled, but Joel was staring at Sidney with a dazed expression.

"Rucker's...dead?"

The question took Sidney off guard. "Well, yes. I'm sorry, mate, I...I had no choice. He was eight feet tall and coming at me—"

"No, don't be," Joel interrupted. "That ogre beat the hell out of me too many times for me to shed a tear. I just...can't believe he's gone. That they both are. I can't believe I'm finally free." He looked around at them in wonder. "I-I really don't know how I can ever thank you all."

"Never mind that," Peter said. "Let's get up the hill to the inn and see what can be done about that leg of yours."

"Is anyone else hurt?" Luke glanced around at them.

"Been better," Peter said with a sardonic smile. "But none the worse for wear."

"Some blackguard had the audacity to cut me on the cheek! Can you imagine?" Sidney harrumphed and touched the scratch gingerly. "You don't think it'll leave a scar, do you?"

"I certainly hope not. That would be a tragedy," Portia teased.

Sidney chuckled, Luke put his arm around Portia, then they all headed for their horses.

"Um, Luke," she said, "I'm afraid Tempo was grazed by a bullet on his hip, but I think he's all right."

He was not at all happy to hear this and went to check on his horse.

Meanwhile, a few feet away, Sidney was helping Joel up onto Axewood's horse. He wouldn't be needing the animal anymore, obviously.

"I say, ol' man," the viscount suddenly quipped, "you do realize you've just gained your uncle's title? You're the new earl, as of this moment."

"Lucky you," Peter drawled as he swung up into the saddle and gave his own mount a pat.

Joel fell silent, gathering up the reins. He nodded slowly. "First thing I'll do is use my new position to make sure this ungodly Carnevale of theirs is stamped out for good."

"Does it help, getting vengeance on your uncle?" Luke asked as he held Tempo's bridle so Portia could climb up onto the stallion.

Joel smiled back at him wistfully. "Oh, I'd say you got the better prize, Your Grace."

Luke smiled back, well aware that it was true.

"I heard of your betrothal while I was in captivity," Joel said. "I confess, I had hoped to be reunited with Lady Portia if ever I got free. But I can see the lady's heart is otherwise engaged. I wish you both happy," he said with a gracious nod, and offered Luke his hand.

Luke stepped over, reached out, and shook it, then glanced at Portia, who spoke up softly.

"Joel, I do hope after all you've been through you aren't hurt by the change in my circumstances. I just want you to know that even after my parents betrothed me to some mysterious duke"—she glanced at Luke, then at Joel again—"I still didn't forget you. That's why I went to Silversmoke and begged him to find you and help you if he could. He kept his promise, as you can see."

Joel nodded. "Heroes always do."

Luke lowered his head, humbled.

"I'm just glad you two found each other because of me. At least it gives some purpose to my, er, adventure of the past year."

"Honorably said." Peter nodded at Joel in approval.

Joel gave Portia a reassuring wink as if to say there were no hard feelings. Still, Luke could tell by his pale countenance the gambler was still in a lot of pain.

"Well, come along, you lot!" Sidney clapped his hands together. "We've got a wedding to get to!"

"It's not for another eleven days, actually," Portia pointed out.

Sidney mounted up. "Nevertheless. I say we rest up tonight and head back to London first thing."

"Civilization?" Joel said, perking up.

"Sounds good to me." Luke swung up onto Tempo's back behind Portia.

"I'll tell you one thing," she said, smiling at Joel. "I know of three trusty servants who are going to be overjoyed at your return."

"She's right," Luke agreed as he slipped his arm around her waist. "That Mrs. Berry cannot wait to have you back so she can fuss over you. She told me so herself."

Joel sighed with pleasure at the mention of a home-cooked meal. "She makes the best puddings in the world."

"Cassius will be so pleased, as well, finally to see you back to your former perfection," Portia teased. "And Denny...well, what can be said about Denny?"

Joel chuckled. "Ah, that Thump's a good lad. Wooden head, maybe, but a heart of oak. I think I'll give them all a raise."

"Come on, you lot. Enough chatter," Peter said from the front of the line. He led the extra horse by the reins. "I don't know about the rest of you, but I could use a stiff drink."

"Hear, hear!" said everybody else.

Bringing up the rear, riding double with Portia on Tempo, Luke let the others pull ahead of them a bit, savoring the comforting softness of her body nestled close to his. She turned a little, and he nuzzled her cheek with his nose, kissing her face with tender intimacy.

"I love you," he whispered.

"I love you too. I'm so glad you're safe." She kissed his lips for a long, lingering moment, then rested her head on his shoulder with a sigh of contentment.

Luke cuddled her against him. She heated his blood, as always, but after all that had happened, the closeness between them as of this moment made his heart swell. He never wanted to be parted from her again.

He continued caressing and kissing her as Tempo walked sedately up the trail. After a few moments of his attentions, he could feel her beaming with happiness, restored to a sense of safety through his doting.

He knew then that the entire purpose of his existence was to love her, but he'd already begun to live that new destiny, holding her, and kissing her now and then about the cheeks and head while they enjoyed a slow, leisurely ride through the moonlit woods.

"I almost forgot," he suddenly said, reaching into his waistcoat.

"What is it?"

"I have something for you. Here." He pulled out the ring he'd been meaning to give her for ages. "Since it looks like this wedding is officially on, allow me to present you, my luscious fiancée, with an engagement ring worthy of the future Duchess of Fountainhurst."

"Luke!"

"It belonged to my grandmother, who handed it down to my mother, and now it belongs to you, if you'll do me the honor of accepting it."

"Oh, Luke, it's beautiful." She took it from his fingers' careful hold. He smiled as he watched her study it in wonder.

"It's a sapphire, in case you couldn't tell in the darkness. I thought it matched your eyes."

She lifted her gaze to his with a heartfelt smile. "Thank you." She put it on her finger and stared at the jewels glistening in the moonlight, then she shook her head. "I can't believe you had this with you at a gathering of thieves."

He laughed.

"I mean it! You could have lost it in the fight! It could have been stolen."

"You worry too much, my dear." He pulled her close and kissed her on the head. "Do you like it?" he whispered.

"I adore it. And I adore you."

Sheer music to his ears. He claimed her mouth and gave her a kiss that told her without words that he felt the same.

When he ended the kiss, she relaxed in his arms, and Luke had to curb his libido.

But a moment later, when the hilltop inn came into view through the trees in all its Alpine coziness, Portia turned her face toward his once more. "Luke?" she said very softly.

"Hmm?" he whispered, besotted.

She flicked her lashes downward. "Stay with me tonight."

His breath caught, but he managed to check his reaction. "My darling, I thought you'd never ask."

EPILOGUE

Wedding of the Decade

Eleven Days Later

*O*n a bright Sunday morning, Portia stood before the cheval glass in her bedchamber, gazing at her reflection.

It was almost time to go. They'd be leaving for the church in a moment. Her heart beat swiftly as she smoothed her white lace skirts, her gauzy veil already pinned in place.

Assessing herself one last time in the mirror, she took in the details of the gown she had agonized over and even helped design. Such care she had put into every decision of this day!

Now that it had come, what surprised her the most was that she wasn't nervous at all. Excited, yes, but there was nothing to be nervous about. Because she was marrying Luke.

Her heart soared with exultation at the thought of spending the rest of her life with him, from this day forward. Oh, how she loved him.

They had barely been able to keep their hands off each other for the past week and a half—ever since that night at the Alpine Inn, after they had rescued Joel.

When they had returned to her hotel room, they had undressed each other in the darkness and, with increasingly frantic kisses, sought comfort for the night's shattering events in each other's arms. But Luke had made sure that his bride could still wear white on their wedding day.

Portia had no idea how the delicious scoundrel had held himself back. But such acts of chivalry were to be expected, it seemed, when one was marrying a bona fide hero. She smiled knowingly at her reflection.

He had the most adorable sense of obligation to her parents. A genteel respect for the proper way of doing things.

One would hardly believe that His Grace was a part-time outlaw.

She, too, was glad they had waited, however. It felt right.

Besides, she had learned in the meantime that Luke had a hundred ways of pleasuring her short of consummation.

That prize awaited her tonight.

But how funny, to think back to when it had been nothing but an arranged match between them. How she used to dread the prospect of the marriage bed!

Now that she'd fallen in love with her soon-to-be husband, everything had changed. Instead of the stoic duty she had anticipated, she knew Luke would give her a blissful experience.

Indeed, it was ironic how he'd turned all her expectations of her future upside down—in the best way possible. All she had cared about when the Duke of Fountainhurst had first proposed was avoiding spinsterhood and benefiting her family.

Now these advantages barely entered into her mind. Nor did she care that she'd be a wealthy duchess by nuncheon. She didn't give a fig for the castle or the coronet.

It was the thought of Luke himself that filled her with joy.

If they had actually been two peasants marrying that day, just like in her fanciful wedding theme, she could not have been happier.

What more could any woman ask for?

Luke had already proven by his actions that what he offered her was the love that gave everything, as Silversmoke had once described it.

Tonight, Portia would prove her love in kind by giving him the gift of her body, her very self.

She looked forward to the day when she could present him with a child, be it daughter or son, to show him that the Fountainhurst line *would* continue on for generations to come.

She knew he'd be a wonderful father…

At that moment, a light tap on the door roused Portia from her reveries, then her own sire poked his snowy head into her chamber. "Are you ready, butterfly? It's time."

"I think so…" Portia took a deep breath and gave herself one last searching look in the mirror.

But she had dragged her feet on this day long enough.

"Yes." She clutched her bouquet, lifted the hem of her gown, and turned to Papa with a wholly confident nod. *"Now* I'm ready."

Then she crossed her chamber, her steps light, to go at last and marry the man of her dreams.

❖

Inside St. Andrew's, Luke stood near the front of the crowded church, greeting guests and nervously waiting for the ceremony to begin.

Amid the buzz of conversation that filled the soaring space, he could hear Tavi's loud trill of a laugh now and then as she milled around chatting with the new arrivals, but most of the guests had already taken their seats.

Flooded with light, the interior of St. Andrew's looked every bit as charming as Portia had promised when she'd described their country-themed peasant wedding she had planned on the day she'd dragged him in here weeks ago, to discuss what he'd considered at the time an array of boring details.

But today, seeing it all come together, Luke found her scheme enchanting. From the pale green fabric runner down the center aisle to the wildflower bouquets stationed everywhere, from the pastel garlands adorning the choir's gallery overhead, to the big fluffy bows gracing the ends of the pews, Portia had indeed created a beautiful day for everyone, down to the last detail.

She was thorough, that one. But little did she know her bridegroom had added a detail of his own without her knowledge.

He could not wait to see the look on her face when she discovered his surprise. The guests seemed to like it, judging by their wonder-struck looks as they glanced all around the church.

Luke's gaze traveled over the gathered company in quiet appreciation. There was Gower, doing much better now. He was seated in the second pew behind the Sedgwicks with Finch, but his new companion, Mrs. O'Toole, was waiting for him back in his quarters at Gracewell.

Sidney was also present, having got up extremely early for the day for a Town dandy. Of course, it was a special occasion.

Idly strolling up and down the side aisle, hands in pockets, the charming viscount chatted with everyone and took care to keep Joel company where he sat in a Bath chair beside the pews.

After a successful operation, the new Earl of Axewood would be confined to his wheelchair for a few weeks to come. Though he'd walk with a limp for the rest of his life, the surgeon had managed to save his injured foot.

His three trusty servants attended their young master and took turns pushing his Bath chair for him when needed. The former Red Carnation seemed humbled by his ordeal, and grateful for the many well-wishes he received from Society.

Everyone had been shocked at his return, and at the tale of how the legendary Silversmoke had saved him.

Luke claimed to know nothing about it, but the story they gave 'round was that Sidney was the one who had hired the famous highwayman to find Joel.

No one could explain how Axewood had ended up pinned to a tree, but the man had been consorting with criminals. A violent fate was to be expected.

As for Luke, his revenge was complete, but he was glad to close that chapter of his life.

This was a day for peace and happiness only—which was why it irked him to see the otherwise amiable Sidney casting icy glances now and then at Portia's brother, who'd arrived three days ago.

Brooding, black-haired Hunter Tennesley, the Earl of Arvendon, ignored the cold looks he received from several in Society, sitting stoically in the front row beside his mother—who wouldn't let go of his arm.

Lady Liddicoat was quite glued to the side of her long-absent son, whether Hunter liked it or not. Portia, too, had been ecstatic at her brother's return, and Luke had been pleased to meet his future brother-in-law. Sidney might've called Hunter evil, but Luke could see no evidence of that.

Her brother might appear to possess a guarded and saturnine nature, but Luke was sure the adventurer's seeming aloofness had more to do with the daggered glances he received in Town than any evil streak on his part.

Luke felt for the man, knowing from experience what it meant to be an outsider. But thankfully, Peter had been gracious toward him—of course.

The major was a fair-minded man and had no quarrel with Hunter himself. Indeed, the two had never met before Luke had introduced them outside of the church a little while ago.

Peter seemed very interested in Hunter's sailing adventures; it turned out that both of them had been to India. They had visited some of the same places and found much to discuss.

At that point, Luke had left the conversation to go and see to his other guests, relieved that Hunter had someone to talk to at the wedding.

Of course, Sidney did not seem to appreciate Peter's ready acceptance of the black sheep, but that did not concern the stoic major any more than did the presence of his recent conquest, Lady Delphine.

Having moved on from her brief dalliance with the major, the mysterious book club hostess had begun to show what Luke wryly deemed an unhealthy interest in Oliver Finch, of all people.

Oliver.

Luke eyed his assistant with disgruntlement where he sat next to Gower. He was still out of charity with the redhead. By all rights, Finch should have ridden down the hill himself to fetch Joel instead of letting Portia do it.

Gower would have to work on training the lad to toughen him up a bit, but Delphine, for her part, seemed to like the young scholar's vulnerable innocence. Of course, it probably wouldn't last long around her, Luke thought, but after what they had been through together, the sophisticated lady seemed inclined to take the hapless quiz under her wing.

At last, Luke heard the announcement he'd been waiting for.

"They're coming! The wedding coach has arrived!"

The news traveled quickly from the back to the front of the church. As the music began, calling everyone to attention, Luke scrambled to get into position, beckoning to Sedgwick to join him.

His arrogant brother-in-law heaved himself up from the front pew where he had been lounging between Bartram and Tavi, who had taken her seat. Luke smiled at his sister. She was already dabbing away tears.

"You owe me," Tavi mouthed at him. *Remember, I found Portia for you, didn't I?* her pert stare seemed to say.

Luke chuckled and blew her a kiss.

Then Sedgwick sauntered over to stand near Luke at the front, his patrician head held high while the vicar and his attendants came out.

Luke's frequent irritation with his brother-in-law perhaps made Sedgwick an odd choice for his best man, but, until recently, Luke barely knew anyone, certainly not well enough to ask for such a significant favor.

Thankfully, that lack was already in the process of being remedied. Without Portia, though, he wondered if he would've gone his whole life without any friends other than Gower and Finch.

Sedgwick elbowed him discreetly. "Last chance to flee the vicar's mousetrap, ol' boy. Run while you still can."

Luke scowled at such sentiments, especially coming from the man who had married his sister. "Honestly, Sedgwick, one more word, and I might punch you."

"Easy! I'm only jesting," Sedgwick mumbled.

Luke gave him a warning look. To him, love was not a joking matter. Then he focused his attention on the back of the church and waited for his bride to appear.

It seemed like he'd been waiting forever to marry this girl, but the day was finally at hand.

His heart beat faster as the wedding party started filing in. The heavy wooden doors opened—it had been important to keep them shut for the time being—but a dazzle of light appeared, and he caught a glimpse of a slender, veiled silhouette.

First, however, came little Katie, their flower girl. His adorable niece looked extremely proud of her pale green gown with a white sash. She had a bow in her golden hair, and a basket from which she began scattering flower petals as she walked.

Just a few steps behind her came their ringbearer, one of the Liddicoats' three grandchildren, a sturdy four-year-old boy called Sam.

Clutching the pillow with the ring attached, Sam was looking around at the doting smiles from all the guests with such an uneasy expression that Luke feared the wee boy might bolt.

Then Sam bumped into Katie, who had stopped in her tracks with a loud gasp.

Luke grinned as his little niece noticed his contribution at last.

"Butterflies!" she cried, looking up and around her into the air, left and right.

The throng of guests began laughing too, because most of them had had the same reaction when they had first arrived.

On Luke's orders, Finch and nearly every other servant in his employ had spent the past two days with nets out in the meadows at Gracewell, carefully catching live butterflies and putting them gently in jars for the big day.

Luke had ordered all the insects released into the church just before the guests began arriving. After all the work Portia had put into making their wedding a beautiful occasion, he figured it was the least he could do.

Now he just hoped that the bride's reaction would resemble the flower girl's, even if the elegant belle was too ladylike to show it on the outside. She would understand the significance of what his gift meant.

Sedgwick beckoned to his daughter to get her moving again, and Katie remembered her duties with a giggle. Little Sam showed no more signs of wanting to flee, absently following Katie—and nearly tripping and dropping the ring as he stared up at the butterflies.

The little boy's mother—Portia's sister Sarah—was right behind him, in any case. The blond matron of honor kept her son focused on moving forward with a discreet whisper.

Portia had chosen to have her elder sister as her witness for the ceremony, for she had so many friends that picking just a few as bridesmaids would've put her in the awkward position of having to play favorites.

Of course, her best friend Serena was seated with her enigmatic husband, Azrael, the Duke of Rivenwood, just behind Portia's family.

In the next row sat the Netherfords, Jason and Felicity, with Peter sitting between his sister and Jason's roguish little son. Simon had been holding out his finger for ages, trying to coax a butterfly to land on it.

The industrious Miss Annabelle, meanwhile, was perched on Felicity's lap, quietly lecturing her stuffed animal.

Trinny, the bubbly red-haired Lady Roland, sat with her husband Gable at the end of the pew, just in case either parent needed to speed out of the church with their now four-month-old son.

So far, the baby had been quiet, content to play with his toes.

Luke had also met Portia's good friend, Maggie, and her Irish-born husband, Connor, the Duke of Amberley, a former military man. The couple had just returned from a month-long honeymoon, but insisted they would never miss the wedding.

Rosy-cheeked Maggie looked far too peaceable, modest, and sweet a creature to carry so grand a title as the Duchess of Amberley, and as for Connor, Luke had liked the Irishman at once for his quick wit and easygoing humor.

Why, Luke thought, if he had known such agreeable folk lived right in his own neighborhood, he would have started coming more frequently to Town a long time ago.

When Katie arrived at the front of the church, she diverted from her path, rushing over to give her uncle Luke a little hug, quite tugging at his heartstrings. She then continued on to stand in her assigned place.

"Lord help me when that one grows up," Sedgwick murmured.

"To be sure," Luke answered with a smile. He was not looking forward to that either.

Then wee Sam marched over to stand beside Sedgwick, and Portia's sister took her place.

There was a pause in the music, and Luke's heart began to pound, for when the next song began, in walked his soon-to-be duchess on her father's arm.

He held his breath, staring at her.

The lady in black had become a vision in white.

Gazing at her, Luke wished he could've seen the expression on her face when she first saw the butterflies for herself, fluttering wild and free throughout the church.

The colorful creatures danced from one wildflower bouquet to the next, passing over the heads of the guests. Some even alighted on the magnificent hats of various ladies.

But, alas, Portia was still too far away for Luke to read her reaction.

With her face veiled in snowy white lace and the sunlight behind her as the church doors slowly drifted closed, he could only see her lithe silhouette.

Then Lord Liddicoat began escorting his daughter down the aisle.

Luke stared, enthralled by the woman. He felt like he'd stepped into a dream. Finally, they could begin the rest of their lives together with nothing else coming between them; Portia had no lingering thoughts about Joel, and Luke was finally satisfied that he'd got justice for his parents.

In fact, he realized as he stood there that his big sister had been right all along. He glanced at Tavi, and she gazed back at him lovingly, tears in her eyes.

He felt the truth of her advice sinking deep in to his bones. It was just as she had said.

The best way to honor their parents was to make a good life and family of their own, passing on to their children all the love that *they* had received from Mother and Father growing up.

Giving his sister a slight nod, Luke could somehow feel their parents' presence in the church. He knew for certain they were there, watching over them, a part of this day. A lump rose in his throat at their memory, but this day was for the future, not the past.

He fixed his stare on his bride as she approached.

Portia had forbidden him from seeing her wedding gown until now, of course. Luke was moved by her beauty as she approached.

She wore a slim-fitting gown of cream-colored lace, with a modest scoop neck and a short train that whispered over the ground behind her, dragging flower petals in its wake.

As she came closer, Luke saw joy radiating from her face behind her light veil, and a rush of tenderness squeezed his very heart.

Ah, she was pleased with his offering.

Her blue eyes danced with humor over the butterflies, and she shook her head at him in chiding mirth as she approached.

Luke grinned in response. He could tell she was holding back laughter.

Exactly the reaction he had hoped for.

After all, it was a bit of a private joke between them, insects in general, and butterflies in particular. She had felt so sorry for them, these bright, beautiful creatures, captured and pinned down on display. How she had reproached him for his alleged hobby!

Well, for one thing, collecting them was actually Finch's hobby, not Luke's. But more importantly, he now understood why it had bothered her so much.

Portia could relate to the butterflies; she had worried *he* might treat her the same way, more or less, when she was his.

Most men marrying a prize like Portia Tennesley probably would.

But the butterflies Luke had released into the church remained free, and so would she. She was safe. She was free. She was loved.

She was so much more to him now than just a prize to be collected for her beauty and her birth.

Indeed, she held his very heart.

Lovingly, he watched her bid her father a wistful farewell. Liddicoat brushed away a tear, then went and sat down beside his wife.

Portia took her place next to Luke at the altar, turning to smile at the guests, while the vicar and the whole congregation waited for the final bars of music to end.

"Do you like your surprise?" Luke murmured as he stood beside her.

"It's perfect," she choked out. "It's just perfect, Luke."

"As are you, my dear," he said in a steadying tone, glancing at her. "Now, let's get married, eh?"

She gazed adoringly at him, her eyes full of trust. "Let's," she whispered.

So they did.

❖

Many hours later, in the velvet deep of night, Portia and Luke flung apart at last in the candlelight and rolled onto their backs. Panting and sweaty, they both stared up dazedly at the canopy over his bed.

"My God," she said, still breathless, her skin aglow from his lovemaking.

With a low, dazzled laugh, Luke glanced over at her, his green eyes mirroring the same flabbergasted satisfaction she felt. *"Damn."*

"So that's what all the fuss is about. Sweet heaven."

With a hint of well-deserved pride in his chuckle, he cast a forearm over his brow. "I'm glad Your Grace is pleased. That was…incredible."

Portia closed her eyes for a moment with a beatific smile.

He'd been so gentle with her, deflowering her as tenderly as possible, but he was a large man, and her body still ached with a curious mix of pleasure and pain from having him inside her.

When she opened her eyes, Luke was watching her.

"Are you sore? Did I hurt you?" he asked, frowning.

"It's a good sore," she said with a caress. Knowing how protective he was, she didn't want him feeling guilty for that glorious experience.

Rolling onto her side to curve herself against him, Portia snuggled under his powerful arm. He wrapped it around her in a warm half-embrace, and she rested her head on that particular region of his chest that she had come to think of as *her* spot.

They fit together perfectly somehow, and Luke sighed as he stroked her hair with a lulling motion. "Ah, if I had known what a little slice of heaven you are, my love, I never would've been able to wait until the wedding."

"Yes! You were such a good boy during our betrothal." She giggled and leaned upward, propping her cheek on her left hand and trailing the fingers of her right over his sculpted abdomen. "But, you know, I must confess, I'm happy you saved your bad side just for me, highwayman."

"Bad side? Me?" He gave her an innocent look. "Whatever do you mean?"

"Ha!" She swung upright onto her knees without warning and straddled him, using a corner of the blanket as a face mask. "Stand and deliver!" she taunted, brandishing a finger-pistol at him.

He laughed, and the slightly scratchy sound of his voice after all their love play heated her blood anew. "I thought I just did. Fairly well, if I say so myself." He bit her finger lightly.

"Ow. Ruffian."

"But you like it when I bite you," Luke whispered.

Portia tossed her head. "That is entirely beside the point."

He lay back, folded his muscular arms behind his head with a broad smile, tousle-haired, devilishly handsome. "Well, at least give a man five minutes to recover, y'vixen."

"Nonsense. Silversmoke is no ordinary man. Now, *stand*," she ordered in a tantalizing whisper. Brazenly, she reached down and grasped his rampant member, and indeed, found it already standing very much at attention.

He shuddered with pleasure at her touch, then captured her about the waist. "What impertinence is this?" Feigning outrage, Luke yanked her mask away as his emerald eyes caught fire.

Portia shrieked with glee as he rolled her off him with a growl, tossed her onto her back, and began stealing kisses of ravishing depth.

And then, to be sure, the highwayman-duke delivered, much to her delight.

Again…and again…and again.

AUTHOR'S NOTE

Dear Reader,

I so hope you had fun reading this story. I certainly enjoyed writing it...*most* of the time, LOL! To be honest, this was the hardest book I ever wrote. Ah well, every author's got to have a hardest book at some point, right? This one was it for me. Don't get me wrong, I fell in loooove with the characters, especially that dreamy Luke (and I hope you did, too!) but he sure made me work for it.

The challenge came about because, for some ungodly reason, I decided to try writing the first draft by what writers call the "pantsing" method — letting the story take you wherever it wants without building an outline first, which I normally do. Sounds nice, doesn't it? Fun. Creative. Artsy. Yeah, I'll never do that again, LOL.

I guess I thought I would shake things up a little just for fun, since 2018 (the year I wrote this book) was my twentieth anniversary as a published author. (Which I can't even believe. Where does the time go??) Zounds, did I have a lot of revision to do as a result—draft after draft—until I got this story to exactly what I wanted it to be. Live and learn! Henceforward, I am resolved to be an outlining nerd for life. Always an adventure. *grin*

In any case, I learned some really cool things while researching for this story that I'd love to share with you. I know a lot of my readers enjoy learning a little of the history behind the book, so here are your fun facts for *Duke of Shadows*, along with some of the most helpful research books I found on the topics, if you wish to learn more.

Highwaymen
Author David Brandon, in *Stand and Deliver! A History of Highway Robbery*, provides countless colorful accounts of real historical highwaymen, but the most famous of them all was Dick Turpin.

Born 1705, (a bit earlier than the Regency period), the legends and myths about Turpin began taking shape even while he was still alive, so history hands him down to us as "the very embodiment of the dashing highwayman." Though totally unscrupulous, this son of a pub owner was trained as a butcher in his youth, but soon realized he could save money on his meat inventory if he just stole or poached the animals instead of having to buy them on the hoof! This practice quickly curtailed his future as a butcher and forced him to have to flee the area, so he went to the Essex coast and got involved in smuggling.

The enterprising young rascal soon took to impersonating a Revenue Officer and holding up his rival smugglers, then making off with *their* loot. This must've become dicey, so he moved on to the outskirts of London, where he took up with 'the Gregory gang.'

Unfortunately, Brandon tells us, these were especially nasty criminals known for cruelty toward the victims. Their penchant for violence made the authorities all the more determined to end their reign of terror, and eventually, they got caught—but Turpin escaped. Legend has it Turpin leaped out the window of the upstairs room where the gang was drinking the night they were busted onto the back of his waiting horse and galloped away!

He worked alone from then on, and his policy was never to use unnecessary violence. After a colorful career lasting several more years, Dick Turpin suddenly disappeared. He wasn't hanged—we'd have had a record of that. There were rumors that he used whatever fortune he'd made over the years to retire to a genteel life in the country under an assumed name, but no one knows for sure. I highly recommend David Brandon's book if you enjoy these kinds of accounts, as well as *The Regency Underworld* by Donald A. Low, another excellent source.

St. Bartholomew Fair

The wicked Carnevale in this story was inspired by London's famed St. Bartholomew Fair, which began in the twelfth century, but was finally suppressed in 1855 for all of the criminality and debauchery associated with it. *The Newgate Calendar* condemned the fair in 1825 as "a school of vice which has initiated more youth into the habits of villainy than Newgate itself." For the purposes of my novel, I combined the St. Bartholomew Fair idea with the world of criminals from my research into the works noted above, as well as the general Regency madness for gambling. Bored gentlemen at clubs like White's would bet on things as trivial as a race between two raindrops sliding down the windowpane on a rainy day!

Thus, it seemed a reasonable leap of fictional world-building that a whole underground festival could spring up devoted to gambling, with at least one twisted attraction that even Turpin's cruel associates in the Gregory gang would've enjoyed (before they went to the hangman).

Picnics

On a much pleasanter note, Lucas's getting-to-know-you "date" with Portia gave me an excuse to research the history of picnics. What a delightful subject! For my research here, I am indebted to *The National Trust Book of Picnics* (1993).

Did you know the first picnic recorded in history comes from the ninth century? An Anglo-Saxon tale recorded in the Chronicle of Reginald, a monk of Durham, tells us: "Some time between 875 and 883 A.D., the monks of Lindisfarne...fled to the Northumbrian mainland to escape the Danes. Sheltering somewhere near Hadrian's Wall, they were provided with sustenance by the local community. One gift was a freshly made cheese." I'm sad to say that, accompanying this, the main dish was "salted horse's head"! Um, no thanks. LOL. Things could only improve from there, presumably.

"By 1802, a Picnic Club was founded by Lady Buckinghamshire and Lady Jersey... Other members included the Prince of Wales and his mistress and secret wife, Mrs. Fitzherbert. The inaugural meeting consisted of private theatricals at Tottenham Street Rooms in London, followed by a picnic supper in a tavern." This almost inspires me with a whole new series idea—!

This book is full of wonderful quotes and anecdotes about picnics over the centuries. The National Trust cleverly provided it to encourage visitors to picnic on the grounds of the great country houses that one can tour throughout the British Isles. I can't think of any more appealing ways to spend a summer afternoon.

The Publication of Pride & Prejudice

"Noooo! Jane, don't do it!!" This was my reaction upon learning that the one and only Jane Austen SOLD all her rights for her second novel, *Pride and Prejudice*, for £110, to her publisher. In other words, she agreed to let her publisher pay her a flat fee of what, in today's money, would be roughly $7000.00 USD, with no further payments due to the author. (Source: http://www.jasna.org/austen/works/pride-prejudice/) *Quelle horreur!*

Because of this contract, neither Jane nor her heirs received any royalties from a book that went on to be a huge hit in her own day and will continue to be with us for centuries to come. To me, as a hard-working woman author, this is just tragic.

I'm no mathematician, but given 200-plus years of successful book sales, movies, plays, TV mini-series, and endless merchandise, what, with compound interest and a good lawyer, I suspect that if the divine Jane had held onto her copyright, her descendants might *almost* be as rich as J.K. Rowling! Very sad. It makes me all the more grateful for how the digital revolution has allowed me and many of my colleagues to publish our own work as independent authors. Heck, if it was good enough for Mark Twain, Charles Dickens, and Edgar Allen Poe, I'm proud to follow in their footsteps. Brilliant as Jane's prose still shines to this day, I wish I could time-travel back in history to warn her not to take that deal.

But, winces for Jane's sake aside, I enjoyed finally introducing you to the Moonlight Square book club that you've seen mentioned in the previous installments of the series.

As for what lies ahead for our Moonlight Square friends, I am happy to report that the series will continue beyond the four dukes on the corners. As you may have gleaned, Major Peter Carvel, as well as Lord Sidney, and Portia's brother, Hunter Tennesley, Lord Arvendon, will all be future heroes in the series. I am unofficially dubbing them The Moonlight Marquesses! I look forward to sharing their stories with you, but I can tell you one thing—I will definitely be outlining those books first! :)

Thank you so much for coming along on this grand journey. Before I go, I would like to invite you to visit my website and join my newsletter while you are there. I would also be delighted if you'd like to follow me on Facebook. I have a small but friendly community there made up of Ladies of Distinction and I enjoy posting and chatting on there on a regular basis. So if you're looking to find some like-minded historical romance readers, just hit like and follow. Lastly, if you really enjoyed *Duke of Shadows*, please consider leaving a review online. That's always very helpful, if you are so inclined.

Again, I thank you from the bottom of my heart for reading. Until next time!

Love,
Gaelen
gaelenfoley.com
facebook.com/gaelenfoleybooks

Previous Moonlight Square Books

One Moonlit Night (Prequel Novella)
At the ripe old age of two-and-twenty, Lady Katrina Glendon just can't seem to snare a husband. Whether her frank tongue or slightly eccentric ways bear the blame, she faces a houseful of younger sisters clamoring for her, the eldest, to marry and move aside before they all end up as spinsters. When her latest suitor defects and proposes to another girl, Trinny throws up her hands in despair of ever finding a fiancé. But sometimes destiny waits just around the corner...and love lives right across the square!

Duke of Scandal (Book 1)
Jason Hawthorne, the Duke of Netherford, made it clear to the young, lovesick Felicity Carvel long ago that nothing could ever happen between them. He has *earned* his reputation as the Duke of Scandal—and she's his best friend's little sister. For honor's sake, he vows to stay away from the lovely innocent. But even now, all grown up, Felicity still wants Jason for her own. And after getting her heart broken once before by Naughty Netherford, does she dare attempt to play with fire again—and this time, can Jason resist?

Duke of Secrets (Book 2)
When shocking family secrets emerge, they turn Lady Serena Parker's world upside-down, sending the bold, raven-haired beauty on a quest to find answers. Her search soon points her right across the street, to the home of her most mysterious neighbor in Moonlight Square—the enigmatic and solitary Azrael, Duke of Rivenwood. He alone can give her the answers she seeks, but at what price?

Duke of Storm (Book 3)
He's the Duke no one expected. She's the Lady he's been looking for. Can their love overcome the dark storm gathering over the House of Amberley? When swashbuckling, Irish-born Major Connor Forbes inherits his English cousin's dukedom, it seems a hilarious windfall—at first. But then Connor learns that the last three Dukes of Amberley all died under mysterious circumstances, and soon realizes that someone is trying to kill him, too! He must unmask the enemy of his family line, all while attempting to survive his new title and navigate life in the London aristocracy. He desperately needs the guidance of a high-society insider, but whom could he possibly trust? Innocent, mild-mannered Lady Maggie Winthrop may be his only hope...

Enter a world of wonder & whimsy, adventure & peril in the Middle Grade/YA series that's as much fun for grownups as it is for kids!

Gaelen Foley writing as E.G. Foley
THE LOST HEIR: The Gryphon Chronicles, Book 1

Jake is a scrappy orphaned pickpocket living by his wits on the streets of Victorian London. Lately he's started seeing ghosts and can move solid objects with his mind! He has no idea why. Next thing he knows, a Sinister Gentleman and his minions come hunting him, and Jake is plunged headlong into a mysterious world of magic and deadly peril. A world that holds the secret of who he really is: the long-lost heir of an aristocratic family with magical powers.

But with treacherous enemies closing in, it will take all of his wily street instincts and the help of his friends—both human and magical—to solve the mystery of what happened to his parents and defeat the foes who never wanted the Lost Heir of Griffon to be found…

"A wonderful novel in the same vein as Harry Potter, full of nonstop action, magical creatures, and the reality that was Queen Victoria's England." ~The Reading Café

About the Author

Noted for her "complex, subtly shaded characters, richly sensual love scenes, and elegantly fluid prose" (*Booklist*), *New York Times*, USA Today, and *Publisher's Weekly* Bestselling author Gaelen Foley has written over twenty (and counting!) rich, bold historical romances set in Regency England and Napoleonic Europe. Since her debut in 1998, her books have been published in seventeen languages worldwide and have won numerous awards, including the National Readers' Choice Award, the Booksellers' Best, the Golden Leaf (three times), the Award of Excellence, and the HOLT Medallion.

A versatile and hardworking writer, Gaelen's passion for the craft of fiction keeps her exploring new creative ground. While continuing to entertain her Regency fans, she has branched out into contemporary small-town romance as well as fantasy romance. Since 2012, Gaelen has also been co-writing fantasy middle grade/children's novels with her husband, a former teacher, under the penname E.G. Foley. The Lost Heir, Book 1 in their Gryphon Chronicles series, was a #1 Amazon Children's Bestseller (and was optioned for a movie!).

To learn more about Gaelen and her books, visit her at GaelenFoley.com.